Beverly Schrader

Resounding acclaim for

HARRI

"CONSISTENTLY GOOD,
NOVEL AFTER NOVEL!...
Segal neatly hooks the reader in the beginning
and keeps the line taut throughout."
Indianapolis Star

"WONDERFUL!...
A writer of quality entertainment."
Evelyn Oppenheimer,
Radio Book Talk, Dallas-Fort Worth

"SPLENDID!...
Segal writes in clear and highly absorbing narrative style"
Nashville Banner

"SUPERB!"
Winter Haven News Chief

"BEAUTIFUL!...
Harriet Segal has a talented gift
in being able to evoke atmosphere
until the scent of flowers or the stench of a market
seems to rise from the pages."
Rosalind Laker, author of *The Sugar Pavilion*

Other Avon Books by
Harriet Segal

MAGNOLIA DREAMS

THE SKYLARK'S SONG

HARRIET SEGAL

AVON BOOKS ◆ NEW YORK

This novel is a work of fiction. Names, characters, places and incidents either are the product of the author's imagination or are used fictitiously. Any resemblance to actual events, locales, organizations or persons, living or dead, is entirely coincidental and beyond the intent of either the author or publisher.

AVON BOOKS
A division of
The Hearst Corporation
1350 Avenue of the Americas
New York, New York 10019

First Avon Books Printing: March 1995

AVON TRADEMARK REG. U.S. PAT. OFF. AND IN OTHER COUNTRIES, MARCA REGISTRADA, HECHO EN U.S.A.

Printed in the U.S.A.

RA 10 9 8 7 6 5 4 3 2 1

This book is for Sheldon
Love is enough

Because the road is rough and long,
Shall we despise the skylark's song?

ANNE BRONTË,
Views of Life

Acknowledgments

Many people were generous with their time and assistance while I was writing this book. I greatly appreciate the help of Diane Moriarty in simplifying the maze of copyright law. I also want to thank: Darlene Sutro, Rensselaer County Historical Society in Troy, New York; Sergeant Major Moon, U.S. Military Academy Band Historian at West Point; Dr. Wright, U.S. Army Aviation Branch History Department at Fort Rucker, Alabama; and Whitney Lucas at Sotheby's in New York.

The staffs of the Greenburgh (N.Y.) Public Library and the White Plains Public Library were, as always, cordial and immensely helpful.

Special thanks to: Beatrice Cooper, who read the manuscript and made many wise editorial suggestions; Ezra Laderman, for shedding light on the language and habits of a composer; and Larry Heller, for answering my questions about his Army experiences in World War II.

I am especially grateful to my son-in-law, Andrew Blum, who looked over the manuscript and attempted to prevent me from playing fast and loose with medical procedures; to my daughters, Amy, Laura, and Jennifer, whose perceptive comments and patience in sharing their knowledge and professional expertise were invaluable.

And without the constant encouragement and support of my husband, Sheldon Segal, I seriously doubt that the skylark would be singing at all.

HARRIET SEGAL

Contents

❧ Chapter 1 ❧

Julia

The fishing fleet leaves port in darkness. It carries rough men with covetous eyes past Palm Island. Past the sleek motor launches and sailing yachts moored at the private docks of Pirates Cove, where their silhouettes are mirrored in the tidal waters of the lagoon.

In the gentle early hours, Palm Island is quite beautiful, faintly reminiscent of the Mediterranean coast. Silvery moonlight etches red terra-cotta roofs and pink stucco walls. Limpid blue swimming pools nestle among appropriately palmy foliage. Tennis courts lie half hidden behind hedges of tall flowering oleander. Across the picturesque inlet, the manicured perfection of an eighteen-hole championship golf course shimmers in the mist, revitalized in the night by automatic sprinklers fed by artesian wells.

If it seems a whit contrived, then it is a tastefully fashioned, subtle artifice. Steel fences, a gatehouse, and a sophisticated security system monitored by guards around the clock ensure that Palm Island remains, in the words of the sales prospectus, "a haven of privacy, a realm of serenity, secluded from an intrusive world."

Julia Rhinehart awoke with a dreadful start. She opened her eyes in darkness and lay perfectly still, conscious of the erratic

1

beating of her heart. She had been dreaming again, the same disturbing, elusive dream, and she tried to hold onto the edge of it. For an instant, there was a clear image, then it vanished, leaving a familiar longing. Clutching her pillow, she pulled the covers around her shoulders and turned over, trying to find a comfortable position, but knew she would not easily fall back asleep. This would be another one of those interminable nights.

Reaching over to the bedside table, she fumbled for the digital clock-radio her grandchildren had given her last Christmas, and turned its face in her direction. It was exactly three-thirty in the morning on the second of November, a scant month past her birthday, and Julia reflected that for the first time in sixty-eight years, she was alone. Completely, absolutely, *permanently* alone.

About a year ago, one wakeful night before the worst of it, George had said, "You're going to hate me for deserting you when this is finally over."

Seized with the raw stab of sorrow, she had protested, "Don't say that. How could I *ever* . . ."

There had been a time early in their marriage when George Rhinehart might have welcomed a display of fervent emotion from his wife, aware that his love for her was the stronger of the two, but on that occasion it seemed to alarm him. Brushing the tears from Julia's cheeks, he grasped her hand. "Scott will take care of you, my love. You know he's the son you can depend on."

"Yes, darling, I know."

When she moved closer, carefully, lest she cause him pain, he had taken her in his arms. "Oh, my sweet, I *so* wanted us to have more time."

Crying together, they had moved beyond pretense that night, and afterward they were able to discuss the future. A future without him. They even considered whether she should return to New York after George was gone, but he reminded her they had chosen Palm Island because it provided convenience, comfort, and security. Everything a couple would need for an active retirement and beyond—to that nebulous, golden old age they had always referred to as *The Rest of Our Lives*.

Obviously, they had known one of them was bound to die first. But it was always easier to deal in abstracts, wasn't it? Well, for heaven's sake, who ever thinks: *What if, after we move to Florida, my husband, who has always enjoyed vigorous good health, should develop a treacherous, lingering illness that drains our finances and leaves me a widow, with my family living at a great distance, and all of our oldest, dearest friends either gone or scattered to the winds?*

She had always been a reticent woman, but it would help now if there were someone to confide in, someone who would understand. Surely not one of her children. Despite what George had believed, they were all immersed in their own concerns and far removed from her. Even Scott. When he and Isobel were not flying to a distant capital for one of his important clients, they were relentlessly nourishing their social position in New York. Scott was the oldest and the most responsible of her offspring, but Julia never counted on him for more than a weekly phone call and sound financial advice.

Deborah then? Her only daughter would seem to be the natural confidante. Because Deborah was the last child and so much younger than the boys, she and Julia had been unusually close in earlier days. A mother and daughter sharing giggles and secrets throughout the years of music and ballet lessons, art classes and orthodontia, Halloween costumes, teenage crushes, and high school proms. Perhaps in the morning she should call Deborah in California.

Julia tried to imagine the conversation. "I am a woman without purpose, Deborah," she would say. "I have no role to play. For all of my life, I have never known a time when I had no responsibilities, until now. And I loathe it."

She could not help but smile at the thought of speaking in this fashion to her youngest child. Their wild-spirited nymph, pampered by all of them since birth, Deborah appeared to be coping with her father's death by pretending he was away on an extended trip, held up by an unforeseen delay in the conduct of a client's affairs, possibly to return at any moment. It was absurd to consider opening her soul to Deborah, who would no doubt recommend meditation.

What she really longed to do was to pick up the telephone and call Neil in Iowa City. But her second son was hard pressed just now to sort out his own life—bogged down in the manuscript of his new book; unhappy, she suspected, in his erratic love affair with Euphemia St. Clair, the volatile Jamaican author-in-residence at the Writers Workshop; and worried also about his son Kit, who was trying to make it as a musician in California. Neil would respond immediately to her call, as he always did, but the possibility of his rushing to Palm Island, most likely with Euphemia in tow, was more than she could entertain.

And yet . . . and yet, the idea had some appeal. Just to unburden herself.

Julia shook her head with impatience at the prospect of bringing her problems to *any* of her children. No, it was impossible. She had an absolute horror of becoming dependent on them. The sooner morning came and she absorbed herself in quotidian activity, the sooner she would put this foolish anxiety behind her. Why was it that everything seemed bleaker at night? "Troubles fade with the dawn," her intrepid grandmother used to say, and Eunice Perkins had been a woman who would have understood something about that.

Resigned that sleep would continue to elude her, Julia pressed the switch on the radio, rotating the knob until she found a station that had often helped them through the nights when George became restless. The announcer's folksy back-porch drawl droned over the air: " . . . there's lots more of your favorite music ahead, friends, but first, the news. The White House has announced a further buildup of American forces in the Persian Gulf. An airlift of reserve units is scheduled to depart from—"

Julia switched off the radio, accosted by unwelcome memories. With the congressional elections almost behind them, it was clear the government was gearing up for war. Were they headed for another Vietnam? If there was fighting in the Middle East, as she felt certain there would be, was it to be the surgical operation the administration was predicting, or would the United States be getting into another endless involvement in a part of the world that would forever despise them?

George, a steadfast patriot, would disapprove of her saying so, but thank heaven none of their grandchildren would have to go to Saudi Arabia. Chip and Ginger were safe at school, and Deborah's two, mere babes. As for her beloved Kit, just turned twenty, he had dropped out of Berkeley after his junior year. Stubborn and impetuous, he was, just like his father. But even if there should be a draft, Kit would never have to serve with American forces, for he was Canadian. Because of Vietnam.

Little had they dreamed in that dreadful autumn when Neil had gone north across the border, that it would be such a long and tortuous journey back. At last, she could think of what happened to him without bitterness, when for so many years it had caused her anguish. His book about the antiwar movement and its effect on his generation, published last year, had revealed the depths of the psychological wounds and had served to heal the rift in their family. She shivered involuntarily, remembering the sleepless nights when she would lie awake with a heaviness on her heart, staring into the dark, as she did now. Sighing with frustration, she forced the mournful thoughts from her mind.

A faint luminosity edged the windows where the drawn curtains met, promising that dawn would eventually come. The mood of the dream from which she had awakened so abruptly lingered on, hazy with disturbing images, like the frenetic frames of an old film. There had been danger; she had been afraid. Searching for her father, she had been unable to call out. Through a maze of corridors, a shadowy figure had pursued her relentlessly, overpowering her, subduing her. *Making love to her.* The skin on her forearms prickled, as her mouth formed a derisive smile. Imagine, an erotic dream at her age.

The house was quiet as a tomb. In the coolness of the November night, there was not even the soft whirr of air conditioning in the background. When they had first moved to Florida, the absence of night sounds had disturbed her. After the street noises of New York, a city that was never silent, the stillness had been unnerving. Even at their country place in Connecticut, if you strained your ears, you would hear the high whine of highway traffic in the distance, the hum of the furnace, the never-ceasing, companionable murmurs of an old house. But here on the Gulf Coast, she had never quite become accustomed to the silent nights.

A welcome feeling of lassitude came over Julia as her thoughts slowed down. She closed her eyes and finally fell into a light, dreamless sleep. At six-thirty, she rose to draw open the curtains. A fresh breeze blew in from the Gulf and she took a deep, grateful breath of salt air. Quickly stripping off her rumpled nightgown, she pulled a black Lycra tank suit over her trim figure. As she emerged from the house in a terry robe, a golden dawn shone on Pirates Cove, promising a glorious day.

At the edge of the pool, she dropped her wrap and snapped goggles in place. Leaning down to brace herself with one hand, she slipped easily into the water. With clean, strong strokes, she swam the first length, expertly maneuvering a kick turn without breaking her rhythm. Invigorated by motion, her body felt firm and loose-jointed, her mind alert. The boys would object if they knew she swam alone, but it had become as necessary as food and drink, this morning ritual, and she had an almost religious devotion to it.

Back and forth she plowed, keeping a steady pace, never pausing, until half an hour had passed. With a lithe movement, she sprang from the water, and tossed wet hair out of her eyes. Wrapped again in the robe, a little breathless, she turned to greet the sun.

The telephone was ringing when Julia stepped out of the shower onto an apricot chenille bath rug. Who would be calling this early, she wondered. Grabbing a towel, she ran across the bedroom and caught the receiver, but whoever it was had hung up.

"You're supposed to let it ring at least six times," she muttered, then laughed as she pictured George saying, *Calm down, honey. If it's important they'll call back.*

To which she would reply, *You know how impatient I am. I can't bear a phone to go unanswered.*

Then she would cross the room to the hospital bed, kiss him good morning, and if it was a good day, he might pull the towel away and begin to caress her. *Let's make out like a couple of horny kids*, he would growl. "Making out" was all he could muster after the second surgery . . .

She shook herself from her reverie. "Enough. I've got to get moving."

Talking to ourself now, are we? George's voice, heavy with irony, seemed to follow her to the dressing room.

The fantasies were becoming less frequent as time passed, she noted with both relief and regret. They were so vivid, these imaginary conversations with George, and there was much comfort in them. Yet she feared for her reason. Raised to keep her own counsel, she had never consulted a psychiatrist, but on her last trip to New York, she had mentioned them to Fred Neiman, their internist of many years as well as old family friend. "Do you think I ought to see someone, Fred?"

"If therapy would bring you comfort, then go ahead, but there's nothing abnormal about this, Julia. It's fairly common when we've lost someone to pretend he's still alive. During a period of denial, it's a way of holding onto the memory of a loved one. As long as you don't lose touch with reality—but I see no danger of that. You've always struck me as an innately sensible woman."

"That's you, a sensible woman," she said with a wry smile at her mirrored reflection as she finished applying moisturizer and sunscreen to her face and arms.

Ten minutes later, clad in khaki slacks and a loose shirt of sky blue Egyptian cotton, her still damp, silver-streaked brown hair brushed back into soft waves, Julia put on a pot of coffee, and went out to collect the morning paper. The sea calls of water birds, the burr of mowers on the golf course, and the distant throb of boat engines reminded her of the first promising year in Florida, when she and George would walk along the shore at sunrise.

A covered terrace fronted the house, with lush pots of bright pink hydrangeas grouped around the columns. Stopping to water them, she admired the splash of color, thinking how they flourished in the subtropical climate. She decided to take a breakfast tray to the screened patio, but no sooner had she settled at the glass-topped table with juice, coffee, and a toasted English muffin than the shrill sound of the telephone interrupted her. This time she reached the kitchen on the second ring.

"You sound rushed, Mother."

"Scott! Good morning, dear. How nice to hear from you." There was spontaneous pleasure in her voice, unexpected as it was for her son to be calling so early. "Don't tell me you're already in the office?"

"No, still at home. I'll be tied up in meetings for most of the morning, so thought I'd catch you now. Am I disturbing you?"

"Just starting breakfast. I have a golf date at nine."

"You're not overdoing it, Mother, with all the golf and tennis? A woman your age—"

"—is old enough to take care of herself," Julia finished crisply. "Don't fuss, Scott. I'm in perfect health and I know my limitations."

His sigh was pronounced; in fact, she suspected he made it especially audible, the way one would with a particularly recalcitrant child. "How are Isobel and the children?" she asked quickly, to divert him.

"Isobel has been talking about opening an art gallery with her friend Cece Bedford, but it's a lousy time to start a new business and I advised them against it. Oh, I forgot to tell you—Chip made varsity soccer at Williams. My son the jock," he boasted, in the hearty back-slapping manner of the clubman. "Ginger's in a sulk, I'm afraid. She wants our permission to spend a year working with Indians in Guatemala, but Isobel is against it."

Ginger, who would be graduating from Hotchkiss in June, was a strong-willed lass, as Julia well knew. "I thought she had her heart set on Princeton next year."

"She plans to defer if she's accepted. Isobel says she's too young to be on her own in a foreign country. I suspect she's afraid Ginger won't come back at the end of the year."

"Would you?" laughed Julia, looking longingly through the door at her cooling coffee. "I can tell there's something else on your mind, Scott."

"Well, yes, actually. I was hoping you might speak to Debbie. She's going through her money at the speed of light. I can't seem to get it into her head that there's a limit to the funds."

"What makes you think I have that much influence on your sister?"

"You certainly have more than *I* do. She was trying to reach me all day yesterday. I was tied up in meetings, but I know what she wants. Just last month she asked for a little something extra to tide her over until the end of the quarter . . ." Scott paused for effect. "Fifteen thousand was her idea of a little extra. Mind you, we have almost two months to go until the quarter ends."

"Whatever does she do with all that money?" mused Julia mildly, feeling the beginnings of a headache.

"How should I know? Supports that aging hippie she's supposedly married to." His voice became more agitated. "You'll never convince me that wedding was legal, Mother. The minister looked like an addict, standing out there in the field half-stoned, with the wind blowing through his dreadlocks."

"Don't work yourself up, Scott. You're never going to change Deborah, so why even try?"

"It's time she acted with some maturity. Debbie's no longer the cute, mod housewife from Scarsdale. She's a thirty-five-year-old woman with two children, for Christ's sake."

Julia massaged her throbbing temples. "You're too emotionally involved. I think George made a mistake when he appointed you trustee."

"She's damned lucky he did. The bank sure as hell would never let her have the extra money."

"So you will agree to send it to her?"

"Not until she accounts for the other payments. That's what I told her the last time she called, and she accused me of being manipulative. *Me*, manipulative! I just want her to demonstrate some fiscal responsibility. I thought if you would suggest that I'm not being unreasonable . . ."

The calm, alert purposefulness of Julia's swim had vaporized like the morning mist. "I'll try to bring it up when I talk to her, Scott. Indirectly. You know how Deborah resents it when I interfere in her life."

"Maybe you should have interfered more often. Debbie's a spoiled brat, Mother, always has been."

Her throat tightened. "But such a *darling* spoiled brat." She kept her voice light, not wanting to end on a controversial note. "Let's not argue about Deborah, dear."

"All right, all right . . ." Suddenly he brightened. "Oh, you'll never guess who I ran into at the museum benefit the other night."

"In that case, you'd better tell me."

"Gerald Ross," pronounced Scott, and Julia slowly sat on the edge of the kitchen stool as the vision flashed through her mind of a certain long-ago night. "He was looking pretty chipper for an old has-been. Must be well into his seventies, isn't he?"

"More like eighty, Scott." Considering her own age, she marveled at her son's choice of words.

"Whatever, he's amazing. Asked about you, sent his warmest regards."

Julia gave a funny little laugh. "Did he really?"

"Why do you say it like that?"

"Oh . . . he's never been one of my favorite people, if you must know. Nor do I believe is he a great admirer of mine."

"Well, you wouldn't have known from the way he spoke of you."

"I wasn't aware that you knew each other."

"Haven't seen him in a while, but we've been on some boards together in the past."

"I see."

"Gerry mentioned something of interest. I guess he assumed I knew. The Knowles Entertainment Group—which is a hot outfit—is backing a revival of *One Night in Venice*. It seems they acquired all those early musical properties when they took over Mitchell Publishing."

"Is that so?" Julia's voice sounded faint.

Scott, paying no heed, charged on. "That really bugs me," he said heatedly. "I'm thinking of consulting our copyright expert."

Her back stiffened. "About what?"

"Michael Shane wrote *One Night in Venice*. Why the hell should perfect strangers have all rights?"

"Evidently Michael sold all rights. I'm afraid he wasn't very businesslike, Scott. That was long before he engaged George to manage his affairs."

"Mitchell screwed him. No one would ever get away with something like that nowadays."

"I suppose not, but it was common practice back then. He was young and he needed the money. You'd be surprised what an unrecognized composer will do to get his work before the public."

"I don't see how you can be so charitable; it makes me mad as hell." Scott's anger vanished as quickly as it had come. His voice took on a casual, offhand note that she recognized. "Mother . . . seeing Gerry Ross got me to thinking. Do you remember when we were young, you used to tell us about a bunch of missing manuscripts, some of Michael's unpublished music?"

"Yes, Michael worked feverishly until the end. He was in such a hurry, he knew he hadn't much time. There were stacks of finished compositions, several notebooks full of musical sketches. More than many composers produce in a lifetime . . ." She caught herself, realizing she was in danger of rambling on. "But I'm surprised *you* remember, Scott. You never seemed to take much interest whenever I spoke of it."

"I was just a kid then, I didn't have the sense to understand." She listened carefully for a hint of his motive, but he sounded innocent enough, lost in thought. "Did you know there are plans for a seventy-fifth birthday salute to Michael Shane at Lincoln Center?"

"Actually, I was told a while ago there might be, but I haven't heard anything definite."

"Well, it's in the works because Gerry is on the committee. There's been a great revival of interest in Michael's music."

"So I've heard." Where was this leading? she wondered.

"I can tell you that Peter Duchin plays Shane medleys, along with Gershwin and Porter, at every affair we attend. Do you realize what an original score with Michael's handwritten notations would be worth today? New stuff, all fresh material." Julia remained silent. "Mother, are you still there?"

"Yes, Scott, I'm here. I don't really see the point of discussing something so hypothetical. I've told you that the manuscripts were lost."

"They have to be *somewhere*. A bulk of work doesn't just disappear. Quite obviously they were stolen, but who do you think took them? What do you suppose happened to them?"

"I haven't the faintest idea." Which was not exactly true, but why get into that?

"You know, Mother, you're not the most organized person. Are you certain they're not among your papers?"

"They're not," she said firmly, struggling not to show her annoyance. Perhaps Scott was entitled to an explanation. "We went through Michael's studio after his death, examining every scrap of paper. In fact, George kept everything for years in the attic in Norwalk. There were dozens of file boxes crammed with papers."

"What happened to the files?"

"After we sold the house, anything worth keeping was stored with the Rhinehart furniture at the Morgan warehouse. George always meant to have Michael's papers catalogued, but when he became ill . . ."

"They're not still at Morgan Brothers after all this time?"

"Heavens, no. You remember when we distributed the family pieces, I think it was about four years ago. You and Isobel took the Japanese screens, the Sheraton table and chairs, and—"

"Yes, yes," he interrupted impatiently, "we love all those things."

"Well, at the same time most of the files were sent to Neil."

"Why Neil?"

"Your brother expressed an interest in Michael's papers and George thought he would be the perfect archivist. After all, he's a historian, and he also knows a great deal about musicology." She could not prevent an edge from creeping into her voice. "Is there a purpose to this inquiry?"

"Just curiosity. It makes no sense that Michael's unfinished manuscripts never surfaced. Why would anyone have taken them unless there was an intention to publish?"

"I suppose we shall never know," Julia said with a note of finality. "Truly, Scott, it's so very long ago, I can scarcely recall the details. I was twenty-seven at the time, with two little boys to care for and so many other problems, that was the least of them. Why bring it up now?"

"I'm sorry, Mother." His attempt to sound contrite did not quite succeed. "It's just that—well, Michael Shane *was* my father. Naturally, his music would mean everything to me."

Julia almost laughed. *Is that so?* she said aloud after they had hung up. *Since when?*

As she spilled out the cold coffee in the sink and rinsed her breakfast dishes she tried to rid herself of a feeling of agitation. The conversation had upset her. Julia knew all of her children well, understanding both their strengths and their weaknesses. She would like to believe it was simply filial devotion that drove Scott, but that was not his way. Scott had something more in mind.

❧ Chapter 2 ❧

Scott

Scott's hand rested on the receiver after he had said goodbye to his mother. A vague mood of disquiet settled on him as he sat at the desk in his study, with the filtered morning light flickering through the curtained windows of his Fifth Avenue apartment.

He was beginning to think that for him, the most ordinary pastime had become riddled with complications. Always he had been the one in command of himself and others, but lately he had the uncomfortable sense that he was losing the advantage. The talk with his mother was just the latest example.

As was his custom when a negotiation went awry, he mentally reviewed the exchange. It had been a mistake to inquire so directly about the missing musical scores. When he had dialed Julia's number before going into breakfast, it was with no intention of discussing Michael Shane's music, but the subject had come up spontaneously. Before he knew it he was asking about the lost manuscripts, and her voice had taken on that careful, skeptical tone. Whenever his mother became frosty and correct, it meant that she had reached the limits of her patience.

Her suspicions were understandable, he was willing to concede. He had probably sounded grasping, solely interested in the royalty considerations of his father's works, when that was *not at all* his primary concern. It was Julia who was his chief consideration. There was also the principle of rightful ownership at stake. But he should have waited for the appropriate moment to raise the issue, or at the very least he should have properly explained his objectives. He prided himself on his subtlety, but—*Let's face it, fella, you blew it.*

It might fairly be said that Scott Rhinehart had seldom in his life made an ill-considered move since the spring of his eleventh year, when he was mugged on his way home from the Buckley School. With the streetsmart instincts of a city kid, he had surrendered his money but unwisely suggested his three attackers should leave the new shockproof, water-resistant sports watch, a birthday present from his stepfather. Knocked down, roughed up, and stomped on for his temerity, he received his first shiner and learned a valuable lesson: Quit when the odds are against you.

As the decades passed, his course became as carefully plotted as the investment strategies for the capital funds and trusts he would govern. His modus operandi was to weigh and evaluate every decision. He had a plan for everything and was accustomed to all going according to plan.

Was it any wonder, then, that the loss of control over the destinies of his children once they passed adolescence dismayed him? His son Chip had been turned down at Yale following a less than stellar academic record at Andover, upsetting plan number one. After all the years of active fundraising for his alma mater, Scott was incensed, and had fired off an irate letter to the director of admissions, accomplishing nothing except the satisfaction of having the last word. The boy had settled for Williams, which Scott considered second-rate, one of those marginal schools on the fringe of the Ivies. But true to the college counselor's predictions, in his sophomore year Chip was becoming a student leader on the small campus, providing his father some measure of pride.

Ginger, at least, was a top student with a forceful personality to match. She was breezing through Hotchkiss, elected president of her class, a "likely" for an Early Decision acceptance at Princeton. But she had thrown them with her latest bizarre proposal to work with a student anti-poverty program in Central America before going to college.

"Will she *ever* do what is expected of her?" cried Isobel who, much to Scott's surprise, was already seated at the breakfast table when he entered the room, a rare morning occurrence. Still smarting from a quarrelsome telephone conversation with Ginger the previous evening, she was in a testy mood. A preview of the season's early debutante parties on the society page of the New York *Times* did nothing to elevate her spirits. "She's as pigheaded about the Guatemala thing as she was about not coming out," she said, slapping the offending news item with the back of her hand.

Out of habit, Scott sprang to his daughter's defense. "Don't start on that again, Isobel. Ginger says only dweebs come out these days."

She gave him a withering look. "Please, Scott, spare me. If you only knew how ridiculous you sound when you try to be hip."

"For Christ's sake, Iz!" He knew it rankled when he called her Iz, but she was forever putting him down. He quickly finished his grapefruit and pushed away from the table.

Isobel's hopes for a debutante daughter had been dashed when Ginger refused to be presented at any of the cotillions or even to allow them to give a small dance in her honor. Most bitter of all, Isobel had been forced to decline *Town & Country*'s offer to do an article featuring Ginger with her mother and grandmother, three generations to have been presented to New York society. "I still say we should have insisted on the Christmas Ball," she continued, following him to the front hall. "It's a big, glamorous event. She would have loved it."

"When are you going to stop bellyaching about a ridiculous dance? What the hell does it matter?"

"That's fine for *you* to say. Your sister didn't make a debut, but it's a tradition in my family. And now this poverty program in Guatemala, of all places. Who is she going to meet in that godforsaken country? What will Mother and Daddy say?"

"Bugger Mother and Daddy," muttered Scott under his breath, as he donned his Burberry topcoat and prepared to leave. Isobel's father was getting on his nerves lately, at seventy-two still butting into everything at the office. When was the old boy going to retire, the way a reasonable man would? Curbing his annoyance, he leaned down to place a perfunctory kiss on his wife's cheek. "I'll see you tonight, dear. Do we have anything on?"

"Dinner with the Burdens, and the Kidney recital. I promised Cece we'd go, so please don't be late. She's giving a reception afterward."

As he rode down in the elevator, Scott asked himself again why his well-ordered life had changed, how there had come to be so much rancor in his household. They never used to quarrel. Until about a year ago he could count on his home to be a center of tranquility, but now it was a constant whirlpool of dissent. Last week they had argued over the art gallery, but fortunately Isobel seemed to have forgotten that foolish idea. She had become impossible lately, restless and irritable, dissatisfied with anything he or the children did or said. Although he took the daily confrontations of the professional world in stride, actually enjoying the challenge of a tax battle, he disliked turmoil in his personal life.

He seemed to be at loggerheads with everyone these days. Especially his sister. Perhaps his mother was right; perhaps his stepfather had made a mistake in appointing him to act as Debbie's trustee. They had seen the world in the same light, he and George Rhinehart. Scott had loved and deeply admired the man who had been a true father to him. Unfortunately, George's one blind spot had been the indulgence of his only daughter.

Debbie was a hellion. Even as a young girl she had chafed under Scott's tutelage, and now he, her elder half-brother, had been given oversight of her assets. If Deborah complained that he was a skinflint, as she was wont to do, it could upset the balance with the rest of the family. Not necessarily with Julia. He got along well with his mother, who was an independent woman. Too independent, in Scott's opinion. Granted, she had built a life for herself in Florida and possessed the virtue of never interfering in the affairs of her children, which was more than he could say for his in-laws. But after what Julia had told him this morning, this was not the time to jeopardize the relationship with Neil, when he needed to stay on his brother's good side. They had grown apart over the years, which was only natural, considering all the trouble Neil had caused. Even when they were boys, they had been careful with each other. A rivalry must always have been there, and Scott admitted to himself that he had taken a certain small satisfaction in hearing that Neil's son had left Berkeley in September without earning a degree. By comparison, Chip seemed less of a failure for not having made Yale.

The elevator doors opened on the lobby, where Enriqué, their cook's husband, who ordinarily waited in front of the building with the Mercedes to drive Scott to his office, was red-faced and gesticulating, embroiled in a heated argument with the doorman. "Is my job on the line, asshole, not yours! You should not permit that they park there, block me in—"

"What," asked Scott, "seems to be the trouble?"

The doorman smiled with relief at the appearance of Mr. Rhinehart, a reasonable gentleman. "Mrs. Chandler's grand-daughters are using her apartment for the winter while the old lady—that is, Mrs. Chandler—is in Palm Beach. They're moving their stuff in and . . . and—well, there you can see for yourself, sir." He threw up his hands in resignation, gesturing toward the entrance.

A green Range Rover with no driver in sight, crammed with Louis Vuitton luggage and T. Anthony leather duffle bags, had apparently disgorged a vast array of cross-country and downhill skis, tennis rackets, stereo equipment, and a veritable rain forest of trailing green plants, usurping the parking area in front of the building and the adjacent sidewalk beneath the awning, and effectively cutting off all access to 957 Fifth Avenue.

"You know the building doesn't permit this, Tony. Why didn't you tell them to park on the side street and use the service elevator?"

"I tried, Mr. Rhinehart, believe me, I tried. They pay no attention. I mean, it's hard, y'know, like it's *Mrs. Chandler* we're dealing with."

"Mrs. Chandler is no different from any of the other owners, despite what she may think. When her granddaughters come down, tell them the president of the cooperative insists they use the freight elevator."

Tony's glum expression brightened. "Here they are now. Maybe you could tell them yourself."

Two most glamorous creatures, with voluminous lengths of wheat-colored hair framing their faces like skeins of silk, burst from the elevator, carelessly pushing the building's ornate brass luggage trolley and causing the other passengers to give them a wide berth. Both wore supple brown leather boots and oversized fisherman's sweaters that stopped just below the hips. In faded designer jeans, their legs seemed endless. Laughing boisterously, they steered the cart across the carpeted marble lobby, casting imperious glances at the three men.

Scott cleared his throat. "I'm afraid, young ladies, you will have to avail yourselves of the service elevator to move your belongings into Mrs. Chandler's apartment. You see, the rules of the co-op are very strict about—"

"Frankly, my dear sir, we don't give a shit about the rules of the co-op," said the taller and more striking of the two.

Scott's jaw dropped as the girls, who looked no older than his daughter, exited through the glass doors, wheeled the cart to the Range Rover and proceeded to unload plants, sporting gear, and suitcases. Suddenly, all the frustrations of the morning blended into one uncontrollable force. He was seized with a blinding, tearing rush of anger. Who the hell were these vixens? Where did they get the gall to address *him* in such a disrespectful manner? He was the president of the cooperative and he would take the matter before the board. It never failed—the richer and more social the family, the worse the breeding. Well, Roberta Chandler, widow of polo-playing ex-ambassador Curtis Chandler, had better tell her fucking granddaughters to wise up. Their behavior was unacceptable in this building.

"Lock the main entrance," he ordered Tony. "Let everyone use the side door until those two are moved in. Any complaints, refer them to me." With that, he left the lobby, Enriqué in his wake, and slammed into the back seat of the Mercedes. Enriqué had to maneuver to get out of the parking space and around the Range Rover. As they pulled away, Scott took grim satisfaction in the spectacle of two blond females shouting through the glass doors at a stone-faced Tony who had locked them out.

"Helluva way to start the day," Scott remarked to his driver.

"Yessir."

As the car moved into the line of traffic crawling down Fifth Avenue, Scott settled back in the seat with the morning papers. He leafed through the Metro section of the *Times*, pausing to glance at the pictures that had earlier captured Isobel's attention. A private dance held at the St. Regis to honor one of the season's debutantes. The father was a banker he knew, and he felt a momentary stab of envy that the man's daughter was fulfilling her parents' expectations in being presented to society. Scott was damned if he would admit he had wanted the debut as much as his wife had. Envisioning himself at the presentation in white tie and tails, graced with the decorations he had received from two foreign governments, he had been keenly disappointed when Ginger refused to make her bow. Of course, the two young women he had just encountered were probably typical of modern debutantes, and he would sooner his daughter walked naked through Times Square than behave like them, but that did not prevent him from wishing he were going to be among the fathers at the Christmas Ball at the Waldorf-Astoria, with Ginger on his arm in a frothy white cotillion gown.

As long as Scott could remember, he had wanted whatever at the moment he did not possess: A brother. His own bedroom. In a cozy house on a tree-lined street in a small town, with a bunch of pals playing catch on the lawn. A father who had time for him. A father.

When he was a nine-year-old lad and George Rhinehart was courting his mother, he had pinned his hopes and longings on that kindly man. In 1952 Julia and George married, and it seemed as if all Scott's private yearnings might at last be met. They moved into the fourteen-room apartment on Park Avenue that George had, until her death, shared with his dowager mother. Scott was given not only his own bedroom but a large playroom for himself and Neil. During the week he attended Buckley, and on weekends they drove to Norwalk where he was quite content with the sprawling old white-pillared country house with a view of Long Island Sound that had been in the Rhinehart family for three generations.

When George adopted the boys, Scott was told—Neil being too young to understand—that they would be considered his sons under the law. "It's for your protection," explained George. "I love you and your brother just as if I were your real dad, and I want to be certain you will always be taken care of." The phrase "under the law" had assumed almost magical implications.

"Will I have the same name as you?" asked Scott, who had a precocious knowledge of stepfathers, considering that fully one quarter of the students at Buckley were living with their mothers' second husbands.

"It's up to you, Scott. Why don't you think about it for a while and if that's what you decide, I'd be honored to have you take my family name."

When he returned to school in the fall, he was registered as Scott Rhinehart, and for a week endured the taunts of classmates, "Shane, Shane, everybody knows your name." Only in his years at boarding school had he become aware that he may not have settled for the better bargain. Rhinehart, while a sound enough name in Manhattan, had another sort of disadvantage. He was forever having to explain that he was not *actually* Jewish himself. By the time he met Isobel it hardly mattered, for in the liberal sixties George Rhinehart was on every important civic committee and a great number of boards, and Isobel Prescott had fallen head over heels for the tall, handsome young summer associate at her father's law firm . . .

Lost in reverie, Scott was surprised to see that they had reached the midtown building where the law offices of Prescott, Spencer & Colwood occupied six upper floors. As he left the elevator on the senior partners' floor and walked down the corridor to his corner suite, the elegant persian carpets and traditional furnishings gave Scott the same sense of solidity they had when he began his career there after graduating with joint law and business degrees from Harvard.

"Good morning, Mr. Rhinehart," Hazel Cassidy, his secretary of fifteen years, greeted him. "Your sister called again last night after you left. I told her to try you at home."

"We were out for the evening," he replied, knowing Deborah preferred to phone him at the office on the off-chance she might have to speak to Isobel if she called the apartment. Hazel was probably cognizant of that, for she knew a great deal about their lives, having kept his appointments calendar, balanced his checkbook, and handled his personal correspondence for many years. Scott took her devotion completely for granted, aware that she was a little in love with him. A few men of his acquaintance were having affairs with their secretaries, but he had long ago determined that there was no place for sex in the office. He had hired Hazel because she was a crackerjack legal secretary, plain of face, dignified of manner, and a solid six years his senior. Their social contact was limited to gifts at Christmas (selected by Isobel), flowers on her birthday, and the offer of a week each June at their Sagaponack house, which she used to treat her similarly unmarried sister.

Hazel handed him a sheaf of messages and an index card on which his schedule had been typed. "Your ten o'clock has been canceled. The conference on the Cartwright stock bequest had to be postponed because Mr. Ehrlander was called back to Virginia."

The meeting could not take place without Enno Ehrlander, treasurer of the Cartwright Foundation, to which Scott was chief counsel and investments advisor. "Did they say why?"

"No, but it was unexpected, I gather."

"I hope it's not the IRS. All we need is another audit." Every major foundation's tax status was constantly under surveillance by the Internal Revenue Service, a legacy of the sixties, when President Nixon's people waged a vendetta against McGeorge Bundy, a Kennedy loyalist, then president of the Ford Foundation.

"You can use the time to finish the report on Rancho American Resorts," Hazel suggested.

"All right," he agreed, but then changed his mind. "No, there's something else I want to take care of. See if the new associate in intellectual properties is free and ask her to come up to my office. What's her name?"

"Jane Downey," said Hazel, picking up the telephone. Scott went into his office, hung his coat in the closet, and set his heavy briefcase on the cabinet behind his desk. Almost immediately Hazel followed, a pad in hand to jot down notes for the day. "Jane will be up in a few minutes."

Scott pulled a sheaf of papers from his briefcase and handed them to Hazel. "Better look these over to be certain my edits are legible. Call Jeff Wheeler, tell him I'll have the appraisal of the art collection in the Girard estate by next Friday. Set up a meeting for that morning, if he can make it, and reserve a table for lunch in the partners' dining room . . ." He consulted his schedule and calendar. "What's this at four-thirty today?"

"Clive Westbrook, the journalist who interviewed you for *Fortune*. You agreed to see him again to answer some follow-up questions about tax exemption for his book."

"Oh yes, I'd forgotten about that." He was reminded of Isobel's parting request not to be late for dinner. "Call my wife and find out what the drill is tonight. If it's black tie, she'll have to send Enriqué down with my dinner jacket . . ." Scott continued giving instructions and dictated the gist of several letters, leaving the wording to Hazel, who was accomplished at legal correspondence. He glanced at his watch. "It's too early to call my sister in California, I suppose."

"I would think so. I'll place the call at eleven, eight o'clock her time. All right?"

"Sure. She ought to be finished paying her respects to the sun by then." Hazel, who shared his exasperation with Deborah's enthusiasm for Eastern religions and communal living, grinned appreciatively at Scott's sarcasm.

There was a soft knock and a dark-haired young woman in a severe navy blue suit appeared in the doorway. "You wanted to see me, Mr. Rhinehart?"

"Come in, Jane." Jane Downey was the first female associate from Fordham Law School to have been hired by the firm. She did not fit the mold of Prescott, Spencer & Colwood, but while a summer associate had proved so capable that Scott, who was serving as hiring partner that year, had said the hell with it and made her an offer in her final term at Fordham. "That'll be it for now, Hazel. See that we're not disturbed."

Hazel left the room and closed the door. "Sit down, Jane," said Scott. "This will be a personal pro bono matter. I'd like you to look into the copyright laws pertaining to musical compositions. The scenario is this: A young composer wrote and arranged songs for a music publisher on a work-for-hire arrangement without any formal agreement. He got paid a flat fee for his songs, which were published as sheet music, for which he received no royalties. A theatrical company formed by the publisher presented one of his first musical plays." Jane was furiously taking notes, frowning in concentration.

"Am I going too fast?"

"No," she said, still writing.

"With time, the composer became successful, was represented by an agent and retained the rights to his works. He wrote a number of Broadway hits, but when he died at an early age, much of his music died with him. Recently an entertainment group has acquired the assets and properties of the original company that published the composer's early works, including the musical play, which they intend to revive—are you following me?"

"Uh, yes, but it would be helpful if I knew where this is leading. What are we after? Also, I need to know when this took place—in what years the composer did his work and which copyright act would apply, 1909 or 1976."

"Right. Most of his music was composed from about 1935 until 1950, when he died. The musical in particular was written around '38, and was performed for a limited engagement in 1939. What I'm looking for is a loophole, if you will, in the law that would give the composer's heirs a right to that or other properties."

"You mean properties for which he did not register the copyright during his lifetime?"

"That is correct. If he didn't actually sign over the rights, who would be the owner?"

"Let's see, if the musical was written in 1938, that's fifty-one years. It could be in the public domain if the copyright wasn't renewed. Under the new law it would be protected for fifty years after his death. When did you say that was?"

"He died in 1950. Forty years ago." Scott's eyes shifted to a group of photographs on his bookshelf. Among them was a publicity shot of Michael Shane that he had once discovered between stacks of old sheet music in George Rhinehart's house.

"Is there existing proof of someone else owning the copyright or of an agreement between the composer and the publisher giving the publisher all rights?"

Jane's question brought him back to the present. "Whatever papers exist are in archives. I can gain access, but meanwhile why don't you see what kind of cases are out there and how the law applies thus far? See if there's precedent for the family recovering rights."

When Jane had left, Scott swiveled in his chair and gazed out the window of his forty-third-floor office at the cityscape of Manhattan looking west toward the Hudson River. By investigating the copyrights of Michael Shane's music, he reassured himself, he was protecting family interests and standing up for the principle of rightful inheritance. He was performing a service for his mother and brother, and preserving

Michael's heritage. Wasn't it his duty as the elder son to do so? His mother was naive to accept the loss of all rights to Michael's early works. He dismissed the possibility that it could be painful for her to dwell on that period of her life. Surely any feelings of sorrow from the death of her first husband had long since dissipated. After all, she had been happily married to George Rhinehart for thirty-eight years.

Scott turned back to his desk. One of the qualities that had earned him a place among the top tax attorneys in the country was his ability to rid his mind of residual matters and concentrate solely on the task at hand. Opening a folder, he put aside all thought of the copyrights to his father's works and became deeply immersed in an estate situation that tapped the best of his talents—the passing of the assets of the last heir to the Cartwright fortune to the foundation that bore the family name.

He had been working for twenty minutes when his buzzer sounded. "Yes, Hazel?"

"I won't have to place that call to California after all."

"Why not?"

"Because your sister is on the phone. Shall I put her through?"

He was not looking forward to this conversation with Deborah, but he had no choice. "Yes, go ahead."

"Scotty?" She spoke with that same breathless rush of energy characteristic of her even when she was a baby.

"Hi, Debs, how are you?"

"Couldn't be better. And you? Still grinding it out in the great stone canyons of the Big Apple?"

"It's not sunny California, but we do manage to see daylight."

"I feel for you, brother dear."

"I heard you've been trying to reach me. We were about to call, but I thought I'd let you get your beauty sleep."

"Thoughtful Scott. I know you've been hoping to avoid me."

"Debbie, that's not true."

"Why is it I don't believe you?" Despite her teasing manner, he felt she had read his thoughts.

"Come on, Debs, don't be nasty. Tell me what it is this time."

"You know very well what it is. I need money, Scott."

"I just sent you a check."

"That was over a month ago."

"Fifteen thousand dollars is a hell of a lot of money to go through in one month."

"Oh, Scott . . ."

"I cannot condone your spendthrift ways, Deb. At this rate the money won't last ten years, and that's not what was meant to happen."

"*I need money!*"

He flinched in the face of her fury. "What do you need it for?"

"That's none of your business. Daddy did not intend for you to be a surrogate parent to me. You're supposed to invest the funds and distribute them to me as needed. *As needed*, Scott."

"*In my best judgment*, Deb. Don't forget that. George relied on me to use discretion to protect your interests."

"What are you supposed to protect me from? No one's taking advantage of me, Scott."

"You wouldn't know if they were."

"I have two children to feed and clothe. Your family goes through fifteen thousand in one spring break on the slopes at Aspen."

"That is not the issue," he said tightly. "What about your husband?"

"What about him?"

"Doesn't he contribute to the support of his family?"

"Of course he contributes. How do you think we live? California is the most expensive state in the country. Everything costs more here—rent, food, shoes, clothing. And don't forget, he's supporting another man's child."

"Brent sends you child support, doesn't he?"

"Not nearly enough. Rich people are the tightest when it comes to someone else."

"All right, Debbie, I get the point. I'm going to have to refuse—"

Deborah interrupted, her anxiety apparent. "Wait, please don't say anything until I explain."

"There's always an explanation, isn't there? If nothing else, I have to admire your powers of invention."

"Are you going to *listen* to me? You haven't even heard what I have to say."

"What did I tell you about giving me an accounting of the last two payments? You've got to stop this crazy spending, Debbie. You're living way beyond your means."

"We are *not* living beyond our means. That money went for necessities. The baby was sick, and we had to pay doctor's bills. Wendy's in private school and she needs braces, our medical insurance doesn't cover orthodontia. Not only that, we've moved—I know I should have told you this before, and I would have, except you're always so preachy. I didn't want you saying, 'If you'd listened to me in the first place, Debbie, I could have told you it wouldn't work.'"

Scott winced at her perfect mimicry of his sanctimonious tone. "Well, you were right," Deborah continued. "We left the ashram. We've been renting a wonderful house in Carmel Valley. The owner has suddenly decided to sell and he's given us an option at a very good price. That's really why we need the money. Jergen is short of cash right now because he's opening another center for holistic healing. It seems crazy to take on an enormous debt when that money is just sitting in my trust."

"What makes you think your money is 'sitting' anywhere? It's *working* for you, Deborah—growing, earning interest and dividends. You do know what those are, don't you? I mean, in your carefree, nonmaterialistic little world out there, you do know that people no longer keep cash under the mattress?"

"Who did you say was being nasty? Of course I know it's invested. What do you think I am, stupid?" Her voice became less strident. "There's so much money there, Scott. It's not as if it doesn't belong to me. It will come to me eventually anyway, but I need it *now*, not in five years."

"You're only entitled to a portion of the assets when you turn forty. The rest remains in trust for your children. Don't you realize you are squandering their future when you deplete the principal? Dare I mention that you receive a regular income—a most *generous* income?"

"I *know*, I know. I meant I need a chunk of my inheritance right now. I can't wait for the next quarterly payment."

"Why not? It's only two months away."

"Because the owner has another offer on this house. Without a down payment we'll lose it, and we adore living here. It's exactly what we want, on a hillside with a long view of the mountains and the valley. So peaceful, so good for the inner being."

"I'll bet it is," he scoffed. "Jergen must sit and meditate all day, staring at the beautiful view."

"That's unfair, Scott, and you know it. Jergen works hard and his healing center is a huge success. Tons of Hollywood celebrities come to Monterey just for a few days at The Well. It's not just another health spa, you know. Perk and Del Hopper swear by it. They claim it's better than going to a shrink or taking tranquilizers."

"Look, Deb, I would be derelict if I released more money before the year end. I'd have to sell securities, you'd lose your earnings. It would be fiscally irresponsible."

"I don't need very much," she said in a small voice.

That waiflike manner always could get to him. "How much?"

"Only fifty thousand."

"*Fifty thousand! Are you crazy?*" He was practically apoplectic.

"We have to put twenty percent down, Scott," she explained in a painstakingly reasonable manner that for some reason made him even more furious. "Jergen has the rest."

"No, Deborah. Absolutely not."

"Scott, *please . . .*"

"Debbie, I cannot do this. It would be questioned by the bank. They are co-trustees and this is not within the guidelines of what George intended."

"I think Daddy was *cruel* to arrange things so I have to come begging to you. How do you think it makes me feel?"

"He did what he thought was in your best interest," said Scott stiffly.

"Well, I'm sure he wouldn't want his grandchildren to be denied a roof over their heads."

"Oh, God, now we'll have a little drama . . . some tears, maybe."

"You're a *shit*, Scott, do you know that? You and Isobel spend more money on one evening of dinner and theater than we do for a whole week of groceries—and you have the nerve to talk to *me* about being extravagant. Where is it written that I have to scrounge like a pauper while you live it up on Fifth

Avenue? You've always been a selfish bastard—"

"Thirty thousand."

"—always cared only for yourself. As long as you—what did you say?"

"I said I'll let you have thirty thousand and not a cent more. I'll advance a personal loan until the dividends come through. But this is it, Deb. I warn you, if you ask again, I'll hang up."

"Oh, Scotty, dear, thank you. That's very sweet of you and I do appreciate it."

"I hope so."

"I do, really. Will you forgive me? I didn't mean what I said about you being selfish. I was angry. How are the kids? And Isobel?"

"They're all fine, thanks. And your children? Wendy and . . . and . . ."

"Ramdas. But you can call him Richard. That's his given name."

"Oh. I didn't know that."

"Well, of course," she said in an injured tone. "You didn't think we were foolish enough to put Ramdas on his birth certificate, did you?"

"To tell you the truth, Debs, I never know what to think when it comes to you. You'll give me an ulcer before I'm through with this." Scott sighed. "Have you any idea how worried I am about you? When are you going to get your life straightened out?"

"I am, Scott. I mean, it's coming together. You'd be pleased, really pleased, if you could see us. I know I did some crazy things, and I'm sorry for the unhappiness I've caused . . ." Here her voice broke, and he knew she was thinking of her dead father, whom she had adored. "Things are much, much better. Great, really. The best they've ever been."

"I wish I could believe you."

"You just wait until we get this house all freshly painted and fixed up. There's loads of room and I'll invite you out, you and Isobel, and you'll see for yourself how terrific everything is."

Scott was not sure that would be a welcome excursion, particularly for Isobel, but he took heart from Deborah's words. She did sound different somehow, more purposeful and mature.

Getting away from the ashram where she and Jergen had been living, with what Scott considered an appalling lack of privacy or amenities, could only be an improvement.

"Remember, I expect a full accounting, Debbie. According to the terms of the trust, you are required to furnish a report on how you spend any funds other than the regular quarterly distribution."

"You'll have it, Scotty, I promise. Just as soon as we wrap it all up with the bank and set the closing. Bye-bye, and thanks muchly."

Scott did not have time to dwell on his difficulties with Deborah because as soon as he hung up, Hazel came in to tell him there was a call from Washington. "It's Burton McKiever."

"McKiever? Do we know him?"

"Sort of. He's the White House assistant who left to form his own consulting firm, says he's calling at the suggestion of Senator Wade."

Scott raised an eyebrow and reached for the telephone, but Hazel stopped him, laying a hand on his arm. "Wait a second until I make sure he's on the horn," she said, her eyes twinkling, "I think they go for that stuff."

Hazel, who enjoyed the fine art of one-upmanship, returned to her desk and picked up the receiver. "Mr. McKiever?"

"Is Mr. Rhinehart on the line?" asked a secretary.

"Just as soon as your boss is," Hazel replied.

Evidently the woman knew when she had been bested. A man with a nasal twang came on, "This is Burton McKiever."

"Please hold for Mr. Rhinehart," answered Hazel, counting to twenty and buzzing Scott. "Mr. McKiever is on the line." She gave a satisfied little smirk before turning back to her word processor.

It was half past five when Clive Westbrook shut off his tape recorder and slipped a notebook and ballpoint pen into the pocket of his tweed sport jacket. "I guess that about covers it."

Westbrook was a respected chronicler of business and politics for major newspapers and magazines. He had written a bestselling treatise on the Japanese automobile industry and was collecting material on tax laws for his next project, a book on American philanthropy. Scott ordinarily avoided reporters, but he found Westbrook an enormously engaging and well-informed man. Despite Hazel's subtle reminder that he had to return phone calls before dressing for dinner, he spent some minutes after the interview chatting with the journalist. "Sorry to break this up," he finally said, "I have an appointment."

Westbrook zipped up the canvas rucksack he carried and prepared to leave. "Thanks for your time. By the way, did Solange Didier get the photographs for the *Fortune* piece?"

Scott nodded. "She came up last week."

"We've collaborated on a number of articles. You'll find her work exceptional."

Modesty prevented Scott from volunteering the information that two days after photographing him in his office, the Didier woman had called with a request for him to come to her studio for a sitting. "I've printed some of the shots we took the other day," she had told him, "and you are unusually photogenic. I'd like to include you in a series I'm doing on men." The photographer's warm throaty voice, intriguingly tinged with a French accent, had been extremely persuasive. Aware that he was succumbing to flattery, Scott had agreed to pose for her.

He ushered the writer to the outer office and was surprised to see that his secretary was still at her desk. "I thought you had left, Hazel."

"Not yet. Your dinner clothes have arrived. I waited to see if you needed anything else."

"Nothing, thanks. You can go home now."

"Don't you want me to place your calls?"

"No, I'll do that myself." Sometimes Hazel could be a pain in the ass. Seemed to think he was incapable of attending to anything without her. In no hurry to leave, she shuffled papers and made a project of clearing her desk. Scott was on the phone when she finally appeared at the door in her coat and waved goodnight.

Enno Ehrlander, the Cartwright treasurer, was explaining that the sudden illness of the foundation's president had made it necessary to cancel the meeting of the investment committee that morning. "What sort of illness?" Scott inquired.

"We don't know. Bob was on his way back from Africa and felt rotten on the plane. He's gone to Hopkins for tests."

"Must have picked up something in the food."

"Probably. We'll have to reschedule our meeting. With Bob out, I'd just as soon stay in Alexandria. Would you mind coming down here?"

"Not at all. What about next Tuesday? I'll have the report on the Rancho American stock."

"Excellent. I'll see you then."

Scott leaned back in his swivel chair and stretched to get the kinks out of his muscles. The firm kept a small exercise room with a few pieces of Nautilus equipment upstairs, next to the partners' conference room. He was preparing to work out for an hour before showering and changing for the evening, when his night line rang.

"Rhinehart."

"Oh, Mr. Rhinehart, I'm glad I caught you. It's Jane Downey."

"Yes, Jane." It did not surprise him that the young woman was still in the office—she probably had a long night ahead of her. The associates put in grueling hours.

"I have some preliminary information for you on that copyright question."

"That was fast."

"Well, I had a little free time at lunch and I dug out several treatises. I haven't given them more than a cursory read-through, but I thought I'd let you know what I've uncovered so far."

Scott reached for a pad and pencil. "Okay, let me have it."

"The situation you described would arise under the 1909 Act, of course, but depending on circumstances, it could come up against the new act. I need some further information about the musical play that was performed in 1939. The old act was very specific about the copyright notice, the manner in which it was attached. It required a definite form and position on the published work." She stopped, sounding embarrassed. "You probably know all this."

"I'm a little rusty on the Copyright Act. Go on."

"Uh . . . let's see. You would have to find out exactly when the work was first published and the form in which the copyright notice appeared. If it did not correspond to the exact code of the 1909 act, the copyright would have been lost and the musical would be forever in the public domain."

"I see. So in other words, I have to go into those archives and find evidence of the original publication?"

"Yes, sir. In fact, unless there's proof of registration, physical evidence would be necessary to determine whether the notice was correctly displayed. Probably original copies of the book and the score."

"All right. It may take a while, but I'll get it. The first step is to see if it's registered with the copyright office, right?"

"Yes, sir."

"Anything else?" He did wish she wouldn't call him sir. After all, he was only fifteen—well, maybe twenty years older than she was.

"That's all I've had time for. We're pretty swamped down here, working on a couple of big cases."

"I'm sorry to have added to your burden," he apologized.

"Oh, I don't mind. I enjoy this kind of detective work. I came across some interesting cases of musical works that were never actually printed and distributed commercially, although they had been performed. Performance per se does not constitute publication, so the CR notice provisions don't apply, but—"

"Wait a minute," Scott interrupted. "Say that again."

Jane repeated herself.

"Hmm . . . that's interesting. Well, thanks, Jane."

Scott did not immediately replace the receiver, but remained with his finger on the button, thinking. Then he punched a speeddial code, glancing at his watch. It was an hour earlier in Iowa City.

"History Department." The girl who answered had a fresh Midwestern voice.

"May I speak with Professor Shane, please? It's his brother calling."

"I'll see if he's in. Please hold, Mr. Shane." Scott shook his head in exasperation at Neil's insistence on using Michael's surname. It caused such unnecessary complications.

In a minute, his brother was on the line. "How you doing, Scott? It's been a while."

They were not in the habit of regular telephone communication, usually receiving news of each other through their mother. Scott chatted with Neil about the family for a few minutes, and then told him why he was calling.

"I haven't sorted through more than half of it," said Neil. "It's important to catalogue everything first and then determine what can be useful."

"Useful?" inquired Scott.

"For my research."

"What are you researching?"

"My book."

"But . . . what have Michael's papers got to do with your book?"

"Well, I'm writing about him."

"You're writing a book about Michael Shane? No one told me." Scott felt a stab of resentment. Why hadn't his mother mentioned it?

"I don't really talk about it very much. In any case, what is it you're looking for?"

"I'm looking for evidence of the dates when some of Michael's music was first published."

"Oh. Well, I can probably tell you that. I've compiled an anthology."

"That could be helpful . . ." Scott debated with himself whether to take Neil into his confidence. He decided it was the only way to accomplish his task. "I need actual proof of publication, Neil. Anything that would help establish the estate's claim to rights for Michael's early works."

He could hear the puzzlement in his brother's voice. "You mean when he was getting started, when he wrote songs for Zachary Mitchell?"

"Yes, particularly his first musical, *One Night in Venice*."

"I thought all that would be in the public domain by now."

"It may well be. Depends on what was done at the time of publication. You haven't seen anything so far?"

"Nothing. But then, I wasn't looking for that sort of information. Have you asked Mother?"

"I mentioned it, but she doesn't really remember, or maybe she doesn't care to remember. I don't want to get her hopes up unless it's feasible, so please don't say anything to her."

"All right." Neil sounded guarded, almost skeptical.

"Anyway, keep an eye open, will you? See if you can find a printed copy of *One Night in Venice*. If you come across any documents or correspondence, anything that seems connected, let me know. As soon as I can get away, I'll come out there and look through Michael's files myself."

There was a silence, then Neil said, "You never refer to him as your father, do you?"

"For Christ's sake, Neil, you didn't even know the man. You were six months old when he died."

"I know, but I still think of him as my father."

"George Rhinehart was my father in every important sense of the word. And if your head were on straight, you'd realize he was yours, too."

"Hey, cool it. I didn't say he wasn't *like* a father to me. He was damn good to me. But that doesn't make him the man who fathered me. Whether I knew Michael Shane or not, his blood flows in my veins."

"All right. I'm sorry. I know I'm touchy about that. There are a lot of unhappy memories . . ."

"I'd like it if you would share them with me."

"Maybe . . . sometime."

When they had finished the conversation, Scott ran up the interior stairway to the forty-fourth floor. There was just enough time for a short workout before dressing to meet Isobel at Le Cirque.

❧ Chapter 3 ❧

Clarissa

Julia leaned on her wood, waiting for the sudden wave of dizziness to pass. A few weeks ago she had mounted this hill on the eighth tee with ease, hardly pausing before swinging her club, but today she found herself breathing hard and was conscious of her galloping heart.

"Are you all right?" asked Joyce Moser, who was five years younger.

"I'll be fine in a minute. Just let me catch my breath."

Joyce bent over to tee up her ball. "This hole is a killer. Maybe we ought to skip it from now on."

"It was nothing, really, just a little lightheadedness. I think it's probably hunger."

"Here, have a peanut butter cracker," said Molly Cunningham, fishing a package from her pocket.

"Thanks, Molly. I didn't have time for breakfast before I left because my son called."

"Is that the professor?"

"No, this is the one in New York, the lawyer," she answered, thinking that hardly described the kind of work Scott did, the trust funds he administered, the huge estates he managed.

She did not often discuss her family with Molly or Joyce. They were new acquaintances, delightful and full of zest for the good life, but vastly different from Sue Winston or Janice

Fried or any of the other friends she had known before they moved to Florida—women she had met at the United Nations Association and the League of Women Voters, or worked with as a volunteer at Memorial Hospital and the Metropolitan Museum of Art.

Molly went next, sending a long, hard drive straight down the middle of the fairway. She was the senior women's division champion, a crack golfer who played every morning, decked out in a succession of plaid bermuda shorts and knit shirts with matching visored hats in hues of pink, coral, and bright green, ordered by the dozen from the C. Wills catalogue. With her tight yellow curls, saucer blue eyes, and perpetually rosy complexion, taut from plastic surgery, no one could guess her exact age, but she was certainly past seventy. Her husband, who had been a bank vice-president in Boston before his retirement, wrote a financial newsletter for seniors, working from his home and selling it through an AARP mailing list. Julia could not imagine the publication would draw many subscribers, but Molly once confided that it was a gold mine. "Fred should have left the bank years ago. Between the newsletter and his investments, he's raking in the money."

The course a life took was a matter of luck or fate, Julia concluded philosophically as she watched her ball hook to the left and land on the edge of the rough. Loath to envision a retirement composed of endless golf games and fishing expeditions, George had made plans to establish a limited practice once they moved to Palm Island. However, after the first surgery, they were always apprehensive about his health. With good reason. Five years later, George had died of metastatic prostate cancer. Five years of hospitals, hormone therapy, radiation, false hopes, and staggering medical bills.

The limits on their health policy had been reached long before the years of expensive care ended. As meticulous as he was about his affairs, George had been caught in the pre-existing illness clause of their supplemental medical plan, and of course Medicare did not begin to cover the gap. When the final costs were tallied, an immense portion of their liquid assets had gone to pay for private rooms, specialists, nursing care, and the newest treatments, some of them considered experimental.

They had been . . . well, if not exactly rolling in wealth, comfortable about money, or so they'd believed. Julia had been left with an ample income, but if she continued to live in the house on Pirates Cove, with its constant assessments, kept her membership in the golf club, rented an apartment in Connecticut every summer, and if she should survive to a venerable old age, which appeared likely, given her excellent health, there would be virtually nothing left in her estate after she was gone.

Scott understood the situation better than anyone, because he helped manage her affairs. George's confidence in him had been natural enough, since trust and estate counseling was Scott's specialty. He was good at what he did and well compensated for it by his clients. Scott was a wealthy man, but with his family's extravagant lifestyle—private boarding schools and colleges for the children, the nine room co-op apartment on Fifth Avenue, the house in Sagaponack, the ski condo in Aspen, the foreign cars, the private clubs, the first nights and benefit dinners, and the designer wardrobe for Isobel that all this required—he had a ceaseless and voracious need for money. No doubt that was on Scott's mind when he had asked about the lost music manuscripts. There was a small income from a trust that distributed the royalties from Michael's estate, but Scott must be dreaming about what those missing scores would bring at auction . . .

Preoccupied by her thoughts, Julia did not play well. They finished nine holes, and Molly went off with another twosome, while she and Joyce stopped in the grill for coffee. Joyce brought a plate of pastries from the breakfast buffet to their table. "Here, Julia, have a danish. I bet you don't eat properly, living alone. Are you still feeling dizzy?"

"No, it passed. I'm sure it was nothing. Truthfully, I haven't been sleeping too well."

"That's only natural, considering . . . but you're amazing, always so upbeat. We all really admire you." Joyce spread butter on a cinnamon bowtie, taking a mouthful. "If anything happened to Jim, why I'd just fall apart. The least little thing, I lie awake and brood. For example, my daughter is pregnant and the doctor says the baby may need a transfusion at birth. They live in Cleveland, and I'm frantic with worry, being so far away. I offered to go up and stay with her until the baby comes, but her husband—well, I guess you could say he and I don't always see eye to eye."

Joyce chattered on about her family, while Julia longed to get away. When two other women joined them, she excused herself. "I have to stop at the bank and do a little grocery shopping on the way home. See you next week, ladies."

"Bye-bye, Julia. If you feel like bridge one afternoon, let us know."

Bridge! I haven't played bridge since 1952. Oh, George . . . was I too awful? I just had to get out of there. Couldn't stand it another minute. I hope they didn't take offense. I know, you always told me I should be more tolerant, that I shouldn't measure everyone by my standards. But I can't help it, I get so restless at times. They're all very nice people, and they think I've made such a wonderful adjustment. That lets them off the hook neatly, doesn't it? No one wants to hear the truth; how lonely I am, how much I miss you . . .

She pulled into a diagonal space in front of the bank. Waiting in line to cash a check, she was struck by the great mops of big hair behind the counter. Did those girls really think that was attractive? Coming out in the sun again, she felt drained of energy. Suddenly she had an urgent desire to be in her house. Rather than go to the supermarket, she decided to pick up a few essential groceries at a nearby convenience store on her way home.

Driving across the causeway, she opened the sunroof to let the slip of warm wind take her hair. The racy red Mercedes SL had been one of their few frivolous purchases. They had been shopping for a more utilitarian car, but George had surprised her on her sixty-fifth birthday when he saw how much she loved this model.

At the entrance to Palm Island Estates, the car came to a halt until the gates swung open. "Isn't it a lovely day, Samuel?" she greeted the guard on duty at the gatehouse.

"Sure is, Mrs. Rhinehart. How y'all doin'?" His face was wreathed in a broad grin as he watched Julia downshift expertly. You didn't see too many seniors tooling around with five on the floor . . . He waved as she drove into the compound.

In the back entry to her house, Julia punched the code to disengage the alarm. Unlike New York, security was not a problem on Palm Island. The elaborate system was monitored at all times by the guards. If she took ill, she had only to touch a button and medical assistance would be there in a flash. Despite the doorman and TV monitors in the lobby of their Park Avenue apartment building, an occasional burglar would slip through the service entrance disguised as a delivery boy. It seemed astonishing now that she had lived most of her life in New York City without giving much thought to safety.

When she and George first announced that they were moving to a planned compound with a gatehouse on the Gulf Coast, their friends had ridiculed the idea. At one of the farewell parties, there had been a rather macabre skit about above-ground interment, and everyone thought it hilarious. They changed their minds once they saw Palm Island. By that time, there was a long waiting list for homesites, particularly on Pirates Cove, the most desirable section, comprised of large single-family homes with private docks. Their best friends, Jack and Sue Winston, had visited them the first winter. Sitting over drinks on the patio at sunset, looking across the lagoon to the bird sanctuary and the bay while the boats returned to their moorings, Jack had said wistfully, "If I didn't know better, I'd think we were in Portugal. You two have found a little piece of paradise."

Only paradise had not lasted long enough.

Home at last. It had been unusually warm on the golf course for this time of year, and the cool restful interior was welcome after the heat of the sun. Except for the muted throb of the refrigerator, the house was quiet. Julia set the bags of groceries on the kitchen counter and poured herself a glass of orange juice. She went into the living room, sinking gratefully in the deep comfort of a sofa.

The generous proportions of this room with its lofty beamed ceilings always gave her pleasure. It was filled with books and pictures and the accumulated jumble of a full and satisfying life. The colors—muted sage greens, soft buttermilk yellow, and a dark, intense midnight blue, with here and there a splash of vivid jade and persimmon—were taken from the chinoiserie chintz that covered plump cushions scattered about on the off-white sofas and chairs. The woodwork was a weathered driftwood gray, the walls a creamy stuccoed plaster, and the floors paved in polished terra-cotta tiles. Once she and George had spent an idyllic month in a Majorcan villa, and Julia had tried to re create that feeling here.

When she stood up, for an instant she felt a passing dizziness again. She made a mental note to phone Dr. Ribera's office for an appointment. Long overdue for a checkup, she had shunned anything to do with doctors or medicine since George's death. Ribera, the local internist who had taken care of George, was a Cuban. Although he had been living in Florida for twenty years, Julia always enunciated carefully when she spoke to him, making certain she left nothing out. In all honesty, she would have preferred a Jewish doctor, trained at Columbia University, but she supposed that was her typical New York bias. Dr. Ribera was a good enough man, the best in the county. Perhaps the lightheadedness was caused by hypoglycemia. She should have something to eat.

After a lunch of yogurt and strawberries, Julia felt better and decided to clip a bouquet of roses for the dining room table. But first she went through the tropical garden room to a side courtyard where an avocado tree grew. Two ripe fruits were ready. One would do for dinner, stuffed with salad from the leftover chicken; the other would keep for tomorrow. Two avocados would have been just perfect if George were here . . . Closing her eyes, she resolved to push the sadness from her mind. Soon, very soon, she would be fine again. It was barely four months, but in some ways it seemed forever.

The roses were beginning to unfurl and she wanted to get to them before they wilted from the heat. They had been warned that the hybrids, which came from their garden in Connecticut, would not survive the fierce Florida summers, but transplanted to a sheltered corner that escaped the midday sun, they were kept well watered and the bushes had thrived. She clipped great bunches of multifloras, setting them in a basket. As she bent over a deep pink Charlotte Armstrong bloom, she pictured how beautiful it would look in the globe of heavy Swedish crystal they had bought on their last trip to Stockholm. It was perfect for roses, they fell just right against the fluted contours of the neck—

"Julia, is that you?" Clarissa Jenkins, her next-door neighbor, appeared from around the tall hedge that separated their properties. Her red hair, a little too brassy for a woman of her years, glinted in the sun. She was wearing a flowered cotton sundress with a halter neck that revealed a generous amount of cleavage. "My, you're an early bird. I came over this morning, but y'all were gone."

"I played golf and then I had to stop in the village."

"I don't know where you find all the energy," said Clarissa, reclining on a lounge chair and putting up her feet.

They had not immediately taken to the Jenkinses when the couple first moved next door. "People down here say New Yorkers are pushy," George complained after Clarissa's husband had invited himself along on a fishing excursion planned weeks ahead with Scott's children.

"Why don't you tell him you'll take him another time?"

"Ah, sweetheart, how could I do that? If I knew him better I might, but I don't want to start out being unfriendly."

Walter changed his mind when he saw the two children and the friends they brought along, and there had never been another opportunity because no sooner had the self-made entrepreneur from Nashville ensconced his wife in their three-bedroom home on Pirates Cove than he started running around with his secretary. A year later, he moved out.

George could not abide what he called a chaser. Sympathetic to Clarissa, he had advised her on the divorce, and she ended with a much better settlement than her lawyer had led her to expect. Forever indebted to George, Clarissa had cooked for him all during his illness, appearing at the door several times a week with homemade breads and stews, delectable fruit pies and jams. "I've been baking and putting up preserves since I was knee high to a grasshopper," she told them when they complimented her on the delicious offerings. "Learned from my granny, who never used anything but a big ol' woodburning stove. That's how Walt made all his money, you know, from my cooking." Clarissa's Downhome Delicacies had started in the kitchen of the Jenkinses' Nashville home and developed into a hugely successful brand of preserves and baked goods famous throughout the South and Midwest.

"Would you like some roses for the house, Clarissa?" Julia asked. "All these have to be pruned before they drop their petals."

"They're gorgeous." Clarissa buried her face in the flowers, inhaling their fragrance. "Come have a drink with me when you finish."

That was another thing, the drinking. "I can't, I have to drive over to Marlin Beach. It's my afternoon at the Admiralty."

"I don't understand *how* y'all can work at that nursing home every week. All those senile old people."

"They're not all senile. Many of them just have nowhere else to go."

"Don't you find it depressing?"

"Not really," Julia answered. "They're very grateful for the attention and the company. They have so few visitors, the volunteers make a real difference in their lives."

"I could never do it," Clarissa shuddered as she pushed herself out of the chair. "Will you come for dinner then? I've been cooking all morning and I hate eating alone."

Julia's first inclination was to say no, but she had to start getting out more. During George's illness, she had devoted herself exclusively to his care and thus cut herself off from social contacts. When he died, she vowed not to become a needy widow, the sort of woman who has everyone feeling sorry for her. It would be easier to remain a recluse, but if she hoped to get back into an active life, she had to say yes to invitations.

"I'd love to have dinner with you, Clarissa."

"Wonderful. I like to eat early, so y'all come over a little before six."

The Admiralty Residence had a pervasive odor of urine that accosted Julia's nostrils as soon as she stepped out of the elevator in the women's wing. Unlike the sterile blend of alcohol, surgical scrub, and anesthesia in hospitals, the stench that permeated the nursing home was a noxious miasma that could never be camouflaged with disinfectant.

Seeking a way to take her mind off her bereavement, Julia had volunteered at the only nonprivate nursing home in the county. After her first visit to the Admiralty, she had been tempted to confine her good works to Planned Parenthood, where she counseled adolescents on Tuesdays. But she had never been a quitter, and this stubborn streak in her nature had compelled her to keep coming back to the Admiralty. Its elderly residents, some of them uncomfortably close to her own age, were pathetically grateful for the smallest attention, and she responded to that need. However, each time she came for her weekly visit, she had to steel herself for the encounter with the sad, leftover men and women who lived there.

Julia walked directly to Marie's room. The elderly woman had claimed Julia for her own and waited for her arrival each week. There were ruffled priscilla curtains at the window, an easy chair with a matching ottoman, and a feminine floral paper covering the walls. Pastel sheets and a printed coverlet softened the institutional look of the hospital bed. But the array of electrical connections and outlets for oxygen and life-support equipment, the monitor that permitted a patient to be supervised from the nursing desk, and the side rails on the bed reminded one that this was a place where people came to die.

Marie was not a beautiful old woman, and from the looks of her had been far from glamorous in her youth, but a gentle energy burned in her eyes, and when she smiled her face radiated loving warmth. Although suffering from arthritis, she was able to get around with assistance, so they went for walks in the garden and then, since her eyesight was beginning to fail, Julia usually read to her. She was especially fond of short stories, and her memory was of sufficiently brief duration that she would often ask for the same story to be repeated. Marie's recall of past events was amazing in its detail, though, and she frequently entertained Julia with tales of her impoverished girlhood on Key Largo, where her father had been a marine carpenter. At an early age she had married a state park ranger, who had vanished one day in the Everglades.

"Never found a trace of him. Eaten by alligators, they said, but I never believed it. More like, it was men he encountered out there. The Glades have always been a sanctuary for murderers and thieves."

Conversation usually stimulated Marie, but today she was lost in reverie. "You never married again?" Julia gently prompted her.

"Oh no-o-o. Lucas was my only love." She smiled and her face contracted into hundreds of wrinkles and furrows. "I worked in a laundry, turning collars and sewing on buttons—don't forget, that was the Great Depression and folks were a lot thriftier then—and I raised young Luke. He was a good boy." She shook her head sadly. "He was killed in the war, you know."

"Yes, I remember you telling me about that."

"Killed on D-day at Omaha Beach. Only eighteen, and such a good boy." Marie sighed. "I lost my job after the war. I was living in Fort Myers then and the only work I could find was cleaning rooms in motels. I always worked, was never on welfare. There was no family to speak of, and moving around I didn't have many friends. Lucky I had my widow's pension and Luke's dependency allotment, and later, after the arthritis set in, my disability checks. So I got along, you see. I was doing all right until a bout of pneumonia put me in the hospital. That was . . . let me see . . . five, six years ago, can't rightly remember. They said I couldn't live alone no more, so they sent me here." Marie smiled again and settled into her chair. "Read the one about the grandmother, Julia."

Marie dozed off before the story was finished. Julia lowered the back of the chair and tucked a blanket around her legs before she tiptoed out of the room. She headed for the elevator, avoiding the lounge where half a dozen old people sat staring with dull eyes at a television screen.

When she had signed on as an Admiralty Friend, as they were called, she had to attend an orientation program for new volunteers. The man sitting next to her had quit after the first session. "We warehouse our old people," he said, looking accusingly at Julia. "Look at that poor old soul over there."

But it's not my doing, she had wanted to say. *She's not my mother.* To recall it now chilled her, and she vowed she would never become sick and dependent.

But what will happen to me when I can no longer live alone? she asked herself as she drove away from the nursing home. Did everyone have this fear? It was terrifying to realize that she was only twelve years younger than Marie.

I lied to Clarissa. I am thoroughly depressed by the Admiralty Residence.

"And so," said Clarissa, helping herself to more wine, "they were sitting right here in this room, and she was telling me about their trip to New York. It was very civilized. Walt didn't say a word, but I wasn't the least bit nervous. I mean, she's not much to look at, kinda skinny and plain-looking, with straight blond hair, if you know the type."

Clarissa lost her balance slightly as she poured wine in Julia's glass. She had been drinking steadily since the two gin-and-tonics before dinner and her words were beginning to slur. "Of course, she *is* a lot younger than me . . . but he'll get tired of that soon enough. He never has married her. I think that says it all, don't you?"

When Julia did not reply, she went on. "So anyway, I said to her, I've known him a lot longer than you-all have, Tina, and I can assure you Walter Jenkins never in his life cared for opera. And do you know what she said?"

"What?"

"She said, 'That's one of the things I've introduced into his life to give it more meaning.' Can you *imagine* her saying anything so *hateful?* And him just sitting there with this sappy expression, hanging on her every word."

Clarissa sniffed and took a gulp of wine. Her eyes moistened, but she raised her chin and smiled bravely. "I know Walter's gonna tire of her, Julia. This is just a passing fancy. Soon he'll realize that he belongs with me and he'll come begging me to take him back."

"Would you? After all you've been through?"

"You bet I would! There's no place in this universe for a fifty-five-year-old woman who's been dumped by her husband." There were tears on her cheeks now. "I gave him my best years, and look at where it's got me. I *devoted* myself to him and his lousy business."

"It's your business, too," Julia said gently.

"That's what you think. Walter put everything except this house and that stinking boat in his name. Just because he named the business after me and used all my family recipes don't mean he gave me ownership. If it hadn't been for your George, I'd have nothing." She stared out the window with dull eyes. "Nothing."

With a sigh, Clarissa reached over to pour more wine, but Julia put her hand over her glass. "I've had enough tonight."

"What's the harm? You never drink, do you?"

"Yes, I enjoy a drink. But I try not to abuse it."

She stopped and turned on Julia. "Do you think *I* abuse it?"

"Perhaps that's too strong a word."

"Are you telling me I'm a drunk?" she demanded resentfully.

"No, Clarissa, but alcohol is insidious, and lonely women are vulnerable."

"Huh. What would you know about it?"

She answered carefully. "Quite a bit, as it happens. I grew up with it. My mother was an alcoholic."

"Go on . . . *your mother?* I figured y'all were from a high-class family. I said that to Walt the minute I met you. That's class, Walt, I said, that's what they mean when they talk about the American aristocracy."

"What makes you think a 'high class' woman can't be a drunk?"

"She really was?"

Julia nodded. "Oh, she wouldn't go around falling in gutters. She just stayed home and spent the day sipping whiskey. A little sherry before lunch. A little something in her tea to pick her up in the afternoon. A good stiff drink or two before dinner, a nightcap before bed. And of course there was always the odd bottle in the night table, under the bed, or in the back of the closet. I assure you, Clarissa, I know all about genteel drunks." She set down her glass, suddenly weary of the conversation. "I really must be going. Thank you for dinner, it was delicious."

"You're not mad at me, are you?"

Julia smiled reassuringly. "Of course not. I'm just tired. I've had a long day."

Clarissa walked out with her. "Look at that beautiful sight," she said, gazing in the direction of the bay where a straggling line of yachts was illuminated against the evening sky. "I might try to find a skipper for the boat."

"Do you plan to use it?"

"Sure, why not? It belongs to me—why shouldn't I enjoy it?"

"It's just that I never thought you cared much for boats."

"That's true," she said ruefully. "Maybe if I had, Walter would never have left."

"Don't torture yourself with such thoughts, Clarissa. For whatever reason Walter ran away from your marriage, it probably had very little to do with you."

"You're very good with people, Julia. I always feel better when I've talked to you." She stumbled on the flagstone walk and Julia steadied her. "I'm sorry I bit your head off before. I know I drink a bit too much now and then. It cheers me up when I'm feeling low. I can stop any time, you understand, so I figure I'm not hurting anyone."

Julia merely smiled and gave her a hug. "Goodnight, Clarissa."

A full moon was rising over the bay when she walked across the lawn. At the dock, the cabin cruiser Walter had named after his wife remained a melancholy reminder of their failed marriage.

Julia let herself in the back way. The house was utterly still. These were always the worst hours, early evenings alone, with nothing and no one to look forward to. She turned on a lamp in the living room and put on a recording of the New York Philharmonic playing Brahms' First Symphony. She sat at the window watching the running lights of the fishing fleet cross the channel under the carmine glow of a harvest moon.

I figured y'all were from a high-class family . . . That's class . . . that's what they mean when they talk about the American aristocracy.

How Eunice Perkins would have relished those words. Her iron-willed grandmother in the outmoded black silk dresses. The grandmother who had deprived a young girl of even the memory of her father.

On an end table was a photograph of Julia with her parents. Perched on her father's shoulders, she must have been about two years old. She picked up the silver frame and peered at the faded picture. Jesse and Ralph, the young and beautiful couple, smiling together in a loving embrace, proudly displaying their child. Looking at them, no one would suspect they were anything but the perfect family. Julia stared at Ralph Tepper's shadowy face for long minutes, striving for a sense of him, imagining the sound of his voice. Imagining the golden time when they had all lived together in the house on the hill and she was loved by two parents.

Long-buried, painful recollections came in a floodtide of remembrance, and she was transported once again to Troy, the industrial city on the banks of the Hudson River, where she had lived and struggled and persevered through childhood. She recalled the drear, dark Victorian apartment building near the river. She pictured the young girl who pitied her sad, weak mother and longed for the father she had scarcely known.

And she remembered with love and gratitude the aunt who had rescued her.

❧ Chapter 4 ❧

Betsy

It was 1940, the summer of her graduation from high school. She arrived in New York three months before her eighteenth birthday. Free of her domineering grandmother. Free, too, of the constant nagging worry of her mother, who had stayed sober long enough to see her off at the railroad station in Troy.

For once not smelling of alcohol, Jesse kissed her and pressed a twenty-dollar bill in her hand. "I'm glad you're getting away, Julia. Don't think about home, don't look back, dear. Go and be the person you've always dreamed of being. That's what I want for you. That will fulfill *my* dreams." Jesse smiled through the edge of tears. She looked young and hopeful, despite the ravages of drink.

"I'll see you at Christmas, Mom."

"*No!* No, you mustn't come back. Not for a full year. Promise me. You need time away to develop your own strength, like Betsy did. Time to forge a shield against *her*." Always between them, the unspoken *her*.

"But Mother—"

"*Mother*," she scoffed. "What kind of mother have I ever been?"

"Oh, but I love you."

"Julia, I don't deserve your love."

"Love isn't something you deserve. You just *accept* it."

Jesse smiled, and for an instant she was beautiful, as she had been years before, the way Julia liked to remember her. "Then I'll accept it from afar. All the way from New York City."

The train arrived and there was no time for more, which was just as well, for her mother was showing that frantic need in her eyes. "I'll write," promised Julia, embracing her once more.

"Be happy, my sweet girl. And give my love to Betsy."

Julia kept waving until her mother faded from view. She continued to stare out the window, blinking back tears as the slowly moving train passed through the outskirts of Troy, gathering speed once more they were in open country. Taking out a book, she tried to read but let it lie open in her lap as she thought about New York and college and the necessity of finding a part-time job to supplement her small savings.

She rested her head against the back of the seat, lifting her shoulder-length hair from her neck in an unconsciously alluring gesture. On the application for Hunter College she had written *brown* for hair color, but that did not begin to describe its luxuriant richness or glossy sheen. The clear, direct look in her wide-set hazel eyes was without guile. Her nose was short and straight, her mouth generous and strong, but with a beguiling sweetness to the curve of the upper lip. Individually perhaps none of these features was remarkable, but the sum of the parts was wholly agreeable.

From across the aisle, a conservatively dressed man with a mustache and neatly trimmed graying blond hair studied her. He had observed her on the platform, saying goodbye to her mother, and thought she was lovely. When Julia's eyes met his, the man said, "First time away from home, young lady?"

He seemed to be a nice gentleman, so she returned his friendly smile. "Yes. How did you guess?"

"It's been many years, but I can still remember the feeling." He moved to the seat next to her. "You remind me of my daughter. Do you mind if I sit here and talk to you for a few minutes?"

The Checker cab stopped in front of a made-over townhouse on East Seventy-fourth Street between Fifth and Madison avenues. Julia could hardly contain her impatience as she paid the driver, who heaved her two heavy suitcases up the short flight of stone steps and set them down in front of a glass door with ornate wrought-iron grillwork.

In the entry there were three doorbells, each with an engraved name card. Julia pushed the button next to Apartment 3, *E. Perkins*. Almost immediately she heard Betsy's voice crackling with static over the intercom.

"It's me, Betsy."

"I'll be right there." A moment later a buzzer sounded, releasing the inner door.

Julia was struggling into the hall with her suitcases, when Betsy came flying down the staircase. "You're here!" She embraced Julia, then held her at arm's length, smiling. Betsy looked beautiful in a heathery tweed skirt and cashmere sweater set exactly matching the blue of her eyes. Her honey-blond hair swung loosely around her face in soft waves. "How wonderful to see you, Jule. How was the trip?"

"Interesting. I met the nicest man on the train, and he offered me a job."

"A *job*? But, you're going to college."

"This would just be part time. I have to earn some money."

"It isn't a good idea to strike up an acquaintance with a strange man. I hope you didn't tell him where you live."

"Of course not, I have more sense than that. He's perfectly safe, Bets. He told me he has a daughter around my age."

"That's the oldest line going," said her aunt reprovingly.

"I don't think it was a line. Look, he gave me his business card. I'm supposed to call him."

Betsy examined the engraved card. "Hopper Associates, Edwin L. Hopper, President. I've heard that name somewhere. What kind of business is it?"

"Drama Agency. It sounds exciting. He knows everyone in show business."

They were by this time in a small elevator cage that creaked upward, grinding to an unsettling stop on the third floor. There was barely enough room to turn around in the tiny alcove outside the apartment door.

"Here we are." They lugged the suitcases into a foyer that was actually a balcony overlooking a high-ceilinged sunken living room paneled in dark oak and furnished with deep, comfortable sofas and chairs. A large fireplace on the left-hand wall was framed by floor-to-ceiling bookshelves. At the front, through broad-silled leaded casement windows, the fading afternoon sunlight played on a tangle of green plants.

"It's beautiful, Betsy. I had no idea a New York apartment could look so homey."

"I was lucky to find this place. It was a private home until about ten years ago. This room used to be the library. Come, let me show you through."

Betsy led the way to a rounded alcove where a dining table stood in a bay overlooking a rear garden. "How charming," said Julia. "You must love having dinner parties."

"I'm afraid I don't do much entertaining, except for my secretaries' club. I work such long hours, I usually spend weekends catching up on sleep."

Julia thought that sounded like a dull life for a beautiful young woman. For the past six years, in her imagination, Betsy had been leading a glamorous existence in New York, dashing from one party to another, with scores of friends and suitors.

She followed her aunt past the tiny kitchen into a spacious bedroom. "Of course it *would* be blue," she laughed, admiring the patchwork quilt, needlepoint cushions, and hooked rug, all in shades of Betsy's favorite color.

"Do you like it?"

"Oh yes, it's exactly right for you." Her eyes roved the room, noticing details of the carved mantelpiece and intricate woodwork, painted a creamy white. A lamp was lit and a book was lying face-down on the chaise longue. There were photographs on a table and dresser, mostly of the family and friends from Troy. Julia bent to look at a picture of her aunt at a social function, with other people in the background holding cocktails. Elegant and poised, Betsy was standing next to a tall, attractive man.

"Who is he?" asked Julia, pointing.

"That's Rodney Barstow. My boss."

"Oh." Julia examined more closely the likeness of the powerful head of the Radio Network of America. "Rather good-looking, isn't he?"

"Yes, I suppose he is," Betsy answered slowly, staring at the photograph for a moment and adjusting its angle. She smiled and held out her hand. "And now for *your* quarters," she said, leading the way through the hall and up a short flight of steps to a sunny attic. It was furnished as a bed-sitting room, with the same taste and care as the rest of the apartment. A large needlepoint rug in shades of lavender, rose, and pale green all but covered the pine floorboards. The walls were papered in an ivy pattern sprigged with lilacs. There were shelves of books and charming framed watercolors of old New York, and on a double bed with spool posts, a fluffy comforter and piles of embroidered pillows made an inviting nest. Two easy chairs and an ottoman, upholstered in a muted green herringbone twill, had been placed in a snug window bay, with a reading lamp between them. To complete the fresh, airy feeling, pots of violets and greens filled the broad sills of the double dormers.

"All this is for *me?*" exclaimed Julia, delighted with the informal English garden comfort of the suite. "And a rolltop desk. Like Grandfather's, only daintier."

"I found it at a rummage sale at the church around the corner. The handyman refinished it for me. You'll need a desk for your studies."

"It's wonderful," cried Julia, flinging her arms around her aunt. "I'm thrilled to be here."

"I *had* to get you out of that house, Jule. And I'm really happy to have the company. It can get lonely in the city." For a moment there was a sober expression in Betsy's eyes, but she quickly smiled. "I'll leave you now to unpack while I start dinner. Have a rest, if you like. You must be tired after your trip. We'll eat in tonight and then tomorrow, since it's Sunday, we'll go see the sights and have dinner at a restaurant."

"Sounds terrific. Don't you want help in the kitchen?"

"Not tonight. Make yourself at home. Let me know if there's anything you need."

When she was gone, Julia leaned against the door and took a deep breath. All this was hers. Her own space, where she would have privacy. A place for her possessions, her favorite books, her porcelain figurines. The sheer luxury of it. She thought of the daybed she had occupied until today in the corner of the dining room in that dark, airless Troy apartment, and was flooded with gratitude for Betsy's generosity.

Opening her suitcases, she quickly laid underwear and stockings, blouses and sweaters in dresser drawers lined with lavender-scented paper, then hung her dresses and skirts in the closet and stowed the luggage. The framed photographs of her mother and grandparents and one of her parents with herself, taken when she was a baby, she set on a table against the wall next to the bed, and placed her books and her dictionary on shelves. Finally she unwrapped the little English china animals and figures of Hans Christian Andersen characters that were her only legacy from her father and arranged them gracefully on top of the bookcase. Touching the rubbed pine of the rolltop desk and the mauve printed blotter set that Betsy had chosen, she looked contentedly around. The room was now hers, and with nothing further to do, she washed up and combed her hair in the white tiled bathroom, with its claw-footed tub and wicker commode, then went downstairs to join Betsy.

Candles in pottery holders and a small vase of cornflowers stood in the center of the dining table, which had been set with blue flowered china. "How pretty everything looks. What are you making? It smells delicious."

"*Suprêmes de volailles aux champignons*," replied Betsy, with a Gallic flourish of the spatula.

"Very impressive." Julia perched on a stool in the small efficiency kitchen to watch.

"How was everything at home when you left?" asked Betsy, as she sautéed the chicken breasts and sliced mushrooms.

"The same," Julia sighed. "Mom seems so sad these days— sadder than usual, that is. And Gran's most disapproving of my leaving."

"I suppose she'd rather you remain at home so she can ruin your life, too," replied Betsy, her voice heavy with sarcasm. "I feel sorry for Jesse, although she has only herself to blame. She should never have stayed there."

Julia looked away. She had no intention of getting into that subject tonight.

"Would you like some wine?" asked her aunt as she poured half a cup into the chicken dish.

"Dare I?"

Betsy stopped stirring and turned to look at her. "You're not afraid to drink?"

"I am, a little. I think of Mom and Uncle Hal, and I wonder if it's hereditary—being a drunk."

Betsy smiled reassuringly. "I'm certain it's not. Hal was just a college boy out for kicks. And Jesse had so much unhappiness. She feels completely helpless, trapped with Mother. Your life won't be anything like that."

"I sure hope not."

"Here, try this," said Betsy, raising her own glass. "Welcome to New York."

"I'll drink to that." Julia sipped the wine tentatively, uncertain of its unfamiliar, fruity bouquet. "Are you sure there's nothing I can do to help?"

"Almost finished." Betsy slid two dinner plates into the oven to warm. "This is a one-person kitchen, Missy."

"Betsy . . ." Her aunt turned to look at her. "Please. Julia is a perfectly good name."

"Of course it is, darling. I'm so sorry. Force of habit, I guess."

"That's okay. It's just . . . that nickname reminds me of everything I want to leave behind."

"I understand." Betsy mixed oil and vinegar for salad dressing. "Why don't you get the rolls out of the oven?"

Julia set warm plates on a trivet next to the casserole of chicken and put the rolls in a bread basket. "Do you still love your job?" she asked as Betsy served dinner.

"Love my job? I'm still married to it, if that's what you mean."

Did Betsy sound a little bitter? "It's what you always wanted to do, isn't it? To work for the head of an important company." Julia recalled the photograph on the dresser, of her aunt standing next to Rodney Barstow.

"An executive secretary is . . . in holy orders. Any day of the week, she's at the beck and call of not only her boss but the boss's wife as well. Or more often, she treads a fine line between the boss and his wife."

Julia's brow wrinkled. "I don't understand."

"These men who are heads of large corporations have little time for family life. Among a secretary's other duties, she's expected to explain absences to the wife and pacify neglect."

"That doesn't sound like much fun. Why don't you quit and find another job?"

"Where else could I make five thousand dollars a year? Besides, they're all the same. I mentioned earlier that I belong to an organization of secretaries. Very special secretaries. We all work for heads of major corporations. We meet for dinner and bridge once a month at each other's apartments, and we trade information—of course, nothing that's confidential about the business. There's not one of us who doesn't have the same complaint: Her life is not her own. You should hear some of their stories—canceled vacations, phone calls at midnight or at six in the morning to take dictation, even being sent to the cleaners with dirty shirts. At least I have a good boss. Rod— Mr. Barstow is great to work for."

There was silence as they ate dinner. "Everything is delicious," said Julia.

"I'm glad you like it." Betsy laughed good-naturedly. "You mustn't pay any attention to my grumbles, Jule. I don't mean half of what I say. It's just been a difficult week." But Julia could not rid herself of the feeling that underneath Betsy's cheerfulness ran a deep vein of melancholy.

Later they got into their nightgowns and sprawled on the bed in Julia's room, talking about family and old friends like two schoolgirls trading secrets. "What has happened to your pal Cathy who lived across the street?" asked Betsy.

"She won a scholarship to the Eastman School of Music. Isn't that great?"

"Marvelous. Is she still so pretty?"

"Gorgeous. Every boy in our class was in love with her."

"She must take after her father. Her mother was sweet but not much to look at."

"I suppose so." Julia reached for a photograph on the night table and studied it gravely. "It's strange, I can't even remember *my* father. Gran destroyed all the pictures of him except this one. Did you know that?"

Betsy stared at her. "My mother did that?"

"Yes. When I was young, Jesse gave me some snapshots she had of him. I kept them in a drawer and I would often look at them."

"I seem to remember that," murmured Betsy.

"One day when I was around eight or nine, I came home from school and they were gone. It hadn't happened that day, because I realized they hadn't been there for a while. I confronted Gran and she said I was crazy. Mom later told me my father used to write to her and she had kept all his letters. Gran found them. She went on a rampage and put them and the pictures in the stove."

"I never knew. I would have stopped her."

"That was during the time you were staying in the dorm at Emma Willard. We could never get in touch with my father after that because Mom forgot the address. She thought it was Pittsburgh."

"Poor Jesse."

"I think she always loved him, don't you?"

Betsy smiled. "Yes, I do."

Julia drew a long breath. "Well, all that's long over. How did we ever get on such a serious subject anyway?"

"I don't know," laughed Betsy. "Tell me, did you have any boyfriends in Troy?"

"Not really. There was one boy who used to ask me to dances, and I went with him a couple of times. But Gran would make it so uncomfortable, it was just easier to say no."

"It was the same with me. That was one of the reasons I left Troy. All through high school and college, Mother never even wanted me to have girlfriends over. Ashamed of our 'reduced circumstances.' I was delighted when the headmistress at Emma Willard asked me to stay in the dorm, even though I was a scholarship student." Betsy stood up and stretched. "We better get some sleep so we'll be full of pep tomorrow. I want to show you the city."

They said goodnight and Julia turned out the light. As she lay in bed before falling asleep, she wondered again whether Betsy had any suitors. There was no sign of a special man in her life, no one evident among the photographs on her dresser. If an exquisitely beautiful twenty-six-year-old woman did not have a beau, there was something wrong. It must not be easy to meet men in New York City.

On Monday morning, Betsy left for work at eight o'clock. Julia slipped on her robe to join her for breakfast, then sat alone at the table over a second cup of coffee, reading the Help Wanted section of the *Herald Tribune*. There were plenty of part-time jobs for waitresses or dishwashers or domestics, she discovered, but most of the secretarial positions were full time.

Not only that, she was told when she called two employment agencies, any reputable employer demanded experience and references.

At eleven-thirty, she summoned the courage to call Edwin Hopper's office. "Good morning, Hopper Associates," trilled a switchboard operator.

"May I have Mr. Hopper's office, please."

"One moment, please." The girl could always make a living with Western Union delivering singing telegrams, Julia decided.

"Mr. Hopper's office," said an efficient-sounding woman.

"Is this Mrs. Kramer?"

"No, it isn't. Would you like to speak to her?"

"Yes, please."

"And who shall I say is calling?"

"My name is Julia Perkins. Mr. Hopper—that is, I met him and he suggested I call Mrs. Kramer." Whew, her heart was racing like a wild horse.

In a moment, the same woman came back on the line. "Is this in reference to employment?"

"Yes, it is." Her voice sounded an octave too high. They would think she was twelve years old.

"If you can come in this afternoon at three o'clock, we'll have time to interview you then, Miss Perkins."

"Oh. Yes. Thank you, I'll be there."

At quarter to three, she entered one of a bank of elevators in a magnificent bronze and marble building in Rockefeller Center and with her stomach doing aerodynamic cartwheels soared to the thirty-second floor. The elevator opened directly into the handsomely decorated reception area of Hopper Associates.

A receptionist wrote her name on a sheet of paper, invited her to take a seat on one of several couches, and picked up the telephone. Julia examined the framed posters on the wall from famous Broadway dramas and musicals. These must be the productions of the clients represented by the agency. How thrilling! Could it be, could it possibly be that she would be fortunate enough to work here? It was too good to be true. One did not meet a complete stranger on a train and end up working for him in a glamorous industry.

"Julia Perkins?" She looked up to see a plump, dark-haired woman with an accent that marked her as a native New Yorker. "I'm Millicent Kramer, Mr. Hopper's personal secretary. Everyone calls me Millie."

Julia shook hands. "Thank you for taking the time to see me, Mrs. Kramer . . . Millie."

"Mr. Hopper is screening scripts at home today, but he called especially to tell me about you."

"That was very thoughtful. I just met him on Saturday, on the train. He was so friendly."

"Never hurts to be nice, I always say."

Julia followed the motherly woman along a corridor past a series of offices to a large area with file cabinets and two rows of desks. After testing Julia's secretarial skills, Millie smiled encouragingly. "Your typing and shorthand are excellent."

"I had plenty of practice in high school. We had to take vocational courses, even if we were going to college, so I chose secretarial."

"What were the other possibilities?"

"Cooking, sewing, and household management. I skipped those."

"You'll learn on the job," said Millie, looking her over. "It shouldn't take you long."

"To learn to cook?"

"I meant to get married. Do you have a boyfriend?"

Julia blushed and shook her head. "I don't know any boys in New York."

"That won't take long either." She handed some forms to Julia. "Fill this out for the accountants. Do you have a social security number?"

"Yes, I had to get one when I worked in the library after school."

"Good. Well, when do you want to start?"

"You mean . . . I have the job?"

"Well, of course you do. Didn't think we'd let a good girl like you get away from us, did you?"

Julia liked Millie Kramer. In addition to being funny and friendly, she was refreshingly honest, a quality often missing in the people she would meet in New York.

The next six weeks passed quickly. At the end of August, Julia registered for classes at Hunter College. She was informed that her courses in Music Library Science and Education entitled her to a state scholarship. Good news seemed to proliferate, for she arranged her schedule so that she was able to work half days on Thursdays and all day on Wednesdays and Fridays.

"Are you sure you can handle all that?" asked Betsy, afraid that Julia was taking on too heavy a burden. "You won't need that much money, especially since you don't have to worry about tuition."

"I love my job, Betsy. I get to see all those scripts and go to readings. I ought to pay *them*."

"Wait 'til you have to write papers and study for exams. You won't say that then."

"I can always take a day off if I get overloaded. They understand."

With Labor Day weekend arriving, the summer was drawing to a close. Betsy's boss was giving a party at his Long Island estate and he had invited his secretary to come and bring her niece.

"Are you sure I should go? I don't want to be a drag on you."

"Don't be silly," said Betsy. "Of course I want you to come."

"I'm not sure I have the right clothes."

"Wear that pretty rose silk and you can borrow my pearls. You'll be fine. The women at these parties spend a fortune on their wardrobes, but they'd give it all up if they could look as young and beautiful as you."

Rodney Barstow sent his car for them on Saturday afternoon. "How are you today, John?" Betsy greeted the chauffeur, a white-haired, florid-faced Irishman who, after a few minutes of friendly conversation, closed the dividing glass window to give them privacy.

When they reached Long Island, Julia found herself disappointed. "It's so ordinary-looking. I thought it would be much more scenic."

"Wait 'til we're further out. This is still commuter land."

The sun was low in the sky when Julia caught her first sight of the Atlantic Ocean. They left the main highway, driving across an inlet. She grew silent as the car moved along winding wooded roads past large fenced estates. They turned in and stopped before an imposing gate. On a discreet brass plaque set in a stone pillar, Julia read *Belle Mer*. A uniformed guard walked out of a little stone building and opened the gates for them.

"I thought you said it was a cottage," she whispered as they pulled around a circle and stopped in front of a huge mansion with white columns.

Betsy's laugh was musical. "That's what they call all these places. Isn't it amusing?"

Julia had never been in such grand surroundings before. Was her dress all right? Despite Betsy's reassurances, she wondered what she would say to the socially prominent, sophisticated guests who were bound to be at this party.

The strains of light cocktail music reached them as they walked through a stately entrance hall to a huge semicircular flagstone terrace covered with a green-and-white-striped canopy. Beyond the terrace, sloping, well-tended lawns edged with flower beds rolled toward the open sea. Betsy looked expectantly across the crowd of fashionably dressed women and suntanned men. As if on cue, a tall, striking man who was beginning to go gray separated himself from a group and walked toward them. Smiling, he stretched out his arms in welcome, seizing Betsy's hands. "You decided to come after all." He leaned down to kiss her.

Betsy turned her head so that his lips brushed her ear. "Hello, Rodney. I'd like to introduce my niece."

"So this is Julia. I've looked forward to meeting you."

"Thank you for inviting me, Mr. Barstow." Pleased that Rodney Barstow knew who she was, she realized he was younger than she had expected and much more handsome than his photograph. With a hand on each of their arms, he steered them toward the bar and ordered drinks, all the while speaking to Betsy in an undertone. Sensing that they were having a private conversation, Julia stood to one side.

Her arm was jostled. "I beg your pardon." A young man turned and smiled at her. "You're a new face, and a very pretty one." There was a plain-folks air to him, a quality she found oddly reassuring amidst all this glamour. His accent was quite Southern and very proper. "I'm Ben Carmichael."

"Julia Perkins."

"What brings you here, Julia Perkins?"

"I came with my aunt. She's Mr. Barstow's secretary."

Astonishment crossed his face, a reaction that Julia had observed before during her few weeks in New York. "You're Betsy's *niece?*"

"She's my mother's younger sister," Julia explained. "I've come from Troy to live with her. We're only eight years apart in age."

"I see. That would make you how old?"

"Going on eighteen."

"The most wonderful age. What wouldn't I give to be eighteen again?"

"You can't be that much older."

"Approaching thirty, my dear."

"You look a lot younger."

"That's my curse. To look forever like a schoolboy. No one ever takes me seriously."

"Boy," cried a woman with an affected manner, coming over and taking his arm. "I've been searching high and low for you."

"You see? It's even earned me that ridiculous nickname. Carlotta, this is Julia. I've been trying to convince her I was a serious older man and you spoiled it."

Her laugh was very New York. "Why should I let you have all the fun? Come with me, darling, there's someone you *must* meet."

Ben gave a helpless shrug and whispered, "Don't go 'way. I'll see you later."

"Here you are, Julia." Rodney Barstow handed her something pink in a cocktail glass. "Having fun?"

"Yes, I am. It's a lovely party, Mr. Barstow."

"Please call me Rodney."

"Oh, but I—"

"You must. Everyone does."

Betsy joined them and exchanged smiles with him. It must be nice to have that easy relationship with your boss, thought Julia. When Rodney excused himself to greet some guests, she whispered, "Which one is his wife?"

Her aunt gazed serenely over the lawn toward the water. "She's not here today. Arden raises race horses. She spends a lot of time at the track." Betsy didn't approve, thought Julia; she probably felt Mrs. Barstow belonged here with her husband.

"Come see the house," said her aunt, leading the way inside.

They were in the solarium when Ben Carmichael found them. "You don't mind if I borrow her, Betsy? I'll show her the gardens."

Betsy gave him her beautiful smile. "Go right ahead, Boy. There are lots of people I have to see."

"What a lovely woman," murmured Ben. "Too bad she's all tied up."

"What do you mean, 'tied up'?"

He studied her briefly. "Not the best choice of words. *Busy* is what I meant to say. Too busy." He tucked her hand under his arm and walked down the steps and across the lawn to the formal gardens. "You should see this place in the spring. They have the most gorgeous weeping cherry trees. And you must visit the pool and the stables."

"I understand Mrs. Barstow raises race horses."

"She does, but not at Belle Mer. Her breeding farm is in Kentucky. They keep hunters here, although no one rides to hounds anymore. Arden rarely shows for Rod's parties." He scrutinized her. "It's not much of a loss, if you ask me."

"The hunt?"

He grinned. "Both."

He told her he was in public relations, specializing in the theater. "Mostly actors, although I do have a few playwrights in my retinue."

"What do you do for them?"

"I enhance their careers. My dear, you would be *amazed* what one mention in Cholly Knickerbocker can do for an unknown." He stopped to sniff a blossom that he had plucked from a bush, tucking it into his buttonhole. "What brings you to New York?"

"I'm starting college and working part time as a secretary for a drama agent, Edwin L. Hopper."

"I know Ed. One of the few real gentlemen in the business."

"He is a gentleman. But why do you say that—one of the few?"

"When you deal with them the way I do, you see another side. Ed Hopper has a reputation for fairness and honesty, which is more than I can say for half of the guests at this party."

"It sounds like you don't like these people."

"Oh, I like them well enough, they're amusing. But the entertainment field—that includes radio and the record industry—is an extremely competitive and somewhat unscrupulous arena. And that is what most of these men do." He took out a handsome gold case. "Cigarette?"

"No, thank you, I don't smoke."

"I hope you don't mind if I do." Ben fitted a cigarette into a holder and lit it with a curiously feminine gesture. "See that couple over there, sitting on the sea wall?"

"The woman is very attractive."

"The *woman* is a call girl and she is, as we speak, making an arrangement with the man, whose name is Lawrence Comerford—"

Julia managed to hide her shock. "*The* Lawrence Comerford?" She could hardly believe that she was at the same party with the famous composer of Broadway musicals.

Ben gave a funny little snort. "I wouldn't be too impressed, if I were you. Larry has seen better days. I think the well may have run dry."

"Meaning?"

"He hasn't had a hit for three years. His last two shows bombed and I hear the new one is in trouble. It tried out in Detroit—they wouldn't let it anywhere near the East Coast— and they're calling in the doctors."

"Doctors?"

"You *are* green, aren't you? Never mind." He laughed, taking her arm again and leading her toward a topiary garden. "Writers who fix up ailing shows are called play doctors. Sometimes they bring in outside songwriters to add new numbers to a musical."

"Is that how new playwrights are discovered?"

"Perish the thought. They get paid off and dumped in the river." When he saw the expression on Julia's face, he laughed again. "You mustn't take me literally, dear girl. What I meant was, the last thing the authors want is to give credit to a script doctor."

"I get it. It's like a ghost writer."

"*Exactly.*" He shook her hand and his voice took on the syrupy accent of deep Dixie. "You're a mighty quick study, honeychile."

They circled through the beautiful grounds, arriving back at the house in time for the buffet supper. "May I take you home this evening?" Ben asked, after he had filled their plates.

"I came with Betsy."

"She won't mind. I'll speak to her." Julia liked him in a way. Or was it that he was non-threatening? He was a little old to date, yet she found him interesting and she was amused by his witty conversation. He seemed to know everyone's secrets. Curiously sexless, he was like another woman, with his gossipy little revelations.

Almost as if Julia were a charge for whom a nanny had suddenly been found, Betsy seemed satisfied for her to go with Ben. "Don't worry if you don't see me until tomorrow," she whispered. "I may stay over with friends."

Ben had a low-slung white sports car that he said was a custom make. "I got it cheap from an overextended movie actor." Only later did she realize he wasn't joking. "You don't have to worry about my driving," he added, as he turned the key in the ignition. "I never drink hard liquor."

He walked her to the door and said goodnight without asking to come up, for which she was relieved. They made a date for dinner the following evening, but he called the next morning to say he would be late and they would be going to a client's party instead.

By noon, Julia wanted to break the date. Betsy came home wearing a borrowed skirt and sweater, looking wan and dispirited. She was uncommunicative, claiming a headache, and retired to her bedroom, not even emerging for the lunch Julia prepared. "Just leave it, Jule, I'll be okay," she called through the door. She sounded so down that Julia hesitated to leave her alone for the evening, but Betsy insisted she should go out.

Thus, at eight o'clock that night, she found herself journeying downtown in a taxicab with Ben Carmichael, who did not seem nearly as clever or diverting as she had first thought. By the time they reached the corner of Sixth Avenue and Waverly Place, she was beginning to weary of his jaded views and constant caustic banter.

"There are more talented and insecure people in Greenwich Village than any place I've ever known," he said, introducing her to the colorful neighborhood that was home to struggling artists and diverse ethnicities. They entered a cobblestone alley near the confluence of Grove and Christopher streets with Waverly Place.

"How charming," said Julia. "I feel like I've stepped through a looking-glass." Ben ushered her past a gate to a quaint two-story building of faded red brick, completely hemmed in by tall tenements. It was a forgotten relic of the past, one of two existing houses hidden in a small courtyard.

"You'll find this gathering amusing," he said, as he led the way up a steep, narrow stairway to a slightly rhomboid-shaped red door that accommodated the ancient doorframe and sloping floors. The party was well underway, people were laughing and talking and having a grand time. Ben handed Julia a glass of beer and promptly disappeared, leaving her to sip the bitter brew and explore her surroundings.

The apartment occupied the entire second floor of the building. It was well insulated from the noise of street traffic, for the windows at the back had been bricked over where the tenements on either side joined. From the dark outside hallway, one entered directly into a cozy living room with built-in bookshelves and a corner fireplace. This chamber ran the width of the house and gave directly onto an open-shelved kitchen with a massive wooden counter dividing the area between parlor and scullery. At the moment, the counter top was littered with overflowing ashtrays, beer bottles, used glasses, and a nearly empty bowl of pretzels. A pair of french doors stood open to a rooftop terrace, where several couples, locked in intimate embrace, were enjoying the mild night air.

Behind the kitchen, a passage led to a rear bedroom with a tiny additional alcove, where another writhing pair reclined on a daybed. Hastily backing out, Julia retraced her steps down the hall to the parlor, which connected to a wide studio through an archway. Piles of music manuscripts, weighted down by large ornamental objects, lay neatly stacked on a wide work table in a squared-off bay that overlooked the courtyard and crooked little alley. Most of the floor space was taken up by a massive grand piano.

A rather pleasant, scholarly-appearing young man with curly brown hair was sitting on the piano bench talking to an earnest girl with long pale hair worn in a dancer's chignon. He had his ear cocked to listen to his companion, but his attention seemed to be on Julia.

Several other people were in the room. A short, pudgy fellow separated himself from a group and came over to her with a broad smile. "Great to see you."

"Hi," she answered. "How do you suppose they ever got that piano up here? The stairs are way too narrow."

"Through the window, of course."

"Oh. Isn't that clever."

He looked at her strangely. "How's Marty?"

She smiled. "A case of mistaken identity, I'm afraid. I don't know anyone named Marty."

Without a word, he turned and walked away. *Oh well, I wonder whom he thought he was talking to.*

The scholarly one on the piano bench continued to stare at her. Feeling uncomfortable, she returned to the living room. Out on the terrace, she noticed Ben in conversation with a tall, dark-haired man with pensive good looks. They appeared to be having a quiet disagreement. She pushed her way through the crowd to Ben's side.

"I hadn't forgotten about you," he said heartily. "This is Michael Shane, who lives in this dump."

"Fuck you, Carmichael. Now it's a dump. You didn't think so when you wanted to borrow it for one of your—" He caught himself as Ben stiffened.

"Charming, Mike. Really charming." Ben walked away and Julia found herself standing alone with this strange, moody, rude, and extremely attractive young man.

"Ah, hell." Shane threw down his cigarette and stamped it into the tiled terrace. "Come on." Taking Julia roughly by the arm, he almost dragged her into the hallway where Ben was leaning against the wall, smoking.

What am I doing here? Julia asked herself. *I don't even know these people.*

"I apologize, Boy. You got to me and I lashed out."

"Look, Mike, either you want honesty from me or you'd better get someone else to act as your agent. I wasn't going to tell you tonight. It could have waited until tomorrow, but you forced it. So don't take it out on me."

"You're right. I said I was sorry." He put out his hand. "Friends?"

Ben looked at the proffered hand, then reluctantly took it. "I really wish I had better news, Michael. We'll keep looking."

"Sure." He seemed to pay attention to Julia for the first time. "What was your name?"

"Julia Perkins," Ben said quickly, "and remember, she's with me."

Julia bristled at Ben's words. True, she had come to the party with him, but he made it sound as if he had a monopoly on her. To her further annoyance, he put an arm around her waist. Shane excused himself.

Ben took a deep drag on his cigarette and exhaled. "God, the things I put up with in the name of friendship."

"Did you say you were his agent? I thought you were a publicist."

"Upon occasion I wear two hats." He smiled, as if he plumbed murky depths she could not begin to fathom.

"Is he an actor?"

Ben shook his head. "A composer."

"That explains the piano."

"That damned piano nearly caused this building to collapse. Mike had to pay for shoring up the floors." Ben shook his head in exasperation. "Michael Shane never does anything the easy way."

"Is he any good?" she asked. "I mean, as a composer."

"I think he's very good. In fact, brilliant."

"Really? Would I know any of his work?"

"Well, he has a song on the current Hit Parade. It's called 'Smiling at Sunrise.'" Ben chuckled at her effort to hide her disdain for the insipid love song from a Hollywood western of the same name, made popular by Roon Daley, the romantic cowboy star. "Michael had a show last year that was probably a little more up your alley. It was called *One Night in Venice*."

She had heard about the musical, performed by a repertory group. "That was his? Then he's well recognized."

"I don't think Michael was too happy with that production. It was done by the Mitchell Theater on a shoestring, and in a way that hardly did it justice. He didn't get the credit he deserves."

"Why not, if he's the composer?"

"He was more than that. It was his idea, the whole concept. He wrote the book and the lyrics, as well as the music."

"Then, why—?"

"It's a long story. When Mike first came to New York, he worked for Zachary Mitchell as a songwriter. That was before I knew him. He got paid, and he gave up all rights to his work."

"Work for hire."

"Exactly. I guess you're learning something at Hopper. Well, Mitchell had *One Night in Venice* but he wasn't doing anything with it, and it looked like he never would. Mike tried to buy it back from him, but suddenly Zach owns a theater and is producing this opus. It's a modest success, but Mike has no rights."

"That's not fair."

"That's show business, my dear. Michael wants nothing more to do with Zach Mitchell's theater, but he's having a tough time breaking out. He needs to team up with the right lyricist, someone established. I tried to help. I thought I had a partner for him, but the man said his music was too avant-garde. I just told him so and that's what ticked him off."

The smoky apartment was by now full to capacity. Ben pushed a path for them to the makeshift bar and opened a bottle. "Beer?"

"No, thanks." Julia leaned against the counter and studied the other guests. They were all young, mostly attractive, all seemingly tense with the need to be noticed. On the opposite side of the room she saw her scholar again, standing against the brick wall with the dancer. He stared back in her direction and she looked away.

"The faces keep changing, but it's the same old story," mused Ben.

"Who are they?"

"Oh . . . mainly musicians, dancers, actors . . . a few artists and writers. All convinced tomorrow will be the day that will change their luck. Half of them will go back whence they came and star in the little theater. Many will hang on, waiting tables and making the rounds for auditions, settling for walk-ons or soap operas. Some will go to Hollywood and a few will become big names on Broadway. Those are the tough ones."

"You're a cynic, Ben," she laughed. "What about Mr. Shane? He seems tough enough, or at the very least rude."

"Despite what I said before, Mike's really a good fellow. I've already forgiven him." He stubbed out his cigarette. "You have to understand creative people. They constantly put themselves on the line for rejection. They throw all of themselves into their art, so to attack their work is to attack them."

Across the room, Michael Shane was talking to a very beautiful, sensuous-looking strawberry blonde. Julia observed them with greater interest. "Who is that with him? She seems familiar."

"That," said Ben, "is the actress Vivienne Tremaine. She had the lead in *One Night in Venice*."

Julia sensed that Ben did not like her. "Where would I have seen her? Is she in movies?"

"She's done several films, nothing memorable. Her latest picture was a romp in the feathers called *Pie in the Sky*, I believe. Dreadful. She's under contract to Metro, but it's said the studio may not pick up her option." His sarcasm was beginning to irritate her.

"I knew I had seen her. She looks different in person, doesn't she?"

"Most film actors do. They're larger than life on screen, and they often get to feel that way about themselves. It's hard for them to accept that they're just like you and me."

"I had rather thought they would be more modest, considering they owe their popularity to being well-liked."

"Some of them are. In my experience, the lesser the talent, the greater the ego." He sipped his beer. "Miss Tremaine, as it happens, has a *tremendous* ego."

It was nearing midnight. The party, which had begun to slow down, ended abruptly with the exodus of the host and an entourage of his friends. "Come on, Ben, bring your girl. We're all going out for pizza," Shane bellowed across the room.

"These people never go to sleep," murmured Ben.

Like a retreating army, they deserted the apartment for a little Italian café on Minetta Lane. "What is pizza?" Julia whispered, when they were waiting to be seated.

"An Italian cheese pastry," said Ben. "You'll like it."

When they were all sorted out, Julia and Ben shared a booth with Shane, while about a dozen of the others filled the remaining unoccupied tables. "Hey, Giuseppe, we'll have three plain pies and two with sausage and peppers," shouted Michael, ordering for everyone. "Whatcha got there, *paesan'*?" he exclaimed when a bottle of imported chianti was brought to the table.

"Only for you," said the owner, pinching Michael's cheek. "Can't get this stuff no more. That stupida Mussolini, he's a ruin my business. Gonna change to some Frenchy name, cook fancy food."

"It's really tough for a hardworking guy like that, getting caught in the middle of a lousy political situation," commented Michael.

Julia, seated across the table, found herself responding to him. There was a magnetic warmth about Michael, a complete lack of self-consciousness. With a word for everyone who wandered by, he was a paradox, slipping easily into alternating personas from moody creative genius to sophisticated writer of popular songs to salt-of-the-earth crony.

He lowered his head and regarded her with brooding intensity. In the light of the restaurant, she saw that his eyes were a deep, vivid blue. "Somehow I get the impression you've never been to the Village before."

"I just moved to New York in July."

"Aha," he said, "a clean sheet of paper, awaiting the first squiggles of inspiration . . ." She felt a rush of pleasure as he smiled at her, his eyes crinkling.

And then Vivienne Tremaine was standing at their table. "Move over, handsome." Michael rose to let her slip inside against the wall.

Julia was surprised at the stab of jealousy that pierced her. Until Vivienne appeared, Michael's attention had been focused on her. But now he was turned sideways, his lazy smile concentrated on the glamorous actress, his long, supple fingers playing with a lock of reddish gold hair.

Hiding her disappointment, Julia tried to keep from staring. How could she ever hope to compete with Vivienne Tremaine? Any man would be bowled over by the chiseled features, that translucent skin, those sexy, luminous eyes.

❧ Chapter 5 ❧

McKiever

"That was," said Isobel, when they were settled in the car after the Kidney Foundation benefit recital at Avery Fisher Hall, "a crashing bore. I simply detest lieder."

"Agreed." Scott yawned hugely and laid his head back against the seat. "As our lovely daughter would put it, I am *totally* wiped out. What do you say we skip the reception?"

For a moment she looked annoyed, then shrugged. "All right. I'll call Cece in the morning and tell her I had a headache."

"Why bother? She'll never notice, with that huge crowd."

Isobel gave him an arch look. "Nothing gets past Cece, darling."

As Enriqué drove east from Lincoln Center to the Central Park transverse, Isobel took out a compact and switched on a little reading lamp to examine her face in the mirror. Scott observed the way she smoothed her blond hair and lifted her chin to tighten the muscles. In a minute, he thought, she will begin to discuss the latest face lift in the luncheon crowd.

But instead she said, "My day is going to be wild tomorrow. Will you need the car?"

"No, you can use it. I have an early breakfast meeting with Burton McKiever."

She looked at him with interest. "The White House aide?"

"Formerly so. He's become an agent for a group of Middle Eastern investors. Calls himself a consultant."

"Talk about revolving doors. That didn't take long, did it?"

"Umm. One wonders, especially since we're about to wage war in the Gulf and there are profits to be made."

"Whatever does he want with you?"

"Don't know. He called and said he was coming to New York and would like to get acquainted. I imagine he's on a fishing expedition. I could have refused to see him, but I'm frankly curious about what he's up to." Scott had loosened his tie and the top button of his starched dress shirt. As they pulled in front of their apartment building, he tucked a white silk scarf around his neck. While he might freely come and go in jogging clothes at any hour, it would look like hell to return home at the end of an evening with an open collar.

"Mrs. Rhinehart will need the car in the morning, Enriqué," he told the driver. "What time, Isobel?"

"Around nine-thirty." She hurried ahead of him.

"What's your big day tomorrow?" he asked while they waited for the elevator.

"I have an appointment to look at some rentals," she answered after a moment's hesitation.

"Rentals?"

"With Cece. We're going ahead with the gallery."

"You told me you had given up the idea of going into business." As he spoke, it occurred to him to question why he was so resistant to the notion.

"I talked it over again with Cece and changed my mind."

"I wish you wouldn't, Isobel. There's something about my wife in sales, even if it is art. As if you *had* to work."

She gave an exasperated laugh. "For God's sake, Scott, you sound like a Victorian husband. I want to be more than a lady who lunches. Everyone is doing *something* these days. Even Lala Barstow has started her own public relations firm."

They rode up to their apartment in silence. As soon as they were out of earshot of the elevator operator, Scott said, "Aren't you busy enough with all your volunteer work? Seems to me you never have a free afternoon as it is."

"I am *bored* with committees. When you don't get paid, no one places any value on your services. Unlike you, I enjoy the idea of rubbing elbows. And making money." She kissed him and ruffled his dark hair in an unaccustomed display of affection. "Oh, Scotty, don't be mad. Turn out the lights, darling, and come to bed."

His irritation vanished at the invitation in her voice. With surprise, he realized he felt desire for her. How long had it been since they had made love? Very.

At some point after the births of Chip and Ginger, sex with Isobel had become a structured activity. Gradually the pleasures of spontaneous lovemaking had receded, to be replaced by a rigid protocol. He soon learned that Wednesdays and Saturdays were her most receptive nights. Then, Saturdays. Never in the morning, and *never* more than twice a week. Once, when they had indulged in a spur-of-the-moment tumble on a Sunday afternoon, Isobel was out of sorts for days.

So although it was Thursday, he quickly shed his clothes in his dressing room and got into bed, impatient with anticipation. There was, however, a ritual delay. First, Isobel must put away all her clothing and jewels. Carefully she removed her makeup and creamed her face. Then she disappeared into her bathroom. With chagrin, he realized she was bathing. By the time she finally came to bed, admittedly fragrant and alluring, the fires of ardor were considerably banked. Half asleep, Scott was debating whether it was worth renewing them—it would take some doing—but once between the sheets, Isobel showed a surprising willingness to lead the way, and soon he was eager and aroused.

"You were a regular tiger," she murmured cozily when they lay side by side, after the fact. "And you claimed to be tired."

Did you like it? he almost asked, but she turned away from him and closed her eyes. Did she still love him? he wondered. Did *he* love *her?* These were questions to which he had once known the answers.

At half-past seven the following morning, while Julia swam the requisite seventy laps in her pool on Palm Island, Scott placed a goodbye kiss on the forehead of his sleeping wife and descended the twelve floors to street level, where he greeted Tony the doorman with the usual hearty, good-fellow egalitarianism he reserved for such individuals. He emerged onto Fifth Avenue to a crisp, late fall day with sunny, clear blue skies, and immediately felt ripe with the vigor of New York and his lofty station in the echelons of power that fired the city.

Walking briskly sixteen blocks south and two east, to the corner of Sixty-first Street and Park Avenue, he was on the minute for his breakfast appointment at the Regency. Half a dozen limousines were double parked in front, their two-digit plates testifying to the prominence of the men inside (they were almost exclusively men), who used the quiet hotel's restaurant as an unofficial breakfast club. Scott was greeted by Marie and ushered to a corner table where Burton McKiever was waiting. On the way, he nodded to David Rockefeller and Henry Kissinger, who were breakfasting together, and raised a hand in greeting to Senator Pat Moynihan. You never stopped to chat, because these breakfasts were all business. He momentarily considered whether anyone would wonder why he was meeting with a Washington insider who had parlayed his position with the Administration into a multi-million-dollar contract with a group of oil sheiks. But Scott's reputation as a respected tax lawyer who counseled blue chip corporations, non-profit foundations, and family trusts made it understandable that he would meet with anyone who had an interest in money or its tax complications. And wholly improbable that there would be anything amiss in the substance of their discussions.

McKiever was younger than Scott had expected. The word around Wall Street was that he stood to make a bundle from his consulting activities, but it was hard to see from his demeanor how he was able to inspire such confidence. A neatly dressed, intense man with a sly, almost simian expression, he had the mean looks of a dyspeptic dirt farmer. A disproportionately small mouth shot off rounds of words like ammunition. When he smiled, his pale eyes became slits between a protuberant brow and high, pouchy cheeks.

Scott found it remarkable that a president would associate himself with the ilk of Burton McKiever. Watching him on "Larry King Live" some months back, when McKiever had resigned from the White House staff to accept an unseemly amount of money for representing Arab businessmen, Scott had at first assumed he was a flunky they hoped to use for his contacts in the United States government. But in the course of answering King's puffball questions in that peculiar, off-putting staccato delivery, McKiever had cited his Mississippi upbringing, his membership in the NRA, and his unswerving devotion to the Right to Life movement, as well as other conservative causes. It had become apparent that he was a zealot and, with direct access to the highest ranks of government, a dangerous man, in Scott's opinion.

As they shook hands, it was evident that McKiever was less comfortable in the power arenas of Gotham than the venue of the Potomac Basin. "You went to Yale," he commented, after they had given their order to the waiter.

"Yes, I did," said Scott.

"That's the politically correct university these days."

"Well, I got my law degree at Harvard, so I'm not all that correct, politically speaking."

"And your MBA."

Scott nodded reluctantly. "And my MBA."

"I'm a Citadel man myself. Went to business school at Austin. A Southerner through and through." McKiever's smile never reached his eyes.

Scott let his breakfast companion do most of the talking as he tried to analyze the conversation. Why had McKiever contacted him? What was he after? They covered such a broad range of subjects that no one topic predominated. His clients were considering forming a charitable foundation, McKiever mentioned. Could they consult Scott on how to set it up?

"I can refer you to a firm that specializes in exempt organizations," he suggested smoothly. "I'm thinking of one in particular—in Washington, since that's where you're based."

"That doesn't sound very enterprising, turning away what could be a lucrative account."

"I must be frank, Mr. McKiever—"

"Please call me Burt."

"Although it might not be a conflict of interest," Scott continued, as if McKiever had not spoken, "I have my fill of non-profits at the moment. In addition to my pro bono work, I am chief counsel to the Cartwright Foundation and I chair their investment committee. That's a major commitment. I think it inadvisable for me to represent another foundation with international scope."

"Ah yes, I had forgotten your involvement with the Cartwright Foundation," McKiever said expansively. "I'm not too familiar with their activities."

Scott was relieved to speak on a subject he could warm up to. "The majority of their grants are in the medical and public health fields. You may have heard of the Russell Fellowships Program for establishing research centers in medical schools. Those receive the largest outlay of funds."

"Where does the money come from?" This man had an irritating effect on him, but Scott sensed he was slowly getting at whatever had been the point of this breakfast.

"From the family, to begin with," he answered patiently, like a college professor giving a class lecture. "The Cartwrights made their fortune during the last century in the anthracite coal business in Pennsylvania. Vaughn Cartwright married a Russell from Virginia. It was his son, V. Russell Cartwright, who inherited the combined family interests and established the foundation in 1920."

"That was early on."

"There are at least a dozen well-known foundations in this country that are older."

"Is that a fact? Tell me, what has been the Cartwright Foundation's impact?"

"Its period of most active domestic influence occurred during the thirties, when it sponsored hundreds of American medical students and teaching clinics. Most of them in the South, by the way—"

"Despite the Depression?" McKiever interjected.

"At a cost. Unfortunately, too much of the corpus was depleted during the Depression years, and as a result the Cartwright has taken a back seat to Ford and Rockefeller in the international arena. However, with a judicious investment policy the portfolio has been enjoying healthy growth."

"What are its present assets, if I may?" He asked the question casually, glancing down and fiddling with the silverware.

"Roughly three billion, although we won't know until the next audit." McKiever's head came up and his eyes widened. "There's been a recent infusion of money," Scott explained. "When the last of the family to bear the Cartwright name passed on without heirs, he left the bulk of his estate to the foundation."

"And who was that?" McKiever leaned forward, intent on his words, and a suspicion began to form in Scott's mind.

"Vaughn Russell Cartwright III. He was called Bunny." Scott watched McKiever's eyes closely as he spoke. They really were beady—there were such eyes—and he knew he was close to the mark in his suspicions. "Bunny Cartwright was the force behind Rancho American."

"The hotels?"

"They're more like an amalgamation of hotel and private club. Think of a cross between a Club Med and the Canyon Ranch. Rancho American has been the phenomenon of resort development in the last decade."

"That's very interesting. What will happen to the company now that Bunny is dead?"

Bingo! The eyes. Scott saw it in his eyes. "It will go on with much the same management, I expect. Bunny, who liked to pretend he was the last of the bad boys, did not remain active in the daily management of the chain, although he was chairman of the board and a major stockholder. Among his other holdings, he left fifty-two percent of Rancho American voting stock to the Cartwright Foundation."

McKiever whistled under his breath. "Controlling interest."

"That's right. By the way, I'm not telling you anything that's not in the public record. This is all generally known."

"Of course," said McKiever. "But it's an interesting idea, isn't it? A foundation that is devoted to medical research and education virtually owning a chain of glitzy watering holes. Must they hold onto the stock?"

"No, in fact, by law they can't. A foundation may not own controlling interest in a commercial enterprise, nor should they. They'll eventually sell it off, but nothing will happen until the estate goes to probate."

"I suppose," said Burton McKiever, speaking with deliberation, as if the thought were just forming, "there are people who would kill to have advance notice when the board decides to put those holdings on the market."

"What exactly is your point?" asked Scott, coming to attention.

"Someone with that knowledge could stand to make a fortune," he said quietly.

Scott stared at him expressionlessly. "That would be pro-viding insider information, Mr. McKiever, and they're sending people to jail for that."

"Oh, I didn't mean—"

"You *do* realize all the stock would not be disposed of at one time? Since by law the financial statement of a foundation is in the public record, if you researched this or any other foundation's divestment of large blocks of equities, you'd see that it's done carefully over a period of time, sometimes decades. The last thing the Cartwright Foundation would wish to do is depress the market for Rancho American Resorts."

"Naturally."

Scott signaled for the waiter. "You'll have to excuse me. I'm expecting someone in my office."

"Allow me," said McKiever, when the bill came.

"Separate checks," insisted Scott, "put mine on my account, please. It's been most interesting, Mr. McKiever." They shook hands. "Good luck with setting up that foundation you spoke of."

Scott had the unpleasant feeling that Washington was rank with players like Burton McKiever, opportunists who used government service to further their own selfish interests, syco-phants who sucked up to anyone who represented money and power. He had few illusions about politicians, but meeting the former presidential assistant was enough to make a cynic out of anyone.

He was reminded of the conversation again over lunch at the Yale Club with Dick Graham, his best friend since prep school days and a fellow partner at Prescott, Spencer & Colwood. "So, Rhino, how was Burt McKiever?"

Scott shook his head in disgust. "A real sleaze."

"What did he want?"

"I'm not sure, but I think I was offered a bribe. He tried to pump me on the Cartwright's plans to sell its Rancho American shares."

"The Saudis want it?"

"It sounds that way. Not surprising. They're always looking for good investments. But I think there could be more to it. McKiever could be thinking of selling short or—I don't know. Bunny held a fifty-two-percent interest, all of which was left to the Foundation. It would be useful to know the status of the other forty-eight percent. Is it held in blocks, by how many individuals, and how many shares have been traded recently?"

"That ought to be fairly easy."

"Yes and no. Depends on whether someone has something to hide." Scott looked at his watch and rose from the table. "We'd better get back. I have a client coming in at two-thirty."

As they walked through the still-crowded dining room, a number of heads turned as people took note of them. "Are we on for squash after work?" asked Graham when they were in the elevator.

"Tonight . . . oh, I can't. I have an appointment. Let's try for next week."

They chatted easily as they walked the few blocks back to the offices of Prescott, Spencer & Colwood in the bright autumn sunshine, two tall, attractive men wearing elegantly tailored gray suits, comfortable in a friendship that had begun in their freshman year at Andover. Back in the office, Scott found a pile of correspondence and telephone messages awaiting him. He just had time to return the most important of the calls before Elizabeth Blackman was ushered into his office for another consultation on the updating of her last will and testament.

Aging widows of wealthy men, Scott reflected, controlled a considerable amount of American capital. The session with Mrs. Blackman took longer than expected. She had found a new pet charity, it seemed, and it took some time for Scott to convince her that before acting, he should first investigate both the scientific and fiscal responsibility of the little-known cancer research institute she proposed to endow.

Since it was Friday, he spent the rest of the afternoon clearing his desk, dictating letters and memos, consulting with Hazel on the arrangements for a dinner meeting of the museum board the following week. Before he realized it, the afternoon had passed. It was after six o'clock and already growing dark when he hailed a cab. Traffic was slow-moving, but as soon as they got below Thirty-fourth Street, Fifth Avenue opened up and it was not long before the driver stopped in front of the commercial building in Soho where Solange Didier had her studio. After buzzing him through a series of locks to the street entrance and the elevator and releasing the deadbolt on a steel-reinforced door, the photographer admitted him to the penthouse suite.

Scott found himself in a spacious, windowed loft that occupied the building's entire top floor. Arrested by the panorama of lower Manhattan and the harbor, with a doll-like Statue of Liberty in the distance, he exclaimed, "Your view is spectacular."

"Yes, isn't it?" Dressed in a severe black tunic over narrow black stretch pants, she was more attractive than he remembered. When she took his coat, a huge Saint Bernard lumbered over to sniff his crotch. "Don't worry, Napoleon is just curious," she assured him.

"As long as he isn't hungry," allowed Scott, and her mouth twitched in a wry moue. Having finished with his investigations, the dignified beast ambled across the floor and settled on the Turkish carpet between a pair of angular white leather armchairs.

"Take a seat. I'll get us a glass of wine," said Ms. Didier, indicating a deep cobalt blue sofa piled with kilim pillows.

He had supposed she would be all business, as she had been in his office, getting down to the photographic session without delay. But with Vivaldi playing softly in the background, she disappeared behind a partition, returning with a tray containing a small terrine of pâté, two Baccarat crystal goblets and a bottle of burgundy. "Clos du Roi," she said, pouring some in a glass. "How is it?"

Scott tasted the wine, savoring its rich flavor. "Excellent."

He glanced around the high-ceilinged room with curiosity. One long wall was taken up by bookcases and a state-of-the-art stereo system, while the space opposite, between high, wide windows, was hung with a series of arresting abstract oil paintings. On brushed steel pedestals in front of the windows were attenuated animal sculptures in bronze, each lit by a pinpoint spot attached to a ceiling beam. The effect was elegant, classic, and restful.

He said, "You're set up for housekeeping in your studio."

"Why not? I live here."

Her accent was charming. Her eyes were huge and gray in a strong-boned ivory face, her black hair styled in a feathery boy cut. He noticed how capable and graceful her hands were as she spread paté on triangles of toast. Fascinated, he watched as she put lemon and cornichons on a plate and handed it to him. "I didn't expect a party," he remarked.

She smiled for the first time and he saw that she was beautiful, a black and wild beauty, like a stormy night. "I was striving for a mood."

"A mood?"

"Look." As she reached behind him to take some photographs from a table, he caught a breath of her perfume, a crisp, intriguing scent. "What do you think of these?"

Scott stared at the pictures of himself, a man he almost did not recognize. An extremely handsome man whose image projected power. He was seated on the edge of his desk, glints from the backlights reflected in his hair, a strong but serene expression in his eyes. His hands were loosely clasped, the set of his shoulders relaxed in his custom tailored pin-striped suit. The suggestion of a smile crossed his lips, the lift of his chin stopped short of arrogance. Solange had done something ingenious with the lighting, casting a soft glow on the shelves of leather-bound books and the paneled walls with the small framed mezzotints Isobel had used to decorate his office. It was a study in self-confidence and privilege.

Solange switched on a light box on a cabinet against the wall and he sifted through a dozen or more color transparencies, then another dozen prints in black and white. She had played with the textures on the black and whites, varying the grain to good effect. He had a strong impression that she had analyzed the character of the man.

He cleared his throat. "They're marvelous. Clive Westbrook said they would be."

She gave him the faintest smile. "The subject was quite marvelous," she murmured matter-of-factly, holding his eyes with hers. Just as he was wondering what to do, she said, "Shall we go to work? Bring your wine. And take off your jacket and tie. I want you relaxed."

He followed her to the rear of the loft, past a kitchen and a sleeping area to a large rectangular space of window walls and skylights, each with blinds that could be manipulated to control daylight. Through the expanse of glass to the right, across the rooftops of Chinatown, the lights of the Manhattan and Brooklyn bridges were reflected in the East River. A series of screens and curtains operated by pulleys served as studio backdrops. Solange busied herself turning on floodlights and angling deflectors while Scott examined the assorted cameras on tripods on the periphery of the set.

She pressed some buttons on a CD player and soft, jazzy blues replaced the chamber music. "All right, have a seat on that stool and drink your wine. Look at the view, listen to the music, think about something nice, pay no attention to me."

"That may be difficult, that last," he said, feeling reckless.

She laughed, a throaty, stirring sound. "You know, a photographer always should be a little in love with her subject," she said, as she moved around him with a Nikon, shooting from different angles.

"Is that a fact?" He was becoming lightheaded from the wine.

"Yes, in portraiture, the camera—and by extension, the photographer—should make love to the subject."

"That, uh . . . that's a very interesting theory."

"Oh, it's more than a theory." Snapping constantly, she crouched, knelt down, stood on a ladder, moving rapidly all the while. "Try to hold that expression. Umm, that's sexy, that's good. Think about going to bed with a beautiful woman. Like *that . . . great.*"

Scott could feel the warmth in his cheeks. The image he saw was of Solange, her head on a pillow. *God, I'd better not drink any more of this wine.*

"Now, we'll do some studies," she said, adjusting the lights and switching to a Leica that was set on a tripod. She peered through the lens, then came over to him, taking the glass from his hand and unfastening two more buttons of his shirt. "Stay as you are and do as I say."

Scott followed her directions, turning when she told him to, smiling, frowning, laughing, looking surprised, completely amazed at how relaxed and unself-conscious he felt. It seemed like a very short time had passed when she said, "That's enough for tonight. We've shot six rolls."

He looked at his watch. "Nine-thirty! How did it get so late?"

"It can be that way, when the energy is right."

That's something Debbie would say, he thought, and it made perfect sense. "I had no idea it would take this long."

Solange flexed her arms and rubbed the back of her neck. "That was satisfying, it felt good." She poured more wine in their glasses. "Would you, perhaps, care to have some supper? I make a rather nice omelette."

"That's very kind, but I—"

"Of course. It's Friday evening and you probably have something special to do," she said lightly. "A black tie gala or some such frolic?" He recognized the defensiveness in her wit and was surprised, for she seemed such an assured, liberated woman.

"No. There isn't much of that going on in the city on weekends. Many people go away."

"Ah, to the country hideaway."

"Yes."

"And do you own such a weekend retreat?"

He gave a reluctant nod. "We have a house in Sagaponack, but Isobel—my wife—doesn't enjoy it once the weather turns cold."

"It's not winterized?"

"Yes, it is. Actually, I much prefer it in the winter, with no people around, the beaches clean and deserted."

"My parents had a cottage in Normandy when I was young. I used to love it in winter, with the cold winds tearing at the roof at night and a roaring fire within. It was wild and primitive. I was an only child, you see, and I had such an imagination—but why am I telling you this? It can't possibly interest you."

"Oh, but it does." At that moment, he could not imagine anything that Solange Didier might say that would not be of interest to him. "About that omelette. If I may just use your telephone . . ."

"Certainly, come in here," she said, leading the way to a small office. "It's private."

He called home, and Candida told him Isobel had gone to an art opening and would be out for dinner. "She say if you want to meet her, you can, but I already cook for you."

"Thanks, Candida, but I have work to do. Will you tell Mrs. Rhinehart if she should call?"

"Well?" asked Solange, when he appeared in the kitchen, where she was arranging various ingredients. "Did you get permission to stay out late?"

"I don't need permission. I'm my own man."

"So. Then open that bottle of wine, my independent man."

How quickly time passed when the company was agreeable and the conversation diverting. The evening seemed slow and leisurely, but suddenly the hour was approaching midnight. The baked omelette had been delectable, more like a soufflé, filled with mushrooms and herbs, served with a crusty baguette, a tangy green salad, and ripe brie. For dessert, there were sliced fresh pears in wine and tiny pecan meringues. Over espresso and cognac, Scott considered Solange. "You are not only a talented photographer, but a world-class cook."

"I enjoy cooking, so long as it's simple. I have no patience for long, complicated procedures."

"It seemed fairly complicated. But not nearly long enough."

"Um, what we call *une petite galanterie*."

"Sincerely meant."

"More brandy?"

"It's rather late. I think I should be going."

She nodded. "That seems sensible. Do you want me to call a radio car?"

"No, I'll walk up to the Village. I should be able to find a cab."

"I'll go along with you for a few blocks. I have to walk Napoleon."

"You shouldn't go out alone at night in this neighborhood. It's not safe."

Solange laughed. "I do it all the time. Besides, I won't be alone, I'll have the dog."

A lone taxi was coming along Prince Street and stopped for them. Scott insisted on taking her back to her apartment building, and after an initial protest, she agreed. They had a little trouble getting Napoleon into the cab, but they shoved the reluctant beast from the rear, and at last he leapt onto the seat, with the two of them crowded together beside him. Laughing, Scott settled back and put his arm around Solange, holding onto her so that she would not fall off the edge of the seat. Soon they were back at her corner.

"Thank you for a wonderful evening," he said, walking her to the door.

"*Vous êtes un homme très fascinant*," she whispered. "*Bonsoir*, Scott."

A dozen times during the next week, she was on his mind. Each morning he would awaken in the dark to a feeling of incompleteness and could not imagine why. And then when he remembered, he would rise and go to his club to work out, arriving in the office before anyone else. After several days of this, he had forced her from his thoughts.

Hazel was out sick the following Thursday and one of the secretaries from the pool filled in. "I didn't quite get the name, but there's someone who sounds like Angela D. Day on the phone, Mr. Rhinehart. I'm not very good with accents."

"Hello, Scott, it's Solange. Am I disturbing you?"

"No. I'm glad you called."

She did not ask why. "I have the prints from last Friday."

"How are they?"

"I'll let you decide that for yourself. Can you come to my studio this evening?"

This evening. Thursday. They had tickets to the new Neil Simon play. "I'm sorry, but I can't."

"Well then, tomorrow? I'm going away on Saturday."

He consulted his calendar. "I think tomorrow would be all right."

"Excellent. I'll see you whenever—and if you like, I'll make dinner. Something more ambitious than an omelette this time."

He closed his eyes. He should not go, he knew he should not. "That sounds lovely."

Tomorrow night. He would see her tomorrow night.

He rode downtown to her studio on Friday evening, filled with doubts about the wisdom of his actions. He realized how eager he was to see her again. The small printing press on the ground floor was alive with activity when he stepped out of the taxi on Thompson Street shortly after five o'clock. The lobby was open, but he had to go through the routine of announcing himself before being carried to the top floor. As he exited the elevator the door to the penthouse opened, and he almost collided with a tall, striking blonde.

"I beg your pardon," he apologized, noting her startled expression. Her hair was tied back with a scarf and she was wearing large tinted glasses, so it was not until she had descended in the elevator and he was inside the loft that he realized it had been the elder of the Chandler granddaughters, the one who had spoken to him several weeks ago in that brazen fashion. Although he had caught an occasional glimpse of her as he entered or left his apartment building, this was the first time they had actually encountered each other. It left him with a distinct sense of unease that someone connected with his place of residence should see him enter the studio of Solange Didier.

"Have you been photographing that girl?" he asked.

"She needs a composite, but I had to tell her I no longer do fashion because it bores me. She didn't want to take no for an answer."

"No, she wouldn't."

"You know her?"

"Not really. Her grandmother lives in my building."

Solange seemed to sense his distraction, and she immediately led him to her workroom to view the pictures she had taken the previous week.

"I'm not much of a judge," he said, after studying them, "but I would think these are unusual. You do the most extraordinary things with lighting."

"It would be even better on location, with available light and natural backgrounds. Would you be willing?"

"I . . . I'm not sure. My calendar is rather full this time of year."

Solange remained silent, shuffling through the eight-by-tens she had developed. There were six sheets of contacts and she had selected several from each roll, experimenting with the grain and cropping. The book was growing, she told him. It could turn out to be an important project, a series on men from a woman's point of view. A major publisher was interested and so was a new gallery. Thus far she had completed photo studies of a black actor, a senator, a farmer, a boxer, and a fisherman. She showed him the prints; they were clearly in the category of art.

But she had reserved her most skillful lens for him. He could see that. It did not take a connoisseur's eye to know that the pictures she had taken in her studio were unbelievably good, and now she wanted to go somewhere on location for an entire day.

"When would we do this?" he asked cautiously.

"Any time, really. It would have to be a weekend, of course, because you could not take a day from your work."

"Where would we go?"

She shrugged, a very French mannerism. "Connecticut perhaps. I have friends who raise horses in Wilton. Or Long Island. Fields, dunes . . . yes, absolutely, dunes. I picture you by the sea."

"My house in Sagaponack," he said quietly. "My hideaway, as you put it."

She smiled. "But of course."

Scott wondered what Isobel would think, but she had left for Boston on Wednesday with her partner Celeste Bedford, who had been her friend since they were at Miss Porter's together. There was a meeting of an art dealers' association and an exhibit to see, she had told him, and they planned to visit some galleries on Newbury Street. From there they would be flying to Chicago for a dealer's auction and an opening at the Art Institute. "It's important to attend these things," Isobel explained, "to become known to collectors and other dealers." Soon after their return, she had added, there would be more trips, to Santa Fe and San Francisco. And in January, they would be going to Europe. In the spirit of the unacknowledged truce between them, he had raised no objections.

Thus, on Saturday morning, Scott and Solange were driving to Sagaponack under a mottled November sky in which the sun played hide and seek with skittish gray clouds. They were out of Manhattan and on the highway by eight o'clock in the morning in the maroon Volvo station wagon his family used for the beach. With cameras and tripod stowed in the wayback and Napoleon sitting contentedly in the rear seat, they headed out the teeming Long Island Expressway, picking up speed once they were beyond the heavily populated commuter towns.

At Manorville, Scott left the main highway, turning south. Solange had been silent on the drive, and Scott was wondering whether it was going to be awkward the entire day, but suddenly she directed him to take a detour. She had a craving for coffee, and not far from Moriches there was a duck farm with a nearby inn that she remembered.

"Take the next right, I'm sure this is it."

They found it, an unlikely Victorian building with displays of faience in the windows and a French proprietor who was also the chef. They ordered café au lait and croissants, and after a while Solange shot some pictures of Scott in a field with a barn in the background, and then they got back in the car and continued on their way. After romping in the grass and barking at a strutting rooster, Napoleon had exhausted himself and fallen asleep. It became more relaxed between them, and the silences were comfortable. By the time they reached Water Mill, there was a cloud cover. Soon they had passed through Bridgehampton and were entering the village of Sagaponack. Scott stopped in Loaves and Fishes to buy bread and cheeses and assorted delicacies for lunch, and then there was only a mile or so to go.

The car bumped along a narrow, unpaved private road, turned right, and came to a stop before a weathered gray shingle structure whose soaring rooflines and chimneys were all but hidden from the road by a screen of cypress trees. Here and there through the evergreens could be glimpsed the rippled waters of a salt pond.

"Here we are," said Scott, turning the Volvo in through an opening in the split-rail fence and driving across crunching gravel past a woodpile and a shed to a parking area.

Napoleon, released from the back seat, went tearing through a stand of cattails to the pond. "He'll jump right in," laughed Solange. "It's all right, isn't it?"

"Yes, unless he tangles with a swan. They're mean bastards."

They walked to the front of the house, where a lawn edged with beach plum bushes gently sloped down from a broad windswept deck. "Too bad the sun isn't shining," said Scott. "This is usually so beautiful."

"Much better this way. No shadows. This weather is perfect for our purposes." She turned to face the house. Seen from this angle, it had great expanses of glass that overlooked acres of tall, plumy marsh grasses, the salt pond, and, beyond that, the sea. "Very nice," she said with a small private smile. "Different from what I expected." Then she returned to the car, opened the rear door, and began unloading her equipment.

Scott followed her, feeling deflated. He realized he had expected Solange to fall in love with the setting on sight as he had fifteen years ago. "Sorry if you're disappointed."

She straightened up, a look of concern wrinkling her brow. "Why do you say that?"

He shrugged. "It seemed that way."

"Well, you're wrong. I sometimes give a different impression from what I mean." She smiled and he felt foolishly happy.

"Come on, let's go in," he said. Taking the bag of groceries, he led the way up to a side deck and the kitchen door.

Napoleon came tearing up the steps, soaking wet, shaking himself and spraying them with salt water. "Bad dog," scolded Solange, pushing him away. She took a long lead from her shoulder bag and tied him to the railing. "You have to stay out here, Napoleon." With an aggrieved look at his mistress, the Saint Bernard settled down on the deck.

"We could dry him off and let him in," said Scott, who had always wanted a dog. Isobel disliked the bother of animals and refused to have one in the house. The only pets their children had ever known were gerbils.

"No, he may have picked up some ticks. He'll be fine for now. We'll let him run on the beach."

Scott unpacked the groceries. "Hungry?" he asked.

"A little, but why don't we get started? I want to take advantage of this light. The sun is threatening to break through."

He cut off a piece of veal terrine and fed it to Solange. "Taste this."

She chewed thoughtfully. "Well, it's not Hédiard, but it will do."

"High praise from a Parisienne." He took a small cooler out of the kitchen closet and put the food in it. "I'll take this along. We can have a picnic lunch."

With Napoleon riding shotgun, they trundled down a sandy path to the beach, Scott lugging the tripod and cooler, while Solange hung herself with cameras and carried a plaid blanket. The ocean was calmer than usual, with gentle waves and seafoam, reflecting a pale gold light that shimmered through the clouds. Napoleon went a little mad when he saw the water. He barked at gulls, dashing into the surf, leaping and cavorting like a playful puppy.

Scott threw a piece of driftwood and the dog caught it in midair, bringing it back to him. "I wish I had a ball."

"I brought one, but if you start now he'll never leave us alone," said Solange. "Go away, you big baby."

They walked along a deserted stretch of beach with no visible houses for about a quarter of a mile until they came to a group of boulders on the edge of a tide pool. Just beyond were some low dunes.

"This is the place," said Solange.

They were cold and damp with salt spray when they returned to the house as daylight waned. Scott laid logs and kindling in the immense stone fireplace and boiled water in a kettle. "Coffee, tea?" he asked, rummaging in a cupboard. "Hot chocolate?"

"Chocolate."

He joined her in front of the fire, carrying two steaming mugs of cocoa.

"What is that on top, white of egg?"

"Marshmallow Fluff. Heaven knows how old it is. It must have been there for the children."

Solange wrinkled her nose but sipped the hot drink. "Not bad. I like it." Her eyes roved around the room. "I also like your house. I had expected something much grander than this, you know. I'm glad I was wrong."

Scott had been immediately taken with the house when they first saw it, because it was unpretentious and informal. The architect had designed it for his young family, but with the completion of the construction his marriage had broken up and the Rhineharts were the first people to look at the property when it came on the market. Isobel had reservations because many of their friends preferred Water Mill or at the very least that private reserve in Wainscot occupied by the exclusive Georgica Association, but in a rare instance of graceful generosity she had agreed it was the house for them. In the days when the children were young she had enjoyed it, sailing and playing tennis, taking Ginger to the stables for riding lessons, entertaining a ceaseless stream of weekend guests, and entering into the chic night life of the nearby Hamptons. But gradually it had palled and Scott, who loved the vaulted ceilings and great stone fireplace, the endless ocean views and the off-season tranquility, could never convince her to come out for fall or winter weekends.

When it grew dark outside, he turned on a corner lamp. "We can stop for dinner on the way back, but let's have something to drink first." He opened a bottle of wine and put on old Edith Piaf tapes.

Ruddy-cheeked from the wind, Solange ran her hands through her disheveled hair. She kicked off her shoes and settled on the sofa, tucking her feet under herself Indian fashion. "This is heaven," she sighed happily. "If I had a place like this, I think I would never leave."

"How would you do your work?"

"I would work here. I would turn one of the unused rooms into a studio."

"And your clients?"

"Since this is *my* fantasy, they would have to come to me. Or I would photograph the sea birds and the dunes."

"You are a romantic."

"Yes, I think maybe so. Does that disgust you?"

He shook his head and smiled. "I doubt anything about you could disgust me."

She drew a skeptical mouth, smiling at him in a way he had come to anticipate. The mood was calm and inevitable. They sipped wine while the flames cast a golden glow on the cedar-paneled walls, and Solange sang along in French with the plaintive throb of Piaf's voice. When the music ended, she moved to the rug in front of the fire and leaned against his legs, turning up her face to look at him. He bent to kiss her and she reached up, drawing him down on the floor beside her. They kissed again, more passionately, and Scott pictured the winter surf of Normandy, the wind and the wildness and the shrieking gulls, and there was a stifling ache in his heart.

"Solange . . ." he began, looking away.

She arched her head back and laughed. "It's really very amusing."

"What is?"

"That I should meet a man I am attracted to who is so very much married. Do you suppose I did it on purpose?"

"Solange, I—" He let out a ragged breath.

She put a finger against his lips. "Don't bother to answer. That was really very gauche of me." With a jolly grin, she jumped to her feet and held out her hands. "I'm starving. Let's go have dinner."

There weren't many restaurants open in the Hamptons out of season, but they found a fairly decent family-style Italian place that catered to the locals. They shared an antipasto for two and a small bucket of steamers. Scott ordered veal milanese for himself, eggplant parmigiana for Solange, and a bottle of Chianti Classico.

"Too much," said Solange, unable to eat more than half her entrée.

Pushing his empty plate away, Scott poured more chianti. "I must have been hungry." They finished the wine and two cups of strong Italian coffee with anisette before heading back to the city.

It was half-past eleven when they reached Soho. Aside from a bar and grill on the corner, the street in front of her apartment was dark and deserted. Scott offered to walk Napoleon before he left, but she refused.

"I can't wait to print these," she said, patting the leather film case.

"When will you have them?"

"Not long. I'll spend all day tomorrow in the darkroom." He envied her focus and dedication. Somewhere along the way, he had lost that excitement for his work.

Solange unlocked the doors to the lobby. "Goodnight, Scott. It was a lovely day."

He spent a lonely Sunday trying not to think of her.

On Monday morning she called him, distraught. "You won't believe this. The film was overexposed. I think it was a defective batch."

"Too bad. What does that mean?"

"All the pictures were ruined. All but one roll. We'll have to do them again, do you mind?"

"I can't get away for a while. My children are coming home on Wednesday for Thanksgiving and we have plans all weekend."

"No problem. How's your calendar for the next Saturday, the first of December?"

"Let's see . . ." Scott consulted his appointment book and noted that Isobel would be leaving for Santa Fe immediately after Thanksgiving. "It looks all right."

"Then it's a date, yes?"

For a moment he held his breath, then let it out slowly. "Yes," he told her.

❧ Chapter 6 ❧

Deborah

The trouble with being the youngest in the family and the only daughter was, it seemed to Deborah Ahlgren, you were never viewed as a serious person.

To her brother Scott she had been, at various stages, invisible, a nuisance, briefly acceptable, and finally an exasperation. Her father, whom she had idolized, had considered her an adorable plaything to be showered with gifts, treated with loving indulgence and limited expectations. To have opinions on anything beyond the choice of a silver pattern or to harbor ambitions above marriage and family was simply not in the picture. His death had perpetuated that view.

Damn Scott! Damn him, damn him, damn him.

She hated asking for money. If it was *her* money, why had her father made Scott the trustee? It amounted to giving him control over her, for she had to beg for every little crumb over the sum distributed to her. And now she had to call to request his signature on the stupid mortgage application, since the trust was her major source of income.

Not for long, though, she reminded herself with a grin as she dialed New York. Not for long.

"Hazel, darling, guess who?" She loved to get a rise out of his old-maid secretary. "Is he in?"

Scott was surprisingly nice, agreeing to fax a letter to the bank immediately and not even giving her a hard time, so relieved was he to hear she was not asking for additional funds. Sounding a little distracted, he gave her a short dissertation on the responsibilities of home ownership and keeping up with mortgage payments.

"I might have known I wouldn't get away without a sermon."

"I was only explaining—"

"Can't you tell when I'm kidding?" Deborah's silvery laugh sounded over the line. "You take everything so seriously, Scott. Poor thing, why don't you loosen up? Let it all hang out, learn to have a little fun?"

"I know how to have fun," he replied truculently.

"I'll bet. One of these days, Scotty dear, you're going to have to let me in on your idea of fun. Well, 'bye, big bro, talk to you soon." She blew a kiss into the receiver and hung up.

Now she would have to dash, since she was late for her lunch date with Tara.

Deborah strode through the crowded restaurant, oblivious to the male eyes that followed her progress across the room. As usual, her costume combined a careless Santa Fe chic with the New Age culture she had so hastily embraced five years earlier. Large silver hoop earrings, a quantity of silver and turquoise bangles and chains, artfully applied makeup, soft and natural. Her heavy shoulder-length hair, the color of polished mahogany, contrasted with the creamy whiteness of her skin and the riotous print of the gypsy blouse she wore with a long denim skirt that fitted snugly over her slim hips and flared to the tops of hand-stitched cowboy boots. A narrow Indian belt of silver coins circled her waist, jangling with a tinkling sound as she moved.

For this meeting she had suggested Tres Pinos, a trendy vegetarian restaurant conveniently located halfway between Monterey and Salinas. She was known as a scrupulous business woman in the upscale establishment, whose management purchased hydroponic vegetables from the communal farm where she and Jergen had settled when they came to the Monterey Peninsula. At this early stage in their joint venture, it would not hurt to give Tara the impression of a woman solidly rooted in the real world.

Tara waited at a corner table, soignée in palomino suede

pants suit and a shirt of washed silk exactly matching her sleek honey-colored chignon. A printed silk Hermès scarf was knotted casually around her neck. She had placed her Ghurka saddlebag on the banquette beside her and was entirely at ease, sipping a frosted glass of lassi and observing the eclectic collection of diners through amber-tinted shades.

"Sorry to be late, it was unavoidable." Deborah touched cheeks and slid into the seat at an angle from Tara. "I'll have a lassi," she said to the waiter, who adjusted the table and handed them menus. "What would you like for lunch? The spinach quiche is divine."

Tara decided on the quiche and Deborah ordered a Mexican plate of vegetable fajitas, refried beans, and salsa.

"How's Jergen?" asked Tara.

"*Manic*," she chortled, then lowered her voice as several heads turned. "This spa thing is really taking off. It's still hush-hush, so say nothing, but after visiting The Well and looking over his books, they've signed a contract to open centers in three of their new resorts—Palm Desert, Santa Fe, and Houston. Can you *believe* it?"

"I think it's fantastic, Debbie. I knew it would all come together for you."

"It's rather daunting. There's so much preparation involved—lawyers to set up a franchise, a designer to create modules and uniforms, trainers for his staff. Jergen is such a perfectioinst, he's determined to maintain quality. Unfortunately he'll need to invest more of his own capital."

"Does that mean you won't have the money for our shop?" Tara asked anxiously.

Deborah shook her head. "Now that he has a contract, Jergen can get a bank loan. Don't worry, there's plenty in my trust. My brother controls it, but I can handle him."

"Have you told him about Treasures?"

"*No*. And I don't intend to, either. Not until we're a going concern. Scott doesn't think I have the brains to run a cookie sale."

"He's dead wrong about that," said Tara. Then she got down to business. "I've seen a store that's for rent. It's perfect, on a quaint little street near the old Mexican marketplace, and there are no other handicraft shops in the immediate area."

"Doesn't that seem strange? I mean, you'd think there would be, if it's a good business location."

"This is a new shopping center. The property is an abandoned cannery that's being renovated by the same developer
who did La Marqueta. It has Mission-style architecture, perfect
for us. They'll give us a two-year lease with an option to
renew, and since we would be one of the first tenants, we
get three months' rent free. I think it's a great opportunity,
Deb. Wait 'til you see it. We're going to meet the agent after
lunch."

"You really want this, don't you?" Deborah smiled. "I sure
hope we know what we're doing."

Driving home after she and Tara had signed the lease on the
new store space, Deborah fought a wave of panic at her daring.
Everything was moving at such a frantic pace. A new house,
Jergen's contract for the spas, and now this. Maybe there were
too many changes at once.

Well, that's what she had wanted, wasn't it? A complete
departure from the life she had known.

She clearly recalled the winter morning six years ago,
when the Scarsdale Adult School brochure had arrived at
the Manndorf house on Overlook Road. It would have been
a Thursday, because her cleaning woman was in the laundry
room ironing Brent's shirts.

Shivering in sweats, Deborah had gone out to collect the
mail . . . she leafed through it quickly, hoping for a letter from
her parents, who had recently moved to Florida, but the pile of
envelopes and cards yielded mostly solicitations and bills, and
she put them aside.

It was starting to snow, which was okay since it meant they
would have good skiing for the weekend, but not so great when
she considered the long drive up to their house in Vermont. If
only Brent would get away from the office when the stock market closed tomorrow, they could start out for Stratton before
dark, but that was unlikely. He usually stayed late on Fridays.
Wrapping up the week's work, he claimed. In her present state
of paranoia, she often wondered whether he wasn't in a bar
somewhere, having a drink with the guys . . . or someone.

At noon the nursery school van delivered Wendy, whiny
and out of sorts, which probably meant she was coming down
with something. Deborah gave her daughter lunch and put her
in her room for a nap, deciding to bag the mother-child art

class at the Y that afternoon. As she sat at the kitchen table, desultorily stirring a cup of alphabet soup and munching on the uneaten half of Wendy's peanut-butter-and-jelly sandwich, she considered how dispiriting it was at twenty-nine years of age to be a suburban housewife.

Until a year ago, they had lived in a light and airy three-bedroom apartment on East Seventy-sixth Street between Park and Lex, and Deborah, happily employed in the market research department of a leading advertising agency, was earning a salary that twice covered her business wardrobe and the cost of the Ecuadorian woman who was their live-in housekeeper. Whatever had possessed her to give it up and go along with Brent's desire to live in the country?

She spilled out the last of the soup and leafed through the mail, which was still lying on the counter. Aside from the usual sales catalogues from department stores, there was the order form for the Lincoln Center theater series, an invitation to a dinner party in Greenwich, several requests for contributions from non-profits, the spring buffet schedule at Twin Oaks, their country club. And the announcement for the Scarsdale adult classes.

Smirking, she skimmed some of the course offerings. CHINESE COOKERY. COMPUTERS: AN INTRODUCTION TO THE IBM PC. CONVERSATIONAL FRENCH. GETTING ORGANIZED: How to Make the Most of Your Time and Simplify Your Home Filing System. Hmm, that could be useful. JAPANESE FLOWER ARRANGEMENTS. JEWELRY DESIGN . . . No, these courses were a waste of time, a way for bored housewives to fill empty hours.

At the next entry, her attention was arrested and a chime seemed to sound in the back of her head.

INNER PEACE: ACHIEVING TRANQUILITY IN A PRESSURED WORLD. Swedish fitness expert Jergen Ahlgren teaches the elements of total mind and body relaxation with his unique method of inner healing. This powerful technique, incorporating holistic practices and principles from Zen, promotes sound physical and mental health, a sense of well being, and results in less stress, better interpersonal relationships. Fee includes an audiotape and copy of Mr. Ahlgren's best-selling book, *The Well of Being: A Guide to Inner Healing.* Class limited to twenty. Eight Thursdays starting March 18th; 2:30–4:45 pm; Quaker Ridge School; $90.

Deborah stood at the sink, her jaw clenched, contemplating the empty chambers of her heart. How long was she to go on this way, she asked herself. She could make it through the pointless and endless days, that was no problem. But how was she to continue to endure the melancholy, panic-ridden nights that had overtaken her?

A thumping turbulence on the basement stairs called her back to reality. "*Annie*," she cried.

The cleaning woman appeared at the pantry door carrying a basket of freshly ironed laundry. "You calling me, Mrs. Manndorf?"

"Yes. Please sit down for a minute, I want to talk to you." Experienced with children and extremely reliable, Annie could be trusted to babysit for Wendy on Thursday afternoons.

Deborah signed up for the course, and by the sixth week she had fallen in love with Jergen Ahlgren.

But such a love! It swept all other considerations aside. Brent argued, then begged; her brother Scott used every lawyerly argument he could muster; her bewildered parents hurried back to New York from Palm Island and pleaded with her in vain. She had gathered Wendy and a few of her possessions, mainly books, and followed Jergen to the West Coast, leaving a stunned Brent Manndorf behind to explain to their friends and cope with two houses, one mink coat, an assortment of expensive jewelry, and an immense walk-in closet full of designer clothes. His pride prevented a messy divorce, and his selfishness precluded demanding custody of their daughter, as she knew they would. But despite her father's law firm looking out for her interests, it was largely Brent's show. After all, she had deserted him.

Admittedly she and Jergen started out a little fringy when they first came to California, but time and success had had a settling influence on them. Two and a half years ago, after she became pregnant, they married. By then her father had become too ill to travel. Her mother and brothers flew to California for the wedding. Julia and Neil managed to enter into the spirit of the occasion, but Scott had looked pained throughout the admittedly unusual ceremony.

Jergen's original holistic retreat, opened four years earlier in Monterey, had become an immediate attraction for the trendy, high-living crowd of the film industry. With the valuable patronage of her mother's cousin, Perkins Hopper, CEO of the largest creative management company in the world, actors, producers, and directors had flocked to the center, named for Jergen's book, *The Well of Being*. After a few days of strenuous hiking, macrobiotic diet, breathing and relaxation exercises, massage therapy, and aromatic herbal wraps and facials at The Well, they came away feeling renewed in spirit and swearing by the restorative powers of the method. The word spread and soon there was a six-month waiting list, with Jergen making plans to open a branch in the hills above Malibu, when he had been approached by a consulting firm on behalf of a chain of exclusive resort hotels.

Meanwhile Deborah's abundant energy had driven her to find something beyond the cooperative farm to occupy herself. Her mother had always been active in Planned Parenthood, and Deborah soon involved herself in giving lectures on family planning to migrant workers. In the course of these activities, while visiting a shelter for Mexican and Indian women whose husbands worked on fruit farms in the valley, she had come upon the most amazing handicrafts sold by the wives to help provide for their many children.

Deborah had been lifelong friends with Tara Williams until marriage placed them a continent apart. In their high school days, the two had haunted New York department stores and spent hours scouting bargains in the out-of-the-way shops of Greenwich Village. Freshly divorced and low on funds, Tara was now living in Century City and managing a chic boutique on Rodeo Drive. When the novelty of ashram living began to pall, Deborah had contacted her friend.

They met for lunch. Deborah, always fond of ethnic dressing, wore a handsome handwoven shawl that she had bought from one of the women at the shelter. "Where did you get that *gorgeous* wrap?" exclaimed Tara, fingering the soft woolen material. Deborah explained about the shelter, which was a place for the women to meet, socialize, and do their handiwork, or to take refuge when their husbands got drunk and abused them.

"I'd love to have one of these, Debbie. In fact, they'd be great in the store."

The result was that Deborah sent Tara the woman's entire

stock, and within ten days the boutique sold out and Tara was begging for more. The shawls were gone but Deborah sent bead necklaces, leather handbags, woven skirts, and baskets filled with potpourri. Those too were snatched up.

Tara came to visit the ashram and Deborah took her to see the women at the shelter. "These are treasures," Tara whispered reverently, holding a pair of Mexican marriage dolls. "*Treasures.*" Her eyes lit up and she turned to Deborah with a cry, startling one of the women who was shuttling her loom.

"What is it?" asked Deborah.

"Wait a minute . . . no, no, don't say anything. I'm *thinking* . . ."

Deborah grinned. That was Tara. Her friend had always been inspired by rash impulses ever since kindergarten at the Dalton School. Suddenly Tara grabbed her and danced her around the room, much to the delighted amusement of the watching women.

"Debbie, I have got the *most fantastic idea*," she cried breathlessly. "We are going to open a shop. The two of us. Together. We'll call it *Treasures* . . ."

Although they had been living in the house before they bought it, Deborah and Jergen were only partly settled. The bedrooms had the essentials and the kitchen was well outfitted with dishes and cookware, but every other room needed furnishing. Deborah realized this could become a permanent state of affairs, since she was spending most of the day with Tara, preparing for the opening of their shop. Luckily they had still been at the ashram with its available babysitters during the months when she and Tara were traveling around to acquire merchandise. Jergen, preoccupied with his burgeoning enterprise, had little time to think about home furnishings; in fact, he could function very well without benefit of tables or chairs.

They did need light, however, and late on a Thursday night she was unpacking an assortment of pottery lamps when the telephone rang. "Hi, Aunt Debbie, it's Kit."

"Kit, darling, I'm glad you called. What's the good word?"

"It's going all right. We've got a bunch of bookings. In fact, we're doing a wedding in Pacific Grove next Saturday afternoon. Any chance we can get together afterward?"

"You'd be history if we didn't. Bring your crew and come stay with us."

"You mean the whole band?"

"Why not?"

"Well, there are five of us, and three of the guys have girlfriends who will probably come along, so that makes eight. Too many, I think."

"You're talking to a woman who's used to group living. I sort of miss all those warm bods since we've moved. Just bring your sleeping bags, because we don't have extra beds."

"Awesome, Aunt Debbie. Thanks a lot."

"Kit, you can drop the 'Aunt.' Just plain Debbie will do. It makes me feel positively ancient to think I have a nephew who's six foot two."

As it turned out, Kit was the only one to spend the night, but the rest of the band with their girlfriends stopped by after the wedding to say hello and at Deborah's insistence stayed for dinner. They were going on to Big Sur that night, and Deborah was just as satisfied because it would give her a chance to visit with Kit, whom she had not seen in months.

Two vans loaded with instruments and amplifiers pulled into the gravel driveway late Saturday afternoon. When she saw Kit with his classically handsome features and deep blue eyes, startling in his sun-bronzed face, she threw her arms around him. "You are *gorgeous*," she cried. "No man has a right to be so good-looking."

"Cut the crap, Deb. You're embarrassing the kid," said her husband.

"Don't be a fool, Jergen. A little flattery never hurt a man. Right, Kit?" Deborah ruffled his dark hair, oblivious of his grinning friends.

Kit blushed and leaned down to hug Wendy, then tossed her little brother over his shoulder while the child shrieked with laughter. They followed Deborah into the huge living room with its raised fieldstone hearth and wall of glass. Facing the fireplace was a large sectional sofa, an assortment of floor pillows, some lamps, and not much else.

"Wow, Debbie, amazing place. What a fantastic view!"

"This room really knocked my socks off when I first saw it," she said. "I knew I would kill to own this house."

To the pleasant background of taped sitar music, the entourage, like most struggling musicians who never turn down a free meal, did not have to be coaxed into the kitchen, where Deborah had set out a generous assortment of vegetarian dishes. Fortified with heaping portions of potato and tofu curry, pilaf, ratatouille, bean casserole, green salad, and freshly baked five-grain bread from the farmers' market, they took foaming tankards of Jergen's home brew and spread themselves on the floor of the big roomy living room at his feet. With his new designer haircut and ruddy beard, Jergen looked more like a film director than a holistic healer. His charisma was legendary and the young musicians came under his spell as he held forth on the merits of self-hypnosis.

Wendy and two-year-old Richie (né Ramdas) were all over Kit, and Deborah noticed how very sweet and comfortable he was with the children. She took a seat on the couch next to him, shooing them away so Kit could eat his dinner.

"Tell us about the band," she urged, including the others whom she feared were too long a captive audience for Jergen. "You guys are making it, I gather."

"It hasn't been all that easy," replied Kit. "We still wait tables and tend bar, but lately we've had a few breaks."

"Our latest album made *Billboard*'s Heatseekers chart," said the drummer.

"Congratulations."

"I'll send you a disc," promised Kit.

"No freebies. We'll *buy* dozens and give them to all our friends," said Deborah. "What's it called?"

"*Down and Out.*"

"Nice title."

One of the girls whispered something to Kit, but he shushed her.

"Oh, go on, tell them."

"Tell us what?" asked Deborah.

"They got a mention in the LA *Times* Calendar section."

"Hey, no kidding. What did it say?"

"Show it to her, Kit," they chorused.

"Knock it off, you guys." Kit flushed, embarrassed.

"Well, if you won't, I will," said the drummer, taking a much folded news clipping from his wallet and handing it to Deborah.

"Listen to this, Jergen . . ." Deborah caught her husband's

eye, silencing him as she read from the column that had a photograph of Kit onstage, playing the guitar:

The Beat Goes On: Oldtimers will remember
the late composer Michael Kittredge Shane

(*Face to Face; Over the Moon; Forgotten Rhapsody*), whose career ended tragically in 1950 with his death. Well, now there's Michael Kittredge (Kit) Shane II, his grandson and namesake, who has been making the rounds of the coffee houses and appears at the Big Dipper this month with the Berkeley Five, a coming group of student rockers with a classical jazz bent. Handsome Kit has star quality . . . he's lead guitar, also sings, plays the banjo and keyboard, and does the group's arrangements. "I never knew my grandfather, but he's been a major influence on me through his music," says the multi-talented performer. Shane confides he has a dream to someday put on a show featuring his grandfather's songs.

"Gee, that's super, Kit."

He grinned, still uncomfortable. "That last bit about the show was off the record. She wasn't supposed to use it."

"Oh well, the more famous you get, the more you'll learn not to trust reporters." When the other band members had gone for second helpings, Deborah asked, "Has Julia seen that item?"

"No, I thought of sending it, but . . ."

"You should. She'd be so proud."

"You don't think it might make her feel bad, I mean, the stuff about my grandfather?"

"She would be thrilled, I'm sure. You know something, I always thought Mother was more in love with Michael than she was with Daddy. She didn't mention him often when I was a kid, but whenever she did, her eyes would get this sort of dreamy, faraway look."

This was obviously a new side of his grandmother to Kit. "Grams must have been a pistol when she was young. She's great, isn't she? I can really talk to that woman."

"There was a time when . . ." Deborah smiled wistfully. "Oh well, I guess maybe the lines of communication skip a generation. Daddy—with whom I could discuss anything, as long as it wasn't serious—used to joke about grandparents and grandchildren having a common enemy."

"I miss Gramps," said Kit. "He was the only grandfather I ever knew. My other grandparents died years ago . . . and of course, my dad doesn't even remember his real father."

"Neil was only a baby when Michael died, but he was the one who used to play his music. I think he inherited the musical gene, and he must have passed it on to you."

Kit traced the Apache design of a cushion cover with his index finger. "Dad doesn't say much about the days when he was growing up. I get the feeling he wasn't too happy."

"You're probably right. When we were kids, I was closer to him than I was to Scott. Even so, he was five years older, so I was still in junior high by the time he went away to college. Neil kept so much to himself, it was hard to say what he was thinking. I know Mother and Daddy tried to understand him, but he made it difficult. Especially when he got involved in the antiwar movement."

"Yeah," Kit said softly, turning his head away.

Dare she ask? Deborah wondered, but she was curious. "Do you ever visit your mother, Kit?"

"Not often." Something painful shifted in his eyes as he looked at her, and she was sorry she had brought it up. "The last time was two years ago. I find it destructive for us to be together. Ursula is a very bitter woman. She drives everyone away. Her second husband left her years ago and took my half-brother with him. That did a lot to make me understand my own situation. I mean, I used to feel there was something wrong with me, because she didn't love me. But now I understand she really doesn't want the closeness or the responsibility for anyone—husband, children, or even friends. She stays in her studio and sculpts. Never goes out, never sees people. It's really weird."

"She sounds depressed. Has she ever been to a psychiatrist?"

"When my stepfather suggested it, she threw him out."

"Oh Kit, I'm sorry. No matter what, she's your mother."

"Hey," said Kit, looking around at the circle of friends who had quietly taken their places on the floor again, "I didn't mean to get everyone down. This is supposed to be, like, a party."

Soon the band was preparing to leave for Big Sur. Deborah

took the drummer aside. "Can you make me a copy of that newspaper column?"

"Keep this one," he said, giving her the clipping, "I have more at home."

"Thanks. I want to send it to my mother. She's very much the doting grandmother when it comes to Kit."

"Hey man," the drummer told Kit when they said goodbye, "your aunt's really cool."

Not a week later, at a quarter past six on Thursday evening, Julia was driving home from Marlin Beach after her shift at the nursing home. Crossing the bay on the series of causeways that connected Palm Island to the mainland, she was aware of the subtle change of season. The days were growing shorter, the air cooler. Migrating birds swooped down in dark waves on the nature preserve across the channel. In the North, she had always taken great pleasure in the beauty of autumn, but without the spectacular color of fall leaves, it had a melancholy aspect.

Or perhaps it was her mood. After spending the afternoon at the Admiralty, she was depressed. Although nothing out of the ordinary had happened, Marie had been less responsive today, complaining that it was too chilly to walk out on the grounds of the nursing home. The old woman seemed disinclined to carry on a conversation, so Julia had given her a manicure and read to her. Finally, holding her hand, she sat with her charge until the supper trays arrived at an unbelievably early hour. Julia's stomach turned at the unappetizing meal, consisting of watery soup, dried-out broiled fish, and soggy vegetables. But Marie perked up at the sight of food and, although it was barely past five o'clock, finished every scrap.

Approaching dusk was casting long shadows across the lawn by the time Julia reached home. The compound's private postman had left a bundle of mail in her box, neatly secured with a rubber band. Oh good! There was a letter from Deborah, heavy enough to contain the pictures she had promised. She put aside the rest of the mail, including an announcement of Janice Fried's one-woman show at the Contemporary Arts Gallery in New York and, dropping her packages on the kitchen counter, headed for the living room. She tore open the thick envelope addressed in her daughter's familiar handwriting and withdrew a quantity of colored snapshots.

The children were as adorable as they could be, Wendy sprouting up and wearing braces, and little Richie with his impish grin. She would definitely go to California this winter to visit them. And on the way, she would stop to see the Hoppers in Scottsdale. It had been so long since she had been with them. Edwin was getting on in years, almost ninety now, but in amazingly good health, thank heaven . . .

She turned her attention back to the pictures of Deborah's family. Even Jergen appeared quite substantial in a white cable-stitch turtleneck sweater, looking considerably more presentable than the last time she had seen him. He was an attractive man, Julia would grant him that. Rather like a modern-day Viking with that full head of hair and his beard neatly trimmed. Deborah, she was pleased to note, looked as young and beautiful as ever, although her hair was a mess, a great untamed mane. Reminded one of that appealing actress with the odd name. In *Moonstruck*. Cher. No doubt Cher's mother occasionally felt an urge to take a brush and scissors to her daughter's tresses. Deborah's smile was radiant as she embraced her husband and children in front of their new home. One of those sprawling California houses, Julia could see, all glass and redwood with a panoramic view that Deborah had included among the pictures.

How nice . . . Kit had come to visit them. Julia finished reading Deborah's scrawled note and unfolded a newspaper clipping. *Oh*, my . . . that picture. It gave her quite a start. Kit looked so much like his grandfather. She read the article through, stared at Kit's photograph, and then read the item again. That was a rather nice tribute to Michael, wasn't it? She put the letter on the desk and sat for a moment, remembering. No, it wouldn't do to dwell on the past.

She simply had to get out in the air. Pushing herself from the chair, she walked through the screened patio to the terrace. Rounding the corner to the garden, she almost bumped into her neighbor. "Oh. Clarissa, you startled me."

"I'm sorry, Julia. I saw your car and was about to knock on the door." Her voice dropped to a whisper. "Come back to the house for a minute, I want you to meet someone."

Julia followed her neighbor through the hedge and along a walk to the carport, where a man was leaning under the raised hood of Clarissa's BMW. He straightened up as they approached, wiping oil-stained hands against his tight-fitting jeans. *Gary* was lettered in red machine stitching on the left breast of his blue knit shirt. Beneath the name was a pair of crossed pennants, with *Brisa* under that, no doubt the name of a yacht.

"Gary is helping out around the property," said Clarissa, making a coy gesture. "This is my neighbor, Mrs. Rhinehart."

Gary flashed a dazzling smile. "Pleased to meet you, Mrs. Rhinehart." Blond and blue-eyed, with golden, suntanned skin and impressive biceps, he was what her granddaughter Ginger would have called a hunk. He exuded a blatant sexuality, and Julia took an instant dislike to him. After regarding her with sharp scrutiny, he slammed shut the hood of the BMW and picked up his tools. "Well, I guess I'll go see to the boat now. See you around, Mrs. Rhinehart."

"Come on in for a minute, Julia," Clarissa said with a high, nervous laugh. When they were in the kitchen, she whispered, "What do you think of him?" There was an edgy timbre to her voice.

"What am I supposed to think, Clarissa? He's your handyman."

"Oh, I know, but isn't he *gorgeous?* I found him at Captain Bart's yesterday, looking for work and a place to live. He's staying on the boat. Sort of like a skipper."

Julia did not bother to conceal her shock. "Staying on your boat? I thought we had rules against that."

"He's considered domestic help."

"Don't you think it's a little risky, letting a stranger just . . . move in?"

"Oh, fiddlesticks, what kind of risk?"

"There's just something about him. For all you know, he could be a . . . a rapist."

"What an imagination you have, Julia. Don't you trust anyone? I checked him out with the man he used to crew for, and he's perfectly fine. Besides, Palm Island's bonding company will investigate him. You know how careful they are, so relax."

Clarissa was probably right; she should learn to take people on trust. *There I go again, making snap judgments*, Julia chided herself. *After five years down here you'd think I would get over my cautious urban mentality.* "Forget I said anything," she laughed good-naturedly.

Still, she thought, locking up after dinner, it was unwise for a woman to have a burly drifter hanging around, living on her boat. There was something unsavory about it. Not that she believed for a minute that Clarissa was attracted to him. That was straight out of D. H. Lawrence. And yet . . . she could have sworn that's what her neighbor had been suggesting. It was dreadfully sad to see a woman of that age who felt only half-alive without a man.

Oh well, she felt sorry for Clarissa, but it wasn't her worry. The dishes washed, she turned out the kitchen lights and, tired from the day's activities, ran a hot bath.

After a good long soak, Julia selected a novel from a pile of books she kept on the library table in a corner of the bedroom. As an afterthought, she also took a volume of essays on mortality sent by a well-meaning friend. Switching on the radio to an all-music station, she piled pillows against the headboard and settled into bed. The entire evening lay ahead with nothing to do but read—until recently an unimaginable luxury.

The novel failed to capture her attention and she put it aside, opening the book of essays, which proved to be heavy going. Soon she nodded off and was drifting into a comfortable slumber, when her mind registered the sentimental strains of "Promises," a country-music version that Michael would have deplored. She turned on her side, fully alert. How strange, the coincidence of hearing one of Michael's songs on the very day she had received the newspaper clipping from Deborah.

She could scarcely remember when she had last heard this piece. From the old sheet music and singles days, like several of Michael's early songs, it had become popular when Republic picked it up to interpolate into a score—in this case *Beneath the Stars*, a completely forgettable motion picture. Far from his best work, "Promises" was straightforward and predictable, one of a group he had written in the mid-thirties before she had met him. Back then, he was composing to satisfy Zachary Mitchell. As one of Zach's stable of songwriters, he had been obliged to fulfill his publisher's demands, giving him material that was sure to sell. Michael's strength had always been in his originality, a classical approach in which the use of half-tones and triplets set new styles in popular ballads. But that had come later, after he stopped working for Mitchell.

The station was playing another early Shane ballad. This

time it was "Sunshine," a lighthearted tune with engaging lyrics, one of his last compositions before his collaboration with Murray Baker. While the simple love songs may not have been among Michael's most memorable compositions, Julia was swept into the mood of nostalgia they evoked. A vision came to her of those electric days after Shane and Baker's first Broadway hit. Much as she hated to admit it, Murray had been good for Michael.

She sighed, coming back to the present. Poor Michael, he had been robbed of the chance to savor his success. Wasn't it ironic that his music was making a comeback after so many years of oblivion? Even Scott, who had a tin ear, had noticed that Peter Duchin and Lester Lanin's orchestras were playing the songs of Michael Shane, with their smooth, clever melodies and sophisticated lyrics. Scott, the intrepid black-tie-benefit-goer, had barely taken notice of his father's music all his life, preferring to think of himself as George Rhinehart's son. Well, that was behind them now.

At nine-thirty she was dozing over her book when the telephone rang. It was Sue Winston calling from New York. "Julia, darling, you weren't sleeping this early?"

"No, no," Julia hastened to assure her, "just reading."

Of all the old friends, the Winstons were the ones who most regularly stayed in touch. Sue usually kept her abreast of events in their circle, and Julia prepared for a long, chatty conversation. But this time Sue did not bother with small talk. There was a strained note in her voice that caused Julia's pulse to skip. "Bad news, I'm afraid. Gerald Ross died last night. I thought you'd want to know."

"Oh dear." She closed her eyes, and let her breath out. "What happened?"

"Heart attack. Late at night. He was working in his study and never came to bed. Florence didn't realize he was gone until early morning."

"Dreadful for her. How old was he?"

"Seventy-seven."

"Funny, I thought he would be older. Scott mentioned seeing Gerry a few weeks ago and said he looked so well."

"With the heart, you never know . . ." she said solemnly.

"I suppose not."

Julia did not remember Sue being especially close to the

Rosses, but she sounded positively mournful. "The body's being cremated. There's a memorial service at Emanu-El on Tuesday at two-thirty, but I don't suppose you would come all the way up from Florida."

"Florida is not outer space," answered Julia with a touch of asperity. "Actually I wouldn't at all mind a trip to New York." She could catch Janice Fried's show while she was there.

"You're welcome to stay with us, although we're leaving for Boston the next day to spend Thanksgiving with Jack, Jr. and the children."

Julia had almost forgotten about Thanksgiving. The Mosers were expecting her for dinner. Joyce liked "bringing people together," and had mentioned that several of the other guests would be widows or divorcées from Naples and nearby Sanibel Island. "Scott and Isobel would be hurt if I came to New York and didn't stay with them," she replied, although she suspected it was far from the truth.

"I ran into Isobel at the Adolfo show the other day. Looking fabulous, as always. She told me about her new venture, the art gallery."

"I just heard about it myself last week. A sudden decision, I gather. I'll probably come up for the opening."

"I simply cannot imagine Isobel in business."

"Why ever not? Isobel has always been a good manager, and she majored in art history at Vassar."

"Oh, she's certainly capable after chairing so many committees, I don't doubt that. It's just unexpected. I think it's wonderful the way these married women are starting careers nowadays. Can you imagine what Jack's mother would have said if I decided to go to work?"

Sue was a little behind the times. Didn't she realize that most women had jobs "nowadays"? After saying goodbye, Julia called Delta and made a reservation for Tuesday morning. Then she dialed Scott's number, but they were out for the evening, so she left a message with his answering service asking to have a car meet her plane at LaGuardia on Tuesday. Slowly replacing the receiver, she wished that Scott had been at home. It would have been reassuring to talk to someone.

She lay still for a moment, trying to collect her thoughts. So . . . he had died. Gerald Ross. She should be feeling something other than surprise. Some depth of emotion. Regret or nostalgia. But all she could feel at the moment was anger.

Throwing back the covers, Julia donned slippers and robe. In the living room, she turned on a lamp and opened the doors to a large custom-made cabinet containing hundreds of old record albums—Decca, RCA Victor, Capitol, Columbia, Vocalion, Brunswick—some of them dating back to the twenties. One section held special master recordings of musical plays with their original casts. Inside of each embossed cover was a copy of the libretto with its published score.

She selected a particular album and stacked the records on the turntable. Leafing through the sheets of music, she stared thoughtfully into space while she listened to the original recording of the Gerald Ross production of *Over the Moon*, the Shane and Baker musical that was Broadway's newest hit in the fall of 1943.

Half a century later, by comparison with modern recordings, the music had a hollow, dated sound. But amplified by the stereophonic speakers, its jazzy, melodic stylishness, coupled with the witty lyrics, remained ageless, and Julia sank down on the floor to listen.

When the first side came to an end, she turned the records over. Opening another cabinet beneath the bookcases, she removed two large boxes from the bottom shelf. Item by item, she began to sift through the contents, stopping to examine a photograph, read a letter, or skim an old newspaper article. At the bottom of the second box there was a brown manila portfolio with a string fastener, the type that law firms sometimes use for client files. Setting this aside, she gathered everything together and replaced the boxes in the cabinet.

Suddenly she could not bear for another instant to listen to the music. She stopped the turntable, carefully replacing the 78-rpm records in their jackets, and returned the albums to the cabinet.

As she turned out the lights, she noticed it had started to rain, one of those sudden unexpected squalls for which the Gulf Coast is known. She had always loved the sound of rain on the roof, to know that she was secure in her house when a storm was blowing. But tonight it made her feel lonely.

Returning to bed, Julia lay back against the pillows and let the memories roll over her. The memories she had been suppressing all evening.

❧ Chapter 7 ❧

Michael

A month had passed since the night she had met Michael
Shane. Although he was often in her thoughts, short of haunt-
ing the crooked alley in Greenwich Village where he lived,
Julia could think of no way their paths might cross.

She had come to know rather more about him than their
tenuous acquaintance would suggest, for she had combed Edwin
Hopper's extensive library of theatrical reference material for
any mention of him. There wasn't much. The transcript of an
ASCAP panel in which he had participated, a brief interview in
Musical America, and a biographical sketch in a new anthology
of contemporary composers. She found a number of reviews of
One Night in Venice. Willela Waldorf in the *Post* had praised
it as "fresh and surprising," although overly ambitious; Burns
Mantle, the *Daily News* critic, was lavish in his enthusiasm
for the "skillful marriage of story and song," while Louis
Kronenberger in *PM* called it "condescending," and Brooks
Atkinson in the New York *Times*, in the biting commentary
for which he had become known, dismissed it as derivative
operetta. Atkinson seemed to lay all blame for the lackluster
state of the American musical theater on Michael's shoulders,
and damned the play with the suggestion that Hollywood would
snap it up.

The critics had been unanimous in their praise of the performance of Vivienne Tremaine.

Julia looked for him everywhere. Since Michael was a composer, you would think he would frequent music copy services, the theater district, Carnegie Hall—all the places she visited constantly for Edwin Hopper. New Yorkers claimed they were forever bumping into old friends on the street, but as the weeks passed and she did not see him, she lost hope. And yet it did not seem possible that she would never meet him again. When you believed in something so strongly, it was bound to happen.

On a rainy Friday afternoon in October, she was standing on the library steps in Hopper's office, cataloging scripts. All the men had left early for the weekend, so she was surprised when she heard footsteps approaching through the outer offices where the secretaries worked.

"Anyone here?"

There appeared in the doorway a tall, rangy young man with unruly black hair and blue eyes. Perched on the topmost ledge of the ladder, her arms full of bound scripts, she felt giddy with instant recognition.

It was obvious he had forgotten her. "Hello. I hope I haven't unsettled you up there."

"No, I'm used to it."

"The door was open, so I came in. No one was at the front desk."

"The receptionist must have gone home."

She climbed down and he came to help her, holding her arm and taking the scripts. "I have an appointment with Tony Regis."

"Mr. Regis has left for the day," she replied before she could stop herself, breaking one of the cardinal rules of a good secretary. Although Regis was not her boss, she was expected to front for all the men. "Are you certain it was for today?"

"Friday at four o'clock."

"I don't work for Mr. Regis, but let me check his calendar. Won't you have a seat, Mr. . . . ?" She felt rather clever, pretending not to know his name.

"Shane," he said. "Michael Shane."

In Tony's office, she looked at his desk calendar. Very faintly, next to 4:00 P.M., she could make out a penciled entry that had been erased.

Tony Regis operated as an independent agent. He rented office space from Hopper and was forever boasting about his contacts. Once he had invited her to the theater, but Millie Kramer, who had a line on everyone, had warned her, "He's not for you, Julia. Too smooth. Unreliable." Trusting Millie, Julia had been cool to Regis. Nevertheless, she decided to cover for him, if for no other reason than to spare Michael Shane's feelings.

"It's not on his calendar, Mr. Shane. Perhaps there was a misunderstanding."

"You're awfully good, but it won't work. Tony and I definitely had a date this afternoon."

Her eyes went to the portfolio he held. "Did you plan to show him some of your music?"

"Yes, I'm a songwriter. How did you guess?"

"Well, actually, you and I have met before," she confessed. "When I came to a party at your apartment."

He smiled in recognition. "I thought I'd seen you somewhere. You were the girl with Ben Carmichael. I don't remember your name."

"It's Julia, Julia Perkins."

"You still going with Ben, Julia?"

"I've never *gone* with him. We're just friends."

"Good," he said. "He's way too old for you."

"He's only twenty-eight."

"Is that what he told you?"

"He isn't?"

"Thirty-four, the last I heard."

"Oh. Well, he looks so young, I guess he thinks he may as well fib a little. Women do it all the time."

He nodded. "That figures."

"I thought Ben was your agent."

"Not really. Mostly I peddle my own stuff."

He was preparing to leave and she wanted to prolong the conversation. "That's why you had an appointment with Tony."

"Yes, and he stood me up. I hate to admit how important this was."

"If you'd like to leave the music, I'll see that he gets it first thing Monday morning."

"You're not *serious?* Give my best songs to a secretary who doesn't even work for him—" He caught himself. "I'm sorry, that sounded rude."

"I promise you, Mr. Shane," she said with all the dignity she could muster, "I shall lock them in the file cabinet and hand them to Mr. Regis myself."

Was it possible to fall instantly and obsessively in love? she wondered months later, when there was no doubt about her feelings for Michael Shane. It seemed trite to imagine she was so impetuously stricken, for clearly there had been a long interval of ambivalence during which she could feel herself slipping slowly and inexorably into that sweetly treacherous condition.

Her first birthday away from home turned out to be unexpectedly festive. On Friday afternoon, Millie and the office staff surprised her with a cake. Betsy gave a small dinner that evening, inviting some of Julia's friends from Hunter College. And on Saturday night, her actual birthday, Ben took her to the Stork Club to celebrate. That morning, a special delivery package arrived from Troy. Julia wept when she opened the gift-wrapped box from her mother containing Jesse's good pearls that had been restrung.

Meanwhile she was discovering the invigorating pleasures of autumn in the city, a time of beginnings, the start of the academic year and a new theatrical season. Her courses at Hunter were interesting and not terribly demanding; her job and the Hopper staff were entirely to her liking. Show tickets were hers for the asking, and she would often treat Betsy to an evening of theater or a concert. It was a way of reciprocating, for her aunt would not permit her to share the rent. Ben Carmichael usually asked her out on Saturday night, and sometimes she would go, but she was seeing less and less of him. One weekend she went apple-picking with friends, taking a scenic drive along the Hudson River to view the fall foliage.

On Thanksgiving Day the apartment was filled with the luscious aroma of roasted turkey, chestnut stuffing, sweet potato pudding, and pumpkin pie. Betsy invited six guests for dinner, and even her grandmother's coldness when they called Troy could not dim the holiday feeling for Julia.

The week after Thanksgiving, Zachary Mitchell, the flamboyant music publisher turned impresario, was throwing a big bash to celebrate the second anniversary of his repertory theater. Edwin Hopper was invited, of course, and he took Julia along. In a short time, a fond familiarity had developed between them. "You'll enjoy this party, Julia," he said on the way over. "There will be lots of glittery people."

When they arrived, Edwin made a few introductions, saw that she had a drink, and then left her on her own while he worked the room. She was talking to Jim Turner, a playwright who was one of Hopper's clients, when Michael Shane walked by and stopped to shake hands with him.

"Good to see you, Mike. Do you two know each other? Julia works for the Hopper office."

"Mr. Shane and I have met," she said quickly.

For a moment Michael looked puzzled, then his smile brightened. "You."

She put out her hand. "Julia Perkins. It's been a while since we've seen each other." Jim edged away to catch the attention of a producer, leaving them alone.

"I was pretty mad that day," said Michael.

"That's understandable."

"I still am."

"Mad at Tony Regis?"

"You bet."

"Why?"

"Never heard from him. I've left messages, but he doesn't return my calls."

"I know he received the scores, because I gave them to him myself."

"I'll remember that if he fails to return them."

"Oh, he would never . . ."

He raised one eyebrow. "He wouldn't? You don't know Tony very well."

"You're right. He really just rents office space from Mr. Hopper, although he'd kill me for telling you that."

Michael looked surprised. "The way he represents himself, you'd think he was a full partner."

"If Edwin knew that, he wouldn't like it."

"You should tell him. But do me a favor, wait until Regis returns my music." They laughed together, and he said, "If you're not busy after the party, maybe we could—"

A tall, patrician blond man unceremoniously nudged Julia aside, addressing himself to Michael with lambent languor.

"Gerald Ross, Mr. Shane. I was planning to call you. We met at the Kaufman party."

"I remember. This is Miss Perkins."

His glance bounced off Julia as if she were a speck of lint on his custom tailored suit. "Can we talk, Shane?"

Michael was cautious, throwing Julia an apologetic sidelong glance. "Now?"

"I'd like you to take a look at a play I've optioned. It's a natural for a musical. I saw *One Night in Venice*, and you could be our man. Interested?"

"Possibly." Julia observed the sudden concentration in Michael's eyes and knew she had lost his attention. She was certain he had intended to ask her out before Gerald Ross interrupted, but the moment had passed.

The two men became engrossed in conversation. Annoyed at being ignored, Julia moved across the room and helped herself to the buffet. A woman wearing an outlandish green Robin Hood hat was piling jumbo shrimps on her plate. Julia nodded and received a chilly stare in response. She wondered whether she lacked a special knack of getting to know people. In this throng of mismatched creatures, everyone seemed to have found someone to talk to. Shouting with laughter, gesticulating wildly, they roared at each other in order to be heard above the din, intent upon furthering whatever singular self-interest they served.

"There you are, Julia." Edwin Hopper came over to her with unusual ebullience. "If you're ready to leave, I'll drop you at home."

"Isn't it out of your way?" she said, aware that he lived in Gramercy Park.

"Not at all, I'm going uptown for dinner."

She could think of no excuse not to join him, although she would have liked to stay long enough for Michael to finish his discussion with Ross. With a backward glance in their direction, she accompanied her boss to the cloak room.

It was good to know that Edwin was getting out in the evening, she thought as they got into his car. Millie was always remarking that he had become a recluse since his wife's death the previous year. When he had given her address to his driver, she asked, "Who is Gerald Ross?"

Hopper looked interested. "Did you meet him?"

"We were introduced."

"Gerry is a young producer with a growing amount of influence. He's brash and he can be difficult, but he's raised the money behind a number of hits. What did he have to say?"

"Not a word. I might as well not have been there as far as he was concerned."

He smiled sympathetically. "It's amazing how many of these people don't take the time to be civil. I'm afraid it's a failing of the industry."

"Not always, Mr. Hopper. When we met on the train, you were so friendly, it gave me a whole different view about coming to New York."

He smiled and patted her hand. "If I hadn't bothered to speak to you, we'd never have hired my best reader."

Julia had a headache and was content to sit back and listen while Hopper related anecdotes about some of the more colorful personalities at the party. He knew everyone's history in the theater world and had the knack of telling a good story. As the car traveled north on Broadway to Columbus Circle, she regretted again that they had left before she had a chance to say goodbye to Michael Shane. If only there had been another few seconds before the producer came along for Michael to finish asking her out—if indeed that was his intention. When the automobile turned off Fifth Avenue onto Seventy-fourth Street, she could still feel her disappointment and the affront of Ross's snub.

"Which building is yours?" asked Hopper.

"Third door on the right." Always gallant, he helped her out of the car. "Thanks again for taking me to the party, Mr. Hopper, that was quite a scene. I hope you have a pleasant evening."

When she let herself into the apartment, Betsy was busy preparing for her secretaries' meeting the following evening. "There's extra chicken à la king if you haven't had dinner, Jule."

"No, thanks. There was lots to eat at the party. I'll come help you just as soon as I get into something comfortable."

In her room, she changed into an old skirt and sweater, then tied her hair back, sponged her face with cold water and took some aspirin for her headache. As she passed through the hallway, the telephone rang and she picked it up.

"Hello?"

"Hi, hon . . . sorry it took so long, but this was the first I could get away." It was a man's voice, low and caressing, and for a wild moment she thought it might be Michael Shane, but of course it wasn't.

"I think you must have the wrong number," she said.

"Betsy?"

"Oh. Just a moment, please."

Her aunt was putting a batch of chocolate nut drop cookies in the oven. "You have a phone call, Bets. A man."

Betsy remained very still, and then she took a deep breath and turned. "Thanks. Will you watch the cookies? I almost burned the first batch."

Julia poured herself a glass of milk and nibbled on an overdone cookie from the cooling platter. Who could be calling Betsy? she wondered. *Hi, hon*, he had said, *sorry it took so long* . . . Intimate words, although people in New York threw terms of endearment around like confetti. It must be someone close to her, though, from his tone of voice. Soothing, melting . . . *seductive*.

Half an hour passed and Betsy had not returned. Julia baked the rest of the cookies, storing them in a tin when they were cool. She put the casserole of chicken à la king in the refrigerator and washed the mixing bowls piled in the sink. Finished in the kitchen, she turned out the light and went to her room to find the script she was reading. The phone was still off the hook in the hall. As she replaced it, she heard a dial tone. Obviously Betsy had completed her conversation but was still closeted in her room. Julia took one of the afghans crocheted by her grandmother from a closet shelf and curled up on the living room couch.

She must have dozed, for when she turned drowsily, the script fell to the floor with a thud, and her eyes flew open. With the clarity that comes upon sudden wakening, she knew something was wrong. Betsy sat in the chair opposite, her eyes red-rimmed and her face puffy from weeping.

"Betsy, what happened?"

"Oh, Jule, can I talk to you? I have to confide in someone."

She sat up and patted the cushion next to her. "Come, sit here." Betsy moved to the couch. "Now, tell me what's the matter."

"I'm not sure I know how to begin."

"Does it have something to do with that telephone call?"

Betsy nodded.

"Who was the man on the phone?"

She sighed and closed her eyes, saying in a barely audible voice, "Rodney."

Julia blinked. "Your boss?"

"Yes." Betsy looked at her steadily. "You may as well know . . . I'm in love with him. We've been having an affair."

Why was she not shocked? In some reserved pocket of her subconscious, Julia realized she had suspected all along, putting it resolutely out of her thoughts when the suggestions were all too clear. The troubled silences, the late hours at the office. Her beautiful aunt's unexplained lonely weekends. The overnight absences, the sudden switches of plans according to the whims of Rodney Barstow, her demanding boss. That odd remark of Ben Carmichael's at Barstow's party: *Too bad she's all tied up* . . .

"You don't seem surprised," said Betsy.

"The only thing that surprises me is that I didn't guess long ago. It must have been such a strain for you all this time with me living here, having to pretend."

"No, it somehow made it easier. It's been a terribly emotional year for me. Having you around has made the last few months bearable."

"Oh, Betsy, I'm so sorry. I'm listening, if you want to talk about it."

"Yes, I need to talk," she said, taking a deep breath. "It started quite innocently. Neither of us expected or wanted anything like this . . . I used to go out to the house on weekends to help Arden with parties. She's hopeless when it comes to people or entertaining. All she's interested in are her horses. I became fond of the family, especially the three children, and they of me. Then, just about a year ago, RNA held a network cruise to Cuba for their broadcasters and affiliate heads. Rod turned the entire project over to me. I planned it, made all the arrangements, and when Arden decided at the last minute not to go because one of her best mares was in foal, he asked me to act as hostess.

"It was a terribly romantic setting. Cruising under blue skies and moonlit nights on a beautiful luxury liner. We were together constantly . . . at meetings during the day, swimming in the pool, each night for dinner and dancing. We left New York on a Wednesday night, and by the time we sailed into Havana harbor I realized I was falling in love with him . . ." For a moment Betsy seemed lost in reverie, but soon she continued.

"I kept fighting it, and evidently so did Rod. It was a constant struggle. I was terribly nervous—having trouble sleeping. One afternoon when everyone had gone ashore, I was taking dictation in Rod's stateroom—he had set up a corner of the sitting room as an office. Suddenly he got up and locked the door and he came to me and pulled me into his arms . . ." Betsy stopped and leaned forward earnestly. "Jule, you must believe me when I tell you I did nothing to encourage him."

"I believe you. Go on."

"He kissed me and told me he was in love with me, that he had been for the longest time. I began to cry like a fool, but that only made him more . . . I don't know . . . tender, I suppose. Well, we didn't make love then. I was afraid and confused and . . . and *moral*. I mean, he was a *married man*, and I thought of Arden as a friend." She caught herself and went on in a quieter voice. "He didn't try to pressure me then, but that night he came to my cabin and my resistance seemed to evaporate . . ." Betsy twisted her handkerchief and looked away.

"If it bothers you to talk about it—"

"No, telling you is almost like explaining it to myself," said Betsy. "I had never slept with a man before. I just . . . I can't describe how it was. So different from the way I imagined. Just beautiful and pure and somehow innocent. And for Rod, too, he felt the same. I said I couldn't continue to work with him, and he absolutely insisted I had to. He promised it wouldn't interfere with our work and that no one would know, but of course people are a lot smarter than that. I imagine a great number of his friends are aware."

Julia realized that was true, for if Ben Carmichael knew, so did the world.

"He said he was going to divorce Arden but he had to wait. He and Arden have been married for sixteen years and there's nothing between them anymore, hasn't been for ages, so it's not like I've broken up a loving marriage.

"The children are still young. The boys would be all right, they're away at prep school. But Elizabeth is only eleven and she's very insecure. Rod wants to wait until she's old enough to understand."

"When will that be?" Julia asked.

"He thinks in another year or two."

"And then? Has he asked you to marry him?"

"Well, not in so many words."

"Has he said anything to Arden? I mean, does she know about you?"

"I'm certain she doesn't. It's a complicated situation. She comes from a very wealthy and powerful family. Her father is the retired board chairman of RNA—"

"Oh no!"

"Oh yes." Betsy heaved a great sigh. "So there you have it. What do you think?"

Julia did not answer immediately, and when she did, it was with caution. "As long as you're Rod's . . . I don't know what to call it—girlfriend, I guess."

"Mistress is the word, I believe."

"Whatever. He doesn't have any *reason* to push for a divorce. If he can stay in his marriage and still have you, he's got the best of both worlds. Why should he bother?"

She nodded despondently. "I know. That's how my thoughts run when I'm feeling down."

"What happened tonight to make you so unhappy?"

"We had planned a vacation together over Christmas and New Year's. Arden was going to take the children to visit her parents in Palm Beach for ten days. Now suddenly she's changed her mind and it's all up in the air."

"But don't you see, that's exactly what I mean. As long as he's married to her, she'll always come first and you'll get what's left."

"I know, I know . . ." And Betsy began to cry again.

Julia put her arms around her. "Bets, I should be comforting you, not pointing out cold, stark truths."

Betsy mopped at her eyes. "No, that's what I love about you. You're honest, and I need someone to give me some straight talk."

"Have you considered breaking it off? Could you bear to?"

"I would have to quit my job. And move."

"Why change where you live?"

She sighed. "You might as well know all of it. Rod owns this building. How else could I afford such an extravagant apartment?"

Julia tried to hide her shock. "Is that why you won't let me pay rent?"

"Partly. I do pay rent to the management office myself, but Rod puts the money in my account, calling it a supplement to my salary." She looked down at her hands. "It sounds pretty awful, doesn't it?"

"Umm . . . well, it sure ain't what I thought, honey."

Betsy hugged her. "Oh, Julia, thank you for being here and listening. Just telling you makes me feel better. I hated living a lie. I hope I haven't burdened you too much with my problems." She stood up and prepared to go to her room. "I think I'll try to get some sleep. I still have to go to work tomorrow."

"Good night, Bets."

Julia stayed in the living room late into the night, alternately staring into space and reading scripts, making penciled marginal notes. She could see a light in Betsy's room, but the door remained closed. Her heart ached for her aunt, whose beauty and generosity deserved better than the leftover affections of Rodney Barstow. It was not a fair world. It was especially unfair to women.

A week later—a week in which she dwelled on the perfidy of men—she was losing a fight with a head cold when she received a telephone call at her office. "This is Michael Shane," said a deep, warm male voice. "I'm in the neighborhood. Are you by any chance free for lunch?"

Lunch was an insurance date, she knew, in case it should not work out. "I'm coming down with the grippe and I'm probably contagious."

"I know just the remedy," he answered. "Meet me in the lobby at twelve-thirty."

Trying to remain calm, she hurried to the rest room to look in the mirror. Her hair was a wreck and her nose was red from blowing. Of all days for him to have called. If only she had worn something more becoming than her green plaid skirt and tan sweater set, but there was no time to go home to change.

When she stepped out of the elevator, he was waiting,

dressed informally in a gray tweed sport coat with a maroon and navy striped muffler wound around his neck. The cold wind hit her as she went through the revolving doors, and she was seized with a fit of sneezing. Her eyes were streaming as she fished in her purse for a hankie.

"That is some cold, baby. You should be home in bed."

"I warned you," she said in stuffed-head tones, blowing her nose. "I hope you won't catch it."

"Not me, I'm tough. Come on, we're going to feed you. It's not very far."

A weak sun was reflected in the brass instruments of the Salvation Army band playing Christmas carols near the skating rink as they crossed Rockefeller Plaza and walked west on Forty-ninth Street. "Where are we going?" she asked.

"To the Stage Delicatessen. I'm sure you've been there."

"No, never."

"You'll like it."

"Hi, Mike," the manager greeted him when they walked into a clamorous, tile-floored establishment, redolent with unfamiliar aromas. He led them to a table against the wall.

"They obviously know you here. You must come often."

"Every chance I get."

Under the sclerotic eye of a sour-faced waiter, Julia perused the menu, which seemed excessively complicated and made her head ache. She was about to order a chicken salad sandwich and a glass of milk when Michael said, "I recommend the hot pastrami."

"I've never—what is pastrami?"

"Stars above, the child doesn't know pastrami," he remarked to the waiter, whose demeanor became even more disagreeable, if that were possible. "Bring us each a bowl of matzo ball soup, two hot pastramis on rye, and two bottles of Cel-ray."

"What is Cel-ray?"

"Take it from me, my girl, if you let on to anyone that you don't know what pastrami and Cel-ray are, you'll never make it in this town."

Before Julia could think of an apt retort, the surly waiter returned with two bowls into which he unceremoniously dumped metal cups overflowing with golden chicken soup, thin egg noodles, and round dumplings the size of golf balls that bore no resemblance whatsoever, as far as she could see, to the flat Jewish matzo of the Passover. Slamming down a bread basket and a platter of dill pickles, he hurried away to the next table.

"This'll clear up your head quicker than any prescription," pronounced Michael. "Now, eat."

There were tiny globules of fat and specks of chopped parsley floating on the surface of the steaming soup. "Umm," she murmured, as the hot liquid soothed her raw throat.

"Like it?"

"It's *delicious*."

"Eat the matzo balls," he prompted, noticing that she was working around them.

Hesitantly, she broke off a small piece with her spoon. "I'm not too adventurous when it comes to food." It was very hot and she waited for a moment before putting it in her mouth. Michael watched intently as she chewed, and grinned at her pleased reaction.

"See what you've been missing? Stick with me, kid, you'll get an education."

She smiled, feeling unreal, remembering her fantasies that he would call her, her disappointment when he came so close to asking her out . . . her conclusion that his interest had been in her imagination. And now here she was, sitting across the table from him in the Stage Delicatessen. If only she were as beautiful as Vivienne Tremaine or as sparkling a conversationalist as Betsy. With her runny nose and throbbing head, she was incapable of anything beyond an agreeable nod at his witty comments.

When the next course arrived, accustomed to the thin, bland pickled ham or egg salad sandwiches in her grandmother's house, she was staggered by the immense quantity of highly seasoned smoked beef stuffed between two large slices of seeded rye bread. Wondering how she would be able to get her mouth around it, she took half in her hands, sniffing the pungent spiciness. Michael watched with a satisfied smile as she bit into the pastrami.

The restaurant was crowded and noisy, with an ambience that was uniquely New York. Surrounded by the clatter of plates and the clamor of voices, Julia sat back contented. She had finished the soup, a dish of coleslaw, a sour pickle, a roasted pepper, and half the pastrami sandwich, which Michael insisted on lathering with mustard. "I can't eat another bite," she groaned, taking a sip of Dr. Brown's Cel-ray. The drink was too sweet and somehow did not seem to fit with the rest of the meal.

"I'll have the waiter wrap up the other half and you can take it home."

"Oh, I've *never*—"

"Do you realize that's the second time you've said that today. Relax. No one ever leaves a sandwich behind at the Stage Deli." The waiter remained impassive when Michael said, "Would you be good enough to wrap this for the young lady. She has a dog who simply craves pastrami." Julia giggled. "Oh, and we'll have two teas with an order of ruggalach."

"Ruggalach! I know what *they* are. My friend's mother used to bake them."

"So you're not a complete dud after all, Miss Perkins." His deep laughter caused a melting flutter somewhere in the lower regions of her stomach. The meal had revived her. By the time tea was served, they were talking easily and she told him that she had grown up in Troy and was working part time while going to Hunter College.

"I imagine it took some courage to come to New York alone."

"I'm not really alone. I live with my aunt."

"Aha, I might have known. A *duenna*."

"Not at all. Betsy and I are like sisters. You'll really like her." And then she was afraid she had presumed too much.

But Michael didn't seem to notice. "Feeling better?" he asked, when they were drinking their second glass of tea.

"Much improved. That was a great lunch. I've never tasted Jewish food before."

"They don't have Jews in Troy?"

"Of course they do, but I never knew many, at least not well enough to—" She stopped suddenly, thinking he might misunderstand. "You're not Jewish, are you?"

The smile left his face. "And if I were?"

She shook her head. "Nothing. I just wondered."

"Well, I'm not, but I find your reaction puzzling." His tone was decidedly cool.

"I guess I'm a little confused on that subject."

"What is it exactly that confuses you?"

This was getting worse by the minute. "Well, it's just—it occurred to me as we were talking that my father was—is—Jewish."

"Your father's Jewish, and it just occurred to you? Now *I'm* confused."

She sighed. "It's complicated. You see, my mother and father eloped when they were quite young, and her family—well, they didn't like Jews. They especially did not like my father. He and my mother were divorced when I was five, and I haven't seen him since."

He stared at her. "That's a long time not to see your father. Where is he now?"

"I don't know. I assume he's still alive somewhere."

"Have you ever tried to contact him?"

Her mouth opened. "Not for years. I wouldn't have the least idea how to begin. *He* was the one who left, after all. If he had any interest in seeing me, he knew where to find me."

Michael took her hand. "I'm sorry. I've made you unhappy with my curiosity."

"Never mind. It's been a while since I've told anyone about it."

"No brothers or sisters?"

"No. What about you?"

"I had a younger half-brother, but he was killed in an automobile accident seven years ago, along with my father and his second wife."

"How horrible. You weren't in the car with them?"

"No, I was at boarding school in New Jersey."

He came from a musical family, he told her. His mother had been the soprano and his father the musical director of a traveling theatrical company. "I was almost literally born in a trunk. My parents were stranded in a blizzard near Shamokin, Pennsylvania, when my mother went into labor. They were able to make it to a hospital. Just. But my mother came down with pneumonia and she died a week later."

Unable to care for an infant son, Michael's father had taken the baby to live with his older sister in Elyria, Ohio. "Aunt Sophie had been what was then called 'disappointed in love' and never married. She was a fine music teacher and she taught me to play the piano. There was a competition going with baseball for a few years there, but I can't remember a time when music wasn't important to me."

"When did you start composing?"

"I can remember making up little pieces when I was in the third or fourth grade, but I really got hooked on musical comedy at the Pennington School. We put on a student show every semester, and we used to go into New York to the theater. When I was fifteen, I saw *Of Thee I Sing* and it changed my life. I mean, here was a musical with a message. It had everything—drama, romance, satire. I decided I would go to Yale or Princeton, major in music, and become another George Gershwin." Michael looked down, laughing softly. "Well, my father's death the following year changed all that . . ."

After graduating from high school, he went back to Ohio to Oberlin College, not far from Elyria. "I didn't realize Aunt Sophie had cancer. She died during my sophomore year, and I had a hard time dealing with that. By then I was getting restless. At Pennington I had teamed up with my roommate, writing and directing all of the student productions. We did some great stuff. Despite its superb music school, Oberlin seemed kind of tame and fusty after that."

Michael's voice was marvelously compelling. Lost in a glow of warmth, Julia could have sat listening to him all day. "So you came to New York?" she prompted.

"Not immediately. I was lucky enough to win a competition to study in Paris. What an incredible experience that was! When I returned, I transferred to Columbia for my senior year."

"And you've been a composer ever since."

He laughed. "You make it sound so simple. After Paris, I was low on funds. The Bank of Elyria managed my father's estate and they went under, wiping me out. I had to eat, so I got a job as a piano player, plugging sheet music for Zachary Mitchell. He owned a string of music concessions in five-and-dimes, and he had started a little publishing press on the side—popular songs, mostly junk. A year later he sold the concessions and put the money into a downtown repertory playhouse. Zach gets his kicks from going out on a limb, but he got lucky this time."

"My boss says you have to be willing to take chances in order to succeed in the theater."

"That's what life's all about, isn't it? Taking chances." He grinned knowingly. "Anyway, where was I?"

"Playing piano in a five-and-dime and going to Columbia."

"Right. It was crazy. I'd go to classes in the morning, play at Kresge's in the afternoon, and then I'd write songs all night. I sold my stuff to Mitchell and I was happy."

"And you dreamed about Broadway."

"Oh sure. I still do."

"But weren't you thrilled when *One Night in Venice* opened?"

"Yes, I was," he admitted. "However, the Mitchell Theater had a very limited audience that first season. I was so naive when I arrived in New York, barely nineteen and green as the grass in Ohio. Not for some time did I worry about copyrights or royalties. Then suddenly Zach was in the theater business, putting on reviews, and . . . well, you know the rest."

Julia had another fit of sneezing and coughing. Michael peered at her anxiously. "Gosh, here I am gabbing away, not even considering you." He laid his hand against her forehead. "You've got a fever. You belong in bed. Let me take you home."

She shook her head. "I can't. There's too much work to do in the office. I forgot to mention that Tony Regis is leaving to start his own agency. I have to pack his files."

"Tough! Let him take care of his own damn files."

"If you promise not to tell, I'm really a spy. Millie, Mr. Hopper's secretary, wants to be sure Tony doesn't steal any scripts or client lists."

"I sure picked a winner to give my stuff to, didn't I?"

"I feel partly responsible, since I'm the one who actually handed him your songs."

"Now, that is ridiculous. I've been around enough to know the score. I got carried away when he claimed to have the inside track with Lawrence Comerford and Dale Hawkins. I heard their new show was in trouble and they were looking for song writers."

"You better catch Tony before he leaves the Hopper agency. Or send a telegram so you have something in writing."

"That's an excellent suggestion. At least you're my witness if he claims not to have seen them."

"Why can't I tell him you called and ask him what happened to your transcripts?"

"That's very kind, but I don't want to involve you in an awkward situation."

"I'm sure I can find a way."

Michael paid the check and they walked back to Rockefeller Center. The clock on the front of the building said five to three. Julia was appalled. "I've never taken so much time for lunch before. Thank you, doctor, for the great medicine."

He laughed. "Here, don't forget your doggy bag."

"Well . . ." It was so late she had to go in, but she hated to say goodbye.

"Will you go out with me on Saturday night?" he said.

"Oh." Hiding her delight was impossible. "Yes, I'd love to."

"Around seven, then." She was halfway through the revolving door when he followed her into the lobby. "Hey, I don't know where you live."

He wrote her address and telephone number in a little red leather book that was crammed full of similar entries.

By force of will, Julia had made a complete recovery by Saturday night. A light snow was falling as they walked along Washington Square toward Minetta Lane, heading for Giuseppe's, the restaurant near Michael's apartment. "Are you sure Italian food is all right? We can go somewhere else."

"No, I really liked this place."

"Good," he smiled, opening the door for her. "So do I."

Julia had forgotten, or perhaps she had been too taken with Michael on her first visit to notice the romantic wedge-shaped room with its red brick walls and beamed ceiling. Plinky concertina music was playing in the background . . . *O Sole Mio* . . . there were red-checked cloths, candles in wine bottles dripping with wax, and jugs of fresh flowers on every table. Passing the booths, they sat at a corner table next to a tiny bar in the rear, where the room narrowed.

Without consulting a menu, Michael ordered a meal of many courses. All the waiters were brothers or cousins, and again he received special attention. Giuseppe himself came to pour their wine and, with a soulful smile for Julia, left them alone. For a moment it brought back the sweet torment of sitting here on the night of Michael's party, knowing another woman had a claim on him. She wondered what had happened between him and

Vivienne. And blushed to think what he would say if he could read her mind. She glanced around the dark, candlelit restaurant, studying the atrocious paintings of Napoli on the walls.

"You're a thousand miles away," said Michael.

"Excuse me. I was just remembering how I used to plan my future when I would live in New York and come to places like Greenwich Village."

"And is New York the way you imagined it would be?"

"Oh, much better," she said, smiling broadly.

As he had at lunch, Michael did most of the talking. She remembered little of what he said that night, much to her regret, for he was, then and always, the most diverting conversationalist she would ever encounter. On any subject he could discourse with a scintillating verve, generating a sense of anticipation and excitement, but he was particularly fascinating on the theater. He did it effortlessly, with an offhand charm. A smile, a wink, a long look of it's-you-and-me-baby here together *now*—all the while pouring wine in her glass or feeding her a morsel of bread dipped in spicy basil sauce. It was penetrating, insightful thought, articulated with a rare mercurial energy. And it left her dazzled.

It was half-past ten when they finished dinner. Passing up dessert and coffee, they wandered through the narrow streets of the West Village, pausing to peer into curio shops and dim cafes. The snow had stopped, and the neighborhood was teeming with a Saturday night crowd of tourists along with more casually dressed Villagers. Stopping to browse at a book stall, Michael came upon a packet of old romances with frayed cloth bindings and bought the lot. "For inspiration," he commented with a grin as he handed the bookseller a dollar bill and slipped them in his pocket. Julia remembered his recent popular song that had faded from glory as quickly as it had risen to a top spot on the Hit Parade. If he culled his ideas from cheap novels, she thought, no wonder "Smiling at Sunrise" was the resulting product.

At a corner bakery, Michael bought cannolis, and they continued along West 4th Street to Grove. "Getting cold?" he asked, as Julia drew in her shoulders against the wind.

"A little."

"Come on, I'll make us coffee. We can't have you getting sick again." He took her hand and crossed to the crooked alley where he lived. The old brick building had once been the residence of a prosperous merchant and was subdivided into flats during the last century, Michael explained on the way upstairs. The present owners, a decorative arts historian and an editor at the *Saturday Review*, lived in an elegantly restored apartment on the ground floor. "The boys are okay, a little cheap. Fortunately they like to keep warm in winter, so there's sufficient heat."

Michael lit a fire in the corner hearth of the living room and put a stack of records on the phonograph. The smoldering voice of Billie Holiday filled the room singing "You Let Me Down," a yearning rasp of a love song. Julia found herself strangely stirred by the passionate rendition of the unfamiliar blues.

As Michael set a pot of coffee on the stove to perk, the telephone rang. "Excuse me, while I get that."

He went back to the bedroom, although there was an extension right there. It was eleven-thirty and seemed an odd hour for someone to be phoning, but by now Julia realized that neither Michael nor his friends led conventional lives.

While a cynical, street-wise Holiday continued to mock love in "A Fine Romance," Julia wandered around the room glancing at Michael's possessions. The apartment had been thick with smoke and the acrid fumes of cheap beer on her previous visit. It came as a surprise to find a clean homelike comfort, chiefly created by a pair of antique oriental rugs and several equally fine-looking pieces of furniture arranged with haphazard order and considerable charm. Examining the walls of books, folios, and prints, she peered at a group of framed photographs on a shelf. Of Michael at the piano; Michael with the cast of *One Night in Venice*; Michael shaking hands with Jerome Kern. Michael with an arm around Vivienne Tremaine . . .

As Billie drew out the final astringent notes of "These Foolish Things," Michael came back into the room. "Sorry to be so long. Coffee will be ready in a few minutes."

Julia hastily turned away from the pictures. "I've been admiring your taste in furnishings," she said.

"Most of this stuff was Aunt Sophie's. Not the books or paintings, though. They're mine."

He brought plates and the box of pastries to the wooden

counter. "Let me do that," said Julia, setting out cups and spoons.

They ate the cannolis and drank coffee while the Mills Brothers crooned softly in the background. When the records came to an end, Michael told her about the show he had agreed to set to music for Gerald Ross. "I remember when he came over to you at the Mitchell party," said Julia.

"Right. We got together the next day, and I read the script. It's a great story."

"Can you tell me about it, or do you not like to discuss your work?"

"I don't mind. It's sometimes helpful to talk about a project." He cradled his coffee cup in his hands and Julia studied his profile as he sipped the strong brew. He was an exceptionally handsome man, especially when he looked serious, as he did at this moment. "The play was written and staged by Stefan Nordberg as his thesis at Yale. It's a fantasy, loosely based on the Viking sagas. He calls it *The Outlanders*. Dreadful title. The hero is a Viking chief who engages in the usual plundering of coastal cities, and on one of these raids he captures a Scottish bride." He paused and flashed her a smile. "And guess what? Lo and behold, he falls helplessly in love with her."

"Of course!" she said, smiling.

"When he returns home he finds his position of leadership has been undermined by a rival chief, and after a meeting of the tribunal he's forced into exile. He takes his loyal band of followers and they set sail for the unknown—the outlands."

"So that's where the title comes from," murmured Julia.

"They reach a distant shore and establish a settlement, which one assumes to be the legendary Vinland, a Utopian sort of place. And there they presumably prosper and grow old." Putting down his empty cup, he turned to her. "Well, how does the idea strike you?"

Without hesitation, Julia answered enthusiastically, "I think it's marvelous. I can see fantastic costumes and stage sets. The story should give you plenty of inspiration—songs about conquest and the sea, heartbreak and love." She lowered her voice dramatically. "The ruthless but handsome and heroic Viking chief subduing the very proud, stubborn daughter of a Scottish laird, who resists but finally falls for him and loves him forever, following him to the ends of the earth and giving him many strong sons."

Michael threw back his head and laughed. "Oh boy, you've really got it down. Are you sure you're not a writer?"

She shook her head. "No, I can't write at all. I'm becoming a fairly good editor, though. By now I can read through a script, see what doesn't work, and suggest how to fix it. But I can't create ideas for the life of me."

"Well, maybe someday you'll take a look at this script. I have some problems with it. It's, uh . . . heavy. I'm crazy about the story, but a musical play is different from a drama. I don't think the playwright has a light enough touch. The guy has never worked on a musical, but he's determined to do the adaptation himself."

Flattered by his confidence, Julia was honest. "I'd love to read it and I'll give you a frank opinion. But although I trust my judgment on drama, I'm not so sure I know what makes a good musical."

"Good music, of course," he responded quickly, giving her a mischievous grin. "And a first-rate director and cast. For me the book is somewhat secondary—no, that's not true, I'm being too subjective. A strong and dramatic story that holds the attention of an audience is the guts of a musical. The dialogue needs pace and wit, and you can't waste a word. But at the same time the story is a framework for everything else—the songs, dances, costumes, sets . . . the *spectacle*. It all has to mesh."

"Yes, I think that's probably right. But I can see a point of conflict. The writer has given you a script and you have to tell him—what's his name again?"

"Steve Nordberg."

"Well, you have to say to him, thanks for the nice story, Steve, but we're going to make some changes because your play is only a vehicle to hang our songs and dances on. Steve, who is very protective of his masterpiece, probably won't like that idea very much."

"Yes," he said excitedly, "you understand *exactly* what the difficulty is."

"So what's the solution?"

"We try our damndest to collaborate. They'll give him a chance to adapt the book. But if it doesn't work—and we should know very soon—Gerry will have to bring in another writer."

"What if Steve doesn't agree? I mean, it's still his play."

"Then Ross won't buy it. None of us has signed a contract yet. At this point, it's still an option." He was silent for a moment, thinking. "We need a lyricist. This score will require a special talent, the kind of Mr. Words who makes the lyrics as integral to the show as the music is."

"And you don't think Nordberg is Mr. Words?"

"Not a chance. It's not even in the picture. Gerry would like to get Oscar Hammerstein, but I doubt he'd be interested in collaborating with a novice. I suggested Murray Baker, my roommate from prep school. I think he's first rate, but I can't blame Ross for not wanting to risk another unknown, considering he's already taking a gamble on me."

Julia admired this unexpected modesty. She stared at his face in the flickering firelight. The bone structure was strong and angular, the skin taut along his jawline. There were long creases in his cheeks, flanking a mouth that looked alternately sensitive and rakish. He turned to meet her gaze. As she lowered her eyes in confusion he reached for her and they fell back against the pillows of the couch. It was the first time she had been kissed by a man—if she didn't count those few groping embraces after school dances. Once their lips adjusted to each other she responded and it was an incredibly wonderful feeling.

Michael drew back and cupped her face with his hand. "You're a very beautiful woman," he said softly.

She smiled uncertainly. No one had ever called her a woman, much less beautiful.

He frowned. "When was your birthday?"

"In October."

"And how old were you?"

"Eighteen."

He let out a shaky breath. Folding her in his arms, he rubbed his cheek against her hair. They remained that way for several long minutes while she wondered whether there was something she should do or say. The strong beating of his heart against her breast caused an unfamiliar sensation deep inside, a rather pleasant, achy sort of longing.

Gently he let go of her. "More coffee?"

She shook her head. "No, but there *is* something I would like you to do."

A wary look came into his eyes. "What's that?"

"Play some of your songs. The only one I've heard is 'Smiling at Sunrise.' "

He grimaced. "That horror. It will haunt me for the rest of my days."

"Horror or not, it's not so terrible to have a song on the Hit Parade."

"No, not terrible."

He stood up, pulling Julia to her feet. In his studio he turned on a lamp over the piano and moved a chair nearby for her. Seating himself, he ran his hands over the keyboard, executing a series of chords and ripples with pliant smoothness. He began with selections from *One Night in Venice*, singing the lyrics in a jazzlike recitative, pulsating and insistent. His voice grew bolder as he played, and she understood that he was building up steam, getting into it. She fell under the spell of the music, with its syncopated rhythms, melodic accents, and sustained cadences.

"Wonderful," she mouthed when by a transitional series of arpeggios he signaled the end of *One Night*, transposing to a higher key and swinging into a light, catchy song with a tricky beat. He da-dada'd along with that, and on the second chorus she joined him, harmonizing. It was a song with a show-tune beat, the kind audiences love and come out humming after a performance. And yet it had a signature of its own, so that if you knew his work you would recognize it as a Michael Shane melody. He followed it with another, and still another in the same vein—jazzy, percussive, melodic. For song after song, she marveled at his ability to create a seemingly endless and wholly original combination of notes and tempos. When there were words, he sang them. Clever words, frequently about love—jaded love, unrequited love, two-timing love. Quick, witty, and sophisticated lyrics, cynically amusing.

Pausing, he said, "This is a piece I'm still working on . . . a concerto for piano and orchestra." With a lift of his head, he closed his eyes and played a lush, rhapsodic Lizstian theme, with minor tonalities and a complicated blues-tinged underpinning. It had an improvisational dimension, and Julia sat spellbound, imagining it in concert with an orchestral background. His marvelous technique enhanced the difficult form, and she realized it was no exaggeration to describe Michael Shane as a genius. At the final note, he executed a rather virtuosic glissando, then lowered his head for a moment, rubbing his hands together. Keeping very still, Julia said nothing, hoping he would go on. As if to throw off the melancholy mood of the piece, he struck up a lively brass band sort of composition with an ostinato bass. When he came to the chorus, he hummed along, inserting a phrase here and there, finally belting it out at the top of his lungs, singing, " . . . I don't have all the words for this one yet . . . except, love, love, love, *love, LO-O-VE* . . ."

There was a sudden hammering from under the floorboards, and a muffled voice yelled, "Knock it off, Shane. It's past midnight."

"Uh-oh, my landlords calleth." He ended with several crashing, dissonant chords, eliciting another furious pounding from below. "I hear you, Malcolm," he trilled, knocking on the floor. Grabbing Julia, he danced her into the next room, yodeling and collapsing with her on the couch in front of the fire, the two of them laughing riotously.

"Thank you for the concert," she said. "I think you might very well become another Gershwin."

He took her in his arms and kissed her again. This time she opened her mouth instinctively and he pressed her down on the sofa and lay on top of her, moving gently against her, his breath coming faster. Finally he let go, saying in a low, gruff voice, "I am not going to corrupt the morals of an eighteen-year-old girl. It's time to take you home."

She wished it were not time to go home. She wished the evening were just beginning.

Michael was banking the fire and she was clearing the coffee cups when the telephone rang again. He gave the instrument a glowering look, then ignored it while he helped her on with her coat and prepared to leave. The phone continued to ring. "Hell," he said and, with an air of resignation, picked up the extension near the kitchen. "Yes?"

Standing in the open doorway, Julia could clearly hear the sound of a woman's voice. "I'm sorry," said Michael, "I'm busy now. I'll have to get back to you."

There was more talking, this time quite agitated. "I'll speak to you tomorrow, okay? Goodbye."

Julia was waiting at the top of the stairs when he came out and locked the door. "Sorry," he said. As they walked down the narrow steps, they could hear the insistent ringing of the telephone in his apartment.

Edwin Hopper gave an annual Christmas party at his Gramercy Park home, to which he invited all of his staff and clients. When the invitations were sent out, Millie said, "Bring a date, Julia. Everyone does. My husband always loves Edwin and Louise's—well, now just Edwin's parties." Julia had thought she would take Ben Carmichael, although she wondered whether that was a wise idea. Ben was not above using a social occasion to further his own interests. She had held off asking him and now she was glad, because she intended to invite Michael.

They had gone out twice since the night he played for her, once to a movie, another time to a Sunday afternoon chamber music concert at a church on Christopher Street. On neither occasion did he take her to his apartment afterward, escorting her home instead and leaving her at the door.

On the Saturday night before Christmas, Michael arrived early. Julia was dressing, having been delayed that afternoon at the Hunter College library researching a term paper. Betsy kept Michael company while he waited, and when Julia came downstairs, they seemed to be getting along famously.

Just before they left, Betsy received a telephone call and when she came back a few minutes later, she was flushed and radiant. Taking Julia aside, she whispered, "That was Rodney. He asked me to go up to Vermont with him until after Christmas."

"Oh. Did you say you would?"

"Do you mind?"

"No, of course not. Go ahead."

"What will you do for Christmas?" she asked, with a guilty look.

"Millie Kramer invited me for dinner, although they don't really celebrate Christmas. It's okay, Bets. Something will come up. When do you leave?"

"Tonight."

"Nothing like last-minute notice," said Julia, not quite keeping the sarcasm out of her voice.

"He only just found out that Arden has decided to stay in Florida after all. I know you don't approve."

"It's not that I don't approve. I just don't want you hurt. I've seen enough of what men can do to women."

"Don't worry about me. You can get hurt only if you count on something. I have no expectations." But Julia knew that wasn't true. She was certain Betsy thought she would win in the end, that if she waited it out she would eventually become Mrs. Rodney Barstow.

Since it was early and the night was pleasant, Michael suggested they take a bus down to Gramercy Park. "Is anything wrong?" he asked when they were walking toward Lexington Avenue.

"No."

"You seem subdued."

"Oh . . . Betsy just informed me she's going away and won't be back until after Christmas."

"You're not going home for Christmas?" He seemed surprised.

"I hadn't planned to."

"Well, then you'll spend it with me. We shall have the ultimate New York Christmas." The bus came at that moment, and they climbed aboard. Michael deposited the fares and the two of them swayed in the aisle as the bus took off down Lexington Avenue. "So is that a date?" he said, when they were seated.

"Are you sure you're not just feeling sorry for me? I have somewhere else to go."

"A better offer?"

She smiled. "No."

"I really want to spend Christmas with you, Julia. I just never realized how much until this moment."

On Christmas Eve they joined a group of Michael's musician friends for caroling, ending at a tree-trimming party on Central Park West where they drank mulled wine and spooned up oyster stew. Back home in her apartment at midnight, they exchanged gifts. Julia had bought Michael a pair of bronze bookends, shaped like treble and bass clefs. He gave her recordings of Beethoven's Fourth Symphony with Serge Koussevitzky conducting the Boston Symphony Orchestra, and selections from Handel's *Messiah*. They played the records on

Betsy's phonograph, and the living room seemed very cheery with the lights of the miniature tree that Julia had bought at a flower stall on Third Avenue.

"I hope you don't have plans for New Year's Eve," he said.

"No, I don't."

He kissed her. "You do now."

She had never been "rushed" before and she feared her expectations were too great. This was the most heady experience of her life. It was gorgeous to awaken on Christmas morning and know that she would be seeing him that afternoon and again on Saturday night, and would be with him to celebrate the dawn of 1941. Her first holidays away from home were the happiest she could remember.

After breakfast, she called Troy. Naturally, Eunice would be the one to answer the telephone. "Merry Christmas, Gran. How are you?"

"I'm not complaining. Where's Betsy?"

"She's not here right now. I expect her later. I'm sure she'll call you."

"Where did she go?"

"Out with friends." Julia did not even mind dissembling.

"Left you home alone, did she?"

"Not really. I'm going to have dinner with some friends of mine."

"You shouldn't be by yourself on Christmas."

"I won't be alone, Gran. I wanted to go with *my* friends."

"A family should be together for the holidays."

"We will be, later on. Let me talk to my mother."

"She's still sleeping."

"Well, *wake her up!* I want to wish her a merry Christmas."

Eunice became huffy, but complied. When Jesse came to the phone, she was thrilled to hear her daughter's voice. Although Julia wrote to her mother every week, sending money, she seldom called home. "Merry Christmas, Julia. Are you having a good time, dear?"

"Yes, Mom, I'm having a great time. I've made lots of friends and I love college, and I have a terrific job. It's the best job in the world."

"I'm so happy for you."

"How are *you?* I miss you."

"I'm just fine. I miss you, too, but it pleases me to know you're there. How's Betsy?"

"Wonderful. She's with friends today and I'm going to a big Christmas dinner in Greenwich Village. There will be more than twenty of us."

"That sounds fun."

It was said wistfully and Julia's throat constricted. "Thank you for the hat and mittens, Mother. I'm going to wear them today. Did you receive my Christmas present?"

"Oh, I forgot . . . thank you, dear. I love the robe. It's nice and warm, and such a pretty color."

"I always liked you in rose. Is it the right size?"

"It's perfect."

When they hung up, Julia could not help crying. The first tear trickled down her cheek, and was followed by an uncontrollable deluge. The sadness of her mother's life overwhelmed her. The thought of the desolate Christmas in that joyless apartment in Troy was enough to dampen anyone's holiday spirit. Finally she dried her eyes and stood under the shower to bathe them, but when she arrived at Michael's apartment, he immediately noticed. "You've been crying."

"Oh, it's silly. I called my mother and I guess I'm a little homesick."

He was terribly sweet. "Sometimes I feel the same way on holidays. It's natural when you're not with relatives. Tell you what, I'll be your family today and you'll be mine. Is that a deal?" He kissed her forehead and she felt very happy as they went downstairs, where they were having Christmas dinner with Michael's landlords.

A more unusual collection of people, Julia had never met. Malcolm Lowell and his housemate, Hugo Miller, had adopted a quantity of strays. All together they were twenty-four displaced children of the hinterlands who had made New York their home but who were in limbo for the holidays. The ground-floor flat was the essence of the Yuletide spirit. Malcolm was the curator of the Museum of Decorative Arts and he had re-created an authentic nineteenth-century Christmas. A profusion of candles and German sugar cookies adorned the exquisitely trimmed tree, and the walls were festooned with garlands and wreaths.

They started at four o'clock with sherry and hot cheese

puffs in front of the fire, and proceeded to a Lucullan feast, which went on for three hours. "The spirit of Christmas past," announced Hugo, the magazine editor, wheeling in an antique English tea table laden with festively decorated silver platters. To the laudatory oohs and ahs of their guests, he lifted a domed cover to reveal an enormous roast goose garnished with spiced crabapples and sprigs of holly. Two tables had been laid for twelve each. The food was set out on the buffet and on an enormous library table—in fact, on every available surface. Hugo had a passion for cooking. In addition to the goose with oyster and cornbread stuffings, he had baked a Smithfield ham, accompanied by every vegetable, potato, and relish imaginable. The variety of desserts defied description—plum puddings, fruit cakes, mincemeat pies, apple tarts, and chocolate-dipped dried fruits.

After dinner there was spiced coffee and chocolate truffles, and everyone joined in singing carols and popular songs, with Michael accompanying on the spinet. Julia made friends with Felicity Lyons, the quiet young wife of an assistant editor at *Saturday Review*, and with Janice Fried, an art student at Cooper Union.

"They're all so nice," said Julia when she and Michael had gone upstairs to his apartment.

"Yes, aren't they? Malcolm and Hugo . . . well, I kid them a lot, but they're really good souls. They've been together for years."

"They're, uh . . ."

"Homosexuals." He smiled tolerantly. "I guess that's a scandalous idea for someone from Troy."

"It would be in Troy," she acknowledged. "But somehow when you know them, it doesn't seem shocking. I mean, they're like an old married couple."

"Probably a good deal more compatible than many husbands and wives," said Michael. "Basically I don't think man is meant to be a monogamous creature."

Her brow wrinkled. "What do you mean?"

"Well, it just seems unnatural to spend your entire life with one person."

"But if you love each other . . ."

He laughed and ruffled her hair. "Ahh, love. Of course."

She pulled away from him. "Don't make fun of me, Michael.

I know what it's like to live without a real family. Is it so wrong of me to believe in marriage?"

"I'm sorry. I didn't mean to offend you," he apologized. "I suppose I'm the one who's out of step. Sometimes I think marriage to the right woman would be wonderful. And then again I think, isn't it absurd to imagine that two people who scarcely know each other—for how can they when they've lived the whole of their existence apart?—that they would love each other *exclusively* for the rest of their lives. Well, it just seems unrealistic, a romantic fantasy."

She gave him a withering look. "Oh, you are really a cynic." Although his words made her uneasy, she dismissed them and pointedly changed the subject.

When Julia reached home that night, a deliriously happy Betsy had returned from Vermont. Rodney had given her a diamond wristwatch for Christmas and was determined to ask Arden for a divorce. "He's flying down to Palm Beach tomorrow and he plans to tell her."

"I thought she was due back in New York tomorrow." That was supposedly the reason why the trip to Vermont had to end on Christmas Day.

"She changed her mind again. He thinks she may suspect that he's seeing someone."

"Is that good?"

"If it precipitates a divorce, it is."

"Golly, I hope you won't be caught in the middle of a scandal, Bets."

"I'm sure not. We've been so discreet."

"Where did you stay in Vermont?"

"At a friend's house. No one was there, no one knows."

"How long will Rodney be away?"

"Only a couple of days. He'll be back before New Year's."

"And then what?"

"I guess he'll move out of their apartment. I don't really know."

"Has he made plans with you? I mean marriage plans."

"Jule! You sound like a prosecuting attorney."

"Yes, that's just what I'm trying to be. Has Rodney asked you to marry him?"

"Well, he said he'll be free . . . that he wants to spend the rest of his life with me . . . that I'm the only woman he has ever truly loved. Is that good enough for you, Madame Prosecutor?"

"No."

"*No?* What do you want from the poor man, for heaven's sake?"

"I want him to ask you to marry him. I want him to say in so many words that you are going to be his *wife*. Just as soon as the ink is dry on that divorce decree."

Betsy threw down the dish towel she was holding. "Boy. You are *tough*, Julia Perkins."

"You bet I am. Someone in this family has to be."

Julia began to believe in clairvoyance when Rodney called Betsy on Sunday afternoon. "He's still in Palm Beach," Betsy admitted. "He may not be able to get back for a few days."

"A few days. What does that mean?"

"Well, maybe not until Tuesday."

"So he will be home for New Year's Eve?"

"Probably, but maybe not."

"Betsy . . ."

"Oh, Jule." Her aunt looked so miserable that Julia hated Rodney Barstow.

"Did he say anything? About his wife and the divorce."

Betsy nodded. "She wants to try to work out their differences. She thinks they should stay together until Elizabeth is older."

"How much older?"

"Sixteen."

"*Sixteen*—that's four years."

"I know." Betsy started to cry. "She threatened to tell her father and said he would call for Rod's resignation from RNA."

"Oh, hell. Does she know about you?"

"He said not. He told her he wanted a divorce because their marriage was a charade and he was tired of being alone. It's true, so she has no cause not to believe him."

The next two days dragged by. Betsy, who had been so jubilant after Christmas, looked pale and wan. She went to the office each day, essentially running RNA as a surrogate for Rodney. There was an enormous staff of assistants and officers who handled all details of network and corporate affairs, and he was in touch with each of them through Betsy, by phone and teletype. Julia thought it must be torture for her aunt to speak to her lover so often, acting as if theirs was an ordinary secretary-boss relationship.

The Hopper office closed early on the last day of the year. Walking home from work, with drifts of snow piled along the curbs, Julia was determined not to allow Betsy's quandary to dampen her own enthusiasm for New Year's Eve.

At seven o'clock, she awaited Michael's arrival in her new black velvet dress with a lace-edged sweetheart neckline. Purchased especially for the occasion at Saks Fifth Avenue, the gown had cost more than she had ever dreamed of paying for one item of clothing. When she answered the door, looking flushed and pretty, Michael whistled and spun her around. "Sensational! You're a knockout."

"Thank you, kind sir," she curtseyed. The truth was that Michael, dashingly handsome in tails, seemed so glamorously remote and unattainable that despite her newly acquired finery, she felt very much the provincial.

Betsy expected Rodney later in the evening, so Julia left the apartment with a carefree heart, wearing a long black velvet cape borrowed from Betsy over her evening gown. They were first going to a champagne reception at the National Arts Club, followed by a gala dinner dance for the benefit of disabled musicians to be held at the Astor Roof.

For the first time, Julia had a chance to talk with Zachary Mitchell, who gave a much kinder impression than she had expected after meeting him briefly at the anniversary celebration of his theater. First-generation son of a coal miner he might be, but over his rough foundations he had acquired an aristocratic veneer with the well-modulated speech and courtly bearing of a cultured gentleman. "I'm very fond of that young man," he informed her, nodding toward Michael, who was engaged in conversation. "I wish him well. He tends to be a little arrogant on occasion, but perhaps that's natural in one so gifted." There was an easiness between them, she observed, and a respectful, almost fatherly light in Zachary's eyes when he glanced at Michael.

It was New Year's Eve as she had always dreamed of it. Straight out of motion pictures, with glamorous women and handsome men and sparkling conversation. She ate food with unpronounceable French names and drank champagne and danced in Michael's arms to the romantic strains of Guy Lombardo's orchestra. And at midnight they kissed, with streamers and confetti flying in the air, to the sound of horns and noisemakers and "Auld Lang Syne."

It was three o'clock in the morning when they crept up the stairs to her apartment. "We'd better not use the elevator," she told him. "It makes too much noise."

She had drunk three glasses of champagne and was feeling silly and giggly, and Michael was amused at her, embracing her in the hallway and taking the key from her hand. "Allow me, fair maid."

"By all means, sir knight."

He unlocked the door and followed her in. Julia let her cape fall and he caught it, laying it on a bench in front of the balcony railing. He stood there, transfixed, looking down into the living room where a dim light burned. "Oh, my God," he uttered in hushed tones.

"What is it?" Julia turned back, following his gaze, and gasped. "*Betsy!*" she screamed.

"No, don't." He grabbed for her, but she brushed by him and flew down the few steps to the sprawling figure on the floor. Michael was there beside her, reaching for Betsy's wrist to feel her pulse. "Thank God, she's alive."

"She looks dead," said Julia, unable to control her trembling. "What's wrong with her?"

"I don't know, but we'd better call a—" Suddenly he began to laugh.

She turned on him furiously. "Why are you laughing? It's not funny."

He picked up an empty glass from the floor and sniffed it. "She's drunk," he sputtered, laughing again. "Passed out. Lord, she gave me a scare."

He was completely unprepared for Julia's fierce reaction. "*Drunk!* How *could* she? She ought to know better—how *dare* she?"

"Hey, hold on there. It's not the end of the world."

"Oh, yes it is, you have no idea . . . Betsy, Betsy!"

By this time, Michael had stripped off his coat and lifted Betsy to the couch. "She's dead weight," he said. "Hey, Bets." He shook her and gave her face a few light slaps, but there was no response. "Whew, she is going to have one hell of a hangover in the morning. I think we better get her into bed. Will you give me a hand?"

Julia, meanwhile, had retrieved an empty cognac bottle from where it had rolled under the coffee table. Michael looked at it. "Well, at least it was good stuff. Have you any idea how much she drank?"

Julia shook her head. "I hardly ever drink, so I don't know how much was in here. Isn't there such a thing as alcohol poisoning?"

"There is, but she would have had to consume the entire bottle, I think." And then he said, "I know you don't drink, but if you'll forgive me . . . does Betsy?"

"No, she never has, but—"

"But what?"

"Her brother did and . . . and her sister. My mother."

He reached for her. "That's why you're so upset."

She nodded and turned away to hide the quick tears that sprang to her eyes.

"Come on," he said, hefting Betsy in his arms. "You lead the way."

Michael laid Betsy on the bed and left Julia to wrestle with undressing her while he went to forage in the kitchen. Betsy had either been preparing to go out or had already come in, for she was wearing a hostess robe over the kind of lingerie and stockings meant for an evening dress. Julia managed to get her into a nightgown and sponged her face with a washcloth. She tiptoed out of the room, leaving a table lamp on.

Michael was making coffee. "Any chance of getting some of this into her?" he asked.

Julia shook her head. "Wouldn't do any good anyway. That's a myth about giving coffee to drunks. The only cure is time. It's best to let her sleep it off. She'll have a terrible thirst in the morning."

He looked at her gravely. "You speak with authority."

"Yes, I do."

"Well, let's you and me have some coffee and some of those scrumptious-looking brownies I see in that glass container."

"You're really a very nice man. You make me feel good . . . almost."

"Almost?"

She smiled. "You make me feel good."

"That's my girl. You are worldly wise. No wonder I was surprised when you told me you were only eighteen. You bear too many burdens for one so young."

"I've never thought of it that way."

"Do think of it."

Julia carried a tray with coffee and brownies to the living room.

"Shall I light a fire?" Michael asked, striking a match without waiting for her reply.

"It's very late—or rather very early."

"I'm not leaving, Julia. I'm going to sleep here on the couch. You shouldn't be alone with Betsy, just in case something happens."

"Oh. Oh, thank you." He held out his arms and she went into them. They stayed like that, with Michael stroking her hair, murmuring softly and planting little kisses on her forehead, and she knew that for now, at least, he was someone she could count on.

Of course Betsy was mortified the next morning when she woke up to find Michael cooking bacon and eggs in the kitchen. Julia was still asleep in her room, and he served Betsy juice and coffee and aspirin.

"You're amazingly chipper," he said.

"For a lush?"

"I must admit, you really tied one on."

"Oddly enough, I feel pretty good. Better than I felt last night." She stirred her coffee. "Do you mind telling me who undressed me?"

"Julia." He grinned. "Not that I wouldn't have enjoyed the prospect."

She blushed. "Explanations are in order. It was a lovers' quarrel."

"I suspected as much."

"I left him at dinner with six other people, and I refused to answer the telephone or doorbell when he came after me."

"You sound proud of yourself."

"I am, rather. It's a whole new me."

"I'm willing to bet he loves the old you."

"The old walk-all-over-me me."

"That's the way it was?"

"Something like that."

"The guy must be out of his head."

"No, not really." She looked at him. "He's married."

"Oh Christ, Betsy, you're too smart to get caught in that one."

"Wouldn't you think so?"

At that moment, Julia walked in. "Well, good morning, everyone. Happy New Year." She looked at Betsy anxiously. "How are you feeling?"

"Better than I deserve."

Julia hugged her. "Good. I'm glad." She turned to Michael. "And you? Did you get any sleep?"

"Your sofa is great. I highly recommend it." He served her breakfast with a flourish. "*Voilà.*"

"You are too good," murmured Julia, "but I'm not complaining."

Michael poured coffee and sat down to have his own breakfast, then insisted on doing the dishes. Shortly after that, he left them. "I'll call you soon," he said at the door. Julia thought she detected a certain disengagement, but she was too preoccupied with Betsy to give it much notice.

She poured herself another cup of coffee and sat at the table. "What happened last night, or shouldn't I ask?"

"Rodney came around eight o'clock. We went to the Pierre with some friends of his from Los Angeles. When we were dancing, he told me Arden refused to give him a divorce. Flat out. I got mad and left. That's all. Oh, and I drank a little brandy."

"Gosh, Betsy, how can you go on working for him?"

"I don't know. I'm not sure I will. But RNA is part of me, and I'm very valuable to the organization. Not long ago, the head of personnel strongly hinted that if I ever want a job as his assistant, it's mine. I may take him up on it."

"Yes, but with Rod being the president . . ."

"It would be difficult but not impossible. I've been at RNA for almost seven years. There are many things at stake: seniority, a high salary, the stock plan. I would lose a great deal if I left."

"You'll lose Rod if you stay."

"What do you mean?"

"I mean that he controls your life the way things are, and as long as he goes on laying the ground rules he'll never be yours. If he sees that you're independent, it may shake him up enough to make him realize he needs you."

"*If* he needs me."

"Well, if he doesn't you might as well know it now so you can get on with your life."

"You're absolutely right," Betsy said with a sigh. "You may be younger than I am, but you're a lot more sensible. How did you get to be so wise?"

"That's the second time someone has said that in the past twenty-four hours."

"Who else?"

"Michael."

"You're crazy about him, aren't you?"

Julia nodded. "I'm afraid I'm falling in love with him."

"Why afraid? He seems to be more than a little taken with you."

"Taken-with is not in-love-with. I sense that Michael is bad news in the love department."

"What makes you say that?"

"Instinct." She thought about what he had said on Christmas night about committing oneself to an exclusive love. She remembered his sudden detachment this morning when saying goodbye. "Michael shies away from involvement. He's a free spirit and I suspect he intends to remain so. Anyway, I have spent a lifetime observing the fruits of an impetuous love affair, and that's not for me, thank you."

"Don't let Jesse's situation make you bitter, Julia. Her biggest mistake was letting Eunice rule her. If she had picked herself up and gone with her husband, sided with him against her parents, it would have been a different story."

"Maybe. We'll never know. Don't forget, my father could have put up more of a fight if he cared. Truthfully, I think they both wanted out. If I hadn't come along, they would never have married in the first place, and everyone could have been happy."

"You are *crazy*. You're the best person this family has ever produced, and just remember that. And while you're at it, remember that you're not Jesse. Whatever happens, you'll be in control."

That was easy for someone else to say.

New Year's Day fell on Wednesday. Julia could have taken

the rest of the week off, but she wanted to get caught up with paperwork before the new college semester began. She was in Hopper's office rearranging files on Friday morning when Michael called to say he had received his music from Tony Regis. The scores, much handled and still in their original envelope, had been mailed with a short letter.

"What did it say?"

"Something like sorry he wasn't able to do anything for me . . . the reaction from quote, the party in question, unquote was that my songs lack originality and are too pretentious for Broadway."

"That was supposed to be from Comerford? I can't believe it. I heard your music. He's jealous. He doesn't want to see anyone come along to compete with him."

"That's sweet of you to say, but he's probably right. I have to take it seriously."

"I'm sorry, Michael. Don't let this interfere with your excitement over *The Outlanders*."

"Not a chance." There was a pause, and then he said, "I'm working hard, Julia. I may not be able to see you for a while."

Her heart sank. Was this his way of letting her down easy? No matter how busy a person was, there was always a free moment to be with someone if you really cared. Maybe he was regretting the time he had spent with her, the closeness that had begun to develop between them. Maybe the only reason he had asked her out in the first place was to get on her good side in case she had any influence with Tony Regis.

"I'll call you soon," he promised.

But it was not until the end of January that she heard from him. They were three of the longest weeks of her life. He took her to a movie and afterward, over a cup of coffee at her apartment, Michael seemed worn out and dejected. "It's not going well," he confessed. "Gerry decided Steve Nordberg could give the lyrics a try, but this guy doesn't understand collaboration. Some composers work independently, but I like interacting with the lyricist—one thing feeds the other; the music helps the words and vice versa."

"How is the book?"

"I think it has serious problems, but I can't push too hard. I don't know Ross well enough yet and he'll think I'm the proverbial difficult composer. He'll have to come to the realization himself. I'm worried about time. He's planning for a fall opening."

Julia knew it took the better part of a year to get a Broadway musical together. A year, and a ton of money.

On a sleety evening at the beginning of February, she encountered Edwin Hopper waiting under the awning for his driver as she was leaving their office building. "Miserable weather," he said. "Let me drop you at home."

"I don't want to trouble you—"

"No trouble at all. East Seventy-fourth, as I remember. It's on my way."

Since Edwin lived in Gramercy, he must be going uptown again for dinner. She wondered whether that meant he was seeing a particular woman. There must be scads of women in New York who would be interested in an attractive widower. At forty, Hopper was charming and youthful, as well as successful. By now she knew quite a bit about him. According to Millie, who tended to romanticize her employer, he had been devoted to his wife. After her death from a long illness he had become somewhat reclusive, especially since his only daughter lived in England with her RAF captain husband and their newborn son. Edwin was constantly worried about their safety during the bombing raids.

When they were in the back of Hopper's car heading up Fifth Avenue, he said, "That young man you brought to my Christmas party—Michael Shane."

"Yes, what about him?" she answered in a guarded manner.

"Millie tells me you gave Tony Regis some of his compositions a while back, when he was still with us."

"That's right. Tony offered to show Michael's songs to Lawrence Comerford, but he forgot about their appointment. I was alone in the office on a Friday afternoon, so I kept the scores over the weekend and gave them to Tony the following Monday. I didn't know Michael very well at the time. I hope you don't think I was taking advantage."

"No, no. On the contrary."

She wondered what he meant. "In any case, Tony sent a note saying he wasn't able to do anything."

"I see." Hopper looked thoughtful. "Do you mind if I ask if Michael is your young man?"

"Not really," she stammered, and felt her face grow warm. "Well, maybe. I mean, we're dating."

He patted her hand. "A little friendly advice, Julia. People in this business are not always what they seem. You might mention to your friend that it's not wise to let a property get into the wrong hands."

She was to remember his words.

❧ Chapter 8 ❧

Isobel

Scott had not yet become accustomed to his wife as a businesswoman. Ever since Isobel had returned from her trip to Chicago, she had been strangely uncommunicative. On the Tuesday before Thanksgiving, at eight o'clock in the morning, she came into the front hall, prepared to leave. Her appearance this morning was uncompromisingly elegant, in a Chanel suit of nubby taupe wool that she wore with a creamy silk blouse and the heavy gold chain and pendant he had bought her in Florence for their twentieth wedding anniversary.

"You're off early, dear," said Scott.

"I'm going over to Cece's. We have a nine o'clock appointment with the contractor." Dissatisfied with the rental properties available, the partners had decided to make over the first two floors of the Bedford townhouse for their business venture.

Scott had not been consulted. "I can't believe Cece's actually willing to knock out walls and tear up all those rooms when you have no idea whether the gallery will be a success. You should be doing this a year from now."

"Thanks for your confidence."

"It has nothing to do with lack of confidence. I'm worried about the economy. We're in a slump and if we don't soon pull out of it, art purchases will be the first to go."

"Oh, Scott," she answered tolerantly, as if speaking to a child. "We're not going to be handling priceless works. We'll be fine. We've already lined up a big corporate account. Cece had a call from CID Associates. They want us to find sixty paintings for the new RNA building."

"That's quite impressive. But I still say you should have waited before an extensive remodeling. You can't possibly open in February with all the work to be done."

"No," she admitted. "They're going to have to scramble to make it by the end of March. But we don't mind. We'll be in Europe for most of January anyway." She looked at her watch. "I really must get going."

"Don't forget my mother is arriving this afternoon."

"I assure you, I haven't forgotten. I suppose she'll be staying for Thanksgiving?"

"Well, of course. She'll want to see the children." He thought he detected a tightening of Isobel's lips. "Good God, Iz, it's only the day after tomorrow. You don't expect me to ship her home before then, do you?"

"Julia is most welcome to stay as long as she wishes, Scott. I just want to *know*. Candida doesn't like surprises."

"One elderly woman is hardly going to put a strain on poor underutilized Candida."

"Shh, she'll hear you. If she quits where would I find another housekeeper who can cook a decent meal?" Then Isobel chuckled. "You *do* have a way with words, darling. I don't think Julia would appreciate being called elderly."

"Oops," Scott grinned, pleased that the tension had eased. "Well, I'd better get to the office. Come on"—he took her arm—"I'll drop you at Cece's."

"Are you sending Enriqué to meet your mother?" Isobel asked when they were in the car.

"I'll go with him so we can drive directly to the memorial service from the airport. You're not planning to attend?"

Isobel wrinkled her nose. "I hardly knew the man."

After leaving Isobel at the corner of Sixty-ninth and Park, they continued to his office, where Scott spent the morning in meetings. Shortly before noon he took the elevator down to the underground garage where Enriqué was waiting with the car. As they headed crosstown toward the Queens-Midtown Tunnel, Scott picked up the phone to get the latest market quotations, then took out a set of contracts to study. He read through the technical language carefully, marking some clauses that needed changing. When he was satisfied, he returned the document to his briefcase and unfolded a newspaper.

Looking out at the crawling line of automobiles, Scott rattled his *Wall Street Journal* impatiently. He found it mildly irritating to be stuck in traffic on the Brooklyn-Queens Expressway on a Tuesday afternoon when he should have been drafting his speech for the January ABA meeting in Chicago. He could have sent the car for Julia, but she might not recognize his driver, and it seemed churlish to let an older woman— not elderly, he reminded himself with a wry smile—struggle through the baggage claim alone.

At last they pulled in front of Delta arrivals. Scott had his hand on the door handle, ready to spring out of the car. "Wait here as long as you can, Enriqué. If a cop comes by, you'll have to circle around and drive back."

Inside the terminal, Scott searched the stream of arriving passengers coming through the gate. The surge of happiness he experienced when he saw his mother's familiar face took him quite by surprise.

At sixty-eight, Julia looked years younger. Her posture was upright, her step brisk. In many ways she felt even better.

Twenty years ago had been Vietnam. Twenty years ago, Neil had fled to Canada and her family had been in turmoil. Deborah, in the full throttle of teenage rebellion, had them worried sick half the time, running around with the wild crowd at Dalton. George, who had never denied her anything, completely reversed course, laying down impossibly strict rules. Oddly enough, this control had produced a tranquilizing effect on their daughter.

Scott, of course, had remained steady as always. With joint law and business degrees from Harvard, the course of his life had already been charted. Newly married to Isobel Prescott, he was to join her father's law firm the following year after completing a brief tour of duty in the judge advocate general's office, where he clerked for a military jurist. George could have secured a clerkship with one of the Supreme Court justices for him, but with the blight of Neil's defection on the family record, Scott had felt honor-bound to serve in the military. Not to the point of getting shot at in Vietnam, mind you, but he *would* wear the uniform of the United States Army. Neil, however, had been lost to them, and it was a constant aching wound.

Yes, all things considered, except for missing George, Julia felt infinitely better now than she had at forty-eight.

She walked up the ramp at LaGuardia, and there was Scott, smiling and handsome. It always amazed her to see him again after a time apart. That this tall, distinguished, immaculately turned-out man with a brush of gray at the temples was her son. The earnest little boy who never seemed to fit in had turned into the consummate insider.

He embraced her with more affection and enthusiasm than she expected. "You're looking absolutely wonderful, Mother."

"Thank you, darling, and so are you. It's good of you to meet me." He took the handcart she wheeled with her garment bag and carry-on case. "Do you have any checked baggage?"

"No, just this. I won't be here that long."

"But you will stay for Thanksgiving and the weekend?"

Julia smiled at her own gratitude. "I'd love to. Will the children be coming home?"

"Of course. They're each bringing someone. I think Chip's may be a real girlfriend, but Ginger has a new flame every time we turn around."

"What fun! You know how much I love young people and romance."

There was just time to stop for a quick sandwich on Madison Avenue before the appointed hour for the memorial service. In the lobby of Temple Emanu-El Julia signed her name to the registry and accompanied Scott halfway to the front of the sanctuary. Amongst the gathering of seven hundred or so, many were widows like herself. Never a woman to wear mink or diamonds, believing display was vulgar, she was simply dressed and appeared younger, healthier, more contemporary than the others. Within this broad segment of New Yorkers who held power and money, Julia was conscious of the heads that turned and the eyes that marked Scott's progress down the center aisle. Swelling minor organ music filled the nave as they found seats, and she ironically reflected that her

own church—Presbyterian, which she hardly ever attended—
was less cathedral-like than this fashionable Jewish house of
worship.

Julia nodded to several acquaintances, smiling and giving a
little wave to Sue and Jack Winston, who were seated at the
far end of the row ahead. "There's David Ross," whispered
Scott, nodding toward the front where the deceased's son
came in from a side chamber, escorting his grieving mother, a stoop-shouldered woman weighted down by a veiled
black hat.

"My dear, how old Florence looks," Julia murmured before
she could catch herself. She turned away so she would not
have to meet Scott's quizzical glance.

On the way back from the airport he had commented, "I
don't understand why you would come all the way to New
York to attend a memorial service for a man you admit you
did not particularly like, Mother. It's too much for you at
your age."

"It's a matter of courtesy, dear. Gerry was someone I've
known for fifty years. I seem to remember they came to
George's funeral."

"I wasn't aware that funerals were like dinner parties,
incurring obligations," said Scott. "Of course, we're always
delighted to see you," he hastily added.

Julia wondered whether that was entirely true. Scott and
Isobel had spent numerous weekends and holidays with them
at the Connecticut house in the old days, enjoying the sailing
and tennis. After Julia and George moved to Florida, they
would often stop for a visit on their way to St. Bart's, or to
drop the children before heading for Gstaad or Ibiza. However, since George's death they had rarely invited her to New
York. Not that she necessarily would have come, for Julia had
never felt at ease in her daughter-in-law's home. Isobel was
an unyielding perfectionist.

The service was interminable, with a dozen speakers, including the son and grandsons, and a number of associates in the
theater, all paying homage to Gerald Ross. She noticed that
the Winstons slipped out through a side exit before the rabbi's
final eulogy.

As soon as the Ross family filed out, to the thundering
accompaniment of the organ, Scott said, "Mother, I have to

get back to the office. Enriqué will take you to the apartment. Isobel isn't home, but Candida will make you comfortable."

"I can take a cab, dear. I have to go downtown, but perhaps Enriqué would drop my bag at the apartment so I won't be encumbered."

"Keep the car. Enriqué doesn't have to get Isobel until five." He couldn't conceal his curiosity. "Where are you going?"

"Oh, just some errands," she answered vaguely, nodding to an old acquaintance.

Scott raised an eyebrow, bending to kiss her cheek. "I'll see you at dinner."

Julia wondered if Enriqué would report to Scott that he had driven her to Rockefeller Center and waited for almost an hour. An hour that she spent with Jack Winston in the law offices of Winston & Rhinehart. When they emerged together through the revolving doors she dismissed Enriqué, and Jack hailed a taxi that took them up Third Avenue to a special climate-controlled warehouse for the storage of archives.

"Let me know what you decide," said Jack when he deposited her at the entrance to her son and daughter-in-law's apartment building at Seventy-seventh Street and Fifth Avenue shortly after five o'clock.

"Thank you, Jack. Won't you come up for a drink?"

"I think not on this day." He smiled indulgently. "Sue always gets a little down when one of our generation departs. She found it difficult to sit through the service this afternoon. I know you, of all people, understand. We're leaving for Boston in the morning, but perhaps you'd give her a call before then. She always likes talking to you."

"Of course I'll call her, but I'm afraid the best I can tell Sue is that those who are left behind go on because they have no choice."

"I think you're a brave and wonderful woman," he said. "Give my regards to Isobel and Scott. I hear he's going to be board chairman at the museum."

"Yes."

"Quite an honor, and well-deserved."

"Well, you know Scott. He works hard, whether or not he's paid for it."

"His father would have been proud."

"Michael?" she said in surprise.

Jack was embarrassed. "I meant George. But of course, Michael was his father. Both of them would have been proud."

In deference to her mother-in-law, Isobel had canceled their plans for the evening; however, exhausted after the long day that had begun at half-past five that morning in Palm Island, Julia had retired soon after dinner. Which left them with three hours before they could even think of going to bed.

They were in the small den that Isobel had made into a home office, Scott reading and she making lists. From the day of their engagement, it seemed Isobel had been making lists. Rarely did Scott concern himself with these rosters, unless he wanted to add a name—a client or an out-of-town visitor—to a party. Every marriage ran its own pattern, and in theirs Isobel attended to the entertaining while Scott contributed by selecting the wines for dinner and seeing to drinks beforehand.

"Who will be coming for Thanksgiving?" he asked.

Isobel, in her robe, was seated at the Edwardian secretary she used as a desk. "The children's friends, your mother, my parents, Cece. And I invited Jeff Wheeler and Uncle Branford."

"Uncle Branford? That old blowhard."

"Scott! Mother wanted me to invite him. Poor thing was going to have Thanksgiving dinner at the Princeton Club." As an afterthought, she added, "Besides, it will even out the table."

"Isobel . . . you're not trying to set my mother up with Branford Morgan?"

"Oh, Scott, don't be childish." That meant he had come close.

Scott sat in an armchair with the New York Law Journal, but he found it hard to concentrate. His thoughts kept returning to the Saturday at Sagaponack with Solange. Ten days had passed since then, and it was distressing how often she invaded his consciousness. He had no illusions about the reason for this, and at forty-seven he was not about to let himself fall into that trap. The sensible thing would be to cancel their appointment for next weekend. He would make up an excuse, say he had to go out of town and that with Christmas coming, his calendar was full. She would not be fooled, but was that important? What *was* important was that he avoid seeing her again.

He watched his wife as she worked, stopping to nibble on the end of her pen, then adding another item to whatever the hell she was doing. The rosy lamplight cast a flattering glow on Isobel. She had scrubbed off her makeup, and her hair, usually styled to perfection, hung loose around her face, making her youthfully pretty. Scott put down his book and went to stand behind her. She ignored him, continuing to write and bending her head lower over the notebook. He leaned down and kissed the back of her neck. Isobel hunched her shoulders, giving an annoyed little laugh. "What are you doing?"

"Kissing you," he said softly, nuzzling her ear.

"Scott, for heaven's sake."

"Let's go to bed," he whispered, reaching to fondle her breasts.

She let out an exasperated sigh, saying in a steady, long-suffering tone, "I'm not in the mood for this."

"Come on, dear, I want to make love to you."

"Not now, Scott. I have to finish this tonight."

"You can do it later . . ." He tried to draw her into his arms, but she pulled away from him. "Isobel, please."

"I told you, no!" She waved her hand, as if shooing away flies. "Go . . . watch television or something."

Stung, he backed away. "This is ridiculous. I'm going for a walk."

He put on an old pair of sweats and some running shoes, and grabbed a parka from the catch-all closet near the kitchen. Annoyed at the cumbersome procedure involved in the simple act of leaving his residence, he jabbed the button three times until he heard the cranking sound that indicated the elevator was on the way.

"Sorry to keep you waiting, Mr. Rhinehart," said Jésus, the night attendant.

Scott nodded, muttering something inaudible. When the doors opened on the lobby, he came face to face with Bitsy and Ned Garrison, who lived on twelve. "Where are you going, Scott?" asked Bitsy, looking him up and down.

He realized how unlike himself he appeared, in gray sweats and Chip's old olive green EMS parka. Very bad for the building's image. What the hell, it was a free country. If he wanted to go out at ten o'clock at night wearing comfortable clothes, he damn well didn't need permission from the board secretary.

"Good to see you." He clapped Ned on the shoulder, smiled at Bitsy, and kept going.

"Evening, Mr. Rhinehart." The night doorman unlocked the door for him, discreetly eyeing his costume.

What an idiotic way to live. You couldn't even escape from your building, for Christ's sake, without getting the fish-eye from half a dozen people. He walked south, noting a woman who approached from the opposite direction with a small, nervous poodle avoid eye contact with him, almost becoming one with the building they were passing. He crossed over to the other side of Fifth. It was darker along the park but had the advantage of uninterrupted sidewalk and little foot traffic. As he neared a bench, two delicate-looking young men rose and skittishly hurried away into the park. Jamming his hands in his pockets, he felt some loose change and a crumpled-up paper. By the light of a street lamp, he saw that it was a twenty-dollar bill, and he remembered that he had no wallet. If he was knocked over the head, no one would be able to identify him. The way he was dressed, they'd probably cart him off to Bellevue with the winos and the homeless.

A professional dog walker passed him by with five canines of assorted sizes and breeds straining at their leashes, and it occurred to Scott that if he had a dog, no one would question what he was up to alone on the street at this hour . . . which naturally led to thoughts of Napoleon and his owner.

The urgent need for a drink overcame him. The way he looked, where could he go? He had reached Seventy-second Street. Jogging across Fifth Avenue over to Madison, he turned north, trying to remember the location of a bar and grill they had once happened on after attending a show at a tiny gallery that specialized in nouveau art. Isobel had hated the place on sight, but Scott convinced her to have a seafood salad and he ordered a hamburger, and it hadn't been half bad. It was somewhere along here on the east side of the street. Yes, there. O'Shaughnessy's Pub and Chop House. It had a green neon shamrock in the window and the interior was all dark wood and rustic rectangular tables. At this hour it was a neighborhood hangout, and no one raised an eyebrow when he walked in and sat on a barstool in the corner.

A burly bartender with a face like gangbusters broke away from three men who were seated at the far end of the bar watching a wrestling match on TV. "What'll it be?"

"I'll have a mug of whatever's on tap," said Scott.

The bartender served the beer and a basket of pretzels and went back to his pals. The light from the shamrock cast a green glow over Scott's hands and he thought it would make an interesting photograph, part of the series on men. The corporate lawyer, slumming with the riffraff. He sighed. Better stay away from that subject. Taking a long swallow of beer, he glanced around the dark restaurant. Only one table was occupied, by a slim young woman with long dark hair and a clean-cut gray-haired man of around fifty. They were deep in conversation. The woman was wearing jeans and a bulky brown Fair Isle sweater. Although the man had a gold band on his left ring finger, you knew they weren't married to each other. Other people's lives . . .

"Another beer, buddy?"

Scott started at the bartender's voice. "No thanks." He extracted the twenty-dollar bill from his pocket and pushed it across the counter. Taking his change, he left the pub and jogged the few blocks home.

Isobel was reading in bed when he came in. "Where have you been? I was worried."

"I told you I was going for a walk."

"Yes, but that was over an hour ago." She noticed his outfit. "What's gotten into you, Scott? You're behaving very strangely."

He did not bother answering and Isobel went back to her book. By the time he came out of the bathroom in his pajamas, she had turned off her lamp and was pretending to be asleep. Pretending, because Isobel never fell asleep quickly. Scott slipped under the covers, sensing she was miffed. Why the hell should *she* be offended? He was the one who had been rebuffed. Maybe she was hoping he would try again, now that they were in bed. Maybe she was waiting for him to make up with her. He started to reach out to touch her, but she was lying on her side facing away from him, scrunched into a tight ball. If body language meant anything, he would be well advised to leave her alone.

* * *

On Thanksgiving Day, Julia stood in front of the new painting, a huge canvas that Chip had hung for his mother. "I could certainly use a handy fellow like you around my house, darling," she said, giving Chip a hug.

"Just say the word, Nana, and I'll come down." Chip flashed his delightful smile, looking so much like Scott at that age. The boy was undeniably handsome and charming, even if he wasn't much of a scholar.

Isobel came over to them. "Thank you, Chip, you did a wonderful job. If I'd waited for the building's handyman to get to it, it could have been weeks." She smoothed back her son's hair. "Now, why don't you put the hammer away and get ready for dinner."

"I'm as ready as I'll ever be." Chip grinned and kissed his mother's cheek indulgently. "Get real, Ma. Jeans are the code of dress." He disappeared in the direction of the kitchen.

Isobel rolled her eyes. "That boy knows how to get around me."

"He's a darling," said Julia. She gestured toward the painting. "Who is the artist?"

"Lance Kohn," said Isobel. "You haven't heard of him. He's going to be part of our Young American Artists series. I first saw his paintings about three years ago at an art show in Saratoga. We'll have several of his canvases at our opening, and I wouldn't be surprised if we sell them all."

"It's very strong work." Julia turned to Isobel. "It must be extremely satisfying to discover an unknown and see his art develop."

Isobel looked at her with surprise. "Then you understand why I'm doing this."

"Of course I understand, Isobel. Did you ever doubt it?"

"I was afraid you disapproved."

"Quite the contrary, my dear. I'm very admiring of you."

Isobel impulsively embraced her. "Thank you for saying that, Julia."

Hardly knowing what to make of so rare and spontaneous a display of affection from Isobel, Julia was quite overcome. "My dear. Oh . . . there are your parents," she murmured.

For all the years Julia had known Victoria and Casper Prescott, she found it difficult to understand what had drawn them to each other. Victoria was a silly woman with frivolous interests and outmoded ideas. Her chief allure had been her beauty, and now that she was losing it she remained, at sixty-five, vain and shallow beyond comprehension. Casper, on the other hand, was a serious man, pompous and full of his own importance. He was a conservative Republican, naturally enough, opinionated and overbearing. George had often commiserated with Scott, who had to work in the same law offices where his father-in-law was a founding partner.

Julia and Victoria went through the usual display of feigned affection with each other. For months after their children were married, Isobel's mother had continued to call her Mrs. Rhinehart. At first offended, Julia came to understand it was to ward off any degree of intimacy, which suited her just fine. What did she need with Scott's in-laws? Uptight WASPs, Deborah called them.

Casper made an effort to be warm and concerned. "How are you managing without George?"

"I'm all right," she replied. "Of course, it's lonely, but I keep busy."

"That's the spirit," he said, giving her an encouraging pat on the shoulder. Having fulfilled this obligation, he fled to the bar.

There was a flurry of greetings in the foyer and Julia looked to see who had arrived. Cece Bedford. Scott's friend Jeff Wheeler, who had been divorced last year. And . . . oh no, there was Branford Morgan, that tiresome friend of the Prescotts. Branford was a bore who fancied himself a charmer. In some way connected by blood to Isobel's mother, he was often included in Prescott family occasions.

He came directly over to her with a big smile and his arms outstretched. "Julia, my dear. How nice to see you. Where have you been keeping yourself?"

"I live in Florida now, Branford. Been there for almost seven years."

"Thought I hadn't seen you for some time. How is Jerome?"

"You mean George."

"Yes, of course. How is the dear fellow?"

"George died five months ago."

"Oh my word, I *am* sorry. Heart?"

"No. Prostate cancer."

"Dreadful. Nasty business." He winced, and Julia could have sworn he reached protectively for his genitals. "Well, you're looking just fine, my dear. It's terribly nice to see you."

"Thank you, Branford."

Ginger came bounding over to give her grandmother a hug. "Hi, Nana." Julia was simply fascinated with her granddaughter. Tall and slim, with thick russet hair grown darker with time, a sprinkling of freckles across her cheeks and a strong, slightly prominent nose, Ginger was one of those fortunate girls who attracts friends and admirers without trying; in fact, she did everything well and seemingly without effort. The new beau, who had arrived with her yesterday, trailed behind.

"How are you, Uncle Branford?" said Ginger.

"Capital, my dear." He kissed her, beaming. "You're as gorgeous as ever. Congratulations on your 'likely' at Princeton."

"Thanks. It was nice of you to have written a letter for me." She gestured toward the youth hovering at her elbow. "Uncle Branford, this is my friend Richard Steinberg. We're going to be on the same program in Guatemala next year."

While Ginger was explaining Guatemala to Branford Morgan, Julia seized the opportunity to speak to her young man. "Where is your home, Richard?"

"I usually say I'm from Erehwon."

"*Nowhere* spelled backwards."

"Right. You know."

"My grandmother is the most well-read person you've ever met," interjected Ginger, who had managed to perplex Branford to the point of his deserting them in search of another drink.

"Why Erehwon?"

"Because I've never really lived in one place. We have a house in Chapel Hill, but my parents have always worked in foreign countries. We lived in India and Thailand when my sister and I were growing up, and now my folks are in Bangladesh."

"How interesting. What do they do there?"

"They're both doctors. Dad heads a medical program for the Cartwright Foundation."

"Isn't Scott involved in some way with the Cartwright Foundation, Ginger?"

"Yes, Daddy's their lawyer."

Young Steinberg reminded Julia a little of Kit, with his longish hair and single earring. Isobel's initial reaction when he walked in last night had been predictably guarded, but she put so much stock in appearances. Richard was certainly friendly and well-mannered, a very nice young man. There was a sweetness about him that appealed to Julia, and she pitied his parents. Imagine, if you were living halfway across the world, summoning the courage to send a child back home to school.

At the dinner table, when Chip got up to pour the wine, Julia made a heroic effort to draw out his girl, Sally Middleton, an anorexic-looking waif with whitish blond hair and large, pale blue eyes. "Tell me about yourself, my dear. Are you at Williams with Chip?"

"No, I'm a freshman at Bennington. I met Chip through a friend from Grosse Pointe."

"Is that your home?"

"Uh-huh. Daddy's an executive with General Motors." Her laugh was a bit cynical for one so young. "Grosse Pointe is a company town." Sally Middleton, Julia observed, was much more Isobel's style.

Cece Bedford, that horsey friend of Isobel's who would be her partner in the new gallery, was seated across the table, somewhat improved in appearance in the decades since she had been a bridesmaid at Isobel and Scott's wedding. With her pronounced overbite, slight lisp and gangly awkwardness, she had been a perfect target twenty-one years ago. Deborah, an irrepressible teenager at the time, used to mimic her cruelly. Cece seemed to have had her teeth straightened, for they no longer protruded, but she still possessed that long-in-the-jaw aspect that results from generations of inbreeding. Isobel had confided that Cece's marriage to a socially prominent ne'er-do-well had ended after a long battle over her family's wealth. Her ex-husband had sued for millions, but fortunately the money was tied up in trusts. He then demanded alimony, finally settling for a lump payment. Julia could not imagine any self-respecting man suing his wife for alimony.

Jeffrey Wheeler was seated with Cece, of course. Isobel's dinners were like the ark, with everyone in pairs.

They joined hands and bowed their heads for a Thanksgiving grace, then Scott made a very warm toast, welcoming the guests to their home. Julia studied her eldest child as he spoke. Scott had changed. It was subtle, but he had lost a little of the stodginess that Deborah so deplored. Yes, he definitely looked less somber. He was wearing a red vest and a red plaid bowtie today under his tweed sport jacket. That was about the extent of informality Isobel could tolerate at her table. Of course the young people were clad in blue jeans, although the boys had put on blazers for dinner.

Julia thought longingly of the Thanksgivings when the entire family and many of their friends would gather at their Norwalk house . . . the morning pony rides, the touch football games, the enormous dinner followed by a sleepy evening, with everyone content and overfed . . . the men clustered around a television set in the den, with the younger children curled in their laps. They'd often had as many as thirty people. How happy those days had been, and how much she had taken them for granted.

This was her first Thanksgiving without George. There would be many firsts. Soon, the first Christmas . . . in February, their thirty-ninth anniversary. As she had told Jack Winston, she would go on because she had no other course.

The dinner was delicious and, thanks to the four youngsters, quite a lively affair. Grandchildren were undoubtedly one of the chief delights life had to offer. Ginger and Chip teased each other unmercifully, but you could tell there was a lot of love between them. Respectful with their Prescott grandparents, they were much more relaxed and demonstrative with Julia.

It was half past nine when Candida and the hired waitress finally cleared away the coffee tray from the living room and the Prescotts said goodnight, taking Branford Morgan with them. The girls had gone to their room and came back wearing long overcoats.

"Where are you going?" asked Scott.

"We're meeting some friends of mine in the Village," said Chip.

"Isn't that Daddy's coat, Ginger?" Isobel's tone was rather sharp.

"It's an old one, Mom. You were giving it away."

"Of course it's old. Just look at it. You don't think your father would be seen with a button off and the hem hanging down in back."

Ginger craned her neck to look at the offending hem. "Oh, I did that, I guess. It gets thrown around a lot at school."

"You took that garment to school?"

"Chill out, Ma," laughed Chip, giving his mother a bear hug. "Don't you know your father's overcoat is the height of fashion on campus? Sally's wearing her dad's old coat."

The signature of the daughter of a senior vice-president at General Motors appeared to put a different light on the matter. Or was it that Isobel had always favored Chip?

After the young people had departed in a burst of raucous laughter, the three of them sat in the study. "They are such darlings," said Julia. "The apartment seems empty without them. Don't you miss them terribly when they're away?"

Isobel smiled. "The first week is always a little quiet, but one gets used to it."

"Funny," said Scott wistfully, "I never do."

"I didn't realize you were such an old softie, darling."

There was a veiled malice in her daughter-in-law's tone that set Julia's teeth on edge. Scott gave no reply but turned on Channel Thirteen to watch a program about Lincoln Center while Isobel chatted with Julia. There appeared to be a coolness between the couple, or was it Julia's imagination? No, she had thought as much last night, but in the excitement of the children's arrival with their friends it had been less apparent. Now, without the distraction of offspring or other guests, Julia realized there was none of that shared warmth between them, the intimate give-and-take that is the mark of a happy partnership. The sort of loving exchange or simply comfortable being together that she and George had known. In fact, in a very civilized manner, Isobel and Scott were barely on speaking terms.

Julia could not imagine anything more uncomfortable than being in the center of a marital quarrel. At least they didn't scream at each other the way Deborah and Brent used to. The first time she had witnessed that, it was enough for her to know the marriage would not last. George had refused to see it and had been completely unprepared for the divorce. After he became ill, Julia had questioned whether the shock of Deborah running off to California might have aggravated his condition, perhaps even hastened his death, because he neglected himself, putting off an appointment with the urologist in order to fly to

New York, trying to save their daughter's marriage. Realizing how irrational and destructive this line of thinking was did not prevent one from having such speculations.

"Listen to this." Scott called their attention to the television.

The director of special events at Lincoln Center was being interviewed. " . . . some other programs on our calendar in the future. In January 1992, for example, there will be a seventy-fifth birthday celebration in memory of the late composer, Michael Kittredge Shane. A special performance at the Metropolitan Opera House will honor the music and the memory of a talent who created some of the most exciting musicals in the history of Broadway. It will be followed by a black-tie gala on the Promenade . . ."

"You'll definitely have to come to New York for that, Mother."

"We'll see, dear." Although her life as Michael's wife seemed another lifetime, the idea sounded rather appealing. Well, there was plenty of time to think about it.

They watched the end of the program and the news, and then Julia pushed herself out of her chair. "This was a lovely day, my dears, and I can't thank you enough. Now I think I will say goodnight."

A lamp on the night table cast a rosy glow in the guest room, where the bed had been turned down. Julia sat for a minute, surprised at how heavy her limbs felt. Yesterday, after visiting Janice Fried's wonderful exhibit at the Contemporary Arts Gallery, she had kept an appointment with Fred Neiman.

"You're in excellent health, Julia," the man who had been their family physician throughout her marriage declared after completing his examination and glancing over the lab report. "Your usual slow pulse, which we agree has always been so; blood pressure one-twenty over seventy-five. A minor change in the EKG, but nothing significant. Blood and urine, normal. Cholesterol's two-ten, a little elevated, but HDLs are good . . ."

"Why do you think I get the shortness of breath and palpitations?"

He shrugged. "Could be stress."

"Fred, I've been under stress for most of my life. Certainly the past five years with George were more stressful than the months since his death."

"Maybe you're having a delayed reaction," he said kindly, patting her shoulder as he ushered her out of his consultation room. "Stop worrying, Julia. I wish half my patients were in such good shape. Try to relax more. Keep eating well and get plenty of exercise. You're in better condition than most forty-year-olds."

Well, tonight I feel my age, she thought as she removed her clothing. Taking her time in the bathroom, she flossed her teeth, used skin cleanser and put on lotion. *Did you ever dream*, she asked the face in the mirror, *when you were swaying to the plinkety-plink blues of Michael's piano at a soirée in Gerald Ross's apartment, that you would one day be this gray-topped grandmother? Could you have pictured this?*

The house was silent when she climbed into bed, grateful for the comfortable mattress and the lightness of the down comforter. She was amazed at her weariness, and yet she knew she would not easily fall asleep. Her grandchildren, out on the town with their friends, would not come home for hours. It was surprising how unspoiled they were, considering the indulged lives they led. So different from the way she had grown up.

Once she had been able to stay out half the night. Once she had been young. But never as carefree as Scott's children.

❧ Chapter 9 ❧

Murray

In early February of 1941, Edwin presented her with a pair of tickets to the Broadway opening of *Her Kid Sister*, the new Lawrence Comerford and Dale Hawkins musical. "For you and your young man, Julia. Since I'll be in California for three weeks, I won't be able to use these. I hope you enjoy the show."

"Oh, thank you! I've never been to an opening night." She was so excited, she could hardly wait to call Michael.

It was a surprisingly mild Wednesday evening when they walked down Broadway and turned the corner on West Forty-fourth Street shortly before curtain time. The lights of Broadway glowed against the darkness of the winter sky and the theater district was humming with eager playgoers. A palpable excitement rippled through the fashionably dressed first-nighters outside the Shubert Theater. Julia recognized a number of celebrities, including Mayor LaGuardia.

As they entered the lobby, someone called, "Mike . . . Hey, Michael." A short, stocky young man with curly brown hair, wearing a ratty trench coat over his tuxedo, pushed his way toward them through the press of bodies. "Sonnuvagun, Shane, if I don't call you, I never hear from you."

"Not true, Squirt," Michael drawled. "Say hello to Julia. This is the famous roommate, Murray Baker."

"Hi, Murray." *Where have I seen him before?* And then she realized, he had been the one who kept staring at her at Michael's party. The scholar. It was a little disconcerting, the way he grasped her hand. Regarding her with twinkling brown eyes, magnified by his thick horn-rimmed glasses, he reminded her of an intelligent teddy bear. Finally he relinquished her hand but kept glancing at her as the line of patrons moved into the theater.

"So what've you been up to, Baker?" asked Michael.

"Since you ask, I've been working on *Kid Sister.*"

"Aha, one of the medical team." Murray smiled enigmatically. "Not talking, huh? I hear they've really beefed up the score, added new numbers."

"I guess it's no secret that Larry and Dale were doing rewrites right down to the wire. The results are worth it, I promise you."

"We'll see," Michael replied. "This is where we go. Where are you sitting?"

"Next aisle. Let's get together at Sardi's after the show."

"Why not?" Michael agreed, after a questioning look at Julia. "We might as well make the whole opening-night scene." With a wave to Murray, they followed the usher to their seats in the fourth row.

"Tell me about Murray," said Julia.

"Well, as you know, we were roommates at prep school. After Pennington, he went to Harvard. He's a Jewish boy from South Orange. His father's a doctor and wanted him to go to medical school in the worst way, but Murray could never get above a C in any science course. He may be a little crazy at times, but he's an extremely talented writer."

The musicians were tuning their instruments. Julia scanned the *Playbill*, although she already knew plenty about the show from the gossip around the Hopper office. For months, everyone in the theater business had been speculating about this opening. Renamed *Her Kid Sister*, it was a complete remake of *Annabelle*, the Comerford and Hawkins musical that had opened in Chicago the previous fall with disastrous results. All the original principal players had been fired, and the producer himself had taken over as director. They had called in a team of play doctors—evidently Murray Baker was one of them—and supposedly sent the composer into exile at his retreat in the

Adirondacks to work on new music. With a rewritten book and half a dozen new songs, the out-of-town tryouts had gone well this time around, but rumors persisted about friction between composer and lyricist. Since the beginning of their association in 1925, the team of Lawrence Comerford and Dale Hawkins had written no fewer than sixteen shows, most of them hits— until three years ago, when they began to experience a run of bad luck.

Despite the troubled history of their latest production, a Comerford and Hawkins Broadway opening was still a theatrical event, and you could feel the anticipation in the audience as the lights dimmed. Michael strove to appear blasé, but Julia sensed that he, too, was excited. The orchestra struck up the overture, and to the accompaniment of light and tuneful melodies, the curtain rose. Julia was immediately captivated by the clever performances of the characters in the rather foolish story about Eloise Lake and her younger sister, Annabelle, who foils a succession of Eloise's romances during the family's summer vacation on the Jersey shore.

The musical moved along at a predictable pace, with a lively dance or two and catchy, tuneful songs—typical Lawrence Comerford fare—until the end of the first act. And then Annabelle and two of her sister's suitors sang the title number, "Kid Sister."

It was a show-stopper. The wildly applauding audience shouted and stamped and whistled, demanding an encore. And indeed, Annabelle sang one chorus more, while the two would-be swains harmonized. As the curtain rang down on the first act, Julia clapped her hands until they stung. She leaned toward Michael without removing her eyes from the stage, where the three players were taking another curtain call. "Wasn't that *terrific?*"

When there was no response, she turned to him. He was staring straight ahead, his jaw set and his face expressionless, oblivious to the people around them who were beginning to file out for intermission.

"Michael?" She touched his arm.

He turned and blinked, as if coming out of a trance. "Sorry," he said brusquely. "I'm thirsty. Let's go out in the lobby."

He was silent as they walked up the aisle, and she wondered what had caused his sudden change of mood. I really don't know this man at all, she thought. I wonder whether I will ever be able to get close to him. When they reached the lobby, Michael went over to the bar and returned with two glasses of champagne.

"What shall we drink to?" asked Julia brightly, trying to restore the festive atmosphere of the early evening.

He pursed his mouth. "I say we drink to . . . my Broadway début."

It seemed a strange remark. "*The Outlanders?*"

"No. I was referring to the song we heard tonight. 'Kid Sister.' "

She looked at him quizzically. "Wasn't that the last number, that great song?"

"That's right," he said, his voice light. "That's my song. Comerford lifted it from my work."

"Oh, Michael . . ." It had to be a mistake. How could the renowned Lawrence Comerford dare to pass off another composer's song as his own? "Are you *certain?*"

His voice was harsh when he answered. "I know my own music, Julia. I wrote that song."

"Then you're saying he *stole* your material?" It was so unbelievable, it took her breath away.

Michael nodded. "He changed the phrasing, added a couple of bars to accommodate the lyrics, but the melodic line is mine and so is the beat—"

"The *beat* is the best thing about it. It's sensational, that quickstep syncopation. Oh . . . what are you going to *do?*"

"I don't know yet." He sighed and looked so dejected that she wanted to put her arms around him and tell him she believed in him.

"Dammit, he didn't have to steal it." His tone turned bitter and angry. "I would have sold it to him, but the bastard didn't even offer to buy it. I wanted to work on the show, sure, but I understand he has a reputation to protect. I would have been content with a mention—I could have been an 'arranger.' There are ways you give credit to someone who helps the score along. But no, he had to say how unsuitable he thought my work was. Didn't even have the guts to confront me—sent the message through that turd, Tony Regis."

"Do you think maybe he didn't know . . . I mean, Tony

could have told him it was someone else's work or given it to him anonymously."

"With my name on the manuscript? Do you really believe that?" He gave her a disparaging look. "Ah hell, what does it matter? Sometimes I think I want to get out of this game. Go teach at Oberlin."

"He can't get away with it, Michael. It's illegal to steal someone else's composition. There's such a thing as copyright." She wished she had not brought him to see *Her Kid Sister*. And yet she was glad she was with him when he found out. The lights flickered for the second act. "We don't have to stay if you don't want to."

"No, I have to see the rest of it. Now I'm really curious."

Three more songs in the final act had been taken from Michael's scores. Julia recognized two of them from among the pieces he had played for her. By the time it was over, he was calm and analytical. "He was a little more inventive with these, but the melodies are definitely mine—that theme in the reprise is exactly as I wrote it, same phrasing, same triplets . . ."

The composer and playwright-lyricist were called to the stage with the cast for the final bows. The audience gave them a standing ovation. It was clear that *Kid Sister* was a hit and would be playing a long run at the Shubert.

"It's not fair, Michael. The best songs in the show are yours. You should be up there."

"That's not the way it seems to work, honey." He looked drained. "Is it okay with you if we don't go to Sardi's? I'm really not in the mood to celebrate."

"Of course not. Come back to the apartment. Betsy made brownies today and we can stop at Schrafft's on the way to buy ice cream."

But Murray Baker cut them off in the lobby. "What'd you think—some show, huh? Is that ever a *smash*! It's gonna break all records. Come on backstage, I want to see the cast."

"We changed our minds about going out," said Michael, trying to beg off. "We're tired."

"Nothing doing. You can't miss all the excitement." He was high on the crest of the show's success, and it was hard to resist his enthusiasm.

Michael gave Julia a rueful glance and whispered, "Oh well, into the enemy camp."

Despite Michael's anger, it was thrilling for Julia to go backstage and see the dancers and members of the chorus still in their costumes and greasepaint, milling around amongst the props. Murray led them to the new star's dressing room. Marie Newberry, who played the part of Annabelle, was surrounded by well-wishers. She had changed to a robe but was still in makeup, seated on a swivel chair in front of a dressing table, speaking animatedly to the thin, sallow man who had just appeared onstage. Julia recognized Lawrence Comerford from her first New York party at Rodney Barstow's Long Island estate. When Marie saw Murray in the doorway, she waved and blew a kiss.

"Come on, you should meet her," said Murray.

"We're already acquainted," Michael replied. Julia turned to look at him, for his tone implied that there was something unpleasant between them.

But Marie greeted Michael with friendly exuberance and he responded in kind, congratulating her on her triumphant performance. Puffed up with the success of his show, Comerford shook hands, giving no indication that he had ever heard of a young composer named Michael Shane.

Leaving the overcrowded room, they headed for Sardi's, where theater people congregated to await the reviews. They were shown to a table in an obscure corner of the second floor. "Siberia," joked Murray, "but at least we're upstairs."

"Congratulations, Squirt," said Michael when they were seated. "Your name is inscribed in the credits of a hit."

"In very fine print, among dozens."

"Well, what'd you expect?"

"I just can't get too worked up about it. Hell, I wrote most of the new lyrics."

"At least you're listed."

Michael's voice was bitter, and Murray looked at him sharply. "What's eating you?"

"Nothing."

"Hey, I'm the guy who lived with you, remember? Something's wrong."

Julia kept her eyes on Michael as he leaned on the table, resting his chin on his hands. "Why don't you tell him?" she said quietly.

"Listen to the lady, Mike."

"I could get deep-sixed for this," said Michael, glancing uneasily around. He hunched forward across the table. "Those are my songs in the show, Murray. Probably the ones you wrote lyrics for."

Murray's expression was incredulous. "What're you talking about? You mean tonight, in *Kid Sister?*"

Michael nodded. "Yes."

"Seriously, Michael, do you understand what you are suggesting? That is a *very* grave accusation."

"I know it is. It's not my imagination. Comerford had some of my music. An agent named Tony Regis sent it to him when he heard they needed help on the score."

"Jesus! When was that?"

Michael looked at Julia. "September?"

"The beginning of October. I gave the scores to Tony Regis myself," she explained to Murray. "I'm with the Hopper agency and he used to work there. He left in December and didn't return Michael's material until the end of January."

"How do you know Larry actually saw it?" he asked Michael.

"How much more proof do I need? Regis sent a letter saying Comerford had rejected my songs. According to Tony, he dismissed them as too pretentious for Broadway."

Murray uttered a curse under his breath. "Exactly how many numbers are yours?"

"Four. The song that brought down the house at the end of Act One. 'Kid Sister'—that was mine."

"Hardly pretentious."

"He changed the tempo and pace, of course, but that can be done with any song. My stuff wasn't written specifically for this show. It was meant to give him a sample of my style."

"And the others you think he stole?"

"Three numbers in the second act—"

Murray interrupted, pointing a finger at him. " 'It's a Crying Shame'—I bet that was yours."

"Right. And the last two songs. Then, of course, the reprise of 'Kid Sister'—"

"In other words, the best numbers in the show. Now that you've told me, I can see it. Christ, you must be boiling."

"Right now, I'm sick."

"What can he do, Murray?" Julia asked.

"I don't know. Talk to a lawyer, I guess."

"Can you see me suing the great Lawrence Comerford? I'd be blackballed for life."

"You have to go about it in a scientific manner, comparing your notation with theirs." Murray was lost in thought for a minute. "Would it help if I could get hold of a score?"

"Can you do that?"

"Why not? I wrote the lyrics. Let me see what I can do. Meanwhile, *say nothing to anyone*."

Abruptly Michael changed the subject. "I've been working on a new show for Gerry Ross. The book is in trouble and they need a lyricist. How'd you like to talk to him?"

Michael and Murray were deep in conversation when the supporting cast began to arrive. One by one, they were seated at tables along the side. Everyone in the restaurant clapped when the producer came in with a large party that included Lawrence Comerford and Dale Hawkins. The stars were the last to appear, and their entrance was heralded by cheers and wild applause. Flashbulbs popped continuously as photographers snapped pictures for the tabloids.

After the enthusiastic reception from the audience, there seemed little question that the reviews would be good, yet there was always that element of doubt. The critics could be brutal and unpredictable, and there was a certain tension in the air. Despite Michael's low spirits, Julia was enjoying the excitement, but she was also uncomfortably aware of Murray's attention focused on her. She was relieved when someone from the cast waved to him and he excused himself to table-hop.

"What time do the reviews come out?" she asked.

"Not for another hour," said Michael. "I think we can break away now. Murray has plenty of friends here."

They said goodbye and left the restaurant just in time to grab a taxi that was dropping a party at the door. "Have you decided what you're going to do?" she asked.

"I'm not sure. We'll see what Murray comes up with."

"Would you mind if I told Mr. Hopper about it when he returns from California? You remember what he said about putting your work in the wrong hands."

"Let me think about it for a few days."

"This was supposed to be a gala evening. I'm so sorry, Michael."

He smiled and put an arm around her. "If it had to happen, I'm glad I was with you." They had reached her apartment. Michael told the driver to wait and took her to the door.

"Would you like to come up?"

"Not tonight. I have a lot on my mind." Holding her by the shoulders, he gave her a chaste kiss. "Thanks for inviting me. Despite everything, it was a great show." He ruffled her hair. "See you soon, kid."

Edwin Hopper added ice to his scotch and joined Julia and Michael, who were sitting together on the sofa in his study. "You'll find George Rhinehart inspires confidence. He's a capable lawyer, solid as they come. I knew his father. Fine family."

"This is awfully good of you," said Michael.

"Regis was working out of my office when he sent your material to Comerford. I hope you believe me when I say I knew absolutely nothing about this."

"That never entered my mind, Mr. Hopper, not for a minute. In fact, I didn't want you to know."

"You mustn't be angry with Julia for telling me, Michael. I had to drag the story out of her."

Julia could only think how lucky it was that after his return from California, Edwin had asked her how they enjoyed *Kid Sister*. Sensing something amiss, he began to question her, and she had been forced to relate how Michael's songs were purloined by the famous Lawrence Comerford. He insisted immediate action was necessary, and as a result here they were, having drinks with him in the booklined room on the second floor of his townhouse on Gramercy Park West.

"I'd like to do what I can to make it up to you," said Hopper.

Michael was leaning forward, hands clasped loosely between his knees. "You already have, by putting me in touch with Rhinehart. I'm going to see him first thing tomorrow morning."

"Good, good. But I can do more than that. Am I correct in thinking you don't have an agent?"

"That's right. I've never really needed one."

"I wouldn't be too sure about that. You'll certainly want one for the new show. Julia tells me you haven't yet signed anything."

"No, I haven't. The contracts are supposed to be ready next week." ·

"Gerald Ross is an innovative producer, has great instincts, and has always been able to raise money, but you should have an eagle eye scanning that contract. If you're willing, I can handle it for you."

"I'd be honored, Mr. Hopper." Michael could hardly believe his good fortune. He realized he needed an agent, but had been too lazy or too preoccupied to go about the business of finding someone to represent him. Edwin Hopper was one of the best in New York, with some of the foremost dramatists in the American theater among his clients.

"That's settled, then. I'll give Ross a call first thing tomorrow." He went to the bar to refill their glasses, ginger ale for Julia, beer for Michael. "Broadway can certainly use some quality musicals to liven things up these days. Have you settled on a lyricist yet?"

"Murray Baker has started working on the book and lyrics. We've collaborated before and I think he's superb."

Julia, who had been content to listen until then, spoke up. "Michael won't tell you this, but the book was in trouble. They had fired two writers when he brought Murray to Gerry Ross."

"That was fortunate," said Hopper. "Well, you've got quite a task ahead, if you plan to open in the fall."

"It's going well, now that Murray's come in. We've been working around the clock. When you get hot, you can't seem to stop. I have high hopes for *The Outlanders*."

Hopper winced. "You've got to get rid of that title, Michael. It's a loser."

"Steve Nordberg is being very stubborn about that. And for some strange reason, Gerry hasn't taken a stand."

"I can't imagine the playwright will prevail, no matter how strong his opinion."

"I suggested *North Wind* or *The Sea Rovers*, which would keep the Viking flavor and have a more appealing sound."

"They ought to go with your instincts. I liked *One Night in Venice*, and I know you wrote the book and lyrics. Too bad you sold it outright."

"I didn't expect to find a producer. Mitchell was my publisher, so when he bought out the theater and said he wanted to put *One Night* in the repertory, I agreed."

"Did you get anything more for it?"

"A little. Zach sent me a check when the show closed. He said it was my share of the profits. It didn't have a very long run."

"No, those downtown things never do. Well, more and more theatergoers are looking for alternatives, so perhaps it will come back someday. You might ask George about recovering rights, although it's probably too late."

It was time for them to leave. "I can't thank you enough for all you've done, Mr. Hopper."

"My pleasure. It won't do for people to walk all over my best reader's beau, now, will it?" Julia felt her cheeks grow warm. "Was I speaking out of turn?" inquired Hopper, looking from one to the other.

"Not at all," Michael replied, hugging her. "She's the greatest."

Edwin accompanied them downstairs and stood on the front doorstep, looking over the brier fenced enclosure of Gramercy Park. "Spring will be a while yet. There's still a nip in the air. Have a nice evening, folks."

"That is one great gentleman," said Michael as they strolled south along the park.

"Yes, isn't he?"

"Do you realize what most people in the theater would go through to get him for an agent? Today was my lucky day, and I have you to thank for bringing us together."

Julia turned to wave at Hopper and saw him standing on his doorstep watching them as they walked toward Irving Place. "He seems so lonely, doesn't he?"

Michael looked at her as if such an idea had never occurred to him. "Do you think so?"

She would have expected a man as creative as Michael to be more sensitive to loneliness, but she smiled up at him. "Where are we going?"

"Just down the block to Pete's Tavern. It used to be the

haunt of O. Henry and such. The food's nothing special, but it's rich in tradition."

Events moved swiftly after that. Michael met with George Rhinehart and gave him the packet of music just as it had arrived from Regis. Within a surprisingly short time, he was back in the law offices of Winston & Rhinehart.

"We came to terms quite easily," George told him. "They're reprinting the program and you'll get credit for the songs you wrote. We're negotiating a financial settlement, which is to include a fair percentage of any royalties."

"I don't know what to say. I feel so stupid."

The lawyer, who was a pleasant fellow a year or so older than Michael, shrugged. "It happens more than you would expect. The other attorney claims his client thought he was working from his own worksheets and was as surprised as you when he was presented with the evidence."

"If the passage of time were greater, I could almost believe him," said Michael. "Most composers make sketches and stash them away to be used again. I never forget my themes, but I suppose it's possible."

"That's rather generous of you," Rhinehart replied, with a smile. "There was nothing to be accomplished by suing Larry Comerford. You've won your point. Too bad we can't go after Tony Regis, though. *Someone* had copies made of your scores, and I suspect it was Regis, who then sold them to Comerford. That doesn't let Larry off the hook, because he must have realized he was trafficking in stolen goods. Our agreement stipulates no litigation, even against a second party. Otherwise I'd really love to get Regis."

"Knowing Tony, we'll be lucky if he doesn't claim he's entitled to an agent's fee."

"Let him try," laughed George. "I'll throw the book at him." He consulted his notes. "As for regaining the copyrights on the work you did for Mitchell Publishing and their subsidiary, Mell-o-dee Records, we'll see what, if anything, can be done about *One Night in Venice*. I'm afraid all the rest is clearly work for hire. Better known as slave labor."

"Those days are long gone, I'm happy to say. I can't really fault Zach Mitchell. He's no worse than most publishers on Tin Pan Alley, and he gave me my first chance."

"We seem to have covered everything for the moment," said the lawyer, rising. "If you have any questions, be sure to call. Good luck with the new show."

"I'll send you tickets for opening night," Michael promised, shaking hands. "Thanks for your help, George. From now on I should be all right, with Edwin Hopper as my agent and you handling the legal end."

Rhinehart had a very engaging smile. "I enjoy working with Ed. You couldn't be in better hands."

"Nice guy," Michael reported to Julia on the phone that evening. "Have you ever met him?"

"I don't think we've actually met, but I've noticed him coming up to the office. Sandy hair, medium height, rather good-looking?"

"I suppose that's a fairly accurate description." She smiled at his grudging reply. Was it possible that Michael Kittredge Shane, ladykiller par excellence, was just the tiniest bit jealous?

Michael always claimed in later years that if it were not for Julia, he would never have put his life in order. George became his legal counsel, investment advisor, and occasional hand-holder. But it was Edwin Hopper who nourished the creative team of Shane and Baker, and to him belonged a large part of the credit for their sudden and remarkable success.

Hopper had so much faith in their first Broadway musical that he invested heavily in the show. It was Edwin who convinced the eminent director Clement Harden to take on the project when Harden was considering a sure thing by Vernon Duke. With Clement in charge, they were able to attract the best talent in choreography, as well as set and costume design. And money.

Although more songs would be added and dance numbers cut during the out-of-town tryouts, the book and music were essentially ready and production underway by the end of May. The costumers, choreographer, and musical director were at work, the sets were under construction, and soon auditions were being held for the more than a thousand singers and dancers from whom a handful would be chosen.

When the casting was complete, in leading roles were Keith Winslow as Rolf, the Viking chief, and Alicia Venning as

Annilde, his captive bride. Understudy for Miss Venning was Vivienne Tremaine, who also was cast in the feature role of Liese, the Viking maid who loves Rolf and plots to get rid of Annilde.

Despite the rigid rules prohibiting outsiders at rehearsals, Edwin assigned Julia the task of sitting in on the first run-throughs and making a report to him. When Gerald Ross raised objections, Edwin told him mildly but in a way that brooked no argument, "She won't say a word. No one will even suspect she's there."

"See that they don't." The aloof producer was no more cordial to Julia than he had been on the occasion of their first meeting, but Hopper was somehow always able to get around Ross.

Julia sat in the rear of the dark rehearsal hall, paying close attention to the action onstage and taking notes for Hopper. She kept her distance from the front of the theater where Ross, the choreographer, the musical director, and at various times Murray Baker and Michael Shane conferred with the director. While Murray and some of the crew involved in the production would occasionally wander back to chat with her during a break, Michael acted as if she were not present.

"He gets totally absorbed," Murray reassured her kindly. "It's nothing personal."

"Don't be silly," she answered, irritated that Murray would think she wasn't strictly professional. "This is my job."

Among the crew was an assistant stage manager named Joe Daley. A former actor who had been with the Mitchell Repertory Theater, he was a great one for sitting and kibbitzing over a cup of coffee. She was certain he had no idea that she was going out with Michael when they had the following conversation.

"Mike Shane and I, we go way back. He's a good guy. Mitchell took advantage of him."

"So I've heard."

"It's something, the way theater people use each other. Nothing just happens in show business. You want to know how Vivienne Tremaine got the part in *One Night in Venice?*"

Julia's ears perked up. She wanted to know.

"There's an actress, Marie Newberry, who had been signed

for it. You know, the one in *Kid Sister*. She's a big star now."

"Yes, I saw her. She's very talented."

"Talented she may be, but she left them high and dry. After a week of rehearsals, she gets an offer to play the ingenue in *Stars in Your Eyes* and quits." He chewed on a toothpick, spitting out a fragment to punctuate his disapproval.

So that explained the ill feeling between Michael and Marie Newberry.

"The understudy couldn't carry the part, and meanwhile they're holding up production. Michael to the rescue . . . he knows Vivienne from when he worked on the score of a picture she did on loan to Diamond Studios. They had a thing going there for a while, a real hot affair."

Julia sipped her coffee, which had grown cold.

"So Mike gets on the horn and calls Viv. She's on the Coast, and she's mad at everyone—the studio heads, the publicity department, her agent—and she agrees to come to New York for the run of the play. A scout's in the audience. He likes her, he signs her for Metro Films, they buy out her contract. Before you know it, she's got a supporting role in a picture with Fred Astaire."

"That's quite a success story." *They had a thing going . . .*

"Vivienne doesn't forget. Things had gone sour for her in Hollywood before *One Night* and she knows if it weren't for Mike, she might be back hoofing it on the boards in Scranton."

"You mean she was in vaudeville?"

"Don't knock it, honey. Those of us in the profession wear that badge with honor."

"I *adored* vaudeville when I was growing up in Troy."

"Troy, New York—no kidding? I used to play Proctor's Theater."

"That's the place. Every Saturday, until we were sixteen and got jobs, my best friend and I would have swim team practice all morning, stop at the drugstore for lunch, and then go to the movies. There was usually a vaudeville show before the picture."

"You probably caught us. I was part of a family act, the Dancing Daleys. We all have show business in our blood. My parents retired to Florida, but my kid sister and my brother went to Hollywood. Faye married a cameraman, thank God, since she never would have made it in moving pictures. But Roon scored big. That's my brother, Roon Daley."

"The cowboy star? The one in *Smiling at Sunrise?*"

"That's him."

Julia gave him a knowing look. "You wouldn't have anything to do with Michael writing the title song for that film, would you?"

He laughed. "You scratch my back and I'll scratch yours. That's the way the business operates, honey."

She shook her head in wonder. "Where does talent enter the picture? No pun intended."

"Look, sweetie." Joe leaned forward, speaking in a confidential manner. "There are three elements on the road to success. One is talent, another is luck, and the third is who you know. That's very important, the connection. For every big player, there are a hundred, maybe a thousand waiting in the wings. You have to be in the right place at the right time and it doesn't hurt to know the right person."

"And what about dedication?"

"They all work hard and they all believe in themselves. It's that extra break that pushes them over."

"Michael . . ."

"Well, Mike's a rare bird. I really think the guy is one in a million. You can't keep that kind of talent down."

"He hasn't really had his big break yet."

"Give 'im time. He's still young. I guarantee you, by the age of thirty, Michael Shane will be at the top of the heap."

"What about Vivienne Tremaine?" She could not resist asking.

"If she doesn't go to hell in a handbasket, she'll become a Hollywood legend."

"She's very beautiful. What do you think of her talent?"

"Viv has what it takes to be a star. Good voice, incredible dancer, and she can act. You have to be totally self-absorbed to be a great actress, and she certainly qualifies there. Unfortunately she has one great weakness. And it could be her downfall."

"What's that?"

"It's not a what, sweetheart . . . it's a who. His name is Michael Shane."

*   *   *

On a cold and rainy night in November 1941, *North With the Wind*, as it came to be called, opened at the Globe Theater after tryouts in Baltimore and Philadelphia. Brilliantly staged by Clement Harden, with sets and costumes by Gene Miles, it was a gorgeous production. A little tony, a bit ambitious for some audiences, perhaps. However, the music was dazzling, the book and lyrics witty and worthwhile, the staging, choreography, and costumes artful and elegant. Three beautiful songs of enduring popularity came out of the show: "Farewell, My Heart," "The Sea Is Calling," and "A Bright Tomorrow."

With few exceptions, the reviews were laudatory. Burns Mantle in the *Daily News* wrote, "*North With the Wind* is a rousing, vibrant evening of musical theater that will stir your blood and tingle your toes . . ." In the *Journal-American*, John Anderson dropped his cynicism for once: "Michael Shane's rapturous score coupled with the catchy lyrics and literate book of Murray Baker have burst upon the stage at the Globe with an effervescence long missing on Broadway . . ."

Howard Barnes of the *Tribune* was less enchanted: "Neither the incomparable songs of Michael Shane, the brilliant lyrics and story adaptation by Murray Baker, nor Arlo Rothmore's lively dances managed to excite this reviewer's interest in the Viking legend . . . in this opulent remake of *Eric the Red*."

As soon as Michael's show opened, the awkwardness between him and Julia vanished. He invited her to bring Betsy to opening night, although they hardly saw him until the end of the play, for he was far too nervous to sit in the audience. Alternately pacing the lobby and the rear of the theater until the final curtain, he was like a fly on a griddle.

Edwin came with a delightful woman named Kitty Montgomery, who was in some way related to his English son-in-law. "I don't think you two have ever met," said Julia, introducing him to Betsy.

He regarded her aunt with an astonished smile. "I used to have an Aunt Betsy, but she was certainly nothing like you."

"You never told me your boss was such a charmer," Betsy remarked when they were seated.

After the final curtain, everyone adjourned to Gerald Ross's luxurious Park Avenue apartment for an opening night party.

They stayed up half the night, waiting for the last of the morning editions, but by two-thirty when the *Times* came out, they knew they had a success:

> This offering shows grace, wit, and originality, just as it introduces a composer with extraordinary talents, and a playwright already finding his voice. The music is brilliant, the book and lyrics are lively, making sport of a ponderous vehicle. Stefan Nordberg's original drama, *The Outlanders*, can cause an audience to nod. This audience did not, as it gave occasionally thunderous applause to the worthwhile effort of a young and talented new team who promise to fill a void left by the Gershwins . . .

Although the show was not a runaway hit, with this accolade from the most influential of reviewers, it had a good solid run of 676 performances, it established the team of Shane and Baker, the angels made money, and everything would have proceeded from there.

If it were not for the small matter of a World War.

Seven weeks after the Japanese attack on Pearl Harbor, Michael Shane enlisted in the army.

Gerald Ross became agitated beyond reason when his music man broke the news that in a few days he would be leaving New York. "You ungrateful sonnuvabitch," he screamed. "You could at least have waited to be drafted."

"We're at war, Gerry. I didn't want to wait."

"I have an investment in you, Michael. You *owed* it to me to stay home as long as possible. Shane and Baker may be a hot ticket now, but if this damned war lasts more than a year or two, the public will forget."

"The only thing about you I find more distasteful than your inflated ego is your colossal stupidity," Michael retorted, and for a week they were not on speaking terms.

He told Julia about the scene that night. "The man's a cretin. The whole world's going up in flames and he's worried about his frigging investment."

Julia had disliked Ross from the moment they met. The days she spent monitoring rehearsals for Hopper had done nothing to improve her opinion of him. "What about Gerry, won't he be drafted?"

"I'm willing to bet he'll find a way out."

"He's hardly in an essential industry."

"Ross is one of those people who think rules are made for everyone else."

On the night before Michael was to depart for basic training at Fort McClellan in Alabama, he took her one last time to see *North With the Wind*. At intermission, he went backstage to say goodbye to the cast. They left before the final act because he had to report to Penn Station at five o'clock in the morning.

With street lights dimmed and Broadway blacked out, the city seemed to be slumbering. By the time they reached her apartment, the sky had the dull metallic cast that meant snow. Betsy had gone to bed, leaving a humorous farewell note for Michael and a fresh batch of his favorite fudge brownies.

Julia poured milk, trying to act as if this were just another evening. As if he weren't going a thousand miles away. "Tonight was the tenth time I've seen your show. It's still my favorite."

"And you're still *my* favorite," he said, taking her in his arms and kissing her. It was a long kiss and very tender. When at last they drew apart, he stroked her cheek. "You're so special, Jule. Have you ever thought about the strangeness of fate . . . there I was, and suddenly you came along. And it changes everything."

I love you so much . . . I'll wait for you. What would happen if she spoke those words aloud? Once said, they could never be unsaid. Instinctively she drew back. Michael was a man who shrank from commitment. And she was a woman afraid of being hurt.

All too soon it was time for him to go. When they were standing at the door, she said, "I've never liked goodbyes."

"Neither have I. Let's just say we'll see each other soon and leave it at that." He kissed her again quickly, then turned and ran lightly down the stairs.

She cleared away the plate of brownies and the milk glasses, straightened the cushions on the sofa, still bearing the imprint of their embrace. Such an emptiness she felt. I am hideously selfish, she thought. With the world at war and people dying, all I can do is feel sorry for myself because I might lose the man I love.

* * *

The city had reacted to war with calm and a determination to rally to the nation's defense. Like most New Yorkers, Julia quickly became accustomed to air raid drills and the dimout. As she drew the shades each night at sundown, it was eerie to imagine German submarines lurking offshore like predatory barracudas, waiting for an American ship to be silhouetted in the night against any glow from the city. They were beginning to experience shortages—rubber, sugar, nylon stockings—and the government was preparing to ration gasoline and foods such as butter and meat. It was amazing how quickly and efficiently wartime activities became organized and citizens responded. Edwin Hopper, who immediately became active in the office of the Coordinator of Civil Defense, was a zone warden for the Gramercy area. Julia enrolled in Red Cross classes at the YWCA on Lexington Avenue and was put in charge of first aid for five floors in their office building. At Hunter she learned to spot enemy aircraft from cards with outlines, although how this newly acquired skill would be utilized she could not imagine.

With all this activity, the days passed quickly. Each night she and Betsy listened to the war news on the radio, reported by Gabriel Heatter and Edward R. Murrow. American troops were fighting against superior Japanese forces in the Pacific. With weakened resistance on Bataan and Corregidor, Japanese strategic gains in Burma and the Bay of Bengal, and the continued bombing raids on England, it was impossible not to feel discouraged about the prospects for an early peace. Only on the Russian front, where the Red Army had stalled a relentless German offensive, was there cause for optimism.

It was a sad commentary on human endeavor that business had never been livelier at the Hopper agency. After a decade of hard times in which half the legitimate theaters in New York had failed, the advent of war brought new energy to Broadway. A deluge of scripts with patriotic themes hit the mail room at Hopper Associates every weekday morning and were duly turned over to Julia, whose job it was to weed out the most promising, relegating the rest to a slush pile from which any of several secretarial assistants who aspired to become readers could help themselves. Julia and Edwin divided the remainder among themselves and the other agents. Perhaps one out of every two hundred playwrights was not eventually turned away.

Edwin had recently formed a partnership with a talent agency. Millie Kaplan was put in charge of running the new Hopper–O'Neil Creative Management office on Broadway and Forty-eighth Street. Given more and more responsibility for screening offerings for the drama group, Julia was always behind in her assignments for her college courses.

"I give up," she announced to Betsy after a night without sleep. "I'm going to quit Hunter at the end of this term. Then I can work full time."

"*No*, Julia! I won't hear of your dropping out. You simply *must* get your degree." It was the first time since childhood that she and Betsy had quarreled, and Julia recalled what a formidable foe her aunt could be.

"Look, I love my job and I'd be happier not going to school just now," she argued. "It seems almost frivolous, with the war, and besides, I'm tired of studying."

"You'll feel differently when summer comes. Don't give up, Jule. It's only two more years, and then you'll have the rest of your life to work."

Betsy had become the dedicated career woman since taking over important administrative duties at RNA after most of the men had been called into the armed forces. An assistant and two secretaries had replaced her in the president's office. Rodney was often away at meetings in his capacity as an advisor to the government—a dollar-a-year man. It was rumored that he had secretly been flown to Europe on special missions. Although their affair continued, Betsy had grown more independent since moving into her new position. She seldom mentioned Rodney these days.

It was Julia who spotted the item in Walter Winchell's column. "What married head of a major broadcasting network has been romancing a glamorous blond woman, not his wife? Stay tuned for further details . . ."

"It couldn't be us," said Betsy, dismissing the gossip with a shake of her head when Julia pointed it out to her. "We haven't gone out anywhere in a year. The only place Rod and I see each other is at his apartment, and as you know, there hasn't been much of that lately." It occurred to Julia, although she said nothing, that the glamorous blonde might be someone other than Betsy.

Despite the changes in their lives, the war itself did not seem real to Julia until a particular afternoon in late March of 1942. She was alone with Edwin in the conference room, seated at a table behind a pile of manuscripts, when a military attaché from the British consul's office was ushered in. Julia started to leave, but Edwin held fast to her hand. No more than a look passed between the two men, but she knew something dreadful had occurred. She felt smothered and wanted to flee the room, but remained rooted to her chair.

Edwin said, "It's Cynthia, isn't it?"

"Yes, Mr. Hopper. I'm so terribly sorry."

Edwin walked to a window and stood looking out on the gray windswept street below. "My grandson?"

Julia was conscious of clasping her hands in entreaty at the English officer. Her heart was hammering and her eyes swimming with tears. He cast a distracted glance in her direction and swallowed as he straightened his shoulders. "I'm afraid, sir . . . it was a direct hit. Many lives were lost. We don't have all the details yet, but you'll be given a full report as soon as possible."

Julia watched Edwin bow his head. "Her husband?" he asked, very quietly.

"Captain Reading has been informed. He's been given compassionate leave for . . . for the church service."

For the church service. Not the funeral. There would be no bodies to bury in a direct hit.

When the attaché had left, Julia lowered her head in her hands, unable to control her sobs. After a moment, she felt a light touch on her shoulder and looked up into Hopper's composed and gentle face. "Oh, Edwin," she cried, rising and putting her arms around him, heedless of the tears that rushed in torrents down her cheeks. It was the first gesture of intimacy that had passed between them, and it felt perfectly natural.

For some minutes they held each other and then he drew back and cupped her face in his hands. "She was just about your age when she married. Her husband and I both tried to convince her to come home before the baby was born, but she preferred to be nearby when Chris had leave." His eyes went to a cabinet against the wall, to the photographs of his dead wife and of his daughter Cynthia with Christopher Reading, the RAF captain she had married. He picked up a more recent snapshot from his desk of the young couple with their infant son. "I worried about them. It was always on my mind, but with the worst of the Blitz over, I had hoped . . ."

Edwin stayed away from the office for a week. Julia went to visit him, bringing food for several meals. She was afraid he would neglect himself, but she needn't have worried. He had a diligent housekeeper named Mrs. Reilly who looked after him and a substantial number of concerned friends, including Kitty Montgomery, the woman she and Betsy had met with him at the theater. Edwin was an essentially private man, discouraging visits or other overt expressions of sympathy from the rest of his staff. Upon his return, he seemed tired and thinner, yet he continued as before, never referring to his tragic loss.

March passed, and April. The fall of Bataan was followed by the surrender of Corregidor. They began to hear of American casualties among people they knew—their butcher's son, a man from Betsy's office at RNA, a distant cousin from Troy.

On a Thursday evening in May it was almost seven when Julia reached home, worn out after a morning of classes followed by six hours in the office. She hoped a letter from Michael would be waiting. After completing basic training at Fort McClellan, he had been sent to OCS at Fort Benning. In his time off, he was working on the score for a musical play he and Murray had sketched out before he went away. He wrote sporadically—short, humorous letters, with just a light edge of affection. No tender endearments, no declarations of love, nothing to give her encouragement. Yet she waited for them as if they were passionate love letters. If she were at all self-protective, she would forget about Michael Shane and turn to one of the other men who showed an interest in her. Ben Carmichael; Joe Daley, of the Dancing Daleys, who had not yet been drafted and had taken over as stage manager of Michael's show. Or even Murray Baker, who had been asking her out ever since Michael went away. Wasn't that an indication of Michael's feelings? Surely Murray, his best pal and collaborator, would know if Michael was in love with Julia.

Her spirits fell when she saw the empty mailbox, but perhaps Betsy had come in first and collected the mail. The elevator cranked its slow way up to the third floor. The lock stuck, as usual, and as she worked the key, Betsy opened the door. "Thanks, Bets. We really have to have someone come change that lock."

Betsy remained standing in the doorway with a smug expression on her face that for some reason caused a feeling of anxiety in Julia. "What is it? You look like the cat who got into the cream pitcher."

Her aunt never said a word, just stepped back and nodded toward the sunken living room, where a tall, lean, suntanned soldier stood near the couch smiling at her.

Michael?

"*Michael.*" It came out a whisper and somehow she was able to control the tears that welled in her eyes. She dropped her purse on the floor, and he sprang up the steps to meet her, sweeping her into a tight embrace, his kiss long and hard, then soft and lingering. Betsy had discreetly withdrawn and could be heard moving about in the kitchen.

"How . . . when did you get here? Why didn't you warn me? I look a fright."

"Not to me, you don't," he said, rubbing noses with her. "I tried to call, but there was no answer. I spent all night on the train."

"Poor dear. How long do you have?"

"Three days. And I want to spend them all with you."

Betsy came in with a tray of canapés. "I think this calls for a drink. Will you fix them, Mike?"

While Michael mixed cocktails, Julia hung up her coat and smoothed her hair at the hall mirror. In the looking glass, her color was high and her eyes sparkling. *Three days. And I want to spend them all with you . . .*

"Where are you staying?" asked Betsy.

"At my apartment."

"I thought it was rented."

"It is, but my tenant is on the road this month. You remember Jim Turner," he reminded Julia. "He writes and directs USO shows now."

Julia had to work the next morning for at least a few hours. Michael spent the time with Murray, showing him the music he had written while at OCS. He came to the office just before noon, and had a talk with Hopper before taking Julia to lunch.

"I was sorry about the tragedy, your daughter and her child . . ."

"Thank you, Mike, I received your kind note," said Edwin, immediately changing the subject and launching into a discussion of the next Shane and Baker musical. He had worked out a system for handling the creative process in Michael's absence. "We can mail you a carbon copy of each scene as Murray finishes the draft. You will have to duplicate your worksheets by hand and send them to us. It may be cumbersome and time-consuming, but I think it will do."

"As long as I'm still in this country. Once I go overseas . . ."

"We'll worry about that when the time comes. Won't be for a while, will it?" When Michael did not immediately reply, he went on. "At the appropriate time we'll get everything over to George Rhinehart for the copyrights."

"Thanks, Ed." They shook hands. "I'll keep in regular touch with you."

"Good luck, Michael." Hopper handed him a pair of tickets for *Best Foot Forward*, the Hugh Martin show with Rosemary Lane and a new actress, June Allyson. "Now, you and Julia go out and enjoy yourselves."

It was a fine spring day, a day such as one encounters only in New York, with a soft breeze and the trees in bud and pretty girls stepping briskly along the sidewalks, clinging to the arms of uniformed men. They stopped for lunch at a restaurant overlooking the park, then continued up Fifth Avenue to the Metropolitan Museum of Art, where they passed two blissful hours wandering hand in hand through the galleries. When they came out it was late afternoon, and they walked the few blocks south along the avenue to Julia's street.

"My feet are killing me," she exclaimed, kicking off her shoes as soon as they were inside. "Shall I make tea?"

"Not for me, thanks. Why don't you soak in a hot tub before we go to dinner? I'll stretch out here for a while. This couch and I are old friends." Julia smiled, recalling that New Year's Eve—was it really a year and a half ago?

"Is Betsy still seeing Rodney Barstow?" he asked.

"Unfortunately, yes. He's in Washington most of the time these days, so they don't get together very often. And when he comes home to New York, they can't be seen in public."

"It never ceases to amaze me that a bright, gorgeous woman like Betsy would get herself into such a no-win situation."

"I know," Julia sighed. "It's ridiculous. She doesn't like to talk about it, so I've stopped asking. Well, I'll see you in a little bit."

Half an hour in a steamy bubble bath revived her and soothed her aching feet. When she came downstairs, dressed for the evening in a two-piece navy and white dress with padded shoulders, Michael was asleep on the sofa. She covered him with an afghan, thinking how young and defenseless he looked.

At forty minutes before curtain time he had not stirred, but she woke him. "I'm sorry, but if you want to see the show, we should leave."

"We haven't had dinner, you'll be starved," he said, rubbing his eyes.

"I'm fine," she assured him. "We can eat afterward."

Michael wolfed down a snack of cheese and crackers before freshening up in her bathroom. They dashed off to the theater, getting there just as the curtain was going up.

Julia was restless throughout the first act and glad when Michael suggested they leave at the intermission. "It doesn't compare to *North With the Wind*," she told him. His show was still playing to full houses, although they were running into problems finding replacements for the male actors who had been drafted. The original leading lady continued in the role, but Vivienne Tremaine had left the cast after six months to return to Hollywood.

Of course they had to go to the restaurant on Minetta Lane, which had become their special place. There was great excitement when Michael walked in. The older boys were all in the army now, Giuseppe told them, bringing a bottle of chianti and joining them for a while at their table.

They lingered over dinner. It was nearly midnight when they came out on the dark, silent street and walked the three short blocks to Michael's apartment. Stifling their laughter, they groped their way through the unlighted hallway and up the narrow stairs. "Be careful," he cautioned, holding onto her, "the boys take this dimout seriously, now that they have a good excuse for saving electricity."

Michael drew the curtains and switched on a lamp in a corner of the living room. Julia noticed that Jim Turner had made some changes. The familiar paintings and books had been replaced, the old sofa pushed back against the book-case, and a wide daybed piled with pillows placed against one wall. Michael's personal belongings, packed in cartons, were stored in the studio. Through the darkened archway, Julia could see the outline of the piano, shrouded with a large sheet.

Although she had come here with him before, there was a difference this time. It felt hushed and still. On the brink. He put on a record, something low and bluesy, she never could remember what. And then he turned to her.

"I want to love you," he said softly, drawing her into his arms and kissing her. "Do you want me, darling?"

All of the aching, all of the longing seemed to be there in his voice. It wasn't necessary to answer. It seemed she had been waiting for him forever. With one motion, he lifted her in his arms and carried her to the daybed. She lay there smiling up at him while he unknotted his tie and opened the collar of his shirt. Lowering himself beside her, he kissed her mouth, her throat, and her closed eyelids. Gently he unbuttoned her dress and pushed aside the clothing, kissing and stroking her breasts.

"I've been waiting so long to do this," he said, his voice urgent with need.

"Michael," she whispered. "Oh, Michael . . ."

Somewhere in the streets there was a siren, but it was an ambulance, not an air raid drill. The record finished playing and repeated itself again and again until he stopped it. Late into the night they made love, falling asleep in each other's arms as the sky began to lighten in the east.

A week later, Julia came out of her office at five-thirty after an especially busy day. She stopped to buy a newspaper before crossing Fifth Avenue to catch a bus uptown. She felt tired and depressed. There seemed to be nothing to look forward to for months, now that Michael's leave was over. She found a seat on the bus and idly glanced through the news. Lost between a war bulletin and a report about the laxity in enforcement of the city's dimout, a small article on an inside page caught her eye.

Arden Barstow Seeks Divorce From Husband, Chief of RNA.

"Oh, my God . . ." What did it mean? She jumped off the bus at Seventy-fourth Street and ran down the block to her apartment building. Not bothering to wait for the elevator, she took the stairs two at a time.

Betsy was not at home. Julia dialed the number for RNA and asked for her extension. "I'm sorry, Miss Perkins is out of the office and I don't expect her back today," said her secretary.

Julia paced the apartment, waiting for her aunt to return. By seven-thirty it had started to grow dark outside, and she drew the blackout shades. She went to the kitchen to prepare something for dinner, although her appetite had disappeared, so unnerved was she at the news. Why had Betsy not told her of Rod's imminent divorce? Surely she had known. Did that mean they would be getting married? Of course it would take a long time for the divorce to become final, but it did seem as if her aunt's long-held dreams were at last about to become reality.

It was past eight o'clock when Betsy let herself into the apartment. "I almost didn't hear you," said Julia, pushing herself out of the club chair where she had been studying for her final exam in French.

Betsy looked fagged out. "Long day. One more marathon meeting about pension plans, and I might resign."

"I waited dinner for you. Chef salad."

"Thanks, Julia." She laid gloves and pocketbook on the console table and removed her hat. Julia noticed a folded newspaper in the outside pocket of her briefcase. "Are you ready to eat?"

"In a minute," said Betsy. "I just want to get out of these clothes."

Julia was mixing the salad dressing when Betsy came back wearing a blue housecoat and slippers. "Iced tea?"

"Fine."

They ate their dinner in silence until Julia said, "I saw the article about Arden Barstow."

"Yes, I saw it, too."

"You didn't know?"

Betsy shook her head.

"Have you spoken to Rodney?"

"He's away. Out of the country, actually."

"I see." She realized that Betsy must know more about Rodney Barstow's secret activities on behalf of the government than she had let on.

"I have no idea what this means, Jule. My instincts tell me not to start shopping for a trousseau."

"But this is what you wanted—what you both hoped for. Isn't it?"

"Yes. It is. But there's something strange about it."

"In what way?"

"It's totally unexpected. As recently as a month ago, according to Rod, Arden said she had no intention of giving him a divorce, not for years."

"Maybe she decided since it takes so long to get a divorce, she should start now."

"Maybe. But then wouldn't you think she would discuss it with Rodney? And wouldn't you think he would discuss it with me?"

"Yes, I would think so."

"Well, he hasn't. Not a word." She threw down her napkin and began to clear the table.

"Don't jump to any morbid conclusions, Bets. Wait until Rodney comes home. Give the poor man a chance."

"Oh, he'll have his chance," said Betsy, running water in the dishpan.

"When does he return from his trip?"

"I never know. I'll just have to wait to hear from him." The door was closed and it was a subject Julia dared not raise again.

Suddenly it was June. Much to Betsy's annoyance, for she was still completely opposed to the idea, Julia would not be returning to Hunter College for her junior year. At the convocation, Julia received honors in her English Literature and Music History courses. Afterward, over a chocolate fudge sundae at Schrafft's, they continued to debate the merits of a four-year college education.

"The world is changing for women, Julia. Especially now with the war, there are more career opportunities. When the men come home, we'll have to compete for positions. Having a bachelor's degree will give you a great advantage."

Julia had been feeling tired and out of sorts all day. "Oh, Betsy, the way you talk, you seem to expect me to work for the rest of my life. Do you think I'll never marry or have children?"

"With the example set by the women in our family," she answered, "I should think you would have learned not to count on those things."

There was no question of telling Michael. He had written only once during the five weeks since his furlough. *Love*, he had said. Not *I love you*, but *I want to love you*. What he had meant was, he wanted to go to bed with her.

She felt serene, strangely detached, yet aware that she must take some action. The logical person to ask for advice was her aunt, but Betsy was sufficiently troubled about her own love affair with Rodney Barstow. Julia decided not to lay an additional burden on her.

On a Friday night, Murray Baker invited her to go down to Greenwich Village to see a play written by a woman friend of his. The few other young men in the audience were mostly in uniform.

"I've been trying to get into the Coast Guard," said Murray, who was 4-F because of his eyesight and deeply resentful of it. "They're such a bunch of dumb asses. So I can't see well enough to hit a target, but there are plenty of jobs I could do." Julia agreed with him. It seemed wasteful not to utilize capable, willing men who wanted to serve their country and were forced to sit out the war because of a slight physical defect.

After the play, they went for dessert and coffee on Bleecker Street. Seated at a corner table in the darkened café, Julia was conscious of how near they were to Michael's apartment. Until then they had carefully skirted any mention of him, but Murray suddenly began talking about Michael and how much he missed working with him.

"Nothing seems to click without him, know what I mean?" When Julia remained silent, he said, "I suppose you miss him too."

She shrugged.

"I got to see him for a couple of hours when he was home on leave," Murray continued. "I guess he'll be going overseas any day."

She gasped. "Did he tell you that?"

"You didn't know?" She shook her head, feeling cold. He reached over and touched her hand. "Take my advice, Julia. Mike's not the kind of guy you want to fall in love with. He's rough on women. He can't help it. Never means to hurt anyone, it's just the way he is . . . not the type to settle down."

Julia traced designs on the table top where the waitress had spilled water. When the long silence grew uncomfortable, she said, "So how is your work going?"

"All right, I guess. I've written a nice story for the idea Mike and I have. I sent him some lyrics, and he left a couple of songs with me. This isn't the way we like to work, but we have no choice." He filled a pipe with tobacco and puffed on it until pungent smoke rose in a plume. "I'm thinking of going out to the West Coast for a while. I can probably get work as a screenwriter."

The room grew quiet. A young woman read poetry, accompanied by a pale, ascetic guitarist. When they finished, Julia said, "Murray, I'd like to ask a favor."

"Sure."

"Remember about a year ago you told me you gave an actress the name of . . . of a doctor who performed abortions?"

He didn't say anything, just stared at her with baleful eyes.

"Murray?"

"*That bastard.*"

She closed her eyes and looked away. "It wasn't like that. You mustn't blame him."

"Have you told him?"

Her eyes widened with alarm. "*No*! And I don't want you to say anything to him or to *anyone*. He's never to know, do you understand?"

Suddenly Murray seized her hands. "Wait a minute. You don't want to have an abortion."

"What else can I *do*? You said it yourself, he's not the type to settle down. Please, *please*, Murray. Help me."

"Listen to me, Julia, and don't say anything until I'm finished. *I'll* marry you. We can be married right away. We'll go to California together. The baby will be mine."

"You're wonderful to offer, but I can't let you. It wouldn't be fair."

"*Fair*." He gave a harsh laugh. "What's fair? I've been in love with you since the day I met you. You must have known."

"That's what I mean. I'm not in love with you. How can I marry you?"

"You *like* me, don't you? I'd take you on any terms. I'd be the best husband, Julia. And father. I love children, I'd be nuts about the kid." He moved over and put an arm around her. "You can't have an abortion, honey. It's too dangerous, especially now. All the decent doctors are in the service, and it's too risky to go to the others."

"Do you think I *want* to have one? I'm terrified. A girl I knew died from a botched abortion."

"Then don't. If you won't marry me, I'll find a place where you can go to have the baby and give it up for adoption."

"*I could never do that*! The thought of giving birth to a child and not knowing where it is, who's taking care of it, whether or not it's happy . . . I couldn't *bear* it."

"You have to do something and abortion is too dangerous. I'm giving you a way out. Marry me, Julia. Please marry me."

She closed her eyes. He was right, she had to do something. "I'll have to think about it. Meanwhile, will you find out about a doctor?"

Reluctantly, he agreed. "Promise you won't do anything without telling me first."

"All right. And I'll think about your offer, about marriage." She kissed him on the cheek. "You're a dear, Murray, a real friend."

She felt sick in the mornings and in the afternoons. In fact, all the time. Wondering whether it was psychological, she bought a box of saltines to keep in her night table and went to the library to read about pregnancy. Using her father's last name, she made an appointment with a gynecologist and told him bluntly that she did not wish to have the child. He was fatherly and quite sympathetic. "Is there no possibility that you can marry the young man?"

That's what happened to my mother. Now I understand what she went through. But I must never let myself get caught that way. She shook her head. "No. It's out of the question."

"I'd like to help you, Miss Tepper," he said, "but as long as it's against the law, there's nothing I can do." He gave her the name of a home for unwed mothers outside of Philadelphia. "It's run by nuns and you'll have excellent care. They'll find a good home for the baby."

She had never felt so alone. Her troubled dreams were filled with threatening images. Drenched with perspiration, she would awaken in the middle of the night and lie with eyes open until dawn, pondering what to do. Finally she made up her mind to give it one more week, and then she would have to act.

On the last Saturday of June, Julia was seven weeks pregnant. She decided she had no choice but to marry Murray Baker, at least long enough to give the baby a name. They were going to see each other that night and she would tell him then.

At four-thirty in the afternoon she was listlessly ironing a dress when the telephone rang. When she answered, she heard the clanging of coins in a pay station.

"Hello . . . hello," she repeated.

It was Michael. She sank down on the bench in the hall, clutching the receiver with both hands.

"I'm at Camp Rucker," he said.

"Where on earth is that?" she asked, trying to quell the trembling in her voice.

"Near Dothan, Alabama."

"Never heard of it. It's been so long since you've written— I thought you were still at Fort Benning."

"I was, but—well, it's a long story. I've been here for a week and it looks like I'm going to stay for a while. I want you to come down, darling."

She wasn't sure she had understood him. "Come down there?"

"Yes. I'll send you a ticket."

"But . . . Michael, I can't do that. Where will I stay, what will I do?"

"I'll get a room. They're scarce as hen's teeth, but I've got a line on one. We'll be together as often as I can get away. They'll give me permission to live off-base with my wife."

"Your *wife*?" she shrieked.

"Well, hell's bells, Julia . . . you didn't think I was asking you to come down here without getting married, did you?"

She felt suddenly frightened and barely coherent. "Oh, Michael, are you sure?"

He laughed. "Of course I'm sure, you silly girl. I've never been so certain of anything in all my life." And he finally said it. "You can't imagine how much I love you, Julia."

After an awkward conversation with Murray, she sat down that night to write Michael a letter explaining that she was pregnant. But when she read it again in the morning, it sounded all wrong and she decided it would be best to wait until they were face to face. The next four days were pandemonium. Julia quit her job, packed her clothes, and by Wednesday night was on her way to Alabama. Betsy went along for moral support and to be maid of honor.

"Can you believe this is happening!" Julia exclaimed, when the overcrowded train finally rolled out of Pennsylvania Station three hours behind schedule. In the coaches troops filled every seat, while passengers were sitting on their suitcases in the aisles, but Betsy had arranged to reserve a compartment for them through Rodney's office. Julia was learning that for people like Rodney Barstow, the game was played with different rules. For the head of the nation's largest radio network, many conveniences denied ordinary citizens were still available.

When she had confronted Rodney on his return to New York, Betsy learned that Arden's suit for divorce had come as a complete surprise to him. It seemed that his wife had fallen in love with a horse breeder from Kentucky and was now in Reno, as anxious to dissolve their marriage as Rod had been. However, nothing had been settled about any marriage plans between Betsy and Mr. Barstow.

It was late the next afternoon when Michael met their train at Dothan, a dusty Alabama farm center that had suffered the full impact of an invasion of the military. Business was booming, the restaurants overcrowded with long waiting lines, public transportation overtaxed, and housing unavailable. Homeowners had turned unfinished basements into apartments that rented for exorbitant sums, and everyone seemed out to gouge the servicemen and their wives.

"I found two rooms with a kitchenette in Daleville, right near camp," Michael informed them, after an exuberant greeting. "It won't be available for a couple of days, so the two of you will be staying on base in the guest quarters for dependents of enlisted men."

"Oh."

"I had to pull some strings. It'll just be for two nights. The wedding is day after tomorrow." He opened the trunk of a maroon Dodge convertible for the porter to stow their luggage. "Bought this car yesterday from a captain who's going overseas. I'm glad the colonel has taken a shine to me. That's why I'm here, you know."

Julia shook her head, confused. "I don't quite understand."

"Colonel Blake takes morale very seriously. With twenty thousand men training here, it's a problem, because the base is brand new and there's nothing—and I mean *nothing*—around except a mudhole they call Lake Tholocco." They were by now seated in the car, with Betsy squeezed into the collapsible rear seat, as Michael drove through town, heading west. "The colonel is a Broadway musical enthusiast, and when he learned there was a composer graduating from OCS at Benning, and it turned out he had actually seen my show in New York—well, he more or less requisitioned me for Special Services. I'm in charge of base entertainment. It's great, I get to spend all my time putting on revues. Not that I tried to avoid combat—in fact, I've put in for an overseas assignment. But this meant I'd be here for a while and we could get married."

It was all too much for Julia. In a daze, she was bewildered by the rapid events of the past week and bedazzled by Michael's highly charged rush of words. They left the suitcases in a barracks-like structure next to the enlisted men's club and went immediately to the chaplain's office to sign for their marriage license.

She meant to tell him immediately, but they were never alone. There was Betsy and Lieutenant Kent, who was going to be the best man. There were the musicians from the band, who idolized Michael and were eager to meet the bride and maid of honor. And there was Colonel Blake, who would give her away and whose wife was planning a small reception in their honor.

Telling a man he was going to be a father was not something one just blurted out without any preamble. The place and the mood had to be right. She lay awake that night in the spartan dormitory room she shared with Betsy, determined that Michael must be told first thing tomorrow morning, the day before their wedding.

Why? asked a sneaky little voice inside. *You're getting married anyway.*

Because it was honest and he had a right to know. Above all, because she wanted candor and trust in their marriage.

"Michael, I have something—there are so many things to talk about," she began, when he came by their quarters the next morning. "Can't we go somewhere alone?"

"Not now, honey, I'm late for work. I just stopped by to see if everything's okay."

"What about later?"

"Oh, didn't I tell you? We're putting on our first program at the officers' club tonight. But you can come over and I'll be with you during intermission. Gotta run now, they're waiting for me." He gave her a quick kiss. "Love you."

And so the day and the evening passed, and Michael did not know.

On Saturday at noon, dressed in a creamy linen suit with a lace collar and a white straw hat with a scrap of veil, both borrowed from Betsy, she took Colonel Blake's arm and followed her aunt down the stairway into the living room of the antebellum-style house. Michael was waiting in front of the fireplace, handsome in his dress uniform, with his best man, the chaplain, and about twenty guests.

The ceremony was over in no time at all. How much can a young minister plucked from his first parish and cast amongst thousands of homesick, love-hungry soldiers find to say about the sanctity of marriage? He said his piece, read from Scriptures, and blessed their union. And they were married.

Julia waited for a triumphant euphoria to overtake her. Michael was ebullient at the toasts of his best man and Colonel Blake. Always good with ceremonial gestures, he made a graceful little speech about his love for Julia and how grateful they were to all of these new friends for being there to share their wedding day. When they begged him to play, he sat down at the piano.

"This is a new song. The lyrics aren't quite right yet. I've written it for Julia." And for the first time, he played the

song that eventually became "Through the Years." It was a
haunting melody, a departure from his earlier style, and Julia
would always adore it, as would the audiences who heard
it with Murray Baker's darkly emotional lyrics in *Over the
Moon*. The verse had a tender, elusive quality, followed by
the quicker tempo of the refrain.

> *I'll sing you a love song*
> *From the depths of my heart*
> *I'll love you forever*
> *Though now we must part.*
>
> *I'll sing you a love song*
> *From the distance of years*
> *Though time may deny us*
> *The solace of tears.*
>
> *You are the wind*
> *Chasing the rain*
> *Kissing the flowers*
> *Easing the pain . . .*
> *You are the sun*
> *Shining on dew,*
> *Casting your warmth*
> *Through the years.*

There was just Sunday for a honeymoon and to set up housekeeping in the furnished rooms Michael had found for them.

On the morning after the wedding, Julia began to bleed.
So astonished was she that she questioned whether she had
ever been pregnant. The doctor had not performed a rabbit
test, depending instead on observation and experience. Could
he have been wrong? She had cramps, but no worse than at
other times. By noon the flow had become so heavy that she
grew alarmed, wondering whether she should go to a hospital.
She felt hopelessly uninformed about what her grandmother
called "female business," and Betsy had returned to New York
immediately after the wedding.

Michael must have thought it peculiar that his bride had
come unprepared for what was for most women a monthly
event. But he was terribly sweet and concerned, running out
to a drugstore for Modess and aspirin and a hot water bottle.

The day was unbelievably hot and sticky. In the late afternoon they went for a walk, but after a few minutes in the oppressive heat Julia felt weak, so they returned to their rooms.

"You need a good solid meal," declared Michael. "You haven't eaten anything since last night." He drove to the PX, returning with food and an electric fan. By the time he had cooked dinner, Julia was feeling vastly better, and by evening she was no longer fearful that she was hemorrhaging. It did not occur to her until they were falling asleep that night that she had completely neglected to tell Michael that she was . . . had been . . . may have been pregnant.

"Michael," she whispered, "are you awake?"

"Mmm?" he mumbled.

"There's something I have to tell you."

She heard him sigh deeply and thought he had drifted off, but he moved closer and put an arm around her. "What is it, honey?"

"I feel rather ridiculous, and it really no longer matters . . ." She hesitated, but it was suddenly urgent that he know all of it. "After your furlough in May, I thought I was pregnant. I think I'm having a miscarriage."

She could feel his body grow rigid with shock. He was fully awake now. "Why didn't you tell me right away?"

"I wanted to, but somehow I couldn't. I didn't know how you would react."

"Didn't you realize I would marry you?"

"That wasn't the way I wanted to be married."

"But, Julia. My darling girl . . ." He pulled her close and cradled her head. "Oh God, to think of you having to bear this alone. What were you thinking? What were you going to do?"

In the darkness, she blinked back tears. "I couldn't come to a decision. Putting the baby up for adoption was a horrifying thought. I wanted to have an abortion, so I went to a doctor, but he refused to help me. He referred me to a home for unwed mothers."

"Oh, my poor darling. I wish I had known. You should have called me, you could have written."

"When I didn't hear from you, I was afraid you didn't love me. I wasn't going to force you to marry me. And I did try to tell you before the wedding, but there was never a chance to be alone."

"I feel like such a negligent fool." His arms tightened around her. "You must see a doctor. First thing tomorrow, I'm taking you over to the base hospital." He planted little kisses all over her face. "God, I love you so."

Suddenly she was flooded with happiness. This was the joy she had wanted to feel yesterday but was unable to, knowing the secret that lay between them. "Oh, Michael. You can't imagine how much better I feel, now that you know. I'll never keep anything from you again, my darling. Let's always be honest with each other about everything."

The sheer bliss of having Michael come home to her each night was even more precious because it was unexpected. To think that a week ago she had been despondent, not knowing where to turn. Somehow she forgot she had been prepared to marry Murray Baker.

It was a long, hot summer. The nights were torpid, the sun not setting until after nine. They lay after love one evening in the rosy half-light, talking of the future. Michael was thirsty and Julia brought him a cold beer from the refrigerator. She climbed back in bed and started to put on her nightgown.

"No, don't," he said, "I want to look at you." She smiled, embarrassed. "Why are you blushing?"

"I don't know. Self-conscious, I guess."

"With me? Why should you be? You're beautiful, Julia. I love looking at you."

She leaned down to kiss him. "I love you, Michael. I've loved you for so long and I never thought you would marry me, at least not for years."

He looked thoughtful. "You're probably right. The war puts everything in perspective. It makes you realize what the vital things in life are. All of a sudden it seemed important to marry you and to have children."

His words pierced her heart. "Do you feel sad about that . . . about losing the baby?"

"No, because it wasn't really a baby. That's what the doctor said, and I agree with him. You're not regretting it, are you?"

"Not really. I wasn't prepared to be a mother. It should be something you plan for."

"Does that mean you don't want to have a baby for a long time?"

"Why do you ask?"

"Because I'd like us to have a child as soon as possible. Is that very selfish of me?"

"Of course it isn't selfish. Whatever you want, my darling, is what I want. But the doctor says I have to wait at least two months before getting pregnant."

"Well, I didn't mean I wanted to knock you up tonight," he laughed. And then he made love to her again.

Michael frequently had to work at night, rehearsing and putting on shows. Julia attended all the performances, but she was often alone after dinner. During the day she occupied herself with fixing up their small apartment. She stitched curtains, and as she struggled with slipcovers she recalled Millie Kaplan telling her she would learn on the job. *Thus far, Millie, I seem to have flunked sewing.*

With more satisfactory results, she tried out recipes for dinner, buying fresh fruits and vegetables from the farm stalls nearby but relying on the PX for their meat and staples. Getting to know some of the other army wives seemed a natural way to make friends, but it was surprising how few officers had brought their spouses to Alabama, and army regulations made it awkward for her to socialize with the young women married to enlisted men.

After visiting the shops and discovering there was no local library, she came to the conclusion that she had exhausted the possibilities of Daleville, Alabama. She put in a call to Edwin Hopper. "I'm going to have lots of time on my hands if you need a script reader."

"I can do better than that," he said. "We're opening a literary department. How would you like to screen book manuscripts?"

Soon after, two fat packets arrived by mail: one a novel, the other a highly imaginative biography of a famous movie actress who had survived the demise of silent films.

❧ Chapter 10 ❧

Solange

They were gone, all of them: Chip back to Williamstown, Ginger to Hotchkiss. His mother—for whom he had arranged a private flight aboard a Learjet belonging to one of his friends, an outrageously successful venture capitalist—was on her way to the airport with Isobel and Cece, who were setting out on their expedition to Boston and Chicago.

As soon as the car pulled away, Scott had felt an easing, a lightness. Isobel's lips barely brushed his cheek when she bade him a breezy goodbye. Julia, always observant, had noticed and he avoided looking her in the eyes when he bent to embrace her. "Keep well, Mother. We'll try to come down to see you soon, maybe after Christmas on our way back from Aspen."

"That would be lovely, dear. Thanks for a delightful visit. I adored seeing the children—such wonderful young people, both of them."

Scott wandered from room to room in the apartment, for once not minding its hollow emptiness. With their son and daughter away, he would ordinarily have hated being deserted by Isobel, but today he welcomed the solitude. The antagonism between them during the past week had been a draining experience. He was certain Julia had sensed a quarrel. She was much too astute and understood them far too well not to have perceived that something was amiss. The crazy part of it was, he failed to understand the cause of the animosity. It seemed to have started the night he had left the apartment, injured by Isobel's rejection. Or had she already been in a snit over something else? His mother's arrival that day might have brought on a mood—the two women had never been close, but there was no actual friction between them. Or could it have been the children? Their homecoming had seemed pleasant enough, although Isobel always found a reason to get on Ginger's back. Their daughter had arrived looking glorious as usual, dragging a duffel bag full of jeans and baggy sweaters. Claiming not to have a dress to put on, she was thus conveniently unable to join her parents at any of the select holiday weekend parties, causing Isobel no end of exasperation. But the root of her anger—if indeed it was anger—was deeper than any of these apparent reasons, and for the life of him Scott could not fathom what it might be.

He had brought a laptop home from the office, intending to finish writing his speech for the ABA meeting, but he was not in the mood and decided it could wait. There was plenty of time—the conference took place in five weeks, and in a pinch he could always wing it. He thought of going for a long walk but instead turned on a football game and settled in a comfortable chair in front of the television with a cold beer and the Sunday *Times*.

After reading the business news, he glanced through real estate, and was snoozing over the sports section, the paper sliding off his lap onto the floor, when the telephone rang. Taking a quick swallow of beer to rid his voice of any grogginess, he reached for the receiver.

"Hello."

"Is that you, Scott?" He recognized his brother's voice.

"Neil. How are you?"

"I'm okay. How was Thanksgiving?"

"It was great. You missed Mother, though. She left a couple of hours ago. I think she had a good time."

"I'm sure she did. Actually, it's you I'm calling, not Mom."

"Oh." He gave a pleased little laugh, feeling a surge of warmth toward Neil. "Well, good. What's up?"

"I've gone through about half of those files we talked about and I think I may have found something you're looking for."

Scott sat up at attention. "Tell me about it."

"There's a folder of material labeled *One Night in Venice*. It contains notes, some correspondence, and two copies of the libretto."

"Is there a copyright notice on them?"

"Nothing that I can see." Scott could hear the sound of papers being shuffled. "They're typed, not printed. One is a rather smudged carbon."

"So there's no sign of the score or the published work."

"Not yet."

"I wonder," mused Scott, "if it was actually published."

"Wouldn't you be able to find that in reference books on American musicals?"

"I doubt that they give that information."

"Why not check with the copyright office in Washington?"

"I have. There's no record, which only indicates it wasn't registered. But as long as the required notice was on the published work, it was protected. If it did not appear, it would be in the public domain."

"Sounds straightforward to me. Boy, there's a ton of stuff here, fifteen cartons full."

"Why so much?" Scott asked in surprise.

"Beats me. Our father was a saver, and from what I can see, Mom didn't throw anything of his away."

"Sometimes that's a virtue."

"I suppose," said Neil. "Michael kept journals."

"Is that what's taking up so much space?"

"Only one box. Most of it is correspondence and personal records. There's a lot of sheet music by other composers, great old stuff. I found his early compositions from his school days at Pennington, but the odd thing is, once he began to publish, there are no original scores. Just a few worksheets, but the complete scores don't seem to be here."

"Perhaps they were sent to the publisher and never returned."

"That sounds reasonable. You're primarily concerned with the score of *One Night in Venice*, right?"

"I'm also very much interested in *any* scores or worksheets that have Michael's handwritten notation. Those are valuable."

There was a silence. "You mean historically speaking."

"I'm talking about monetary value, Neil. Michael Shane's music has had a renaissance, and I believe any music papers in his hand will be worth a lot of money one day."

"Imagine that," said Neil. "I guess I don't think along those lines."

"Old college professor, huh?"

"Guess so." Neil laughed amiably. "Well, what do you want me to do? I would ship the files to you, but I hate to let them go until I've catalogued everything and finished taking notes for my book."

Scott thought for a moment. "You hang on to them. Just be sure they're in a safe place with no fire hazards. I have to be in Chicago the first week in January, so I'll come to Iowa City from there."

"*All right!* I knew I'd get you out here someday."

The next morning, Monday, Scott was late getting to his office after a breakfast meeting. Hazel waited at her desk with the usual stack of memos and messages. "Burton McKiever rang not five minutes ago. Says he would like a word with you."

"If he calls back, tell him I'm not available."

"Okay, boss." She followed him into his office, leafing through pink message slips. "The ABA asked for a copy of your speech for the Chicago meeting."

"Uh-oh. I'd better write something."

Hazel laughed. "Guess so." When she had finished going through the day's schedule and making notes, she left the office, quietly closing the door. Scott settled at his desk with a yellow legal pad and a holder full of sharpened pencils.

A few minutes later, the buzzer sounded and he depressed a button on his speaker phone. "Yes, Hazel?"

"Mr. McKiever is calling again and he insists I tell you he's following up on your discussion of November second."

Scott cursed under his breath. "I should have known better than to meet with that character. I don't want to talk to him. Get rid of him." Before he could clear his mind and begin writing again, she was back on the intercom. "*Now* what, Hazel?"

"McKiever says, and I quote, You tell him he'd rather hear it from me than read it in the Washington *Post*."

"What is that, some kind of a threat?"

"Sure sounds like it to me."

"What do you think, Hazel, is he bluffing?"

"There's only one way to find out."

Scott scowled at the thought of having to speak to the former White House aide. "Okay, put him on, but you'd better monitor the call."

"Right-o."

McKiever's take-no-prisoners voice came over the wire. "How are you, Scott?"

"What can I do for you, Mr. McKiever?"

McKiever laughed. "You've got it wrong. It's what we can do for each other."

"There's nothing that I can think of."

"You be the judge," he said confidently. "Have you given any thought to the matter I raised at our breakfast meeting?"

"I wasn't aware there was one."

"Come now, Scott. I made a suggestion and you agreed to think it over."

"I *agreed*? I'm afraid I don't know what you're talking about."

"You were going to consider a certain idea that was to our mutual benefit—"

"I don't have time for guessing games, McKiever," Scott interrupted. "Why don't you get to the point?"

"Very well. Let me refresh your memory. We had an understanding that you were going to consider my request for information on the Cartwright Foundation's divestiture of certain securities. In exchange for that information, I assured you there would be an unspecified but substantial reward for your services."

Scott was seething but managed to control his rage. "We had no such understanding, McKiever. I never agreed, as you put it, to think over your suggestion. There's nothing further for us to discuss."

"I don't think so," he said. "Why don't we talk about The Well of Being."

Although there was a familiar ring to the words, Scott was puzzled. "You like riddles, don't you?"

"You don't remember The Well? I rather doubt that Jergen Ahlgren would appreciate your forgetfulness."

At those words, Scott was seized with apprehension, but there was hauteur in his voice when he replied, "Just where is this leading?"

"Y'know," said McKiever, suddenly lapsing into a cornpone drawl, "I am fas-ci-nated, simply fascinated by you Ivy League types. You sat in that phony New York power scene coupla weeks ago, givin' me the fish-eye, so high-and-godalmighty *ethi*cal. 'Fraid to dirty your hands with the likes of this uppity redneck . . . and all the time you playin' pokey with the billions. I love it, I really do."

"What in the hell are you talking about, McKiever?"

"As if you didn't know."

"Well, I don't. So you'd better start stating your business in plain English, or I'll hang up."

Again, McKiever was spitting bullets. "I'm talking about collusion and the use of influence to allow a member of your family to profit from your position as counsel to a tax-exempt organization. Which amounts to the same thing as betraying a public trust, since the American taxpayer is footing the tab."

"You'd better explain that."

"It won't do you any good to bluff, Rhinehart. I happen to know that your brother-in-law, the guru, has just signed an exclusive contract with Rancho American Resorts to install his health spas in their premier hotels."

Scott tried to ignore the sick feeling in his gut. "Do you mind if I ask where you came by this information?"

"I have my sources. Thought no one would make the connection, didn't you? Of course, the contract would have absolutely nothing to do with your place on the investment committee of the foundation that now owns controlling interest in Rancho American . . ."

"I don't suppose you would believe me if I told you I know nothing about this."

"You're right. I wouldn't believe you." He laughed. "When I think of you reading me the lesson on insider information . . . I must say, you really had me fooled. For a while there I thought I'd come up against the patron saint of incorruptibility." McKiever paused. "Ready to talk business now, Mr. Rhinehart?"

"What is this, a shakedown? You have a hell of a nerve. What you're doing is attempted blackmail—"

"Calm down, Scott. It's pointless to get so emotional. Look, I understand these things. As a businessman I realize it's the bottom line that counts. And . . . as a stockholder in Rancho American, I'm not overly concerned about any sweetheart deals, as long as they're to the benefit of the corporation." That answered one question, at least; McKiever had an equity in Rancho American. But his tone of voice suggested a more serious problem, just as Scott had anticipated. "It may be that other stockholders wouldn't see it that way, though— or officers of the corporation, not to mention members of the Cartwright Foundation board. Especially if it should be leaked to the press."

"Goodbye, Mr. McKiever," Scott said softly. And hung up.

Hazel came in. "I got it, boss. Every word."

Scott leaned back in his swivel chair and stared at the ceiling. "This is just what I needed. How the hell did it ever happen? No one will believe I didn't know."

"If you say so, they'll believe you. I can always swear you didn't. After all, I know everything about you—well, almost everything."

"You better see if Dick Graham is available. I have a feeling I'm going to need counsel." He stood up and walked to the window. "Shit!"

"Aren't you going to call your sister and find out if it's true?"

"No. I want to be able to say that I never discussed it with her. Deborah never mentioned Rancho American Resorts; the subject never came up. The only thing I knew was that Jergen was opening a second holistic center near Malibu."

It took Graham only hours to confirm the news. Rancho American Resorts was preparing an advertising campaign to announce the spring debut of their state-of-the-art health spas designed and operated under the guidance of Jergen Ahlgren, whose famous Well of Being was the most talked-about retreat in California. The first spas would be featured in Rancho American's newest and most lavish hotels—in Palm Desert, Santa Fe, and Houston.

"Get Enno Ehrlander on the phone, Hazel."

"I'm glad you called, Scott," said the treasurer of the Cartwright Foundation. "You'll be happy to know they finally tracked down that bug Bob picked up in Ghana. It's a specific bacteria and is responding to medication."

"That's good news, Enno. How's he feeling?"

"Coming around, although he's been going through hell. They were looking for everything from cholera to colon cancer."

"Can I call him?"

"No phone calls or visitors for a while. He's still very weak."

"I'll drop him another note." He hesitated, wondering how to begin. "Enno . . . something rather unusual has come up. I don't know all the details, but I'm going to recuse myself from discussions or committee action on the Rancho American bequest. In fact, it may be advisable for me to drop off the investment committee altogether."

There was a stunned silence. "Scott. That's about the worst news you could have given me. You *are* the investment committee, as far as I'm concerned."

"Well, when I tell you what happened, you'll understand my dilemma . . ."

When he had finished, Ehrlander said, "I see no conflict of interest here, Scott. First of all, you have had no personal contact with the management of Rancho American Resorts. Secondly, the Cartwright Foundation is not yet in actual possession of the shares left by Bunny, since the estate has not gone to probate."

"It's a question of propriety, Enno. There must be no *appearance* of conflict. If McKiever gives the story to the *Post*, he'll put whatever spin he wants on it. Let's face it, it sounds like hell."

"Have you spoken to your brother-in-law to get the facts?"

"No, I thought that inadvisable. My colleague, Dick Graham, represents me. He's conducting an investigation—getting names, dates, who made the contact, when the contract was signed, and so forth. It may take a while, but I'm hoping it will be a clear picture of no possible collusion. Meanwhile I am withdrawing from deliberations on the Rancho American shares."

Enno sighed deeply. "I wish you weren't so damned ethical."

"I'll be very honest with you, Enno. As embarrassing as this is to me personally, there's another factor involved. It's the first real break my sister's husband has had. I don't want to do anything to jeopardize that."

In the ensuing days, the conversation with Burton McKiever kept preying on Scott's mind. He valued nothing more than his honor and reputation. Both could be tarnished, as well as his standing in the firm, if the unscrupulous lobbyist should start circulating rumors. Once accusations were made they were always remembered, even if untrue. The week seemed to go on forever, and by Friday evening, with Isobel away and no social plans on his calendar, Scott found himself looking forward to the next day's excursion with Solange Didier.

Saturday, December first, dawned a raw and wintry morning. When they reached the Hamptons, the ocean was stirred up and angry, crashing onto the shore in great rages of foam.

"It will be a different mood today," said Solange, when they were unpacking the car, "but perhaps that's as well."

It was past noon when they headed for the beach, carrying the hamper of food that Solange had packed for lunch. As before, after several hours of shooting, they returned to his house in the late afternoon, this time cold and wet. The blackened sky became redstreaked at sunset and the angry steel sea quieted.

Scott turned up the heat and built a fire. "Cocoa? Wine?"

"Both," she smiled, rubbing her damp hair with a towel. "The same as last time, but let me make the chocolate."

"You just add boiled water to these envelopes."

"No, not like that. It needs cream, or at the very least, whole milk."

"We don't have any. There's no fresh food in the house."

"See what I've brought." Solange ferreted in her food hamper and produced a container of half-and-half, a bar of French chocolate, and a vanilla bean. Scott watched as she heated the cream with a piece of vanilla bean, melted the chocolate in hot water, and whisked them together. "Sorry I have no fluffy marshmallow," she said, handing him the rich brew.

They finished the chocolate and he poured wine. With her legs drawn up like a little girl, her hair curled and disheveled, she was very beautiful. He watched her sip wine and stare into the fire, and he was seized by an intense desire to take her in his arms.

She put down her glass and rose. "I shall find my way to the bathroom. Don't disturb yourself."

Scott stirred the fire and threw on another log. He sat down again on the couch, filled with a sad, tugging need. He was sitting with eyes closed and hands cupped over his brow when Solange returned, quietly padding across the room in stocking feet. She stood behind the sofa and lightly touched his shoulder. "You're very tense," she said softly, sitting on the back of the couch and kneading his neck.

He let out a long sigh, leaning back to look at her. She bent her lips to his and he reached up to pull her down into his lap, kissing her deeply. Her mouth, ripe with the taste of wine, opened under his. She turned and fitted herself against him, taking his hand and guiding it to her breast.

Scott lost himself in caressing her. "I want you so much," he said, his voice husky with desire.

"Then you shall have me," she assured him. "But not here. Where shall we go? A room you don't ordinarily use."

"This way." He led her to a small pastel guest room with a double bed and a woolen dhurrie on the floor. Quickly they removed their clothes and she stood before him, slim-hipped and small-breasted, looking incredibly young. She wrapped her arms around him and drew him down on the bed next to her. "Come, my darling, let me remove that look of misery from your face."

He would not have believed love could be so sweet or so satisfying.

Afterward she said, "How long have you been married?"

"Twenty-one years."

"And you have never done this before? Made love to another woman?"

"No. I am—have been committed to my marriage. What about you?" he asked. "Have you been married?"

"No, never."

"Remarkable. How have you managed to escape? It can't be for lack of opportunities."

She smiled. "I actually came close a few years ago. I was engaged to Alan Fairchild."

"The foreign correspondent?"

"Yes," she answered, a look of amusement crossing her face.

"He's quite a guy. I just saw him on the news last night, reporting from Baghdad."

Her laugh was rueful. "Alan is always *somewhere*. We lived together for three years, and I usually had to turn on CNN if I wanted to see him."

"Do I hear a touch of bitterness, Ms. Didier?"

"I hope not. I respect Alan and I think I was in love with him. But we decided to call it off. Partly because of his career, but to be perfectly honest, I found the idea of that kind of commitment—attaching myself to a man for the rest of my life—rather frightening."

"And I thought nothing could scare you. How long since you broke up?"

"About two years."

"There's been no one since then?"

"Not really. One doesn't enter easily into new relationships . . ."

"No," Scott admitted, sighing.

"You are," she said slowly, "a magnificent lover. I hope your wife appreciates you." She knelt over him and began to kiss his body. He closed his eyes, allowing the ecstasy to wash over him.

Later, much later, they left the house and drove to a nearby inn for dinner. Scott was hungry, but after a few bites he hardly touched his food. "Have you lost your appetite?" Solange teased.

He nodded. "I seem to have."

"You are suffering from an attack of conscience, I believe." She laughed softly and cast her eyes at the ceiling. "American men. You know, a Frenchman thinks his life is not complete until he has a mistress."

"So I've heard, but I've never really believed it."

"It may be a bit exaggerated for purposes of national pride, but for the most part I would say it is the truth."

Well, he argued with himself over the ensuing weeks, he was not French and he did have a bad case of guilt. Isobel made it too easy, staying away for long stretches, informing him there would be additional trips for acquisitions after the New Year. Something else, especially strange, he thought. She had mentioned when she returned from Chicago that Jeff Wheeler, his good friend and client, was investing in the gallery.

"You never asked *me* to invest," Scott said querulously.

"I wanted to do this on my own, completely independent of you," she answered.

During Isobel's absences he spent most evenings and every weekend with Solange. She was uncannily perceptive, sensitive to his every change of mood, and he found it natural to unburden himself, sharing his concern about Burton McKiever and the Rancho American conflict of interest—a subject he had avoided mentioning to Isobel on those brief occasions when they were together.

In the serene environment of the loft, Scott and Solange talked endlessly of art and politics and their families, listened to music on her stereo system, ate the delicious food she prepared with the expertise of a French chef. And made love. In her vast bed, he found a deep contentment that had somehow eluded him. In the dark of night he would lie awake and realize that he wanted it to last forever.

Gradually he learned more about her, for she was not a woman to reveal herself easily.

"How long have you lived in this country?"

"Eighteen years, although it seems longer. I came to Smith on a scholarship and I never really went back to live again in France. My parents were elderly; they had married late. My father passed away when I was fourteen and my mother lived half a life after that. She died nine years ago, while I was here."

"That must have been difficult."

"Yes. I regretted leaving her, not because she made me feel any remorse but because she was alone when she died . . ." Her eyes were speculative and troubled. "I have told you I was an only child."

"Yes."

"I have no relatives. None at all."

"How is that possible? There must be someone, distant cousins."

"No, I don't think so. My parents were the only survivors in their families. All the others were killed in the war, either fighting in the Résistance or in concentration camps."

He frowned. "They were French and they were put into concentration camps?"

"French, yes. But they were also Jews, you see."

"Oh. I'm sorry."

"That makes you uncomfortable?"

"No, not at all."

"You probably don't know many Jews."

"On the contrary. My stepfather, whom I considered my real father, was Jewish. And my college roommate—my closest friend, Dick Graham—is a Jew."

"Graham. That doesn't sound like a Jewish name."

"Neither does Didier," he answered.

"*Touché.*" Solange laughed and the tension eased a little. "I thought because you are a socialite you would be anti-Semitic."

"Well, I'm not. And that's not a fair statement. You shouldn't stereotype people." He knew he sounded irritable, but she had touched a nerve.

She placed her hand over his. "I'm sorry, Scott. Forgive me."

He took her hand, placing a kiss in the palm, then rubbed it against his lips. "Nothing to forgive," he said, pulling her into his arms.

The time passed too quickly. In a few days it would be Christmas, and his family was to meet for a ski vacation in Aspen. On his last night with Solange, he said, "I must see you again. I'll work it out somehow."

"I won't use the pictures I took of you," she told him. "Not for the book, not in a show. I knew after the first time in my studio I would not."

He nodded. "I'm glad you said that. They're too—"

"They say I love you, and that is something I do not wish the world to know."

"Oh, Solange . . . Solange." He gathered her against himself and buried his face in her neck. "I don't know what we're going to do."

"I never meant to fall in love with you," she said in her husky voice.

❧ Chapter 11 ❧

Kit

The message on the answering machine brought a smile to Julia's face. A short burst of ghostly percussive music followed by a melodramatic voice that she recognized as Kit's. "Count Dracula speaking. Leave your name, rank, and blood type and I'll catch you at the first full moon." There was laughter in the background, then, "Di, if this is you, call me at the Dipper."

"Count Dracula, indeed." Julia could not suppress a chuckle. "And I thought you were a vegetarian. It's your old granny calling, dear. It would be nice to hear from you. You know the number."

Oh my, she thought after hanging up, I do hope that dear boy will be all right. Neil was right: no matter what Kit wanted to do, he should have a degree. He was such a fine young man, with so much talent, but he had to go back to college.

One was not supposed to have favorites. She adored Chip and Ginger and Deborah's children, who were sweet and affectionate, but there was no denying the special bond of love that had formed the first time she had held Kit in her arms. She remembered the night Neil had called from Toronto to tell them he was a father. "We're naming him after Michael," he said, and she had been terribly moved.

To her delight, she was the baby's godmother. They had met Neil's wife only once before and it had been a disaster, so that when Julia and George arrived for the christening, it was with some trepidation. "Ursula's mother and father wanted a church ceremony," Neil explained. "She's inclined to indulge them, especially since we didn't have much of a wedding. I—I guess we weren't very thoughtful of our families." Neil would never come right out with an apology, but knowing her son, Julia realized this was his way of making amends.

As she held Kit while the minister blessed him, he fixed wide, intelligent eyes on her, wrinkling his tiny forehead when he was sprinkled with water. "Michael Kittredge Shane II," she whispered, stroking his cheek. "Your granddaddy would have been so proud."

But was that true? she asked herself on the trip back to New York. In moments of complete honesty, she could admit that Michael had displayed a limited interest in his children. By the time their second son was born, Michael was dying. Scott had been a lonely little boy, wary of the father who paid less and less attention to him as he grew older. George was the only father the boys had really known, and a more loving and forgiving parent did not exist. Neil had hurt him dreadfully, but thank heaven they had made their peace.

Six years after Kit's birth, Neil came home alone to the States, heartbroken to leave his son behind. George had moved heaven and earth to gain custody of the boy. Ursula's parents were by this time dead, and she was living with another man, pregnant by him. Canadian law was rigid, favoring the mother regardless of her fitness. Kit's half-brother had been born before the divorce was final, and only when Ursula reached a point of desperate lack of control, where she was in danger of abusing her children, did she agree to give up Kit. By that time, two damaging years had passed. Neil was committed to running a program for American students in London, so the boy had stayed in New York with Julia and George.

That had been the most trying, remarkable, and exhilarating year of Julia's life. Kit, a frightened and withdrawn child when he first came to them, had been a bedwetter with peculiar habits in food and clothing. At first he stiffened whenever they tried to hug or kiss him. But within six months—a miracle in brevity, upon reflection—he had been transformed into a smiling, happy little boy, secure in their love for him. When Neil returned from England, he observed the closeness between Kit and his parents and took a job at the University of Connecticut so his son could continue to be with them. For four years, until he was twelve, Kit had virtually lived with Julia and George. And then in 1982 Neil had been offered a tenure professorship at the University of Iowa.

It was like losing a son all over again when he took Kit to Iowa City. "Maybe," said George, standing in Kit's empty room that autumn, "we should think about moving to a warmer climate. I've never liked the idea of retirement, but a change might be good for us."

It had taken five months to find the right place, longer to complete the house, but by the following Christmas, they were taking their sunrise walks along the beach at Pirates Cove.

Kit Shane drove through the electronically controlled gates of the estate as the last crimson rays of sun disappeared over the Pacific and a panoply of lights twinkled on in the valley below. Unaware of the eyes that observed him from a window, he parked in a paved area behind the white mansion, pausing for a moment to admire the spectacular view.

The woman who watched had not been seen in public for more than two decades. She kept the shades drawn in daylight, leaving the house by night in a black and silver Bentley to tour the winding, deserted canyons of the Hollywood hills. There had been a time when no face was more familiar to the rapt audiences of the motion picture screen. Now, all but a few old-timers had forgotten her name.

Kit had never heard of Annette Heublein. His agent, Leonard Gold, had booked him for a solo gig. The woman, a former screen actress, had read about him in the Los Angeles *Times*. Although he preferred working clubs with the group, this was not the first time he had played alone for a small party in the home of a wealthy patron. It paid well and you never knew who might be there. Lots of jazz artists had been discovered this way, or so Len told him.

Kit's long, gangly body unfolded from the interior of the van. Clad in an eccentric getup of studded blue jeans, white dinner jacket, and cowboy boots, he was wearing a ponytail and one earring. He looked young and nervous and exceptionally handsome. With a toss of his head, he unloaded keyboard and speakers from the rear compartment and, with practiced grace, hoisted them onto his shoulders. An unruly lock of dark hair fell across his brow as he carried the equipment to the front entrance. Before he could press the bell, the imposing door swung open and a stern-visaged butler admitted him.

She was waiting alone in a cavernous living room. Poised before the mantel, she had lit candles, and although the evening was mild, a fire burned in the hearth. Her figure was slight, even girlish, in the Fortuny pleated gown of gauzy midnight blue silk. It was difficult to make out her face, for her head was swathed in a long flowing scarf of silvery chiffon that covered her hair and shoulders and was artfully wound around her throat, obscuring the neck and chin. Her eyes, huge and lustrous, seemed to pierce the gloom and held him frozen at the door. For an instant, his gaze flicked away from her to the portrait hanging above the fireplace. An exquisite girl, an ethereal titian-haired beauty, had been depicted in a pose both innocent and abandoned. Kit swallowed and searched for something to say.

"Come closer," demanded the woman, beckoning him.

He settled the instruments on the floor and approached her. As he drew nearer, something in the set of his shoulders and the outline of his brow drew a look of puzzlement from the woman. When he smiled, the corners of his blue eyes crinkled in such a way that her breath caught in her throat. With one hand, she steadied herself and then closed her eyes.

"It's not possible," she whispered. "*Michael . . .*"

The next morning, Kit called Julia. "Hi, Grams. Got your message, foxy lady."

"I thought you'd forgotten your old grandmother."

"Never! You're still my best girl."

"That's not what I hear."

He groaned. "You've been talking to your spies. What did Dad tell you?"

"Nothing much, just that she's pretty and sweet."

He laughed. "She is all of that. Maybe I'll bring her to visit you one of these days. I'm supposed to go to Palm Beach to meet her family soon. They're from Boston, but they live down there during the winter."

"Palm Beach isn't far. You can fly one of those little local lines to Naples," said Julia excitedly. "When would it be?"

"For Christmas, maybe. I'm waiting to hear from Diana. She's with them now."

"This sounds a little like wedding bells," she commented, thinking that Kit was far too young for marriage.

"Could be, but not for a while. Diana is a junior at Berkeley and her parents insist that she graduate first. And I . . . well, I guess I have to go back next year. I talked to Dad and it makes sense. He understands why I had to try this."

Julia's eyes closed in relief. *Thank heaven.* "Deborah sent me that wonderful clipping from the Los Angeles *Times,*" she told him.

"Hey, what did you think about that?"

"I'm impressed. Is it important?"

"It's a pretty influential column. My agent got quite a few calls after it appeared." There was a click on the line. "Oh gosh, that's my call waiting; could be Diana. I'll let you know when we're coming, Grams."

"Can't wait to see you, dear. You'll have to tell me all the news when you come to Palm Island."

Despite the festive party at Clarissa's house and the annual holiday buffet Joyce Moser insisted she attend at the golf club, Julia spent a lonely Christmas. Scott and his family were at their ski house in Aspen, and she was almost sorry she had not gone to California to see Deborah, who had begged her to come out for a visit.

She thought it wise to keep to herself this first Christmas without George, fearing that she had become too maudlin of late. She seemed to weep at the slightest bit of nostalgia these days. Letters from old friends, Christmas carols, even those sentimental Hallmark commercials on television, with their cloying scenes from America's heartland, brought tears to her eyes. Imagining herself in a red clapboard farmhouse with smoke curling from every chimney and fires roaring in every hearth, surrounded by her huge, multigenerational family, she pictured a team of Clydesdale horses pulling a sleigh over fields blanketed in virgin snow . . . on Christmas morning half a dozen rosy-cheeked grandchildren tumbling out of tester beds to gobble up Granny's hotcakes . . .

What nonsense! Was there any such place left in this world? But she did question why she had not become one of those contented white-haired ladies who had mellowed into old age.

Christmas was as bad as she feared, but at last it was over. She awakened the next morning, went for her usual swim in the heated pool, and spent the early part of the day paying bills and catching up on long-neglected correspondence.

Around ten, Kit called. "We're at the airport in Fort Lauderdale," he said, sounding subdued, and she could tell immediately that there was a problem. "Is it all right if I bring Diana there?"

"Of course it is, darling, I've been expecting you. I thought perhaps you'd changed your mind."

"It hasn't gone exactly the way we planned." The strain in his voice was evident. "Anyway, we're on the next flight to Naples, due in an hour. We'll rent a car."

"Don't bother, I'll meet you at the airport. Kit, what's wrong?"

"Nothing . . . no, that's not true. I just can't tell you over the phone."

"Perhaps I can help."

"I can't talk now, we have to board in ten minutes. Diana isn't feeling well, that's all."

"Poor child, bring her here, I'll take care of her."

It was a short drive to the airport and the plane landed on time. One look at the pale young woman on Kit's arm was all Julia needed to know that she was truly ill. "You should be seen by a doctor."

Diana shook her head vehemently. "She's already been to a doctor," said Kit. "He gave her antibiotics."

"Well, don't worry, my dear," Julia assured the pretty blond girl, "we'll get you right home to bed, and you'll soon be feeling much better." Saying nothing further, she got behind the wheel.

"I see you cut off your ponytail," said Julia, trying to make conversation.

Kit gave her a bleak smile. "I thought it would be a good idea." All the way home he sat in the front seat, turned sideways, watching Diana, who lay in the back with her eyes closed.

Julia had debated about whether to give them the guest room or to go through the charade of assigning separate bedrooms and shutting her door to whatever nocturnal traffic might go on. With Diana looking so unwell, there was no question of her need for a room of her own and Julia put her in the queen-sized bed, leaving her with Kit, after seeing that there were enough pillows and a quilt to make her as comfortable as possible.

"How is Diana?" Julia asked, when Kit came into the kitchen where she was preparing lunch.

"Okay, I guess." He took a sandwich from the platter. "Actually, she's feeling rotten. All she wants to do is sleep."

"That's the best thing for her. If she doesn't feel better in a few hours, though, she really must be examined by a doctor, Kit. She could develop complications."

He flushed. "Complications?"

She smiled sadly. "You don't think I believe the story about this being a virus." Before he could reply, she put up her hand to silence him. "I've been a volunteer at Planned Parenthood clinics for many years, dear. It's clear to me that Diana has had an abortion. I can only hope it was done by a competent doctor under sterile conditions."

His façade crumpled. "She did it before I got there. I don't know why she didn't wait." He leaned his forehead on his hands. "I wish I had known. She didn't have to do this."

"Oh, Kit . . ." Julia wanted to take him in her arms, but instinct told her to get more facts. "Do you mean you would have wanted a baby?"

"God no, but she should have told me. She knows I would have married her."

"Have you considered that Diana might not have wanted to get married yet? Maybe she isn't ready to be a mother."

"No more than I'm ready to be a father. But if it meant her health—what if she—"

"There is absolutely no reason for a woman to have an unsafe abortion in these times, even in Florida, where they're trying to make it difficult. Where did she go?"

"To some doctor in Miami. I don't think he was the best."

"If she had consulted Planned Parenthood, they would have referred her to a safe woman's health clinic where she could have received proper care."

"She did have an appointment at a clinic, but when she got there a group of right-to-lifers was picketing. They were getting pretty violent and had shut the place down—"

"Those *damned* hypocrites. They claim to be pro-life, but it doesn't bother them when women die from back alley abortions. Where are they when child abuse is the issue? They're against sex education, they block any program that will benefit women or children . . ." Julia could feel the heat of anger in her cheeks. "What did Diana do then?"

"She called a woman she knows in Miami who took her to a doctor down there. Di was back in Palm Beach the same day." Kit ran his fingers nervously through his hair. "That was Saturday. I arrived two days later on Christmas Eve, and by then she had a fever. So yesterday we went to a hospital emergency room in Fort Lauderdale."

"What about her parents? They don't know?"

"No, she refused to tell them." He sighed and shook his head. "I can understand why. This was the first time I met them, and they're pretty unapproachable."

"The meeting did not go well, I gather."

"To put it mildly. It's quite apparent that I am not what they have in mind for their daughter. Not now or in the future." He rubbed his eyes. "Shit, what a mess. Excuse me, Grams."

"Well, now." Julia became practical. "I know a terrific woman gynecologist who volunteers at the Planned Parenthood clinic. She has a private practice, and I'm going to call right now and ask her to see Diana."

"You can't, Grams. Di doesn't want you to know."

"That's ridiculous, Kit. She needs medical attention. A woman should not be running a fever after an abortion. She has an infection and that can become very dangerous—even life-threatening."

Kit rose. "I'll go talk to her."

Diana was lying curled up in bed with her eyes closed, but she stirred when Kit came into the room. "How are you feeling?"

"Not so great."

"Pain?"

She nodded. "Like very bad cramps."

"Listen, Di, my grandmother knows."

She began to cry. "You *promised* you wouldn't tell her."

Sitting on the edge of the bed, Kit put his arms around her. "I didn't have to say anything. She guessed, and she wants to call this doctor she knows from Planned Parenthood." He stroked her forehead, alarmed at how warm she felt. "I think she's right, Di. The antibiotics aren't working."

Diana shivered and turned on her side away from him. "We're going to make that call. I can't let you—you're *sick*, Diana!" She did not answer, and Kit left the room.

It was late in the afternoon when Dr. Janice Borden finally came into the hospital waiting room, still wearing scrubs. "Diana should improve within a few hours," she told them. "There was a nasty infection. We did a D&C and she's receiving infusions of broadspectrum antibiotics. I want to keep her here until her temperature remains normal for twenty-four hours."

Kit had almost worn a path in the floor from hours of pacing. "Is she—will she—?" he stammered.

"There's a good chance she'll be able to have future pregnancies, if that's what you're asking, although it's too soon to say for sure." The doctor was surprisingly young, with an approachable, no-nonsense manner. "Tell me, why didn't she go to a reputable physician? There's no need for a woman of her background to resort to substandard care. She could have gotten a referral to a reliable clinic."

"She *did* go to a reliable place—" Kit shook his head and turned away.

Seeing how agitated he was, Julia explained. "It's the same old story, Janice. When Diana reached the clinic, the zealots were demonstrating and she didn't have the courage to run the gauntlet."

"Operation Rescue?"

"Who knows? One of them. They intimidated her, so she called a friend. And this is the result."

Dr. Borden shook her head in disgust. "Those people are criminals. They're breaking the law. I'd like to see them all in jail. But surely there were other clinics. It's very discouraging when an intelligent, privileged woman gets herself into a situation like this."

Kit had recovered his composure. "Di wasn't thinking straight. She was feeling alone and threatened. I was in California and I didn't find out until it was over."

"Well, she's lucky. A few more hours could have meant disaster."

After Dr. Borden left them, Kit went in to see Diana, who was still groggy from anesthesia and sedation. When he returned, he said, "I'll take you home, Grams, and come back to the hospital later."

On the way to Palm Island, Kit was hungry, so they stopped at a McDonald's. Julia had not been in a fast-food restaurant since the days when she and George used to go on road trips. She toyed with a dry salad and sipped decaffeinated coffee from a Styrofoam cup, while Kit wolfed down a Big Mac, a large order of fries, and a chocolate shake. The sight of the food turned her stomach.

An hour later she was in bed, drained from the anxiety of waiting for Diana to come out of surgery. What an enormous responsibility this was! A dozen times she had thought that she ought to call Diana's parents in Palm Beach. Should they not have been informed if their daughter was ill, perhaps in danger of dying? But Diana was nineteen, no longer a child, and she was adamant about not telling them. Julia knew she did not have the right to break faith with her, but what a terrible dilemma.

She remembered her own experience with an unplanned pregnancy. The panic, the desolation of feeling abandoned. Abortion had been outlawed and dangerous then. Fortunately society had changed, but Diana's experience proved that women were still paying the price of loving. Even with abortion legal, their lives were in danger, thanks to the fanatics. Sighing, she adjusted her pillows and fell into a restless sleep.

Julia awakened early on the third morning. Kit was already in the pool when she came out. He heaved himself out of the water when he saw her. "Good morning, Grams. I called the hospital. Diana had a good night and she can be discharged anytime after eleven o'clock."

"That's wonderful news, Kit."

"How can we ever thank you? I don't know what we would have done without you."

"You would have managed, I'm sure. You would have taken her to a good doctor or another hospital."

"Yes, but it might have been too late."

"Well, thank heaven it wasn't." There was a cool wind and she wrapped her terry robe tighter. "I believe I'll skip my swim this morning. Come into the house, let's have breakfast."

Kit brought Diana home from the hospital in time for lunch. They spent a quiet evening together, and Diana returned to San Francisco the next afternoon. She wept when she said goodbye to Julia. "I could never expect such understanding from my own family, Mrs. Rhinehart."

"You know, Diana, it was easy for me to be objective because I'm not as emotionally involved. I'm sure your parents would have done everything in their power to help you, no matter how much they disapproved."

Kit was not leaving for Los Angeles until the next day, and when he returned from the airport to find Julia working in the garden, he was obviously in low spirits. "I think it might be over," he told her, popping open a Coke. "Nothing definite was said, but I have that feeling."

She came to sit next to him, putting aside her tools and removing her gardening gloves. "If you're both in love, it will work out."

"I don't know . . . Diana's parents have a lot of influence on her. By the time I get back to Berkeley next fall, she'll probably have found someone else."

"This was a dreadful ordeal, Kit. Diana is bound to have a reaction. Even if she didn't want the baby, the body's natural response is a letdown."

"I know. It's unfair, isn't it? I mean, that the woman is the one who takes all the risk."

"Yes, it is unfair. Diana is fortunate that you're sensitive and caring enough to realize that. Not every man is."

"It's strange, Grams, I think about the way it used to be. I mean, back when you were young—"

"You mean, in the olden days?"

"Yeah!" He grinned. "No, really—how did you know you could marry someone without, you know, having sex? Is it wrong for me to ask?"

"It's a perfectly fair question." She settled back on the chaise longue and pondered the answer for a moment. "Well, first of all, many couples *were* having intercourse before marriage. They just didn't talk about it. But I suppose most women were virgins when they went to the altar, while the majority of men were not. We actually believed that was preferable— that it was good to marry a man who had experience. Sexual experience, by the way, was a loose term. A woman could indulge in anything short of actual intercourse and technically remain a virgin."

"I know, but it seems hypocritical."

She laughed. "Americans are hypocrites when it comes to morality. You must remember, there was a very good reason for these practices. We didn't have effective birth control, and that was a mighty powerful deterrent. A girl who got in trouble, as we called it in those days, had her reputation ruined forever. I don't say it wasn't inconsistent, but it worked. And when I see the latest statistics on teenage pregnancies and AIDS and other sexually transmitted diseases, I'm not so sure that it wasn't better in some ways."

Kit took a long swallow from the can of soda. "When I was growing up, Dad was always reluctant to talk about sex."

"That's surprising. I would have thought Neil, of all people, would be perfectly candid on that subject. He certainly has no hangups about having his own affairs, does he?"

"I think that may have been part of it. How could he tell me not to have sex when he was with a new woman every time I looked around."

"Oh dear, I see what you mean. Maybe I didn't do my job so well if my son is unable to sustain a lasting relationship."

"No, Grams, I don't think it has anything to do with you. Dad's never found the right partner. But if he really wanted to settle down, why would he keep choosing unstable women? He's searching for something that's unattainable."

"You sound as though you have it all figured out," she laughed, ruffling his hair. "That's enough serious talk for one day. You must be hungry."

After dinner, when they went into the living room, Julia removed a manila portfolio from a drawer. "Kit, I recently came across these few pieces of your Grandfather Shane's—some compositions that he never finished orchestrating. They're all I have out of a great number of unpublished works that disappeared from his studio after his death. I'd like you to take them. Perhaps you'll decide to arrange them for that revue of Michael's music . . ."

"Oh, *wow!*" Kit seized the packet eagerly. "*For my wife, Julia Shane,*" he read, slowly turning the leaves of music paper.

" 'Julia, Julia,' 'Blue Memories,' 'Love in the Morning,' 'Walking Alone,' 'So Little Time . . . ' " He sighed. "Gosh, Grams. These are actually his, the very sheets he worked on."

"Scott tells me those manuscripts may be valuable, so take good care of them."

"You bet I will. Look, see how angular his notes are."

"Yes. He had a strong characteristic style. Notation is as distinctive as handwriting. Anyone familiar with Michael's work sheets would be able to recognize them as his."

"Amazing," said Kit, running his fingers reverently over the composition paper.

"I'm reminded of an interesting story," said Julia. "When I first met Michael, he was just three years older than you. A famous Broadway composer stole some of his songs. In the days before Xerox machines, all copies were made by hand. You couldn't always tell when someone had made a duplicate, but if a piece was duplicated by one of the regular copy services, usually it was possible to track it down. Michael was able to prove those songs were his from the original worksheets."

"What happened?"

"In order to avoid an embarrassing lawsuit, they made a very generous settlement. Incidentally, that's how Michael met George. Uncle Ed sent him to Winston & Rhinehart because he needed a lawyer."

"And that's how *you* met Grandpa George, isn't it?"

"So it is," she replied, laughing, although her eyes felt misty. "I suppose there's a lesson in there somewhere. Some good comes out of everything."

"Nothing is ever wasted—"

"Every cloud has a silver lining—oh, listen to us. Aren't we silly?"

"We're fun," he said, hugging her. "I'm really very lucky. I've always been able to bring my problems to you."

"I'd prefer that you didn't have problems, dear. But I hope you know you can always come to me."

Once Kit had left for California, it seemed lonelier than ever. His presence lingered in the house. Julia straightened the spare bedrooms, stripping the beds of linens and putting a load through the washing machine. The maid would be coming in tomorrow, but she needed to keep busy. When all was in order, she spent the rest of the afternoon rearranging bookshelves and cupboards. At the end of the day, after a light supper of soup and a mushroom omelette, she felt weary enough to shower, put on a fresh nightgown, and settle into bed.

It had been a sobering experience for Kit. Youth was meant to be a time of joy and laughter, not sorrow. Julia believed that, although her own youth had hardly been free of burdens.

All her life, it seemed, she had taken on other people's problems. She stretched out in the bed, longing for sleep, but every muscle was taut. Instead she lay awake remembering an almost forgotten time, nearly fifty years ago.

✣⦿ Chapter 12 ⦿✣

Jesse

Troy. The sign loomed ahead under an overhanging lamp at the end of the railroad shed. Stepping down from the last car, Julia had to walk the length of the platform through six inches of newly fallen snow. A bitter wind gusted, driving stinging icy sleet into her face. She clutched her suitcase and pulled the coat closer around her swelling figure.

In front of the station, she joined a line to share a taxicab. A stout ruddy woman looked her over. "When is your baby due, dearie?"

"In July."

"Husband in the service?"

"Yes, ma'am."

"Gone overseas?"

"Yes, he has." Julia's reply was short; she did not much care for inquisitive strangers.

Just then her turn came, and she hurried to join an elderly man and a nun in a taxi. As they drove over unplowed streets, the clinking tire chains did not prevent the cab from sliding on the slippery hills. At last they stopped in front of a turreted building that loomed in the stormy night. She paid the driver and walked up the familiar stone steps. In the front window she could make out Gran's silhouette peering through the curtains.

"I waited dinner for you," said Eunice by way of greeting. Her grandmother never kissed anyone.

"Thank you, Gran." Julia removed her coat and galoshes. "Where's Mother?"

"Up in her room."

Julia hurried up the stairs, her heart tripping with anxiety, dreading what she would find. Jesse was dozing in a rocker, wearing the rose bathrobe Julia had sent several Christmases past.

"Mother."

Jesse awakened, looking around with a startled expression. "Oh." She held out her arms. "Julia, darling, you're here. Is it really you?"

Julia knelt beside the chair and hugged Jesse, kissing her sallow cheeks. A sweet, sickish odor emanated from her mother. "Of course I'm here. If I hadn't been so far away I'd have come a lot sooner. How are you?"

"I'm all right, honey. Don't worry about me." She struggled out of the rocker and held Julia at arm's length. "Let me see you. To think you're going to have my first grandchild." She smiled and Julia felt her heart turn over, for her mother had the wrinkled flesh and discolored teeth of an old woman. "My Jule, you look so well and happy."

"Oh, Mom, I *am* happy. I wish Michael could be here with me. You would love him. There wasn't time before he went overseas."

"I understand. When he comes home to you, we'll get to know each other."

"Dinner's on the table, come eat," Eunice called from downstairs.

Dinner consisted of a fried pork chop, home fries, and canned lima beans. Julia was appalled. Her grandmother, who had been married to a doctor, surely knew the elements of nutrition. How could she feed Jesse this unappetizing mess? No wonder her mother looked emaciated.

Julia spoke to Eunice when they were sitting in the parlor after Jesse had retired for the night. "Mom's not eating enough, Gran. She needs wholesome food, green vegetables. She doesn't look well."

Worn down by the years, her feisty grandmother seemed

to be losing her bite. "She has no appetite, Missy. I worry about her."

"Has she been to a doctor lately?"

"Dr. Whitley looks after us. He was an intern at the hospital when your grandfather was alive."

"Well, what does he say about Mother?"

"He pays a house call now and then, gives her vitamins, tells her she should get out more, eat to keep up her strength . . ."

"And that she should *lay off the booze*? Does he tell her *that*?" Julia spoke between gritted teeth. "I saw what she drank after dinner."

Eunice made a helpless gesture with her hands. "What can he do? What can anyone do? You don't know what it's like when I take away her drink. That's all she has." Then in that long-suffering voice Julia so well remembered, she said, "But it's my cross to bear and I do it willingly, without complaint."

"Oh, for God's sake, I can't *believe* this!" Julia paced the parlor, holding onto herself, knowing she had to keep from screaming at Eunice, from making a scene that would upset her mother. "All those years . . . all those long, awful years when you could have *done* something to help her. I was only a child, but even I knew what was going on. You let it happen. *You!*"

"No, Missy. You are not going to put the responsibility on me. Let me tell you, when Ralph Tepper walked into that big house on the hill, he saw our pure and beautiful daughter and he made up his mind to *corrupt* her. It's too late for blame, but if you're looking for somewhere to place it, look no further than your father."

"No, Gran, that's not true. Don't forget, there were witnesses. Betsy saw what happened, and young as I was, so did I. My father left us because of *you. You* drove him away. You took away the letters he wrote to Jesse and the photographs and every happy memory she had. If it hadn't been for you, she could have had a decent life. We all could have. I am sick of standing by and letting this happen. My mother belongs in a hospital! If she doesn't get help soon, she'll die. I am taking her tomorrow."

"No!" Eunice sprang out of her chair. "No, you can't take her away. She has to stay here with me. Without me, she'll die."

Julia drew herself up. "Don't you mean, Gran, that without her, *you'll* die?"

A black expression crossed Eunice's face. Without a word she turned and climbed the stairs to her room. Julia sat on a bench in front of the fireplace, angrily jabbing at the smoldering logs. The radiators clanked as the furnace shut down for the night. Shivering in the chill, she made up the daybed in the dining room and, wearing socks and a fleece robe over her flannel nightgown, huddled under the covers.

The next morning she took Jesse to Dr. Whitley's office. After finishing his examination, he invited Julia into his private consultation room. "Your mother is anemic and suffering from malnutrition," he told Julia gently.

"Dr. Whitley . . . my mother is an alcoholic. Why won't you just come out and say so? Why this conspiracy of silence?"

After an astonished moment, he said, "I do whatever my patients require, Mrs. Shane. Your grandmother has made it quite clear that she will tolerate no mention of alcoholism."

"My grandmother has no right . . ." Controlling herself was an effort, but Julia realized that venting her anger at the doctor would accomplish nothing. In a contained voice, she asked, "If you were to treat my mother for alcoholism, what would you do?"

"The only treatment is to withhold alcohol and improve nutrition. I could commit her to a sanitarium, but knowing the history, I'm afraid that would be more inhumane than allowing her to remain as she is." He sighed and looked at her steadily. "There's already damage to her liver."

What did he mean, *the history?* "Can't you do *something?* I'll pay for medicines."

"There is no medication for this."

"Well then, give her vitamins, prescribe a special diet. You should see what my grandmother cooked for dinner last night—all fat and starch. No wonder Jesse looks like a scarecrow."

"I'll have a talk with Mrs. Perkins," he promised.

That was it, then. There was nothing else to be done. "Dr. Whitley, what will happen to her?"

"She'll get along. I'll keep an eye on her." Seeing how despondent Julia looked, he put a hand on her shoulder and said kindly, "You mustn't worry too much, Mrs. Shane. With a baby coming, you have other, more pressing responsibilities."

She stayed in Troy for a week, laying in a supply of groceries, cooking wholesome meals, dusting the house and polishing the furniture. The weather improved. Dressing warmly, they went for long walks in the park, and Jesse began to show some color in her cheeks. One afternoon Julia took her downtown to a beauty parlor to have her hair styled and, inspired by the resulting improvement in appearance, they shopped for clothes. Over her mother's embarrassed protests, Julia went wild, buying a quantity of dresses, skirts, sweaters, blouses and stockings and two pairs of shoes, as well as underwear and nightgowns and a new bathrobe to replace the stained rose wool. Eunice had refused to accompany them, calling the whole expedition frivolous, and Julia was just as happy not to have her along. But she did buy a warm blue cardigan for her grandmother and, knowing her secret craving for sweets, a box of chocolates in the ice cream parlor where they stopped for lunch.

"I don't know when I've had such a good time," sighed Jesse, smiling happily as she dabbed her mouth with the scrap of paper napkin. "You spoil me, Julia."

"Oh, Mother . . ." She had to look away to hide the tears that came to her eyes. To think that such ordinary pastimes were an occasion. Jesse had eaten all of the tuna fish sandwich and was making her way through a chocolate milk shake. That just proved her appetite would be normal if she were offered tasty food. The new hair style was enormously becoming, and most important of all, the animation on her face made her look like a different woman from the pathetic wraith who had greeted Julia on her arrival. All she needed was a little stimulation in her life . . .

The idea came swiftly, a sudden inspiration. "Mother! I want you to come to New York. I want you to live with me."

Jesse stopped sipping the milk shake and stared at her. "You don't know what you're saying."

"I do, I do. I think it's the most *wonderful* plan. We can move into Michael's apartment in April when his tenant leaves, and you'll be there when the baby is born. You can help me and keep me company until Michael comes home. It would be so fantastic, Mother. Don't you think so?"

Jesse shook her head. "No, it . . . I couldn't . . . it wouldn't work."

"It *would* work. We'll *make* it work," Julia insisted. "You don't have to come right away, although I'm sure it would be all right with Betsy. Her new apartment has two bedrooms, so there's plenty of room." Jesse was beginning to look as if the proposal had possibilities. "You just have to get used to the idea. Please say you'll come."

"I'll think about it. Maybe in the spring. I couldn't leave your grandmother in the winter."

"Gran would manage just fine without you. You'd be surprised."

"Do you think so?"

"I most certainly do."

They took a bus home because there were no taxis available. Not unexpectedly, her grandmother managed to put a damper on their high spirits. Laden with parcels, they arrived at the house in a holiday mood, only to find Eunice scowling and uncommunicative, hunched next to the radio for her daily dose of "Stella Dallas."

"We had a great time, Gran. Doesn't Mom's hair look beautiful?"

"Her hair always looks nice. I can do it just as well."

"It needed a good professional cut and shaping. I think it's extremely attractive," said Julia, undeterred. She began opening the bundles. "Look, we went shopping. All those are for Jesse, and . . . these are for you."

"For me? What for?"

Julia laughed. "Can't I buy you presents if I want to?"

"You're wasting money."

"Well, it's *my* money, so what do you care? How often do I come to Troy, and why can't I give you something nice if it brings me pleasure?"

All her life this woman had managed to take the joy out of even the most delightful event. How could any one person hold such power over others? Julia noticed the immediate effect on Jesse, who became skittish and jumpy. As far as she could tell, her mother had not been drinking since that first night, yet now she began fidgeting and her eyes darted nervously around the room.

"Well," said Julia, forcing a smile. "I think I'll go start dinner. Why don't you come help me, Mother?"

Jesse's eyes came into focus and she started to rise, but

Eunice stopped her with a loud, "No, let her rest. She's had too much excitement for one day."

"I'm not at all tired, Mother," protested Jesse meekly.

"Do as I say. I know what's best for you," snapped Eunice. "It's almost time for 'Portia Faces Life'."

Julia kept up an attempt at conversation throughout the evening meal, trying to recapture the relaxed pleasure of their afternoon. "Downtown was busy today, wasn't it, Mom?"

"Oh yes," said Jesse, "busier than I've ever seen it."

"I suppose there's lots of war-related industry here now."

"I don't know," Jesse replied doubtfully.

"I didn't mean guns. Things like uniforms, maybe tents or other equipment . . ."

"Maybe."

"Do you know anything about that, Gran?"

"No," responded Eunice frostily, "I'm afraid I don't."

Julia passed the platter to Jesse. "Have some more chicken and rice, Mother."

"Oh, I couldn't eat another thing, dear, after all I had for lunch."

"Spoiled her appetite," said Eunice smugly. "Probably ate all sorts of junk."

"No we didn't. We had a very healthful lunch and Mom finished everything on her plate," answered Julia. *Don't argue with her*, she told herself. "Would you like seconds, Gran?"

"No. The green beans and carrots aren't done enough."

"Vegetables are better for you and have more flavor when all the life isn't cooked out of them."

"It's a waste to buy fresh vegetables in winter. I use canned."

Julia cleared the platters and dishes from the table. In the kitchen, she gripped the edge of the sink, closing her eyes. *I cannot stand it. How did I grow up in the same house with that woman?* Poor Jesse, having to live here with her.

Returning to the table with fruit salad and date cookies, she asked, "Who wants tea or coffee?"

"Tea," said her grandmother.

"Maybe some milk, if you don't mind," Jesse suggested timidly.

"Good idea, Mom. I'll have some, too. The doctor said I'm supposed to drink a quart a day. It's good for the baby."

This had the happy effect of introducing the subject her mother most liked to discuss, the expected grandchild. It kept them going through dessert and after dinner, when Jesse sat at the kitchen table while Julia washed the dishes. Eunice had gone to the parlor to listen to "Amos 'n' Andy."

"That was a delicious meal," said Jesse. "Shall I dry?"

"Sure, if you want to. But you can just let the dishes drain."

Jesse took up a kitchen towel, preferring to keep her hands occupied. "You look sad, honey. Is something wrong?"

"Oh," Julia sighed, "I was just missing Michael. I hope there's a letter waiting when I get back."

"Are you worried about him overseas?"

Julia frowned. "I try not to be. He's not a combatant, but I suppose he'll be in some danger. They'll spend a lot of time putting on shows for wounded men in hospitals, but they'll also be entertaining troops near the front lines. I'll never know where he is at any one moment, but it makes sense that he'll go to Africa soon."

"Africa?" said her mother.

"Yes, Mom. That's where we're fighting the Germans right now."

Jesse looked puzzled. "Not England?"

"The Germans have dropped a lot of bombs on England, but it's quieted down a bit and there's no actual fighting on English soil. The war's going on all over Europe and Asia and now Africa. Our troops aren't fighting in Europe—not yet. But someday they will be."

"I never did understand politics too much."

They smiled at each other. "Maybe you should listen to the news every night on the radio. If you read the newspaper, you'll be able to follow everything."

"Maybe I will. Now that I have a son-in-law who's over there." She gave Julia a beseeching look. "You mustn't be too angry with your grandmother. She doesn't mean half of what she says. Some people just can't seem to back down."

"I'm not trying to get her to back down on anything. I just don't understand someone who takes no joy out of life and who can't seem to bear it when other people do. She never smiles, she never looks happy."

"That's because," said Jesse, "she never is happy."

Again, Julia waited until her mother had gone to bed. Eunice was sitting in the living room near the radio, crocheting a small shell-patterned afghan in lovely pastels. "This is meant for you," she said tersely, "for your baby."

Julia was filled with shame at the bitter feelings she had expressed toward Eunice. This was her grandmother's way of showing love, perhaps the only way she knew. "Oh, Gran, it's beautiful. Thank you." She spontaneously threw her arms around the old woman's neck and gave her a kiss.

The wrinkled cheeks flushed, but the hard bony body stiffened in a rebuff of physical affection. How awful to be incapable of displaying sentiment toward the people you love, thought Julia. For of course Eunice loved them. Her heart had been broken not once, but three times. When her beloved daughter had defied her to marry a man Eunice despised; when her son, her favorite child, had died in a tragic drunken driving accident; and when her position as wife of the town's most respected physician was reduced to that of a penniless widow. She may not have been able to help her daughter, but she hadn't caused Jesse's condition. It *was* her cross to bear, in a way, for she had to live with it, witnessing the daily deterioration of her once lovely child, helpless to do anything to prevent it.

"Gran, I want to talk to you about Jesse." Julia drew up a chair. "In just these few days she seems so much better, doesn't she? She's eating well, I don't think she's drinking—at least not as much. And she seems happy."

"Well, of course she's happy when you're here. We're all happier when our children are with us."

"No, I don't mean that. She's better because she's been more active, getting out and walking, helping with the housecleaning. She has an appetite because I take some pains to prepare meals she likes. And she's smiling and lively—you must admit that."

Eunice gave a grudging grunt.

Julia moved closer to her. "I know it's hard for you," she said earnestly. "It must be tedious and frustrating, day in, day out, the same problems, the same routine. I don't blame you for feeling sick and tired of it all. You're so tied to the house with Mother here. You probably never get together with your friends any more."

"Friends forget about you."

"Not necessarily. Perhaps they feel you're not interested." This was getting off the track. "Anyway, I have what I think is a splendid idea."

Eunice listened in utter disbelief as Julia outlined her plan for Jesse to live with her in New York. " . . . so you see, it would only be until Michael comes home, a year or two at the most. It could even be sooner. I mean, how long can the war last? She'll receive excellent medical care, I'll see to that, and she can enjoy her first grandchild . . . What do you think?"

Eunice unraveled pale blue wool with furious tugs at the ball. "I think you've taken leave of your senses."

"*Why*, Gran? Give me one reason why it wouldn't be good for her."

"One reason, eh? I can give you a dozen reasons." The crochet hook flashed in the firelight as her fingers kept up a constant rhythm. "You think you're so clever. You don't show up for months at a time, then within one week you're reorganizing our lives, coming up with the perfect solution."

"It's a plan that will work, Gran. I was never in a position to do this before. I'll have my own home now and enough money to take care of Jesse."

"There are a few minor problems you haven't thought of, Missy, with this brilliant idea of yours." Eunice let the needlework rest in her lap. She spoke with sudden savagery. "What will you do when she drinks herself into a stupor? When she embarrasses you with your fancy New York friends, coming out in the parlor stark naked and using obscene language . . . when you're eight months pregnant and you have to pick her up off the floor, bathe off the vomit, change her stinking underwear because she's made a mess in her pants, just like that baby you're going to have . . . when she decides one night that life isn't worth living and she tries to slit her wrists and you find her bleeding like a stuck pig all over the bathroom . . . *what will you do then, Miss Julia?*"

"Stop it!" she cried, holding her hands over her ears. "I don't want to hear this."

"No, of course you don't want to hear. Neither does Betsy. You both prefer a clean, well-ordered life as far away from this house as you can get. Playing the career girl, going out in the evening to the ballet or a concert, attending opening nights."

She laughed. "Dinner at '21' . . . Isn't that the place Betsy calls her favorite restaurant? Well, if you take your mother to live with you, Missy, there will be no more dinners at '21.' Those days will be over. Finished."

Julia brushed tears from her cheeks. "She really slashed her wrists?"

"Three times."

"You never told me. Does Betsy know?"

"No, Jesse didn't want either of you to know. I promised never to tell."

"But . . . but she's been so good this week. She was excited about New York, I mean, she was hopeful."

Eunice looked up. "You spoke to her about it?"

"Yes, it just came out. I got the idea at lunch when we were talking, I don't even remember about what."

"Did she say she would go?"

"She said she would think about it. She was afraid to leave you alone. I told her you could manage for a while. It isn't as if she's going forever. We could do it just until the baby's born." She gave Eunice an imploring look.

Her grandmother shook her head slowly. "It will never happen, Julia. I wish it could. I wish she could get away from here for a spell, and I know you want to help her. But I also know it's hopeless. Jesse's sick. There's nothing can help her."

"How do you account for this week?"

"She can hold out for four or five days, ten perhaps. It couldn't last much longer. Sooner or later she'll need a drink."

"Why do you have liquor in the house?" she asked tearfully.

Her grandmother rose. "Come with me." They went into the kitchen and out to an enclosed back porch. Eunice unlocked a door. She turned on a light and led the way down steep wooden steps to the basement. "See those shelves?"

"Yes, what about them?"

"One night a little over two years ago, a few months after you left for New York, I woke up and the house just didn't feel right. I went out in the hall and Jesse's door was open, but she wasn't in her room. I looked everywhere—in the bathroom, the living room, the dining room. When she wasn't in the kitchen I got really worried, especially as I felt a draft and realized the porch door was open. Well, I found her down here in the cellar, passed out. There was an empty container of wood alcohol lying on the floor next to her. It had been there on the shelf with old cans of paint and turpentine. Had been there for years, came from some work I had done, you know how I never throw things out . . ."

Eunice's usually sharp voice sounded feeble, echoing off the concrete walls of the basement. Beneath the harsh overhead light, Julia saw that her grandmother appeared even more elderly and frail. The pink scalp shone through her gray, straggly hair, and the withered skin seemed almost transparent where it stretched over her cheekbones.

"I couldn't get her up the stairs, she was dead weight," Eunice continued. "I called an ambulance and they took her to the hospital, pumped her stomach. Jesse almost died that night. Since then, my feeling is if she needs a drink that badly, she's better off sticking to wine and whiskey."

"Oh God." Julia put her face in her hands.

"I'm sorry to tell you this, Julia. Your mother would never forgive me. But you had to understand why it's impossible for her to live anywhere else but here."

"What will I tell her?" Julia's voice was thick with emotion. "I don't want to go back on my word. She said she wouldn't leave you in winter, but maybe in the spring."

"Well, there's nothing wrong with that. Let her think about it. I know my Jesse, and she never would have gone." They walked upstairs and Eunice shut the basement door. When they were in the kitchen, she said, "Oh, Julia, in so many ways, I wish I could do it all again. I've made my mistakes . . ."

Never had she thought she would hear those words from her grandmother. For Eunice Perkins to admit to being even the slightest degree wrong . . . "Gran, we all make mistakes. Sometimes things happen and it's not anyone's fault. Maybe no one's to blame."

On the long train ride back to New York, Julia felt she had been through a firestorm. Aching with fatigue by the time she reached Betsy's new apartment on East Fifty-second Street, she tried to explain everything at once, but she was barely coherent. The range of emotions she had gone through with her mother and her grandmother was almost too complex to describe.

Finally Betsy said, "That's enough for tonight. We'll talk about it tomorrow. You should have something to eat."

"I'm not at all hungry," insisted Julia. "I had dinner on the train."

"Well, I'm going to make you some warm milk with honey, and then you are going to take a bath and go straight to bed. Sleep as late as you can in the morning. You have a baby to think about."

"I'm fine, Bets, really, and the baby doesn't know the difference."

"I don't believe that," she answered. "I'm sure in some way a baby senses when its mother is under strain. If you want a calm, secure child, you have to experience a serene pregnancy."

Julia laughed. "That sounds a little like voodoo to me."

Nevertheless she was happy to have a relaxing soak in the big roomy bathtub. The modern tile of the guest bathroom was a marked change from the ancient Victorian fixtures in the old apartment. Betsy's move to this twelve-story building near the East River had taken Julia completely by surprise. In Alabama, a month after her wedding, she had received a letter from her aunt saying she had given notice at the Seventy-fourth Street address. Betsy gave no explanation for the decision, but in the early fall she wrote that Rodney Barstow had suddenly announced he was marrying the daughter of a senator—a very beautiful blond divorcée he had met in Washington. Was this the blonde Walter Winchell had been referring to in his gossip column, Julia wondered as she struggled to digest the shocking news.

"You tried to warn me," Betsy had said ruefully when Julia returned to New York at the end of January immediately after Michael's departure for overseas.

It had been their first opportunity in ages to talk, and by then Betsy had become accustomed to the idea that Rodney Barstow would never be hers. She was angry, but mostly at herself. "I think I must have known all along that Rod would never marry me. I just didn't want to face the truth."

"How could this have happened so precipitously?"

Betsy arched an eyebrow. "Precipitously?"

"Do you suspect he was seeing her at the same time you two were . . ." Julia groped for the proper word.

"Sleeping together?" supplied Betsy. "Yes. Yes, I do. Especially because that was what our relationship had come down to."

"Oh, Bets." She felt such sadness for her beautiful aunt.

"For more than two years it was perfect, Jule. Our attraction was based on companionship and common interests. We had so much fun together, and sex was only part of it. But in the last year, since the beginning of the war, it began to change. When Arden divorced him, instead of bringing us closer together it seemed to place a barrier between us. Rod was away so often, and when he returned to New York we never talked any more, particularly about marriage. He had become extremely reticent. I thought he felt pressured by his position at RNA and the demands of his work for the government. Now I believe he was already involved with Margaret."

"I hate him for hurting you, for betraying you," Julia blurted angrily.

"I hated him, too, for a while. But I have only myself to blame. I should have recognized what he was. You see, toward the end I learned things about him I had never suspected."

"What sort of things?"

"His façade, for one. Rod is a phony. His impeccable social background was a fiction. His family are plain folks from Des Moines, Iowa. Not that there's anything wrong with that, but he's ashamed of them." She looked away. "I'm not very proud of this . . . I learned some unsavory facts about him when I took the job in administration, and I ignored them. I discovered he's been quite ruthless in his climb to the top. A number of people were hurt in one way or another. One man's career was destroyed. I know many important men have reached their positions at the expense of others, and perhaps it was naive of me to have thought Rod was any different."

"When you love someone, it's natural to make excuses for him," Julia had said sympathetically.

"But I should have realized that when a man compromises his principles to gain power, why wouldn't he do the same in order to get what he wants in a wife?"

"I'm not sure I follow your meaning."

"Margaret Reynolds is another Arden. A wealthy woman

from the right social background. The only kind of woman Rodney Barstow could ever bring himself to marry."

Two weeks ago, on the night of that conversation, Julia had been afraid that Rodney Barstow's perfidy might turn her aunt into a bitter woman. But while it might be a long time before Betsy trusted another man, Julia had confidence that her innate resilience and good humor would prevail.

Julia twisted the tap to add more hot water to her bath. She lay back in the tub, considering what the future would hold for Betsy.

At twenty-nine she had already made great strides in her career. At the end of 1942 she had given up her job at RNA, accepting an offer at twice the salary to take charge of affiliate relations at a rival network, the Empire Broadcasting System. EBS was a young, innovative outfit, quite different from the stodgy, old-line Radio Network of America. Empire had begun television broadcasts in 1939, but the war had put a temporary halt to this promising experiment. As soon as hostilities came to an end, the network was prepared to resume telecasting on a regional basis, and after that there were no limits to the potential. For anyone connected with EBS, the future held challenge and opportunity. If romance was lacking in Betsy's life, career possibilities were not.

Julia stepped out of the tub and dried herself with a fluffy blue bath sheet. Looking at her reflection in the long mirror, she marveled that a new life was contained in her expanding abdomen. Michael's child. She felt the baby move and she thought of Betsy's theory about a serene pregnancy. Could she be right? It sounded like an old wives' tale, but certainly a little serenity could never harm the baby, and it might be a good thing for its mother.

After putting on a warm flannel gown, she brushed her hair a hundred strokes. When she opened the bedroom window, snow was falling steadily outside. She stretched out her hand to catch the thick white flakes spiraling in the wind off the river. Settling back in bed against the pillows, she closed her eyes. It seemed a long way from Troy, another universe from the life in her grandmother's house.

Whiteness, enfolding the world in a cover. Her father, large and gentle, wrapping her in a scratchy plaid blanket. What

*safeness there was with him! Secure in the sled, padded against
the wind, she was unable to move. He was her steed, galloping
down the hushed, drifted street, leaving the first tracks in
virgin snow. Crystalline pinpoints of light sparkled on silvery
branches overhead. She lifted her face to the skyglow, fingers
of snowspray brushing her cheeks. Warmed by his laughter,
she laughed too, for the joy of the snowswirled night and the
inner warmth of this fragile, enveloping fatherlove.*

*Shattered into a thousand splinters by the coldness of the
woman's voice . . .*

It was half past ten when Julia awakened on Sunday morning.
She had slept the sleep of the dead, stirring once from a dream
she tried to remember but falling back into a deep slumber
before she could recapture its feeling. It had snowed heavily
all night, and through her window the city was wrapped in the
silent stillness that she loved. It was a blissful feeling to be
snowbound in a snug and comfortable nest. There would be
coffee and breakfast waiting and the Sunday papers with the
crossword. And today she would call Edwin Hopper at home
to tell him she was back in New York and ready for the next
manuscript. This inviting prospect got her out of bed and into
the bathroom.

She found Betsy at the breakfast table, reading the Magazine
section of the *Times*. "You must be starved, Jule. There's
orange juice, coffee, eggs—or would you rather have pancakes? I didn't want to waste coupons on bacon. Hope you
don't mind."

"No, that's all right. The doctor at Camp Rucker told me
to avoid fatty foods while I'm pregnant. Which reminds me,
I have to find an obstetrician."

"There's a really nice older couple who live next door.
We've said hello in the hall. The husband's a doctor, and I
can ask him to recommend someone."

"Wait until I call this woman who had a baby last year, Felicity Lyons. We've known each other since my first Christmas
party with Michael, where I met Janice Fried. Remember, the
time you went to Vermont—oh, I'm sorry."

Betsy laughed. "There's going to be a lot of that for a while.
When I think about it, there was nothing else in my life except
Rodney Barstow. You'd be amazed how many friends I've

made and interesting things I've done since he jilted me."

Julia gave her a hug. It was such a relief to find that Betsy was not at all a tragic figure. "I'm glad to see you've got your sense of humor."

"It's been my saving grace. Now . . . your breakfast order, Madame."

"I'll fix it. After all, if I'm going to live here until April, it won't be as a house guest. In fact, I insist on sharing the rent."

"We'll talk about that later. Actually I was hoping you'd stay until the baby's born. It really makes sense. I have air conditioning for the long, hot summer when you will be the size of a dirigible. And I would really love the company."

"Oh, Bets, I don't know. I hate to get too dependent."

"I think it's the logical thing to do, but maybe it's too soon for you to make a decision."

"There's another reason, too, but I'll tell you about it later."

After breakfast Julia called Edwin Hopper, but there was no answer at his house. "Where could he have gone on a stormy day like this?"

"It's Washington's Birthday, so maybe he went away for the weekend. As I recall, he's an attractive man. He must have lots of friends."

"Actually I think he keeps pretty much to himself these days. When his daughter and grandchild both died in the Blitz, it took a lot of the starch out of him."

With a blizzard raging outside, they built a fire and lounged in the living room, reading. "You know," said Betsy, stretching languorously, "I really like this apartment much better than my old place. It may not have as much charm, but everything's so clean and new, and it's a lot airier with all that daylight coming in through the big front windows. You can catch a glimpse of the river from here and my bedroom. It's also more convenient, with an elevator that works and a doorman for deliveries. The heating system is more efficient, too, and don't forget about the air conditioning. Oh, Jule, you just *have* to stay until the baby's born. Please say you will."

"Okay, okay," laughed Julia, "you've convinced me."

"What was the other reason you mentioned? Why you couldn't?"

"Well, I asked Jesse to come live with me until Michael gets home from overseas. However—"

Betsy's jaw dropped. "Are you out of your *mind?*"

"What is it about this family? That's another variation of what everyone else said."

"Who's everyone else?"

"Jesse and Gran. Only Gran puts a lot more animation into it. A little vitriol really adds some color." The words came out headlong, with biting sarcasm. "Jesse, on the other hand, came around to my way of thinking after a bit. At least, she agreed to consider it. Unfortunately, that was before I talked to La Perkins. Did that ever puncture my balloon. But now the dilemma is, what if Mom says she's ready to come? I mean, what can I say to her after such a big buildup? I still want her, but I'm afraid. If everything Gran said is true, I'd be terrified all the time. Now I understand what Dr. Whitley meant about Jesse's history—"

"Whoa!" called Betsy. "Back up there, Dobbin. You're losing me. Maybe you had better start from the beginning."

"Sorry," Julia apologized. "I'll take it day by day. The night I arrived, Mom was sober, I think. But she was in terrible physical shape . . ."

Half an hour later, she was still talking. "I discussed it again with the doctor the day before I left. He wasn't much help. He didn't think putting her in a sanitarium would be wise, but he didn't recommend that she come live with me either."

"Jesse was in a sanitarium once, you know," Betsy commented.

That was news to Julia. "She was?"

"Don't you remember?"

"No. When was that?"

"Years ago. I was seventeen, so that would have made you nine. It turned out to be a catastrophe, and it was all my doing. I arranged for her to go to a mental disease clinic in Albany that specialized in alcohol and drug addiction. She was supposed to stay for a month, and she went willingly, signed herself in. After about ten days we received a call late one night to come as soon as possible. Jesse was in a coma. We left you with Mrs. Johnson across the street . . ."

"Oh, I remember now. I tried to get in touch with Mrs. Johnson when I was in Troy, by the way, but she had moved. I stayed there for a couple of days that time. It was the only occasion that Gran would allow me to sleep over at Cathy's house."

"You were there for a week," said Betsy. "We didn't think Jesse was going to live, but she came out of it. It took a long time for her to regain her strength. Mother used to tell me that she was never the same afterward. As if I had personally caused it . . ." Her voice faltered.

"Don't, Bets. You did what you had to. I know just how you felt. It's horrible to sit by and think that no one is doing anything to help her."

"That's exactly why I did it. I didn't know the treatments were dangerous."

"Dangerous? What did they give her?"

"Insulin shock."

"Insulin shock! Why?"

"It was all the rage in Germany. In those days that's where the best medicine was practiced."

"Now I understand why Gran had a fit when I said Mom should be in a sanitarium. Did you know about the suicide attempts?"

"No," said Betsy, "I never guessed."

"Imagine how desperate she must have been to try to take her own life." Julia shook her head sadly. "I still can't accept that there's nothing I can do to help her."

"I don't think living with you is the answer, Jule. For once I agree with my mother."

"What about Alcoholics Anonymous?"

"Ha!" Betsy threw back her head. "Are you kidding? Eunice Perkins's daughter hanging out at some tacky Baptist church with a bunch of drunks?"

They talked in circles, and Julia realized they were going nowhere. She tried Edwin again, but he had not returned. Late in the afternoon the snow stopped and the wind ceased howling. Out in the street were the stirrings of a city coming back to life. The scraping of shovels against pavement, the laboring whine of an automobile engine turning over, like a great beast waking after months of hibernation.

"Let's get dressed and go for a walk," suggested Betsy.

"I'd love to, but I'm not sure I have any snow gear that will fit me."

"I should have something for you to wear. There's a whole box of ski clothes in the hall closet."

Julia found a man's red plaid lumberjack shirt and a red woollen sweater. Outfitted in Betsy's old red ski suit, she secured the baggy snow pants around her middle with safety pins and twine, but the jacket hid everything. More rummaging uncovered a pair of stout reindeer boots that fit perfectly over wool socks. Her own red and white knit hat, scarf, and mittens gave a jaunty fillip to the outfit.

"You look like Nanook of the North," she said to Betsy, who was wearing a fluffy white fur parka.

"And you look like one of Santa's elves."

"A rather rotund elf. I am so *fat*."

"But for such a lovely reason," answered Betsy.

The block they lived on was a cul-de-sac where Fifty-second Street ended high above the East River. It was alive with children romping in the snow, shouting gleefully as they made angel wings and snowmen, built forts and stacked supplies of snowballs in preparation for battle. A number of mothers and one or two civilian fathers were pulling their young children in Flexible Flyers down the middle of the road, sure in the knowledge that no motor traffic could get through.

"Isn't the city beautiful, all covered in white," exclaimed Julia, scooping up a handful of snow and tossing it in Betsy's face.

"I'll get you for that," laughed her aunt, brushing the wetness out of her eyes. "It's beautiful now, but just wait a few days until it's all gray and slushy."

"Spoilsport."

As Betsy made a snowball, turning around to hurl it at some teenagers who had scored a hit on her back, a tall, Nordic-looking man in a white sheepskin coat came bounding toward them over a bunker of snow. "Hello there, Miss Perkins, I thought I recognized you under that disguise." He had the hearty air of a ski instructor. His accent was European, his manner patrician.

"Oh, hi. How are you?" Betsy looked slightly flustered, unusual for her. "This is Julia Shane . . . Robert Schild."

He came to attention and bowed his head slightly. "Delighted, Miss Shane." His eyes took her in. "Or is it Mrs. Shane?"

"It's Mrs. Shane," said Julia, with a smile. "How do you do, Mr. Schild?"

"Julia is my niece. She's staying with me while her husband is overseas."

"Ahh. What branch of the military?"

"Army Special Services."

That seemed to capture his interest. "Special Services . . . does that mean intelligence?"

"Oh no, nothing so mysterious. Michael is a composer and they have him putting on musical revues to entertain the troops."

"Fascinating," said Schild. "And where does he do this entertaining?"

"I don't know exactly where he is. I expect he moves around, wherever the soldiers are."

Schild smiled. "Are you ladies out for a constitutional?"

"Yes," Betsy answered, "we were feeling housebound after two days of snow."

"Well, I won't keep you." Again, he gave a correct little bow. "I hope we shall have the pleasure of meeting again, Mrs. Shane."

"*Who* is that impressive man?" inquired Julia as soon as they were out of earshot.

"He's my new neighbor across the hall. We met one night when he came over to borrow a light bulb."

"At least that's more original than a cup of sugar," laughed Julia. "Is he married?"

"I don't think so. No one else is living there."

"What is he? I mean his nationality."

"Swiss. He's in banking."

"I expected you to say he was a refugee. I could have sworn he was German."

Betsy gave her a puzzled look. "Why do you say that?"

"His accent. And the Prussian manner in which he acknowledged your introduction and then said goodbye. He all but clicked his heels."

"Isn't that just a European custom?"

"I don't think so. It's specifically German or Austrian."

"How do you know such things?"

"You'd be amazed at the amount of trivia I have picked up with all the reading I do. Especially these days. Every novel that Hopper gives me seems to be about Nazis."

"Well, Robert Schild is from Zurich, so he's Swiss-German."

"I suppose that explains it." She spied some little girls across the street holding onto an iron rail and making ice slides. "Oh look, remember when we used to do that in the schoolyard? More than anything, snow makes me think of being young."

"If you weren't pregnant, we could go ice-skating in the park tomorrow. I don't have to go to work on Washington's Birthday."

"Maybe I could. What would be wrong with it?"

"I'd be afraid. What if you fell?"

"Yes, I suppose . . . too bad. If this baby only knew what I'm giving up for its benefit."

"Do you want a boy or a girl?"

"I don't care, just so long as it's a healthy child. I think Michael wants a daughter, though. He's already picked out a name."

"What is it?"

"Jessica Kittredge. It was his mother's name."

"What if it's a boy?"

"Then he will be named Scott, for Michael's father."

❧ Chapter 13 ❧

Edwin

Scott Shane was born at three o'clock in the morning on the Fourth of July. The baby weighed in at a hefty eight pounds, four ounces, and was viewed through the nursery window at Doctor's Hospital that same afternoon by Murray Baker, who had returned from California in March after cranking out two screenplays for Metro Films.

"Uncle Murray is pleased to report the heir comes equipped with all the proper accessories," he announced at the threshold of the jubilant mother's room.

Julia was sitting in bed on an inflated rubber tube but otherwise feeling marvelous. "How could you tell? Wasn't he all wrapped up?"

"Smart kid, knew I was watching. He did his business so the nurse would have to change him."

"Oh, Murray . . ." Julia winced, trying not to laugh.

"Yesiree, this Yankee Doodle Dandy's all balls. Just like his daddy."

"Don't . . . you'll make me split my stitches."

"*Stitches*." He looked horrified. "I thought . . . I mean, doesn't nature take care of the whole thing?"

"Not when the baby's that large. Hey, you look kind of green. Come here. Don't worry, I'm all right."

Murray leaned over gingerly to plant a kiss on her forehead.

"This is for you," he said, presenting her with an enormous oval box lavishly upholstered in pink satin.

"Chocolates," she smiled in delight. "So *huge*—are you sure a chorus girl won't pop out? And thanks for the flowers. They just came a little while ago. Look, aren't they beautiful?"

"Beautiful," he agreed, not taking his eyes from her, "just like Scott's mother."

It was an extremely warm summer Sunday, and the city had the quiet air of a holiday weekend. Murray stayed on through the afternoon, released from the grueling discipline of casting and staging sessions for the beleaguered collaboration he and Michael were calling *Over the Moon*. With relish, he related the most recent peccadillos and indiscretions of the theater world. Although she had been somewhat removed from that milieu during the past year, Julia was familiar with the personalities, and she listened in amusement while he gossiped about who was sleeping with whom, which director had passed over a veteran character actress in favor of an undiscovered ingenue, and which playwright—whose nails, as she could plainly see, were bitten down to the quick—was feuding with a certain producer well known to them both.

"I swear," declared Murray, "if Gerry Ross is ever found strangled to death, they'll be vying to take credit, and I'll be at the head of the line. The guy's impossible to deal with. I'd sooner take on six Hollywood producers."

"So why stay with him?" she asked, broaching a subject she had long wanted to raise with Michael.

"It's not that easy. Our productions are expensive. Ross is willing to assume the risk, but he takes his pound of flesh."

"Michael's missing out on all the fun this time, isn't he?" Then she thought better of it, realizing Murray had to stand up to the imperious Gerald Ross alone. Although Edwin Hopper had negotiated the contract and Julia had power of attorney for her husband, Murray had to take the day-to-day guff from the producer. "I think Michael's afraid they'll butcher his songs when he's not around to protect them," she said.

"Mike doesn't have to worry. I'm looking out for his interests."

In more ways than one, she thought fondly. Ever since his return to New York, Murray had assumed the role of big brother, showing up at unexpected moments, insisting she accompany him to dinner, a movie, the theater. He made himself useful in a hundred ways, helping to clean and paint Michael's apartment, installing extra shelves in the kitchen. When Jim Turner finally moved out at the end of April, it was Murray who put new locks on all the doors and windows, assembled a crib for the baby, lugged home the Victorian rocker Julia had bought in an antiques shop on MacDougal Street and refinished it for her.

By the end of May, Michael's books and paintings had been taken out of storage, unpacked, and properly arranged, with her few belongings added to his. Betsy had given them several nice pieces from Seventy-fourth Street that had been in storage— a bed, the rolltop desk, a pair of armchairs, some end tables, and a coffee table. Julia had sewn new curtains and turned the small windowed alcove off the bedroom into a nursery. With the apartment freshly painted and all repairs complete, Murray had polished and buffed the floors, and since the smell of wax made Julia ill, he waited a few days to roll out the oriental rugs and, under her direction, rearrange the furniture. Although she would not move in until after the baby was born, everything was in place.

There were no constraints between them, for which Julia was grateful, for she would hate to have lost Murray as a friend. In all these months, however, nothing had been said about the circumstances of her wedding, until one night in June, almost a year to the day that Murray had offered to marry her. Prompted to celebrate the fruits of their labor, Julia had invited him to dinner in the refurbished apartment. She served spaghetti Bolognese and poured a glass of red wine for Murray.

"Aren't you having any?"

She shook her head. "It upsets my stomach when I'm pregnant."

Murray sipped the wine with a thoughtful expression. "Julia, do you mind if I ask a personal question?"

"No, go ahead."

"What happened last year?" When she did not immediately respond, he went on. "You said you were pregnant, but the baby won't be born until long after . . . uh . . ."

She sighed. "I've often thought I should explain."

"If you don't want to . . ."

"No, it's okay. I had a miscarriage, Murray." She hesitated, then went on. "Michael and I weren't married because I was pregnant. In fact, he didn't even know until I lost the baby."

At first he found that hard to believe. "You mean, you got married without telling him?"

"It all happened too quickly. We were never alone until after the wedding, not even for five minutes."

"Did you tell him I knew?"

"No, I . . . well, it just seemed unnecessary."

His relief was obvious. "I'm glad. Mike might not understand. About me wanting to marry you, I mean."

"You were very sweet. I never adequately thanked you." He looked thoroughly uncomfortable, breaking off little pieces of bread and rolling them into balls.

Julia wound spaghetti around her fork. "Do you have a girlfriend, Murray?"

"Yeah." He grinned. "Great-looking actress. We've been going out for almost three months."

"That's some kind of a record for you, isn't it?"

"Actually there was one in Hollywood that lasted for eight months, but it didn't work out in the end." He gave a helpless shrug. "What can I say?"

They washed the dinner dishes and Murray dropped her at Betsy's before going to meet his girlfriend after her performance. "She's in the chorus of *Oklahoma!*," he said in parting. "Maybe you'd like to go see it some night."

"Oh, I'd love to." But she had not spoken to him again until this morning, when she called from Doctor's Hospital to say she had become a mother.

He was still regaling her with outrageous tales about their new show when Betsy walked in carrying a bouquet of cut flowers. In a blue cotton dress and sandals, with her hair tied back, she looked fresh as a summer breeze despite having stayed at the hospital half the night, going home to catch a few hours of sleep only after Scott was born.

"I just saw the baby again. I think he's actually grown overnight. He's so adorable, I'm dying to hold him." Betsy gave Julia a hug. "How are you, Murray? Have you seen Scotty?"

"Cute little bugger," commented Murray, nervously fiddling with the basket of flowers. "Well, chums, I think I'll be shoving off now." He squeezed Julia's hand, kissing her cheek. "I'll call you soon," he promised.

Betsy's gaze followed him as he left the room. "That man is in love with you," she said.

"Oh no. He used to be, but I don't think he is any longer. He has a girlfriend, an actress."

"Maybe so, but he's in love with you. If ever I saw a man look at a woman with adoration . . ."

Julia was distressed at Betsy's words. "What should I do? Murray is not only Michael's writing partner but his best friend. He's never done or said anything out of line."

"I suppose there's nothing you *can* do. He's been so generous, I don't see how you can stop being friends with him. Just be on guard." She changed the subject. "I sent a priority cable to Michael and I called Troy. Jesse is so thrilled, she can't see straight. Even Mother sounded enthusiastic."

"Tell me, what did they say?"

"The usual. How big is Scotty, who does he look like, how were you feeling. I told Jesse you would phone in a day or two."

"I'll call them tomorrow morning. By then I ought to know Scott a little better. The nurse brought him for me to feed, but my milk hasn't come in yet. She said he's a hungry baby because he's big. He's not fat, just long." She giggled. "You should see his feet, they're tremendous. Reminds me of a puppy. You know, all paws."

"Oh, Jule, that doesn't sound very maternal, comparing your son to a *dog*."

This somehow struck them as hilarious. Like schoolgirls, they were seized by a laughing jag. "Would you say he was a retriever?"

"Maybe a cocker spaniel, with those big eyes."

Again they went off into peals of laughter. Doubled over, grimacing in agony, Julia almost failed to hear the knock. Gasping for breath, she called, "Come in."

Betsy had jumped up, prepared to go to the door, when in walked Edwin Hopper. For some reason, this got them going again, and they continued to laugh, Betsy leaning against the wall and Julia clutching her sides, while Hopper stood with a befuddled expression, holding a gift-wrapped package and looking from one to the other.

"Oh," gasped Julia. "Oh, Ed, forgive us. What idiots you must think we are. I can't even remember exactly what I said to set us off, but we couldn't stop. We were helpless."

"Julia said," Betsy told him, wiping her eyes, and fighting for control, "she said . . . the baby reminded her of a *puppy*, all paws."

"Just as long as he's not covered with hair," he quipped. "Well, I've certainly come to the right place if I wanted to be cheered up, haven't I?" He handed Julia the package. "A small offering for the new mother."

"How kind you are. I'm going to open it right now. Do you remember Betsy?"

"I never forget a beautiful woman," he replied with a smile.

As a concession to the heat of summer, or perhaps to the military influence of the times, Hopper's hair was shorter than usual, and he had recently shaved off his mustache. In a blue and white seersucker suit with a light blue shirt and a navy polka-dot bowtie, he looked more handsome and youthful than ever.

Julia removed the white satin ribbon from a blue Tiffany gift box. It contained a hinged sterling silver picture frame with her monogram on it. "How beautiful. Thank you so much, Ed."

"I thought it might hold photographs of the two men in your life."

"That's just what I'll do with it. We'll have to take pictures of Scott as soon as we get home from the hospital."

"When will that be?"

"I feel well enough to leave right now, but the doctor says not before a week."

"Will you have someone to help you?"

"Julia and the baby are coming back to my apartment until he's at least a month old," said Betsy.

"Two weeks," demurred Julia. "Our place is all ready for us."

"It's a matter of practicality," Betsy explained to Edwin, as if he were the one to make the decision. "Michael's apartment has a very steep stairway. It would be so difficult, trying to manipulate a baby carriage up and down and lugging bags of groceries home. I know she's anxious to get settled in her own nest, but they should stay with me for as long as possible."

"That sounds sensible to me, Julia," Hopper agreed. "I was going to offer my housekeeper's services, if you need someone to relieve you in the afternoons. Mrs. Reilly has a wealth of experience, with five children and eleven grandchildren."

"That's so thoughtful, Ed. I may take you up on it." She opened Murray's box of candy. "Have some of these before they melt in this heat."

Edwin helped himself to two squares of dark chocolate fudge. "My weakness. Fudge and brownies."

"Then you'll have to taste Betsy's," said Julia. "I think Michael misses her brownies more than he does me."

"Is that so?" He turned to Betsy with a teasing smile. "Any time you want to invite me up to sample your brownies, I'd be delighted."

Julia was surprised to see her aunt, who was usually in command of any situation, blush. "When Julia and Scott get home, you must come to dinner."

"I'm going to hold you to that," he said with a twinkle in his eyes.

Although the windows were open to the river breeze, the room was warm. "With your permission," said Edwin, removing jacket and tie and rolling up his shirt sleeves.

Betsy took his coat and hung it in the closet. Julia noticed his eyes follow her across the room. When she pulled a chair closer to him, his smile was shy, almost boyish. The blue of Betsy's embroidered cotton chambray dress almost exactly matched Edwin's shirt, and he said something to that effect. She laughed softly. For the next few minutes it was just the two of them, as if no one else were in the room.

There was a sharp rap at the door and a merry-faced nurse with a frilled cap and an English accent popped her head in the door. "Baby's here!" she chirped. "I'm afraid your guests will have to leave, Mummy. No visitors when Baby's in the room."

"Oh dear," sighed Julia. "It seems they just got here. I wish they didn't have to go."

"You know you want to see the baby," chided Betsy. "I'll come again tomorrow. It's already past five. I had no idea it was so late." She handed Hopper his suit coat from the closet.

"May I take a peek at the baby on the way out?" he asked.

"As far as I'm concerned, it's fine. It's Nurse you'll have to convince," said Julia, glancing at the uniformed woman who bustled into the room, wheeling a bassinet.

"Here he is, the little love," cooed Nurse, lifting a blue-wrapped bundle. "Isn't he just the most perfect lamb?" She held the baby aloft before depositing him in Julia's arms.

"He's a fine-looking boy," observed Edwin, as the baby squirmed and gnawed on a fist.

"Shoo, shoo," Nurse waved the visitors out the door.

"Thanks for coming," called Julia.

"I'll phone you later," said Betsy from the threshold.

They came out on East End Avenue, moving aimlessly along the block, reluctant to part. Across the street in the park, a grove of birch trees was stirred by a fresh breeze from the East River. The sun in the western sky cast a late afternoon glow over the city.

"Such a lovely time of day, the hours before sunset," remarked Edwin.

"Yes, isn't it? I so enjoy summer in New York. Especially on quiet weekends like this, when everyone's gone somewhere." Betsy lifted her face to the breeze, inhaling the summery fragrance of a flowering vine hanging from a tall wrought iron fence.

A tenderness softened his mouth as he watched her. "May I . . . that is, are you . . ." He stopped, at a loss for words.

She smiled at him. "What is it you are trying to say?"

"I want in the worst way to spend the evening with you. Will you have dinner with me?"

"I'd like nothing better," she said, looking down at her bare legs and sandals, "but I'm not very dressed up."

"I know a quite casual Hungarian restaurant. You'll be fine." When he smiled he was especially attractive, she thought, with his teeth so white and even. He hooked his jacket over his shoulder with one hand and took her arm with the other. "Let's walk, shall we? It's not too far."

They fell into step, strolling west on Eighty-seventh Street. Clamorous children were playing hopscotch or jumping rope on the sidewalks under the watchful eyes of fleshy women in baggy cotton housedresses who sat on the steps of their brownstones gossiping in broken English. Even in this ethnic community, no one wanted to be caught speaking German on the streets, with Hitler laying waste to all of Europe.

Edwin said, "Yorkville was the center of the German-American Bund."

"This neighborhood?"

"You bet. Swastikas, Heil Hitler and all. There are probably a lot of them left. The FBI can't have routed them all."

"How much harm can they do?"

"Enough. Sabotage, for one thing. They could gather information on civil defense, I should think. The Germans must have had plans to invade this country, and their agents were prepared to operate as a fifth column. Now that the Allies have them engaged on two fronts, those dreams of conquest will most likely not materialize."

"It's rather unsettling, though, to think they might be right in our midst."

"Never fear, Mademoiselle, you are safe with me," he said, with a Groucho Marx growl, and Betsy laughed. He stopped to put on his jacket, tucking her arm closely under his when they resumed walking. At Second Avenue they turned south. "It's another ten blocks. Getting tired?"

"No, I love to walk."

On a side street in the seventies they went down some steps to Cafe Duna, a family-run restaurant with a small number of tables inside and a garden in the rear. It catered to a neighborhood clientele, serving Middle European fare with a heavily Magyar flavor. As in most provincial cultures, Madame did most of the work, while her husband gossiped with his friends and entertained the diners with classical guitar selections. From time to time one young woman or another, draped in scarves and dangling earrings, would lament to the accompaniment of a gypsy violinist. The candlelight was so low and romantic that one could only hope the tableware was clean.

"Delightfully schmaltzy, isn't it?" Edwin remarked, as vast portions of goulash and chicken paprikash with mashed potatoes were served by a daughter.

Madame made certain their glasses were filled and the bread basket replenished. They sipped wine and they talked. He asked about her job, her family, what she liked to do in her leisure time. It was very natural and easygoing, yet Betsy was aware that she had that shivery feeling of anticipation called butterflies. Edwin revealed something of himself and his work. He had started the agency with a partner in 1930 after working as a writer and drama critic. When the partner relocated to the West Coast, Hopper had toughed it out, living off a small inheritance from his parents during the lean years. He came from Glens Falls, he told her, although he had lived in Manhattan for over twenty years, and the only family left upstate now was an older sister who was married to a doctor. They rarely saw each other, since she and her husband almost never came to the city and Edwin seldom visited Glens Falls.

"It has unhappy memories," he explained. "My wife is buried there."

"How long ago did she die?"

"It's been a little over four years."

"Is her family still in Glens Falls?"

"No one close. Louise was an only child and both her parents are gone. It just seemed the right place for her to be." He swirled the wine in his glass, looking down. "Truthfully, I avoid going back. Three years ago was the last time. My sister had an operation, so I went up to visit her." He smiled brightly. "That's how I happened to meet Julia. Coming back to New York on the train, there was this lovely young girl sitting across the aisle from me. I knew just by looking at her that it was her first time away from home."

"I remember I scolded her for talking to a stranger."

He laughed. "I don't blame you. She was so unspoiled and appealing, and clearly vulnerable. The wrong person could have taken advantage of her."

"I'm not so sure," mused Betsy. "Julia is a lot tougher than you'd expect. She has carried her share of burdens. I was very disappointed when she didn't finish college. As you know, she's extremely intelligent, so I hope she'll find the time to go back, now that she has returned to New York."

"That won't be easy with a baby to care for."

"No, not easy. But she can take one or two courses a semester, and eventually she'll have her degree."

"That's important to you, isn't it?"

"Oh yes."

"Why so? It's nice to be educated, of course, but a woman usually doesn't have to support a family."

She looked him steadily in the eye. "That is the first disappointing thing you have said to me. I should think you'd know better."

"I'm sorry. I've obviously touched a nerve."

"Yes, I suppose you have. You see, I had to work so hard to get an education. I went through both Emma Willard and Russell-Sage on scholarships because my mother couldn't afford the tuition. My father had been a much admired doctor, and no one would ever have suspected from the way we lived that there was no money. When he died, we lost everything— our house, the furnishings, his valuable collection of books. My mother has never recovered from the shock of it. Instead of picking herself up and finding a way to support her family, she hid away, living off her widow's pension and becoming a bitter and mean-spirited old woman." Edwin was looking at her with a mixture of surprise and admiration. "Sorry if I bit your head off, but as you can see, I was determined that nothing like that would ever happen to me."

"What I can see, Betsy Perkins, is that there is more to you than your beautiful face." He smiled again and it broke the tension.

The conversation turned to less personal subjects: the war; the city's civil defense, in which Hopper was involved; the theater, about which he was passionate.

"Now you're a literary agent as well," said Betsy.

"Yes. It came about quite naturally. Several of my playwrights wrote books and asked me to handle them, and it grew out of that. The surprising thing is, it's getting almost as big as the drama department."

"Are they so different?"

"Oh, very. World of difference, dealing with publishers as opposed to producers."

"Which interests you more?"

He thought about her question. "I'm not certain. Perhaps because it's new, I'm getting a kick out of talking to editors, watching a book come together, then waiting to see what will happen. The theater is a lot trickier, I think, but at least there's an immediate reaction. On opening night you have either a hit or a flop. On the other hand, with out-of-town tryouts you have a chance to salvage a play, which isn't true of a book."

"What about the other office, your talent agency?"

"Hopper-O'Neil is an entirely separate operation. I don't

have much to do with it. My partner plays the major role and Millie Kaplan, my former assistant, runs the office," He signaled the waitress. "I've been talking about myself long enough. Will you have dessert?"

"Why don't we go back to my apartment for coffee and that'll give you a chance to try my brownies."

"That's the best idea I've heard all evening."

There were no cabs in sight, so they caught the Second Avenue bus and walked east on Fifty-second Street to Betsy's address. When they reached the canopied door, a dark-suited man wearing a gray hat stopped them from entering the lobby.

"Do you people live in this building?" he asked.

Betsy glanced at Edwin questioningly.

"Who are you?" Hopper replied in answer.

The man flashed a badge. "FBI, sir. I repeat, do you live in this building?"

"I do," said Betsy. "This man is my guest. What is the FBI doing here?"

"Official business, ma'am. What floor do you live on?"

"The tenth."

"I'm not sure you'll have access to that floor, ma'am."

"What do you mean? That's my *home*. I want to go up there."

The agent opened the glass door and signaled another man who was standing in the lobby. "These folks want to go to her apartment on ten, Walters. Is it okay?"

"Which apartment?"

"Ten-D," said Betsy.

The dial above the elevator indicated that the car was stopped on ten. "Just a minute." He pressed the button three times and the car immediately started its slow descent. When it reached the lobby, the doors opened to reveal the doorman, the elevator operator, and another FBI agent.

"Hello, Miss Perkins," said the doorman, scarcely able to contain his excitement.

"Joe, what's going on?"

"Never mind," said the first agent. He spoke to his associate. "Take these people to the tenth floor and make sure they get into Ten-D."

"Right."

"You better stay here with me," the agent told the doorman.

They rode up in silence, the operator looking at them with round, scared eyes. He was a little old to be working, but all the younger men were at war. When they reached ten, the FBI man ordered him to keep the elevator there while he escorted them to the right-hand corner of the large square hallway. There were four apartments on each floor. As Betsy turned the key in her lock, there came a stream of invective from across the hall, and the opposite door opened to a shocking scene. Her cosmopolitan neighbor, Robert Schild, with his hair and clothes in disarray, was led out of the apartment in handcuffs by two men who could only have been federal agents. Looking straight ahead, his face was a stony mask. Betsy watched in open-mouthed wonder, while Edwin looked on with interest as the three men entered the elevator and descended to the ground floor.

"*What in the world is going on?*" asked Betsy when they had finished gaping.

"You'd better go in, Miss," said the agent who was still standing with her and Hopper.

"But I *know* him. Tell me what happened."

"How well do you know him?" asked the agent, paying sudden attention.

"Not well at all. We're neighbors, we say hello when we meet in the hall."

"Have you ever noticed anyone else enter or leave his apartment?"

"No . . . wait a minute. Yes, one night when I came home late, I saw three men leaving."

"Did you get a good look at them? Could you identify any of them?"

"I don't think so. I didn't pay much attention. Will you *please* tell us what this is all about?"

"He's a German agent, Miss. He was running a spy ring."

"*Here?* In this building?"

"Yes, ma'am."

"But he said he was Swiss."

"Did he, now?"

The elevator came up again. The agent tipped his hat and said goodnight. One of the other men got out and took up a post in front of Schild's apartment. Edwin closed the door and put the chain lock on.

"Well," he said, "I hadn't expected quite this much excitement when you invited me home for brownies."

"I'm in shock."

"How well *did* you know him?"

"Just to say hello, as I told the agent. For some reason he made me uncomfortable, with his formality and his patronizing manner. He was always cordial, but except for coming over to borrow a light bulb one night when he first moved in, he never attempted to become better acquainted."

"Well, thank the Lord for that," said Hopper with understated humor.

"Oh, Ed. I am really shaken by this. It's like having the Bund in your own backyard."

"Didn't I tell you?" He peered at her closely. "You do look a little pale, at that. Is there any brandy in the house?"

"That's a very good idea. In the first cabinet next to the fireplace. You get it while I put on coffee."

He poured two generous tots of pre-war Hennessey's. "I'm depleting your stock, but I thought we could both use a drink."

"It brings it all so much closer, doesn't it? Up until now, spy stories were just that—stories."

"Well, don't let it upset you too much. War is a serious business and this is a part of it. Will you be nervous here alone tonight?"

"I don't think so. Nothing more can happen, can it?"

"They appear to have posted a guard across the hall, so you'll be well protected, I'm sure."

She looked at her watch. "It's after eleven and I forgot to call Julia. Too late now. I'll have to wait until morning. She may not be too surprised about our neighbor. Believe it or not, the first time Julia met Mr. Schild, she thought he was German. Something about the way he clicked his heels." Betsy returned to the kitchen and brought out a plate of brownies and poured the coffee. "We hardly ever use sugar, so I don't feel guilty about baking every now and then."

"These brownies are exquisite. What do you do to make them so fudgy?"

"I combined a recipe for fudge with the Fannie Farmer brownie. Have another."

"Thanks, I will."

"They're even better with ice cream and hot fudge sauce, but I don't have any right now."

"Maybe you'll invite me another time."

She smiled. "As often as you like."

"You may be sorry you said that. You'll find me on your doorstep every day." He got to his feet. "But right now I think it's time I went home and let you get some sleep. You must be tired after last night's vigil."

"Actually, I feel rather invigorated. It must be the coffee."

At the door, he said, "Is tomorrow a holiday for you?"

"Yes, that's the advantage of not being in broadcasting operations. I don't usually have to work on weekends or holidays."

"What plans do you have?"

She shrugged. "Nothing much. I thought I'd visit Julia."

"Would you spend the day with me?"

"The entire day?"

He nodded. "And the evening. We can both see Julia and then do whatever we do together."

"Sounds wonderful. What time shall I be ready?"

"How late do you want to sleep?"

"Oh, ten-ish, I guess. Why don't you meet me at the hospital around noon?"

"Perfect. I'll take you to lunch. If it's a nice day we can go out to the country."

Although she was tired, Betsy did not fall asleep easily. She dreamed of the enemy, of spies and goose-stepping invaders. And, at the center, a circle of warmth and safety.

When she reached the hospital late the next morning, Julia was just finishing a conversation with her mother. "As soon as the baby's old enough to travel, I promise to bring him to Troy. I do wish you'd reconsider about coming down here, but I understand."

"What was that about Jesse coming to New York?" asked Betsy.

"Don't worry, it was just for a visit. But she says she's not up to traveling." A look of concern clouded Julia's brow. "I think she's getting worse. Her voice fades every now and then, as if she's been making an effort just for me."

Betsy nodded in agreement. "I noticed that yesterday. I

asked Mother about it and she said Jesse has her good and bad days."

"I thought Gran seemed a little weary, too. In fact, neither one of them sounded in great shape."

"Well, Mother's getting old. We have to accept that. Come on, Jule, cheer up. You have someone else to worry about now." She opened a tin that had once held saltwater taffy. "Look what I brought for you."

"Brownies," exclaimed Julia, immediately helping herself to one. "Just in time for my milk."

"Better not let any of the nurses catch you eating sweets in the morning."

"I know. They're so intimidating, they make me feel two years old. It's like having a dozen Grans bossing me around." She munched on a fudgy square, washing it down with milk. "Mmm, Bets, these are unusually good. Have you done something different?"

"I added a touch of strong coffee," said Betsy. "Edwin Hopper loved them."

Julia stopped chewing. "Ed?"

"Yes. We had coffee and brownies after dinner last night."

"Dinner . . ." Her eyes widened. "You had *dinner* with him?"

"Well, it was time to eat when we left here and it just sort of happened." At the expression on Julia's face, she hastened to say, "Don't get any grandiose ideas. He was just being a gentleman." Then she told Julia about Robert Schild.

"I *knew* that man had to be German. But I must admit it never entered my mind he was a Nazi. I assumed he was a refugee and didn't want to admit it." Her eyes sparkled with excitement. "Tell me what happened."

"There's not much to tell. They took him away last night and now there are agents in his apartment collecting evidence, although the superintendent thinks they're really waiting for some of his contacts to show up. He said the FBI borrowed a passkey to enter and surprised Schild before he had time to warn anyone."

"Aren't they afraid someone else might tip off the other members of his ring?"

"That's what I asked, but the super said he and all the staff were sworn to secrecy. I'm the only tenant in the building who knows about it. Practically everyone was away for the weekend or had gone out for the evening. I promised the agents I wouldn't say anything."

"You've just told me about it," Julia reminded her.

"Well, for Pete's sake, you live with me."

"And what about Ed Hopper?"

"What about him?" asked a familiar voice as Hopper entered the room through the open door.

"Edwin, what a nice surprise." Julia looked at Betsy, who didn't seem the least bit astonished to see him.

"I was just telling about our neighbor, the spy," Betsy explained. "The FBI swore all the building staff to secrecy, and Julia implied that since *you* know all about it our national security is in grave danger."

"A fine way to speak about your employer," Hopper said with mock severity. He carried a vase of anemones and ferns. "The nurse put these in water for me. Where would you like them?"

"Thank you. How lovely—so colorful. What about over there?" She motioned to her aunt, who took the flowers and placed them on the window sill.

"So now I'm a security risk, am I?"

"Oh, Ed. Betsy said the other members of the spy ring won't be forewarned because no one knows about Robert Schild's arrest. I reminded her that she had told me, and you already knew. I'm sure the doorman and the super couldn't resist telling their families and friends. It just proves how impossible it is to keep information from getting out."

"If you think that's a problem," said Edwin, "consider launching a surprise invasion of Europe."

"You're right, the Germans must be expecting one. I wonder when it will come."

"Could be any time. That's really what someone like your neighbor was nosing around for. Odd information that would tip them off about when and where."

"Now that I think of it, when he heard my husband was overseas, he asked about him. Wanted to know if Special Services meant intelligence. I guess it's important that families don't know where their men are."

Hopper took a seat next to Betsy. "I just had a good look at your son, Julia. He's a handsome child, but I can't see much of a resemblance to either you or Michael."

"I think maybe he looks like my father," said Julia. "Don't you, Bets?"

Betsy looked startled. "It's much too soon to tell. Ask me in a month."

Sensing an awkward moment, Hopper began discussing Michael's new musical, *Over the Moon*. "They've almost finished casting."

"So Murray told me," said Julia. "That's the only way I'd get any information these days because Gerry Ross completely ignores me. I haven't wanted to interfere, but it sounds like the two of them are having a problem getting along."

"Anything I can do to help?"

"Maybe. I'll ask Murray."

Edwin exchanged a lingering glance with Betsy. "Well," he said, "I promised to take this lovely lady to lunch. Will you mind very much if we desert you?"

"Oh. Of course not. They'll be bringing Scotty in a few minutes, anyway."

"Are you sure you won't be lonely this afternoon?" asked Betsy.

"Not at all. I have lots to read, and Millie Kaplan is coming to see me. So is Janice Fried. You remember, she's the artist I met through Michael . . . we've become rather good friends. And Murray said he might stop by later with his girlfriend."

"Good, then you'll have plenty of company. I'll call you tonight if I get home early enough. Otherwise I'll see you tomorrow after work."

It occurred to Julia when they left that Betsy must be planning on a very long lunch.

Julia came home from the hospital two days after the Allies landed on Sicily, the first step in the onslaught of Fortress Europe.

Scott was an easy baby. She had no trouble nursing him, and other than one middle-of-the-night feed, he kept quite civilized hours. The doughty Mrs. Reilly came twice a week to help take care of him and clean Betsy's apartment, which proved an ideal arrangement.

Hopper was spending more than a little time there himself, coming by after work on the pretext of bringing a manuscript for Julia, then chatting over a martini until Betsy came home, and usually staying for dinner. More often than not, Julia found herself drifting off by nine o'clock and would say goodnight, leaving him to Betsy. She would fall asleep to the murmur of their voices, waking late at night to squint at the clock, amazed that he was still there.

Despite a lack of sleep, Betsy seemed full of boundless energy, imbued with a zest for life and her work. On most evenings she arrived in time to help with Scott's bath and see him put to bed. But as the days passed, she would sometimes call to say, "I won't be home for dinner tonight, sorry it's so last-minute." If no explanation was forthcoming, Julia felt reluctant to pry. This had gone on for about two weeks before it occurred to her that on the nights Betsy did not show up for dinner, neither did Edwin Hopper.

Am I dense? Am I an idiot, or what?

"Betsy," she said at breakfast the next morning, "where were you last night?"

"Umm, I went out for dinner and to the theater."

"I see. May I ask with whom?"

Betsy busied herself with the breakfast dishes. "With Edwin."

"You . . . why didn't you *tell* me?" she shrieked. "You've been seeing him all this time, haven't you?"

Betsy's face was flushed, but she looked extremely happy. "I didn't want to say anything. It seems too good to be true."

"Do you like him?"

"Yes."

"Are you in love with him?"

"I think so."

"Oh, Bets. Is he in love with you?"

"I don't know," wailed Betsy, and she burst into tears. "I know he likes me, but I'm afraid. I trusted my heart once, and I'm frightened to do it again."

"Don't be. Ed is *nothing* like Rodney Barstow. They're as different as night and day. He would never hurt you."

"He might not mean to, Jule . . . but what if he doesn't love me?"

That was always the problem, wasn't it? Julia sighed deeply, remembering that she had waited almost two years for Michael, convinced until the very last moment that he would never marry her. All Betsy could do was to hope that Edwin returned her feelings and would one day declare his love.

The rest of that summer passed swiftly and magically for Betsy. Despite the strictures of wartime regulations and the demands of her job, there was the opportunity to get away for weekends to visit Edwin's friends in Maine, in Connecticut, or on Long Island. They went to concerts at Lewisohn Stadium, took picnic lunches to the park, wandered through the Cloisters listening to Gregorian chant.

There was a surfeit of tickets to the theater, on Broadway and off. Part of Hopper's work was to discover promising new playwrights, and he took her along to scout summer stock, university drama productions, or experimental repertory companies in union halls and high school auditoriums. In the living rooms of wealthy patrons of the arts, they attended a reading of a drama in manuscript by Lillian Hellman and a full-length presentation of a Vernon Duke musical. After an offering he would seek her opinion, giving the impression that he valued her judgment.

All this time he treated her with affection yet never attempted to make love to her. Once, when they raced back to his house after getting caught in the rain, he embraced her passionately, but as his arousal became urgent he checked himself, as he had on other occasions. Despite their closeness and his obvious delight in her company, there remained a wall of reserve beyond which she could not penetrate. She suspected it had to do with the difference in their ages.

"April and September," he remarked one night when he was confronted by their mirrored reflections in the foyer of her apartment.

"Thirteen years doesn't seem so great a difference."

"Almost fourteen," he said gently. "I'll soon be forty-three."

"A very youthful forty-three."

He took her in his arms, murmuring, "When I'm with you, I feel like a boy again."

In the last week of August, Julia and the baby moved to Greenwich Village.

Betsy had to admit it was a snug and charming apartment, but she voiced her concern to Hopper about the hazards of living in an eighteenth-century building without a fire escape.

"That rickety stairway is the only way in and out of this place. What if there should be a fire downstairs and their only exit is cut off?"

He promptly went shopping at Hammacher-Schlemmer, returning with two strong rope escape ladders that he installed in the bedroom and living room. At Betsy's insistence, Julia practiced using them, descending not once but twice with a blanket-wrapped pillow in her arms to simulate the baby—first from the roof terrace and then the bedroom window.

"You know how I hate heights," she complained. "This Alpine exercise is giving me vertigo."

"I'll sleep a lot better knowing you have a way out of here," Betsy retorted.

"Well, you would have quite a time explaining to Michael how the mother of his child broke her neck," snapped Julia with acid tartness.

"Now, now, ladies," said Hopper.

By noon that Saturday, Betsy and Edwin left Julia nicely settled in, with Scott asleep in his new nursery and a supply of groceries in the larder. "Promise you'll call if you need anything, no matter what time it is, day or night."

"All right," laughed Julia, practically pushing them out the door. "You're worse than an anxious mother."

"Do you think they'll be all right?" Betsy asked, when they were on their way to Connecticut in Hopper's Chevrolet. At the beginning of the war his chauffeur had been drafted, and he had traded in the limousine for a more sensible car. Since he seldom drove, he had a surplus of gas coupons.

"Julia will do just fine. I have confidence in her," he said, taking her hand. "You mustn't worry about them."

They were on their way to look at a restored farmhouse near Darien. George Rhinehart, before leaving for overseas, had learned of Hopper's interest in buying a country place and told him about a friend's property that was for sale. It was not too far from the Rhinehart family estate.

The old stone house was beautiful. It had been completely modernized and was in pristine condition, having recently undergone the ministrations of an interior decorator. "Well, what do you think?" Edwin asked after they had gone through the rooms and toured the gardens and barn.

"It's a dream of a house. I'm sure you would find it relaxing on weekends. The barn could easily be made into a guest house or office."

His eyes smiled as he looked down at her. "It's especially important to me that you like it." He went around jiggling windows, turning on faucets, and kicking the stones of the foundation, as if doing so would help him to make up his mind. "It's not the best time to be buying a weekend house . . . on the other hand, this is an unusual opportunity. George says the owners are anxious to sell. I should probably look around a little more, but I'm inclined to make them an offer."

After stopping for dinner at a seafood restaurant in Greenwich, they drove back to the city. "It's still early," said Hopper. "Why don't we go to my house?"

"All right."

In his upstairs library, Betsy took a seat and looked around admiringly at the tasteful furnishings.

"Do you want to call Julia?" he asked.

"I'll wait until tomorrow. I'm afraid she'll think I'm interfering."

"May I fix you a drink?"

"A little sherry, please." He handed her a glass with a delicate design. "What beautiful crystal."

"There's a complete service for sixteen. Since Louise died, I've had little use for it. I had planned to ship everything to Cynthia after the war . . ." He drew a deep breath as he poured a brandy for himself. "Might as well use it," he said philosophically.

There was a long silence.

"Forgive me if I'm intruding . . . but you so seldom speak of them. Louise and Cynthia. Is it too painful?"

He nodded. "Partly that. Pity has always made me uncomfortable."

"Pity?" she protested. "Is that what you imagine I feel?"

"I suppose so."

She shook her head. "You're much too strong a man for pity. I'm not sure what to call it—sympathy, perhaps. Or maybe just a desire to know more about you."

He sat on the sofa next to her and took her hand. "What is it you'd like to know?"

"Oh, everything. I want to know *all* about you. The way

you grew up, the things you dreamed about, the kind of boy you were . . ."

"Your usual American variety. I was fond of sports, especially basketball and ice hockey. My parents were well-to-do and they sent me away to boarding school when I was fifteen." He chuckled. "I wasn't a deep thinker in those days, but I liked my studies and got good grades . . . what else?"

"When did you fall in love with Louise?"

"That's not easy to answer." He looked thoughtful for a minute. "We had known each other all our lives. Our families had been friends forever. When I was at Yale, we had an understanding. We became engaged in my senior year and married a week after graduation." He took a sip of brandy. "Louise was nineteen and I was not quite twenty-one. Doesn't that seem impossibly young for the responsibilities of marriage?"

"Oh yes, it does," Betsy smiled. "And were you divinely happy?"

He frowned. "Perhaps not divinely, but we were happy. Our daughter came along the first year, and truthfully, Louise wasn't prepared for that. Emotionally, I mean. It might have been better for her if she had been more mature before becoming a mother . . . as it happens, we had no other children. I'm not sure why; we did nothing to prevent it, but Louise never again conceived. It was probably just as well, since she had limited reserves of strength. You see, she'd had rheumatic fever when she was a girl. Her heart was weak and it eventually killed her." He cleared his throat. "Well, since Cynthia was our only child, you can imagine how precious she was to us . . ." His voice faltered, and he was unable to go on.

Betsy put her arms around him and he laid his head on her shoulder and wept. She held him, stroking his head and neck, uttering soothing sounds, placing small kisses on his brow and whispering, "It's all right, darling, it's all right."

At length, he sat up and took out a handkerchief. "I never thought I would do that. I'm dreadfully sorry."

"Never apologize, not to me. You've lost so much. A wife, a child . . . a grandchild. You *have* to grieve for them. If you keep it bottled up inside, it will make you ill."

"Oh, I've done my grieving, but in private. It's always

been difficult for me to display my feelings in front of others."

"Then I feel honored that you did so with me."

After a few minutes, he was composed again. "You hold back, too, I think. You've had your losses. And your secrets."

"Nothing to compare with yours. It was painful when I lost my brother and my father, but other than that, there has been just one disappointment. Or secret, if you will. I think you know about that."

"Rodney Barstow?"

"Yes."

"He's the reason I never called you after meeting you the first time at the theater. I asked Mike Shane about Julia's aunt and he said you were more or less engaged to Barstow."

"That was a gentlemanly way of putting it." She sighed. "I was such a fool. I have no excuse for my stupidity."

"You were in love."

"Yes, I was in love."

"And he was in love with you?"

"He said he was." She sighed again. "I thought that meant we would be married, but he met someone else. She was rich, glamorous, and social. And I wasn't."

"You mustn't be bitter, Betsy. Don't let one bad experience spoil it for you."

"Spoil what?"

"Love."

She quickly turned away. "I wanted never to fall in love again."

"Please don't say that. You leave me with no hope." She looked at him to see if he was teasing. He was a little, but not really. Taking her hand, he brought it to his lips. "I'm in love with you, Betsy. Deeply in love. And I'm afraid it's a permanent condition."

"Oh, Ed . . ." As his lips came down on hers her eyes closed, and they kissed as if they were lovers reunited after a long separation.

"My love, my dearest," he whispered, holding her close. "Take a chance with me, Betsy. A new love, a new life together . . ."

In the first week of October, the new Shane and Baker show *Over the Moon* opened at the St. James Theater to rave reviews. A month after the surrender of Italy, the musical's lighthearted optimism seemed the most successful formula for Broadway as the second year of war was coming to an end.

The book and lyrics were clever and amusing, and the music was sheer delight. Michael had polished the songs in that brief halcyon period following their marriage, claiming that Julia was his inspiration. Everything he wrote during those heady months in Alabama was golden, and in no time at all he finished the score, but he was sent overseas before there was time to complete the orchestration. Murray and Gerald Ross almost came to blows over the musical arrangements, but finally Hopper successfully intervened, saving the show.

Edwin's participation far surpassed the usual role of an agent. Without saying so, it was apparent he did not trust Ross. Among other tricks, Gerry had tried to cut Michael's percentage, claiming that since he was not available to do the arrangements nor consult during rehearsals, he was not entitled to his full share. Hopper prevailed, but Ross had acted badly and Julia disliked him more than ever.

Although the rehearsals were fraught with controversy, none of these conflicts was apparent on opening night, and early the next morning Julia read the reviews with gleeful satisfaction. Burns Mantle was lavish with praise in the *Daily News*: "A funny, speedy, sophisticated romp, brilliantly executed by a superb cast." Lewis Nichols, replacing Brooks Atkinson who was in Russia for the duration, wrote in the *Times*: "A happy, uproarious evening of lively entertainment in the best sense of the Broadway musical comedy," while Louis Kronenberger in *PM* welcomed it as "the first smash hit musical comedy of the season."

Hoping the mail would get through with all the insertions, Julia sent the clippings to Michael. She received a wonderful letter in return, telling her how thrilled he was with the notices. His letters these days were long and loving, and she awaited each one eagerly, keeping them together, reading and rereading them countless times. They were often reflective, revealing parts of her husband she had not known.

. . . How I wish I had been there with you on opening night, my darling! We both know that if I were, the seat next to you would have been empty, for I'd have been pacing a hole in the carpet at the rear of the St. James, just as I did two years ago at the Globe. Do you remember how nervous I was the night *North With the Wind* opened? I was practically sick to my stomach, and I seem to recall that I behaved abominably toward you throughout those weeks of rehearsals and tryout jitters. That's one of my weaknesses, taking it out on the one I love when I'm confronted with my own inadequacies. Is it too late to ask your forgiveness?

I think of you constantly, my darling girl, and of the baby. I dream of being with you to share all the everyday domestic happenings that will never seem ordinary again. I know you're lonely and I think you are doing such a fantastic job on your own. Between your wonderful letters and the great reviews, I've got just the boost I needed to tackle *Kick Up Your Heels* . . .

That was the working title of their next project. With his sure wit and acid pen, Murray had come up with an original story about a ballerina and a Rockette who meet in the waiting room of a podiatrist. The doctor has a large practice among dancers, and is constantly becoming romantically involved with them. The ballerina falls in love with him, but after much vacillation he chooses the Rockette. Murray had a history of a long string of girlfriends who were dancers, and the idea for the play was actually based on a true story.

Edwin had devised a clever system for receiving the music sheets from abroad. Michael would make three hand-notated copies of every piece, mailing one to Murray and another to Hopper while keeping the third himself. He never sent more than one work in the same envelope. In this way, the chances of a song being lost were minimalized, and although throughout his time overseas several envelopes actually did go astray, at least one duplicate of each composition made the journey intact.

Julia jealously guarded Michael's interests and insisted on being consulted at each phase of production. Now that they had a major hit, it was easier for her to assert herself, for she recognized that Michael's value to the producers was directly related to the box office receipts. Entranced with Scott, however, she began to lose touch with the progress of

Kick Up Your Heels. The chief focus of her life now was their child, and Michael assured her that was his first priority, too.

"The snapshots are wonderful," he wrote. "I can't believe that little fellow is actually my son. I can see he's changed since the baby pictures. I'll miss all of his firsts—first tooth, first word, first steps. We'll have lots of catching up to do when I get home."

She was overjoyed at Michael's response to the baby. He wanted to know everything about him, and she was happy to report the slightest detail in Scott's development, any change in his daily routine.

"Scotty won't walk for many months, darling," she replied, "I pray you'll be home by then . . ."

Suddenly it was November. Betsy and Edwin were getting married, barely four months from the afternoon they had discovered each other in Julia's hospital room. Eunice and Jesse journeyed to New York for the wedding, as did Edwin's sister and brother-in-law from Glens Falls. It was startling for Julia to see her mother, who had become an old woman since she had visited her in February. Aging was a natural process and had to be accepted, but the deterioration in Jesse's appearance was heartbreaking to observe. Her complexion had a yellow, waxy cast, and her hands had developed a tremor. Thankfully, she remained sober throughout the visit, enthralled with her grandson, playing with Scott for hours at a time, and singing to him as she rocked him to sleep. While the newlyweds traveled to the Shenandoah Valley of Virginia on their honeymoon, the two women stayed in their Gramercy Park house, coming daily to visit Julia and the baby.

"I hate to say goodbye," said Jesse when she and Eunice departed for Troy. She stroked Scott's cheeks and kissed his chubby hands.

"I'll bring him to see you soon," promised Julia, filled with a tugging sadness. She would never rid herself of the feeling that she was somehow responsible for the tragedy of her mother's life.

By the spring of 1944, Julia was beginning to feel the war would never end. She saved tin cans and foil and cooking fat, and tried to be diligent about the dimout. The apartment was stifling at night, yet she kept the shades and curtains tightly closed when the lights were on. She was still reviewing book manuscripts for Edwin. When Scott was napping, and in the long, lonely evenings, she was grateful for anything that relieved the boredom. Reading about the killing and the horror each day in the New York *Times*, hearing news broadcasts of bombing raids on the French coast or tank battles on the outskirts of Rome did little to bring the war closer. It was the tedium of food rationing, the sameness of each day, that made her reality. And the loneliness.

Her need for Michael was so intense it was almost palpable. Was his longing for her as great? she wondered. How had she lived the first twenty years of her life without him, when it seemed he had been part of her forever?

Just as she thought nothing encouraging would ever happen again, Betsy announced that she was going to have a baby. Edwin was so happy he could scarcely contain himself. "I think he wants a girl, but he's afraid to say so," Betsy confided. Julia wondered whether a son might not be easier on his emotions, but it was a joy to see that dear man free of the careworn expression and so obviously besotted with his lovely wife.

On the sixth of June, the Allies landed in France. Americans were jubilant, confident that in no time their soldiers would be marching through the streets of Berlin. But in a radio address to the nation, President Roosevelt dashed their hopes for a quick victory, warning of a long and difficult struggle ahead.

Scott's first birthday on the Fourth of July was an unexpectedly festive occasion. They spent it with the Hoppers at their country house in Connecticut. Edwin had bought the farmhouse for Betsy as a wedding gift, and they usually invited Julia and the baby to join them for weekends.

"Poor Scott," said Julia. "All his birthdays will be overshadowed by a national holiday."

"Not if you play it right. Let him think the whole country is celebrating his day," suggested Edwin.

They went to the Independence Day parade in Darien, and Scotty bounced up and down in Uncle Ed's arms as the high school band marched along playing "The Stars and Stripes Forever." With the bright uniforms, the drum majorettes twirling batons and the locals waving flags, drinking soda, and eating ice cream, one could almost forget that American men were fighting and dying overseas. Until the disabled veterans came along in a motorcade at the end of the parade.

At the beginning of August, Betsy, well into her fourth month of pregnancy, was outraged when the president of EBN called her into his office and informed her she would soon have to give up her job. "This isn't the nineteenth century," she argued. "I'm not supposed to go into seclusion just because I'm giving birth."

"I'm sorry, Mrs. Hopper, it's company policy. If you decide to come back after the baby is born, we'll be happy to consider you for another opening."

"And I thought I was so vital to them," she scoffed. "They've got a man all lined up to take my job."

"How do you know that?" asked Julia.

"The chief of operations told me. He's a pal. The word is the new director's salary will be half again as much as they paid me."

Before marriage and pregnancy, Betsy had thought her future at EBN was unlimited. As one of a few women executives in the broadcasting industry, she had felt secure in that position. Without a job to go to every day, she began doing volunteer work for the Red Cross and New York Hospital. The Hopper agency could have benefited from her skills, but Edwin thought it might be intimidating for the staff to have his wife in the office. Accustomed to working hard, Betsy tried to fill the empty mornings with useful activity. And she spent many afternoons in the Greenwich Village apartment with Julia and Scott.

They were there together on the rooftop terrace in the last week of August. It was Monday, a few days after victorious Allied forces had liberated Paris. Julia thought that Michael might be in the French capital, for his most recent letter had been headed "Somewhere in France," but as usual, she had no way of knowing his exact location.

It was four o'clock, nearly time for Betsy to be getting home to see about dinner. The Hoppers usually dined out before going to the theater, but tonight was free and Betsy was telling Julia how much she looked forward to a quiet evening with her husband, when the doorbell rang.

"I wonder who that can be," said Julia, leaving Scott with Betsy and going to the door. She went out in the hall and stood at the top of the stairway, waiting to see who had come.

An adolescent youth entered the dark passage and came halfway to the foot of the stairs. He was wearing the billed hat and jacket of a Western Union messenger and carried a bag with a strap over his shoulder. After stopping to shuffle through its contents, he withdrew a yellow envelope. Looking up, he saw her standing there and slowly began to climb the stairs.

"Telegram for Mrs. Julia Shane."

Silently she held out her hand as his head came level with hers. His eyes flashed with compassion and she wanted to assure him it was not necessary. Not for her.

Playing with Scott on the terrace, Betsy heard Julia come back into the apartment. There was a very long silence. Then a stifled cry. She put Scott in his playpen, and ran to see what had happened.

Julia was leaning against the brick wall with her eyes closed, clutching the yellow Western Union form. Betsy took it and read:

FROM DEPARTMENT OF ARMY LT MICHAEL KITTREDGE SHANE PREVIOUSLY REPORTED MISSING FOUND ALIVE WOUNDED STOP CONDITION FAIR STOP ADMITTED MILITARY HOSPITAL REIMS FRANCE STOP

"Oh God . . . Julia, darling, come sit down. Come on, dear." Through the open French doors, they could hear Scott prattling away in his playpen. Betsy poured some scotch into a glass. "Here, drink this."

Julia swung her hand, knocking the glass to the floor. "Haven't you learned by now that's not a *remedy?*"

After a moment of shock, Betsy said, "I'm sorry, Jule." She sat on the sofa and put her arms around her. "What can I do? Shall I call Ed?"

Julia nodded mutely. Half-listening, she heard Betsy speak to Edwin at his office and explain what had happened. She wanted to feel something, but she was numb.

The next hours passed in a daze. Edwin arrived at her apartment and insisted that she should not be alone. "We're taking you and Scotty home with us right now."

"But what if they try to contact me here? If Michael should get worse—" He went downstairs to see Malcolm Lowell, who offered to stay in the apartment to receive mail and answer the telephone.

By the time Scott had been fed and bathed and was asleep in the extra crib Betsy kept for him in the guest room, Julia had partially recovered from the shock. "What do they mean, *found alive?* They never informed me he was missing."

"Sometimes there's a snafu. The telegram may have been sent but for some reason never reached you. Considering the outcome, it's just as well."

"How do you suppose he was wounded? He doesn't go into battle."

Edwin made inquiries through his contacts in Washington and learned that Michael's unit had been caught near the front lines on the banks of the Marne, less than a hundred miles from the Belgian border. They had been bombarded by the retreating enemy, and in the ensuing melée Michael had disappeared. For eight days he was listed as missing, until it was revealed he had been in the hands of the French Résistance and transported to the hospital in Reims.

As soon as Ed called him, Murray Baker came rushing down to Gramercy Park. He was so distraught at the news that Julia spent considerable time calming him down, despite her own agitation. Even after a cable arrived from Michael, assuring her he was not seriously wounded, she could not rid herself of anxiety. Only when he was home in her arms again would she believe he was truly whole.

For the past year, Murray had been preoccupied with *Kick Up Your Heels*. First he got bogged down in the opening scene, then having crossed that hurdle, the third act proved no less dull and flat. The mechanics of collaboration were problem enough, but for composer and playwright-lyricist to be separated by an ocean and a war was an almost insurmountable obstacle. That vital give and take, the spark of flint on stone, was a necessary part of the fascinating creative process. Julia remembered the running fire of comments when the two men were sharpening an idea, and she marveled that they had been able to get even one show on the boards with this cumbersome, unwieldy method.

By October, as Murray continued to polish the script, auditions had begun. He told Julia that they liked a young dancer named Marcia Hunter for the role of the ballerina, although she would have to leave the cast of *Song of Norway*. "She's perfect for the part. Beautiful, with an ethereal quality, and she's classically trained," said Murray. "I think we've got her. Keep your fingers crossed."

Rex Bolton had been signed for the part of the doctor, but the leading female role had yet to be cast. The director favored a young unknown who had understudied for Mary Martin in *Dancing in the Street*, but Gerry Ross insisted they needed a name. With the musical about to go into rehearsal, Murray told Julia they had finally agreed on Marie Newberry.

Julia expressed her concern. "It's a sexy part. I thought she played ingenues."

"She's matured a lot," Murray assured her. "I was there for her audition and it was impressive."

On a blustery fall day, Julia dressed Scott warmly and took him to Washington Square Park. Although he could play on the terrace in the fresh air, she thought he needed the stimulation of being around other people. The morning passed quickly, and as lunch time approached she wheeled his stroller to the greengrocer on Sixth Avenue. After purchasing a bag of tart Cortland apples and an assortment of vegetables, she stopped at the dry cleaners to pick up her woollen jacket.

Back at the apartment, she was disappointed that there was no mail from Michael. It had been a week since his last letter. Although he repeatedly affirmed that he was well cared for in the hospital, she worried about him. She had hoped he would be sent home as soon as he could travel, but Michael had written that his injuries were not serious and he would return to Special Services.

Julia gave Scott his lunch and put him down to sleep. Having staggered around the park all morning holding onto her hand, he would take a long nap. It was exhausting trying to keep up with an energetic sixteen-month-old and she considered napping herself, but decided there was just enough time to finish evaluating the latest book for Hopper.

Settling herself in a comfortable chair with the boxed manuscript, a notebook, and pencils, Julia had found her place and begun to read when there was a loud rap on the apartment door. It could only be her landlords—anyone else would ring the bell. She opened the door, expecting to see Malcolm or Hugo.

Standing in the hallway was Vivienne Tremaine.

After her initial surprise, Julia invited the actress in. Vivienne sauntered across the floor, glancing around with curiosity. "You've made some changes, I see."

"Well, that's only natural. We've been living here for over a year, ever since Scott arrived."

"Scott?"

"My little boy. Our son."

Vivienne seemed to recoil. "Oh, yes, I heard you had a baby. May I see him?"

"If you're very quiet. He's napping." Acutely aware that Vivienne knew her way around the apartment, Julia led her through the bedroom to the alcove where Scott was sleeping.

"Oh." It was an involuntary exclamation. Scott was a handsome boy, with silky brown hair and rosy cheeks. He grimaced in his sleep and his cheeks indented in much the same way Michael's did. A tender expression crossed Vivienne's face as she bent over the crib, her hand outstretched to hover over the sleeping child.

With a touch on her arm, Julia indicated that they should leave. They returned to the living room. Vivienne's hands were trembling when she fitted a cigarette into an ivory holder. "He doesn't really look much like Michael, does he?"

Julia ignored the remark. "Would you care for some tea or a Coke?" she asked, wondering again why the actress had come.

"Actually, I'd prefer a drink, if you don't mind. Do you have any gin?"

Containing her surprise, Julia checked the liquor cabinet. "I'm afraid not. There's scotch, bourbon, and sherry."

"Bourbon, then. One ice cube and a splash of water."

Julia poured herself a Coke and sat on the couch.

Vivienne took a drag of her cigarette. "I suppose you're wondering why I'm here."

"Well, I . . . yes."

"I came to tell you I saw Michael."

The room was suddenly very still. For a moment Julia could not find her voice. "You *saw* him? *Where . . . how?*"

In France, I was on tour with a USO show and we went to the hospital in Reims. I had no idea Michael was there until he sent word to the company."

"Oh, my heavens! How *was* he? Tell me about him."

"I'll do better than that," said Vivienne, fishing in her purse and taking out an envelope. "You can keep these."

There were two snapshots. One of Michael alone, with an arm in a sling and his leg in plaster. He was smiling into the camera, looking thin and drawn but sound. In the second photograph, Vivienne was perched on the edge of his bed. They were both grinning broadly and Michael's free arm was around her waist.

"He looks fairly well," said Julia faintly.

"He'll be good as new," Vivienne assured her. "Those casts look worse than they are. His tibia was shattered when he caught some shrapnel from a shell. The arm isn't broken, but the muscle was torn."

"He wasn't in pain?"

She gave Julia a long look. "Does it look like he was in pain?"

Julia met her gaze. "No. It doesn't. But then, Michael has always been very good at concealing his feelings."

Vivienne downed her drink in one gulp and gathered her purse and gloves. "Well, I'd better be getting along. Just thought I'd let you know Mike was okay."

"It was really very thoughtful of you," said Julia politely. "Are you on your way back to Hollywood?"

"Why, no." The actress paused, stage center. "I'm rather surprised you haven't heard. I just signed a contract for *Kick Up Your Heels*."

As soon as Vivienne left, Julia dialed Murray's number, but there was no answer. She kept trying until late that night, when he finally picked up the telephone.

"Murray? I've been trying to reach you . . . how is it that Vivienne Tremaine has been signed for *Kick Up Your Heels* and no one informed me?"

"Gosh, Jule, I thought Gerry would let you know."

"Well, he didn't. Who, may I ask, decided Vivienne should have the part?"

"Well, actually . . ." He sounded acutely uncomfortable. "Mike and I had her in mind for the character when we wrote it. Did you know she saw him in—"

"Yes, I know."

"Michael thinks she's right for it, Julia. She brought a note from him."

"I see."

"Why? Do you have any objections?"

"No, of course not. It's just that I thought the part had already gone to Marcia Hunter. Vivienne doesn't particularly look like a ballerina."

There was a pause. "Viv's not playing the ballerina. She's the Rockette."

"You mean . . . she has the leading role?"

Julia missed the opening night of *Kick Up Your Heels* because in the middle of November an urgent telephone call came from Troy. Her mother had collapsed into a coma and was not expected to live. Leaving Scott with Mrs. Reilly, Julia joined Betsy and Edwin on the train to Troy. They went directly to the hospital where Jesse lay in an oxygen tent, attached to intravenous drips and a urinary catheter.

"She has diabetes and cirrhosis," the doctor informed them. "Even if she comes out of this, she will be terminally ill."

Jesse died two weeks before Christmas without regaining consciousness. Standing at the graveside while the minister read the burial service, Julia felt a deep, unending sorrow for her mother. Not for her death at the age of forty-two, but for the tragedy of her life.

Her grandmother seemed to have shrunk to half her size. "She was all I had," she kept saying over and over, until Julia thought she would go mad. They knew that Eunice could no longer live alone. Her bones were fragile, and with her fading eyesight she could stumble and break a hip or shoulder with the slightest fall. They arranged for her to go into the Presbyterian Home for the Aged outside of Albany. It was a pleasant rambling building on thirty acres of a private estate that had been donated to the church.

Julia, Betsy, and Edwin returned to New York in a somber mood. Betsy's baby was due in a month. The doctor could not be certain, but he thought he might have heard a second heartbeat. As far as they knew, there had never been twins in their family.

"You must come stay with us for Christmas, Julia," said

Edwin. And she was grateful, because the thought of another holiday without Michael was more than she could bear.

At the end of January, Betsy gave birth to a healthy baby boy and a sickly female infant, who lived for less than a day. There were complications during the delivery. Betsy began to hemorrhage, and the doctor had to perform an emergency operation to remove her uterus. She would never be able to bear more children. So relieved was Edwin when, after a long vigil, he was finally convinced that his wife was out of danger, that he was more than content with their son, who was named Edwin Perkins Hopper.

By April, Julia's natural optimism had returned. Everyone believed the war in Europe would soon be over, and she waited to hear that Michael was on his way home.

She hummed as she pinned sheets and towels to the clothes-line she had strung up on the back half of the roof, behind a wooden lattice. Scott liked to help with the clothespins. He was running all over now, never at anything but a breakneck gait, and she was forever dashing after him to prevent his falling down or crashing into furniture.

The utility area was further screened from the terrace with plants and vines and potted evergreens. She had scraped and painted half a dozen Adirondack chairs and a heavy round table that she had found at a salvage store on Bleecker Street, and the results were quite professional.

"Mommy needs another clothespin, Scotty."

Julia bent down to pick up a pair of his wet overalls from the basket. She glanced over at Scott and noticed he was sucking on a clothespin. "Don't put that in your mouth, baby," she said automatically.

"Soldier man," said Scott, pointing, and went lurching over the terrace toward the french doors.

"Careful, Scotty," she called as she pinned the last of the laundry. She turned in time to see Scott toddle headlong across the roof, straight into the arms of a smiling army officer who was stooping in the doorway.

It was Michael.

❧ Chapter 14 ❧

Neil

She awakened before dawn, still drugged with sleep. Cold, damp air streamed in through the open window, parting the curtains to reveal an expanse of silvery sky.

The tiredness was still in her limbs, settling there as if it had taken permanent hold. Late into the night she had allowed herself to travel back through time, recalling memories long buried, reliving the past as if it were yesterday. The war years had come alive with startling clarity. Voices, laughter, tears . . . the scent of warm flesh. The joys and sorrows as sharp and fresh as ever.

But now with the approach of a new day, the images grew dim and faded. Jesse and Eunice and Michael, all of them long dead. Murray, too. Scott was no longer that stumbling little toddler, but a dynamic, self-confident man with grown children of his own. Edwin, thankfully alive and amazingly spry at eighty-nine, was enjoying a prolonged retirement in the sun-filled Arizona house where he and Betsy had recently celebrated their forty-seventh wedding anniversary together. Perkins Hopper, their only son, for sixteen years now head of Hopper Creative Management, had built his father's business into the largest talent agency in the world.

And finally here was Julia on Palm Island. Once again, alone. An aging widow, with children and grandchildren who no longer needed her . . . Impatiently she sat up. She despised self-pity. Getting out of bed, she glanced automatically at the clock. It was six-thirty on Monday morning. The final day of a year she would be glad to leave behind.

Instead of her customary swim, she took a brisk walk along the shore, then spent the morning gardening. Despite the staff of groundskeepers at Palm Island, she would allow no one else to tend her flowers and potted plants.

Around noon, the telephone rang. It was Neil. "Happy New Year, Mom."

"Thank you, darling, and the same to you. How's everything in Iowa?"

"Freezing. I've been indoors by the fire, though, grading final papers."

"That doesn't sound like much of a holiday."

"I don't mind. Kit called a little while ago and he said you had a great time together."

"Yes, it was grand to see him." Her antennae went up. Just how much had Kit told his father?

"That was pretty brave, letting him fall in on you with the girlfriend."

"Nonsense, I loved having them. You know how I thrive on company, and I haven't had much lately." She went on quickly, in case she sounded too wistful. "I assume he reached home safe and sound."

"Yes, but he's feeling down. He and Diana broke up last night."

That was not surprising news to Julia. "She seemed like a sweet girl."

"Were they fighting when they were there?"

"Not that I noticed. You know how young people are. Kit is still feeling his way. Don't worry, he'll find the right girl in due course."

"Let's hope so." In faintly embarrassed self-deprecation, he quipped, "It would be terrible if he followed in the footsteps of his old man."

"His old man sets a very fine example, Neil," she was quick to say.

"Aside from matrimony, you mean?"

"Well . . . I rather hope you will eventually marry again. I do believe we are meant to spend our lives with someone."

"Oh, I believe that, too," he said lightly. His voice dropped. "It's all over with Euphemia."

"I suspected as much. You haven't mentioned her in a while."

"She left Iowa City at the end of the semester."

"Back to Jamaica?"

"No, she's giving a seminar at Bennington and then heading for Europe."

"You'll miss her."

"Not really."

"Then it wasn't meant to be," she said in her practical manner.

She could hear the smile in his voice. "Oh, Mom, you always have a comforting aphorism to offer."

"You mean some hackneyed old cliché."

"From you it sounds like wisdom."

She laughed gently. "What are you doing for New Year's Eve?"

"There are a dozen parties in town and an unattached man gets invited to all of them."

"That doesn't surprise me in the least," was her pithy reply. "I was always of the opinion that women don't get a fair shake."

"Those are pretty cynical words, Madame. How about you— are you going anywhere?"

"Not tonight, dear. I'll get in bed early, turn on the television and watch the ball drop in Times Square." Lest he feel sorry for her, she hastened to add, "That's really what I prefer. There's a gathering at the club, but New Year's Eve parties depress me."

"I know what you mean. They always seem phony, with everyone trying to act like they're having the time of their lives."

"Yes." *The time of their lives* . . . She had a sudden vision of a gala New Year's Eve at the Astor Roof. So many years ago.

"I won't be staying out all night, that's for sure," said Neil. "Have to clear my desk because I'm expecting Scott next Wednesday."

"How nice. He was supposed to visit me this week, but he phoned from Aspen the other night to cancel. Something came up and he had to rush back to New York."

"What a rat race that guy leads," Neil said with some spirit. "Don't know how he stands it. There's a meeting of the bar association in Chicago next week, and he's coming here afterward, since it's practically around the corner."

It was lovely that the brothers were getting together, she thought, after she had said goodbye to Neil. They didn't see nearly enough of each other.

Two days earlier, at the time that Julia was commiserating with Kit on his faltering love affair, Scott Rhinehart had boarded a corporate jet in Aspen, bound for New York's Westchester County airport. With a year-end crisis facing Nordco Industries, one of his most important clients, Scott had been forced to abandon his family halfway through their annual ski vacation.

Nordco, makers of high-technology electrical equipment, with the encouragement of the U.S. State Department—which was interested in strengthening ties with the government of Saddam Hussein—had signed a contract the previous year to build special electronic generators for the government of Iraq. Despite advising government officials that the equipment could be adapted for military purposes, the company had received assurances from Washington that the generators would be used solely for peaceful ends and were urged to go ahead with the deal. The order had been on the docks ready for shipment when the American government had halted all exports to Baghdad and frozen Iraqi assets in the United States—including the millions of dollars held in escrow in a special account meant to pay for the custom-made generators.

Stuck with a potential ten-million-dollar loss, Nordco was filing suit for payment from the frozen assets. Suddenly, two days before Christmas, the company had been notified of a December 31st deadline for submitting a petition to the Treasury Department, including full details of the tax implications.

While the rest of his family was out on the slopes, Scott had been tied up on the telephone in his condominium for most of Christmas week. Despite his reluctance to cut short the holiday reunion with his children, he finally had no choice but to call an emergency meeting at his client's corporate headquarters before the year ran out.

Forcing his eyes away from the gorgeous spectacle of the snowcovered Rockies below, Scott tried to concentrate on the confidential report that had been awaiting him when he came aboard the company plane, but his thoughts kept returning to the last few days in Aspen.

Isobel had taken the news of his departure cheerfully enough, but the children, especially his daughter, had been crushed. "Oh, Daddy," Ginger cried, when he announced the change in plans, "I thought you promised this would be a holiday without interruptions. You've been on the stupid phone all week, and now you're leaving."

"I know I promised, and I can't tell you how sorry I am. It was completely unexpected and unavoidable."

"But this might be our last Christmas vacation together!"

"Of course it won't. Where did you ever get that idea?"

"Well, who knows what will happen in the future? I'll be in Guatemala next year, and after that there's college, and—and—well, *you* never spent holidays with your parents."

"We always celebrated Thanksgiving and Christmas with them, Ginger. You just don't remember." How to make your dad feel rotten, he thought ruefully.

Chip had been more understanding. Or maybe he had learned to expect less of his father. Certainly there was ample reason, Scott reflected, when he considered the broken promises over the years—the school programs missed, the games unattended—all because of his work. Lately he was becoming more aware of lost opportunities to cultivate a closeness with his son.

On the first day in Aspen, the two of them had spent the morning skiing together. Back at the house for lunch, Chip said casually, "I was elected president of my class."

Scott was ecstatic. "That's phenomenal, Chip. Why didn't you tell me? I'm really proud of you."

Chip's eyes misted. "That's got to be a first. I don't think I've ever heard you say anything like that before."

The remark wounded him. "Then that's my fault. I've always taken pride in you; I couldn't ask for a more wonderful son."

Chip looked down. "I know you were bummed when I didn't make Yale."

Scott answered honestly. "I was. But I was wrong. Parents can be wrong, you know."

Chip lifted his head, all earnestness. "I wish I could have gone to your college. It's always been my dream to be like you, to do what you've done."

"Chip . . ." He was at a loss. "You have to be your own man. I'm not even sure I'd want you to be like me. There are lots of things I would do differently if I had them to do over."

Chips eyes widened. "Your life is *perfect*."

Unable to meet his gaze, Scott put an arm around his son. "The only perfect thing about my life is my family."

All that afternoon Scott had thought about Chip's words as they skied together in companionable closeness. Late in the day, Ginger joined them with a friend who had been a year ahead of her at Hotchkiss and was now a freshman at Connecticut College. Lindsay McGraw was her name.

"Lindsay and I met by chance at the top of the gondola. We haven't seen each other since last year," Ginger explained.

Scott noticed that Chip took an immediate interest in the attractive McGraw girl. For the last two runs, Scott's skiing buddy stuck close to Lindsay, while Ginger paired with her father on the lift. Ginger was a beautiful skier and it had been a joy to skim down the mountain in her wake, watching her graceful turns. When Isobel flew in from San Francisco that night, their social calendar immediately filled up. The following day brought the first of the Nordco phone calls, leaving him little time for leisurely pleasures with his children.

This morning, when he said goodbye, Ginger had hugged him, whispering, "I'm sorry I bit your head off last night, Daddy."

"It's all right, pumpkin. I know you're disappointed. I'll make it up to you, I promise."

"I'll see you in New York on my way back to school. Happy New Year."

Perhaps Ginger had been right. How many more of these long holidays would they have together, the four of them? Both children were becoming independent adults. He could worry about them and take pride in them, but ultimately they belonged to themselves and would grow away from him. As their father he would always be there for them, but he wasn't at all sure they would need him. His acceptance of this came as a revelation. Not long ago his lack of control over the course of their lives had dismayed him, but now he almost welcomed the change.

At least we had that marvelous day together, he reassured himself. Before Nordco pushed the panic button. Before Isobel arrived.

As soon as the plane landed, Scott was driven directly to the Nordco world headquarters in Purchase. For the next two days, sequestered in conference rooms with accountants and department managers, he pored over inventories and tax records, spending endless, grueling hours trying to solve the complex problems created by a flawed government policy.

He was staying at a nearby hotel instead of going into the city. Hazel came up to help and brought the client files and a garment bag with two of his suits. By Sunday evening, Scott was drained of energy. In a few more hours, the job would be all but finished. The financial analysts would work all night, and by the next morning, the last day of the year, he would dictate the final report. With the year end requirements completed, a young assistant would fly down to Washington to deliver the documents by hand.

It was almost midnight when he returned to his hotel room. Bone weary, hopped up from countless cups of coffee, he felt exhausted but too taut to sleep. He picked up the telephone and dialed. It rang four times, then an answering machine clicked on and he heard her voice. "Hello. This is Solange Didier. I'm not able to take your call—"

"Hello," said the real Solange, and suddenly his weariness evaporated.

"It's Scott. I'm glad you're there."

"I walked in this minute," she said breathlessly. "Where are you?"

"In Rye, at the Hilton."

"In *Rye*," she wailed. "I just drove past on my way home from Connecticut. *Damn*. I thought you were supposed to be in Aspen."

"I am, I was—ahh, I'm too tired to explain. Had to come back to bail out a client. I've been working round the clock, I'd be absolutely no use to you tonight."

"I can always find a use for you," she purred.

He chuckled. "What are your plans for tomorrow night?"

"Nothing that can't be changed," she assured him.

"I have to finish up here tomorrow, but I'll come take you to dinner for New Year's Eve."

"No, no, I'll make dinner," she said quickly. "Just to see the New Year in together. That's an especially promising sign, don't you think?"

All the next day, she occupied a corner of his mind. Whenever he paused in his work he would think of her, savoring the sense of anticipation. It seemed forever since they had been together. During the time in Colorado, when there had been no possibility of seeing each other, he had been able to forget about her, but now that he would be with her in a few short hours, he was as impatient as a race horse.

Before leaving Nordco, he slipped into an empty office and called his house in Aspen, not really expecting anyone to be there. He was prepared to leave a message when Ginger answered. "I pulled a muscle in my calf," she explained. "No more skiing this week."

Immediately he began to worry, as he had when she was a little girl. "Are you sure it's not torn? Have you seen a doctor?"

"The paramedic at the first aid station examined me and he said it was just a strain. It was dumb. We were jumping moguls and I landed wrong."

"Maybe you should have an x-ray."

"I don't think so, Daddy. It's not that bad. I'm keeping it iced."

"Why are you alone?"

"Lindsay was here all day. She and Chip went to buy food because we're having a party tonight."

"That should be fun." He wondered why Isobel wasn't with Ginger. "Where's your mother?"

"Over at the Aspen Club, getting a massage. Cece Bedford is staying there."

"Cece's in Aspen?"

"Yes. There was room for her here, but I guess she likes her privacy. Lindsay moved in yesterday because the people she was visiting went home."

"I thought she was with her family."

"No." There was a forlorn quality to Ginger's voice. "Her parents are getting a divorce."

"Well, that does happen, pumpkin," he said kindly.

"I know, Daddy, but they've been married for *twenty-five* years. Lindsay is miserable. She was crying last night. I feel terrible for her."

While he showered and dressed in his hotel room, the conversation with Ginger lingered, causing a dull ache in his chest. *Lindsay is miserable . . . I feel terrible for her.* Scott sighed deeply. No matter what was happening between him and Isobel, he could never do that to his children.

A Nordco car was waiting in front of the hotel to drive him to the city. He told the driver to drop him at the Yale Club. After stopping at a wine shop to buy champagne, he took a taxi to Soho.

The door to the loft opened and he was clasped in Solange's eager embrace. Napoleon leapt up to lick his face, tail wagging and body aquiver with excitement. "I don't know when I've received such an enthusiastic welcome," laughed Scott, patting the ungainly beast and planting his front paws firmly on the floor.

"You look all in," said Solange sympathetically, smoothing his brow. "Come and sit down, dear man, and I'll bring you a glass of wine."

Outside her windows, the city sprawled, cold and wintry. Inside it was warm and softly lit, with the tantalizing aroma of spices and herbs in whatever epicurean delights she had prepared for them. He heard the heels of her mules clicking on the tile floor of the kitchen. She came in, carrying a tray with two frosted glasses and a bottle of white wine on ice. Setting it down, she disappeared briefly, returning with a platter of smoked salmon garnished with onions and capers.

"Now," she said, settling next to him, "tell me everything. What have you been doing?"

A Mozart string quartet played softly in the background. From the depths of a canine dream, Napoleon sighed. The tightness inside Scott began to ease. The cares of the past week faded away as he reclined on the deep-cushioned sofa, surrounded by her books and paintings and spare sculptures. There was the muted sound of traffic in the street below. Out there, the frantic tempo of metropolis went on, driven people going through the paces of a life he had thought important.

When had he changed? How long ago? They had known each other for less than three months, but time had no meaning. This was another world. This was the only place he wanted to be, where he belonged.

Solange leaned over to kiss him.

"Will dinner be ruined if there should be a slight diversion?" he asked.

"It is very patient, this meal." She smiled. "Come with me, my love."

Solange undressed him and pushed him back on her big, sprawling bed. She sat astride him, removing her clothes. In the darkened room, he put his hands on her breasts and saw her arch her back as she began to stroke him. The hot warmth spread from his belly, coiling down through his groin and thighs and upward to his chest like liquid tongues of fire. "Oh, Solange," he breathed, thrusting up into her. "Oh God, I've missed you . . ."

The duckling roasted in apricot and almond sauce, if perhaps a bit more crisp than called for, suffered no loss of flavor from the delay. The dessert of warm chocolate soufflé was perfection, followed by espresso in fragile Sèvres cups. They had finished dinner, and the bottle of Salon le Mesnil Blanc de Blancs that Scott had brought stood chilling in an ice bucket, to be opened at midnight.

"You're distracted," said Solange.

"Momentarily."

"You seemed worried. Tell me what's wrong."

"You're much too prescient," he sighed. "I was wondering what will happen to us."

"Why do you wonder tonight?"

"Perhaps because it's the beginning of a new year. Perhaps because I've been with my children this past week . . ." He took her hand. "You've become so important to me."

She looked away for a moment, then met his gaze squarely. "You are everything to me."

"What shall we do, Solange?"

She smiled sadly. "Nothing. Just continue to love each other, for as long as we are permitted." She stood up and began to clear away the coffee cups. "It's almost time to open the champagne," she said, looking at him through tear-bright eyes.

Scott pulled the cork and poured the foaming pale liquid, handing her a frosted crystal flute. "Happy New Year, darling."

She sipped the champagne and kissed his lips. "For me, there has always been something a little sad about New Year's Eve," she said. "I remember when I was young, wondering on this night what sorrows the coming year would bring."

The first weeks of a new year always seemed to Neil Shane like a good time to assess one's life. Other than his chronic worries about his son, the thought that he would never make History chair was uppermost in his mind this wintry January day. Aside from the limitations this placed on his salary, it was probably just as well for the department, he acknowledged regretfully as he waved a hasty farewell to the graduate student whose thesis proposal he had approved. Administration was not his forte. Neither was diplomacy. Two essentials for an academic who aspired to departmental leadership.

Leaving his office for the cleaning woman to lock up, Neil hurried through the hall to a side door and ran down the steps to the lot where his car was parked. He was on his way to the airport to meet Scott. Late as usual—a habit that came from a reluctance to say no. Rather than disappoint a friend or colleague by refusing the invitation to dinner, the bid to serve on a committee, the request to submit an article for a journal, he was constantly fending off frantic editors who threatened to go to press without his manuscript, rushing in just as his hostess, having given up on him, was serving the overdone leg of lamb, or sliding into place as the chairman brought the budget discussion for the symposium to a close.

An unfortunate penchant for overloading himself with commitments had been a stumbling block since prep school. "If only Neil would learn to concentrate on one or two activities instead of spreading himself thin, he might excel and have sufficient time to devote to his studies," a succession of advisors had commented on his term reports. Or words to that effect.

His inability to refuse a friend had eventually landed him in jail.

The summer after his sophomore year at Michigan, he was working as a political reporter on a suburban weekly, assigned to cover the student view of the Democratic convention, when he interviewed two seniors from Ann Arbor who were activist leaders of the antiwar movement. Later he realized they had used him, but who would ever have expected the Chicago police to come down like stormtroopers? He believed the war was immoral and when the protesters urged him to help get their message across . . . well, with all the TV cameras present, it was an irresistible temptation. And so he had joined them in what was to have been a peaceful demonstration. By the time his stepfather flew in from New York the next day to bail him out, he was vomiting and seeing double. He had collapsed in George's arms with a hairline fracture of the skull. Three months later, reclassified 1-A, he had headed across the border to Canada.

What you're doing will kill your mother . . .

You'd rather I went over there and murdered someone else's mother, is that it? Or maybe they'd kill me and that would satisfy everyone. . .

At the wheel of his Land Rover, he groaned aloud. No use raking over all that again. The wasted years, the shame. Not that he thought he should have gone to Vietnam. The war was *wrong*. But there had to have been another way. An honorable way. He had tried to explain it in his book, *A Burden of Guilt*—as much to himself as to others. In some measure he had succeeded, judging by the supportive letters he received, many of them from veterans. But there was the hate mail, too.

During the bleak years in Toronto, he had worked out his frustrations in the pursuit of knowledge, and by the age of twenty-seven had acquired a doctorate with distinction, a five-year-old son, and a failed marriage. After leaving Canada, he had led a rootless existence until Kit was restored to him. Eight years ago, when they settled in Iowa City, he had built them a home and Kit had been the central focus in his life ever since.

Neil was regarded as an iconoclast and somewhat of an enigma even by his friends. Well liked and respected by the university faculty, he had gained a following among the students, who flocked to his lectures on the Vietnam War. Of medium height and build, he had the muscular leanness of a youthful athlete, although his longish brown hair and neatly trimmed beard were now lightly sprinkled with gray. A reflective man, with a slow, warming smile, his appearance only added to the mystique and held enormous appeal for women.

He drove carefully. There had been a heavy snowfall the night before and the roads were treacherous. The flight from Chicago was due at five-fifteen, and he parked in the airport lot, reaching the terminal building just in time to see his brother stride through the gate, carrying an attaché case and a carry-on, with a suit bag slung over one shoulder. Scott looked terrific, he thought, tall and masculine in a handsome shearling coat and leather boots. All he needed to complete the image were the Western hat and the cigarette.

The brothers embraced. "Great to see you, Neil."

"I never thought you would make it to Iowa City," grinned Neil, taking the carry-on.

"It's not exactly on the beaten track, is it?" The bitter air hit them as they left the terminal. "Christ, it's cold!"

"This is nothing. You get used to it after a while."

The Land Rover crunched along snowy, sanded roads, passing through town and crossing over the Iowa River to a wooded bluff not far from the university. Parking in the garage attached to his rustic ranch-style house, Neil led the way in through a back entry and hung their coats in a hall closet.

"This is yours," he said, opening the door to Kit's room. "Why don't you take off your jacket and tie and get into something comfortable. I'll fix us a drink."

When Scott came into the oak-floored country kitchen, he was wearing a navy plaid flannel shirt and a gray cardigan sweater. "Smells great," he said, sniffing the scent of garlic, herbs, and wine.

Neil's kitchen was the heart of the house. Open cupboards were filled with colorful pottery platters and bowls. From an overhead rack hung an assortment of copper pots and saucepans, and a marble counter adjacent to the Garland range was laden with professional equipment, including a food processor, coffee grinder, and an enormous stainless steel mixer. At the far end of the room, facing a well-used brick fireplace, were comfortable couches and chairs and a long maple-block table for dining. "It looks like a photograph out of *Gourmet* magazine," said Scott as he watched his brother sprinkle chopped parsley over the top of a casserole and place it in the oven.

Neil smiled self-consciously. "Cooking's sort of a hobby with me." He plunked ice cubes into oversized old-fashioned glasses. "Glenlivet on the rocks all right?"

"Yes, that's fine," said Scott, settling on a sofa facing the fire. An appetizing assortment of cheeses was arranged on a board on the low table in front of him.

"Try this," said Neil. "It's a goat cheddar called Capricorn. Made here in Iowa." He cut a generous slice of the firm white cheese and laid it on a croustade.

"Umm, nice," said Scott. "So is the bread. You must have a first-rate bakery in town."

"I bake my own. There's nothing but spongy white cotton out here."

"You really are a serious cook. I had no idea."

"I guess we don't know each other all that well, do we?"

Scott gave a half-smile and sipped his drink, glancing around at the paneled walls and beamed ceiling. "This must be your favorite room."

Neil nodded. "I spend a lot of time in here when I'm not working."

"You live alone?"

"I do now. There was a woman, but that's over."

"I'm sorry."

"Don't be. She wasn't the first, and I imagine she won't be the last. It just wasn't right."

"How did you know?"

Neil gave him a lopsided smile. "I've had some experience with a bad marriage, if you recall."

Scott grunted. "That was rather insensitive of me." He focused his attention on his drink, swirling the liquid. "I just meant . . . with a new woman, how do you know if it will last?"

"You've been married for so long, I should think you could tell me how it works."

"Isobel and I . . . we were young when we met. I'm not sure we thought beyond the initial attraction. We each represented what the other was expected to marry."

Neil frowned. "But you *are* happy?"

"Oh . . ." Scott shrugged, "of course."

Dinner was a hearty beef bourguignon accompanied by a

full-bodied burgundy wine, a fresh loaf of homemade sour-dough bread, a green salad with tomato and basil, and finally an open-faced apple pie. "Man, that was good," groaned Scott, as they left the table. "If Isobel knew what I just ate, she'd put me on lemon juice and water for the next week."

Neil laughed. "Nouvelle cuisine hasn't quite made it to Iowa."

Over coffee and brandy, they sat again in front of the fire. They wondered aloud when the first shots would be fired in the Persian Gulf. Neil brought out some of the letters he had received about his book, and for the first time they talked about Vietnam and the years he had spent in Canada. Which led to reminiscing about the days of their youth, the winters in the New York apartment and the long, lazy summers and holiday weekends in Norwalk.

"That house was like a mausoleum after you went away to school," said Neil. "When you came home the first summer, we were almost like strangers . . ."

"Andover was a great change for me. I loved it, but I'm not sure I like what it did to me."

Neil did not comment. "Do you remember the time you went sailing and got becalmed out on the Sound?"

"I haven't thought about that in years," said Scott. "George called the Coast Guard."

"Right. You and Perk went out with two girls, it got really late, and you weren't back. I had never seen Aunt Betsy so upset or furious, and I thought Uncle Ed would have a heart attack."

"As I recall, there wasn't enough gas in the outboard. We sailed out too far and the wind died."

"I was pissed at you that day, because you refused to take me along. Then I felt guilty when I thought you'd drowned."

Scott laughed, remembering. "I really caught hell for that."

"Yeah. One of the few times you got grounded. It was always me they were punishing."

"Ah, come on."

"It's true. I'm not saying I didn't deserve it. I was a trouble-some little bastard and you were always doing the right thing."

"You make me sound like a real prick."

Neil laughed. "You were, kind of. But I always envied you in a way, wished I could be more like you."

Scott stared at him, remembering Chip's very similar words in Aspen. "Why would you?"

"Everything seemed easy for you. I was always struggling with my demons, and I thought no one gave a damn about me."

"I never realized . . ."

"Well, it's not something you talk about when you're a kid." He poured more coffee.

"I won't sleep tonight," Scott protested.

"Don't worry, it's decaffeinated," Neil assured him, sitting down again. "If anyone ever needed a mentor, it was me. When I was at Michigan and got caught up in the antiwar movement, I wanted so much to confide in you. I came back East early for your wedding, but soon realized it wasn't the right time. Then . . . Chicago." He made a fist and hit the palm of his hand. "I was rotten to George. And to Mom."

"It was a long time ago, Neil," Scott said softly. "Forget about it. They did."

"I know, but I wish I could take back some of what I said."

"We all say things in anger."

"It seems a lame excuse," said Neil. He stared into the fire, sadness etching his face. With a sigh of resignation, he stood up. "Well, we should turn in, it's getting late. Classes don't begin until next week, but I have a couple of conferences with grad students in the morning." Carrying the tray to the sink, he rinsed the cups and brandy glasses. "Help yourself to breakfast. I leave early to work out. You're welcome to join me if you like."

"No, I don't think so. If you'll show me where the files are kept, I'll get to work first thing."

"Everything's downstairs." Neil led the way to a recreation room, little used since Kit had left for college. Eight cardboard file boxes had been placed side by side on top of a ping-pong table, while eight more were neatly stacked along one wall. "They're arranged more or less chronologically. These cartons contain files and journals from the thirties. This is the folder I called you about; I put it aside. I've flagged everything I found pertaining to *One Night in Venice* with red stickers. The worksheets have blue stickers and . . ." Neil opened a library log. "This is a record of what I've catalogued so far."

Scott flipped through the notebook. "You've done an incredible job. This should be very helpful. It'll probably take more than two or three days to go through all of this, but at least I can get a start."

"You really believe this stuff is worth something?"

"I'm certain of it. A letter, a worksheet, or an original score could bring quite a decent sum at auction."

"How much?"

"Well, I'm no expert, but a friend of mine collects art and rare books. He told me an offering of music notebooks signed by George Gershwin went for a hundred and ten last year."

"Thousand?" Scott nodded and Neil whistled. "But, that was Gershwin. Michael Shane isn't as well known."

"At one time he was, and he may be again, after the seventy-fifth birthday salute next year."

"I had hoped my book would be out by then, but there's not a chance."

"How near finished are you?"

"It'll take more than a year to complete the manuscript. It's an expensive production, with photographs and plates. They'd never get it out in time. Too bad. Publishers always go for a tie-in with a special event."

"There may be another opportunity. I've been told an investment group is planning a revival of *One Night*."

"I see," Neil said slowly. "So that's why you're interested in the copyright."

Scott always slept poorly the first night in a strange bed. He heard Neil moving around early in the morning and hurried out to the kitchen in time to say goodbye. After showering and dressing in jeans and a sweater, he pulled on a pair of boots and went for a walk. The frigid morning air was still and hushed. It had snowed a little during the night and a few lazy flakes still came drifting down. Back in the house, he poured himself a cup of coffee and heated a cinnamon bun. Then, with no further excuse for procrastination, he went downstairs to attack the first of the file boxes.

Accustomed to reading intricate legal treatises, he had developed the knack of scanning documents quickly. By eleven o'clock he had covered the papers from 1937 through 1939. There was no sign of either an original score or a published copy of his father's first musical comedy. Although he was curious about Michael's journals and gave them a hasty examination, he put them aside for later and began to leaf through the correspondence files stacked against the wall. Some of the papers were crumbling with age, triggering his old dust allergy. By noontime he was sneezing, his eyes watery and itching, which sent him to his room in search of an antihistamine tablet. While rummaging through his toiletry kit, he heard his brother at the back entrance.

"It's starting to come down out there," said Neil, stamping snow off his feet and throwing a load of logs in a bin. "We don't usually get a lot of snow, but according to the weather report we're in for a blizzard. When were you planning to leave?"

"Day after tomorrow. I have to be in New York Friday night."

"It should be all right by then, if they get the roads plowed. The forecast is for six inches."

"If only you had a mountain around, you could ski."

"We sometimes go cross-country on the golf course," said Neil. "How'd you make out this morning?"

"Quite a pile there. It will take a professional appraiser to catalogue it properly. Some of the journals contain sketches, like music notebooks, and might be of interest to collectors. I haven't yet come across a score of *One Night in Venice*."

"So what does that mean?"

"Nothing, really." Scott shrugged philosophically. "It's probably in the public domain, anyway. I don't believe in fairy tales."

"Well, don't give up. I'll lend you a hand this afternoon."

They went for a walk after lunch. The wind was high, driving the snow into their faces, and they soon turned back. All afternoon they worked, dividing the file boxes between them. Scott went through the letters and memos rapidly, but Neil read more carefully, labeling folders and making notes as he went along. "Sorry to be so slow," he apologized, when he noticed Scott glancing over at him. "I might as well save myself double work later on."

"That's all right. I probably should be doing the same thing, but I thought I'd try to cover as much as possible in the short time I have."

By the next afternoon they had made a cursory examination of the contents of all but two boxes. It was growing dark outside the high, narrow basement windows when Neil suddenly exclaimed, "Hey, look at this."

"Wait a minute," said Scott absentmindedly, continuing to read. "This is fascinating stuff. Gerry Ross is telling Michael that his vanity is getting in the way of his judgment and he has to stop trying to direct his own shows."

"Scott," said Neil impatiently, holding up a sheet of paper, "read this letter."

Scott slipped the Ross memo into the file and reached for the document Neil handed him. Addressed to Lt. Michael Shane, it was typed on the letterhead of Winston & Rhinehart, Attorneys at Law, and signed by Jacob Winston:

March 10, 1943

Dear Michael,

I hope this letter finds you well. When George went overseas, he turned your files over to me. In his absence, I will be looking after your interests.

The contract for the new musical play titled *Kick Up Your Heels* has been finalized and was co-signed on your behalf by your wife and Edwin Hopper. If you would like a copy of the contract, please advise me and I will have one mailed to you. Mr. Hopper thought it was not necessary, since you and he had thoroughly discussed the terms of any agreement before you shipped out.

We have heard from Zachary Mitchell about the work entitled *One Night in Venice*. He advises us that he has no plans for publication or recording in whole or in part. However, he would like to retain first option on any theatrical production of the work for a period of ten years . . .

Scott quickly scanned the rest of the letter. "That's all it says. This sounds like Zachary Mitchell gave up the right to publish but retained entertainment rights."

"For ten years."

"Correct."

"Then the investment group that bought Mitchell Publishing would not own *One Night in Venice?*"

"Probably not, but they can still put on a production without paying us royalties, unless we can prove that Michael's estate owns it. If there was a copyright when that letter was written, it would have expired by now—unless it was renewed." Scott placed the letter in a folder. "I wonder why Mitchell had no interest in publishing the music."

"I don't think the show was very commercial," said Neil. "It was rather avant garde for the time. The songs weren't especially melodic, and that's what people liked back then."

"I just wish we could find something more on it . . . a letter between Michael and Mitchell, even a marginal note. With all the parties deceased, it's impossible to establish anything definite without proof."

Scott went back to work, while Neil seemed to be lost in thought. "Scotty . . ."

"Hmm?"

"Jack Winston isn't dead."

The flight was late taking off from Cedar Rapids-Iowa City, and Scott almost missed his connection in Chicago. He reached the gate just as the ground crew was closing up. At his insistence they let him board, but they had given away his first-class seat, and rather than raise a fuss he was stuck in the back between two passengers. The plane had to be de-iced twice while they sat on the runway waiting to take off, and he was reminded of why O'Hare was his least favorite American airport.

Eager to speak to Jack Winston, he had called the offices of Winston & Rhinehart yesterday to make an appointment with his stepfather's partner, only to learn that the Winstons were in the Orient on an extended cruise. He would have to be patient until their return.

The archives had given him the opportunity to spend time with Neil again, after all the years of hasty meetings. If they had not been brothers, and if there hadn't been a history between them, he thought he might have been drawn to him as a friend, for Neil was good company—humorous, smart, a straight-shooter, and a natural sportsman. Last night they had talked into the early morning hours and Scott was now unable to shake the memories their conversation had dredged up.

The mind of a six-year-old sometimes compensates for pain

by blotting out a particular event. But although the details were hazy, Scott had never quite forgotten the dreadful day when Neil was born. The terror was indelibly imprinted on him.

They had been living in Gramercy by then, in a large apartment near Aunt Betsy and Uncle Ed Hopper. Scott spent most days playing with their son, his cousin Perk, yet despite the closeness of family, he remembered being a lonely little boy.

Fascinated by his father's work, he was never allowed into the studio alone—neither the room at home where Michael sometimes composed, nor the suite in Greenwich Village that he preferred. On this particular morning, Julia had gone out and their housekeeper was busy. Scott had stolen into the big sunny front room to play the piano. He picked out tunes with one hand but soon tired of that, and climbed onto a chair next to the massive composing desk where stacks of music papers—their staffs partially filled with the cryptic hieroglyphs of notation—were neatly aligned, just as his father had left them. Reaching for a tuning fork, Scott knocked over an ink bottle. As he watched in helpless dismay, the black liquid splashed across the composition sheets and dripped onto the oriental carpet . . .

His most terrifying memory: being locked in a closet, paralyzed with fear of the dark, choking from sobs and dust and camphor. His father's loud voice, shouting at his mother, and Julia crying, "He's only a *child!*"

Peeking through a crack in the door, he had seen them struggling. Michael, in the wheelchair, seemed to be twisting Julia's arms, hurting her. Her face contorted in pain as she doubled over. Scott heard a sharp cry . . . he could no longer see them. Hoarse from weeping, he had fallen asleep and awakened hours later, still trapped in the dark, airless closet.

Soon after, his mother appeared with a baby in her arms. His new baby brother. When Neil was four months old, their father had been taken to the hospital where the doctors attempted to remove the deadly growth from his brain. He never came home again . . .

They were about to land in New York. Shaking off the melancholy mood brought on by his memories, Scott stretched his legs in the cramped space on the airplane.

Enriqué was at the gate to meet him and handed him an envelope from Hazel. Amongst the mail and messages, there

was a memo from Dick Graham: *Hope you had a good trip.
It's taking more time than I thought to get the background on
your brother-in-law's Rancho American deal. Everyone in the
world was gone over the holidays, but I'm on the case, and we
should have some answers soon. See you on Monday.*

Whenever he thought about Burton McKiever and the threat
he posed, Scott had a sense of dread. More than once he had
awakened at night in a cold sweat. Dick had urged him to
be patient, but it was difficult to sit back without taking
action when his good name was in jeopardy. He knew that
a lawyer could be ruined by nothing more than circumstantial
evidence.

When he reached home, Isobel was on the telephone in the
study. She waved an indifferent greeting. In a week, she would
be leaving for Europe—a long trip this time, her longest yet.
To acquire paintings for the gallery, which would have its
grand opening in March. An uneasiness still lay between them.
Clearly they were trying to avoid a confrontation.

The time had passed quickly. Isobel was expected to return
from Europe tomorrow.

She had flown to Paris with Cece on the very eve of the
Gulf War. As he'd watched the surrealistic spectacle on television of Scud missiles lancing the skies over Riyadh and
Jerusalem, Scott had worried that Americans abroad might be
threatened by terrorists. But Isobel called to assure him that
it was business as usual in Germany and Italy, as well as in
France.

During his wife's absence, Scott had virtually moved in with
Solange.

They were lying in bed after making love. Solange rested
her head against his shoulder and his arms were around her.
The soft lamplight cast shadows across the wall. He was very
still, staring at the ceiling, his eyelids blinking rapidly.

Suddenly Solange spoke. "This is the last time, isn't it?"

She caught him by surprise. "I . . . I don't know . . . I can't
think."

"It is. I can feel that it is."

His arms tightened around her. "I wish there were a way
we could be together always. I've considered divorce . . . but
I love my children. I care enough for Isobel to feel a . . . a

loyalty, a responsibility." He sighed deeply. "I wish we had met in a different time, a different place."

She raised herself on one elbow and looked at him. "You think I don't understand, but you're wrong. I know you love me. But sometimes love isn't enough."

"It should be."

"But it isn't."

He closed his eyes in despair. "I can't bear the thought of not seeing you. I wish it didn't have to be this way."

"Wishing will not change anything," she said practically. "Now we shall make love one last time and then you will leave. We shall not see each other again. You will not call. And if we should meet by chance, you must promise not to speak to me."

"How can I promise such a thing?"

"Because you love me."

❧ Chapter 15 ❧

Jergen

Richard Graham unbuttoned the jacket of his three-piece suit and seated himself in an armchair in the corner of the office. "You look like hell," he said, regarding Scott with affectionate concern.

"Thanks, you're a real pal." Scott rubbed his eyes, which felt gritty and were ringed with dark circles. "I have to leave for Tokyo tomorrow."

"Why don't you spend a few days in Hawaii on the return trip. A little R&R would do you good."

"Well, actually, I was thinking I might stop in California to see my sister and try to resolve this matter." He gestured toward the documents lying on the table between them.

"Don't push yourself, Scott. We're not getting any younger, as my mother would say."

"You needn't remind me."

It was the end of a bleak and interminable week. Scott had been pushing himself to the point of exhaustion, working long hours at the office, returning home in time to fall into bed. And still he was having trouble sleeping. All the joyful sense of anticipation had left him since he and Solange had parted. He was glad to be going to Japan. He hoped a change of scene would help him to forget her. However, before he departed, there was the issue of Burton McKiever's charges to deal with, and the potential conflict of interest with Rancho American Resorts, a matter that had been on the back burner since before Christmas.

"You've heard nothing further from Mr. McKiever?" asked Graham.

"Not a word. I didn't really expect to. Hazel's been combing the newspapers in case he planted an article, but nothing has turned up so far."

"Here's what I've got," said his colleague, opening a folder. "The company that initiated the contact with your brother-in-law is a consulting firm called the Sunbelt Group, based in Dallas."

"Never heard of them."

"It's an aggressive outfit; they do some lobbying for the hotel industry. The most interesting fact I've uncovered is that one of the partners is Burt McKiever's sidekick, Tom Peck."

Scott took the blue-covered report Graham handed to him and began leafing through it. "Tom Peck," he mused. "Haven't I heard that name? There was something unsavory about him."

"Right. He made a run for Congress several years back, but lost in the primary. It was a dirty campaign; they were accused of circulating rumors about his opponent's sexual orientation."

"Yes, I remember now." It did not surprise him that McKiever would be linked to an unscrupulous politician.

"At any rate," Dick continued, "Peck seems to have lived that down. His firm was hired by Rancho American to come up with an image-enhancing marketing plan. They decided on a theme of physical fitness and conducted a survey of existing health resorts, with an idea of buying one out. It narrowed down to four of the most popular spas in the West and Jergen Ahlgren's came out on top."

"Where does Burton McKiever fit in? I don't believe in coincidences, Dick."

"Neither do I, but that's harder to pin down. He bought his Rancho American shares before the deal, probably on the basis of a tip from Peck. He contacted you after the contract was signed. Somehow he got a line on Jergen's relationship to you and your position as counsel to the Cartwright Foundation. My guess is he put two and two together and came up with nepotism, because that's the way he would operate. What his motive is in trying to blackmail you is another question.

"To get hold of a large block of Rancho American stock, I would think. It's closely held and not usually available on the open market."

Dick shook his head. "Burt McKiever doesn't have the money for that. He owns a few thousand shares in a numbered account."

Scott looked at him sharply. "If it's numbered, how did you find out the account was his?"

"Better you don't know," laughed Graham. "McKiever is most likely a front for his clients. It's well known that the president and founder of Rancho American, Charles Bronstein, has an aversion to doing business with Arabs."

Scott scrutinized his friend with exaggerated disbelief. "You missed your calling, Graham-cracker. You should've been a private eye."

Dick grinned. "It's never too late."

"So where does this leave me?"

"You're clean, Rhino. I advise you to spell it all out in a confidential memo to Enno Ehrlander and the board. Of course, these things never remain secret, but the story can't do you any harm if it circulates."

"What about my serving on the investment committee?" asked Scott.

"Because of your brother-in-law's connection with Rancho American, as long as the shares are held by the foundation, you would be wise not to involve yourself in any decisions on divestiture. But there has clearly been no conflict of interest up to now."

"Good." He breathed a sigh of relief. "I'm glad that's settled."

"By the way," said Dick, "I wouldn't be surprised if Bronstein makes an offer to buy back the Cartwright Foundation's shares."

"Is that so? Mind telling me why?"

"He seems to have gotten wind of the fact that a certain group of investors is planning a raid on his hotels. He doesn't take kindly to the Saudis moving in on his territory."

Scott raised an eyebrow. "You wouldn't possibly have anything to do with that bit of information reaching his ears?"

Graham put on a face of offended innocence. "I'm surprised at you, Scott. Just because my cousin Stanley happens to play golf with Charley Bronstein?"

The foreshortened flight over the pole to Tokyo gave Scott a false sense of the enormous distance traveled. Resetting his watch in his room at the Imperial Hotel, he realized it was the fourteenth of February in the States. Thirty-nine years ago today Julia had married George Rhinehart. It would be a lonely day for her, this first anniversary without her husband. The last thing he did before going to sleep was to cable his mother a dozen roses.

After twenty-four hours in his hotel suite Scott was caught up on jet lag and as prepared as he would ever be for the grueling week of conferences with the officials of the Japanese multinational that was seeking his advice in striking a tax accord with the IRS. Each night a different set of executives would take him to dinner, plying him until midnight with enormous platters of sashimi and lethal amounts of sake, so that by week's end he was wasted while his clients remained fresh and vigorous. Remembering Dick Graham's suggestion, he seriously considered a few days at a small, exclusive resort he knew on the island of Kauai. It was an appealing prospect. Complete privacy, no telephones or fax machines—just snorkeling and tennis and unwinding in a palm-thatched hut while smiling Polynesian maidens served long, cool fruit drinks on the beach. But the thought of being alone with the endless skies, vast blue ocean, and balmy, perfumed nights of Hawaii caused an ache in his heart. There was only one person he longed to share it with, and she would never be with him again.

He placed a call to his sister and made arrangements to pay a long-overdue visit to Debbie and Jergen.

Deborah had felt a thrill of excitement in the second week of January when the workmen at last hoisted the green and gilt sign above the scaffolding on the row of cannery shops. The carved letters settled in place, glittering in the noonday sun: *Treasures of the Sierra Nevada*.

"This calls for a toast," announced Tara, appearing at the door of the shop in a voluminous canvas apron with the Treasures logo printed across the front. With her usual abandon,

Tara had ordered twelve dozen of them in assorted colors, as well as coordinated kitchen towels and barbecue mitts to feature with the glazed terracotta dinnerware they had commissioned from the Morales family.

Deborah joined her partner, who had set out a bottle of chardonnay and wine goblets of sea-green Mexican glass on one of the newly installed display platforms. After pricing slatted crates from design studios, they had enlisted a local carpenter to create their own store fixtures at a fraction of the cost.

"To us," Tara toasted, "still a duo."

"To a long and successful partnership," echoed Deborah, clinking glasses.

With satisfaction she surveyed the colorful wares that lined each wall, representing weeks spent trekking through the hills and valleys of California and the Southwest to track down merchandise. Hand-loomed rugs and blankets, beaded and embroidered jackets that could be paired with denim or chiffon, gauzy Mexican dresses with lace insets in the vivid hues of a tropical garden . . . baskets of every imaginable size and shape, wrought iron candelabra, fireplace tools, trivets . . . Everything had been handmade of natural materials by native craftspeople. With no wholesalers involved, prices could be kept low enough to attract trade while ensuring a fair profit for the skilled artisans, as well as the shopkeepers.

"We'll have calls for *thousands* of these," exclaimed Tara, indicating her favorite hand-thrown dinnerware with its luminous doublebaked glazes, beautiful and sturdy enough to go from oven to table. "Every bride in Southern California is going to want a set."

"They couldn't possibly fill that many orders," Deborah answered, concern wrinkling her brow. "The factory isn't a mass production outfit. I don't think we should contract for any deliveries we can't guarantee within ten weeks."

"You're right, as usual," Tara acknowledged with a wry grin. "You'll have to keep reminding me we're not Bloomingdale's West."

From the day of its opening, the shop had done a brisk business. The two women had devised a division of labor, with Tara taking the primary responsibility for balancing the books and keeping inventory records, while Deborah was in charge of displays and advertising as well as direct contact with the craftspeople. They had hired part-time sales help for weekends, but both worked behind the counter, believing they would learn more by meeting and talking to their customers.

Balancing the demands of marriage, children, and household with entrepreneurship, Deborah soon discovered, required the skills of a juggler. She was always rushing from home to store or school, wedging in Richie's play group or Wendy's appointment with the orthodontist while setting up a new window display at Treasures, with never enough time to spare for the house. Jergen, consumed with the opening of the first of the Rancho American spas, was no help at all, for he was hardly ever at home, even in the evenings.

When Scott called from Tokyo, little more than a month after the grand opening of Treasures, to say that he would be arriving in Monterey in three days, she experienced a moment of complete panic. *It's too soon*, she thought. She wanted everything to be under control when her brother paid them the first visit. "Wonderful," she answered, "I can't wait to see you." All the while picturing her suave, cosmopolitan brother in the half-furnished house and the turmoil of their frenetic life.

"I've booked a room at the Carmel Inn," he told her.

"Nonsense, you'll stay with us," she said automatically. Suicidally.

"Uhh . . . we'll see."

Partly elated and partly terrified, she spent the next two evenings pulling the house together, borrowing rugs and pillows and pottery and wall hangings from the store to give the rooms a more inhabited look. "What is all this fuss about?" her husband finally inquired, when he became aware of the frenzy of activity.

"Oh, Jergen," she confessed, worn out from what seemed a hopeless effort, "it's going to be a disaster. You know what a fussbudget Scott is. You've seen their apartment—it's Mark Hampton heaven. Can you picture him staying here in the midst of chaos?"

Jergen was very understanding. He tucked her in bed and brought her a cup of herbal tea, massaging her neck and shoulders to soothe her jangled nerves. He smoothed back the hair from her forehead and said, "What would you think if we put him up at The Well?"

"The Well?" She looked at him dubiously. "Scott's not exactly into holistic healing . . ."

He laughed. "We're not freaks, after all. Nor are we a killer spa like the Ashram. He'll have peace, quiet, privacy, and the run of the place. We'll bring him here in the evenings, and I'll even promise to come home for dinner every night. How's that?"

"Fantastic, if you really mean it."

"Trust me, my darling." He turned her face to his and slowly began to make love to her, and she was reminded of why she had been willing to throw over an enviable life to brave the uncertain future with this remarkable man.

"Welcome to Monterey, Mr. Rhinehart. I'm Dennis. I hope you had a good flight."

Blond and blue-eyed, he was disgustingly healthy-looking, exuding fitness and the spiritual well-being that Deborah was always nattering about. In the blue and yellow aviator's jacket with The Well's logo emblazoned on its chest, Dennis looked like a testimonial to clean living, making Scott feel even more dissipated and played-out.

Sixteen hours aloft in the stale air of the United 747 had been the coup de grace after a week of late nights and painfully polite marathon meetings. All he wanted was to crawl into bed at the Carmel Inn and sleep for twenty-four hours, but Jergen insisted he had to stay at the damned healing center, as they called it . . . Just what he needed. A screwy, New Age Canyon Ranch, without the worldclass chef. He had visions of sleeping dormitory-style on rope cots, surrounded by bearded yogis and subsisting on raisins, pine nuts, and carrot shavings. But he was stuck. If he refused, his sister's husband would take it as a personal affront.

Dennis escorted him to a sky-blue station wagon. *The Well of Being, J. Ahlgren, Director* appeared in discreet buttercup yellow lettering on the door. A small replica of the blue and yellow Swedish flag was painted underneath.

"Debbie said to tell you she'll see you tonight for dinner," Dennis informed him after stowing Scott's luggage in the rear and taking a seat behind the wheel. "She couldn't come to the airport because she had to work at the store today."

"Thanks," said Scott. *Work at the store?* Had Deborah been forced to take a job? Jergen's business must not be doing as well as Dick Graham had led him to believe.

He nodded off on the ten-mile drive from the airport, awakening when the car came to a gravel road that wound up wooded hills crisscrossed by hiking trails. They turned into a circular driveway in front of a sprawling buff-colored Mission-style building with a pink tile roof.

Another amazing physical specimen with great biceps, wearing a blue knit shirt and yellow shorts, came hurrying out to greet him. "Welcome to The Well, Mr. Rhinehart. I'm Randy." With a dazzling smile, he hoisted Scott's heavy suitcase as if it were filled with cotton balls, grabbed the two smaller bags with one hand, and led the way into a lounge that was simply but comfortably furnished in the now-familiar colors of the Swedish flag.

Scott wandered over to a big picture window from which he observed he was in the center section of three connected wings. Surrounded by lawns and gardens, the building nestled around a swimming pool where half a dozen people were playing water volleyball. Other men and women, presumably guests, clad in The Well's shorts or jogging suits, were seen entering or leaving smaller buildings that lay half hidden among a grove of trees. On a lower terrace were the tennis courts and a second lap pool with six lanes for serious swimmers.

"Not bad," Scott said to himself. "No wonder Debbie needed all that money."

"Scott." He turned to see a handsome, well-groomed man with crisp russet hair and neatly trimmed beard walking toward him. He scarcely recognized Deborah's husband.

"Jergen," he said levelly.

"Welcome. Forgive me for not being here to greet you, but I was in a meeting." They shook hands, Jergen rather more effusively than Scott. "How was the trip? You must be tired."

"I admit to that," answered Scott. "It's been a rough week."

"Come, I'll show you to your room. We'll give you a bit of lunch and then allow you to sleep it off."

The room was unexpectedly commodious, allaying his fears of a spartan few days. It had every amenity—king-size bed, large marble bathroom with Jacuzzi, and private patio.

"It's quite a place, Jergen." Scott could not manage to keep the irony out of his voice.

"When you're over your jet lag, I'll show you around," his brother-in-law said in a cordial tone.

There was a knock at the door. A sturdy, golden-skinned girl in blue and yellow sweats entered, bearing a tray with a large bowl of salad, thin wheat bread, fresh fruit, goat cheese, and a bottle of Evian water. "Set it outside on the table, Astrid," said Jergen. "Lunch is usually vegetarian, Scott, but if you'd prefer cold chicken or shrimp salad, I can order it."

"No, this looks great. I had way too much food in Tokyo. These business trips are eating and drinking orgies."

They sat on the patio while he sampled crisp crudités dipped in a tasty tofu dressing. "The Well grows its own vegetables and herbs," Jergen explained when Scott remarked on their freshness. "I own fifty acres and, in addition, have the use of the adjacent land for our hikes. It goes all the way down to the sea."

"It's a magnificent piece of property."

Jergen nodded in agreement. "This building was the main house of a large estate."

"How were you able to get hold of it?"

"Karma," said Jergen, and Scott inwardly winced. "I went to an auction intending to bid on a small farm and happened to meet the woman who owned this land. Her father had left everything to her, but the only way to sell such a large piece of real estate was to break it up into small parcels. She's an environmentalist who couldn't bear to see the property developed. Since she had read my book and believes in my method"—Jergen drew in his breath sharply in the characteristic Swedish way—"I got it for a very good price."

"Lucky for you." *The least you could do is say "we," considering you bought the damn place with my sister's dough*, he thought. "I guess you're not too busy this time of year."

"We're *always* full," Jergen replied. "We have eighteen suites with a maximum capacity of thirty guests and there's a six-month waiting list."

"How does this room happen to be free?"

"We usually set aside accommodations for special guests. We have to, with our clientele." He smiled thinly. "We try not to cater. Everyone is treated the same at The Well. We use first names and no one is supposed to talk shop—but it's inevitable that a film star or studio head will call and insist on coming. If we turn away someone like that, it could hurt our business."

Scott glanced at a printed card of The Well's amenities. *Cuisine fraîche by master spa-chef, Sven Brule* . . . "So you are . . . uh, you're making a success of it."

"Yes," said Jergen, "I am satisfied with what I have thus far accomplished."

Scott waited for him to go on, perhaps to mention the Rancho American deal, but Jergen remained silent.

"It seems rather quiet. Where is everyone?"

"Taking part in the program . . . hiking, working out at exercise or yoga classes, or having various therapies. Part of the routine is the quiet. Most of our guests are stressed when they arrive. The last thing they want or need is the stimulation of noise or competitive activities."

"I see."

"By the way, I bring regards from Perk and Del Hopper. They spent last weekend with us. Perk would have come back to see you, but they left for Paris on Monday."

"Too bad," said Scott. "I would have liked to get together with them, it's been a long time." He rubbed his eyes. "I'm really bushed. I'd better catch up on my sleep."

"Deborah will be terribly disappointed if she doesn't see you this evening. Shall I have you woken for dinner?"

"Please do." He stood up and stretched. "I think I'll try the Jacuzzi. My muscles are in knots."

Jergen brightened considerably. "May I suggest a therapeutic massage? They're most restorative." When Scott offered no objections, he said, "I'll send our therapist to your room. Shall we say in twenty minutes, after you've had a bath?"

When Scott accompanied Jergen home that evening, it was with a complete change of outlook. After a massage that could only be described as sybaritic, he had fallen into a long restful sleep, waking to feel rejuvenated and ready to tackle the world.

The Well was really an amazing place. He appreciated good management, and Jergen's spa or healing center or whatever he wanted to call it was as beautifully organized as any resort he had ever seen. Yet another hale, well-conditioned member of the staff had knocked on his door at five o'clock and conducted him on a brief tour of the treatment rooms. Twenty minutes in the sauna, followed by a plunge in the lap pool, had cleared Scott's head of sleep before dressing for the ten-mile drive to his sister's home. So carried away with enthusiasm was he that at Jergen's suggestion he agreed to attend the sunrise yoga class the following morning.

Scott could understand why Deborah had been intent on buying the house. It was smashing, with the view of the valley all that she had described. He was amused at the profusion of pillows and throw rugs of native design—a riot of color, suited perfectly to Debbie and her outrageous taste. The effect was rather pleasing, actually. Solange would adore it . . . *Solange*.

"It's so *marvelous* to see you, Scotty, it's been ages," Deborah greeted him exuberantly, throwing her arms around him and kissing the side of his mouth. She had always been the most demonstrative member of the family, and it warmed him to know that the harsh words between them had been forgiven. "What do you think of your niece and nephew? Come kiss Uncle Scott, kids."

After dinner—fresh corn, asparagus, and grilled tuna steaks that Jergen cooked on the outdoor barbecue, which wiped out two of Scott's misconceptions: that his sister's husband was a total vegetarian and a male chauvinist—the children grew sleepy and wandered off to bed, with no one paying them much attention.

Jergen lit a fire and took out a bottle of brandy. "Whenever you're tired, Scott, I'll take you back to your room."

"Thanks. I feel great."

Deborah returned from kissing Wendy and Richie good night and settled on the sofa next to him. "Has Jergen told you about the new spas?"

"No, Debbie, I haven't had a chance." Jergen jumped on it quickly, before Scott could reply. He cleared his throat. "I've—ah, I've signed a franchise agreement with a chain of resort hotels. We'll be opening three new health centers in the next several months."

Scott hesitated, but he decided to be open. "Actually, Jergen, I had heard something about that."

"But that's impossible, it hasn't been announced yet!" Jergen looked chagrined that Scott had known about his surprise, casting a questioning glance at his wife.

"I'm counsel to the board of the foundation that has inherited controlling interest in Rancho American Resorts," he explained. "It was called to my attention—more or less inadvertently."

Jergen immediately got the picture. "I hope this hasn't caused you embarrassment. If I had known of your connection—"

"No, no," Scott hastened to assure him, "there's no problem. It was an unlikely coincidence. I was surprised, I must admit."

"Now I see that we should have told you, but I didn't want you to think we expected anything of you. That is, in the way of money." He drew in a sharp breath. "There have been a number of sudden changes in our family. This house . . ." He glanced at his wife. "And of course, Deborah starting her own business."

"Debbie . . . has started a business?"

His sister affected an expression of guilt. "I was going to tell you about that, Scott." She filled him in on all the details of Treasures.

"You two," said Scott, dumbfounded, "certainly have been busy. I had no idea you knew anything about running a store, Debs."

"I'm learning on the job," laughed Deborah. "Tara has the retailing experience, and I'm picking it up fast. Oh, Scott, I can't *wait* to show you Treasures. You must come see it first thing tomorrow."

There was a mother with two young children on the flight to New York. She reminded Scott of Deborah in her casual attire and the offhand way she allowed the boy and his sister to fend for themselves throughout the trip. They were well-behaved youngsters and seemed perfectly happy to draw pictures, eat their lunch, and then put on the earphones to watch the movie. He recalled how diligent he and Isobel had always been with Chip and Ginger, making every experience into a learning opportunity. Perhaps children were happier when left to their own devices.

He was astonished at his misconceptions. It was obvious that Deborah's marriage was happy—a good deal happier than his own had ever been. Jergen was actually well suited to her, a considerate husband and, in his unique way, a charming man. Why hadn't he seen this before?

They were a tolerant couple, nonjudgmental, accepting of other people and of opinions different from their own. If Scott were to leave Isobel and marry Solange, he knew Deborah would embrace Solange as a sister. So would Neil, he realized. Even his mother would understand. But he could not leave his marriage, because his children would never accept it and he could not bear to hurt them.

He leaned his head back against the seat and closed his eyes, filled with desolation at the thought of spending the rest of his life with Isobel.

℀ Chapter 16 ℀

Vivienne

In the summer of 1945, Michael Shane's creative discipline had deserted him. The passion, the hunger burned in him still, but the years of war had left him with unchanneled energies and an inability to focus his drive.

Instead of settling into the productive collaboration that had given birth to *North With the Wind* and *Over the Moon*, he fed on his restlessness. A new dissatisfaction ruled his life, impeding his work and nourishing his private fears that he would never finish another score.

This was astonishing to Julia, who had fallen in love with a man who thought nothing was beyond his reach. She tried to meet his unfulfilled needs, but she was helpless in the face of Michael's frustration. He refused to schedule a working session with Murray. He grew angry when she suggested he talk to Edwin. Unable to concentrate on his music, he blamed her. How did she expect him to compose, he asked, with a wife and child in the apartment?

She began spending the days at Betsy's, working on manuscripts while Mrs. Reilly took charge of Scotty. At night, when their son was asleep, instead of seeking her company, Michael would sequester himself in his studio or disappear for hours, wandering the Village jazz clubs. He often came to bed with his breath smelling of liquor, and he would be in a foul temper the next morning.

Julia was terrified that he was on the verge of a break-down. The dread of alcoholism—always in the back of her mind—haunted her. At all costs she was determined to avoid a confrontation, but she desperately needed advice. Embarrassed to reveal their problems or Michael's weaknesses to Edwin, she confided in Murray, who had recently returned from Hollywood, where he had written another screenplay.

"Be patient," he counseled her. "Mike's gone through bad patches before. I've learned from experience that he can't be pushed. Give him time; he'll find his muse again."

"The apartment is too small for the three of us, but Michael doesn't want to move. He's superstitious—he says if ever he can get going again, it will be there." Her voice trembled. "Oh, Murray, I'm so worried about him."

Gently he stroked her hair, then withdrew his hand, his eyes dropping. "The rent's low, you can afford to keep it for a studio. Find another place to live."

Well, of course. Why hadn't she thought of that?

Never having gone apartment-hunting before, Julia set about the task with alacrity, concentrating at first on Greenwich Village. After being shown a succession of dreary walk-ups in undesirable locations, she concluded that they would have to look further uptown, although it would be less convenient for Michael.

They were discussing the endless possibilities of Manhattan—Julia liked the Upper East Side, while many of Michael's theatrical friends lived on Central Park West—when Edwin happened to strike up a conversation with a doorman in his neighborhood. Soon the Shanes had signed a lease on a spacious flat at the corner of Lexington Avenue overlooking Gramercy Park, diagonally across from the Hoppers.

The positive step of moving had an electrifying effect on Michael's outlook. The day after Labor Day, standing in the half-empty rooms, he opened a bottle of champagne to toast a new beginning. Julia reminded him that it was the anniversary of the night they had met, five years earlier.

"Only five years," he said with wonder. "Doesn't it seem much longer?"

In an optimistic frame of mind, Julia ordered furniture, had curtains made, rooms painted, floors sanded and stained. This was their first real home, the first place that she considered truly their own. She appropriated Aunt Sophie's oriental carpets from the Village apartment, as well as some of the better upholstered pieces, paintings, and books. The front parlor became a music room, intended as a place for Michael to work at home. An extra bedroom was outfitted as a library where Julia would work on manuscripts in the afternoons. She could glance out the window to see Scott playing in the park with Betsy's son, Perkins, under Mrs. Reilly's watchful eye.

Michael stopped drinking. Now the only thing that kept him from his family at night was his music. Murray quickly reinstated the habit of working with him at the studio, and soon the sparks of their collaboration were flying again.

In the next two years they wrote *Her Majesty* and *Ring Loud, Ring Clear*, both of them hits presented by Gerald Ross. Tired of clashing with the producer about staging, by the middle of 1947 composer and lyricist were planning their first independent venture, *A Light in the Sky*. Ross was furious when he heard, but Edwin persuaded him that Michael and Murray deserved to try it on their own, suggesting that Gerry might be involved in future productions.

It was a daring idea, going it alone. George Rhinehart was largely responsible. "For all of your efforts, you're getting a relatively small percentage of the profits," the lawyer had told Michael. "You have a family now. You have to start building an estate."

A week before casting for *A Light in the Sky* was scheduled to begin, Rhinehart was invited to their home for dinner. He brought along a date, Rosalind Lehman, a tall, very attractive blonde who had graduated from Radcliffe and did volunteer work at the Henry Street Settlement. Betsy and Edwin came too, and the talk, as usual, was about the theater.

"The basis of every musical is a love story, trite though that may sound," remarked Michael, and Edwin agreed.

"There must be a more serious theme," Julia insisted. "Your plays always contain a main plot that has nothing to do with the love story."

"True," acknowledged Michael.

George joined the argument. "You can't get away from boy meets girl, Julia. Love is a very powerful force in the human condition."

Coming from a bachelor, that romantic notion intrigued her.

She studied his strong, even-featured face and engaging smile, finding him a very attractive man. "Is Rosalind his girlfriend?" she whispered when she and Betsy were clearing away the cocktail glasses.

"I've seen them together a few times, but he goes out with other women, too," her aunt replied. "I understand that any time he gets serious, his mother breaks it up."

"What sort of mother would do that?" Betsy cocked an eyebrow at her. "Okay, Bets, Eunice Perkins—but what kind of man would *let* her?"

When they were seated at the dinner table, Betsy asked, "How's the new production going, Michael?"

"We're a little nervous," he confessed. "Arlo Rothmore is doing the choreography, which is a great relief. He always gets the best out of his dancers, and he understands our insistence that the dance numbers don't get off the track. This time Murray and I have total control. Every song and every dance routine is an integral part of the story. The complete concept was in our minds when we wrote *A Light in the Sky*, and that's why it will be all of a piece."

The following month, when auditions were over, Metro Films announced that Vivienne Tremaine had been given a leave of absence to appear in the leading role of Amelia Earhart in Michael Shane's new Broadway musical.

The night Julia heard the news, she tried to quell her dismay and the nagging unease that gripped her. With all the talented actresses in New York, couldn't they have cast someone other than Vivienne in their show? Yes, she was beautiful and could sing well enough—and she danced like an angel. But she was not the type to play a plucky aviatrix. Surely she did not intend to crop that glorious titian hair.

"*You are jealous*," she hissed at her reflection in the bathroom mirror. "Admit it. A jealous wife."

An hour later she lay in Michael's arms after making love and chided herself for worrying about Vivienne Tremaine— or any woman. No one could take Michael away from her. Not when there was this incredible, this unbelievable miracle between them.

"My darling," he whispered against her lips, "I love you *so*, Julia. I hope we made a baby tonight."

For two years they had been trying to have another child,

but she could not seem to get pregnant. They had consulted specialists, endured examinations and tests, and learned nothing. Her doctor speculated that she was having very early miscarriages, considering her previous history.

By March, with two months to go before spring tryouts, *A Light in the Sky* was in rehearsal. A musical in progress was a tight conspiracy, excluding outsiders. Julia was extremely careful not to create the slightest distraction. Michael's moods were by turn edgy or despondent, depending on the day's work, and tensions mounted as the opening approached. The show would have limited engagements in Philadelphia and Boston, with time allowed for changes before coming to Broadway. More than usual was at stake with this effort, for the outcome would determine whether Shane and Baker could make it as the producers of their own musical plays.

It was late in the afternoon and already growing dark when Julia finished with the doctor. Immediately she dialed the studio, for she knew Michael was working on arrangements that day. Ordinarily she would never have dreamed of interrupting, but this news could not wait.

The line was perpetually busy, and she suspected he had taken the phone off the hook, as he was wont to do when concentrating. This gave her pause, but she was so excited that she hailed a cab and went straight downtown to Waverly Place. In the back of the taxi, she could not help grinning as she hugged herself.

The doctor had been all smiles and reassurances when she was shown into his consultation room. "Congratulations, Mrs. Shane. There's no doubt this time."

She was overjoyed. "When will it be?"

"If all goes well, you should deliver in early October."

"Just in time for my birthday," she smiled, delighted.

"A wonderful gift. I understand how much this baby means to you and your husband." With the usual words of caution about eating well, getting plenty of normal exercise, and avoiding strenuous activities, he had dismissed her.

Julia entered the old building through the courtyard. It had been months since her last visit to the flat. They had hired a woman to clean once a week, so there was really no reason for her to come here. Before ringing the bell, she checked her purse. The key was still on the ring, along with those to the Gramercy apartment and their safe deposit box. She climbed the steep stairway and let herself in quietly, relishing Michael's happy reaction when she surprised him with the wonderful news.

The apartment was silent. She tiptoed to the studio, but it was empty, although a lamp was burning. Music papers were spread across the desk and there was a stack of sheets on top of the piano.

She noticed two glasses on a table, one with melting ice. It was obvious that Michael had been working until a short time ago. He must be taking a break, unless he had quit for the day. But it wasn't like him to leave his studio in disarray; he was always meticulous about organizing his papers at the end of a session.

Puzzled, she walked down the hall toward the bedroom. The door was slightly ajar, and for a moment she paused. For no apparent reason, she was seized with foreboding. If he was in there napping, maybe it would be better to wait to break the news tonight when he came home. Hesitantly she pushed the door in a few inches.

Michael was lying in bed with his eyes closed. In the shaft of light from the hall, his tousled hair and handsome features looked touchingly young and defenseless. At his side, with one bare pearly arm thrown across his body, Vivienne Tremaine lay asleep, her newly shorn head pillowed on Michael's chest.

The bile rose in Julia's throat. Waves of dizziness swept over her and the room began to sway. A groan escaped her lips as she fell against the door frame. Michael's eyes flew open. As her head cleared a bit, Julia turned and ran, stumbling as she went, desperate to get to the door. She heard him call her name, but kept on going.

In the outer hallway, as she rounded the newel post, her coat caught on the metal latch to the gate she had installed when Scott began to walk. Wrenching at the fabric to free herself, she lost her footing. Desperately she clutched the balustrade, trying to regain her balance, but it was too late. Down she tumbled, down the steep, narrow stairs, slowly turning. Down into a bottomless well of darkness.

Julia regained consciousness in the ambulance. A siren was shrieking and lights were flashing. She tried to move, but she was immobilized, with her head, arms, and legs strapped into restraints. The pain was excruciating.

She moaned and a young man in a white uniform leaned over her. There seemed to be two of him.

"You're on your way to St. Vincent's," he said loudly. "I've given you something for the pain. Don't try to move." Too dazed to answer, she closed her eyes again.

The next time she opened them, it was many hours later. She was lying in a hospital bed and her arm was in a cast. Michael sat at her side, looking haggard and terrified. "Jule," he whispered, his voice cracking with emotion. "Oh, God, I'll never forgive myself."

For a moment, she had no idea what he was talking about or why she was there. And then gradually it all came back. She had no control over her tongue. Try as she would, the words would not come out. "The baby . . ." was all she could manage.

Michael's mouth trembled as he shook his head, fighting back tears. She turned away, hating the sight of him. He stayed at her bedside for hours while she drifted in and out of sleep. Whenever she awakened, he was there in the dimly lit room, but she never spoke to him. The nurse made him leave at midnight and Julia lay awake staring into the darkness, more miserable than she had ever been.

"I have always hated those stairs," were Betsy's first words when she arrived at the hospital the morning after the accident. "You're lucky you weren't killed!"

With her left arm broken in two places, Julia was incapacitated for six weeks. Miraculously, there had been no additional injuries—other than the miscarriage. When she came home from the hospital, Michael had engaged a niece of Mrs. Reilly's from the Pennsylvania coal regions to help in the house and take care of Scott, who had been staying with the Hoppers in Julia's absence. Regina O'Brien was the second of ten children, and had been taught to clean, cook, and sew by the nuns. She was to stay with the family for thirty-three years.

Julia told no one, not even Betsy or Edwin, the circumstances of her fall. The show must go on, she observed cynically, for *A Light in the Sky* was scheduled for out-of-town tryouts with a new Amelia Earhart, played by Jane Lawson, the understudy who had replaced Vivienne. Privately, Julia thought Jane the more suitable actress for the part, but still she refused to accompany Michael to the opening.

The weeks since the accident had passed with no more than a few perfunctory words between them. "I can't go on this way," Michael finally despaired on the eve of his departure for Philadelphia. "*Please*, Jule. *Talk to me*."

"There is nothing I have to say to you," she cried, her voice bitter with self-righteous anger.

"*What do you want of me?* I've fired Vivienne. I won't ever see her again."

"You've lied before. You'll do it again."

"No, I swear." He came to sit next to her on the small settee in their bedroom. "I know there's no excuse for what happened, but if I could make you understand how dejected I was . . . The rehearsals were lousy and I was having such self-doubts. We revised some of Vivienne's songs. She suggested we rehearse them alone, without the rest of the cast. And it worked. Suddenly I began to feel confident again. We had a drink . . . and it happened."

She closed her eyes. "Nothing just happens."

He took her hand and kissed it. "I love only you, darling. She means nothing to me. It was purely physical, a moment of weakness."

"How many such moments have there been, Michael?"

"None before, I swear."

"Do you expect me to believe you? You must imagine I'm an even greater fool than I've proven to be. When I think how naive and trusting I was, picturing you at work in your studio. I would never call or disturb you, for fear I would interrupt the creative process. Only because I was so thrilled about the baby did I come down there unannounced. I thought maybe you'd be excited, too."

"I would have been. I'm heartbroken about losing our baby. Honestly, Jule, I would give anything if I could change things." Seizing her other hand, he kissed the palm. "There will be other children, darling, as many as you like. Please say you forgive me." He put his arms around her and pressed her head against his chest. As he stroked her back, despite her anger and sorrow, Julia felt the hard bitterness inside begin to melt.

If only she did not care so much, she told herself. If only

she were not powerless against her love for him.

Gradually they resumed their life together, although it would never be the same as it had been before. Julia worried that Michael's firing of Vivienne had appeared unprofessional. They made the usual excuse about artistic differences, but she was certain the true story would get around. The theater world was an environment that nurtured gossip.

In her heart she knew the problem was Michael, not Vivienne. She wondered how many others there had been. How many more there would be.

A Light in the Sky broke all records for box office receipts when it opened in New York. Jane Lawson was heralded as the brightest new star in the musical comedy firmament. She was radiant in the role, and Michael admitted that they should have cast her from the beginning.

Michael and Murray were among the most sought-after dinner guests that season. They were taken up by patrons of the arts, as well as café society. Michael in particular became the darling of every fashionable hostess, and Julia, who at one time had reveled in his celebrity, now wearied of the endless dinners and receptions at which she was merely the woman who arrived on his arm.

On New Year's Eve, after several stops at other parties, she found herself at, of all places, Gerald and Florence Ross's Park Avenue triplex. Ross had decided to let bygones be, once it became evident that Shane and Baker were the hottest team on Broadway. He was trying to talk them into co-producing with him, offering to take on the financial responsibility while giving them free rein with the artistic side of any production. Michael had asked Edwin to sound out his offer.

It was the usual scene at the Rosses'. Florence threw a good shindig, and a parade of show people had come and gone, including Ethel Merman, Irving Berlin, Moss Hart, Bea Lillie, and Anita Loos. At two hours past midnight the gathering was still going strong, whittled down to the hard core of partygoers. Julia, bored with the repeated toasts to the new year, sought a moment of respite in the library.

Nineteen forty-nine. She was pregnant again, but she felt little of the delirious joy of last year. When she held this new baby in her arms, she was certain that would change.

She desperately wanted another child; in fact, she hoped for several more.

Scott was a lonely youngster, a sweet, serious little boy who was extremely bright. They had enrolled him in kindergarten at Friends Seminary. She worried that he did not mix easily with other children. He always seemed to stand on the fringe of a group, watching with a wistful smile the rough-and-tumble of his classmates. Her heart often ached for him. He had a pathetic need for a more involved father, but as much as Michael loved him—and she knew that he did—he made so little time for any other person in his life. His music was his life.

He was at the piano now in the Rosses' huge living room, surrounded by a circle of guests. Michael could play anything from the classics to jazz, improvising at will. With some of the most outstanding talent in America at this party, he was the center of attention.

She was standing at a window, looking down on the string of lighted trees that divided Park Avenue, when Gerald Ross wandered in. "I see you're all alone, Julia. As usual."

"What's that supposed to mean, Gerry?"

"Poor little neglected wife of the great man," he simpered drunkenly, patting her cheek.

"Why don't you shut up," she said, turning her back on him.

Suddenly he grabbed her and kissed her full on the mouth, a wet kiss. She could taste the whiskey on his probing tongue as she fought him, beating her fists against his chest and arms.

Just as suddenly, he released her. "Happy New Year, Julia," he taunted her.

She scrubbed at her mouth, shuddering. "Ugh! You disgusting man. How dare you . . . how *dare* you! You are *vile*."

Ross frowned, as if at a minor annoyance. "You know what I think, Julia? You're frigid. No wonder Mike chases anything in skirts." He walked out of the room.

A minute later, Murray came in and found her close to tears. "Jule! What's wrong?"

She shook her head. "Nothing, nothing."

"Gerry was in here—what happened?"

"He . . . he . . ." She couldn't go on.

"*Tell* me. What did he do?"

"He made a pass at me and when I fought him off, he said the most awful thing about Michael."

"The bastard. Just wait 'til I get him—"

She grabbed his arm. "No, Murray, please, leave it alone. I don't want everyone to know." He handed her his handkerchief and she wiped her eyes. "Thanks, I'm okay now."

"What was it he said about Mike?"

Why shouldn't she tell him? After all, this was Murray, who knew so much about them. "That he chases 'anything in skirts,' as he put it. Is it true, Murray?"

He did not answer immediately. "Look, a man like Michael is very . . . attractive to women. They chase *him*, Julia, not the other way around. He has a hard time dodging some of them."

"Then he's—he *does*—"

"No! He's not running around. He doesn't get involved with any of them. Sometimes it just doesn't look so good."

For a moment, Julia closed her eyes, and then she said, "I'm going to have another baby, Murray."

She saw the play of emotion on his face. "That's good. Scotty should have a little brother. Or sister."

"Yes," she answered bitterly. "He should also have a father who pays attention to him. I wish Michael would spend more time with him."

"He's not a domestic animal, our Michael. I think you always knew that."

She sighed. "People change when they have new responsibilities."

"I think Mike *has* changed a great deal. If he became too different, he wouldn't be the guy you fell in love with, would he?"

Reluctantly she smiled. "You're right. I don't know why I let Gerry Ross get to me. He was drunk, but he's still a revolting man."

Murray pulled a tough face, making a fist. "I tell ya, I'd like to beat the hell out of him."

She hugged him. "My champion. Save it for the important battles."

He smiled fondly at her. "I'm starved, aren't you? Let's go see what they have to eat." Arm in arm, they strolled across the hall.

"There you are, Julia," said their hostess. "I was coming to find you. Michael isn't feeling well."

In the living room, Michael had stopped playing. He was still seated at the piano, leaning forward with his elbows on his knees. Several people were standing around looking concerned and Jane Lawson was bent over him, her arm around his shoulders.

Julia rushed to his side. "What's wrong, darling?"

His hands were gripping his head. "I have a splitting headache."

She stroked his forehead and he closed his eyes. "How bad is it?"

"Bad," he said.

"Did you drink too much champagne?"

"Hardly any. I've had a dull pain all evening, but it suddenly got much worse." He rubbed his eyes. "My vision was cloudy before."

"It sounds like migraine," commented Jane. "I sometimes get them so badly, I can't see at all."

"Really?" replied Julia. "What causes them?"

"My doctor says it's from tension."

"I guess Mike has plenty of that," said Murray. "Come on, pal, you'll feel better when you get home."

Florence Ross returned with a glass of water. "Here, Michael, take some aspirin before you leave." When he tossed the tablets in his mouth, the motion made him wince.

Murray dropped the two of them at their building and went on in the taxi. Going up in the elevator, Michael's pain was so intense that he sagged against the wall.

"I think we should call the doctor," said Julia when they were inside the apartment.

"Don't be ridiculous," he snapped irritably. "It's just a headache."

He slept fitfully. Julia kept waking to pull the blankets over him. His body felt hot and he was drenched with perspiration. *It must be the flu*, she thought. *I hope Scotty doesn't catch it.* Around five-thirty, Michael asked for water, still complaining that his head hurt. She found a vial of aspirin with codeine from when she had broken her arm, and she gave him one. He fell asleep, this time not stirring until noon the next day.

Julia had called Betsy earlier to tell her they would not be coming to the Hoppers' New Year's Day open house, but Michael awakened fully recovered and insisted on going.

"I thought you were ill," exclaimed Edwin when they walked in.

"You know how Julia exaggerates things," Michael laughed. "It was nothing but a simple headache."

Midway through March there was a severe winter storm. The radio predicted at least eight to ten inches by nightfall.

Julia sat by the fire in the living room, winding a skein of soft yellow worsted yarn for a baby sweater and enjoying the enforced leisure of a snowy Sunday afternoon. Smiling, she thought of what Eunice Perkins would say if she could see her with knitting needles in hand. For all the years her grandmother had encouraged her to do handiwork, Julia had resisted out of a perversity that Eunice had always brought out in her. Poor Gran had slipped away in her sleep last year at the nursing home in Albany, recognizing no one in the final months of her life.

Michael was in the music room, going over and over a passage on the piano. He would try it with one set of chords, then another, changing tempo and key until it suited him. Most of the time he never went near an instrument when he orchestrated, for the notes were in his head, but when he experimented with different arrangements, she never tired of listening.

She was not surprised that he had not held to his promise to take Sundays off. The doctor believed that the frequent headaches were caused by tension and advised Michael to relax more, to learn to pace himself and form outside interests. For a few weeks he had taken the advice seriously, setting out on long cross-country walks with her and Scotty when they were at the Hoppers' house in Connecticut on weekends. But it was clearly a chore for him, and they had not gone hiking for weeks.

The studio always beckoned. He seemed driven more than ever, consumed with orchestrating the score for *California*, their new musical about the Gold Rush, while composing songs for the next project, *Magic Island*, a fantasy based on the life of Gauguin. At the same time, he was working on "Forgotten Rhapsody," a suite for symphony orchestra, while planning a spring concert in Carnegie Hall and writing the score for a documentary film series. The ideas appeared to spring endlessly from his imagination, tumbling over one another in their need to emerge. There were never enough hours in a day for Michael. If Julia did not remind him to eat, he would work straight through mealtimes. As it was, on nights when they were not going out to the theater or a concert, he usually retreated to the music room after dinner, staying until long after midnight—

Her thoughts were interrupted by the crash of a dissonant chord, and a moment later Michael appeared in the doorway. He was frowning, while absentmindedly massaging his right hand and flexing the fingers.

"Are you finished?" she asked hopefully.

"No, I am *not* finished. I smelled something burning."

"Burning? Oh my God, where's Scotty?" She jumped up and ran into their son's room where he was playing with his Erector set. Grabbing his arm, she hurried to the front hall, opened the door, and then stopped, aware that she smelled nothing out of the ordinary. "Michael . . . what burning? What are you talking about?"

"I smelled burning rubber. You didn't?"

She sniffed the air. "No."

He rubbed his eyes. "It's gone now. It was just a whiff."

"It could have been the incinerator." She hurried to the kitchen and opened the door to the service hall, but the air was clear. "Whatever it was seems to have dissipated."

Michael rubbed his eyes again. "I'm feeling strange all of a sudden."

She stood still, hardly daring to breathe. *There is something wrong.*

"Go lie down, dear. You've been working too hard. Remember what the doctor said."

"Can I go back to my room, Mommy?"

She had forgotten about Scott. "Oh . . . yes, darling. That was just a fire drill."

There is something wrong, she thought again. This was the second time.

She recalled the afternoon several weeks ago when Michael had come home early . . . "I thought I'd take a nap before tonight's show," he said, and she had noticed how fatigued he looked. He tossed his coat and hat on a bench in the foyer, and she went to hang them in the closet.

"Smells good, what are you making?"

She looked at him, puzzled. "Nothing. I haven't started dinner yet."

"I smell frying onions. Regina must be cooking."

Regina had taken Scott to play with a friend and was doing the grocery shopping. Julia went to the kitchen, just to be sure, but it was empty . . .

Instinctively now she connected the imagined odors to the headaches and she was alarmed.

So in a way it should not have been surprising a month later when Murray called her from New York Hospital. It was April, Julia was in her fifth month of pregnancy, still plagued by nausea, and she later blamed herself for neglecting the signs of illness in Michael.

"There's nothing to be alarmed about, Julia," said Murray, and she knew that meant there was everything to be alarmed about. They had been working on *California*, getting ready for tryouts. "Michael . . . well, he sort of passed out, and then he was, uh, confused. I called his doctor and he told me to bring him here to the emergency room. He's examining him now. Mike didn't want me to tell you, but I was sure you'd want to know."

"Absolutely, Murray. You did the right thing. I'll be there as soon as I can get a taxi."

She was so nervous, she was shaking. *There is something terrible, I know. I've known it for a while. Oh, God, please let him be all right. Please. I won't be able to bear it if anything happens to Michael.*

They said the tumor was not malignant—a benign meningioma. How long it had been there was impossible to say, but the doctors felt they had interceded early and there was a good chance of complete recovery. The growth was small, slow-growing and elusive, the symptoms not presenting in a straightforward manner. Oh, the habits of medical expression: *The symptoms not presenting.* As if headaches and imagined odors and fuzzy vision and sudden weakness in an arm or leg were so many little ballerinas parading themselves center stage and taking a bow before performing.

Don't be bitter, everyone advised her. How could she not be bitter? To see her handsome husband with his head swathed in bandages, mouth drooping, shuffling along the hospital corridor with a walker. Who would not be bitter?

It brought tears to her eyes to witness his struggle to regain his speech and the full use of his hand. Each minor victory became a cause for celebration. The doctors and nurses were amazed that three weeks after the surgery he was walking with a cane and speaking in complete sentences. Occasionally he searched for a word, but his thoughts were clear.

Michael's ability to compose was totally unaffected. If anything, in an odd twist of the circuitry of his brain, it was enhanced. Without the headaches and the eye problems, he was better able to concentrate. But he did tire easily, and at the end of an afternoon, as much as he hated it, would resort to the wheelchair.

Scott had been upset when Michael first came home from the hospital, but he soon grew accustomed to the sight of his father in the chair. They installed a stair elevator in the Greenwich Village building, and at Michael's insistence, Murray would take him to the studio. More often he worked at home, composing rapidly, the notes dashing across the lined staffs of music paper, flags flying like those of a charging miniature army.

With each passing month of her pregnancy, Julia noticed Michael's strength returning. His hair had grown in, thick and wavy, covering the scar in his scalp. His speech was almost natural now, growing hesitant only when he became weary. Although he tired easily, Julia could do nothing to prevent him from working all day. He was in a frenzy of creativity, as if he were in a race against time. Each week he was able to work for longer stretches.

One afternoon late in July, fatigued by the summer heat, Michael came home from the Village to find the compositions he had left on his desk in the music room drenched in black India ink. The bottle was tipped over, its contents running over the edge of the desk and spilling onto Aunt Sophie's Kermanshah rug. The carpet was permanently stained and several days' work obliterated.

Obviously Scott was the guilty party. His yo-yo was found on the floor next to the desk—incriminating evidence. Michael was furious. Irritability had been part of the tumor, but this was his first display of temper since the operation. "I'll tan that kid's hide," he shouted when he discovered the mess.

"Don't upset yourself, Michael. It's not good for you."

"Not good for me! I suppose it's helpful to see a whole week's work down the drain, the little bastard."

"That's a *terrible* thing to say about your son, even if it's in jest!"

"The boy has been told a hundred times to stay out of my studio. He should be punished."

"He's only a *child*," she cried. "Don't be so hard on him."

Michael seized the sheets of compositions, some of which Julia thought could have been salvaged, and began ripping them apart.

"Don't! Don't do that. It hasn't soaked through." She reached for the papers, but he pushed her away. She held onto his arms and wrestled with him.

Suddenly he laughed and pulled her down on his lap. "You would take advantage of a cripple, wouldn't you?"

"Oh, darling, I'm sorry he ruined your work. I know he didn't mean it."

He kissed her and put his arms around her. "I love you," he whispered.

From his hiding place in the cupboard, Scott could see his parents through the crack where the doors met. They were angry at each other, and they were shouting.

It's all my fault. They're arguing over me.

Now his father was ripping up the sheets of music and Julia was trying to stop him. Michael took hold of her arm and was twisting it. It looked like they were fighting. His father pulled his mother down on his lap and the wheelchair moved back so that he could no longer see them.

Scott strained his ears, but he couldn't hear what they were saying. Were they *laughing*? How could they have been trying to hurt each other and now they were speaking sweetly, lovingly? Grownups were strange.

Suddenly his mother screamed. "*Oh God, Michael!*"

"What? What's wrong?"

"Pain . . . terrible pain," Scott heard her gasp. "Oh, please . . . *do something*. It's too soon."

His father was shouting for Regina and then there was a confusion of voices. Julia was moaning. Every so often she would cry out. Scott cowered in the cupboard. It seemed to go on forever, and then the doorbell rang. Strange men came in and Michael was explaining something to them. There were loud clanking noises and the sound of something being wheeled away. And then there was silence.

He waited for a long time. They seemed to have forgotten about the spilled ink. Well, he could probably come out now.

He reached for the latch, but there was nothing there. Frantically he ran his hands up and down the wooden panels, but there was only a stationary handle. With all his strength Scott pushed, but the cupboard remained solidly closed. At the top of his lungs, he called for Regina and pounded on the doors, but no one came.

He began to cry and soon he was in a panic, unable to breathe in the stifling, dusty, camphor-smelling cabinet. After what seemed like hours, he cried himself to sleep and dreamed that he was suffocating.

He woke crying. The door was flung open. Sudden light from the room blinded him. He was sobbing with fright.

"*There* you are, Scotty," exclaimed Uncle Ed, scooping him up. "We've been looking high and low for you. There, there, young fella, it's all right."

Regina was holding her arms out to him, but he shrank from her. "Mommy . . . I want my mommy."

"Your mommy went to the hospital, Scotty, to have a little—"

Edwin shook his head warningly and put his fingers to his lips. "That bad old closet," he said, "keeping you locked up in the dark. It was just like being in jail, wasn't it?"

Neil was three months old. The baby nurse had left and there was just Regina to help with the children and the housework now. Julia was exhausted all the time. Neil proved to be a fretful baby, often waking at night. She was attuned to the first faint wail, leaping out of bed to rush to the nursery before Michael's sleep was disturbed.

She watched her husband furtively, looking for signs of illness. Had he forgotten a word? Was that mannerism he had of rubbing the space between his eyes a habit, or did it mean he was having headaches? She thought one pupil was slightly larger than the other . . . he seemed more irritable of late . . . he was restless at night . . .

And then when it happened she was unprepared.

In the last week of October, Michael had an appointment for a routine checkup. "I'm not a hundred percent satisfied with the EEG," the neurologist told them when he saw the results of the electroencephalogram. "It could be edema from the previous surgery, but just to be on the safe side I'm going to refer you to a specialist at Memorial for a consultation."

Julia felt a wave of panic. Memorial was a *cancer* hospital. "Not necessarily," said the doctor. "There just happens to be an excellent neurosurgeon there. I have a lot of confidence in his judgment."

"Don't worry, honey, I feel fine," Michael tried to reassure her. "I'm getting better every day."

The new doctor, whose name was Phillips, repeated all the tests—the Wassermann, the colloidal gold reactions, the uncomfortable lumbar puncture, and the excruciating lumbar air injection. This entailed withdrawing some cerebrospinal fluid by spinal tap, injecting several cubic centimeters of air into the ventricles of the brain, and then taking x-rays of the head.

Afterward Michael was stuporous with fatigue. "Why am I going through all this?" he moaned. "It's a waste of time."

Dr. Phillips did not see it that way. He ushered Julia into his consultation room while Michael was recovering from the procedure. "There is definitely something there. I see a slight deformation of the ventricle in the left hemisphere. It could be a blood clot or fluid collection at the site of the former surgery"—he paused and gave her an apologetic smile—"but it could also be a recurrence of the tumor."

Julia took a deep breath, certain she would suffocate. "I thought—I thought benign meningiomas did not recur."

He drew in his lips, considering his words. "I'm not convinced this was benign. I want to examine *all* of the slides."

"Haven't they sent them to you?"

"A hospital always hangs on to some slides in case the others get lost. On the basis of what I've seen thus far, they could have missed some suspicious cells."

"But he's been so *well*!" she protested. "There's so much improvement. He hardly ever uses a wheelchair now. He even walked up the stairs to his studio last week."

"I understand what you're saying, Mrs. Shane. And these are all very good signs. But I would be doing him a disservice if I did not try to rule out even the shade of a suspicion."

The next few days were an agony of suspense. Without planning to, they skirted the subject, finding it easier to pretend that everything was normal. Michael was edgy but in especially good humor. He spent many hours playing with Scott and holding little Neil.

At six-thirty in the evening on the tenth of November, Dr. Phillips telephoned. Fortunately, Julia was alone in the study when she took the call. Because it was the worst possible news.

"I'm afraid we see malignant cells in the slides, Mrs. Shane. I want to operate immediately."

Her heart stood still. "They told us there were none."

"It's easy to miss, a very difficult diagnosis." He was trying to be kind, but that changed nothing.

"It's been seven months since his first surgery," she cried. "Seven wasted months!"

"No, they haven't been wasted. Dr. Gregory took out all the tumor he could see. It's always a judgment call. There really wasn't anything else he could do at the time without sacrificing critical brain regions and causing significant physical impairment."

She could hear the panic in her voice. "Does—does that mean that he will be greatly impaired this time?"

The doctor sighed. "Well, there is that possibility. I can't tell you what or how much. It all depends on what we find when we get in there. However, you should be prepared for that."

"But he feels fine now! What would happen if you did nothing?"

"I'm concerned that his tumor is growing, and in time there could be more loss of function from the disease itself. If we don't operate, it could become life-threatening. With surgical treatment there's the possibility of recovery. There are no guarantees, of course, but at least he would have a fighting chance." She listened mutely as he went on to explain what would happen. "I can't tell you how sorry I am. Michael Shane is—well, he's our most brilliant composer."

When she hung up, she broke down and sobbed. All their hopes, all their prayers—all in vain.

By force of will, she made herself stop crying. She was glad that Michael was taking a nap before dinner. *How am I going to tell him?*

There was no need. The moment he saw her, Michael knew. "You've heard something, haven't you?"

She nodded, trying to keep her voice steady. "Dr. Phillips called. He—he thinks one of the slides looks suspicious. He wants to operate as soon as possible."

Michael shook his head. "I am not going to have more surgery. I refuse to go through that again."

"*Michael, you have to!*"

"I don't *have* to. No one can force me."

"But, darling, he says there's a good chance for a *cure*!" And as he continued to shake his head, she cried, "Without it, you'll—you have no chance."

On the following Tuesday morning at seven o'clock, Julia walked alongside the gurney when they wheeled Michael down to the operating room at Memorial Hospital. He was premedicated and affected a sort of woozy bravado. "Take one last look, sweetheart. I'll be a mummy when I get back."

"The most handsome mummy since Ramses the Second."

"You think Ramses was better-looking, huh?"

He could still make her laugh. "They say he was a lady-killer." She bent over to kiss him. "I'll be waiting for you, my love. Hurry back."

Michael smiled and closed his eyes, and that was the way she pictured him throughout the long hours of surgery and the even longer afternoon when she waited with Betsy while he was in the recovery room. Betsy had gone to a pay phone down the hall to call Edwin when the surgeon came to find Julia in the early evening. He looked weary from an entire day spent in surgery.

"I'm sorry I couldn't get here earlier, Mrs. Shane," he said kindly. "Tough case this afternoon. I hope the resident came to see you."

"Yes, Dr. Phillips, he did. Thank you for your concern." She held her breath. "Well?"

"Sit down," he suggested, but she shook her head. "First of all, he came through the surgery very well. It *was* a tumor—we think we got it all. That's the good news."

Whenever anyone said that, inevitably there was bad news. "We were operating close to his speech center, so he may have some speaking difficulties as a result of the surgery. With time, this can improve."

She nodded, regarding him steadily.

"Also," he continued, "we found considerable vascularization."

"What does that mean?"

"There's more chance of bleeding into the surrounding tissue. The next few days will be critical. I'm keeping him in the surgical recovery room so that he can be constantly monitored. Someone will watch him every minute."

She felt numb. "May I see him?"

"Yes, for a few minutes, if you're sure you want to. He may not be conscious, and if he is, he may not know you. Do you think you're up to that?"

"I'm up to it," she answered evenly.

He went with her to the recovery room. Michael lay behind a curtain, hooked up to machinery, intravenous drips, and a urinary catheter.

It was worse than she had expected. Far worse than the last time. His head was elevated. His eyes were bruised and his features so distorted that he was barely recognizable. Protruding from the swathes of bandaging were drains to relieve the accumulation of fluids in the skull.

"Those will be removed once the swelling recedes," a nurse assured her.

When she held Michael's hand his grip tightened slightly in hers, but his eyes remained closed and he did not respond when she spoke his name. The minutes passed with no change, and finally she went out to the corridor where Betsy and Edwin were waiting.

"Come on, Jule, we'll take you home now," said her aunt.

Julia shook her head. "I'm staying here tonight."

"That's not sensible. There's nothing you can do and you need your rest. The children are waiting for you."

"The children are perfectly fine with Regina," she argued. "They'll let me in to see Michael every two hours, and I am going to be there. Just in case he knows."

When they saw that she would not budge, Edwin insisted on staying with her. "We'll go somewhere in the neighborhood for a bite to eat. Don't worry, I'll have you back here in two hours."

In the middle of the night, the third time she went into

the recovery room, Michael opened his eyes. They were mere slits between his swollen, bruised lids. He stared at her uncomprehendingly for a long moment and then slowly his lips formed the semblance of a smile. "Mummy . . ." he muttered.

At first she could not think what he meant. But then she remembered. "A whole lot better-looking than Ramses," she said, kissing his hand. "You're going to be fine, darling."

He smiled again. "Wanna bet?" he whispered, and closed his eyes.

Blinking back tears, Julia held his hand until the nurse told her it was time to leave.

Murray was devastated, a man in anguish. He seemed to have shriveled to half his size, holding himself huddled, as if he were warding off painful blows. In addition to his customary winter pallor, his face had become haggard. Julia noticed for the first time that his hairline had begun to recede and he had a perpetually wrinkled brow. If he had once made her think of a teddy bear behind the horn-rimmed spectacles, he now resembled a wizened owl.

And yet he was a bulwark for her. *California* was in production, scheduled to open in a matter of weeks, and in Michael's absence the full responsibility for artistic guidance fell to Murray. Despite this, day after day he would come to the hospital for a brief visit on his lunch break, returning at night to keep a vigil.

One afternoon he asked her to accompany him to the studio. Before the operation, Michael had been working on minor last-minute changes in some of the solos, and Murray wanted to pick up the scores.

"Don't you have a key?" asked Julia.

"I don't know . . ." He fumbled through his pockets. "I think I lost it." Murray was notoriously disorganized about his belongings.

"You can use mine."

"I'm sorry to ask this of you, but I'd rather you went with me. I don't want to go through his worksheets alone."

Silently they rode downtown.

The apartment already had an uninhabited feeling. The radiators had been turned off and Julia shivered in the cold. Exploring the kitchen, she found a quart of sour milk in the refrigerator. She spilled it out and rinsed the bottle, setting it to drain on the counter.

Murray was turning the pages of a composition book when she returned to the studio. "Look at this stuff!" he exclaimed. "I had no idea what he was doing."

She took the notebook and read, "*Honest Abe*." The pages were crammed with musical sketches, a scenario, and narrative notes for an ambitious work based on the life of Abraham Lincoln.

"Can you believe this!" Murray handed her another folio. "He's finished the score of *Magic Island*. How can he have produced all this? Where did he find the time?"

He was so keyed-up he could scarcely contain his excitement—snatching pages, throwing them aside, and grabbing for more, as if he were a starving man and they were sustenance. "*Look* . . . look at *these*, Julia. There must be fifty pieces. God, what I could do with all this! There's enough material for I don't know how many plays. And I can take all these songs and write half a dozen more."

There was a look of ecstasy on his face. "Do you realize what this means? His work will live! Even if Mike can't compose—" He checked himself, horrified, realizing what he was saying and how unfeeling he must seem to Michael's wife. "Forgive me, Jule. I didn't mean that the way it sounded."

Julia was gripping the edge of the piano, breathing harshly. "I know, I know you didn't." She brushed at the tears that seeped out of her eyes. "You're right. His music is the most important thing in the world to Michael, and he would want it to live on."

He put his arms around her and she rested her head on his shoulder. "I love him, too, Julia. I can't imagine life without him."

She sighed deeply, longing to get away from the studio. "Have you found what you came for?"

"No. I got sidetracked looking at this treasure trove." He went to a small table Michael kept next to the piano. "Here they are." He picked up a sheaf of papers. Next to them, lying flat on the table, was a brown manila portfolio. "This seems to be for you."

"For me?"

"It says *For my wife, Julia Shane*."

He held the folio out to her. Uncertainly, she took it, loosening the cord and opening the flap.

There were nine songs.

Slowly she turned the pages, repeating the titles in a hushed voice. " 'Julia, Julia,' 'Blue Memories,' 'Sea Change,' 'Love in the Morning' . . ." Stifling a sob, she pressed a clenched fist against her mouth.

" 'All I Want Is You,' " she continued. " 'Love Passed Me By,' 'Walking Alone' . . . 'For the Rest of My Life,' 'So Little Time' . . ."

At last her voice broke and she burst into tears. Murray was crying, too. He rocked her in his arms.

"Oh God, Murray. He's going to die. What will I do without him? How will I go on?"

"I'll always be here for you, Julia," he told her. "You'll never be alone."

At the end of the week Michael's condition was sufficiently stable for him to be moved to a private room. He had periods of coherence, but intermittently he lapsed into a state of semi-consciousness in which he was barely responsive.

Regina was singlehandedly running the house and caring for the children. Julia felt guilty for neglecting them, especially Scott, who was almost seven and old enough to be disturbed by events around him. But she could think of nothing except Michael and being there when he needed her. Betsy looked in on the boys several times a day, and Edwin would stop by every evening on his way home from the office. They wanted Scott to stay at their house with Perk, but he clung to the security of Regina and his own room.

Julia would arrive early each morning at the hospital and stay until late at night. Any improvement, no matter how slight, was a sign to be seized, examined, and held close. The nurses had orders to stimulate Michael so that he would remain as alert as possible, and a physical therapist exercised his limbs daily to prevent thrombosis or atrophy of the muscles. Julia regarded these ministrations hopefully, for were they not an indication that the doctors expected him to eventually recover? To leave his bed, to walk again and get around on his own?

"He really perks up when you come in, Mrs. Shane," the nurse remarked one morning, and Julia was all the more determined to be there whenever he was awake.

She wanted to tell him that she had found the portfolio of songs, that she had tried them on the piano, picking out the melody with one hand. She wanted him to know how much she treasured the songs, yet she was afraid. They were his last message to her, and to acknowledge them was to accept the end. She still had hope, no matter what she had admitted to Murray in a moment of anguish.

Murray Baker entered the dingy tile-floored lobby of the West Side apartment hotel he had called home for the past ten years. After collecting his mail from the wino desk clerk, he rang for the creaking, wood-paneled elevator. As the car slowly rose, the fumes from an assortment of culinary traditions wafted through the elevator shaft. Onions frying in chicken fat on two, garam masala on four, corned beef and cabbage on seven, garlic and peppers on nine.

The car jolted to a stop on the tenth floor. Unlocking the apartment door, Murray dropped his briefcase on the floor of the combination foyer-kitchenette and threw his wrinkled trench coat over the back of a chair. After a cursory glance at the mail, he tossed it on the pile of unopened envelopes on the counter and poured himself half a tumbler of scotch.

He hated the taste of liquor, preferring wine or beer, but they didn't give him enough of a lift. In the past, to achieve that lift, he had popped amphetamines, to which he proved violently allergic, or resorted to women, dozens of them, until he got a dose of the clap. He had on one occasion even considered trying men but finally concluded that he was incurably heterosexual.

He poured himself another scotch, this time adding ice. Picking a copy of *Variety* from the stack of unread journals, he sat on the couch and drank deeply from his glass. He was still waiting for that kick.

There was always a letdown after the opening of a new musical. For months you pushed yourself to the limit for rehearsals and tryouts, gave up sleep to rework the problems. You rode the high of a Broadway first night, sweated the reviews, grew dizzy with the thrill of a hit. Then, nothing.

Murray had grown to hate the flatness of the aftermath. He had become dependent on that edge that goes along with taking chances, stretching himself to the limit. He needed the heady mix of nauseating uncertainty and soaring possibilities.

He needed Michael Shane.

It was Mike who had the ideas, who generated the excitement. Oh sure, Murray knew he could write great lyrics and create fabulous scripts. But only with concepts from the mind of a genius. To the inspirations of Michael Shane—the melodies he composed so effortlessly, the tales he spun from the air—Murray could apply the final glittering touches. With Mike he had always been able to capture a unique spirit and weave a web of fantasy. Without him, he was wooden. He could no more create the inspired ideas or original stories of their collaborations than he could compose the music or orchestrate the scores.

He knew it, even if others did not. Murray had learned about himself during the war. It was Mike's creativity that kept him going, and when the compositions stopped coming in from overseas, he had dried up. Lacking inspiration between shows, he had gone to Hollywood, where he had written scripts.

When Michael died, part of him would die, too. The only time he felt alive was when he was writing the lyrics to Michael's songs, the book to his sketches. Shane and Baker were a *team*. With Mike, he was the full partner of genius. Without him, he would become a hack.

His glass was empty again. Going to the kitchen to pour another drink, he looked with distaste at the furnished rooms. This place was a dump. The shade fell off a lamp when he pulled the chain, the sofa springs sagged. He could well afford Sutton Place now, or an apartment overlooking the park, and he often thought of moving. But the fact was he was a slob, and any apartment he lived in would soon look the same. He spent as little time as possible at home, because when he was alone he had to confront himself and his misery.

Murray hated living alone. He wanted a wife, he wanted a family. Every time he met a new woman and thought she might be the one, they would start an affair and that would be the beginning of the end. All his women wanted marriage, but none of them was right for him.

One woman. For ten years he had been in love with one woman. Love at first sight. And second sight—and on and on and on. It never let up. Even before he had known her name, he had fallen in love with the lovely girl he noticed across the room in his best friend's apartment. He could remember every time he had seen her, every word they had ever exchanged since that night at the Shubert Theater when he had run into Michael with the girl he had dreamed about.

If he couldn't have her himself, he was curiously content that she was with Michael. Because Mike's having Julia was almost like Murray having her. And now that his alter ego was leaving him behind, Murray felt his tenuous connection with Julia slipping away. Without Michael, he would no longer be the best pal, the almost-brother, the fond uncle. When Mike had been injured overseas, Murray had fantasized taking his place. For one brief moment he had pictured his dream come true, then lived in terror lest it did.

What was the use? What was he going to do when the music was gone, when the magic spectacle would no longer appear? *I'll always be here for you, Julia. You'll never be alone.* But half of him would be dead when Michael was gone.

The bottle was empty. With a furious snarl, Murray slung it across the room, where it bounced against the wall and shattered. Going to his desk, he opened a small drawer and removed a key. He put on his trench coat and took the elevator down to the lobby. It was sleeting outside. The streets were wet and slick, and there were no cabs in sight. Murray walked to the subway and took the Seventh Avenue local to Christopher Street.

How many times had he walked into this alley, savoring the sense of expectation, the pleasure he derived from working with Michael? Never to know that thrill again, the elation that came from their uniquely inspired partnership. Sliding on the slippery pavement, he stumbled against the gate. A garbage can tipped over, making a terrible racket as the lid went rolling across the brick courtyard. His head felt woozy. He thought he was sober, but maybe he'd had a little too much.

Can't do that. Have to go to work. Mike was counting on him. Murray laughed aloud as he tripped on the bottom step. *Shhh . . . have to be quiet. Better not wake the boys.* That's what Mike always called them. *The boys.* By now they were getting to be old men. Malcolm and Hugo, still living together in harmonious amity. Even two queers could make him feel deprived.

Shit! These damn stairs, they were treacherous. No wonder Julia almost killed herself. Got to be careful, Murray. Very, very careful. Don't fall down the stairs. You'll kill yourself—ha, that's very funny. You'll kill your goddamn self and wake goddamn Hugo and Malcolm. Or Malcolm and Hugo.

The key. Christ, don't drop the goddamn key! Easy . . . easy. There we go. Now, close the door . . . slowly, so it doesn't slam. Light switch. Goddamned light is burned out. Bright enough to see. Light from alley, shining through the windows. Light shining, shining light . . . Shining, shining through the windows . . .

Lamp. Good, it works. Cold in here. Turn on radiator. Thought we left it on—cheap fags must've turned it off. Cranking's gonna wake them. Who the hell cares. Have a right to be here. Perfect r-r-right.

Promised George . . . work on *Magic Island.* Promised Hopper, too. Mike would want me to . . . that's what Mike would want.

I need a drink.

No scotch. Bourbon . . . phew! Brandy. Need a glass. Where the hell's a glass? Hell, the damn glass *broke.*

Ah, that's good. A little pick-me-up. That's what we always did when we finished, Mike and me. Had a little pick-me-up.

Where's the score? So much stuff here. Cou—Could write a dozen shows. Dozens. One a year—keep me going. That'll keep us going, Jule. One a year. You and me, we'll do it. I'll get an arranger. Ed will help.

It'll work. *I tell you, it'll work*! He'll live on. Together we can keep him alive. Just let me be with you. Lean on me, let me take his place. That's all I want. All I ask. Is that too much? Stand in his place . . . Take care of her, love her.

I'll do it. With these, I can do it. A dozen shows . . . dozen. *Honest Abe. Honest*—'sbout Lincoln. Good idea, great scenes. These—these good—

Jesus, careful! Don't burn the goddamn place down. Cigarette out . . .

Tired, gotta sleep. Take a little nap. Bed . . . good bed. Julia's bed. Just a little nap . . .

She lost track of the weeks. *California* had opened to rave reviews and was sold out for months, but Julia had not seen the show. Christmas and New Year's passed, but she was hardly aware of them. She had dreamed of taking Michael home for the holidays, but he was too sick to leave the hospital.

In January, the day after his thirty-third birthday, Michael was more alert than usual when she came into his room. He was sitting up in a chair and, except for his stubbly head, looked almost normal. The turbanlike bandages had been removed and now there was just a small dressing to cover the scar.

"Good morning, darling. You look wonderful today."

"I . . . w-walked," he said. His speech was halting, his manner subdued.

"Michael, how marvelous! That is the most fantastic news." She noticed how he smiled and his eyes lit up when she spoke to him. "I just *know* you're getting better."

With Julia and the nurse supporting him, Michael walked once more, the two steps to the bed. Sinking against the pillows, he seemed utterly debilitated.

Julia sat quietly, letting him rest. She tried to read but was unable to concentrate.

"Have . . . you . . . g-gone to . . . studio?" he asked in the slow hesitant monotone that had become his speaking voice.

She nodded. "Yes, I went with Murray just before *California* opened."

"Did you find . . . ?"

"The songs you wrote for me? Yes, darling, I have them at home. They're beautiful. I adore them."

"L-last ones," he muttered.

"Don't say that, Michael. There will be more—many, many more."

Slowly he shook his head. "I c-can't . . . hear my music anymore. It's gone . . . whatever it was."

There was a trembling in her throat. "You believe that now because you're not completely well yet. Just wait until you come home. You'll work again, you'll hear your music again. You're going to be *wonderful.*"

Michael smiled sadly. "You n-never were . . . a good liar."

His eyes closed and his hand became flaccid in hers.

And that was the way he remained for the next three weeks. Until he died.

❧ Chapter 17 ❧

Jack Winston

"Twenty by Ten" opened at the Museum of Modern Art in early March. The MOMA exhibit was a carefully selected show, the works of ten contemporary photographers on the American scene.

The Rhineharts, naturally enough, were going to the reception for sponsors. Despite her preoccupation with the imminent opening of her own gallery, Isobel would not have missed the preview. Scott thought of every excuse not to accompany her, but in the end his curiosity persuaded him to attend.

"Solange Didier's work is the most powerful of the ten," commented Isobel, mispronouncing her name. Scott was tempted to correct his wife, as she stood gazing critically at a black-and-white study of a Maine fisherman mending his nets, one from the series on men.

"Great strength. So uncompromising." Isobel leaned into the dispassionate photograph. "What an inspiring face, Scott. Look at the expression, the wrinkles around his eyes. Can't you just sense the harshness of his life in those hands?"

They moved along the display of Solange's photographs, some of which he had viewed before. But many were new. A portrait of two blind children was particularly tender and poignant. The work was mature, touched with melancholy and a down-to-earth lyricism.

He stopped to examine the picture titled *Sea Birds*, a composition of three gulls on a rock in the surf. The dark silhouette of a man seated on the sand loomed in the right foreground. The texture of his sweater and windblown hair were detailed in relief while his face remained lost in shadow.

A prickly sensation crept across Scott's neck as he realized he was looking at himself. Solange had taken this shot on that second Saturday in Sagaponack. The day they had first made love. She had cropped most of him out of the frame and darkened the image by exposing the negative to produce the widest tonal range, but she must have known he would recognize it. Quickly he glanced to his right, seeking Isobel among the viewers. She was about ten feet away, standing in front of a mounted photograph, transfixed. His uneasiness increased as he walked toward her.

"Magnificent," she whispered reverently. "I find this profoundly stirring. Look . . . look at the plasticity. There's a sculptural quality. It reminds me of the Sistine ceiling."

For perhaps the first time in his life, he knew what it meant to have one's breath taken away. The photograph was indeed a work of art. *Early Morning, After Love* was inscribed on the margin in the photographer's spiky European script. Again, Scott was the subject, but he had never seen this picture before.

Solange had photographed him in the silvery hours before dawn as he lay sleeping. He was naked, in a state of complete relaxation. One arm cradled his head, the other was thrown across an abandoned pillow that still bore the imprint of his lover's head. The face, turned to one side, was obscured, but it was no accident of light or angle. Solange had intensified the grain so that his features and the hollows of his neck and chest muscles were deeply shaded, and this accounted for the sculptural quality that so entranced Isobel.

"If only we can acquire this! I must meet the photographer. We should have her for the gallery."

"That's simply *absurd*," he expostulated, alarm coursing through him. "Photographs of this sort with the pieces you'll be offering?"

"Oh, Scott," she passed him off with a dismissive gesture, "we need a photographer to round out the collection. We've been looking for the right artist. I wonder where Cece is."

Isobel left him, and headed toward the area where cocktails were being served.

Scott fervently wished that he had stayed at home.

"Hello, Mr. Rhinehart." It was Clive Westbrook, whom he had not encountered since their interview in November. "I see you're admiring Solange's work."

"Good to see you, Clive." He shook hands with the journalist. "And call me Scott, please."

"What do you think?" Westbrook inclined his head in a gesture that included all of Solange's photographs. "Incredible, isn't she?"

"Very talented."

"In my opinion, she could be the next Stieglitz," said Clive. "By the way, after many postponements, the *Fortune* piece is coming out next month. I'll see that you get an advance copy."

"Congratulations. I hope you're pleased with the article."

"They actually did a decent job. Not too many cuts, and they messed up only one paragraph. You look great, by the way. They've used your photo for the lead."

"Have they really?" he answered guardedly.

"I can see you're uncomfortable with that. It's only natural. Most people are uneasy at the thought of publicity."

"In my field we tend to shy away from it."

"You won't be unhappy with this, I promise. Very tasteful and dignified. The color quality is terrific." Westbrook moved closer to the picture of the sleeping lover and examined it carefully. He glanced once at Scott, then his eyes returned to the photograph.

"How would you like a drink?" Scott hastily suggested.

"Good idea. I can take only so much of photography exhibits. What about you?"

"I almost never go, but my wife is involved in MOMA." He steered Westbrook away from the section labeled DIDIER in huge block letters.

At the bar, Scott stood chatting with Clive while he scanned the crowd and waited for their drinks. And then he saw Solange. She was standing with her profile to him in a cluster of people that included the museum director, Cece Bedford, and Isobel.

At precisely that moment, Clive exclaimed, "There's Solange, come on!" Before Scott could protest, the journalist seized his arm and headed for the group. "Didier, you're magnificent," he boomed, grabbing her in a bear hug until she groaned with delight. "You've surpassed yourself. I am so proud of you."

"I've been looking around for you, Clive. I was afraid you hadn't come."

"Wouldn't have missed this for the world." He indicated Scott, who was trying to edge away. "You remember Scott Rhinehart, don't you?"

"Yes I do," she said politely.

Scott's mouth was dry, but he had to say something. "Congratulations on the show. It's very fine work."

"Thank you," she murmured, her lips barely moving. In the fraction of time that her eyes touched his, a light was kindled, flickered briefly, and died. Deliberately she turned her back on him.

There was a thundering in his head as he moved to his wife's side. "I believe you know Frank Mason, Scott," prompted Isobel, when he stood there, mute.

"Nice to see you." Aware that he was talking babble, Scott launched into a pointless discussion with Mason, a MOMA trustee. When he looked up, Solange had disappeared.

"Are you all right, Scott?" asked Isobel, when they had a moment alone. "You look so pale."

He took out a handkerchief and wiped his brow. "Strange, but I feel like I'm coming down with something. Do you think we can go home now?"

"Of course. Just let me say goodbye to Cece."

When they were in the car, she peered at him anxiously. "You've been overdoing it lately. You really must go for a checkup."

"I'm just worn out. It must be jet lag."

"You've been home for over a week. How can it be jet lag?" She glanced idly out of the window.

As if the fates were conspiring against him, one of the Chandler girls—he never could distinguish between them—was waiting for the elevator when they reached the lobby of their building.

"Hello," said Isobel, friendly as could be, "you're Roberta Chandler's granddaughter, aren't you?"

"Yes, I'm Kristen. You must be Mrs. Rhinehart. I already know your husband." She actually giggled. "Sorry I didn't say hello when I saw you at Solange Didier's studio, Mr. Rhinehart. I was so surprised. I *never* expected to run into *you* there."

The effrontery of the young never ceased to amaze Scott. He mumbled something incoherent and the elevator arrived.

As soon as they reached the apartment, he went straight to bed. Isobel brought him a tray with broth and a soft-boiled egg. He could not remember her ever having done such a thing before, even when they were first married. When they were happy in their small two-bedroom apartment, with no live-in help.

"I wasn't aware that you knew the Didier woman," she mentioned suddenly.

He paid careful attention to peeling his egg. "She took my picture for *Fortune* magazine," he replied, as nonchalantly as he could. "I was talking to Clive Westbrook tonight. He told me the article's coming out next month."

"She's terribly independent, that photographer," Isobel continued irritably. "She wasn't the least bit interested in showing her portfolio."

When he made no comment, she sat on a chair and watched him eat. "Do you want the lights out?" she asked, taking away the tray when he had finished.

"No, leave a lamp on. I'm not quite ready to fall asleep yet."

"I'll be in a little later. Call if you need anything."

"Thank you, dear." She looked at him oddly, almost with pity.

He lay back against the pillows, his mind in turmoil. A feverish confusion seemed to grip him. Seeing Solange had forced him to admit the depths of his torment.

Until now, he had imagined that her devotion was as passionate as his. But he had been shattered by her lack of warmth for him. Can that have been feigned, or had she stopped loving him so quickly? Her coldness had pierced him like a steel blade. Yet what could he have expected? *If we should meet by chance, you must promise not to speak to me,* she had insisted. And he had promised. At least on this occasion, with Westbrook and the others looking on, they had been forced to acknowledge each other.

Her appearance tonight had been subtly different. It might have been a trick of the lighting, but her edges seemed softer, the hollows in her cheeks less pronounced, making her even more desirable in his eyes.

He was obsessed with his longing for her, consumed by his memories of their time together. It was impossible to quell the tearful ache in his heart. *Not ever to be close to her again. Not ever to touch her, to hear her voice.*

He yearned to hold her in his arms once more, to kiss the love back into her eyes.

The Bedford-Rhinehart Gallery opened in the last week of March. Julia flew to New York in time to attend the press party.

Isobel and Cece had gathered an impressive array of painters for their first showing. The main floor and half-basement of Cece's spacious townhouse had been transformed into a series of arcades, each devoted to an individual artist. A colorist from San Francisco, in her first New York appearance, was the star of the show. The young abstract artist whose work Julia had admired at Thanksgiving was also well represented. She liked him even more when she saw half a dozen canvases grouped. The attenuated, skillful sculptures of a Neo-Expressionist from Barcelona pleased her less, although he was generally regarded as brilliant and original. In addition, the partners had assembled a fine collection of lithographs and monotints, as well as a selection of rare antique miniatures. They had been wise in offering enough variety, yet it was not an overly ambitious first effort.

The reviews were generous and the gossip columns full of knowing tidbits. Isobel and Cece were launched. As if there had been any doubt.

Scott and his mother walked the short distance to his Fifth Avenue apartment from the Carlyle, where they had stopped for a light supper after the press party. Isobel had begged off, claiming she and Cece must make further preparations at the gallery for tomorrow's opening.

Scott offered Julia an after-dinner drink in the study. "How long will you be staying, Mother?"

"Until the end of next week," she told him. "I want to get together with a few old friends while I'm here. Janice Fried is having a party at her new studio. And of course I must see the Winstons. They've just returned from a cruise."

"That was a long vacation," remarked Scott. "I tried to get in touch with Jack in the middle of January. I wanted to ask him about his recollections of some of Michael's music."

Julia's surprise was evident. "Why Jack?"

"I discovered that he took care of Michael's legal work during the war, when George was overseas."

"I don't remember, but I suppose he did. What is it you wanted to know?"

Scott told her about the trip to Iowa City, mentioning in particular the letter that he and Neil had found among the archives. "The original score seems to have been lost. In fact, none of the originals is there. We may not need a score if we can prove that Mitchell gave up the rights to *One Night in Venice*—or that the work was never published."

"The score is not lost, Scott," Julia said quietly. "We have it. In fact, we have all of them."

He was astounded. "I thought you—where are they? And who do you mean by *we?*"

"They've been in a vault leased by Winston & Rhinehart. Jack and I removed them from the firm's archives several months ago. Truthfully, I had forgotten all about them until you reminded me. At the moment they're in the hands of a dealer for appraisal."

"But . . . why didn't you tell me?"

"You never asked."

Scott was nonplussed. "I feel rather foolish, having gone off to Iowa on a wild goose chase."

"You're angry. You feel I've deliberately kept something from you."

"Well, haven't you?" he asked bluntly.

"Yes, I suppose I have," she admitted. "But as long as we're being honest, Scott, I questioned your motives. You had never shown the least interest in your father's music until several months ago. When you inquired about the missing scores, I thought you were . . . avaricious. Perhaps even scheming."

Scott would not have believed he could be so wounded by her words. He was considered an honorable man by his friends and associates. Did his own mother have such a low opinion of him?

"It wasn't for myself I was doing this. I'm not in need of money. I was thinking of you—and of Neil. You know how impractical he is—I can't imagine how he gets along on his university salary." Too agitated to remain seated, he paced the floor. "I worry about *you*, Mother. I know how much of the estate went for George's medical care. With all the bequests he made in the years before he died, setting up trusts for Debbie and all the grandchildren, the corpus has been greatly depleted. What if something happened? Well, I worry. You're so independent, you never allow me to do anything for you. I felt it was my duty to look out for your interests. Certainly that's what George would have wanted."

"If I was wrong about you, Scott, then I offer you my heartfelt apology. I probably should have taken you into my confidence."

Still hurt, he shook his head. "It doesn't seem to matter now. You and Jack have taken over."

"Who else would it be? I am the custodian of Michael's works, and with George gone, Jack represents Winston & Rhinehart."

"I realize that. I suppose I earned your skepticism, considering how I've ignored anything to do with Michael Shane all these years." He sighed. "It wasn't that I had no interest. It was just that when I was young, I always associated unhappiness and fear with—with my father."

"Fear? I don't understand. Of what were you afraid?"

"Of him," Scott said simply. "I was terrified of Michael when I was a child. My most vivid memory of him is the time he locked me in a closet and I saw him abuse you. It was the day Neil was born, when Michael knocked you down and you had to go to the hospital."

Julia was open-mouthed with astonishment. "*Knocked me down?* Scott. Where did you *ever* get such an idea? Michael may not have been a model husband, but he never struck me. And as for locking you in a closet, that never happened, I'm certain."

"I remember it distinctly," he insisted. "All my life there's been a clear picture in my mind of that day."

"Absolutely not," she said firmly. "I can't imagine what gave you that impression."

"I couldn't have made it up, Mother. I was locked in a closet in my father's studio. Uncle Ed let me out."

Julia shook her head, puzzled. "Honestly, Scott, you are mistaken. I seem to recall that you once hid in a cupboard in the music room. It had a self-latching door that couldn't be opened from the inside, and you were stuck in there. But no one *locked* you in. I assure you, your father would never have done anything so cruel. Michael adored you."

"But all these years . . . that's the way I remembered it."

"Children's minds invent fantastic explanations sometimes. You must be connecting unrelated episodes. I once fell down a flight of stairs and broke my arm. Perhaps that's what you remember."

He shook his head. "I have no recollection of you breaking your arm."

"Well, I'm certain you're confusing events. If only you had talked to me. I always felt that you were troubled when you were young, that something prevented you from being completely happy, the way a boy should be. Even before your father died, I tried to understand what it was, but whenever I would ask, you said there was nothing wrong."

Scott shook his head. "I *was* happy, Mother. Particularly after you married George. I've always felt that was the real beginning of my life."

"George was a loving and generous parent to both you and Neil. But you had a real father, Scott, and he truly loved you, even if he was often preoccupied with his work. Michael was a wonderful man. *Wonderful.*" Her voice faltered and she blinked back tears. "I was very much in love with him."

Deeply touched, Scott took her hands in his. "Now I'm the one who should apologize. I didn't mean to upset you."

He observed the gray in her hair and the familiar lines around her eyes. She suddenly appeared frail to him, and it struck him for the first time that there would be a terrible void in his life if Julia should die. At that unhappy thought, a shadow crossed his face. In the indirect lighting of the study, his weariness was evident.

"You look drawn, Scott. Is anything wrong?"

"No, I'm fine. Just a little tired." As he rubbed his eyes, his expression plainly denied his words.

A meeting was arranged for the next afternoon in Jack Winston's office. The older lawyer confirmed that *One Night in Venice* had never been published.

"Zachary Mitchell died in the sixties without exercising his performance option, and we know he never disturbed the music," Winston reported. "His heirs eventually sold the business to developers, who wanted it for the value of its real estate. There was never a buyer for the music inventory until the Knowles Group picked it up last year."

"Who owns the copyright on *One Night?*" Scott asked him.

"All rights belong to the estate of Michael Shane, and any company staging a production of the musical would need permission from his heirs. Under common law copyright, an unpublished work is protected for fifty years after the composer's death. That would take us to the turn of the century."

"What now?" inquired Julia.

"The Knowles Group appears to be unaware that *One Night in Venice* is not part of the inventory they acquired. We shall inform them immediately by registered letter."

Winston & Rhinehart had meanwhile received appraisals of the Shane scores from the foremost American dealer of rare books and manuscripts. The values were astonishing.

"I can hardly believe such figures," said Julia.

"Their worth is likely to increase next year, after the seventy-fifth birthday salute," Scott told her.

Winston agreed. "We should wait until then before offering them at auction."

"That sounds awfully commercial," she answered in a worried tone. "I don't know whether Michael would approve of their falling into the hands of private collectors. Shouldn't they be available to the public, to students and musicologists?"

Scott looked thoughtful. "We have time to think about that, Mother. What about Michael's journals and the letters, Jack?"

Winston had never been told about the files, and Scott explained what Neil had in his house in Iowa City. "Some of them are certainly valuable, but they should be released slowly," Winston advised. "You don't want to inundate the market. There is a certain *éclat* to rarity."

Satisfied with the outcome of their discussions, Scott was content to have his stepfather's partner shepherding the Shane estate. "There's something I'd like to discuss in private as soon as possible," he said quietly, when Julia had gone to say hello to some of the staff who had worked with George. "May I call you?"

"By all means," Winston replied. "If it's a matter of importance, perhaps we should have lunch early next week."

His secretary was impatiently awaiting his arrival when Scott reached the office later than usual on Monday morning.

"Have you seen today's *Wall Street Journal?*"

Hazel had highlighted a front page story about the savings and loan scandals that were rocking the country. Scott gasped as he read that Burton McKiever was facing indictment in Texas for violation of federal banking regulations.

"Wouldn't you know that he'd be involved in this loathsome business?"

"No wonder we never heard from him again," remarked Hazel. "I guess that's the end of McKiever."

He shook his head dubiously. "I wouldn't be too sure. You know what they say about the proverbial bad penny."

At noon that day, Scott met Jack Winston for lunch at the University Club. Over appetizers, he briefly outlined what he wanted to do, and then they spoke of other things.

They conferred again on Friday afternoon at the Fifth Avenue offices of Winston & Rhinehart. When they had concluded their rather lengthy discussions, Jack looked over his notes. "This ought to take no more than a few weeks. I'll attend to everything and let you know as soon as the papers are ready to be signed."

"Thank you. Meanwhile I'll arrange for a transfer of the funds. Remember, Jack, they are not to be told. I don't want anyone in the family to discover who the buyer is."

"You can be certain of that," Winston assured him. "Just out of curiosity, why must it be anonymous?"

"I feel more comfortable this way. I know it complicates the process, but once it's done no one need ever know."

"You're the boss. It's a rather noble thing you're doing."

Scott shook his head. "I'm not doing it to be noble. This seems to be the best way to accomplish my objective and satisfy everyone concerned."

"As you wish," said Winston, rising. "We should have a talk soon about what will happen in the future. There's the matter of who will take over here in the firm when I retire.

I'm approaching my seventy-eighth birthday in August. Sue and I are rather keen about Palm Island, if any of those homes should come on the market."

"My mother would be delighted. It would be wonderful for her to have you nearby."

Scott and his mother had a quiet meal together, served by Candida in the dining room. Neither of them spoke of his absent wife. There had been a message from Isobel that she was dining with an important out-of-town client.

Julia would be leaving for home in the morning. "Do you know of any houses for sale at Palm Island?" Scott asked her.

"They have a listing, but I never pay much attention. Why do you ask?"

Too late he realized he had blundered. "Well, I ran into Jack Winston at lunch and he mentioned that he and his wife might be interested."

"In Palm Island?" She sounded surprised. "They never mentioned it when I saw them the other evening."

"I think it may have been a new idea. Maybe after seeing you. He was more or less thinking aloud about retirement. I'm sure they'll call you if they're serious. You'd like having them there, wouldn't you?"

"Of course," she answered. "Wouldn't George have loved that?"

After leaving the table, they went into the study. "Something to drink, Mother?"

"No, thank you. I'll just ask Candida for another cup of coffee."

Scott poured himself a brandy and sat in his favorite club chair. With a sigh, he put his head back and closed his eyes. When he heard Julia returning he straightened up, but not before she had noticed his dejection.

She put a hand on his shoulder. "Something is troubling you, Scott. I can always tell."

"It's nothing important."

"I sense that it is. Can't you talk to me?"

Suddenly he wanted to unburden himself to her. He needed to confide in someone. There was no one else he could tell. Not Dick Graham, nor any of his other friends.

Searching for the right words, he blurted, "I'm in love with another woman."

He winced at the shock on his mother's face. She sat down slowly, leaning forward to face him. "I thought you and Isobel had a good marriage."

"At one time, perhaps. But things have not really been happy for the last several years. Ever since Ginger went to boarding school. Once both kids were out of the house, I discovered that we hardly knew each other. We have so little to talk about, we—oh hell, Mother, it happened. It just happened."

Julia's tone was cool. "Tell me, is your . . . is she a younger woman?"

He nodded. "A little. Thirty-six, almost thirty-seven."

"Are you sure you're not making excuses for yourself? Now that your wife is middle-aged and perhaps not as attractive to you, you need a reason for having an affair."

"No, I don't think so. And I'm not having an affair—at least, not any longer. It lasted for a very short time. We broke it off some months ago. Except for a single accidental encounter, we haven't seen each other since January."

Julia pursued what was beginning to sound like an interrogation. "Does Isobel know about this woman?"

"I'm certain she doesn't. Isobel and I have barely occupied the same house for months. She's been traveling most of the time since you were here at Thanksgiving."

"You're feeling neglected. Are you sure that isn't the reason? Are you perhaps jealous that Isobel has a new interest, a career that keeps her away from you?"

He shook his head adamantly. "Absolutely not. It's true that at first I wasn't in favor of the gallery, but the situation between us had already become sufficiently strained. It was actually a relief when Isobel began to travel. Now that she's back in New York, we'll stay together. But when I think of all the years ahead . . ."

"Oh, Scott. I'd like to be more sympathetic, but I don't approve of a man cheating on his wife."

He flinched at the harshness of her words. "I don't approve of it, either. It didn't seem that way. There are problems between Isobel and me that you couldn't possibly understand. No one could."

"There are problems in every marriage. You have two marvelous children. Even though they're grown up, they are still your children and Isobel is their mother. Have you thought of them?"

"Of course I have, Mother." Scott closed his eyes wearily. It was an effort to keep the irritation out of his voice. "It's mainly to spare Ginger and Chip that I won't consider divorce. I probably shouldn't have told you. But now you know."

Julia's tone became more understanding. "I'd like to offer words of encouragement, dear, but I'm not sure what they are. Some marriages seem to grow stronger with time. That was true of George and me, but it was not true of my first marriage."

Startled, he looked up. "You just told me the other day that you were extremely happy with Michael."

"No, Scott, that is not what I told you. I said I was very much in love with him. More 'in love' in a romantic sense than I was with George. But love isn't always enough." She took a deep shuddering breath, and he recalled Solange speaking almost the identical words. "When the dust had settled, I was really much happier with George." She smiled wistfully. "How I wish he were alive to hear me say that."

"Surely he must have known."

Slowly Julia shook her head. "If only I could be certain."

❦ Chapter 18 ❧

George

The moment they walked in, it was obvious that someone had been there before them. Filled with dread at the prospect of returning to the studio, Julia had steeled herself for the impact as she accompanied George Rhinehart downtown for the purpose of going through Michael's effects.

"Who did all this?" she demanded.

Standing in the doorway, her eyes took in the scattered books and the overturned chair. An empty brandy bottle lay on its side on the wooden counter, a broken glass on the floor. In the bay window of the front room, Michael's worktable loomed, strangely bare. It was not until she had gone through the rest of the apartment and seen the rumpled bed and the ransacked dresser drawers that she realized what was missing.

The sheets of music paper were gone from Michael's composing table. All the new material—the entire score to *Magic Island*, the treatment for *Honest Abe*, and the dozens of songs that she and Murray had discovered that bleak afternoon six months ago—had vanished.

At first she could not believe it. "Where *are* they? How can they have disappeared?" She darted from one corner of the room to the other, snatching at sheet music and catalogues, frantically searching through stacked folders of papers. "Someone has taken them!"

George tried his best to calm her. "Don't panic, Julia. They must be in a drawer or one of the bookcases. I'll help you look for them."

"You don't understand," she cried. "They were here on his composing desk. The apartment was in perfect order. It never looked like this. Someone has gone through everything."

Julia had put off coming here as long as possible. Living in the apartment on Gramercy Park for all these months since her husband's death had been unbearable enough, but she had little choice. This was different. The studio had become a shrine to him. It was the essence of Michael, the dwelling-place of his soul. The task of entering these rooms where he had worked, of seeing his concert grand, touching his papers, of reliving all the shining moments and the pain she had known here, had been so onerous that she had been unable to face up to it.

Ultimately it had to be done. It was time to vacate the apartment for a new tenant. Michael's will must be processed, the estate appraisal finalized and tax papers filed. George would send a young associate from the firm to record the inventory, but he needed Julia to help him organize the contents of the flat.

"Are you certain they were on this table?" he asked.

"Positive. Murray and I were here together the week after Michael's operation to pick up the last-minute revisions for *California.* Murray was actually the one who came upon all the new material. I'd never seen him as excited. He got so carried away, he kept saying he could write a dozen musicals with all those songs, that Michael's work didn't have to die with him—" She stopped abruptly, breathing hard.

George was looking at her with a questioning air. "Are you thinking what I'm thinking, Julia?"

"That Murray has them."

"It makes sense. Especially since he told Ed Hopper he was working on *Magic Island.* If I'm not mistaken, he had the score."

"He did? But . . . he never told me, he never *asked.*"

"I imagine he didn't want to disturb you when Michael was so ill, or afterward, when you were grieving."

"But it's not right. It's deceitful."

"Oh, I'm sure he didn't mean—"

"No, don't defend him, George! He has a lot of nerve taking Michael's work without my permission. Murray had no right to remove *any* of the worksheets from this studio, much less *all* of them." She was lost in thought for a moment. "He hasn't called me once since he left for California. He's been working on a script out there since the beginning of March. Do you think he took the music with him?"

George threw up his hands. "I have no idea. We're just surmising that it was Murray. We don't know that for a fact."

"Well, who else could it be? Who else would have any use for it?"

"No one," he admitted. "I must say, it seems peculiar that he would just walk off with the scores. I can understand his thinking, though. On the one hand, *Magic Island* was half his. He and Michael started the project together. They talked it through. Murray already had a first draft of the book. He was waiting for the music to finish the lyrics, so I guess he felt he had a right to take it and work on it."

Julia was shaking her head in protest. "Wait, hear me out," said George. "While there's a good case for his taking *Magic Island*, he has absolutely no right to the rest of the material. That is your property; it belongs to Michael's estate. And it presents a real legal problem."

Julia crossed her arms and paced the floor of the studio. "I am so angry. They're like vultures, all of them! Gerry Ross, Arlo, Mitchell Publishing—all they want is to milk the last dollar they can get out of Michael's work. I thought at least I could trust Murray. I should have realized the day we were here. It was obvious he was itching to get his hands on those songs. Of all people, to do something so underhanded!"

"Well, now, we mustn't jump to conclusions until we find out what really happened. Let's wait until we speak to him. Perhaps there's another explanation. It could have been a burglar."

Julia heaved a sigh of exasperation. "That doesn't make sense, George. The door wasn't forced, the windows are locked. What would a burglar want with music manuscripts?"

"Does anyone else have a key to the apartment?" he asked.

"Only the landlords. Malcolm Lowell and Hugo Miller. They live downstairs. They'd be at work now."

"I'll talk to them," said George, making a note. "What about a janitor?"

"No, we stopped the cleaning woman when Michael went into the hospital. She gave Malcolm her key." Julia put her face in her hands. "Michael's music, his marvelous songs. They're all I had left of him."

"I don't like to see you upset like this."

"*Upset?* My husband is *dead!* How the hell would you feel if everyone was trying to take advantage of the person you loved even after he was gone?" She was crying openly now, and George patted her shoulder awkwardly. Julia took the handkerchief he handed her and blew her nose.

"Now," he said, clearing his throat, "why don't we go in the other room and sit down." He brought her a glass of water from the kitchen and took out a pen. "Try to recall what compositions were here that day, the ones you say are missing."

Drawing a deep breath, she made an effort to collect her thoughts. "In addition to the orchestrated score for *Magic Island*, Michael had written a detailed treatment with musical sketches for a work based on the life of Abraham Lincoln. There were also extensive notes for several musical comedies. I don't recall exactly how many, but I think at least five or six. And then, he had written many songs—an extraordinary number. There was a thick stack of music sheets, all of them complete songs." George was writing rapidly in a tight, neat script. "Let me see what else . . . oh, his ticklers were on the table. Michael jotted down ideas—melodies, themes, and storylines. They were often quite detailed, with suggestions for sets and costumes. He was actually pretty good at drawing, and he was in the habit of illustrating his concepts. All of these were recorded in a series of blank books."

"Like diaries or journals?"

"No. He did keep a journal when he had time, but those are at home. These notebooks were an inspirational thing. He called them 'ticklers' because they more or less got him going when he was stuck. He claimed he could always flip through a tickler and come up with the kernel of a new idea. Once he made use of something he would draw a diagonal line through it." She hesitated because George had stopped taking notes and was staring at her. "Am I not making sense?"

"Oh," he said, catching himself, "you're explaining it beautifully. I am absolutely in awe of the artistic mind. I have no facility for creativity."

"Nor have I," she answered. "But let me tell you, after living with Michael, I know it doesn't just spring from the air. He worked *hard*—harder than anyone I've ever known. That's why this infuriates me so."

"I really do understand how you feel. It makes me angry, too. If I seem unemotional to you, remember that I have to keep a cool head in order to handle this in a dispassionate way."

"Oh, God," said Julia despairingly. "On top of everything else, now I'll have to fight Murray."

"No you won't. You needn't concern yourself about Murray. That's what I'm here for. I'll take care of everything."

"What are you going to do?"

"I'll get in touch with him and straighten it out. It does seem odd that a writer would not understand that those compositions are private property and must be respected as such." George had put away his notebook and pen. He bent down to pick up the shards of broken glass from the floor, and began putting the books back in the bookcase. There was a reassuring calm to his manner. "I'm certain it was just a misunderstanding. Murray probably thinks he was doing you a favor by developing Michael's ideas."

"I hope you're right. After all these years I would hate to think that he would steal Michael's work," she said sorrowfully. "But I can't forget how he reacted that day. Almost as if this was his salvation. As if Michael had provided him with sufficient inspiration for the rest of his life."

"Try not to think about it. You have enough on your mind, taking care of your two sons. How are they, by the way?"

"They're fine," she smiled. "It's amazing how quickly a child forgets. Scotty was heartbroken when Michael died, but he doesn't seem to miss him at all."

"I doubt that very much. He's probably hiding his feelings." George snapped his briefcase shut, preparing to leave. "You must be tired. I think we should attend to this another time."

When they were in a taxi, Julia apologized. "I'm sorry I carried on so. It's been horrible. I would never have believed that people could be so grasping, so unfeeling."

"I have discovered in a decade of practicing the law," said George, "that when money is involved, sentiment is easily forgotten."

George called Julia the following week and made an appointment for Saturday afternoon. He came to the apartment and seemed disappointed when she told him that Regina had taken the children to the park.

"I was looking forward to seeing them," he said before revealing the reason he had come. "I've had a talk with Malcolm Lowell and Hugo Miller."

"You have? When?"

"This morning. I arranged to see them on the weekend, since their working hours seem to be rather erratic."

"To say the least," she laughed. "Hugo's always got some kind of deadline at the magazine, and Malcolm sets up his exhibits at night."

George took a seat on the sofa, refusing her offer of something to drink. He looked more casual today in his weekend attire of gray herringbone tweed jacket, blue buttondown shirt, and jaunty bowtie in a red paisley print. In the last few weeks, she had begun to feel extremely comfortable with him.

She looked at him seriously. "Well, what did they tell you?"

"As we suspected, it was Murray. He came there at night, a week or two before Michael died. He was evidently drunk, because he made a racket in the courtyard and they looked out to see what was going on. He staggered into the building and tripped on his way upstairs. They were going out to help him, but he let himself into the apartment before they could get up the nerve."

"Didn't they question why he was there?"

George shook his head. "Hugo said they knew he had a key. They've seen Murray come and go regularly for thirteen years—as long as Michael had been renting from them. It never occurred to them to stop him. Their main concern was that he'd fall down the stairs and break his neck."

"Was that all?"

"No. They heard him knocking around for several hours. Something shattered—probably the glass we found—and a number of heavy objects fell to the floor. At one point they thought he went sprawling. Still, they didn't go up, which I think was a mistake. But I guess you can't blame them; it really wasn't their business."

"What happened then?" asked Julia.

"For a while he was picking out tunes on the piano in a very amateurish way. Then he played records, and when it grew late, they were tempted to tell him he was making too much noise. But suddenly everything became quiet, so they went to sleep. The next time he appeared it was morning, around six o'clock. Actually it was only Hugo who saw him; he gets up early to write. The window in front of his desk has a view of the front entrance and the courtyard."

"What did he see?"

"Murray left the building, unshaven and in a disheveled state. He was carrying a large portfolio under his arm. Hugo assumed it contained musical scores, and he didn't see anything particularly unusual about that, because Murray often came and went with papers when he worked with Michael." George stopped talking and smiled apologetically. "So that's it."

"There's no doubt, is there? It *was* Murray." Julia drew a shaky breath, fighting tears. The confirmation that Murray Baker had stolen Michael's work was so appalling that she could find no words to express her disillusionment. "I just— I find it so unbelievable, so outrageous. No wonder I haven't heard from him. He has violated Michael's memory, our friendship, everything that was between us. I never want to see or speak to him again."

"You don't have to. I told you I'd handle it, and I will. I'm sending someone to obtain a sworn deposition from Malcolm and Hugo, and I will deal with Murray as soon as I can get hold of him. My office has been trying to reach him, but he's on location with a film crew in some remote spot—the Yucatan, I believe."

She nodded, not trusting her voice, overcome with sorrow. Her grief was fresh and raw, more keenly felt because she had begun to recover from the numbness of mourning. Not for herself did she care, or even for her children. But she could never forgive Murray for his betrayal of Michael. Twenty years of friendship that had been closer than a blood relationship. Did the memory of all they had shared mean so little to him?

"I can't tell you how sorry I am, Julia," George said softly as he was leaving. "I realize this is terribly distressing for you. You have a right to feel outraged. But you mustn't make yourself ill over it. You've been driving yourself too hard. Learn to lean on other people. Let me assume some of the burden."

He was so comforting, so reassuring. "Thank you. Not just for this, but for everything you've done. I don't know how I would have gotten through the past year if it weren't for you."

From the day Michael had become ill, George had been there to help them in every way possible, far more than could be expected of an attorney. Whenever a tangle arose with the production of *California*, George would handle it. If anything at all went wrong with Michael's hospital records, the medical insurance, their finances, it was George she had turned to. Their special treatment at Memorial had been not so much the result of Michael's celebrity, she discovered, but of George's influence with the hospital administration. Before his death, George's father had been on the board for many years; the family donated large sums of money for cancer research. The Rhineharts, as Edwin had remarked on more than one occasion, were an influential and wealthy clan.

Julia was often alone, but she did not particularly mind the solitude. For much of her life, she had been alone. Michael had attracted legions of friends and hangers-on by the force of his personality. They had come by the hundreds when he died. *We hadn't realized how sick he was,* they murmured with tears in their eyes, stricken at the finality, the absence from their lives of his youth and vigor and aura. *All that talent and creativity . . . a tragic loss. We'll keep in touch . . .*

But of course they hadn't. They had come for Michael, not Julia, and she had never expected it to be any other way.

It was some of his close associates, however, who had disappointed her most of all. Arlo Rothmore, who was suing for a share of the profits from *California*. Gerald Ross. If she had any illusions left about Gerry, they had been shattered by the story in *Look* magazine.

"Working with Michael Shane was always a roller-coaster ride," Ross had been quoted as saying in the article about his current revival of *Over the Moon*—a contract that the Hopper agency had negotiated when Michael was apparently healthy and riding high on Broadway. "I discovered him, you know. He was a remarkable talent, but I credit myself with pulling Michael in line, disciplining him, keeping him off the booze and away from women."

And now Murray . . . George was right. Dwelling on the bitterness of betrayed friendship could make her ill. When Michael died she felt her life was over, and yet she had forced herself to go on. She was determined to put the pain behind her, for the sake of her children. During the days it was easy to keep busy and not brood over her predicament. But at night she would awaken with anxiety, wondering how she would get through the years that lay ahead. In the past she had managed on her own, but now she had two little boys to care for. The responsibility was overwhelming. They must be taught about life. They must be guided and nurtured and shown how to be good men. How would she do it alone?

Time passed slowly, and she found herself gradually seeking life again. Summer came, she enrolled Scott in a day camp during the week, and they often spent weekends in the country with Betsy and Edwin. She heard nothing further from George about Murray Baker, although she consulted him frequently on other matters.

Seven months after Michael's death they were still sorting out the details of his affairs. Usually she went to the Winston & Rhinehart offices, but now and again they would meet at the Hoppers' townhouse to go over royalty statements with Edwin. One late summer evening, finished with their conference, they sat on the vine-covered balcony outside the library, having a gin and tonic with Ed and Betsy. Afterward George walked her home. He lingered in front of the building, and she considered inviting him up for an impromptu supper but immediately thought better of it.

"How are the children?" he asked, as was his custom.

"Wonderful. They both had birthdays in July."

"They're great kids. I really enjoy talking to Scott. Would it be all right if I stopped by sometime to visit?"

"Oh, George . . . how thoughtful of you. We'd like that very much."

"Perhaps Sunday afternoon, then. We could take them to the park."

She turned to wave at the door and he gave her a half salute as he swung across the avenue.

I must remember not to count on people. I must remind myself not to build my expectations. To say that I would inconvenience myself on their behalf is not sufficient reason to place myself in a position to be disappointed. If I anticipate nothing, then I will not feel let down.

George had promised to come by, but it was past one o'clock and he had not even phoned. Well, maybe he hadn't exactly *promised*, but he had made it sound definite. It was obvious now that he was just being kind. Why would an attractive bachelor want to waste a Sunday afternoon with a widow and her two children anyway? Poor man had witnessed so many of her sporadic displays of temper and tears all these months, he would have been mad to subject himself to more.

She had actually looked forward to seeing him. Regina had the weekend off, Neil was napping, and Scott was playing quietly in his room. Betsy and Edwin had left for the country yesterday morning, inviting her to come along, as usual, but she had told them she had things to do in the apartment.

It would have been nice to have had company; she was feeling lonely. Well, no matter. It was important to remember that George Rhinehart was her lawyer, and that was the extent of their friendship.

As soon as Neil woke up, she would take the boys for a walk, maybe to the playground. Scotty was bored with the neighborhood park. *I suppose it was silly of me not to go up to Connecticut with Betsy and Ed. Scott would have had a playmate all weekend, and it would have been good to get out of the city on such a lovely day.* She longed for some physical activity. For so many months, she had wanted to do nothing. Only her responsibility for two little boys had forced her to keep going.

Her desk, which had been moved into the music room when Neil's crib was put in the study, was piled high with papers. There were bills to pay, the checkbook to balance. She had to be very careful with expenses now, because her future income was uncertain. Michael's shows had made a great deal of money, but most of the profits had been invested in the expensive productions of *A Light in the Sky* and *California*. Additional funds were tied up in the road companies for sets and costumes, rents and salaries. Until the final audit was complete, there was no accurate estimate of their net worth. They had never lived extravagantly, but they hadn't worried about saving money either. With four hits in a row, they had thought the royalties would keep rolling in for years to come. No one had expected a talented composer to die in the prime of life.

Michael had set up a trust for the boys, but whatever capital was there had to be conserved for schools and colleges in the future. Scott and Neil had a lifetime of needs ahead of them. If she went back to work, her salary would never cover all of their expenses. They could probably manage without a housekeeper now, but the boys were so attached to Regina—

The house phone buzzed sharply, startling her. The doorman's voice sounded hollowly over the intercom. "Mr. Rhinehart is here to see you, Mrs. Shane."

"Oh." Her hand automatically went to her untidy hair. Not expecting him to appear without calling ahead, she had paid no heed to her appearance. "Please ask him to come up."

She hurried into the bathroom, ran a brush through her hair, and hastily applied lipstick. There was just time to smooth her skirt and tuck in her blouse before the doorbell rang.

Scott came dashing out of his room. "I'll get it, I'll get it," he shouted.

George was standing in the hallway, looking rather collegiate in khaki slacks and a sport shirt. He carried a gigantic bunch of garden flowers and a shopping bag from F.A.O. Schwarz. "Hi," he said, stepping into the apartment. "I know I'm late. I was in Connecticut and I stayed to have brunch with my mother. She's not been well."

"I'm very sorry to hear that. I hope it's nothing serious."

"Old age is usually serious," he replied drily. "I've been calling you since ten o'clock. Is your phone out of order?"

So he *had* tried. A flood of happiness surged through her. "I don't think so," she answered, "I spoke to Betsy this morning." Her hands flew to her mouth. "Oh, I switched phones— I wonder if I left it off the hook. Excuse me." She went into her bedroom and sure enough, the receiver was lying on the night table.

When she returned to the living room, Scott was opening a big box. "A chemistry set," he exclaimed. "I always wanted one!"

"I was afraid you might already have one," said George.

"No, my friend Roland does, but this kind is *much* better." They all laughed. "I brought a stuffed animal for Neil. And these should go in water," he said, handing her the flowers that were lying on a table. "They're from our garden."

"Thank you," she murmured, "you're awfully kind."

She was glad to have an excuse to leave the room, glad that George could not see the tears that welled. He'll think I do nothing but weep, she admonished herself, wiping her eyes. In the pantry, she quickly unwrapped the flowers and arranged them in a tall white ceramic jug.

"Don't they look beautiful," she said, carrying the generous bouquet to a console table against the wall. In answer, his brown eyes crinkled at the corners. He had a square, decidedly pleasant face that creased agreeably when he smiled. She found herself smiling back at him. *This is a man who really takes pleasure from making people happy.*

Just then they heard Neil. "Oh my, he always cries when he wakes up from a long nap. I have to josh him a bit to get him in a good mood. Will you excuse me for a few minutes, George?"

"Scott and I will keep each other company, won't we, sport?"

The boy drew his breath in delight. "Would you like to see my room?" he asked shyly.

"I'd like that."

Julia took a bottle from the refrigerator and went into the temporary nursery Regina had set up in the study. The children were meant to share a bedroom, but Scott had been waking up lately when his brother cried at night.

At thirteen months, Neil was a handsome little boy. He had so much of his father in him. The deep blue eyes and wavy dark hair, the cleft in his chin, the way he frowned, and a certain expression around the mouth that Julia could never define but had always loved in Michael. Maybe that was why she had infinite patience with this child's moods.

"Hello, sweetheart," she crooned, adoring the feel of his warm, sturdy body in her arms. "Don't cry, Neil. Mommy brought you some juice. I'm going to change you, and then we shall go for a walk in the park with a very nice man." She laid him down on the changing table. "See what he brought you? Look at the teddy bear."

George had parked his car, a dark green Chrysler convertible, out front on Lexington Avenue. The top was down, and Scott knelt in the back seat while Julia sat in front with Neil on her lap. It was a fine bright, sunny day, cool for August, with a fresh breeze stirring the trees. A day for going on an excursion with someone you liked. As they drove up Fifth Avenue to the sixties, Julia glanced sideways at George, who rested one elbow on the door, his hands lightly holding the steering wheel. The wind ruffled his neatly groomed sandy hair as he turned to smile at her. His face had a glow of sun and the outdoors, and his arms, where the turned-back sleeves of his open-collared Madras shirt exposed them, were sinewy and tanned, covered with fine golden brown hair that caught the sunlight.

They parked near the entrance to the Central Park Zoo and he put up the top before taking Neil's stroller out of the trunk. Scott skipped ahead, turning to wait for them to catch up. They had visited the lions and tigers, the elephant, the bears, and the monkey house when Scott heard hurdy-gurdy music. "The merry-go-round," he cried, his face lighting up.

Grinning, George bought a rash of tickets, and they rushed on board to find the perfect horses. Scott's was huge and went up and down, while right beside it was a smaller one for Neil, who became quite entranced with the mane and the reins, jiggling ecstatically when the carousel began to turn. At George's insistence, Julia mounted a horse while he stood next to the baby and held him.

After the third ride, they managed to tear the boys away and headed for the ice cream parlor. Scott was as animated as she had ever seen him, applying himself to a chocolate ice cream cone and talking a mile a minute, while Neil for once was smiling and contented. Julia tried to remember. *Did we ever do anything like this with Michael?*

By five o'clock, Neil was getting cranky. "I'll drop you at

home so you can tend to him," said George, "Scott and I will go pick up some Chinese food for supper."

"Are you sure? You don't have to if there's something you'd rather do."

He looked at her with an amused smile. "What makes you think I'd rather do anything else?"

She had finished bathing Neil and was preparing his dinner when they returned. Scotty came into the kitchen, very importantly bearing the cartons of Chinese food. "We went to Chinatown," he announced.

"You did? All the way down there?"

"I have a favorite place," said George. "We'll have to go there sometime."

Julia concentrated on pouring hot water into the warming pan of Neil's feeding bowl. "Dinner certainly smells wonderful."

"Where are the baking dishes? I'll put it in the oven to keep warm."

"In the cupboard next to the stove."

While she fed Neil, George spooned shrimp in lobster sauce and dumplings into Pyrex casseroles. Scott had signs of the day's indulgences around his mouth. "Go wash your face and hands before dinner, Scotty."

"Do you think he'll like this food?" asked George, heating won ton soup in a pot. "I got some chop suey and chicken chow mein, just in case."

"Scott enjoys new experiences."

"He's a wonderful boy and very smart," said George, settling on a stool next to the counter.

"If you'd like a drink, everything's in that cabinet."

"Do you have any beer?"

"I'm not sure. Look in the fridge."

"Two beers," he said triumphantly. "Will you have one?"

"No, thanks. I'm not crazy about beer, but I'd like a glass of wine. I think there's some open from the other night."

George found a glass and poured wine for her. Neil was humming contentedly, rhythmically thumping his foot against the high chair while he chewed cut-up chicken and swallowed the carrots she spooned into his mouth. Scott, who was going into second grade and loved to read, had brought a book and was lying on his stomach on the hall floor. It was a very domestic scene, and for the second time that day Julia realized that this was new for them, this family tranquility and harmony. Whenever Michael was at home the atmosphere had been charged with high energy. The apartment had reverberated with the sound of his voice and his music and the constant ringing of the telephone. They were always either on their way out to a performance, a concert, a party, or expecting people in. This peaceful, soothing contentment was something she had seldom experienced with Michael.

They ate at the kitchen table. Julia spread a green and white checked cloth over the scrubbed wood and set out white crockery. She placed the steaming baking dishes on straw trivets and poured more beer for George and a glass of milk for Scott. Neil sat in his high chair, eyeing them sleepily as he guzzled milk from a bottle. When his eyes looked ready to close, she carried him to his crib and he promptly turned on his tummy and fell asleep.

Regina returned while they were still eating dinner. She reminded Julia that some of her delicious rice pudding was left in the refrigerator for dessert. There were fortune cookies, too, and Scott, who had never seen one before, took great delight in them.

"*A very important person is about to come into your life,*" he read slowly and seriously. "I wonder who it will be? How soon will it happen?"

George smiled broadly at Julia. "Maybe it has happened already. Did you ever think of that?"

"But it doesn't *say* that," Scott insisted, while Julia avoided George's eyes. "Let me see what yours says, Mom. *Great pro-sper-ity will be yours.* What does that mean?"

"Prosperity means wealth," explained George. "It seems your mother will be rich."

"Oh," Scott replied, sounding disappointed. "What does yours say, Mr. Rhinehart?"

"*The gods that smiled when you were born are laughing now,*" George read from the slip of paper. "Someone seems to have a sense of humor."

Scott wrinkled his nose. "I don't like that one."

Julia looked at the clock. "It's time to take your bath, Scott. Camp day tomorrow."

"Okay," the boy said reluctantly. "Are you gonna be here when I'm done?"

"Yes, I'll stick around for a while," George assured him.

He cleared the table and helped Julia wash the dishes. Afterward she made coffee and they sat in the living room talking until Scott came to say goodnight. They accompanied him to his room and George tucked him in.

"I had a good time today," Scott told him. "Will you come see us again?"

"I'd very much like to, if your mother will invite me."

"Please, Mommy, will you?" he pleaded.

Julia was embarrassed, but she said, "Yes, I will."

"When?"

"One day soon," she replied briskly. "Now go to sleep."

"We all had a very good time today," she told George when they were back in the parlor.

"I think I enjoyed it more than anyone. Those are two terrific little boys."

"Thank you." There was a silence.

"It's been so very pleasant that I hesitate to bring up a business matter . . ." he began.

She studied him and saw that his expression was grave. "You've talked to Murray Baker."

"Yes I have. Yesterday."

"Did he have anything unexpected to say?"

He nodded. "Actually he did. The score of *Magic Island* he freely admits to taking. He claims you were aware of that, that you expected him to work on it."

She frowned. "That may have been his understanding. I really don't remember."

"He also took three of the unrelated songs, he says. He was somewhat embarrassed about that, and apologized but says he thought they would fit into the score of *Magic Island*. It evidently needed more music."

"Why didn't he ask?"

"He said you were too distraught and so was he. For him, he claims, working with Michael's music was therapeutic, but he couldn't expect you to understand."

"What about the rest of it? The treatments, the other songs?"

George drew in his lips and raised his eyebrows, indicating there was a new wrinkle. "He swears he doesn't have them."

"And you believe him?"

He made a futile gesture. "I don't know, Julia. He sounded very convincing."

"But why hasn't he called me? Why hasn't he answered any of your letters? You've been trying to reach him since April."

"He said he was in the Yucatan for three months, working on a Metro picture called *The Conquerors*. And then they went down to Argentina. As soon as he returned to Beverly Hills, he found my messages and called immediately."

"I don't believe him, George. There is something very strange about this. He would have written to me or telephoned, no matter where he was. I haven't received so much as a postcard from him. For all the years I've known Murray, he's never remained out of contact for so long." She waited for a moment, but George said nothing. "My husband has died and I'm alone with two children. It's not like Murray to be so out of touch—unless he has something to hide."

"Maybe—maybe he's distracted by someone. A woman."

"Why would that stop him from calling me?"

He scratched his forehead self-consciously and placed his hand over his mouth. "Murray has become . . . involved with the star of *The Conquerors*—Vivienne Tremaine. He thinks you hate her."

"Oh, brother!" She threw back her head and laughed. There was an edge of hysteria to her laughter and she could not seem to stop. "Am I a fool? He's taking us for a ride. Murray has always wanted to step into Michael's skin and he's doing everything he possibly can to pull it off. That music is sitting in his apartment, or safe deposit box, or his mountain cabin. I *know* it. Isn't there *something* you can do? Get a search warrant?"

"He said we were welcome to search his residence, but I can't advise you to do that. Not on the flimsy evidence we have. I could put a private detective on it, but that gets messy. I don't know, Julia . . . I'm afraid this will never come to light. There's no way he can ever try to publish any of it."

"Why not? No one's ever heard that music—no one but Michael. Murray could collaborate with another composer, pass it off as his work."

"He'd never get away with it," said George. "Not now, when he knows we suspect him. I wouldn't be surprised if tho music just turns up on your doorstep one day in a plain brown wrapper."

"You agree with me, don't you? You think he took them."

He looked at her squarely. "I honestly don't know."

Julia closed her eyes and leaned back against the sofa. "I will never believe that he didn't. Nothing will ever convince me."

George took her hand. "I'm sorry I didn't wait until tomorrow to tell you. I hope I haven't spoiled the day for you."

"No, it was a lovely day. One thing has nothing to do with the other."

He stood up. "I guess I'd better be going now." At the door, he said, "*Will* you invite me again?"

She smiled. "Yes, of course. Any time you say."

"How about next weekend?"

"It's Labor Day. I promised Betsy and Ed I'd go to Darien for the long weekend."

"That's perfect. I can see you up there. My house is twenty minutes away from them."

"I remember now—Ed found their place through you, didn't he?"

"That's right. I was overseas, but my partner handled the closing."

"It all seems so long ago, doesn't it?"

"Not so very. About seven years, that's all."

She sighed. "I feel as if I've lived two lifetimes in those years."

He took her face in his hands and gently kissed her forehead. "You have."

George came by the Hoppers' house on Saturday afternoon. He and Edwin took Scotty and Perk to a nearby stable for pony rides, and he stayed to have dinner with them. Afterward, they went to the movies in Westport.

The next morning he appeared unannounced, carrying a bag of bagels and smoked salmon. "I forgot cream cheese. I hope you have some." Betsy did, and they sat out on the terrace, eating a second breakfast and reading the Sunday *Times*.

That night the four of them had dinner at a country inn, leaving the children at home with Regina and Mrs. Reilly. The next day, Labor Day, Betsy packed a picnic basket, and

George joined them again. They all piled into the station wagon, driving to the local park to see the parade and play softball. At night, after the children's baths, the grownups took them in their pajamas to see the fireworks, then drove back to the city and put them to bed.

Julia and her sons saw George frequently after that. On a Saturday in the city he would take Scott, and often Perk, for a game of catch in the park. Sometimes he came for supper, helped Scott with his homework, and read stories to Neil. Whenever they went to the country with the Hoppers, he would drop by for brunch and end up spending the day. Betsy invited him to join them for Thanksgiving dinner, but he said he had to be with his family. There was a large assortment of aging Rhinehart aunts and uncles, as well as cousins, according to Betsy. George promised to stop by afterward, and arrived just as Ed had finished carving the turkey. Julia was as happy as the boys were to see him.

Scott especially had become attached to George. Even Neil, always more reserved than his brother, had warmed up considerably. At Christmas he brought them the most outrageous presents. "You'll spoil them," Julia protested.

"Children should be spoiled. When else will life be as perfect?"

He presented her with a necklace of square links of carved antique jade strung on silk cord. "Oh, George, it's so beautiful," she said uncertainly. "But you really shouldn't . . ."

He placed a finger against her lips. "Don't spoil my pleasure," he said. "I enjoy selecting gifts for my friends. I knew when I saw this that I wanted you to have it."

There was a quiet New Year's Eve at Betsy and Edwin's with just a few good friends. And then it was 1951 and the month of January to be endured. The month in which Michael had died. An entire year gone by without him. She gazed at his photograph, and her grief was still sharp and unrelenting. She leafed through the scrapbooks and reread his letters once again. *I wish there were some sort of ceremony or ritual to mark his passing,* she thought.

George did not call her at all that week, but on the anniversary of Michael's death, he sent flowers.

February and March seemed endless. At last it was spring again. *Kick Up Your Heels* was soon coming out as a motion picture. Before the movie was released, there was to be a private screening in New York.

It was dreadful. Julia hated it. They had changed the story until she hardly recognized it, turning the clever, sophisticated plot into a typical Hollywood farce. The musical arrangements were all wrong. Worst of all, they had interpolated a banal love ballad and other mediocre music for some of the dance numbers, and she feared that audiences would believe they were Michael's.

"Never again," she declared when it was over. "That is the last one of Michael's shows that Hollywood will ever get hold of, if I have anything to say about it."

"Don't fret, Julia. It will make money and keep his work before the public," Edwin argued. "How many Americans do you suppose get to see stage shows?"

On Memorial Day weekend George took her to meet his mother. "My grandfather bought this place from a railroad tycoon who had it built as his seaside cottage," explained George when they were approaching the residence along a driveway lined with stately oak trees.

This was the first time Julia had seen the house that the Rhinehart family kept as a country retreat. It lay southeast of the town of Norwalk in an area of grand old estate-farms, a large graceful country colonial of whitewashed brick and wood, with a columned terrace on the water side. The gardens were informal and beautifully tended by a caretaker who lived in a cottage on the property. There was a private beach with a boathouse on the Sound, as well as a tennis court and swimming pool that the neighbors were welcome to use at any time.

"I spent all of my summers here, except for when I went to camp in Maine," George told her, pulling to a stop across from the pillared front entrance. "It was called Oakwood when my grandfather was alive, but Dad discontinued the custom. He thought it sounded too much like a Southern plantation."

"It's very beautiful. You must have been happy growing up here."

"Actually," he said, "it was not a particularly joyous house. It should have been. It should have been filled with children and laughter, but . . ." He came around to open the car door for her. "Let's go in."

The interior was polished and silent, with the faint scent of lavender and pine. "I'd like to throw open all the doors and windows, but Mother is afraid of drafts." He looked suddenly tense. "I hope she's up to meeting you. She was fine when I left, but she has spells of feebleness that come on unexpectedly."

They found Mrs. Rhinehart in the morning room, sitting in a wheelchair, gazing absently through the windows. A uniformed nurse hovered nearby.

Annabelle Rhinehart was wearing a rose-colored silk kimono, with diamond earrings and a triple strand of pearls around her neck. Julia could tell that she had been a beauty in her youth. The regal, even features and flawless bone structure were evident beneath clear, fragile skin. Not a freckle or an age spot marred her face. Her snow-white hair was immaculately arranged in an upsweep that had been fashionable perhaps forty years ago.

"I was calling you, Georgie," she said in a high, well-bred voice when he walked in, with Julia lagging behind.

"I told you I was going over to the Hoppers, Mother."

"Who are the Hoppers?"

"That nice couple who came to dinner not long ago. Mrs. Hopper brought you the needlepoint pillow that you liked so much."

"Oh, yes. Wasn't her husband that handsome man who talked about Herbert?"

"Yes, Edwin knew Father quite well." George took Julia's hand. "Mother, I've brought a friend to meet you. This is Julia Shane. She's related to the Hoppers."

The imperious scrutiny was all too familiar. My heavens, she's just like Gran, thought Julia. That same look of entitlement, as if the world owed her homage.

"How do you do, Mrs. Rhinehart." She took one frail white hand in hers. "It's a pleasure to meet you."

The alert brown eyes closed briefly in affected refinement. "Miss Shane," she said.

"*Mrs.* Shane," George corrected her.

"You are married?"

"I'm a widow," said Julia gently.

"Julia's husband was Michael Shane, the composer. You remember, Mother, I've played the records of his Broadway shows for you You especially liked *California*."

"Wasn't he a *client?*"

Julia saw the hardening of George's jaw and she quickly spoke up before he could reply. "Yes, Mrs. Rhinehart, George was my husband's attorney. He has been extremely helpful to me and my two little boys since Michael's death, and we are most grateful to him."

Annabelle Rhinehart gave her a polite, wintry smile. "Will you have tea?"

"I think not today, Mother," George said firmly. "We have to be going. I just wanted to bring Julia by to meet you and to show her my boat."

"When will you be coming back?" asked his mother.

"Later. After dinner." He smiled indulgently and kissed her cheek, but it was clear that in what had been a battle of wills, the elderly lady had lost.

George was quiet as they filed down a path to the beach. "She's very difficult," he finally said, "but I try to be patient. She's had a sad life."

"Why sad?"

"She lost two children when she was young. I had an older sister and a brother whom I never knew. They both died of childhood illnesses—diphtheria and rheumatic fever."

"How dreadful. When was that?"

"Early nineteen-hundreds, years before I was born. Mother was forty-five when she had me. Then my father died just before the war. It was particularly hard on her when I went overseas."

"I don't think she liked me very much."

"She liked you as well as she can like any woman I—well, I was going to say go out with." He smiled.

"Is that what we're doing—going out?"

"Not yet," he said, "but when you're ready." He took her hand. It felt safe and comfortable in his. "You haven't asked about the other girls I've brought home, but maybe I shouldn't talk about them."

"Tell me!" she laughed.

"Well . . . there was Victoria Converse, whom I met in my senior year at Yale. Very pretty, rather desirable. She came from a fine New Haven family . . . but they weren't Jewish."

"I see. And?"

"And . . . there was a long string of attractive young women when I was at Harvard Law School. One after another, I would bring them home. Mother could always find something to criticize or object to. She excels at picking out the minor flaw. I wasn't in love with any of them, so it was simple enough to lose interest." He paused to tug at some beach grass. "Then in my last year of law school, I met Elyssa Maier. She was a brilliant and beautiful Radcliffe senior. I fell in love for the first time in my life, and I hoped to marry her. Her parents were refugees from Germany, her father a distinguished scholar and her mother a talented violinist. But here in America, you see, they were just poor, struggling Jews who spoke with an accent." He chewed on a blade of grass. "Well, by this time, I was a lot wiser. I became engaged to Elyssa, despite my mother's attempts to discourage it." He pulled at another strand of grass. "I'll never know exactly what happened, but while I was overseas Elyssa married someone else. A professor at Columbia. Much more suited to her, as Mother said in the letter she wrote to inform me of the wedding."

Julia remained silent. She really didn't know what to say.

"I tell you this so you will understand that there's nothing new or unusual about my mother rejecting the women I see."

"What about the girl you brought to our house for dinner that night? Rosalind Lehman. You haven't mentioned her."

"Aah, now *there* is a woman of whom my mother approves. Right background, ideal family. The perfect wife for Annabelle Rhinehart's son."

"So?"

He shrugged. "So I wasn't in love with her. For a long time, Julia, I really tried to please my mother. But I'll be damned if I marry someone I don't love for her."

They had reached the boathouse. Under the shed was a shiny motor launch, a skiff, and two canoes. They walked out on the dock. A sleek mahogany-hulled sloop was tied up alongside.

"This is the *Limerick*. She's my baby," said George, laying a fond hand on the gunwale. "Come on, I'll show you around." He sprang on board and extended a hand to help her.

Julia knew little about boats, but she had always loved the water. In high school she had been on the swim team, and whenever she had the chance she swam long distances. From the moment she stepped on the *Limerick*'s deck, she knew she would adore sailing. She was fascinated as George explained the rigging and showed her below deck, where four could comfortably eat and sleep. Everything was made of teak or mahogany with brass fittings, and it was as immaculately kept as the kitchen of a fastidious housewife. The metal was polished, the woods oiled and varnished, the ropes, which George told her were called sheets, bleached white and neatly coiled.

"How do you like her?" he asked when they were standing close in the main cabin.

"She's *wonderful*," said Julia, her eyes shining.

Without warning, he took her in his arms and kissed her. His lips were firm yet gentle, nothing like the wanton, demanding insistence of Michael's kisses. At first she was stiff and unyielding, but the soft pressure of George's mouth on hers, the warmth and comfort of him, unleashed a flood of tenderness and wanting, and she gave in to it, returning his kiss and circling her arms about his neck. She was surprised at the surge of feeling that ran through her. When he let her go, she touched his face. His eyes closed and he rubbed his cheek against her hand. Grasping it in his, he turned it over and impulsively kissed the palm. Again he took her in his arms and kissed her, a strong, deep, sensuous kiss this time, holding nothing back.

"You can't imagine how long I've wanted to do that," he said when at last the kiss ended.

"I think maybe . . . I've been wanting you to." Frowning, she unconsciously shook her head in denial.

George gave her a wise smile and said lightly, "Shall we go for a sail now?"

She heard nothing from him for the next two weeks, and she began to wonder whether Mrs. Rhinehart might not have more influence on her son than he realized.

Early one morning in the middle of June, Betsy called. "George Rhinehart's mother died yesterday. She's been in the hospital. Did you know?"

"No, I hadn't heard. What should I do? Go to the funeral?"

"Yes, I think you should. We'll go together. Ed will find out the details."

The burial was private, but Julia went with Betsy and Edwin to the memorial service for Annabelle Rhinehart. It was the first time she had entered Temple Emanu-El. The magnificent Fifth Avenue synagogue was filled to capacity with an extraordinary number of prominent men and women, many of them elderly. The governor of New York State, the mayor, the presidents of Yale and Columbia universities, and many other leading citizens were in attendance. After the service a long line of people waited to pay their respects to the family. George, looking handsome and distinguished in a dark suit, gravely shook hands, exchanging a few words with each of them.

When he caught sight of Julia, his eyes lit up. "She died very peacefully in her sleep," he said, holding onto her hand tightly. "Thank you for being here. I'll be at home afterward. Will you come by?"

She had never seen the family apartment on Park Avenue that was George's city home. The fine period pieces, the antique persian carpets, and the oil paintings hanging on the walls of its many rooms rather overwhelmed her. Although she was not a connoisseur of museum-quality furniture, her eye was acute enough to recognize its excellence.

"George lived here with his mother," Betsy whispered when they were helping themselves to the platters of food in the dining room. "I don't imagine he would choose to furnish a home like this."

"It's magnificent," said Julia, looking over her shoulder to be certain they were not being overheard.

"A little stuffy, though, don't you think?" continued Betsy. "I mean, for children?"

Julia gave her a long unsmiling look. "Please, Bets, let's not jump the gun."

"You could do a lot worse," said her aunt, a most uncharacteristic remark for Betsy.

"I have no intention of doing anything," she replied tartly, "and I'll thank you not to mention it again."

George and Edwin together had negotiated a complicated arrangement for the stage production of *Magic Island*. They managed to convince Julia that Gerald Ross was the best person to produce Michael's posthumous musical, the last of the Shane and Baker collaborations. Murray was in favor of it, Edwin told her, and it really was the right decision, both artistically and in a business sense. Despite his obvious drawbacks, Ross had experience with Michael's shows and offered the most attractive financial arrangement to the trustees of the estate.

Feeling badgered but glad to have the decision behind her, she agreed. Murray called George when the contract was signed, saying he wanted to make peace with Julia, but she never heard from him directly. She knew his affair with Vivienne had ended, for the simple reason that the newspapers had been full of Miss Tremaine's marriage to Mortimer Axelrod, the powerful head of Metro Films. After the success of *The Conquerors* and her first major dramatic role, Vivienne had become Hollywood's leading female star.

As far as Julia knew, Murray had not come to New York for rehearsals of *Magic Island*, but whether or not he had, he made no attempt to get in touch with her. She felt that was significant. If he really had not absconded with Michael's manuscripts, she was certain he would have the courage to face her rather than rely on intermediaries.

She saw Murray one final time, at the opening night of *Magic Island*. He had gained weight and looked rather well turned out—for Murray. They came face to face, nodded civilly, and exchanged a few words. Very few. Then she took George's arm and moved down the aisle to their seats.

The production was magnificent. The music was exquisite, the book brilliant, the sets and costumes extraordinary. *Magic Island* won every award that season. But for Julia, sitting through the show was an ordeal. She left immediately after the final curtain and asked George to take her home. Betsy and Edwin stopped in at the cast party afterward and reported that both Murray and Gerald had asked for her.

The next morning, a box containing two dozen long-stemmed roses was delivered to her apartment. Tucked under the ribbon was a note:

Because the road is rough and long
Shall we despise the skylark's song?

I miss him too.
Murray

Julia was asleep, burrowed under the covers, breathing deeply and evenly. She had forgotten to draw the shades the night before, and sunlight streamed through the bedroom windows, waking her. There were sounds of activity below: a car pulling into the gravel driveway, the boys' laughter out in the garden, Mrs. Reilly's voice speaking to someone from the doorway of the Hoppers' old farmhouse. Stretching luxuriantly, she squinted at the clock.

And then she realized what day it was. It was her birthday and she felt old. *Old. That's ridiculous,* she told herself. Twenty-nine was not old.

Padding across to the open window, she raised the screen in time to see a florist's van pulling out of the driveway. In the rear of the garden Edwin was raking leaves, making neat mounds. Scotty and Perk tossed a football back and forth, running to tackle each other. Neil, a few months past two and frustrated at not being able to keep up with the older boys, was crying, and Ed distracted him by tossing him into the piles of leaves.

Leaning out the window, Julia called, "Good morning, everyone. Look who's an old sleepy-head."

"Mommy, Mommy, look at me!" cried Neil, half buried in a mountain of leaves.

"Happy birthday, Mom," shouted Scott, racing over to the house and standing beneath her window.

"Happy birthday, Aunt Julia," echoed Perkins, who called her aunt even though they were cousins.

"Thank you, darlings."

Edwin waved. "George called a little while ago, Julia. Betsy went to the market. I waited to have breakfast with you."

"Give me ten minutes. I'll be right down."

She quickly showered and pulled on gray wool slacks and a burnt-orange Shaker knit sweater. As she came downstairs, a gorgeous basket of fall flowers greeted her on the hall table. With a secret smile, she withdrew a sealed note addressed to her:

To my favorite birthday girl. May today and all the days of your life be filled with love and happiness.

Devotedly,
George

She closed her eyes and thought about last night at his house . . .

They had been there alone. Once summer came to an end there was no staff, except for the caretakers who lived in a separate cottage.

George had taken her in his arms and kissed her. "You know how I feel about you." His voice was husky with emotion.

Smiling uncertainly, she nodded.

"Do you think you can ever love a short, not terribly good-looking Jewish lawyer?"

She laughed gently. "You're quite tall enough for me. And I've always thought you were rather handsome."

"Come on . . ."

"Truly, I have. As for the Jewish part, I guess you don't know my father was Jewish."

"No-o! You never told me that."

"He left us when I was very young, so I don't remember him. I was raised a Presbyterian, but I'm half-Jewish."

He cocked his head equivocally. "Being Jewish is really more a matter of experience than blood." He took her hand. "Anyway, getting back to my question . . ."

"I already love you in many ways, George. You're everything to me—my best friend, the one I depend on for so many important things."

"But?"

Her eyes dropped. "Michael has been dead for almost two years, but he's not yet dead for *me*."

"Maybe he never will be."

She looked at him in astonishment.

"You were married to a remarkable man, Julia. Michael's presence, his personality, made him that—even without his talent. As for his talent, he may have been the most gifted composer this country will ever produce. How can I not understand what you've lost?" He touched her face tenderly. "But you're young. You have a whole lifetime ahead of you. Do you propose to spend it alone?"

"No, I don't want to be alone."

He drew her into his arms. "If you marry me, I know I can make you happy. All I want is to take care of you. You and the boys. I already feel as if they're mine." She had wondered at times what George knew about her marriage with Michael. He said something next that answered her question. "You'll never have cause to doubt me, Julia. I'm a one-woman man."

It would be so simple to marry this gentle, self-confident man and know that she would be loved for the rest of her life. "I want to love you, George, but I'm afraid. There's this frozen place inside me and it's always there. As if it's keeping me from being hurt."

"Let me warm you, darling. Let me love you," he murmured softly.

He kissed her again, and she had taken his hand and let him lead her upstairs to his bed . . .

Standing in the front hall of the farmhouse with the morning sun shining brightly through the Dutch door, she felt a tremendous sense of release, a shedding of the past. Last night had been a new beginning. George was everything that was good in a man. Strong, honest, and loving. She felt safe and contented with him. And she *did* love him. It wasn't the way it had been with Michael, and she knew it never would be. But who could subsist on champagne and caviar? In all the years with Michael, she had never been sure of him. There were always uncertainties. What would be his mood, was he still hers, was he with Vivienne . . . or with someone else? With George she would never have that worry. When he gave her his love, it would be completely. Always and forever.

She and Edwin were still eating breakfast when George's new maroon Buick convertible pulled into the driveway. They heard him talking to the boys and looked out in time to see him toss the football high in the air. It sailed above the maple tree and plummeted down, straight for Perk, who caught it and fell backward on the grass.

"Wow!" shouted Scott.

"See you later, guys. I've got a date with an aging woman."

"I shouldn't speak to you after that remark," said Julia, kissing his cheek. "Thank you for the beautiful flowers."

"Happy birthday." He gave her a very tender look, fondling

her hair, then helped himself to coffee and took a bite of her pancakes. "Mmm, delicious."

"Mrs. Reilly, have you got more flapjacks for Mr. Rhinehart?" called Edwin.

"No, no, I've already had breakfast." George straddled a chair. "I came to take Julia away for the day, if that's all right with you."

"Oh, but—" she began.

"It's fine," said Ed. "Try to be back in time for an early dinner, though. The boys are full of plans. Please don't let on I told you."

"All right," she answered. "It looks like I'm outvoted."

It was a magnificent golden harvest day. They went to an antiques auction in Westport and George came away with an old flatiron to use as a doorstop, a set of handwrought fire irons, and a handsome captain's chest with leather straps and brass nailheads. They stopped at a roadside stand for a bushel of Pippin apples and ate two each, then skipped lunch because they weren't hungry. It was mid-afternoon when they returned to his house and walked through autumn woods, down along the Sound, which sparkled under sunny blue skies.

"The water is so beautiful today!" she exclaimed. "It seems like summer."

"Come on," he said impetuously, "let's go out."

The *Limerick* was already in storage, but the launch's motor had not yet been winterized. George turned the winches, lowering the craft into the water, and they spun out across the Sound, raising a foamy wake. There wasn't another boat in sight. Julia flung out her arms, loving the speed and freedom of the open waters. They made a broad sweep south and circled around for half an hour. A sudden wind churned up whitecaps, drenching them with cold salt spray. George turned back to shore, and they ran laughing for the house, to dry off in front of a fire in the small den.

They were sitting close together on the sofa, Julia wearing one of George's sweaters, when he went to the desk and took a small box from a locked drawer. Inside, resting on ivory satin, was an exquisite rose-cut diamond ring.

"I'm scared to death," he told her. "I was going to keep this until Thanksgiving, but I can't wait that long."

His expression was so earnest, she couldn't help smiling. "Oh, George. It's the most beautiful ring I've ever seen."

He slid it onto her finger. They both looked at it and at the same moment said, "I love you."

They laughed and fell back on the couch together. His lips came down on hers and she was melting inside. She opened her mouth to him, drinking deeply of his kisses. "I love you . . . I love you," she breathed, and saw the ecstasy in his eyes.

Exultantly, with complete abandon, they made love. Last night had been strained. She had been alone so long and felt unsure of herself. But now it was as if they had been doing this for all of their lives together, and she embraced him eagerly. They were joined in a communion of body and spirit. When he moved inside her, she felt his driving strength and slow sensuality. He called out her name, arching above her, and she was seized by searing swells that crested higher and higher until they exploded like a fireball, lighting up the sky in a shower of sparks and then slowly drifting down to earth.

Afterward he pulled her against him, holding her until the frantic beating of his heart had quieted. "Unbelievable," he whispered. "Absolute magic."

"I'm so happy, George. I feel almost guilty, as if I had no right to be this happy."

"Life was meant to be full of joy, my darling. It's time to forget the pain. There's a long road ahead of us. And it will be beautiful."

❧ Chapter 19 ❧

Jeffrey

On a Friday afternoon in April, Scott was waiting for Jack Winston to return to the book-lined conference room at Winston & Rhinehart.

He remembered the first time George Rhinehart had brought him here. He had been nine years old, and his mother and George were engaged to be married. Getting off the elevator in the empty reception room, he had felt special to be spending Saturday morning alone with the man who was going to be his stepfather. While George took care of business, Scott had twirled in the leather desk chair and amused himself by drawing on a legal pad. Afterward they had eaten lunch at a Horn & Hardart, then ridden down to Thirty-fourth Street on top of a double-decker bus, to take an elevator to the top of the Empire State Building. It was a day that stood out in Scott's memory.

Over the years he had paid many visits to the office. Although there had been a place for him in George's firm when he graduated from law school, he had been seduced by the old-line prestige of Prescott, Spencer & Colwood. Yet each time he returned to these law offices, George Rhinehart's spirit seemed to hover here.

Jack came back into the conference room, interrupting Scott's reverie. "Here's the official letter from the Library of Congress, Scott. You might want your grandchildren to read it someday."

Scott took the document and read it through. "Very impressive. Thanks, Jack. I appreciate the delicate way you've handled this."

"Your mother was overwhelmed when I informed her. I wish you could have heard her."

Scott smiled. "I can imagine what she said. 'Whatever shall we do with so much money?'"

"Words to that effect."

"She'd better not give it all away to one of her charities."

Winston laughed. "Wouldn't that be an irony? There's little danger of that. It's in the trust and I'm the co-trustee. Since you've waived your share, that part will be reinvested."

When he was young, Winston had always been Uncle Jack to him, but as close as his parents had been to the Winstons, Scott had never felt completely comfortable with his father's partner. Their son Jackie, near his age, had been a spazz, in the parlance of the time, and whenever the families had gotten together—usually at the Rhineharts' Connecticut house—it had been his chore to entertain Jack, Jr. Jackie couldn't play tennis, was afraid of sailing, and wanted to do nothing but walk through the woods looking for insects. Scott and Neil had been pretty awful to the kid. As a result, Scott had never formed a particularly close friendship with father or son. Well, lo and behold, the nerd had grown up to become a professor at Harvard Law School and one of the country's outstanding Constitutional scholars. Furthermore, he had married gorgeous Olivia Nugent, an eye surgeon at the Mass General, from a social Boston family. They lived in a restored Victorian house in Cambridge with their four good-looking, smart, and well-behaved children. And Scott did not have to take his mother's word for all this, for he had once stayed with them when he went to give a tax seminar at the law school.

Jack poured them both a drink and sat down opposite him, prepared to talk.

"There's another matter I'd like to discuss with you, Scott. As I mentioned, I plan to retire at the end of the year. That means there will be no partner with the name of either Winston or Rhinehart."

"I never thought of that. There's no chance of Jack, Jr. joining you?"

"Afraid not. We've discussed it at great length, and he intends to remain in academia."

"I can understand that. In fact, I envy him a little. It's certainly a more attractive way of life, living in Cambridge and being a law professor than working for a New York firm."

"He's happy there. I don't begrudge him the choice he's made. But I wonder whether you would consider coming in yourself? I know you've turned us down in the past, but circumstances have a way of changing."

Scott realized, with some surprise, that he was not inclined to dismiss the offer. "I'm immensely flattered by your confidence, Jack. I'd certainly like to hear more about it."

Winston described at length the organization of the firm, referring to several of their important clients. Through the years, Winston & Rhinehart had greatly expanded, taking over several adjoining suites of offices. It had changed from a firm that concentrated on copyright and estate work. They now had lawyers who specialized in corporate law, litigation, exempt organizations, and health care, among other areas.

"There's a real need for a tax expert here. We would attract some prestigious clients if you joined us."

"I'll give it serious consideration, Jack. In twenty-three years I have never imagined leaving Prescott, Spencer."

"It would be a decided wrench. Take all the time you want to deliberate. You don't have to come to an immediate decision."

It was after five when the two men finally shook hands. Scott called Hazel and decided his messages could wait until Monday morning. There was no point in returning to his office this late on a Friday afternoon. After a brief stop at Brooks Brothers to order some oxfords (he would never entrust his bespoke shirts from Turnbull & Asser to hotel laundries) he continued up Madison Avenue. Passing the Bedford-Rhinehart Gallery, he did not bother to stop in. Since the opening, Isobel and Cece had secured two more corporate accounts. Their solvency was assured, even if private sales were a little slow.

As he walked, Scott thought about Jack Winston's offer. It was true that he was thoroughly entrenched at Prescott, Spencer. On the other hand, he was not a name partner and was not likely to become one as long as Isobel's father remained there. If he left, it would certainly shake up the firm and some of their most important clients, some of whom might follow him. Jack had told him that if he joined them, the firm's name would immediately become Winston, Rhinehart & Rhinehart. Would George have loved that!

When he reached home, Candida informed him that Isobel would be out for dinner. She was never there in the evenings lately. Scott alternated between dull anger and bouts of wondering whether this was what marriage meant for most people, merely a way of existing without really being together. He usually dined with friends on weeknights, but he had no plans for this evening, which meant he would be eating a lonely meal in the apartment.

He changed into jogging clothes and went for a run in the park, then showered and put on slacks and a knit shirt. He had turned on the evening news when the telephone rang.

It was his mother. Julia had been calling often in the three weeks since her visit. He knew she was worried about him, and although he appreciated her concern, he felt oddly irritated by her sympathy.

Tonight he heard excitement in her voice. After his falsely lighthearted replies to the inevitable questions about Ginger and Chip, Julia said, "The most wonderful thing has happened! Someone has bought Michael's scores and donated them to the Library of Congress."

Scott smiled to himself. "That's terrific news, Mother. When did this happen?"

"In the last week or two. The minute it was known they were being offered, there was a buyer. Jack called me on Tuesday. I had to agree to the sale. He's been waiting to receive an acceptance from the Library. They had to examine them, of course. There will be a little ceremony sometime around Michael's seventy-fifth birthday."

"That's very fitting. Are you pleased?"

"*Thrilled.* I just didn't feel right about Michael's scores becoming the private property of people we don't even know. They might easily have turned into commodities, peddled around from one collector to another. This way, they'll be where they belong, in the archives of the American people."

"If you're happy, then so am I."

"And Scott—the trust did not lose money, I assure you. The donor paid a very substantial amount for the lot." She paused. "Three million dollars!"

He tried to keep the amusement out of his voice. "Three million dollars . . . Imagine! Who is the donor?"

"That's the most amazing part, dear. He insists on remaining anonymous."

"Why do you say *he?* It might be a woman."

"I suppose that's true. We'll never know. Why would someone want to remain anonymous?"

"Various reasons. Probably doesn't want to be bugged by other organizations. I'd love to know who it is."

"So would I, but I guess we should count our blessings. You won't have to worry about Neil any longer. There's plenty of money in the trust now."

"I never thought of that. It was a good thing, then."

By the time they said goodbye, the news broadcast was over, except for sports and the weather. He had turned to Channel Thirteen for MacNeil-Lehrer when Candida announced that his dinner was on the table.

On Saturday morning, Isobel walked in while he was eating breakfast. She had not come home the night before, calling very late to say that she was staying at Cece's. That seemed ridiculous, like two high school girls having a sleepover, but Scott cared so little that he had not bothered to object.

"I must talk to you," she said, and he could tell by her tone that it was going to be a Serious Conversation. She led the way into the bedroom, where they were unlikely to be overheard.

Of all the things she might have told him, it was the least expected.

"I don't know how to put this in a way that won't hurt you, Scott," she began. "I guess there *is* no way, except to say it. I want a divorce."

He blinked. She could not possibly mean it.

"Well, aren't you going to say something?"

"Why? What have I done?"

"It's nothing you've done. I simply don't wish to be married to you any longer."

"Isobel," he protested, "that's not a reason."

"Sit down, Scott," she said, "I know this is a shock for you. I'll try to explain." She composed herself in a graceful position on the settee and folded her hands. "Over the past months, I have come to realize that I have been claustrophobic in our marriage for quite a few years. Being apart from you during this period has made me realize how much I need to be independent. To be permanently free of this stifling existence."

He shook his head in disbelief. "I don't know what to say . . ." *Claustrophobic?* Isobel, whose days had until recently revolved around lunch at the Colony or Mortimer's, whose dearest wish had been for her daughter to become a debutante, now claimed she had been stifled by marriage. Stunned, Scott could not even argue with her.

Was this not what he had secretly wanted, to be free of his wife? Such was the contrariness of his nature that for days he refused to accept it.

Isobel insisted that he sleep in the guest room, and then she told him he would have to move out of the apartment.

"But this is my *home!*"

"You can have the Sagaponack house. You've always loved it."

"Isobel, why a divorce? There are plenty of marriages that go on with an understanding. If it's freedom you want—" Suddenly a thought struck him. A thought so outrageous that it had not occurred to him before. "Is there someone else? Are you having an affair?"

"I was wondering whether you'd ask." He would like to have slapped the smug expression from her face.

"You are, aren't you? These trips—Cece's nothing but a front. All this time you've been with a man, haven't you?"

But she would not give him a straight answer. "Even if there *were* someone, I have no plans to marry again."

It was like a physical blow. "*Who?*"

She shook her head. "Scott, it really has no bearing on us. Can't you accept that?"

"I *know*," he shouted triumphantly, "I know who it is. I should have known all along, that son of a bitch!"

"Who, then? Who's a son of a bitch?"

"Jeffrey Wheeler. It's Jeff, isn't it?"

Isobel merely smiled.

Incredulous, he sputtered at the monstrousness of it "He's my *client*. We just had lunch this week at the Metropolitan Club."

She gave him a puzzled glance that seemed to ask what that had to do with anything.

He felt diminished. It was impossible for him to think clearly. Scott Rhinehart, the great organizer whose life had always been in well-oiled working order. He was paralyzed. What should he do next? Inform the children, tell his mother, get a lawyer?

But when he asked Dick Graham to handle the divorce, his bosom buddy of thirty-one years said, "I've already had a talk with Isobel, and we agreed it would be wrong for me to act for either of you."

"You're my best friend, for God's sake. Why shouldn't you represent me?"

"I'm also a friend of Isobel's, and she and Nancy are close."

"Friendship didn't stop Jeff Wheeler from sleeping with my wife, Dick. To hell with both of you." He called a divorce lawyer he knew outside the firm. Maybe it was just as well not to have his personal affairs in the files of Prescott, Spencer & Colwood. He took a room at the Yale Club and became one of those disconnected, rootless men, eating alone in restaurants at night, wandering around the city on weekends.

He would not have believed how quickly the hostesses tracked him down. The stacks of invitations jammed his mail slot and rapidly accumulated on his desk in the office.

His mother was shocked when he told her about the separation, but Scott was saddened at the lack of emotion when he spoke to his children. He and Isobel had agreed to call them together. Ginger cried a little. Chip acted sullen but unsurprised, as if he had expected nothing better of his father. *But I'm not the one,* he longed to say. However, it sounded ungentlemanly and petty since he and Isobel had agreed to a no-fault divorce.

The room at the Yale Club depressed him. He chafed to get out of the sterile atmosphere. Hazel contacted a real estate agent who lined up a number of condos and co-ops. In the sluggish market, she told him, there were bargains to be had, great apartments going begging. "Of course, if you want a really large place, the kind you're accustomed to, the prices haven't come down that much."

Hazel had taken over and was central to his new life. Accustomed to paying his bills, balancing his checkbook, and managing his appointments schedule, she now kept track of his social calendar as well. Fussing over him like a maiden aunt, she knew far too much about his every move. "I'm too old to have a housemother," he groused one morning when she remarked that he looked peaked and must not be eating or sleeping properly. When he saw how offended she was, he apologized. "Forgive me, Hazel, I know I'm not easy to get along with these days. It will pass."

They had been separated for three weeks when, at the end of a long day, Scott decided to work out in the gym at the Yale Club before having dinner in the grill. He had just picked up his messages at the front desk and was waiting for the elevator when he ran into Jeff Wheeler.

"Scott. Where the hell have you been? I've been trying to reach you. Don't you return your phone calls?"

I cannot believe the nerve of this guy. He's responsible for breaking up my marriage, and he actually expects me to answer his phone calls. Without speaking, Scott entered an empty elevator.

Jeff followed him, squeezing in just as the doors closed. "What the hell, Rhinehart. What's gotten into you?"

"You bastard, you have the gall to ask what's gotten into *me?*"

Wheeler looked like the breath had been knocked out of him. "What the fuck are you talking about?"

"As if you didn't know."

"I *don't,* so how about telling me." They had reached the sixth floor. With a withering glance, Scott left the elevator and headed for the locker room with Jeff on his heels.

"Get lost, Wheeler."

"I think you've gone off your rocker. I have no intention of leaving until you explain what this is all about."

Furious, Scott turned on him. "Why don't you ask Isobel?"

"What has Isobel got to do with it?"

"Don't give me that shit, Jeff. You've been screwing my wife, you've broken up my family, and now you're acting like my innocent pal. What a phony."

"I honestly don't know what the hell you are talking about!" shouted Jeff, then lowered his voice as a freshly showered man walked out of the locker room, giving them a disapproving glance. When they were alone again, Wheeler said, "You are crazy, do you know that? I've never been *near* your wife."

"You think I don't know about the trips to Boston and Chicago? And Paris—I suppose you're going to tell me you weren't together at L'Hôtel in January?"

"Well, for crying out loud, I'm a *collector*. Of course we see each other at shows. If that constitutes being together, then we were—just Isobel, me, and five thousand others."

Scott finished changing into sweats and slammed his clothes into his locker. "Knock it off, Jeff. Isobel has told me everything. In case you haven't heard, she's asked for a divorce."

"What are you saying? Are you trying to tell me that Isobel told you she and I are having an affair? That I'm the reason she's divorcing you?"

"You got it, buddy." Throwing a towel over his shoulders, Scott headed for the exercycle.

Wheeler followed. "Look, I don't know what Isobel is up to, but you've got it wrong. I am *not* sleeping with your wife. Furthermore, at the risk of sounding ungallant, I haven't the slightest desire to go to bed with her."

Scott stopped pedaling and leaned on the handlebars. "You know, you missed your calling. You'd have made a hell of an actor."

"Scott, you have to believe me. There is absolutely *nothing* between Isobel Prescott and me."

"Isobel Prescott *Rhinehart*, may I remind you? I know for a fact you had dinner together in London. Don't bother denying it, because you were seen."

"I'm not denying that, but we weren't alone. Cece Bedford came along with the graphics guy at Christie's. There were a ton of people around. Ask anyone who was there. Christ, I have nothing to hide. Ask Cece. She and Isobel travel together. If Isobel has a lover, you can bet Cece knows who he is."

Scott considered him silently. "You actually mean it, don't you?"

"Yeah. Because it's the truth."

"Hell, Jeff, I guess I owe you an apology."

"Hey listen, I've been there myself. There's nothing as awful as a divorce, even when you want one."

"Well, I didn't want this. I don't believe in divorce."

Jeff put an arm around him. "Come on, Rhino, bag the gym. Let's go have a drink."

Scott realized he had rushed to judgment. It lightened his burden to know he had not been betrayed by a friend.

But by her own admission, Isobel was having an affair. There was no doubt that she had a lover. But if not Jeffrey Wheeler, then who?

Chip

Hotchkiss commencement. Ginger was the class speaker.

Scott and Isobel sat in the third row with Chip between them, acting as a buffer. After the exercises they would endure the civility of the headmaster's reception together, followed by a class luncheon. Ginger was refusing to stay through the evening for a farewell dinner with her friends and their families. Now that the shock of her parents' separation was behind them and the reality had set in, her distress was evident.

They were scattering immediately after lunch. A family diaspora. Chip had to get back to Williams for his final exams. He and three friends were driving cross-country next week, planning to get summer jobs when they reached the West Coast. Scott had rented a car for the trip back to New York, since Isobel and Ginger were using the Mercedes. Enriqué would follow in the station wagon loaded with Ginger's belongings.

The rites of passage became unpleasant ordeals in a broken family, Scott reflected. *A broken family*.

He remembered once remarking on the sensible if spartan manner in which a neighbor in Sagaponack had raised his children, requiring them to earn all their spending money. "Imagine, those kids get no allowance after the age of fourteen."

"Oh, but they're not an intact family," Isobel had replied smugly. Visions of ruptured fathers and mothers with little cracked boys and girls had danced in his imagination.

We are not an intact family.

On the parental permission form for Ginger's Guatemalan program, he had circled *Divorced*. They were not yet divorced, of course, but there seemed to be no special category for the legal quibbling known as separation.

Ginger was avoiding him. She had kissed him hurriedly when he arrived, pretending to be distracted, chattering about her friends and their various summer plans. Whenever their eyes met, hers would slide away.

In three days she would be flying to Guatemala. "I hope we'll have a chance for a talk before you leave," Scott told her when he was saying goodbye.

She bit her lip. "There's so much to do, Daddy. I haven't finished packing."

"You'll be gone for a year," he answered quietly. "I won't take much of your time, pumpkin." She seemed to flinch at the childhood endearment.

Shopping and dentist appointments occupied Ginger's only free day in New York, and she was having dinner with her Prescott grandparents on the last evening. Scott had to be satisfied with taking her to the airport on Tuesday afternoon. At least the two of them would be alone on the trip to JFK, since Isobel maintained it was too busy at the gallery for her to get away.

When he brought up the subject of the divorce, Ginger began to cry. Feeling helpless, he gave her his handkerchief and put an arm around her. "You know I'll always love you," he finally said. "Nothing will ever change that."

Her classmate Richard Steinberg was waiting for her at the terminal, where the group assembled. Seeing the two of them together, Scott had the most certain premonition that this boy was going to sleep with his daughter. If he hadn't already.

What had Isobel taught Ginger about birth control? he wondered, distraught. *About AIDS?* What kind of mother was she? A mother who would use the excuse of business to keep from seeing her daughter off on a year's journey.

The plane was two hours late taking off. Scott waited until they boarded. On the way back to Manhattan, he felt sick with his powerlessness to protect Ginger. He spent a sleepless night, imagining every disaster that could befall her, from plane crash to rape.

The next morning when he reached the office there was a message from his son. Chip was at the apartment after arriving from Williamstown late the night before.

"I pulled two all-nighters in a row to finish my term papers," he said. "I wanted to get here in time to see Ginger off."

"She understood. I took her to the airport."

Chip seemed to be struggling for words. "Dad, I need to talk to you."

"Okay. How would you like to meet me for lunch?"

"Swell, but can we go somewhere, y'know, casual?"

They met at Ray's Pizza on Madison. Chip needed a shave and looked as if he had slept in his clothes.

"Do you have the keys to Sagaponack?" he asked once they had ordered.

"I left my keys at the apartment. I haven't got all my stuff out of there yet. No place to put it."

"Oh," said Chip, looking glum.

They ate in silence.

"Is there an extra bed in your pad?"

"Yes," Scott answered, surprised. "You're more than welcome to stay with me, but the room's pretty small. You'd be a lot more comfortable at home."

He shook his head. "I'm not going back there. I won't stay with her."

"Chip, you mustn't speak of your mother that way. Our differences should have no effect on your relationship with Isobel."

"I can't help the way I feel," his son replied. "I'm sorry if you thought I blamed you, Dad. I didn't understand. I guess this is pretty tough on you."

"It's difficult to get your life reorganized," Scott admitted. "We've been married for almost twenty-two years."

"I know." Suddenly Chip grimaced and pounded a fist on the table. "How the hell could she *do* it?"

Scott sighed deeply. "Isobel has changed. It's all this women's identity stuff, going into business . . . I don't understand her anymore. I'm not sure how it happened or when it happened, but . . . well, your mother has evidently become involved with another man."

Chip just stared at him without saying anything. With a look of disgust, he pushed his pizza away.

"Aren't you going to finish that?"

"No, I'm not hungry." He fiddled with the straw in his soft drink.

"You said you wanted to talk to me."

Chip seemed relieved at the change of subject. "I've decided I'm not going out west this summer after all."

"What do you propose to do instead?" asked Scott.

"If it's all right with you, I'd like to stay in the Sagaponack house and get a job out there. Maybe as a waiter."

"That's fine with me, son. But are you sure that's what you want? I thought you were looking forward to the trip with your friends."

"It seems like a waste of time now. I'd rather save some money."

"I could help you get a summer internship on Wall Street. You'd get a decent salary and some good experience."

"Thanks, Dad, but let me see what I can do on my own first."

"Well," said Scott, "come on up to the office. Maybe there's a set of keys in my desk."

Hazel made a big fuss over Chip, whom she had known since he was a little boy. He tolerated her effusiveness rather well, noted Scott, as he rummaged through his drawers. "I could have sworn we had extra keys to the beach house, Hazel."

"I threw the old ones away when you changed the locks last year. The caretaker was supposed to have sent another set."

"Call your mother and see if she has the keys, Chip."

"I'd rather not," he said tightly.

Sensing the tension between them, Hazel left and closed the door.

"What happened?" asked Scott. "Did you and Isobel have an argument?"

"Yeah, I guess you could say that."

"About what?"

"Nothing—nothing important. Anyway, I don't want her to know I'm going out there."

"Your mother has to know where you are, Chip."

"I said I would be staying with you. You can tell her in a few days, after I'm settled."

Scott shook his head dolefully. "All right, but I don't like it. The situation's bad enough without the two of you on the outs." Chip was Isobel's favorite. They had never had trouble getting along. What had happened between them?

Scott called the caretaker and arranged for the house to be opened for Chip. "I'll come out on the weekend. Do you need any money?"

"No, I have enough."

Scott hugged his son. "Keep in touch with me. I'll see you on Saturday."

On Saturday morning, he went up to 957 Fifth Avenue to pick up his car. "Why, Mr. Rhinehart, how are you?" The doorman's eyes widened when Scott parked the Mercedes in front of the apartment building and walked into the lobby.

"Fine thanks, Tony. Yourself?" Scott marched past him to the elevator. He hardly needed permission to go up to his own co-op, for Christ's sake. It was his money that had bought the place, dammit, and he still paid the maintenance.

He waited for the elevator to descend before ringing the bell. His key was still in his pocket, but he knew Isobel would resent his walking in, and he was not feeling up to a confrontation. He rather hoped she was at the gallery and Candida alone in the apartment.

After what seemed like an inordinately long delay, the door opened. Instead of the housekeeper, Scott was surprised to find Isobel in her dressing gown. But not nearly as surprised as she was to see him.

"Scott!"

"I was expecting Candida," he said.

"She has the weekend off."

"I hope I'm not disturbing you."

"Why are you here?" she asked hostilely.

"I came to get some things from the study."

With a sigh of exasperation, she said, "Must it be now, Scott? I'm busy."

"You needn't bother about me, I won't disturb you. Don't you have to be at the gallery soon? I thought Saturday morning would be a good time."

"Well, it isn't. You should have called first."

He eyed her robe. "Were you still sleeping?"

She looked strangely defensive. "Of course not. I was just doing some paper work."

"Well, it will take me ten minutes to find what I need. Are you going to keep me standing out here forever?"

She stepped aside to let him enter. He went directly to the study and began opening desk drawers. Isobel followed him, standing in the doorway with her arms folded. "What are you looking for?"

"The keys to Sagaponack, among other things."

She went to a cabinet and opened a false panel to a compartment where they had always kept passports and certain other valuables. "They're in here," she said, handing him the keys. "Why the urgency? Are you going out to the house today?"

"Yes. Chip is staying there. He wants to get a summer job in the Hamptons."

A look of annoyance crossed her face. "He really intends to cancel his trip?"

"So he informed me."

"This is your doing, isn't it?" she said angrily.

"No, it is not. It was Chip's idea."

"I don't know what's gotten into that boy. He had such a wonderful summer planned."

"Maybe *we* spoiled his summer. Did that ever occur to you?" he snapped. "It's not exactly fun having your family ripped apart."

"That's precisely why he should get away," argued Isobel. "If he's traveling with other young people, he won't dwell on himself so much."

"Oh, that's a fine lesson for him to learn. Running away from problems."

"Better than sitting out there in that house alone and brooding."

Scott was silent as he removed folders from a file cabinet. He had opened his briefcase and was fitting them inside when there was a clinking of glasses and the sound of someone walking in the hall.

"Is that Candida?" he said absently. "I thought you told me she had the weekend off."

Isobel's lips moved, but she did not answer.

Scott looked up. "Who's in the other room?"

She shrugged. There was a guilty expression on her face. Scott moved toward the hallway in time to see the door to the master bedroom suite closing.

In an instant it all became immensely clear to him. His unexpected appearance at the apartment this morning had interrupted a lovers' tryst.

Brusquely he pushed Isobel aside. "Scott, let me explain—"

With a purposeful stride, he walked to the bedroom door and flung it open. At last he would learn the identity of Isobel's lover.

He walked through the alcove of closets and drawers that had once contained his wardrobe. He entered the bedroom and stared in confusion.

Cece Bedford was sitting on the edge of the unmade bed, wearing a terry-cloth bathrobe. A coffee tray with two cups had been placed on the bedside table next to her.

"*Cece!* What on earth are *you* doing here?"

Isobel had come up behind him and was standing in the room, her hands in the pockets of her robe. She shook her head dubiously. "Scott, you wouldn't recognize a freight train if it mowed you down."

"What the hell . . . ?" A very strange, creepy feeling was coming over him. He swallowed. "What is going on here?"

Isobel nodded at her friend.

"What does it look like?" Cece asked patiently.

"It looks like something I can't believe . . . something I don't *want* to believe." He turned to face his wife. "Isobel, tell me this isn't so."

She made a futile gesture, looking troubled. "Scott, I've tried and tried to let you know. You never would see it."

"Oh God, don't tell me this. You're my *wife*. You've been my wife for twenty-two years."

"Let's go in the other room."

Obediently he followed Isobel to the study. "Sit down," she said, closing the door. She went to the bar and poured him a scotch. "Here, you look as if you could use this."

He slung the liquor back in his throat and put down the glass. He was feeling ill. "It's true?" he asked, his eyes pleading with her to deny it.

"It's true, Scott. I'm sorry. I know what a shock this is for you. I never meant for you to find out this way."

He began to weep. He couldn't help it. The tears rolled down his cheeks and his breath came in harsh gasps. Isobel put her arms around him. Like a mother soothing her child, she cradled his head against her shoulder.

"I'm sorry, I'm so sorry," she murmured, kissing the top of his head. "Please don't be sad, Scott."

Sad? There was no word for the way he felt. He was heartbroken. It was the end of his life. This happened to other people, but not to them. Not to their family. *"The children! What will we tell them?"* he sobbed.

"Oh, Scotty . . . the children *know*. They've known for weeks. Ginger was worried about how to tell you. Chip doesn't even realize you don't know."

That explained Chip's reaction at lunch the other day. *She's involved with another man*, Scott had told him. Poor kid, must have thought his father was pathetic, a cretin. *How the hell can she do it?* Chip had said. So he knew.

"Is this what you and Chip had a fight about?"

She nodded.

"That doesn't do anything to you? Having your son know his mother is a dyke?"

"Scott, please!"

"Well, what the hell else do you want me to call it? My wife goes to bed with another woman and I'm supposed to just accept that as normal, everyday behavior? Hey, it's okay. Twenty-two years of marriage down the drain so Isobel can make it with Cece. What is it—you were bored with plain old hetero sex, you had to go looking for kicks?" He began to cry again. She rubbed his back until he took out a handkerchief and blew his nose.

"What if I told you I've loved Cece since we were at boarding school together?" she said calmly.

"You mean, you and she—*all these years?*"

"No, not all these years. But long before I knew you, before I went to college. Then I met you and I married you. Cece got married. It was the way things were supposed to be. I really thought I was in love with you, but it changed. I don't know why, Scott . . . I care for you deeply, but it hasn't been good for us for a long time. Don't tell me you haven't felt it.

I wouldn't have blamed you for having an affair."

"You never loved me," he said hoarsely.

"Yes, I *did* love you. I still do, I always will. You're a part of me, part of my family, like a dearly loved relative. But I'm no longer *in love* with you. And I'm sick of pretending, sick of denying what I am, what I want." He saw tears in her eyes. "The world is different now. You of all people should understand, with all your causes. All your pro bono work—AIDS research, sex education, Gay Men's Health Crisis. You're the one who used to tell *me* I had to be more accepting of gays and sexuality and alternative lifestyles. Can't you accept this?"

"None of those ever affected my marriage. My life is a shambles, and you expect me to be understanding?"

"I'm sorry your life is a shambles. But it won't always be. You'll be all right. You'll find some nice, sweet woman who will adore you and be everything you want that I never could be."

"What about your parents?"

For the first time, she looked uncertain. "What about them?"

"Do they know?"

She shook her head. "No. I tried to tell Mother, but she doesn't even realize such things exist, as far as I can tell. And Daddy—well, it would kill him."

"New York is a small place for people like us, Iz."

"I realize that, and it scares me to death. Mother just told me last night that Daddy has decided to retire finally and they're thinking of moving to San Diego. I wonder whether he hasn't heard something."

"This is some mess you've created."

"I know," she said disconsolately. "But it will all settle down as soon as the divorce is final. I might go to Nevada, just to get it over with. I'll probably move in with Cece."

"And sell this apartment?" He could not imagine Isobel giving up the home she had taken such pride in.

"Do you mind terribly? It's in joint ownership. Would you want to buy me out?"

"I don't think I could bear to live here now. Too many sad memories, after all that has happened."

"Yes. Oh, Scott, I *am* sorry. I know I keep saying that, but it's true. For you to have to face our friends, to live it all down, must be a daunting prospect. I wish I could spare you that."

"What about you? You don't care what your friends think?"

"Of course I care. But my *real* friends will understand. As for the rest—to hell with them."

Raising his head, he let out a long, shuddering breath. "I have lived with you for all these years and I hardly know you. What other people think has always been important to you. It *ruled your life*, for Christ's sake!"

"I know," said Isobel. "Isn't it a crock?"

The blue Rabbit was parked in the driveway when Scott reached Sagaponack, but the house was empty. He walked out on the deck, calling his son's name. A momentary fear gripped him as he recalled how low in spirits Chip had sounded on the telephone yesterday. Scott had thought it was because he was only able to find part-time work, but now he realized that Chip was brooding about his parents. It was essential for them to have a talk. Kids did irrational things when they were depressed. What if, in an act of despondence, he should try to take his life? Yesterday Scott would have felt foolish letting his imagination run away with itself, but now he was thrown into a panic.

Shading his eyes, he scanned the marsh. In the distance, near the far side of the salt pond, he spotted a rowboat. He fetched his high-powered binoculars from a cabinet in the living room and focused them on the boat. It was Chip, fishing, oblivious to his presence. He raised a red pennant on the flagpole—their old signal for the children to come home. A spasm of pain went through him as he thought of summers past and the splendid hopes they had held for the future.

When he replaced the binoculars, his eyes lingered on the framed family photographs on the bookshelves, of the children with Isobel and himself. Vibrant with love and laughter they were. *Oh God. Was it all a lie? Was he being punished for breaking his marital vows?*

A sudden memory of his stepfather flashed through his mind. George had been conscientious about his paternal responsibilities to his adopted sons, and before Scott went off to Yale he had dutifully delivered a homily on sex and women. In his vaguely old-fashioned, genial way, he had been a man of the times. After repeating previous warnings about respecting women and protecting himself against disease, he had told Scott something very wise.

"Reserve a special part of yourself for love," he had counseled. "There's love and there's sex. Don't confuse them. You will feel lust for many women. But you will fall in love with only one. When sex is combined with love, it can be sublime. But they are not the same. Learn to recognize the difference."

What would George Rhinehart have made out of Scott and Isobel and this appalling situation?

He went out on the deck again and peered through the binoculars. Chip had seen the pennant. He was putting up his fishing pole and began to row toward shore.

They played two sets of tennis; Chip won both. On the way home, they picked up lobsters for dinner. They sat out on the deck, eating cheese and crackers and drinking cold beer. Just that morning, Chip had landed a job as a waiter at the Sandpiper, a trendy restaurant in the Hamptons, but he would not start work until the following week.

"Aren't you lonely all by yourself out here?" asked Scott.

"A little, but I read and listen to CDs, and I can always find company down at the beach or various joints around. I'm doing my best to avoid the club and the other families. I don't want them asking about . . . things."

Scott took a deep breath. "I had a talk with your mother this morning. I went to the apartment. Cece was there."

Chip looked at him uncertainly. "What exactly do you mean?"

"I mean that for the first time, I understand everything. It was a shock, to say the least."

Chip sighed. "Now you know why I don't want to see her."

"You mustn't feel that way. It's not the end of the world, Chip. Although for a while today, I thought it might be."

"I can never face anyone again."

"Of course you can. If *I* can—" Scott's voice broke. "How do you think I feel, knowing my wife has left me for a *woman?* But you have to be understanding. Isobel must have been under enormous pressure for a long time. You have to view the total picture. She was a good wife for many years, and a wonderful mother to you and Ginger."

"She should never have allowed it to happen! All my life I've been lectured to about controlling myself. Don't give in to temptation, don't cheat, don't cut corners, don't take advantage of other people, don't sleep with a woman just because you can get away with it—" He was blinking back tears. "Mom had *no right* to do this. She had a responsibility to us. We're her family. We depend on her."

"Everything you say is true, Chip, but there's nothing you can do to change it. You must learn to accept it."

"*Never.*"

"What can I say to convince you?"

He spoke slowly. "I don't think you can, Dad. I'm feeling too hurt and angry to be convinced."

"If I can accept it, why can't you?"

"You're an admirable man. I can never be like you. I don't understand how you can forgive her."

There had to be some way of making Chip come around. Perhaps it would just take time. "You know, we haven't been happy in our marriage for a long while. I thought we would just go on like a lot of couples, staying together for the sake of harmony, not really engaging. But maybe that wasn't right."

Chip stared across the marsh at the salt pond. Everything was bathed in the rosy glow of the setting sun. "It's none of my business, Dad," he said, "but have you ever, well, had other women?"

Oh, boy. Scott rubbed his eyes. He had to handle this in the right way. So much depended on it. "One. One other woman. I fell in love with her."

Chip looked downcast. "You did?"

"Does that disappoint you terribly?"

"Well, at least it wasn't a man . . ." He turned his head away.

"Oh, Chip. This isn't fair to you. Ask me anything about her. I'll tell you."

"How did it start?"

"I met her when she took my picture for a magazine article."

"The *Fortune* article?" he asked, looking at his father in surprise.

"Yes."

"So it wasn't very long ago?"

"It was in November."

"Are you still seeing her?"

"No. We stopped in January. I couldn't leave my wife and family, I told her, and she decided we should never see each other again."

"What about now? Your wife has left you. You no longer have a family."

"We're *still* a family. The three of us, and Isobel too. She will always be your mother."

"You know what I mean, Dad. There's nothing to keep you from this woman now."

"I don't think that would be fair," said Scott. "From her point of view, I'd be using her. I wasn't willing to give up anything for her. To expect her to take me back now would be arrogant and selfish."

"Yeah. I guess so. But if you really loved her . . ."

"I still do."

"Does she love you?"

"She did. I have no idea how she feels now."

"Maybe I shouldn't tell you this, but I think you should find out."

Everywhere Scott went, he thought he saw her. Once going into the Condé Nast building, another time hailing a taxi. When she turned profile to him, he realized it could not have been . . . It was definitely Solange on a sunny Tuesday after lunch, coming out of the International Center of Photography. He was on the other side of Sixth Avenue, but when he ran across the street and hurried after her, she had vanished. Something about their last meeting at MOMA tugged at the recesses of his mind. He tried to grasp what it was, but the image eluded him.

On a Saturday afternoon he was browsing in a bookshop in Greenwich Village, pretending to deny why he had chosen to come so far downtown. He soon found himself walking south on Thompson Street. When he reached her building, there were lights in the ground floor printing plant, which meant the doors would be open. He entered the lobby and rang for the elevator.

Her voice came over the speaker, "Is that you, Jimmy?

You're early, but come on up." Scott held his breath as the elevator slowly ascended.

She opened the door at his knock, and gasped when she saw him. "Oh, I thought it was—what are you doing here? You're not supposed to be here." She folded her arms and turned away from him, but not before he saw the tears that sprang to her eyes.

He grasped her shoulders and turned her around. "I had to see you. I had to know . . ." His eyes moved over her. "I was right."

"I didn't want you to know. Oh, *why* did you come here?"

He pulled her against him, conscious of the rounded curve of her belly. "Because I couldn't stay away. Because I love you. Because this is where I belong." He kissed the tears from her cheeks and covered her mouth with his own. She closed her eyes and clung to him, her kiss hungry with need.

Finally he let her go. "Why didn't you tell me?" he whispered.

"It was something I was going to handle myself. It didn't concern you."

He blanched. "It's my child, isn't it?"

She stroked his cheek. "Yes, of course. I haven't been with another man for years, since I stopped living with Alan. That's why I wasn't careful. It's so easy to forget, and a day or two without the Pill, that's all it takes." She smiled ruefully.

"Do you want the baby?"

She nodded. "At first, I thought I would go to France, to take that drug, RU-486. But suddenly I realized, abortion is for women who don't want to be pregnant, who have no desire to have a child and can't support one. I want this baby, Scott, and I can afford her."

"What were you planning to do?"

"To give birth to her, probably in France—"

"Why do you keep saying *her?* You're so sure it's a girl?"

"There's no doubt. I had a sonogram to be certain everything is normal and the baby is definitely female." She smiled happily. "I'm thirty-seven years old, Scott, a little old to be having a first baby. That's why I want her. I'll probably never marry and there might not be another chance. Certainly not to have your child."

The telephone rang, but she made no move to answer it,

listening to the caller on the answering machine. "Hi, Solange, it's Jimmy. Sorry I can't make our appointment today, something came up. I'll give you a call this week and we'll reschedule."

"That's a photographer I know. He wants to rent my loft when I go to Paris."

Scott realized the living room was bare of ornament and there were cartons lined along one wall. "You're packing. You're really going away?"

"Yes, I'm putting my things in storage. I should leave soon. It makes sense to prepare while I can still get around."

He drew her to him and looked into her eyes. "Don't go, darling. Stay here. Let me be a part of this."

"You don't know what you're saying. Your wife, your family . . ."

"My wife has asked for a divorce."

"Because of me!"

"No, she knows nothing about us."

"That's not possible." Incredulous, she questioned him again and again. "How can you be sure?"

"I just am."

"I don't believe it. A woman knows. She may not know who, but she must suspect there's another woman."

"She hasn't said a thing."

"No, she wouldn't. There's her pride. Better for you to think she has found someone."

"The French, the French . . . they know so much about men and women." Frowning, he said, "But it is Isobel who has found . . . someone else."

"Oh, Scott, your pride is hurt."

He could not keep the truth from Solange. "It's not exactly the usual situation. I found her in our apartment with a woman."

She shrugged. "It happens."

"You don't even seem surprised."

"I'm not. The thought had crossed my mind when I met her."

Now he was incredulous. "You're not serious!"

"Yes really. It's fairly common knowledge among my artist friends that her partner in the gallery, Celeste Bedford, is a lesbian."

"Well, I'll be damned. That's the woman."

"You had no idea?"

"Of course I didn't. Why would I suspect that she and Cece were anything but friends?"

"Poor Scott. You've had a terrible blow."

"Not nearly as terrible as my children. This has been awful for them, especially my son. He's always been close to his mother, and at this point he won't speak to her."

"But that's cruel. Why punish her for something she can't help."

"You're sympathetic. That surprises me."

"I can understand how a son would react, but I do feel compassion for her." She caressed his cheek. "How long have you been separated?"

"Almost three months."

She did not ask why he had waited until now to come to her. "What will happen?"

He kissed her. "As soon as my divorce is final, you and I will be married."

"*Married?* Scott, it's too sudden. I can't make such a decision now."

He was stunned. "Surely you want to be married? The baby—"

"That's not a reason to marry. I never expected this."

"You're no longer in love with me, are you?"

"Oh, you foolish man, of course I am. I love you very much, more than I've ever loved anyone. But I'm not sure I *want* to be married. Even to you. You must give me time, Scott."

Time? They didn't have that much time. The baby would be born in October.

It took half the morning to get a call through to Chimaltenango, Guatemala. Hazel had convinced the official at the exchange program that there was a family emergency of sufficient magnitude to warrant a call to Ginger, who was working at a rural outpost.

"Daddy, is everything all right?" Ginger said anxiously, when she came to the phone.

"Everything's fine. I just wanted to talk to you. You can tell them I'm in the hospital with a broken leg or something."

"Oh, Dad." He could hear the relief in her voice. "I miss you."

"I miss you, too, sweetheart. It's wonderful to hear your voice. How are you, Ginger?"

"I'm okay. How are *you?*"

"I'm doing fine, honey."

"Really?"

"Cross my heart. I don't want you to worry about me."

"Mom wrote to me. She said you know. About her."

"Yes. Yes, I know."

"Dad, I—" Her voice broke.

"Don't cry, pumpkin."

"I can't help it."

"Ginger, listen to me. This is not the worst thing in the world. We're going to be fine. We're still a family. We still love one another. It'll just be different now. Life changes, but one thing never changes. And that's how much I love you."

"I love you, too."

"Promise me something?"

"What?" Her voice was still tearful.

"Promise me you won't dwell on this. I know it makes you sad, but I want you to try to put it behind you. Don't let it interfere with this year. I want you to get the very most out of being there."

"I will. I promise."

He was all choked up. "I want to say all the things to you that I should have said before you left. For some reason, I wasn't able to."

"That was because of me. I shut you out, and I'm sorry. I just didn't know how to react."

"I don't wonder." For a moment, he felt an unreasoning anger at Isobel for bringing this on his family. He realized there would be even further changes ahead for his daughter. "Well, how is Guatemala?"

For the first time since they said hello, she sounded like the old Ginger, full of zest. "It's really wonderful here. I feel like—oh, I don't know—like I've found what I want to do with my life."

"Tell me about it."

"I've been working with a nurse in a clinic, helping with mothers and children. We teach them about sanitation and nutrition. It's such a good feeling to help people."

"I'm very proud of you. I always have been." He hesitated. "How is your friend Richard?"

"Okay, I guess. He's not with my group now. They sent six of the guys to another village near San Juan to help with construction work, so I won't see him for a while." She giggled. "They're pretty strict about men and women. We're not supposed to be together."

"Is that so? Well," he laughed, "I suppose customs differ. It's a responsibility when they bring young people down there."

"Yeah. You don't have to worry about me, Dad. I'm really doing great."

"That makes two of us. Write to me, sweetheart."

"I will, Dad. I'm awfully glad you called."

Scott stood gazing out of his office window after talking to Ginger. There were a dozen important matters that claimed his attention, but his mind was elsewhere. His family. They were his first priority now. Ginger and Chip. Soon they would have to know about Solange. She was part of his family now. Solange and their unborn child.

Scott called her first thing on Monday morning, as soon as he saw the apartment. "Can you meet me for lunch today?"

She sounded distracted. "At what time? I have to pick up some transparencies at the lab and drop them at Lintas. I promised them by this afternoon."

"Surely you don't do these things yourself. Why not use a messenger service?"

"Because I recently had a disastrous experience with a messenger. He ran down a pedestrian with his bike and my acetates went flying all over Third Avenue. Half of them were ruined. If anything happens to this work, I've lost an entire week, and I'm in no shape these days for scrambling over rocky trails in the Adirondacks."

"I will have a car in front of your building at whatever time you say, to take you wherever you want to go, as long as you meet me at one o'clock. Is that a deal?"

"Where shall I come?"

"The driver will know. Just put yourself in his hands."

And so, only five minutes past the appointed hour, Solange

was delivered to an address in the East Forties and took the elevator to the top, where Scott was waiting with the keys to a duplex roofhouse that had been constructed on top of a nondescript pre-World War II apartment building.

"What is this place?" she exclaimed. "Why are we here?"

"Just come with me." He showed her the living room with sliding glass doors leading to a terrace. On one side were a dining room and a kitchen, on the other a library and master bedroom suite.

"There's more," said Scott. "Follow me." He led the way upstairs, where three smaller bedrooms were situated adjacent to a huge empty space lined with windows. It would be perfect for a photography studio, and there was a storage area that could be converted into a darkroom.

Scott watched her, not daring to say anything.

Solange turned to him with a guarded expression, raising one eyebrow. "So now you are tempting me with treasures beyond my wildest dreams."

"I was hoping that you would come live with me. I swear I won't put any pressure on you. Later you can decide—after my divorce is final, even after the baby is born, if you like." He looked so defenseless as he waited for her to reply.

"But if I move in with you, what is there left to decide? For me that is just as binding a commitment."

"You've lived with a man before."

"Yes, for three years, and it was pure misery when we separated. I never want to go through anything like that again."

He took her in his arms. "I want to spend the rest of my life with you, Solange. Married or not." He rubbed his nose against hers. "Even though you are the most infuriating female I have ever known."

She smiled her radiant smile. "Well, at least you must admit it won't be dull."

They moved in immediately. Scott signed a lease with an option to buy. The owner, a corporate executive who had lost his job in a hostile takeover, had left New York for the Southwest and was eager to sell, but it was a buyer's market. Solange signed over the lease on her Thompson Street loft to Jimmy Spoletto, a coming young fashion photographer whose work was appearing regularly in *Vogue*.

"I must be out of my mind," she wailed the first night, exhausted from a day of unpacking camera equipment and negative files. "I've given up my studio without any idea of whether this is going to work."

"Go take a warm shower and get into a robe," Scott ordered cheerfully. "I'm cooking dinner."

"No one would believe this," said Solange, as he served veal and mushrooms with brown rice and a green salad. "I'll bet you never cooked before in your life."

"Not true. I did most of the cooking in Sagaponack. It was Isobel who had an aversion to the kitchen." Then he worried that she might be put off by his reference to his wife.

But Solange allayed his fears. "We both had a life before we knew each other. It would be terrible if we couldn't speak of the past."

"I feel as if my life is just beginning," he said, kissing her.

After dinner, Solange became practical. "Will you come shopping for baby furniture next weekend?"

"I can't. I have to go to Tokyo on business. In all the excitement, I forgot to tell you."

"It can wait until your return," she said.

Exhausted by the day's activity, Solange fell asleep as soon as they got into bed. But Scott lay awake. In the core of his happiness, there remained a hard nugget of anxiety. He knew what he had to do.

As soon as he returned from Tokyo, he would have to go to Florida. It was time to explain himself to his mother.

❧ Chapter 21 ❧

Cathy

Leonard Gold was Kit's agent, and he could be a pain in the ass. It was sometime in May when he called.

"Kit, you know that gig you did back in December? Annette Heublein. The crazy dame on Mara Vista Drive."

"What about her?"

"She wants you again next Sunday."

"Nothing doing. That place was weird, Len. I mean, I don't need a vast audience, but it makes me self-conscious, putting on a performance for one lone woman."

"Whatta you care if the pay is good?"

"I don't know, it really spooked me. That room with the candles and those big eyes staring at me, like she was hexing me."

"*Hexing* you?" Leonard snorted. "Your imagination is working overtime. The woman's lonely. She likes music."

"There's something about her, I tell you. She's psycho, man. Kept calling me Michael, even after I told her I use my middle name."

"Kiddo, if some dame was willing to pay me five hundred bucks to sit in her living room for a couple of hours and play for her, she could call me anything she wants. It's not as if she asked you to do kinky sex."

"Yeah, well, she's so far out, I'm afraid that might be next. Anyway, I have a date on Sunday."

438

"You can change the date," he argued.

"I don't get it, Len. Why me?"

"Beats me. Can't be your ugly puss, so it must be your music. Do this one, kid. For me."

"Why for you? What do you get out of it? A lousy fifty dollars."

"Look, the guy who asked me is a personal friend. A very influential friend. I can say no more."

"See, it's even weirder than I thought," said Kit.

"I promise you, on my son's head, nothing bad is going to happen. The lady doesn't do drugs, she's not into S&M. All she wants is a little private concert. Please, Kittredge," he pleaded, "do me a favor. When did I ever ask anything before?"

"Okay, Len," Kit sighed. "But remember, you owe me one."

This time he arrived in the middle of the day. The tall iron gates were closed, and he had to get out and announce himself on a speaker before gaining entrance. As he climbed back in his van, he noticed the name *Axelrod* carved into the stone of the vine-covered gateposts.

The woman was waiting for him on a large terrace under an awning. She was wearing a clinging white jersey caftan with a matching hooded turban that ended in a long scarf wound around her throat. Although the afternoon was warm, she was drinking hot water.

"Will you have something?" she asked.

"Coke, please." The butler remained impassive. "I meant Coca-Cola," Kit hastily added.

"Sit down for a moment and talk to me." She indicated a chair next to her chaise longue. "Tell me about yourself. Where did you grow up? How did you become a musician?"

What an unusual woman, he thought, intrigued despite his misgivings. She spoke deliberately in a deep, melodious voice that seemed to give her words added weight. Although her eyes were hidden behind the dark glasses, he felt them intent upon him. At first this made him uneasy, but as he answered her questions he sensed that she was not really listening to what he said so much as trying to get a handle on him.

"Is it true that you do your own arrangements?"

"Yes."

"And you compose?"

"I wouldn't go so far as to call myself a composer," explained Kit, "but I have written some songs. Like for my group, the Berkeley Boys."

Abruptly she said, "Play for me now. Not your usual repertoire. Do you know any show tunes?"

"Yes, I cut my teeth on show music."

He set up the keyboard and launched into what he cynically termed his geriatric cocktail-party routine. Numbers his father had taught him when he was learning to play pop piano. It was music he adored—although he would have been hard pressed to make that admission to some of his fellow musicians. He did not quite get its bittersweet, self-deprecating, once-in-a-lifetime message, but he suspected that his generation was utterly incapable of creating anything remotely approaching it in value.

He began with Sondheim, segueing into Bernstein—songs from *West Side Story* and *Candide*. Instinctively he reached back to the era of Richard Rodgers and Cole Porter, to Kern and Gershwin. He played well, with an elegant ease, swaying over the keyboard, occasionally turning toward his listener to sing the lyrics. Finally it was only natural to move into some of his favorites of Michael Shane's music: "Through the Years," "Twilight Melody," "Violets in the Rain." And best of all, "A World Apart" and the haunting ballad "Wild Flowers," from *Magic Island*.

As he sang the pensive melodies from his grandfather's last show, Annette Heublein removed her dark glasses and closed her eyes. When she rested her turbaned head against the back of the chaise, the scarf that swathed the lower part of her face momentarily fell away. Before she could readjust it, Kit caught a glimpse of the hideous scars that puckered her neck and chin.

He had been playing for more than an hour, but she gave no sign of wanting him to stop. She was staring at him. The way her eyes devoured him was unsettling. This old woman treating him as if—well, almost as if she might want to have sex with him. The notion caused him to shudder inwardly.

She gestured and immediately the butler reappeared, taking

some sheets of music paper she handed him and bringing them to Kit.

"Can you play those?" she asked.

He ran through the first composition, improvising the bass. There were four pieces in all. They were old-fashioned stuff, but with a timeless quality. There was an elusiveness to them, and yet they seemed familiar. It was almost as if he had played them before.

Kit paused to flex his hands. "Thank you. That's enough for today," said Annette Heublein, as if she were suddenly too bored for words.

"These are good. I could work on them," he told her. "You know, arrange them so they sound better. I'd need some time, though."

"Take them," she said negligently.

He nodded and began folding his keyboard.

"Come with me." With an imperious lift of her hand, she led the way inside to a library. She handed him a folder thick with music. "See what you can do with these," she ordered. "I'd like you to play all of them when next you come."

What had he done, what had he said? His mouth opened in protest. *I won't be coming here again.* But he was unable to get the words out.

As he was stowing his equipment in the van, he glanced up at the house. Annette Heublein was standing at a window, watching him. *That is one strange female*, he said to himself as he drove down the mountain from the estate, maneuvering the hairpin curves of Benedict Canyon.

Weeks later the music was still untouched, buried amongst piles of papers in his apartment. Len had asked him to go out to Annette Heublein's house the coming weekend, but fortunately the Berkeley Boys were scheduled to cut some preliminary tracks for their new video at a sound studio, so he was able to say no without a hassle. However, that reminded him that he had not even glanced at the sheaf of papers in the folder since playing for Heublein on the terrace of her home. She had asked him to have the material ready the next time he came. He knew there had to be a next time, if only once more.

Tired as he was at the end of the evening, he sat down

at the keyboard with the sheets of ruled staff paper. He ran through several pieces with melodies so buoyant they seemed to float on the air. His left hand automatically improvised, and he was gripped by an inner excitement as he played. These were really good. The beat was surprisingly modern, kind of bluesy, with those half-tones and triplets. He could hear this one as a heart-tugging ballad . . . or maybe in a jazz arrangement, with that *daa-da-dum* . . . he snapped his fingers and nodded his head, as he tapped out the rhythm.

Something about the fourth and fifth songs bothered him as he ran through the rough scores. A particular quality. He stopped to bring the lamp closer, adjusting the shade to shine the light directly on the worksheets. They were obviously old. The paper was yellowing along the edges, and the notes were faded with time but legible. More than one person may have worked on them, he thought. There were marginal notes, penciled lyrics under the lines, and smudges wherever the composer had erased and rewritten a phrase. Here and there, entire lines had been crossed out. As he struggled with the phrasing, Kit had a sense of *déjà vu*. The texture of it . . . the flags, the way they charged across the page like knife slashes. Angry, hasty. He could not rid himself of the eerie sensation that he had seen this score before.

His eyes were closing. He caught himself as his head nodded forward. Maybe he would sleep well tonight. The only way he got any rest these days was to force himself to keep going until he crashed into bed. After all these months, he still thought about Diana. He would not go back to Berkeley in September. It would be too depressing to be in the same place without being together.

It was nearly dusk when Kit waved goodbye to the band and left the studio. He headed home to Brentwood along Sunset Boulevard. It was Monday, and after the weekend without commuter traffic, the skies were clear overhead.

Today's recording session had sucked. They would have to recut two tracks for the demo they were doing for Epic. The interview in *Rolling Stone* had boosted the sales figures for their last album, and Len thought they had a good shot at getting a video on MTV. They needed to hook up with the right director, though. Someone new and innovative who would complement their sound with good visuals and grow with them.

He had reached Westwood. On an impulse, he parked and walked over to the UCLA campus.

A student assistant was sitting at the reference desk in the yellow building that housed the Arts Library. She had long, shiny, reddish gold hair. When she looked up, her brilliant smile was not the only thing that struck him. It was her eyes. One was brown and the other was blue. Heavily lashed and tilted at the corners, they sparkled with friendliness.

"Hi. Can I help you?"

He stopped staring and took a deep breath. "I'm trying to find some information about an old movie actress."

"How old?"

"Oh, really old. She must have been in silent pictures. Probably back in the early forties."

She suppressed a smile. "More like early twenties, if she was in silent films. What's her name?"

"Annette Heublein."

"Never heard of her."

"Hey, do you know every woman who was ever in movies?"

"Probably," she said, with a confident grin. "Come on, I'll show you the reference section."

Kit followed her into the stacks, admiring the way her nicely faded jeans fit her nicely shaped derriere. "Are you a student here?" he asked. It never hurt to be friendly.

"Yes, I'm at the Film School."

"It never fails, whenever I make a dumb remark."

She laughed. "You, I take it, are not studying filmmaking."

"No, I'm not."

She frowned. "But you are a UCLA student, aren't you? I mean, you're supposed to be, if you check out books."

"Well, technically, not yet. I'm transferring from Berkeley next fall."

She shook her head. "That's a nice story, but it's not good enough."

"No kidding. Here . . . look." He took out his wallet and showed her his student I.D. from Berkeley and the receipt from the UCLA admissions office for his transfer application fee. "I wouldn't try to con you."

"You can't check out books until you're registered," she said, "but reference materials don't circulate anyway."

She handed him a volume. "Start with *Star Stats*. If your actress isn't in there, you might have trouble finding her." She moved along the stacks. "That section is all encyclopedias of theater and film, and on these shelves are the biographical references. Let me know if there's anything else I can help you with. My name's Cathy."

"Thanks, Cathy."

After searching through every film encyclopedia in the Arts Library, he had drawn a blank. He moved to the biography section and looked through half a dozen biographical dictionaries, consulted *Who Was Who in Hollywood*, and the *New Century Cyclopedia of Names*. Nothing. As far as film history was concerned, Annette Heublein had never existed.

"How'd you make out?" asked Cathy when he walked up to her desk.

"Not so good. Haven't found a thing."

"Is this important?"

"It could be. Right now it's a big mystery."

She pushed a book request form toward him. "If you'll write down her name, I'll see what I can do. There's a lot of stuff on microfilm, and we may have some old reference books stashed away in the archives."

"Gee, thanks. That's very nice of you."

"It might take a while. You better tell me how to reach you, in case I come up with something."

He jotted down his name and telephone number. "Since you have my vital statistics . . . I think it's only fair that I have yours," he said, trying his most charming smile.

A faint blush colored her cheeks. "The name's Cathy Wallace. You can reach me here on Mondays and Wednesdays. Just leave a message if I'm not at work."

All the way home, he smiled, thinking about Cathy Wallace. If she didn't get in touch with him, maybe he would give her a call.

The Berkeley Boys were finishing a three-week booking at the Big Dipper. Kit liked the popular coffeehouse, which was a hangout for students, but he would be glad when it was over. He needed some time to himself before going back

o college. He was actually looking forward to a new start
at UCLA. It wasn't only because Di was at Berkeley. If he
stayed in LA, he could continue to play with the group on
weekends.

Their demo was on hold. The songs were terrific. They
finally got the mixing right and had cut the album, but the
staging for the video was all wrong for them. He hated that
smoky, strobe-laced retro style, but he didn't want them to
end up looking like the Beach Boys, either. This album was
too special to take a chance on a mismatched production.

His phone was ringing when he came in the door. He caught
it just as the answering machine was picking up.

"Hello."

"Hello, is this Kit?" It was a pleasant female voice.

"Yes. Who's this?"

"It's Cathy Wallace." When he didn't react, she quickly
said, "We met two weeks ago at the Arts Library."

"Oh, yeah. Hi, Cathy. I'm sorry, I wasn't connecting."

"That's okay. I wanted you to know that I looked for
Annette Heublein, but I can't find her."

"Well, it was nice of you to try."

"If I had a little more information, it would help. What do
you know about her?"

Just then, his call-waiting beeped. "Hold on a sec," he said.
No one was on the other line. "Cathy? I'm back. Listen, are
you still at work?"

"I'm just finishing up. I work late on Wednesdays."

"Would you like to get something to eat?"

"All right."

"How's Hamburger Hamlet?"

"That's fine."

"Meet you there in twenty minutes."

"I'll be there."

He was waiting when she walked in and slid into the red
leather booth opposite him. "How hungry are you?" he asked.

"Starved. I haven't had dinner yet."

They ordered taco burgers. Kit had a beer and Cathy a diet
Coke while they waited for their food. And they talked.

She told him she came from Scarsdale, New York, and had
transferred to UCLA after her freshman year at Brown. "Ever
since I was a kid, I've wanted to direct films. That was a

little unusual on the East Coast. Everyone I grew up with was going to be a lawyer or an investment banker. I tried to do the expected thing to please my parents. They think everyone in Hollywood is depraved."

Kit grinned. "They're right."

"Shh, don't tell!" Lovely things happened to her face when she laughed.

"Was that important to you?" he asked. "Pleasing your parents?"

She paused before answering, seeming to consider his question. "Yes, I think it was. They're exceptional people and they've always tried to do what was best for us. They weren't like the other parents. I mean, they weren't running in a popularity contest. If they thought we shouldn't do something, even if all the other kids were allowed to, we weren't."

"You have brothers and sisters?"

"Yes, one of each," she said happily. "An older brother and a younger sister."

"What are they doing?"

"Tim, that's my brother, is twenty-three. He's going to grad school in Colorado, studying geology and conservation. And my sister Jill is a freshman at Brown. Unlike me, she loves it. She wants to go to medical school."

"Did your dad go to Brown?"

She grinned. "How'd you guess? He went to Brown and Columbia Law School, which is where he met my mom. She was getting her master's in social work."

"It sounds like a nice family," he said, consciously suppressing any trace of envy. "Did you have fun growing up?"

"Oh, yes. We had the *best* times together."

Once again, he had to keep from staring at her. Her smile was wide and open, with an unblinking directness in those mysterious eyes. She wore no makeup and needed none. Her skin was smooth and healthy, with a few freckles across the bridge of her intelligent nose. She was not beautiful, really, but radiantly attractive.

"You haven't told me about you," said Cathy.

"I'm a musician, part of a group. We're called the Berkeley Boys."

"Oh, my gosh! I heard them at the Dipper last week." Her brow wrinkled. "But I didn't see you."

"I kind of wear other clothes and stuff when we play at a club. You know, to look the part."

"Which one were you? I mean, which instrument."

"Keyboard and guitar."

"I can't believe I didn't recognize you. Of course, it was dark in there, and if you dress differently . . ."

He smiled. "Yeah. I also wear a fake ponytail."

"You're kidding! Why?"

"I used to have a real one, but I cut it off. The guys thought I shouldn't have, so I wear a switch. That's what they called it at the place where I bought it. Crazy, huh?"

"I'm looking at you with different eyes," she said, cocking her head. "No earrings?"

"I usually wear one of those, too." He smiled sheepishly. "I cut my hair and took out the earring last Christmas when I went to meet my girlfriend's parents. I figured there were enough strikes against me."

"Oh." Her face fell. "Well, did it work?"

"No. They were uptight proper Bostonians. They hated me on sight."

"That's too bad."

He shrugged. "She's not my girlfriend anymore. I'm not even sure why I mentioned it."

The waitress brought their order, which was a relief, because he was feeling uncomfortable talking about such personal things to a perfect stranger. The taco burgers were messy, dripping with onions and sauce. Cathy cut hers in half and took small bites. He had devoured his burger and fries before she was half finished.

"Where did you grow up?" she asked.

"Here and there, like a tumbleweed." Kit made circles on the table with his glass. "I was born in Toronto. My parents were divorced when I was six. Dad came back to the States—he was an American—and when I was eight, he brought me to live in New York with my grandparents. We were there for four years and I was very happy. My grandmother gave me the only real mothering I've ever experienced."

"What happened after four years?"

"Dad took a job as a history professor at the University of Iowa." He drained his glass of the last of his beer. "We moved to Iowa City and my grandparents retired to Florida."

"My grandparents retired to Florida, too. All four of them. My father's parents live in Fort Lauderdale and my mother's are near Sarasota."

"My grandmother lives on an island a little south of Naples. She's all alone now. My grandfather died last year. Well, actually he was my step-grandfather. My real grandfather died when Dad was a baby." He laughed then. "I have a very complicated family, compared to yours."

"It sounds that way. Why are you transferring to UCLA?"

"If I'm down here, I can play with the band. We're getting good notices and we're going to do a video. That is, if we can ever find the right director."

She blinked her brown-blue eyes and put down her taco burger. "I've always wanted to direct a video."

"Well, I don't think . . ."

"No, really, I mean it. I can do it."

"C'mon, Cathy, be serious. This isn't a hobby with us. It takes special skills to do an album. It's not a miniseries, and yet it has to have drama—"

"Of course it does," she said impatiently. "It needs fantastic lighting, great camerawork, primary focus on the musicians, integrating the soundtrack with a fantasy background that dramatizes the music." Her voice was rising with excitement. "I know all about it. I took a course in videos. I was the creative director on our class project. Would you like to see my tape?"

"No."

"What do you mean, *no?*"

"No, I would not like to see the tape from your class project. Look, Cathy, we're professionals and we need an experienced director." He had forgotten all about his conviction that they should find someone young and creative who would grow with them. "What we do not need is a college student who thinks it would be fun to work on a video."

"That's insulting! And unfair. How can you make a judgment unless you've seen my work? I've got lots of tapes of things I've produced and directed. I'm a terrific director. I know lighting, I do great visuals."

Kit looked around self-consciously. Several people were glancing their way. In a quieter tone he said, "I'm sure you're very talented, Cathy. We just can't afford to fool around. It costs a lot of money to rent a studio and hire a cameraman and a production crew."

"Please, Kit, just give me a chance. Let me show the tapes to you."

What harm was there in screening a couple of tapes? he asked himself. After all, she had been nice enough to look for Annette Heublein. "Okay," he sighed, "I'll look at your tapes. Now, eat."

Kit sipped his second beer while Cathy ate in silence. She left half of her burger and insisted on paying her share, and they walked out into the warm summer night. The sidewalks of Westwood were crowded with groups of young people, mostly UCLA students.

They drove the few blocks to Cathy's apartment in an off-campus building owned by the university. Her three roommates were using the VCR to watch a rented movie. They looked up with interest when Kit walked in.

"We can take the tapes to my apartment," he said. He noted her hesitation. "You don't have to worry. I promise to behave."

"Don't be silly, it's not that." She gave him a withering look. "If I'm there, I'll just feel self-conscious. Let me give you a couple of tapes. Take them home and look at them when you have time."

"It's a deal."

She walked downstairs with him. "We never talked about Annette Heublein. What do you know about her?"

"Nothing really. My agent sent me to her house on a gig. He told me she was once a star and has powerful connections. There's a mystery about her. She has these terrible scars all over her neck and she tries to hide them."

"How much of a star could she have been if she's not listed in any of the reference books?" said Cathy.

He was in bed, half asleep, when his phone rang.

"It's Cathy. I just thought of something."

"What?" This young lady was getting to be a bit of a problem.

"Maybe she used a stage name."

"Who?"

"Annette Heublein, stupid. You know, like Cary Grant. His

name was Archie Leach, but if you looked that up, you wouldn't find him." She sounded quite pleased with herself.

"What good does that do us, if we don't know what it is? *Stupid*."

"Oh." She sounded deflated. "It was just an idea."

"Goodnight, Cathy."

Kit had improvised a large desk from a flush door and a pair of sawhorses. Each night when he came home, the music Annette Heublein had given him was there on the desk, an irritating reminder. He turned the sheets over, examining all sides, wondering what it was about them that pricked his curiosity. On a sudden inspiration, he went to a chest of drawers in the hall. Removing a brown manila portfolio, he carefully laid it open on the desk. One by one, he leafed through the contents, comparing them to the pages that were lying next to them.

A thoughtful expression came into his eyes. He glanced at his wristwatch. It was past ten o'clock in Florida, but his grandmother had always been a night owl. He picked up the telephone and punched in Julia's number.

Chapter 22

Marie

Julia was taken by a spell of coughing as Clarissa Jenkins backed through the door carrying still another dish, this time a chicken pot pie. She stared helplessly at the containers of food crowding the kitchen counter.

"I can't possibly finish all this alone, Clarissa," she protested between sips of warm tea and honey to soothe her throat.

"Have as much as you like, then, and freeze the rest. Y'all need to eat more. You're still weak as a kitten from that bronchitis." She disappeared briefly, returning with a sweet potato pudding and a fresh batch of zucchini bread.

"This is ridiculous," said Julia laughingly as she took the casserole from her. "You've been wonderful, cooking all my meals, but it's no longer necessary. I'm really feeling much better."

"What else have I got to do?" Clarissa muttered as she began putting the containers in the refrigerator.

Julia looked sharply at her friend, noting how drawn she appeared. Except for the past two weeks, when Julia had been laid up with flu and severe bronchitis, they had seen very little of each other lately. "What's troubling you, Clarissa?"

Her neighbor shook her head despondently. "I'm about at the end of my rope."

Julia took her arm. "Come sit down for a minute. Let's have a talk." She carried the teapot and a plate of cookies to the sunroom. "Now, tell me what's wrong."

Clarissa was stirring sugar into her tea. "*I'm* what's wrong. I wish I could be more like you, Julia. You're so busy all the time, you never seem to be bored. I've been living here for almost six years and I haven't made one real friend outside of you."

"It's not as easy to form friendships when we get older."

"I guess." Clarissa nibbled on a cookie. "These are delicious. Who made them?"

"Joyce Moser. She brought them over yesterday."

"See what I mean," she pointed out. "You don't have trouble making friends. If I were sick, nobody outside of you would pay any attention to me. I get so lonely, sometimes I think I'll go crazy."

Julia passed the cookies again. "I get lonely, too. That's why I make it a point to keep occupied."

"Well," said Clarissa emphatically, "I've come to a decision. I'm going back to Nashville to take care of my baby sister. Her husband died a couple years ago and she just found out she has MS."

"Oh, Clarissa, that's terribly sad. It's the right thing for you to do, but I shall be sorry to see you go."

Her eyes welled with tears. "You really mean that, don't you?"

"Certainly I mean it. You're a wonderful person and a very generous neighbor. I'll miss you."

Clarissa sniffled and wiped her eyes. "I'll miss you, too. No one ever treated me as nice as you and George."

Remembering the many times she had avoided Clarissa's company, Julia felt a twinge of guilt. "How soon do you plan to leave?"

"The minute I can get rid of my house. You know me. When I decide to do something, I don't fool around."

"I am well aware of that," said Julia drily.

"Oh, you . . . are you still thinking about that Gary? You are, aren't you?"

"Well, you must admit it was a bit impetuous, hiring a skipper you met at the marina and giving him the run of your property without knowing anything about him."

"You're right. But as soon as I caught him padding the marine supply bills, I fired him."

Julia laughed. "Meanwhile he lived on your boat for months and took you for a lot of money."

"I was very disappointed in that boy," she said, with great dignity. "Well, I better get going. There's a lot to do, planning a move." She took the Pyrex dishes from last week's pot roast and lasagna. "By the way, if you hear of anyone who might want to buy my house, be sure to let me know."

When Clarissa had left, Julia cleared away the tea things, carrying them to the kitchen. Something had been triggered at the back of her mind, but whatever it was escaped her. It was not until after she had eaten some of Clarissa's chicken pie and sweet potatoes for dinner and was watching the evening news on television that she thought of what it was. She immediately went to the telephone and dialed the Winstons in New York.

Perhaps Sue and Jack would want to look at Clarissa's house if they were serious about retiring to Florida. In any case, it wouldn't hurt to give them a call.

In the middle of the night, she was startled out of a deep sleep. It was black and misty, with no moon. For a moment, she had trouble getting her bearings in the dark, then gradually the dim, familiar outlines of the room swam into shape. A spasm of coughing seized her and she sat up, reaching for the glass of water she kept on the night table. Although she had fully recovered from the flu, she was still wracked with a dry cough that always seemed to grow worse at night.

She puffed up the pillows and lay back, closing her eyes. There had been that dream again. That old, baffling dream. She had thought she was rid of it, but since her last trip to New York and the disturbing news of Scott and Isobel's separation, her nights had often been visited by the fleeting images, familiar and yet intangible. She was searching for her father, fleeing through a maze of corridors and stairways, and hunted by an unknown man; no matter how she tried to cry out, her voice remained mute. Tonight it had been more intense, more within her grasp. She tried to summon the hazy impressions. Of running and wind and a voice calling her name. Of pursuit and capture . . . and ecstasy. She focused all her concentration, and in a sudden insight she understood.

The man in her dream had been Michael . . .

Why, after forty-one years, was she dreaming of Michael? It was impossible to explain the workings of the subconscious mind.

But it was not the dream that had awakened her. It was something else. A vestigial reflex, a sense of impending doom.

There was the slightest alteration in the stillness of the Palm Island night. Sitting up, Julia strained her ears to listen. Had she heard a noise? She slid out of bed and reached for her robe. A night light in the hall gave enough illumination for her to move about. She was unafraid. With all that had happened, what was left for her to fear? After checking the doors and the alarm panel, everything seemed in order. She took a cup of spring water from the cooler and went to the sunroom, cranking open a louvered window to let in the warm, moist breeze. Through the darkness came the wash of lapping water. She settled on the couch, drawing her legs up under her. On a night like this, it was hard to keep her mind off her family.

All three of her children had failed at marriage. What did that say about her as a mother? It seemed she was forever to be troubled about one of them. As a rule, it had been Neil or Deborah she worried about, but now it was Scott, the son she had thought was beyond need for concern. When he had called to say goodbye before leaving for Tokyo, he insisted that Isobel was the one who wanted the divorce.

"Did she find out about your love affair?" Julia asked, unable to imagine what else would cause Isobel to leave Scott.

"No," he said curtly. "I'll explain it fully to you another time, Mother."

It broke her heart to think that their marriage was at an end. While it was true that she had never been especially close to her daughter-in-law, Julia had to admire Isobel's style and newly discovered independence. She thought Isobel, in her own undemonstrative fashion, had also held her in high regard.

And now Scott was living with the woman he loved. Solange Didier. Soon he intended to bring her to meet his mother.

It was all too much. She closed her eyes and leaned back, exhausted by the roiling in her mind. *I am weary beyond words of other people's problems.*

Suddenly she sat up. She had heard a high, thin sound echoing across the water. It seemed out of place in the serenity of Pirates Cove. How silly, she told herself impatiently. *When George was here, I never listened for noises in the night.*

But there was positively something out there. She heard a dull thunk, followed by the low muffle of an inboard diesel. *A boat,* she thought, relaxing. Sound was deceptive. It was hard to tell direction or distance over water, especially in the dark. Although it was most likely a fishing craft, it had seemed to be in the lagoon.

She loved the throb of a marine engine at night. It reminded her of the excursions with George in the old days. They had kept *Limerick IV* until the end, because Scott used to take them sailing every time he came down from New York. One of the first matters she had settled after George's death was to sell the ketch. She could not bear to have the last of his sailboats there, waiting for him.

The hum of the diesel was much too close and distinct for the commercial fleet. There was definitely a boat in the lagoon. One of her neighbors must be leaving on a fishing trip. The motor swelled and then settled into a low drone and moved steadily away until it faded on the wind.

There were hours to go until morning. She should go back to bed, and try to get whatever sleep she could. Tomorrow she had to put in a full day at the nursing home.

As she drove out the gate the next morning, Samuel nodded without his customary cheer. "I see you're goin' out early, Mrs. Rhinehart." He handed her a memorandum printed on official Palm Island stationery.

"What's this, Samuel?"

"Oh, that's nothin' but a silly bit o' never-mind," he said. "You heard about that jail break in Tampa last week?"

"Yes, I remember reading about it."

"Well, this dude up and tells the state police he seen them two convicts on Route 41. Got himself on TV 'n' ever'thing. How some folks like to show off. Anyways, jus' as a precaution, the management's suggestin' all our folks keep their doors locked and be sure to use the alarm." As Julia frowned, he said, "I *tole* Mr. Ramirez printin' a notice'll just upset our people. Now, you're not to worry, ma'am. That jail's near two hundred miles from Palm Island. I don't for a minute believe they headin' south, and even if they was, they ain't gettin' in Palm Island. Ain't *no way* anyone gettin' past these gates."

"I do feel that the management is being overcautious, Samuel, and I assure you the notice doesn't upset me in the least."

Samuel smiled reassuringly. "Have a nice day now, ma'am."

Julia recalled hearing about the prison break and seeing photographs of two men, life-term murderers and drug traffickers, on the evening news, but she had paid little attention. Jail breaks and worse had been daily fare in New York. She and George had always avoided watching the local TV stations with their emphasis on murder, rape, and mayhem, preferring the deliberative, in-depth coverage of world and national events on MacNeil-Lehrer.

Not for a minute did she believe the convicts posed a threat to her sheltered community. Fugitives from the law would head straight for a large city where they could blend in with the population. They would avoid a closely guarded compound of homes where there would be no place for them to hide and no way out. Palm Island was as well protected as a fortress. Surrounded by water and electric-eye fencing, there was only one way in, and that was through the heavy steel gates.

Driving across the causeway, Julia was filled with reasonless optimism and a great sense of well-being. What a magnificent day! Far out on the bay, a three-masted schooner heeled in the wind, sails billowing, forming a perfect picture against sea and sky. *God's in his heaven*, she hummed, *all's right with the world . . .*

"Well, well. It's been a long time since we've seen *you*," said the coordinator in the volunteer office at the Admiralty Residence. "Three whole weeks."

Julia had never liked this woman. "I've been sick. I assumed you knew, since I called."

"It's not good for our patients when the volunteers don't come regularly, you know. They forget people."

"It's also not good for them to catch the flu," she responded frostily.

When she walked into the room, she found Marie strapped into a wheelchair. "What happened? Why are you tied in that way?"

Marie began to cry. She was bewildered and almost incoherent. "I . . . can't . . . they won't . . . go away," she finally said.

Greatly concerned, Julia went to find the nurse in charge. "Why is Marie Barnes tied into a wheelchair?" she asked.

The nurse looked regretful. "I'm afraid it was necessary, Mrs. Rhinehart. She fell and injured herself."

"Poor soul. She seems so confused. Three weeks ago when I was here, she was alert. Can her condition have deteriorated so quickly?"

"Yes, it happens all the time. They reach a point where they can no longer be permitted to wander around. We can't allow our patients to injure themselves, can we?"

"No, but it seems too cruel, to be tied in that way."

The nurse shrugged. "All I've been told is the new supervisor ordered her confined. She's become incontinent, you know."

"Incontinent! The last time I was here she was able to get to the bathroom with just a little assistance."

The telephone rang. "If you'll excuse me, Mrs. Rhinehart, we're very busy."

When she returned to Marie's room to read to her, Julia was greeted by the strong odor of urine. "Oh, Marie," she commiserated.

Marie began to cry, a pathetic, mewing sound. Like a child, she rubbed her eyes with the back of her hand. The volunteers were not permitted to move a patient who was confined—something to do with the insurance—so Julia rang for a nurse. After five minutes, she rang a second time and finally went down the hall again, dreading an encounter with the same nurse. Fortunately Jeanie, a young nursing assistant and one of Julia's favorites, was on the desk.

"Marie Barnes had an accident. She needs to be washed up."

Jeanie clucked sympathetically. "I'll do it, Mrs. Rhinehart, just as soon as someone relieves me here. I'm not supposed to leave the desk unattended."

"I can't get over how quickly she has deteriorated," Julia whispered to Jeanie, once Marie was washed, powdered, dressed in a clean nightgown, and resting comfortably in her bed, with the rails up.

"There's more to it," said Jeanie, looking around cautiously. "This is my break. Would you join me for a cup of coffee?"

"I'd like that," said Julia. She needed to relax for a few minutes. The incident had upset her more than she had realized.

When they were seated in a quiet corner of the staff cafeteria, Jeanie leaned over and said, "You understand what's happening with Mrs. Barnes, don't you?"

"You mean she's becoming senile?"

"That's the final result of it, but no, that's not what I meant."

"What, then?"

"She had a little bladder infection; they were treating it with antibiotics and sulfa. Naturally she had urinary frequency." Jeanie lowered her voice even further and Julia had to move her chair closer in order to hear. "She rang so often for a nurse and, you know, they're busy. Especially at night, when there's a smaller staff on duty. They wouldn't answer every time she called. So she got up one night to go to the bathroom herself. She was woozy from the tranquilizer they ordered so she would sleep—" Here, Jeanie gave Julia a meaningful look. "Well, she fell and hit her head on the corner of the night table. One of the aides came in and found her. She wasn't seriously hurt, but she had a big bruise on her forehead. So they ordered her strapped in at night. The next time, she wet the bed. After that happened they said she was incontinent, ordered diapers, and she's tied into the wheelchair. It doesn't take long to become incontinent and senile once you reach that stage."

Julia was aghast. "I've never heard anything so horrible in my life. It's inhumane! It should be reported to the administration."

"Don't you think they know? This goes on in every nursing home. There aren't enough nurses or aides, especially at night, and lots of them really don't care."

"But the Admiralty is supposed to be a good facility, it's well recommended."

"It's better than most," said Jeanie. "Don't forget, this is the only state-run senior residence with total Alzheimer care in the county. Most people who can afford it send their elderly to one of the private nursing homes."

Julia persisted. "I just can't accept this. Are you sure nothing can be done?"

"Listen, I could get fired if anyone found out what I told you, and I really need this job. I want to go to nursing school as soon as I save a little more money."

"You'll make a wonderful nurse, Jeanie."

"Thank you, Mrs. Rhinehart." She touched Julia's hand affectionately. "You mustn't blame them too much. They're very short-staffed and there's just so much each person can do." She looked at her watch. "I guess I'd better get back."

Late in the afternoon, Julia drove home, feeling exhausted and depressed. She could not rid herself of the image of Marie Barnes tied into her wheelchair, wet and soiled and whimpering like an infant.

Oh God, under no circumstances will I ever go to a nursing home. I'd sooner die.

There was a police car in the driveway when she reached her house. An officer was at the wheel. A second man in civilian clothes approached her.

"Mrs. Julia Rhinehart?"

Her heart fluttered. "Yes, I'm Mrs. Rhinehart."

He displayed a badge. "Detective Carey, County Sheriff's office. We'd like to talk to you for a few minutes, ma'am. Is it all right if we come in?"

"May I ask what this is about?"

"There's been an intruder in the area, ma'am. We'd just like to ask a few questions, if you don't mind."

"Certainly, come in." He sounded just like a character on television. She suppressed a smile as she disengaged the alarm and led the way into the living room.

"This is Officer Fry, ma'am."

Julia nodded to the policeman, who had joined them. "Please have a seat, gentlemen."

The detective sat on a side chair, but Officer Fry chose to stand all the while, looking curiously around the room.

"Do you know a Mrs. Clarissa Jenkins?"

"Why, yes, of course. She's my next-door neighbor."

"When did you last see your neighbor?"

Alarm coursed through her. "Is Mrs. Jenkins all right?"

"Please, Mrs. Rhinehart, would you just answer the question."

She pursed her lips. "I saw her yesterday afternoon."

"And where was that, ma'am?"

"Right here, in my house. I've had the flu and Mrs. Jenkins has been coming over almost every day to bring me hot meals."

Carey was making notes in a small looseleaf binder. "And what time of day was it?"

Julia tried to collect her thoughts. "Somewhere between three and four o'clock in the afternoon."

"How long did she stay?"

"Not very long. She brought dinner, we talked for a little while and then she left because she had errands to run." Again Julia asked, "Won't you please tell me what this is about? Has something happened to Mrs. Jenkins?"

"I'm afraid so, ma'am."

"Well, *what*? Where is she?"

Just then, Mr. Ramirez, the Palm Island manager, came running up the front walk and pounded on her door. Officer Fry let him in. Ramirez's usually florid complexion was almost gray, and although it was a comfortable afternoon, he was sweating profusely. "Mrs. Rhinehart, I apologize for the intrusion. I asked you *not* to disturb the residents until I notified them, Detective Carey."

"Sorry, this couldn't wait," said the detective, dismissing him with a look of contempt.

"Please! Will *someone* tell me what's going on?" cried Julia. "What has happened to Clarissa?"

Detective Carey did not look up from his notebook. "She's been taken to the hospital, Mrs. Rhinehart."

"Oh, my heavens!" Her pulse began to race. "What happened?"

"She was the victim of foul play, ma'am."

"Foul play?" When had she last heard anyone use that archaic term? "I wonder whether you would mind being more explicit."

"She was tied up and struck on the head with a heavy object. We won't have the full details until we can question her further."

Her heart was galloping again. "Did this happen in her house?"

"Yes, ma'am. But the house wasn't broken into. It appears that she admitted someone who then overpowered her."

Julia could feel the blood drain from her cheeks. She had never in her life fainted, and she did not intend to do so now. "But who could get in through the gates? What about her alarm?"

"These are questions we can't yet answer."

"Could it be someone from inside?" she asked, and Mr. Ramirez looked pained.

"That is a theory we're considering."

For a moment she felt weak, and then her head cleared. "Gary. You should question Gary."

"Gary who?"

"I don't know his last name. He was a sort of handyman who used to take care of her cabin cruiser. She fired him about six weeks ago. He was living right there on the boat for four months."

"I don't recollect seeing any boat," said Officer Fry, who had not spoken until now.

"It's moored down at her dock."

"Go check the dock, Fry," ordered the detective.

"Will Mrs. Jenkins be all right?" Julia asked Carey.

"Yes, ma'am. She's shook up some." He looked at her. "You look a little pale yourself."

Everything had suddenly begun to spin. The next thing Julia knew, she was leaning back on the couch with Carey and Ramirez bending over her. "Are you all right?" asked the detective.

"If I could just have a glass of water, please. I'll be fine in a moment."

Just then the policeman returned. "Ain't no boat down there."

Julia slowly sipped ice water while the detective asked dozens of questions. Was Mrs. Jenkins in the habit of picking up strange men? "No, of course not," she answered indignantly.

Had Julia noticed anything at all suspicious around the neighborhood? Had she heard anything unusual? At first she said no, then she recalled the odd, high sound, and the boat in the lagoon late the night before. She told him about it.

"Did you go over there this morning?"

"No. There seemed to be no reason to. I left early for Marlin Beach, where I work in a nursing home. I'd forgotten all about hearing anything until now."

"So you didn't go by at all today, just to say hello?"

"I told you I didn't. I'm not in the habit of dropping in on Mrs. Jenkins uninvited."

"In other words, you are not friends."

She did not at all care for his tone, and her answer showed it. "I wouldn't say that. We are quite neighborly; however, we respect each other's privacy. I like her very much, although we are not *close* friends. You understand how that is, I'm sure."

"Who *are* her close friends?"

"I'm not aware of any, at least not around here."

"Husband?"

"They're divorced. He lives in Coral Gables now."

"Children?"

"None. They lost a little boy many years ago."

"Well, it appears that she let the burglar in. He may have had a gun or maybe it was someone she knew, like this Gary. The house has been ransacked, but we have no idea what was taken besides the boat. They're dusting for fingerprints. There's some indication that there was more than one intruder."

"It's ironic that this should happen now," said Julia. "Mrs. Jenkins is planning to move back to Tennessee to live with her sister, who is ill."

"Do you know how to reach the sister?"

"No. I don't even know the family name."

Clarissa remained in the hospital under observation for a week. Julia visited her daily, but her neighbor was barely able to speak. Although she had recovered from the trauma to her head, she was so terrified by her experience that she remained in a state of near hysteria.

When she came out of shock, Clarissa had told the police that it was indeed Gary who rang her doorbell, claiming he needed to talk to her. Against her better judgment, she had opened the door, whereupon a second masked man forced his way in and hit her over the head. When she regained consciousness, she had found herself bound and gagged, and the men had vanished. She remained there throughout the night, fearing for her life, until late the next morning, when the maid arrived to clean her house.

Contacted by the police, Walter Jenkins came to Palm Island to cooperate with the criminal investigation. In a surprisingly

hort time he had made a complete inventory of the house
and its contents and arranged for it to be put on the market.
He thought it advisable for Clarissa to depart immediately for
Nashville. So taken aback was Julia at the unseemly haste
with which he dispatched his former wife to Tennessee that
she could barely be civil to him.

"Clarissa told me last week that she had decided to sell
the house, Walter. Friends of mine from New York made
an appointment to see it. They're supposed to fly down this
weekend."

"That's just fine with me," he answered. "If they're friends
of yours, we'll give them a real good price and there won't
be a broker's fee."

"Perhaps you'd better speak to them beforehand, because
Clarissa has already given them a price."

"Well, now, we'll have to see. I can't be expected to be
bound by the word of a woman who isn't able to speak for
herself, can I?"

Julia was appalled. What a loathsome man. But worse than
her shock at Walter's callous behavior was the horror of
Clarissa's ordeal. The thieves had entered Pirates Cove by
the only unguarded route—the water. If it was not safe here
in the protected environment of Palm Island, where was there
to go?

A week after Clarissa's departure, Julia made herself a chef's
salad and was sitting in the screened patio to have lunch. There
had scarcely been time to bid her neighbor a proper farewell.
Julia was haunted by the idea that she had actually *heard* the
criminals leaving Pirates Cove. If only she had called the
police or the Coast Guard that night, they might have been
apprehended. It was unnerving to think they might still be
at large.

She heard a car turn into the driveway. Who could it be? The
gate always announced visitors. She went out on the terrace
and saw that it was a patrol car. Detective Carey waved and
walked across the lawn, followed by Officer Fry.

"Good afternoon, gentlemen."

"How are you today, Mrs. Rhinehart? Feeling better?"

Julia shrugged. "Yes, thank you. It takes getting used to,
having a friend attacked in her own home."

"Believe me, I understand. That's why we're here. We thought you should know that the sailor is dead."

"The sailor?" She looked puzzled. "Do you mean Gary?"

"Yes. His body was caught in a shrimper's net in the Gulf, just south of Key West. He had been trussed with nylon line and tossed overboard. Death by drowning."

Julia shuddered. "How cruel. Why do you suppose they killed him?"

"They were drug runners. That's why they stole the boat. Splitting the proceeds two ways instead of three could have been the motive. They may always have intended to get rid of him. We'll never know. These criminals are the cruelest people on earth, ma'am. Other lives have no value to them. Anyone who makes money in the drug trade basically doesn't care about human life."

"Was it definitely the escaped convicts, then?"

Carey nodded. "There's no doubt. Fingerprints in Mrs. Jenkins's house match those of one of the men. The sailor's prints were also found. His name was Kevin Gary Willis. He had a record—served time for dealing drugs and burglary. Of course, that was petty stuff compared to the men he was messing with."

"Do you think Gary intended to steal the boat all along?" she asked.

"Yes, it was probably his objective from day one. This has the profile of a planned operation."

The police speculated that after the convicts had killed Gary and dumped his body overboard, they headed for a rendezvous in the Caribbean. Based on past experience, Carey told her, the *Clarissa* would never be found.

"They steal yachts all the time, use them in drug trafficking, and then scuttle them. It's unusual for them to come into a private marina such as this one, though."

"We thought we were safe from any intrusions here," said Julia ironically.

"I realize how upsetting this has been for you. We wanted you to know there's no reason for you to worry about it happening again."

The police were not insensitive after all, even though it had seemed that way the day they came to question her. "That's very thoughtful of you," said Julia. "I appreciate your coming ɔy. Would you care for some coffee or a cold drink?"

"No, thank you, ma'am. We've got to be going." She walked across the lawn with them. "You'll be having a new neighbor, I guess. I heard that Mrs. Jenkins's house has been put up for sale," said the detective.

"It looks like friends of mine from New York may buy it. They came down last weekend and they liked it."

"That's where you're from, New York?" asked Officer Fry, who she had decided was the strong, silent type.

"Yes." She waited for his eyes to take on that familiar guarded look that came over people who had been born down here whenever you mentioned New York.

But he surprised her. "My wife hails from Yonkers. Her folks usually visit us every winter. They like to get away from the cold."

"That's why we moved here when my husband retired. We thought a warmer climate might be nice for a change. That, and all the violence in Manhattan—" She stopped, giving them a wry smile. "I guess there's no place in the world that doesn't have crime."

Carey shook his head. "It's the drugs. Drugs are at the root of most violent crime."

After the men had left, Julia dumped the half-eaten chef's salad in the disposer. Taking a glass of iced tea and the New York *Times*, she went into the sunroom. She sat on the couch and tried to concentrate on the editorial page, but her mind kept wandering. Detective Carey may have assured her that there was no further need to worry, but she knew it would be a while before she felt completely at ease in the night.

Betsy had been terribly concerned when she heard what happened to Clarissa. "Why don't you come out here for a few weeks, Jule? You know both Ed and I would be thrilled. The weather is lovely. We're high enough not to get that oppressive desert heat, and the nights are cool."

"You're a darling to ask," she had replied, "but I'm not in the mood for traveling. I was supposed to have gone to New York for Janice Fried's retrospective, but I caught the flu. I'm still feeling a little washed out."

"It would do you good to get away. The trip wouldn't be so bad. You fly straight to Phoenix and I'd meet you. It's been almost four years since you were here."

"Yes, I know." She longed to see Betsy again. Except for brief visits during George's illness, they had not been together for ages. Betsy didn't like to leave Ed alone. Of course, they had both come to New York for the funeral. "I'll think about it," she said. "Maybe I'll feel more like myself by next week."

At ten o'clock that night, she was reading in bed when the telephone rang. It was Kit calling from California, and she was delighted to hear from him because they always had fun conversations that picked up her spirits.

"What's new with you, dear?" she asked.

"I've decided to transfer to UCLA. I realized I don't have the slightest desire to go back to Berkeley."

"Because of Diana?"

"Partly that, but it isn't the only reason," he assured her. "I like it here. I've gotten used to it."

"As long as it's right for you. Happiness is the bottom line."

"*Love* that philosophy," said Kit. "Hey, Grams, I want to ask you something. Have you ever heard of a movie actress named Annette Heublein?"

"No," she said thoughtfully, "I can't say that I have. But you're asking the wrong person, darling. I haven't been a movie buff for the last thirty years. Is she someone new?"

"No, she's very old. Well, that is, not young."

Julia laughed. "Perhaps you mean she's around my age?"

"Umm, I put my foot in it that time."

"The answer is still no. Annette Heublein? It's not a very glamorous name for an actress. In my day, she would have been called something like Dorothy Lamour."

"Dorothy Lamour . . . wasn't there a movie actress by that name?"

"Oh, my heavens, I'm glad she can't hear you say that."

"Big-time star, huh?"

"The biggest. Used to co-star with Bing Crosby and Bob Hope. In all those pictures they used to run on TV when you were young—The Road to This and the Road to That."

"I remember now. The lady in the sarong, with the flower in her hair."

"That's the one. Who is this actress? Why do you want to know about her?"

There was a note of hesitation before he answered. "Just curiosity, really. I had a gig at her house not long ago."

"For a private party?"

"Uh . . . yes. She lives in a great big movie-star mansion. Like something out of, well, out of the movies!"

Julia laughed. "I didn't think anyone lived that way these days."

"You'd be surprised. They keep a low profile, but there are plenty of those old places tucked away behind tall fences in the Hollywood hills."

Julia reflected that the tall fences would not keep anyone out who was determined to find a way in. "What does your father think about your transferring to UCLA?" she asked.

"He seems satisfied. He's just relieved that I'm going back to college."

"I'm sure he is. Have you spoken to him lately?"

"Not since last week. He told me that Uncle Scott and Aunt Isobel are splitting."

"Yes, I'm afraid so."

"That's too bad. Is Scott all broken up about it?"

"I would have thought so, but no, he isn't." She might as well start telling the rest of the family. "He seems to have found a new love."

"*No kidding!* Hey, that's pretty cool."

She raised her eyes to the ceiling. "The one who's broken up, as you put it, is Chip. He's taking this very hard. Perhaps you could give him a call and cheer him up a bit. He's staying out at their beach house."

"Sure. How do I reach him?"

She gave Kit the telephone number in Sagaponack. "That's my sweet boy," she said. "Sorry I wasn't able to help you with that movie actress. What did you say her name was again?"

"Annette Heublein."

"Annette Heublein," she repeated slowly. "No, it doesn't ring a bell. Take care of yourself, Kit. I think of you often."

"You are always on my mind," he crooned.

"Goodbye, darling."

"Ciao, Grams."

What a dear boy! She did love him so.

Chapter 23

Annette Heublein

It had been a long time since Kit had talked to his cousin.

During the four years he lived in New York, he and Chip had been pals, often spending weekends and holidays together at their grandparents' house in Norwalk. Chip was a year younger, but big for his age. The two boys got along well, playing tennis together and sailing with George Rhinehart, who had delighted in teaching them to handle the *Limerick*. Kit retained cherished memories of holidays in the gracious old Connecticut house. Those wonderful Thanksgiving and Christmas dinners with aunts, uncles, cousins, and assorted friends gathered around the table had given him his first real taste of belonging to a family.

And now part of that family was disintegrating. He called Chip, not because he had promised Grams he would but because he wanted to. He thought he could help. In their younger days, Chip had looked up to him.

"I know how you're feeling because I've been there," he told his cousin, who sounded really down. "It was a long time ago, but I remember. Time will help. At least your family was together in the important years, when you were growing up."

But he was hardly prepared for what Chip had to say. All things considered, it was pretty heavy. There was no question in his mind what he should do.

"As soon as we finish taping this video, I'll have some free time. How would it be if I came to stay with you for a couple of weeks?"

"That'd be great," said Chip, suddenly sounding more cheerful. "Thanks, Kit. With Ginger in Guatemala, you're about the only one I can talk to."

His call-waiting had signaled during the long conversation, but not wanting to interrupt his cousin when he was pouring his heart out, he had let the answering machine pick up. The message was from Cathy.

When he returned the call, she said, "Guess what! I found Annette Heublein."

"I don't believe it. Where?"

"In a tattered paperback anthology that was in the archives with the out-of-date journals. I made a copy of the article."

The Berkeley Boys had finished at the Dipper and it was his first free weekend in a month. "Let's have dinner," he said, happy at the thought of seeing her.

This was their fifth date. They met at the Stratton Grill, which was always crowded. The streets in Westwood Village were closed to traffic on Friday and Saturday nights. It took Kit half an hour to find a parking space, and Cathy was waiting in a booth when he arrived.

"I was right," she said immediately, "she used a stage name."

"Let's see." She handed him two sheets of paper stapled together. He squinted at them in the dimly lit restaurant. "I never heard of *her* either."

"She was famous."

Kit glanced over the long listing, but it was hard to see. "Does it say anything interesting?"

"I didn't really have time to read it."

He folded the papers and stuffed them into his back pocket. "I'll look at this later."

After dinner, they walked around the village for a while before going back to his apartment. He showed her his keyboard and guitars, and the new sound equipment. They sat on the couch and watched a rerun of "Star Trek" but could not get into it. Kit flipped channels to a baseball game and put on some CDs. "Do you like 10,000 Maniacs?"

She gave an equivocal shrug. "They're all right."

"Who do you like?"

"John Coltrane . . . R.E.M. I don't know, I like lots of different kinds of music, except I hate heavy metal."

With the television on mute, they watched the Yankees beat the Red Sox, and listened to the Indigo Girls and Suzanne Vega. Cathy seemed tense, and he thought she was waiting for him to mention the video.

Kit had been blown away by her tapes. They weren't professional quality, but he hadn't expected them to be. In fact, his expectations had been so low that he had delayed running them for over a week. When he finally got around to viewing the videos, it was apparent that what they lacked in slickness they more than made up for in ingenuity. He had told her he thought they were sensational and there might be a chance. "It's not really my decision. I have to clear it with my agent."

That was before Leonard Gold had broken the news about the "influential friend" who had contacted him on behalf of Annette Heublein. The man turned out to be none other than Foster Dale, president of the hottest production company in town. Heublein had evidently put in a good word for him, and Dale was going to produce their video.

Now Kit would have to tell Cathy it was no go, and he dreaded the task. He turned off the TV and lowered the volume of the CD player.

"I have some bad news," he said. "I guess it's good for me, but I know you'll be disappointed."

Without making excuses, he told her the entire story. "I didn't realize it, but he came to the Dipper to scout us and he said he'll work with us as a favor." She sat listening, not saying a word.

"You have some fantastic concepts, Cathy, but there's no way we can turn down an opportunity like this. Our agent has already told him we'd do it."

"I knew there wasn't much of a chance, but I kind of hoped," she said in a subdued voice.

Kit had never seen such a pathetic expression on anyone's face. She looked like a lost kitten. "Hey, come here." He put his arm around her. "Maybe you can come along as our assistant. Would you want to?"

"Yes."

The other band members had girlfriends who went with the

group when they were on the road and occasionally sat in on their taping sessions. Cathy wasn't exactly his girlfriend, but something was evolving between them.

He lifted her chin with his hand and leaned down until their lips met. His eyes closed as her arms went around his neck. He was kissing her, and suddenly the world had a whole new dimension. From there, things just seemed to naturally progress.

"I didn't plan this," he said softly, when they were in bed.

"I know you didn't."

He sensed her hesitation. "What's wrong?"

"It's not you." She seemed embarrassed. "You're not going to believe me, but I've never done this before."

He was very still. "You're kidding."

She shook her head. "I'm not kidding."

He rolled onto his back. "Cathy. I'm sorry."

"Don't be sorry. There has to be a first time."

"How old are you?"

"Twenty-one."

"You've really never?"

"No." She became quite indignant. "I'm not going to apologize! Women are always being pressured to go to bed. Guys all think they're such studs. Most of them are a real turn-off."

"Well, don't get mad."

"I *am* mad! Why should I be ashamed of not having had sex? That's all it would have been. I never felt like it before. I never met anyone I—I liked that much."

He moved closer and took her in his arms again. "Do you like me?"

"Yes."

He smoothed her hair back from her forehead and kissed her again. "Well, I like you, too. I think we're very good together."

"You do?"

"Umm . . ." he murmured, kissing her and stroking her breast. His hand moved down over her hips and through the triangle of russet hair, slipping between her thighs.

She let out her breath in a long sigh of pleasure. "Show me what to do," she whispered.

"Just relax. Do whatever comes naturally."

"But what about—I'm not on the Pill. I don't want to get pregnant or anything."

He reached over and opened a drawer in his night table. "There better be a condom in here." There was.

Much later, he said, "I don't want you to think this is the usual routine for me. I haven't been with anyone for a long time. Not all men have to go to bed with every woman they meet."

Very early the next morning he awakened and remembered he had forgotten to read the reference Cathy had given him. He turned on a light. His chinos were lying across a chair, and he fished the folded pages out of the pocket, smoothing them out. There was a note in Cathy's loopy handwriting:

Holland, J. L., *Holland's Guide to the Stars: An Anthology of Screen Personalities from Silent Pictures to the Modern Age of Film*. New York: Hawthorn Books, 1973, pp. 167, 630–31.

On the first sheet, she had highlighted two lines of the small print:

HEUBLEIN, ANNETTE MARIE The birth name of the actress Vivienne Tremaine (See Tremaine, Vivienne).

The second entry, alongside a photograph of a glamorous young woman, filled more than one page:

TREMAINE, VIVIENNE, actress, b. Camden, N.J., May 10, 1918; d. Otto and Maria (Schmidt) H.; m. Mortimer Axelrod, 1951, div. 1953, m. (2) Marvin Long, 1955, div. 1956, m. (3) Robert Hayland, 1957, div. 1962; member vaudeville troupe Dance Capades, 1934–36; contract player, Republic Pictures, 1936–39; female lead *One Night in Venice*, Mitchell Repertory Theater, 1939; contract player, Metro Films, 1939–49. Broadway musicals: *North With the Wind*, 1941; *Kick Up Your Heels*, 1944. Films: *The Muffin Man, 1937; Dolly's Dilemma*, 1938; *Pie in the Sky*, 1939 . . .

There followed a long list of motion pictures of which Kit had never heard. At the end of the film credits was a narrative summary of Vivienne Tremaine's career. His eyes ran down the column and stopped abruptly. A name leapt out of the page at him.

He sat down to read, his excitement mounting as he scanned the long summary.

Vivienne Tremaine began her stage career as a vaudeville dancer at age fifteen . . . became romantically linked with the composer Michael Kittredge Shane . . . leading female role in his musical drama, *One Night in Venice* . . . Hollywood scout in the audience . . . signed a long-term contract with Metro Films . . . motion picture roles were disappointing . . . Broadway debut in 1941 in *North With the Wind*, the musical that made the reputation of Michael Shane, with book and lyrics by Murray Baker . . . In 1944, the actress starred in another Shane and Baker hit, *Kick Up Your Heels* . . .

Following a mysterious falling-out with Michael Shane in 1948, returned to Hollywood . . . a drama filmed in England . . . recognition as a dramatic actress . . . Over the next decade, Vivienne Tremaine starred in a dozen important films (see above).

In 1951, she married Mortimer Axelrod, the powerful head of Metro Films . . . marriage lasted a short time; however, the two remained close friends and associates until Axelrod's death . . . Two subsequent marriages ended in divorce. Vivienne Tremaine's career was abruptly curtailed in 1963, when she was severely injured in an automobile accident. She now lives in retirement in Hollywood.

Kit slowly laid down the paper. Then he picked it up to read again. His mind was whirling. What did it mean? Annette Heublein/Vivienne Tremaine had been "romantically linked" with his grandfather!

Following a mysterious falling-out . . . in 1948 . . . Michael had been married to Julia for years by then. Neil was born the following year. Scott would have been five or six years old . . . what had been going on?

He looked at the two packets of music on his desk. One, the

manila portfolio of nine songs that his grandmother had given
him when he had visited Palm Island in December. Signed and
dated from August to November 1949, they were love songs
that Michael Shane had written "*For my wife, Julia Shane.*"

The other was the thick folder of rough compositions by an
anonymous composer, handed to him by the woman who called
herself Annette Heublein. Their distinctive notation exactly
matched that of the songs that Grams had given him.

There was no doubt that the scores he had taken from
Annette Heublein were the work of Michael Shane. Were
these the missing manuscripts his grandmother had described
to him? If so, how did Annette/Vivienne gain possession of
them? Had she realized that Kit was Michael's grandson when
she gave them to him?

He had to know the answers.

Kit was going to do this on his own, without involving
Cathy. He spent Saturday afternoon at Powell Library, the
main library at UCLA. There were hundreds of entries under
"Vivienne Tremaine" in the Los Angeles *Times* Index for the
years 1945 to 1965. Painstakingly he copied the dates until
he grew tired. Scanning the microfilms, he impatiently ran
through film reviews and coverage of the Academy Awards
ceremonies, pausing to read and make copies of straight news
stories.

Vivienne Tremaine's three marriages to and successive
divorces from a studio head, a director, and a handsome younger actor were given ample space. The gossip columns often
mentioned her romances with wealthy and powerful businessmen. Although she was often escorted by her various leading
men, she reportedly did not become involved with them. And
then, on March 17, 1963, the huge black headlines:

VIVIENNE TREMAINE SURVIVES
FATAL CRASH
Film Star, Severely Burned,
Hovers Between Life and Death.
Screenwriter Perishes.

In a dense fog this evening, a sports car driven by playwright-
lyricist and screenwriter Murray Baker went out of control on a

curving section of Benedict Canyon Road and burst into flames, killing the driver and leaving his passenger, Hollywood actress Vivienne Tremaine, in critical condition with burns over thirty percent of her body.

Miss Tremaine was a long-time friend and associate of Baker, who had dined with the glamorous film queen at her luxurious mansion on Mara Vista Drive earlier in the evening. It is not known where the two were headed, but police said the vehicle was traveling at high speed on the winding road, which was made even more hazardous by fog causing low visibility. It appears that Mr. Baker lost control of the vehicle, a low-slung Jaguar convertible, on a curve. The car crashed into the side of the mountain and burst into flame. Baker was trapped in the vehicle, but passing motorists were able to free Miss Tremaine, whose clothing was on fire. Both parties were rushed to Cedars of Lebanon Hospital by ambulance. Baker was pronounced dead on arrival. Vivienne Tremaine was admitted to the burn unit in critical condition . . .

The article went on to give the history of Vivienne Tremaine's career on stage and in film, mentioning in detail her three marriages and rumored love affairs, including her long romantic attachment to Michael Shane. She allegedly had gone into seclusion at his death . . .

At his death! Julia had been married to Michael for almost eight years when he died. Why would Vivienne—or Annette—mourn for him after all that time?

Kit read on. The article said that Murray Baker, who had collaborated with Shane on his musicals, came to Hollywood as a screenwriter after the composer's death in 1950. He was a victim of the McCarthy era blacklist when he refused to testify before the House Un-American Activities Committee. Although he had never been a communist and was later cleared of all wrongdoing, as the article pointed out, he was cited for contempt and received a suspended sentence. For years he could not find employment as a writer with the film studios, although it was later revealed that he wrote many scripts under an assumed name. Vivienne Tremaine insisted that he work on all her films, and a quiet arrangement was made. The two remained fast friends and were reportedly planning to produce a major motion picture together when Mr. Baker died.

After the accident, it was disclosed in further newspaper

reports that Murray Baker had died almost without assets
There were occasional small bulletins about Vivienne's medical progress, with one photograph showing her released from
the hospital wearing dark glasses and a hat with a thick veil.

After that, nothing. Vivienne Tremaine disappeared. Annette
Heublein was reborn.

Her telephone was unlisted, but Kit managed to get the number
through Leonard Gold. He called on Sunday morning. It took
some convincing for the butler to put her on the line.

Without any preliminaries, Kit said, "I would like to see
you, Miss Tremaine."

There was a silence, and then in a controlled voice, she
replied, "This afternoon at five."

She was waiting for him, standing in the middle of a large
tile-floored solarium that was furnished with brightly upholstered wicker couches. For once not swathed in all-enveloping
garments, she wore elegantly cut taupe pants and a simple
open-necked shirt of sea green silk.

Every visible part of her, except for her hands and the right
side of her face, had been ravaged by the fire that had engulfed
her on that fateful night. In the late afternoon daylight, her neck
and chin were pink and ridged. Her left cheek was horribly
distorted by scar tissue. The perfectly arranged auburn hair
looked strangely incongruous until Kit realized it was a wig.
Of course, her hair would have caught fire, too.

She noticed how he tried to avoid focusing on her disfig-
urement. "The plastic surgeons did their best, but skin grafts
have their limitations," she commented matter-of-factly.

Kit was filled with pity despite his growing anger. "You
must have suffered terribly."

Her eyes softened and her lips curved in a sad smile. "But
you didn't come here to talk about that. In fact, you find
yourself confused, don't you? You want to hate me. Because
I am the enemy."

He was irritated with her for understanding him so well.
"How did you get my grandfather's music?" he demanded.

"Oh, you are so very like him! That same scowl, those same
brooding, deep blue eyes. Full of laughter one moment, angry
at the world the next . . ."

"Answer my question."

"All right," she said quietly, as if he were a colt who needed gentling. "All right. Sit down and I will tell you a story. Please have patience, for it's a rather long story."

From years of practice, she composed herself with her damaged left side turned away from him.

"I met Michael Shane in Atlantic City, in the month of May. It was nineteen thirty-eight, and I was just turning twenty. He was the most beautiful man I had ever seen, and I fell in love with him instantly. Oh yes, we did that in those days. We weren't nearly as cynical as your generation. Each expression, each glance meant something, and great romantics that we were, we allowed ourselves to be swept away on a tide of ecstasy . . ."

Kit listened, mesmerized, not the least embarrassed to hear a woman old enough to be his grandmother confide in him her passions. On a table he noticed a large photograph of an exquisite young Vivienne Tremaine. A woman he could imagine his grandfather or any man falling madly in love with. And yet, Michael had married Julia. Lovely, down-to-earth, steadfast Julia. He had chosen wisely in a wife, spurning the glamorous actress.

" . . . when I heard that Michael was dying, I simply could not believe it. He was larger than life, stronger than the flesh. It was impossible that the world should be robbed of his spirit.

"I was in England, making *The Property*. You wouldn't have heard of it, but it was my first dramatic role in an important picture. It was a tragic role, and I played it thinking of Michael, lying on his deathbed. I was rushing against time, hoping to finish in order to get to New York before he was gone. I had to see him once more; I had to speak with him . . ."

She stopped talking and closed her eyes, sighing deeply.

"He died the day before my ship docked in New York. I went to the funeral wearing a wig and dark glasses. No one noticed me. I sat in the back of the church and saw all of them. Your grandmother and her little boy. A nurse was carrying a baby . . ."

"That would have been my father," said Kit. "He was six months old when Michael died."

She nodded slowly, as if this was of importance. "I saw how tragic Julia was, how brave . . . and yet all I could feel was my own agony. I could not accept that Michael was no longer alive, that he was forever lost to me."

The actress in her had taken over. It was spellbinding to listen to her hushed voice. Kit could actually visualize the scene.

"It was heartbreaking. His widow all in black, looking almost too young to be a mother. Murray Baker was there, constantly hovering over her and the little boy—"

"My Uncle Scott."

"She was surrounded by people who loved her. People I had known well, before I was banished. Betsy and Ed Hopper. Gerry Ross. Arlo Rothmore. All the theater crowd. And George Rhinehart, the lawyer. Oddly enough, as if I were clairvoyant, I sensed at the time that Julia would marry him. I doubt either of them dreamed of such a thing, but I knew. Murray was in love with her, of course, but he never had a chance."

There was a long silence, and Kit said, "When did you take the manuscripts?"

"That same day. I still had a key to Michael's studio. I kept it with me always. I never gave it back when he sent me packing." Her lips curled in a self-deprecatory smile. "I was certain he would have changed the lock. But no, it was the same. Either he hoped I would come back, or else he damn well knew I wouldn't."

She sighed again. "I went down to Greenwich Village, never intending to steal his music. You see—I was looking for my letters. I didn't want Julia to find anything, anything at all, that would hurt her or destroy her memories of her husband. Or perhaps my intentions were less noble . . . one forgets after forty years.

"I went through every drawer, every closet, every inch of that apartment. I even looked behind the books in the shelves. There was nothing, not a photograph, not a trace of me. Michael had obliterated any reminder that we had been lovers for so many years."

Her eyes flashed and she became quite agitated. "That made me angry. Had our love meant so little to him? I had never stopped loving him, and I could never forgive him for wanting me out of his life. His manuscripts and notebooks were lying on a table in the studio. On an impulse, I took them. It was out of spite. From feeling remorse for what I had done to Julia, I suddenly experienced a complete change of heart, becoming wildly jealous of your grandmother. She had Michael all those years, she had his sons, and I had nothing. So I took the most precious part of him—his music.

"I thought I would use it someday. I was going to make a film based on Michael's life and I was in possession of the last music he ever wrote!" She gloated at the words. "Of course, it could never have been done. I wasn't thinking rationally. I believe I was a little mad at the time. I went to his funeral, you know . . ."

"Yes, you told me."

"Oh. Did I?" She seemed suddenly vague. "I was making a film in England, you see, and they told me he was dying . . ."

Kit shifted uneasily.

"Eventually I realized what a horrible thing I had done."

"Why didn't you send them back? You could have done it anonymously, once you knew you weren't going to use them."

"Oh, but I hadn't given up that idea yet, you see. I still could not let go. Julia had remarried, I knew she was happy and well taken care of. Murray told me what had happened to her. But he never confided in me that Julia thought it was *he* who had stolen the scores! We had a brief affair—more to comfort each other than anything else. But he was always in love with Julia," she said, repeating herself. "I guess she knew that."

"I don't know. She's never mentioned him."

"He loved her until the end of his life. That was another reason why I didn't send them back. Murray was down on his luck in the fifties, blacklisted. I somehow thought that if I could devise a way to give him Michael's music without admitting that I had taken it, he would write the book to a brilliant new musical and I would star in it, and he would be on top again."

"But instead he died."

"Yes, he died. I can still recall everything that happened that night, every single detail. As if it were yesterday . . ."

"You look like hell, Murray."

"I feel like hell." He drained his brandy glass and went to the bar to pour another.

"You drink too much."

"Lay off, Viv. I don't need a nursemaid."

"What *do* you need?"

"Nothing. I don't need anything or anyone."

"Everyone needs someone. Even *I* have needs." Her laugh

was bitter. "It's time for you to pull yourself together, before there's nothing left to salvage."

"I'm going back to New York," he said suddenly. "I'll never get anywhere in Hollywood. This industry is brutal. They don't want writers. They want hacks who chew up other people's ideas and spit them out in digestible segments."

"Oh, Murray. What makes you think it will be any different in New York?"

"I'll go back to Broadway. I'll find a composer to team up with. Hammerstein did it. They said he was finished, he hadn't had a hit in ten years, and look what happened."

"There will never be another Michael Shane. You might as well face it."

"No. But he wasn't the last songwriter. I'll find someone."

"What if I told you I have some scores that are as good as any Mike ever wrote."

He looked at her quizzically. "By whom?"

"An unknown. You never heard of him."

"Where are they?"

"Right here in my house. I'll get them." She hurried out of the room and returned with a heavy tapestry carryall. Removing a folder from the bag, she handed it to Murray.

He took it with a puzzled expression on his face. Laying it down on a console table, he began leafing through the contents, one by one. When he was about a third of the way through, he looked up. Vivienne recoiled at the fury in his eyes.

"Where did you get these?"

"I told you, a young composer brought them to me."

He grabbed her wrist. "Where did you get them?" he shouted.

"You're hurting me!"

"I'll do a helluva lot more than hurt you if you don't answer my question."

"Murray, calm down. This young man—" His hand slammed against her shoulder and she fell back, stunned by the blow. "Murray!"

"Tell me how you got hold of these scores! They're Michael's work. You know they are!"

She saw that there was no sense pretending any longer. "He gave them to me. A long time ago."

"*Liar!* They were in his studio two weeks before his death. I saw them there. You stole them. *You!*"

"I didn't—"

"Stop lying to me," he bellowed, gripping her by the scruff of the neck. "How? How did you get hold of them?" He shook her. "You had a key to his studio, didn't you? You went to New York. You told me you were in England, but you came to New York. *Answer me!*"

"All right. Please, let go of me." She stepped back, afraid of him, rubbing her neck. "Yes. Yes, I was there. I came in time for his funeral. No one was paying attention. They didn't recognize me. Afterward, I went to the studio. I never intended to take anything. I wanted to see it one last time. I wanted to be sure nothing of mine was there."

"And you stole his songs."

"Murray, they're for you. You can write the book for his musicals. Everything's here—his notebooks, his scenarios, all the ideas and sketches and rough scores. Take them. Do it!"

With one violent gesture, he swept the portfolio off the table and the sheets of music went scattering across the room. "You're crazy. Do you know that? A crazy woman. Because you couldn't have Michael, you stole his legacy from Julia and his children."

"No, Murray—"

"Julia thinks I took them. She cast me out of her life because she thinks I stole her husband's music. I *loved* her. I wouldn't have done anything to hurt her." He began to cry. "I hate you, Vivienne. I hate you."

"Murray, please. Take the music. It's yours."

Suddenly he grabbed the tapestry bag. "I'll take it! I'll give it back to Julia. Now she'll know I wasn't the one."

He ran out of the room toward the huge front door. "No, Murray," she screamed. "No, you mustn't tell her I took them."

"It's too late, Vivienne. You should have thought of that before."

She ran after him as he flung open the door to the mansion. His Jaguar was parked at the foot of the front steps. As the motor roared to life, Vivienne jumped into the passenger seat. The car tore around the circle and down the driveway. Murray stopped at the gate.

"Get out, Vivienne."

"No!"

"All right, have it your way."

With a screech of brakes, he careened onto the road. It was misty and damp and the surface was slick. The tires squealed as they came around the curve onto Benedict Canyon.

"Slow down, you'll get us killed," screamed Vivienne.

"Your precious life isn't that valuable," he cried, "and God knows mine isn't worth a damn."

"Murray, for God's sake, listen to me."

"I've listened to you for the last time, Miss Tremaine."

He was going faster and faster. They hit a patch of dense fog. Vivienne closed her eyes and prayed. He was a maniac. He had completely lost command of himself.

"Stop the car. Let me out," she begged.

"You should have gotten out when you had the chance," he yelled.

Vivienne was terrified. How much had he had to drink? Three brandies, wine with dinner, two scotches beforehand. They hurtled around a hairpin curve so steep that the car turned on two wheels. She gripped a strap above the door to keep from falling against him, too frightened to scream. The road twisted again in the reverse direction. Murray lost control of the wheel at the apex of the curve. Instinctively he braked. Vivienne's heart stopped as the car skidded toward the sheer drop at the road's edge. Desperately, Murray battled the steering wheel, trying to gain traction. The rear wheels screeched as they were thrown into a complete circle, hurtling across the road toward the mountain.

Through the fog, she saw rock and earth and trees coming straight at them. And then everything exploded in a blinding flash.

"Do you think he tried to kill you both?" asked Kit.

"I don't know. I don't believe he started out with that intention. He said he was going to take the notebooks and scores back to Julia. But then something happened when we were in the car. He was in agony. I think he thought it was a way out. He was testing fate or God or something. If he came out of it alive, then it would prove that he was meant to go on. I don't know why I believe that, but I do. It wasn't suicide. Murray was testing the grand design. He died and Michael's music died with him, destroyed in the flames. The only pieces left are those I gave to you, those he had thrown on the floor." She was panting. "That's how Murray died."

"But you lived."

"Yes," she said bitterly, "I lived. If you consider this living. Look at me, young man. Michael . . . Kit . . . whatever you call yourself. My beauty was more important than my talent. I can assure you, my life has been more horrible than his death."

"I'm sorry, Miss Heublein."

"What will you do now, dear boy?"

"What do you mean?"

"I mean, am I a criminal? Will you have me charged with grand larceny?"

His breath was taken away. "I—it never occurred to me."

"It's not your decision to make, of course. You will tell your grandmother. It is Julia who must decide."

⅋∾ Chapter 24 ∾⅋

Officer Fry

It was a clear, bright morning. The air was surprisingly fresh for July. Julia went out through the sunroom, stepping onto the terrace and crossing the lawn to the swimming pool. Her lungs filled with the mingled scent of dewy grass and sea as she stood for a moment, gazing across the lagoon to the nature conservancy. Soon she would be leaving this behind, going to Connecticut for the remainder of the summer.

She dived into the water, hoping a vigorous swim would wash the cobwebs from her brain. She had not slept well last night, waking and tossing for hours. Finally she had fallen into a stuporous sleep from which she awoke at daybreak, feeling not at all rested. She rolled over into a lazy backstroke, kicking steadily for several turns, then resumed a slow crawl. It usually took a few laps for her to warm up, but even after ten minutes her arms felt strangely heavy. Back and forth she continued, waiting for that smooth, restorative surge, but it never came. Hoisting herself out of the pool was an effort.

After breakfast, she tended her flower beds. As she clipped and cultivated, she could hear hammering next door and the buzz of a power saw. The contractor had already begun working on the renovations of Clarissa's house. At the end of the year the Winstons would be moving in. George would have enjoyed so much having Jack and Sue as neighbors.

She straightened up, a little short of breath. That was enough
ardening for today. When she entered the kitchen, sunspots
anced before her eyes. She felt momentarily disoriented and
eld on to the counter to steady herself. The feeling passed.
he drank a glass of cold spring water, swallowed a vitamin
ill, and took up a note pad to make a shopping list.

Perhaps she would bake a chocolate layer cake for Kit and a
atch of his favorite Toll House cookies. He would be arriving
n three more days, on his way to New York to spend some
me with Chip. Wasn't it just like that darling boy, to drop
verything in order to cheer up his cousin. He said he had some
ather dramatic news for her, something that would come as a
omplete surprise. She wondered what it could be.

Opening the pantry cupboard, she checked the shelves. She
vas out of flour again. Living alone, she was forever throwing
ut half-used packages of grains before they became mealy.
Ier supply of staples was running low, and with Scott coming
o visit next week on his way back from Tokyo, she might just
s well get a head start on the shopping. She needed sugar and
anilla, butter, eggs, nuts, soft drinks, olives, a few cans of
hat delicious madrilene . . . and she would pick up some good
odka and a bottle of Glenfiddich. Scott liked a drink before
linner.

It was almost time for her 11:30 hair appointment. She
ad better wash up and get herself looking more presentable.
Changed into a crisp Liberty print blouse, a blue denim skirt
nd navy espadrilles, she was soon on her way, heading across
he causeway to the village.

The midday sun was beating down when she emerged from
he hairdresser, with her newly shorn head shampooed and
•lown dry in a becoming shorter style. She stopped to pick
p her white linen dress at the dry cleaners and hung it in
he car. She loathed money machines, preferring to stand in
ine at the bank to cash a check. As she walked toward the
•ost office, the heat waves rising from the pavement were
•ppressive. After buying a roll of stamps, she paused in the
ool interior before going out in the sweltering air again.

The floor seemed to tip sideways and it occurred to her that
he was about to faint. In an instant it was over. She felt normal
gain. Last November, when Fred Neiman had given her a
horough checkup, he said stress was causing the occasional

dizziness. There was no doubt that she had been under greater tension than usual lately. Nevertheless, she would make an appointment to see Dr. Ribera.

Twenty minutes later, Julia was reaching for a can of Bumble Bee water-pack tuna, when she blacked out in the middle of Aisle Twelve of the Winn-Dixie supermarket on Ponce de Leon Avenue. Unable to read the labels clearly, she had bent down to get a closer look and was overcome by a wave of weakness. She made a mental note to add this little spell to the list of symptoms she was recording for Dr. Ribera. And then everything went blank.

When she opened her eyes, a ring of faces peered down at her. Someone—she hoped a woman—had arranged her skirt so that her knees were covered. Knees became so ugly as one grew older. For an instant, she could not remember her surroundings, imagining that she was back in the Gristede's on Lexington Avenue.

The manager had called an ambulance. Over her feeble protests, she was placed on a stretcher, covered with a blanket, and rolled out of the store to the parking lot where a curious crowd had gathered. The humiliation of being wheeled out of the Winn-Dixie with all those strangers watching! Trailer-camp women in shorts and halters, their hair in rollers. Ne'er-do-well men in overalls.

"My purse!" she suddenly cried in panic.

"It's right there under the blanket with you, ma'am," the manager assured her. "The cop has your I.D. over there in the patrol car, but everything else is just the way it was."

If this had happened in New York, her purse would have been gone, grabbed by the first addict or homeless person who happened along. *But she wasn't in New York. She was in Florida . . . She was a sixty-eight-year-old widow a thousand miles from home, and she was all alone.*

"Mrs. Rhinehart." A shadow fell across her and she turned her head, squinting up at the dark silhouette against the brightness of the sky. His voice sounded familiar. "It's Grady Fry, ma'am. Remember me?"

"Oh, Officer Fry, I'm so very glad to see you."

"Now, don't you worry, Mrs. Rhinehart," said the policeman reassuringly. "You're going to be just fine. We're taking you to County Hospital. If I can have your keys, ma'am, I'll get ny partner to bring your automobile over there."

He was very kind, following the ambulance in the patrol car. "Y'all must be a real VIP," the paramedic drawled, "gittin' your own po-lice escort."

At the hospital, Grady Fry accompanied her into the emergency room and helped get her through admissions. What would they do if I were having a heart attack? she wondered, as the young woman painstakingly entered her social security number, Medicare number, major medical insurance coverage, next of kin, and countless other statistics into a computer.

That lengthy process completed, she was taken through a pair of double doors and wheeled down the hall to an examining room. They transferred her to a table, and a nurse came to cover her and take her blood pressure.

She caught a glimpse of the police report as Fry handed it to the nurse, and was startled to see herself described as an elderly woman. She had never thought of herself as elderly. Older, perhaps. But *elderly?* Elderly women did not golf and play two sets of tennis, or drive red Mercedes sports coupes . . . Elderly was white hair, wrinkled flesh, lapsing memory, halting steps. Elderly was Marie at the Admiralty Residence, half blind and incontinent.

The second patrolman showed up with her car keys and told her where he had parked. "Well, we'll be going along now," said Fry. "They'll take real good care of you here."

"I am so grateful to you, Officer Fry." She felt as if she were saying goodbye to an old friend.

The emergency-room doctor was a Pakistani. Were there no Americans working in hospitals anymore? She had the most difficult time understanding him.

"Your pulse is very slow," he said so rapidly she had to ask him to repeat it.

"It has always been slow. My normal pulse is fifty-two."

"This patient has brachycardia," he commented to the nurse.

Alarmed, Julia asked, "What is brachycardia?"

"A slow heartbeat."

She was by now in an upright position on the examining table. They had attached electrodes to her chest, and she was hooked up to monitors that recorded her vital signs and electrocardiogram. There was an oxygen tube in her nostrils and an intravenous shunt in her left hand.

"What's that for?" she asked.

"In case we have to give you medication in a cardiac emergency," the doctor replied, and the EKG monitor spiked ominously. "Your heartbeat is irregular."

She hardly needed him to tell her that. She could feel her heart skipping a beat as it palpitated. "Am I having a heart attack?"

"Don't worry about it." He wagged his head sideways. "Dr. Ribera is just coming."

Dr. Ribera had called in a cardiologist, Dr. Marciano. The admitting diagnosis was "accelerated idioventricular rhythm with AB dissociation and fusion beats," and Dr. Marciano wanted to implant an artificial pacemaker immediately in order to prevent heart block.

Julia was panicky at the prospect of undergoing surgery—even minor surgery—in a small county hospital in southwestern Florida, and she told them so. They had put her in the Intensive Care Unit for observation, and once her heartbeat had stabilized, they agreed to wait. Until they completed all the tests, though, she would be kept on intravenous fluids.

During the night, she slept sporadically. She had been given a sleeping pill, and it had an odd effect on her. She was in a twilight zone, half dreaming, half hallucinating. Jesse was there. And Eunice in a tirade, with her crocheting needle darting in and out of an endless afghan that stretched beyond the room, out of the house, and across the river to the mountains. *Ralph Tepper corrupted our pure and beautiful daughter*, she ranted. Jesse huddled in a corner, crying. *You had no right! I always loved him, I always loved him*. It was snowing and Julia was running through a forest, calling for her father. She suddenly came to the top of a long stairway and she was falling through space while the void around her was filled with her mother's lament.

Her eyes opencd. Jesse's voice, young and anguished, still rang in her ears . . . *I always loved him*. Even at this great distance, the tragedy of her mother's life filled her with grief. The monitor cast an eerie green light in the darkened room. Above her head, the slow drip of the I.V. marked the passage of time like an hourglass.

The sudden memory of a cold winter day at the end of 1968 came to her. It had been little more than a month after Neil had left for Canada. Julia had not yet recovered from the painful scene of her son storming out of the house, flinging angry words at them. When she returned from a long walk, she had found Betsy in the library talking to George.

"I have something to tell you," said her aunt. "You had better sit down."

"*Neil!*" Julia cried, reaching for her husband's hand.

George had gripped her shoulders, bending down to kiss her. "No, darling, nothing to do with Neil. Something rather unexpected has happened, that's all."

"I received a call from the Veterans' Administration," Betsy had explained. "They traced me through the nursing home in Albany where Mother lived."

Julia frowned. "I don't understand. What would the Veterans' Administration want with you?"

"They were actually looking for you." Betsy chewed her lip, deliberating. "Ralph Tepper is in a VA hospital in Pennsylvania. He has cancer, Julia. He wants to see you."

She had been speechless. Through five months of anguish and sleepless nights over her son, she had managed to hold back her tears, but she wept then for her father.

George had driven through the snowy Pocono Mountains to the Veterans' Hospital in northeastern Pennsylvania. He had stayed at her side, steadying her when they approached the bed. The man lying there had borne no resemblance to the father she remembered, the father in the photographs. His hair was white, his skin wrinkled and jaundiced. A tangle of tubes and catheters hung from his wasted body. There were tears in his eyes.

She wanted to hate him, but all the long-forgotten love and need crowded aside the bitterness. Once the emotional reunion was behind them, she had sat alone at his bedside, holding his hand. "I don't know what to call you. I'm too old to call a man Daddy."

He had managed a smile. "I used to hunger to hear your voice. I longed so much to see you."

Even knowing how cruel the words might sound, she had been unable to stop them. "Why didn't you come, then? All those years we needed you, Mother and I."

He had drawn in his breath, and she saw the pain on his face. "I couldn't take it any longer. Your grandmother hated the sight of me. When she ordered me out of her house, Jesse had to make a choice, and she chose her mother."

"But still you could have visited. Later on."

He had closed his eyes, remaining silent a long time before answering. "I had another wife by then, Julia. A wife and a child . . . a boy."

She had been stunned. In all her fantasies she had never imagined that he would marry again. Which, when she thought of it, had been ridiculous. "You mean, I have a brother? Where are they?"

"Both dead. They lived in Pittsburgh. There was a fire, and they died of smoke inhalation. It was during the war, when I was overseas. My son was ten years old."

"I'm so sorry." More seemed to be called for, but she could think of nothing else to say.

"There was no one to go home to," Ralph explained, his voice growing weaker. "I stayed in the Army Engineers. I went to Troy once after the war and learned that Jesse had died and her mother was in an old-age home. No one seemed to know what had become of you, though. They told me you had married, but they had no record of your husband's name or where you lived. When I heard that, I decided not to inquire any further. I had done enough damage."

His strength was ebbing. They left soon afterward, promising to return.

"Thank goodness for you," she had murmured to George when they were in the car on their way back to New York. "I could never have gone through that alone."

She had seen her father once more before he died. He had been in a coma by then.

This room in the ICU, with its greenish light, reminded her of the Veterans' Hospital in Pennsylvania.

By the second day, she was irritable and famished. They had taken her off the I.V., but Dr. Marciano had ordered a no-salt, low-cholesterol diet. She was fed up with fruit salad and boiled chicken. What she wouldn't do for a corned beef sandwich on rye and a kosher dill pickle!

Her first act that morning was to call Kit and tell him not

bother coming, since she was in the hospital. He insisted
e would be there on schedule.

Julia was still hooked up to a monitor and unable to move far
om the bed. She was dozing when Alice, the pretty Australian
ay nurse, came into the room. Her long, straight brown hair
ung halfway down the back of her white pants suit. You'd
ink all that hair would interfere with her nursing duties. And
hatever had happened to those nice perky caps nurses used
wear?

"We finally spoke to your son in Tokyo last night, Mrs.
hinehart. He won't be able to get here until tomorrow."

"Thank you," said Julia.

The nurse looked at her reprovingly. "You never told us
ou have a daughter. We lost a whole day trying to locate
our son when all that time we could have been in touch with
our daughter. She's on her way from Los Angeles."

The monitor started going crazy. Wild green peaks and
alleys etched their way across the screen. "I don't want
y daughter to come," gasped Julia. "Why did you have to
all her?"

"There, now, don't excite yourself," soothed Alice as anoth-
r nurse rushed into the room. "Your son gave us her telephone
umber. Someone will have to stay with you until you're on
he mend. Won't it be nice having your daughter taking care
f you for a while?"

"Heaven forbid," said Julia.

arly that afternoon Deborah breezed in, wearing a fringed
e-dyed blouse of indeterminate ethnic origin over slim, faded
lue jeans. Her earrings swept her shoulders, and Julia thought
er feet in their sandals could have been cleaner. Was this the
ame sleek daughter who used to have weekly pedicures at
lizabeth Arden?

Deborah stooped to kiss Julia's brow. "Hello, Mother. How
re you feeling?"

"I am absolutely fine, dear. I wish they hadn't bothered you.
id you have a comfortable trip?"

"Not bad, except for the passengers. I'd forgotten how awful
eople back East can be."

Julia knew better than to take the bait. "How are the chil-
ren?"

"Thriving." She smiled proudly. "Wendy is learning to ride and play the flute, and Richie will be starting nursery school in September."

"And Jergen?"

Deborah beamed. "Just terrific. The new healing centers are a huge success. They're going to open two more—in Michigan and Vermont."

"That's splendid." Now that Deborah was here, Julia was really thrilled to see her. She shifted her position in the bed. "Come sit over here. Scott told me wonderful things about your shop. He couldn't stop raving."

"Did he really?" She looked extremely pleased. "I thought he was just being polite when he came to see it."

"Not at all. He was truly impressed."

Deborah opened her purse. "The children drew pictures for you. They're in here somewhere."

Julia watched her daughter rummaging through the huge pouchy carpetbag. "Your hair could use a good brushing, dear."

Deborah laughed. "Same old Mother. I guess you're not as sick as you look. All that electronic equipment is rather upsetting."

"I don't think I'm sick at all. I just had a little dizzy spell. It was probably the heat."

The fact was that she did not feel the least bit ill. A bit frightened, perhaps, by the experience of fainting and being carted off to the hospital in a wailing ambulance, but who wouldn't be? Her heartbeat had settled down shortly after they moved her from the emergency room. She had walked from the stretcher to the bed and when they hooked her up to the new monitor, everything was back to normal and had remained so for the past twenty-four hours.

There was a clattering in the hall and a nurse's aide came in with a wheelchair. "Moving day, Mrs. Rhinehart. They're sending you upstairs to a private room."

"Oh, wonderful! I hope that means I'll get some decent food to eat," she said hopefully.

The aide shook her head. "The diet doesn't change until they finish all your blood work and you have an echocardiogram."

Julia made a face. "Darling," she said to Deborah, "while they're moving me, why don't you run over to my house and get settled in. When you come back, I can use my toilet articles. And would you bring a couple of nightgowns, a robe, and some slippers?" She wrote down the alarm code and driving directions to Palm Island. "I'll call the gate so they know you're coming. My car is down in the parking lot . . . here are the keys."

The private room was very pleasant, with a distant view of the Gulf. Since she was on a portable Holter monitor that recorded her heart function around the clock, she was permitted to go to the bathroom, walk in the halls, and actually encouraged to be active.

Scott arrived the next afternoon, bringing Dr. Sidney Marvin, a renowned heart specialist from New York. The doctors had a long consultation and it was agreed that whatever had caused the irregular heart rhythm had corrected itself. Dr. Marciano wanted to put in a pacemaker in case it should happen again.

"I don't agree that you should have a pacemaker," Dr. Marvin explained to Julia. "For some reason, your normally slow heartbeat decreased even further. When that occurred, the heart's own natural secondary pacemaker kicked in, causing an irregular ventricular rhythm. Ever since it stabilized, the EKG has been normal. Hemodynamics are fine, echocardiogram shows no abnormalities. Given your asymptomatic condition, I think you should be discharged for periodic follow-up."

"But why did this happen?" she asked. "What caused my heartbeat to slow down?"

He shook his head and gave a perplexed shrug. "I don't know why it occurred, but that may be moot. It may never happen again."

"The dizziness?"

"It could be the inner ear, Meniere's disease—although I doubt it because of the pattern. You're a swimmer, so we can't absolutely rule out labrynthitis. Since it's an infrequent complaint, I'm inclined to agree with Dr. Neiman's diagnosis. Stress. You might try some relaxation techniques."

"You mean . . ." She could hardly believe her ears.

"You should come to The Well, Mother." Deborah had been sitting quietly near the window, listening to every word with a satisfied smile. "My husband owns a chain of holistic healing centers," she explained to the doctor. "He teaches meditation and relaxation therapy."

"There are various names for it," said Dr. Marvin. "Bio-feedback, self-hypnosis, meditation. Alternative therapies can be helpful in the right circumstances."

The great Dr. Marvin departed for New York shortly there-after. Dr. Marciano, however, insisted that Julia have an exercise stress test before she was discharged. "You'll have to remain in the hospital one more night," he said. "It's too late to schedule for today."

"I think he's a little miffed," remarked Julia, when Marciano had left. "His pride is hurt."

"He's probably more concerned about liability," said Scott crisply.

Deborah went back to the house to bring Julia a pair of sweatpants and Nikes to wear for the stress test, which was scheduled for eight o'clock the following morning. Scott hung his jacket over the back of a chair and loosened his tie. Julia thought he looked extremely tired after his long flight from Tokyo but much happier and more relaxed than he had in many years.

He took her hand. "I was so worried about you. I can't tell you how relieved I am. Please don't wait until August. Come back to New York with me now."

"We'll see."

"It's all settled, Mother. I want you to meet Solange. You'll stay with us."

It was very tempting. She remembered how alone she had felt without her family, on the way to the hospital in the ambulance. "Well, perhaps I will. But I won't be able to come immediately. I'll need a few days to get myself together."

Kit arrived at five o'clock, just as Debbie was returning with a suitcase containing her mother's clothes and a picnic basket full of hors d'oeuvres and wine. As usual when Kit was around, the mood picked up.

"Hey, what's going on around here?" he exclaimed, after an exuberant greeting. "I expected to see a pale-faced patient, and I walk into a party."

"We're celebrating," replied Julia gleefully. "I get sprung in the morning."

Her dinner tray arrived. Deborah lifted the plastic covers to reveal plain boiled rice, boiled chicken, fresh orange sections, and Jello. "That looks *disgusting*," she gagged. "Here, Mother, have some more caviar."

There was a knock on the door. When it opened, Neil walked in. Julia could not believe her eyes. "Oh," she gasped, overcome with emotion. Wordlessly she held out her arms.

They were all here now. All her children.

They stayed until long after visiting hours. Finally Julia sent them on their way to have dinner. "This isn't New York. If you don't eat soon, all the restaurants will be closed."

"You mean there's not even an all-night diner?" asked Kit incredulously.

She laughed. "I haven't checked out the diners lately."

They kissed her goodbye. Kit lagged behind after the others had left.

"What is this remarkable news you said you have to tell me?" Julia asked curiously.

He gave her an enigmatic smile. "It's a long and complicated story, Grams. There'll be plenty of time for it when we get you home tomorrow."

"Can't you give me even a tiny hint?" she teased.

"Well," said Kit cryptically, "I suppose you could say it has to do with a ghost from the past."

❧ Chapter 25 ❧

Juliette

January in New York.

The bustle of pavements at dusk, the glitter of lights against pink skyglow, the sharpness of frosty air had always held enormous appeal for Julia. She reveled in the vitality of the city. Each time she returned, she realized how much she missed its energy and tempo. The crowds, the frantic pace, had never lost their allure. New Yorkers might be jaded by political scandals, the latest outrage on the streets, or the rantings of an electoral campaign, but for her Manhattan held the same fascination as it had the first time she had stepped off the train from Troy.

After an exhilarating day of shopping and museum-going, she was exhausted. She had sent home four dresses and three pairs of shoes from Saks, then met Janice Fried for lunch at Jo Jo, a new restaurant recommended by Scott. With reckless abandon—for the prices were absurd—they ordered champagne in honor of the recent acquisition of one of Janice's paintings by the Museum of Modern Art.

"This is in the category of All Good Things Come to Those Who Wait," Janice commented archly when Julia toasted her stunning achievement. "I wish you had been here for the retrospective."

"I know. It was a terrible disappointment to me. I *never* get the flu, so why then?"

Mellowed by champagne and nostalgia, they reminisced about their more than fifty years of friendship, since the party where they had met on Julia's first Christmas in New York. After their extravagant lunch they walked over to MOMA so that Julia could view the work of art. It was an ambitious piece—an immense canvas with active brushwork, a strong example of Abstract Expressionism.

"What a satisfying feeling it must be," said Julia, remembering all the years of struggle Janice had gone through for this recognition.

It had started to snow when they came outside and they were lucky to find a taxi. Back at Scott and Solange's stylishly appointed roofhouse, all Julia wanted was to sink into the comfortable rocker in the nursery and hold her newest little grandchild.

"Juliette Micheline Didier Rhinehart. What a ponderous title for a little wisp," she murmured softly, kissing the infant's dimpled cheek.

Juliette waved her arms and kicked her feet, cooing and babbling as if she were conveying the most important news imaginable. Three months old, and you could already tell she was going to have a strong personality.

The baby yawned hugely as her grandmother laid her against her shoulder, where she promptly snuggled down and went to sleep. Julia had almost forgotten what a blissful feeling it was to hold a tiny body in her arms.

Juliette. What a complicated world you have inherited, little one.

Scott and Solange would be fine together, she was convinced. Scott had recently joined Winston, Rhinehart & Rhinehart, as the law firm was now called. Solange was balancing motherhood with working on a new book about experimental photography. There was a good feeling in their home, and Julia felt extremely comfortable with them.

She had been far less surprised than anyone anticipated when she first met Solange to find her pregnant with Scott's child. None of them had expected Julia to accept it so readily. It helped Chip enormously to know that his grandmother wasn't propelled into a tailspin. From the first day, she and Solange got on famously, as if they had been friends for years. They thought so much alike it was uncanny. The only matter on which they seemed to hold opposing views was Solange's decision not to marry Scott before the baby was born. But perhaps that didn't matter. The simple ceremony had taken place two weeks later in the Winstons' apartment. There had been ample time for a wedding before Juliette's birth, since Isobel had gone to Nevada for the divorce.

Isobel . . . now *that* had been unexpected. To imagine that Victoria Prescott's daughter was openly living with a woman who was her lover. Well, it simply boggled the mind.

Julia did not recall there being such a marked difference between her generation and her mother's . . . the world around them was changing at an ever-increasing rate, as if accelerated by jet propulsion. Life took so many unexpected twists and turns. The wonderful part of it was that if you lived long enough, almost *anything* could happen.

When Kit had brought Michael's lost compositions to her and related the incredible circumstances of their coming into his hands, she had been simply astounded. It was on the day after her discharge from the hospital, and they had all been gathered at her house—Deborah, Scott, and Neil, as well as Kit. Her grandson had waited for a quiet moment alone with her and then very gently related the story of Annette Heublein.

In all her years, Julia had experienced every possible emotion and imagined she was immune to shock. But on that occasion she had been truly dumbfounded. Her immediate thought was, *George! I need to tell George.*

Vivienne Tremaine, a pathetic and bitter woman who had suffered a great deal, according to Kit, had put her fate in Julia's hands. She could understand the actress taking Michael's music. Women performed monstrous acts when driven by jealousy and love. But she would never be able to forgive Vivienne for making her reject Murray. He had died tragically, believing Julia despised him. Her heart ached to think of the misery he had suffered. Blacklisted in Hollywood, unable to salvage his reputation as a screenwriter, Murray had been denied the scores and inspirational ideas Michael had prepared for him. For of course that had been in Michael's mind when he was composing feverishly during those final months. He had realized better than anyone else, even the doctors, that his days were numbered, and he wanted to leave a legacy. But he needed Murray to do it.

Murray had been as necessary to Michael's art as Michael had been to his. Together they had created magic.

Even in death, Murray had been robbed of the glory. Last week in Washington, there had been an official ceremony commemorating the anonymous gift of Michael's scores to the Library of Congress. Julia and her family had been received at the White House, where the President awarded a special posthumous medal to Michael Kittredge Shane.

Tomorrow, on the seventy-fifth anniversary of his birth, there would be a concert at Carnegie Hall to raise money for a Michael Shane Scholarship at the Juilliard School of Music. And on Saturday night, the gala Seventy-fifth Birthday Salute to Michael Shane would take place at the Metropolitan Opera House at Lincoln Center.

They were all present tonight.

Well, not quite all. George wasn't here . . . nor Michael. And, of course, Murray. But all the others had come.

Imagine that Edwin had traveled from Scottsdale! He was indestructible, so dignified and erect, walking slowly down the aisle on his son's arm. Betsy, radiant and still lovely, followed with Perk's wife.

And the rest of them. Scott and Solange, already seeming to belong together. Deborah and Jergen with Wendy, who was adorable in blue velvet. Neil, alone tonight. She worried about him, but in her heart Julia felt he would be all right. The boys looked handsome in their formal dinner jackets. Kit, resembling Michael so much that it quite took her breath away, had come with lovely Cathy Wallace, who seemed much more mature and interesting than the last young lady. And Chip appeared happy again, holding hands with Ginger's friend Lindsay MacGraw, who was obviously very taken with him. Julia wished that Ginger were present, but her oldest granddaughter was still in Guatemala and having a remarkable experience, from all reports.

Oh, and there across the aisle were Isobel and Cece. That would take some getting used to. But she would make the effort. After all, Isobel was the mother of her grandchildren.

She turned her attention to the program. It included a discriminating selection of Michael's music. Beginning with songs from *One Night in Venice*, it went on to chronicle the years of Shane and Baker's Broadway hits.

*North With the Wind; Over the Moon; Kick Up Your Heels;
A Light in the Sky . . . Ring Loud, Ring Clear; Her Majesty;
California.* And *Magic Island,* the last show, the one that
Michael had not lived to see. They had even included a few
numbers from his World War II army revues—*Cast Off, She-
nanigans,* and *Crackerjacks.*

What a wealth of music! It seemed impossible that one
person could have created it in the short span of years allotted
to him.

The musicians were tuning their instruments. An expectant
ripple ran through the crowded opera house. It had the feverish
excitement of an opening night, and Julia felt it all over again,
just as if it were the first time. The thrill of anticipation. The
sick feeling in the pit of the stomach. The anxiety of not
knowing how the audience would respond.

There was a burst of applause as the conductor took his
place and bowed. He raised his baton.

The great crystal chandeliers ascended, the house lights
dimmed. As the orchestra struck up the overture, the haunting
strains of "Forgotten Rhapsody" filled the vast auditorium.

Her heart beat faster. The curtain rose.